SHADOWS & FLAME

BOOKS 1-4

DEMONS OF FIRE & NIGHT

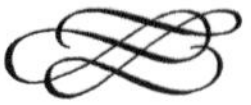

C.N. CRAWFORD

COREY PRESS INC

C.N. CRAWFORD

SHADOWS
&
FLAME
SERIES

INFERNAL MAGIC

A DEMONS OF FIRE AND NIGHT NOVEL

CHAPTER 1

If Ursula had been able to plan her eighteenth birthday, the evening would be going very differently. First, she wouldn't be working in a nightclub owned by her ex. Second, she wouldn't have this weird fever burning her cheeks, setting her nerves on edge—like she was blazing from the inside out. And third, she definitely wouldn't be pushing through an unruly crowd to break up a fight between two hammered university students.

In an ideal world, she'd have called in sick and taken the whole night off. Of course, in an ideal world, she wouldn't be worrying about the rent that was due in two days.

"Excuse me!" She said, squeezing between a gawking couple, arms raised. *That shows authority, right?*

Two young men squared off on the dance floor, bathed in District 5's pulsing orange and pink lights. A pounding bass rumbled through the room.

Part of her wanted to let these two knobs stab each other with broken bottles, but she had a mission tonight, fever or not. She was going to prove to the world that she had her life together, that she was a valuable asset to the club—or at least, she was going to prove it to her ex. Granted, Rufus was an idiot, but he was her boss and she was hanging on to this job by a thread.

A small crowd gathered around the potential brawlers, and she tried to suss out the bigger threat—possibly the red-faced giant who swayed in place. His platinum hair, bushy eyebrows, and full lips gave him the appearance of a Muppet—a murderous one who might crush someone with his giant, meaty hands.

"I told you to watch where you step. You scuffed my shoe!" The Muppet screamed, a vein popping in his forehead. "Arsehole!"

His opponent, a stocky guy with a bushy beard, jabbed a stubby finger. His voice boomed over the music. "Oh, is that what I am, you fat-faced donkey?"

Oh, good. A totally rational argument over a scuffed shoe. Sweat beaded on Ursula's skin, and she wiped the back of her hand over her forehead. God, it was hot in here. She couldn't be the only one who felt like the room was on fire. Maybe that was what was making these guys act like lunatics.

The two drunks circled each other, and Ursula squeezed between them, ignoring the heat burning through her. "Everyone take a step back," she said, trying to project as much authority as possible.

Muppet was definitely the real threat here. He sloshed the remnants of his beer from his pint glass, baring his teeth. "You know your girlfriend still wants me," he growled at Stubby.

Of course. It didn't matter if the argument was about shoes or football, every bar brawl came down to one thing: a fight over some girl. Whatever the case, no one was civilized after five pints of Bombardier.

Stubby grinned. "She said you only lasted for two—"

"Okay!" Ursula cut in, holding up her hands. "Seems like you've both—"

The tall one lunged past her, trying to smash his pint glass over Stubby's head. With a reflex so fast it shocked even her, Ursula's hand shot out, gripping the man's wrist. Warm beer splashed all over her white shirt. *Bollocks. Now I'm getting really annoyed.*

And, incidentally, so was the giant Muppet. He clawed at the shorter man. "I'll rip your hairy face off and shove it up your arse."

Ursula needed to get control—now. And despite her petite size, she had one thing on her side: a surprising amount of physical strength.

Still gripping Muppet's wrist, she twisted his arm behind his back, wrenching it up high and forcing him over.

"Get off me!" He shrieked. "Stupid bitch!"

Not the B-word. It was one of those insults that really burned her up, and she was already way too hot. In fact, her body felt like some kind of inferno, and she could think of nothing but white hot flames.

"She's burning me!" Muppet shrieked.

Her attention jolted to his shirt—which, incidentally, was on fire. *What the hell?*

Panicking, she released him. The man threw himself to the ground, frantically rolling to put out the flames. Within moments, a girl doused him with a pitcher of water, and the air filled with the scent of burnt cotton.

Ursula stumbled back, staring at her hands. Was it just her mind, or were grey tendrils of smoke curling from her fingertips? *This fever must be rattling my brain.* She really needed to go home and lie on the sofa.

She clenched her fists, trying to ignore the rising panic. She stood in the middle of Rufus's club, her shirt soaked in beer, having lit a customer on fire. Her plans to prove her worth to her boss had back-fired just a bit.

Muppet rose, his hands shaking, and pulled out his mobile phone. "I'm calling the police."

Her pulse raced. *Time for damage control, Ursula.* "I'm very sorry about the fire. It was a complete accident."

Just as Muppet put the cell phone to his ear, another man stepped forward—someone she hadn't even noticed before, though she had no idea how she'd missed him.

At the sight of him, a shiver crawled up her spine. If she'd thought Muppet looked aggressive, this guy screamed pure malice. It wasn't his appearance: rich chestnut hair, sharp cheekbones, and perfect lips that could charm the knickers off a nun. No, it was the feral way he moved, and his piercing green eyes that bored right into her soul when he slid a glance her way.

His gaze flicked to Muppet. "I don't really think that's necessary." He spoke in a commanding voice, his accent posh as hell. "Give me your phone, and take your friend to another bar."

Wordlessly, the Muppet handed over his phone, and the green-eyed stranger pocketed it. Muppet and Stubby grasped each other's arms, staggering toward the exit.

A small crowd still stood, gaping at the stranger as he closed his eyes, muttering. As he spoke, goose bumps rose on Ursula's flesh, and the hair on the back of her neck stood on end. *What the hell is he doing?*

Whatever it was, the crowd seemed to lose interest, and when he opened his eyes again, the onlookers had drifted back to their tables.

Ursula stared at him, stunned. In the past few months, there had been rumors about witches in London, but... *No, that's insane.*

Whatever this stranger's secret was, his stunning physique now drew her eyes. A bespoke suit accentuated an athletic body, and a gold watch flashed on his wrist. *Definitely rich.* The way he had spoken wasn't just confident; he was entitled, too. Probably a total knob.

Still, he'd helped her out, so it wasn't like she was going to complain.

He turned to her, green eyes lingering on her drenched T-shirt. "You work here?"

"Yes." Despite her fever, she shivered again. There really was something *lethal* in those eyes.

"I'll have two fingers of the Glenlivet 21. Neat. A glass of water on the side."

Irritation simmered. Apparently, no one had ever taught him to say please. But it was more than just annoyance that unnerved her. There was something *strange* about him. *Am I losing my mind, or do his movements seem... otherwordly?*

She was losing her mind. That was the only explanation. She had a fever, and she was rattled by... whatever the hell had just happened.

She cocked her hip. "Well, since you just bailed me out, I guess I won't insist that you say please."

He stared at her, his lips a thin line.

Heading back to the bar, she cringed. She shouldn't have said that, but something about him really irked her—probably the rich-boy attitude that reminded her of Rufus.

This club was just one of the ways her ex invested his father's money. He was studying business at University College London, planning to build himself some kind of financial empire—a testament to his genius, of course. Frankly, she was getting a little sick of rich people thinking they were better than everyone else just because they'd been born lucky.

Ursula slipped behind the bar, reaching up for the Glenlivet. When she turned to pour the drink, he'd taken a seat.

She filled the tumbler with two fingers of Scotch and slid it over, glancing at the fifty-pound note he'd left on the bar. She didn't often see fifty-pound notes, but this guy probably had plenty. In fact, she could imagine him lighting them on fire in front of a homeless person for a laugh.

Then again, maybe she wasn't in any position to accuse others of pyromania. The bar smelled of burnt Muppet, and her stomach was still turning flips from the whole debacle. *What in God's name happened? Hell of a birthday.*

"What's your name?" the stranger asked, his deep voice resonating.

His intent gaze made her pulse race, but she needed to get a grip and focus on trying to salvage her job. "Ursula."

He unnerved her, and she could feel her chest flushing.

She turned, catching a brief glance of herself in the mirror with a shiver of distaste. Even on a shoestring budget, Ursula normally prided herself on her sense of style. Tonight, she'd chosen a white shirt with tight maroon trousers that could *almost* pass for leather. She'd accessorized with her favorite boots and a chunky black bracelet. But the look wasn't working out so well right now. Her ginger hair was a mess, and her soaked shirt clung to her body, showing off the pink bra underneath. Only her black eyeliner remained in place.

With any luck, she'd get the chance to clean herself up before Rufus saw her again. Otherwise, it would only confirm every terrible thing he'd said about her when he'd dumped her.

From behind, the stranger said, "Miss?"

She spun around. "Yes?"

"Pour yourself a drink, on me. It is, after all, your first night at the legal drinking age."

Her blood went cold. *How the hell does he know that?*

Just as she was stammering out a response, she caught sight of Rufus striding up behind him, a stormy look on his face. Her ex leaned on the bar, immaculate in a pressed white shirt.

"Ursula," he said. "We need to talk about what just happened."

CHAPTER 2

"In my office. Now." Rufus inclined his head toward an open door behind the bar, his face pink with rage.

Flinching at his demanding tone, Ursula followed him through the door. She shoved her hand into her pocket, gripping her good luck charm —a smooth, white stone. Right now, it was doing fuck-all in the luck department, but touching it had become a nervous habit.

She plopped down in a chair. It wasn't much of an office. Since it was a former storage closet, there was only room for the bare essentials: a dingy desk and two chairs. Rufus took a seat behind the desk.

The room was oppressive—either the lack of windows or the wanker behind the desk. *Probably both.*

Rufus pushed his blond hair back, appraising her with cool, blue eyes. Maybe his Nordic good looks had somehow fooled her into overlooking his serious personality problem.

"What the hell happened out there?" he snapped. "We could get sued. *I* could get sued."

"There was a fight, and I was just trying to calm them down. That's all."

"By lighting a man on fire?"

The fever blazed behind her temples. She *really* should have stayed at home tonight. "I don't know how…" She trailed off. She had no clue what had happened. "One second, I was trying to stop him from hitting some guy, and the next thing I knew, his shirt was on fire."

"Was he smoking a cigarette?" Rufus narrowed his eyes. "Were *you* smoking?"

"Neither of us were smoking, as far as I know. I just looked down at my hand, and it looked—hot." No idea why she'd said that last part. She realized it made her sound insane, and quickly corrected herself. "He probably *was* smoking, now that you mention it."

"Did you say your hand was *hot*?" He winced. "You do realize what you could be accused of?"

Witchcraft. He was talking about witchcraft.

It would have sounded completely crazy a few months ago, but the world had changed, ever since a group of mysterious men had been caught on American TV slaughtering people in a Boston park, before disappearing into thin air in a whirl of demonic activity. Now half of London was talking about witches and magic. For her part, Ursula had no idea how they'd disappeared, but she liked to believe *magic* wasn't the culprit. There was enough shit to worry about without adding in a supernatural threat.

She loosed a sigh. "Look, all I said was my hand was hot. I have a fever. You know, I think I should go home."

Rufus leaned back in his chair. "It's not as crazy as you might think. Madeleine knows all about witches. She's been doing a lot of research since the attacks. She works with a professor at UCL."

"I'm not a witch, for God's sake. I don't even believe in them. And who is Madeleine?" His new girlfriend, no doubt. Poor lamb had no idea what she was in for.

"Never mind that." He gave her his puppy-dog eyes. "Oh, Urse. Why is it so hard for you to get things right? Why do you always feel the need to mess everything up?"

Somehow when he was trying to be nice it was worse than when he was just an arsehole. "That's what you think of me? That I can never get anything right?"

For a moment, he pressed his lips into a thin line. "You always look so lovely, and that's an asset in my club, though tonight you haven't even managed that. You've achieved remarkably little with your life. You never managed to get into uni. You nearly got evicted last month. Again."

She gritted her teeth. "We talked about this when you dumped me, and I told you, those are both the kinds of things that happen when you've got no money."

He leaned over his desk. "It's just that you've got no plan for success. No goals. I've been building an empire, investing money—"

"Your *father's* money." *Shit.* She shouldn't have said that out loud. It would hit a nerve, and that wasn't good for her employment prospects.

"Whatever," he snapped, cheeks reddening again. "I'm building *something*. Just because you were famous once, you think you've made it." He stood, throwing his shoulders back. "Honestly, you're just a sad cow who won't make anything of your life."

It took all of Ursula's willpower not to slap his smug face. Rufus had brought up that tidbit up all the time when they were dating, as if her former celebrity status was some kind of personal affront to him.

"I never asked for my fifteen minutes of fame. The press showed up as soon as they found me. And besides, after that fourteen-year-old gave birth to sextuplets, I was pretty much forgotten." She was desperate to tell him to sod off and head home, but she needed this bloody job.

A knock on the door interrupted their conversation.

"Rufus, honey? Are you in there?" A neatly-coiffed blonde poked her head in, smiling for only an instant until her eyes landed on Ursula. "What are you two up to?"

Rufus blinked. "I... I didn't know you were coming by now, Madeleine."

"The lecturer let us out early." She eyed Ursula warily, running a hand over a pink silk blouse. A week's wages right there—and Ursula couldn't even imagine how much her fat diamond earrings cost.

Rufus cleared his throat. "Madeleine is my girlfriend, Ursula. She's studying mythological history and cryptozoology. She's very accomplished."

"That sounds really *interesting*," said Ursula, trying—and failing—to mask her irritation. "Looks like it's time for me to go."

Madeleine's eyes lingered over Ursula's soaked shirt. "Did something happen?"

"Beer accident," said Ursula. It was all the explanation she needed.

Madeleine's hand flew to her throat. "Oh. Well, I stopped by so you could escort me home, honey. You don't know what sort of creatures are lurking on London's streets these days. Professor Stoughton said the city's been *filled* with magical activity in the past few months. Witches, demons, all sorts of horrible things. He has a meter to measure it." Madeleine blocked the exit, her voice laced with jealousy. "What *were* you two talking about, anyway?"

"I was discussing Ursula's future here," said Rufus.

"Oh?" Madeleine plastered on a saccharine smile. "There's a future?"

"Well, that's just it," said Rufus. "I simply can't keep someone employed who lights people on fire. It's a liability."

Ursula could feel herself heating up again, and the fever that had been quietly throbbing behind her temples turned into a dull roar. She held onto the door frame for support.

"Well, chin up. I'm sure you'll be able to find another job," said Madeleine, barely containing her glee. "It'll be exciting. A new adventure." She didn't move from the doorframe, obviously savoring the moment.

Ursula felt her temper flare, and she gripped the wood by Madeleine's side. "Are you going to let me leave? Or do you plan to keep blocking the door all night?"

Madeleine gasped, jumping back. She gaped in horror at Ursula's hand —and the smoke that curled from beneath Ursula's fingers.

"Oh my God! What did you do to the door?" Her eyes froze on Ursula's face, and she whispered one word: *"Witch."*

CHAPTER 3

$\mathcal{U}$rsula skulked along Bow Road, her hands jammed in the pockets of her leopard-print coat, fingers curled up for warmth. With the beer-drenched shirt plastered to her skin, the winter air was brutally cold. At least her feet were warm in her boots, though she'd probably have to sell them soon for cash. She had only one more paycheck coming in, and it wouldn't cover the rent that was due in two days.

Disappointment crushed her. If she didn't figure something out, she'd be homeless soon, sleeping on the streets through the freezing winter. How long, exactly, did it take for a landlord to evict someone? And how long would it take for another homeless person to rob her of her leopard-print coat?

A biting wind nipped at her ears. She could have used a bit more of that fever now. Skint and unemployed, she'd chosen to walk from Brick Lane back to Bow—nearly two miles. She wasn't spending the last of her money on a bus. And, more importantly, it had given her time to think. Well, time to stew, really. Her chest ached with a familiar hollow feeling.

She could have done without meeting Madeleine, with her beautifully coiffed blond hair, French-manicured nails, and all the letters she'd have after her name when she graduated.

Ursula shivered. *My eighteenth birthday.* This should have been a night for a celebration, but apart from her flatmate she hardly had any friends left. After her breakup with Rufus, he seemed to have taken her whole clique with him—probably because he could lavish them with champagne and pick up the tabs at fancy restaurants.

Or maybe it was just like Rufus had always said: she wasn't very good with people.

She pulled her coat tighter as she passed the warm lights of a pub, wishing she'd had the foresight to wear a scarf. Break-up aside, she'd been expecting something a little more momentous for her eighteenth birthday. This was the night something big was supposed to happen—she just had no idea what.

Apart from her birthday, there weren't many things Ursula knew about herself. Her background was so outlandish, it was like something out of a soap opera: a rare case of amnesia that had rendered her childhood a complete blank slate. There was simply nothing in her memory before the age of fifteen.

What she knew for certain was that a few years ago she'd turned up in a burnt-out church, with a strange, triangular scar on her shoulder and a piece of paper in her pocket. The paper had read:

On your 18th birthday,
March 15, 2016,
ask for a trial.
- Ursula (You)

SHE'D STARTED to think of herself as two people: Former Ursula and New Ursula. Former Ursula was a complete mystery, and her one link to Former Ursula was the white stone in her pocket, its surface now worn smooth from constant rubbing. It was a strange little anchor to her old life.

Occasionally, glimpses of a bygone life appeared in her dreams: fields of wild thyme and orchids, skylarks and adders. She had no idea what it meant, except that she'd probably grown up in the countryside.

Here she was, waiting for her life to change by some sort of magic on her eighteenth birthday, but that was obviously a sad joke. At what point in this disaster of a day was she supposed to have asked for a trial? On the crowded bus she took to work, burning with a fever? Midway through losing her job? Or while meeting Rufus's new girlfriend? The whole day had been a series of ordeals, one trial after another, but none of them particularly momentous.

It didn't matter. She'd been gradually losing faith in the idea that her fortunes would magically turn around, that someone or something would waltz into her miserable life bearing a gift of a diamond or a secret bank account.

And now, she had to figure out how to save herself from complete destitution.

She shivered, hugging herself tighter. A normal life would be nice: a family and a steady income. Maybe some childhood memories, and hands that didn't spontaneously ignite.

She stalked past a row of crooked Victorian homes, warmly lit from within. She didn't even want to think about what had happened with her hands. Madeleine had called her a *witch*, for crying out loud. Maybe there *was* a trial in her future.

Her door came into view—the one she could always pick out from the rows of identical houses, by the chipped red paint on the doorframe. She jammed her key into the lock. *Thank God I'm home.*

She stepped inside, hoping to hear a welcoming *Hello* from her flat-mate Katie, but the flat was as dark and quiet as a grave. She flicked the switch by the door, but the lights didn't turn on. *Shit.* The electric key must have run out. It would remain dark and cold until she got to the shop tomorrow. She shook her head. Maybe the point of the note was that her whole life was a trial.

Sighing with frustration, she steadied her hand along the wall as she crept down the carpeted stairs.

It wasn't a stunning place—a one-bedroom basement flat—but it was home nonetheless. Katie had the bedroom, since she paid more in rent, and Ursula slept in the living room, tidying up an air mattress every morning. With Katie's help, she'd brightened up the woodchip wallpaper with canary-yellow paint and some posters of wildflowers—forget-me-nots and golden aster—that reminded her of her most soothing dreams.

Ursula pulled out her phone, flicking open a text from Katie.

Happy Birthday Ursula! I'm coming home soon. Let's go out.

A pit opened in her stomach. She was going to have to tell Katie about her little rent problem. She dropped her phone on the sofa, then peeled off her leopard-print coat and the beer-soaked shirt and bra, still shivering, before yanking a black shirt and bra off the drying rack. *Might as well have an outfit to match my mood.*

She slipped into her dry clothes, then crossed to the kitchen, a cupboard-sized space with a tiny vinyl countertop. As she flipped open the blinds, she let a little light in from the streetlamp outside. Crouching before a kitchen drawer, she rifled around for a box of matches.

After lighting two tea candles by the stove, she felt her stomach rumble. When was the last time she'd eaten?

Yanking open the fridge door, she grabbed the last smear of butter. *Bread and butter for dinner.*

Just as she reached for the loaf of bread, the hair on her neck prickled. Someone was watching her. She could always tell when she was being observed. And right now, someone was most definitely lurking in the shadows of her tiny flat.

Slowly, she turned, and her heart nearly leapt from her chest. Moving silently through the living room was a broad-shouldered man, his face hidden in the gloom. Probably her flatmate's latest conquest, but better safe than sorry. She slid open the knife drawer.

Carefully, so as not to alarm the stranger, she gripped a knife's hilt, her hand hidden in the drawer.

The man prowled closer, his movements smooth and almost inhuman.

Ice licked up her spine. Just outside the doorframe, the stranger paused in the shadows.

She swallowed. "Who's there?"

His green eyes seemed to glow in the dark, and the word *witch* flitted through her mind.

"My name is Kester." His deep voice slid through her bones.

When he stepped into the flickering candlelight, she gasped in recognition. Rich chestnut hair, sharp cheekbones, and perfect lips. The hot bloke from the club. *What the hell is he doing here?*

Cold fear tightened her chest. Ursula tightened her fingers around the knife's hilt. "You followed me." A tendril of horror curled around her heart. "Did you just watch me take off my shirt?"

"I averted my eyes. I'm not here to disturb you. I'm just here for your signature." He raised his arms over his head, holding on to the door frame. Candlelight flickered over his golden skin, dancing in his green eyes. Despite his beauty, there was something predatory in the way he stared at her, like he was about to devour her.

"Signature? What are you on about?" Any fast movements, and she'd fling the knife at him. "If you don't leave now, I'll call the police." She couldn't call the police, since she'd just chucked her phone across the room, but he didn't need to know that.

His gaze slid over her, as if he were memorizing her. "I won't linger any longer than you want. I just need you to sign the contract. You must have been expecting me."

"What contract?" Slowly, she lifted the knife in front of her. Only instead of looking at the tip of a blade, she was staring at the soft silicone paddle of a spatula. *Bloody hell.*

He smiled, and white teeth gleamed in the candlelight. "If you want to make me pancakes first, I won't object."

"I don't have the ingredients," she said lamely.

Where are the kitchen knives? They must be dirty. If she could inch over to the sink, she could get a proper blade, one with an edge that could slash his throat.

"Look, I can see you're having a bad night. And I'd truly love to help you." Dropping his arms from the doorframe, he widened his eyes, all sincerity. "But you committed yourself years ago, and it's your eighteenth birthday. All you need to do is sign the contract, and I'll be on my way."

There it was again. How did he know it was her birthday? She didn't know him. Hell, she didn't know anyone remotely like him. There was a strange edge to his plummy voice, one that reeked of old money and private clubs with three-hundred-year-old mahogany bars. Not exactly Ursula's sort of crowd.

She eyed the stove to her right. A dirty cast-iron pan rested on the nearest burner. Perfect for frying sausages, or for smashing skulls, depending on the occasion.

"Ursula. You don't need to be scared," he soothed, his emerald eyes drinking her in. "I'm not here to hurt you."

If he weren't such an obvious nutter, the guy would be seriously seductive. She laid the spatula down on the countertop with feigned casualness. "Look, I've had an awful day. I'm tired, and I want to finish my bread and go out for one little drink with my flatmate, who will be here any minute." She paused. "And she's huge, by the way, and lethal. I'm sure you've got somewhere better to be. I'm advising you to leave me alone. I can be a little... unpredictable when I'm irritated, and I wouldn't want you getting hurt."

He cocked an eyebrow. "Unpredictable? Sounds exciting. But I'm afraid I cannot leave until I get your signature. For Emerazel. Then I'll leave. Unless you want me to stay to attend to your other needs, of course."

"I have no idea who *Emerazel* is. But if you're here because you think I owe you something for helping me out at the club, that's not going to happen. I don't have anything. I can't afford electricity. I can't afford *socks*. My boyfriend just dumped me last week, and then fired me. So on top of all the other shit, I'm unemployed. I'm eating sodding bread and butter for dinner on my eighteenth birthday. So if you're planning on robbing me, have a wonderful time. Take the spatula. Take my threadbare socks. Take the moldy shower curtain. Whatever you desire." She could feel her cheeks burning as anger flooded her. "Then fuck right off."

"I'm not here about the club, and I'm not here to rob you."

"So what are you? Some sort of pervert?" Her body grew hot, her pulse quickening. Pure strength surged through her muscles, and she wanted to break something. If he thought he was going to get his hands on her, she would choke the life out of him.

He opened his palms, eyes widening, all innocence. "Ursula, you're not listening. I'm not here to hurt you. I'm here about that triangular mark you carved somewhere on yourself, the one that gives you the fire. You *do* understand the bargain you made, don't you?"

My scar. So he did see me without my shirt on. There was no air left in the room. "You said you looked away."

"I did. Emerazel sent me, and that's how I know you have a scar. You owe her your signature. It's fine. There's nothing to panic about," he murmured, stepping closer, his voice a dangerous caress. "Everything will be fine, Ursula."

She shook her head. Who was this Emerazel he kept talking about? She had no idea where the scar had come from, or what it meant. All she knew was that only stalkers and serial killers followed women home from work.

Her heart raced faster, adrenaline surging. For some reason she wanted to believe him, but he'd trapped her in her own kitchen. If there was one thing she hated, it was being trapped. She balled her hands into fists, overcome by the need to fight.

She pulled back her arm for a punch, but with a lightning-fast motion, he clamped his hand on her wrist, fingers piercing her flesh. *Not fingers,* she realized with growing terror. *Claws. He has claws. What the fuck?*

Her blood roared in her ears, and she could feel fire run through her, hot and molten. With her free arm, she grasped his shoulder. Her palm glowed. Somehow, her body knew what it was doing—knew how to burn him—and she waited to hear him cry out in pain.

Instead, he stared deep into her eyes. No longer a bright green, his irises now blazed a deep, smoldering red. Terror ripped her mind apart. *What the hell is going on?*

His gaze trailed over her body. "Ursula, my dear. There's no need for fighting. Emerazel's power won't burn me," he purred in a velvety tone. But underneath the softness, there was an edge to his voice—a sharp command. Kester was used to getting what he wanted. "The goddess's fire runs in my veins just as it does in yours. You can't fight me."

His voice was husky, a lethal lullaby. His beautiful gaze hypnotized her, rooting her in place.

A part of her felt tempted to do whatever he wanted just to make him happy. "What do you need me to do?" She rasped, half hating herself as she said it. What was happening to her?

"I'm not here to hurt you." He leaned in closer and whispered, his breath caressing her ear. "Sign," he commanded.

He seemed so sure of himself. Her hand relaxed on his shoulder, and she stared into his fiery eyes. She should be terrified of those preternatural flames, but something about his masculine scent and his beautiful lips was intoxicating. *But the strange fire in his eyes... Is that magic? Do I care?*

His claws retracting, Kester reached into the pocket of his trousers and pulled out a fountain pen the color of bone. Her gaze landed on a tiny symbol carved into the pen—an encircled triangle, just like her scar.

Holding her gaze, Kester popped off the cap, revealing a razor-sharp nib, and gripped her palm. "This will only hurt for a moment," he said, his voice seducing her, sliding over her skin.

As she stared into his beautiful eyes, he pressed the pen into her hand. A sharp pain pulled her attention down, and she watched as the point depressed her skin. Something in the back of her mind rebelled at this imposition. He pushed the nib further, into her flesh, and she snapped out of the spell he'd woven. *What was I thinking, mooning over this posh twat?*

"Ow!" She yanked her arm backward, gripping the cut. Blood dripped between her fingers.

"Apologies for that, Ursula." A seductive smile played over his lips, but she wasn't falling for his act anymore.

He produced a small, yellowed piece of parchment from his other pocket, pushing it toward her along with the blood-inked pen. "Please. I need you to sign."

Her hand throbbed, and she shook it, trying to focus her thoughts. Everything about this man was alluring, but right now only one angry thought burned in her mind: *This entitled wanker thinks he can get whatever he wants. Just like Rufus.*

She blinked, trying to clear her mind. Of *course* she shouldn't trust the psycho who'd stalked her into her kitchen. And did he want her soul? She wasn't signing that away. She had no idea what a soul was for, or even if it was real, but she didn't want to find out what happened when you gave one away.

She glanced down at the parchment, at the faded beige writing. Only a few words were legible in the candlelight, and though the language wasn't English, the looping letters looked strangely familiar. She almost had the sense that if she concentrated hard enough, she could read it. In fact, she could translate a few of the words: *soul, contract, eternal.* The longer she looked at it, the clearer the words became.

"What's this language?"

"Angelic."

"What?" She glared up at the towering stranger. "What happens if I sign it?"

"You've really never been told this?" He seemed genuinely curious. "How did you come to carve yourself in the first place if you don't know who Emerazel is?"

"I have no idea." She nodded at the parchment. "It says something about an eternal contract."

His brow shot up. "You can *read* this?"

"Yes. Don't ask me how. Is this some sort of pact with the devil?"

He exhaled slowly, pinching the bridge of his nose as though marshaling an extreme amount of patience. "No. There is no devil." He gazed up again, a charming smile playing about his lips. "I understand this must be confusing for you. I will leave you as soon as you do what I ask."

She crossed her arms. "Look, I have a little memory problem. I don't know anything about the first fifteen years of my life. You may have heard of me; it was all over the news after I turned up in a burning church in London. The tabloids called me the Mystery Girl." Wherever the scar had come from, that was a secret only Former Ursula could unravel. Not the clueless, unemployed girl trying to eat bread and butter for dinner.

"Mystery Girl? Never heard of you." He studied her carefully, the candlelight flickering over his smooth, golden skin. "I can tell you this. Emerazel is not the devil. Some mortals call her that, but she is a goddess. Her domain is the volcanic magma in the center of the earth and, when angered, she destroys cities. She is neither good nor evil. She is love, power, rage, and light. You cannot fight her. You cannot win this." All signs of softness left his face, and his gaze grew fierce, almost feral. "Do not fight her, and do not fight me. You will not win."

The hair rose on the back of her neck. "Right. According to the crazy bloke who followed me home and broke into my house, I owe my soul to an all-powerful goddess of rage and power." She clamped her hands on her hips, trying to ignore the chill running up her spine. "I'm not signing your stupid paper."

"That's really a shame." Kester tilted his head, almost apologetic. "Then I must reap your soul for Emerazel now."

Ursula forced a smile onto her face. "Whatever that means, it's not happening either." She grabbed the tea candles from the counter, flicking the hot wax in his face.

Kester hardly flinched.

Her panic rising, she grabbed the cast-iron skillet and swung for his head. He reached up to block it, and it slammed against his arm with a crunch. He emitted a low, inhuman growl that rumbled through her gut. As he glared at her, eyes blazing bright green, his forearm swung down at an awkward angle, a mangled mess that should have had him screaming in agony.

She steadied her breath. "I'm not signing your devil's pact tonight. I don't care if you work for Satan, or Emerazel, or if you've escaped from a psychiatric hospital. I'm not giving up my soul. Whoever you are, you need to leave now before I shatter your skull."

Kester's eyes slid to his arm, and he whispered softly—words at once strange and familiar. A chill licked up Ursula's spine.

She stared as Kester's arm straightened with a cracking sound. With the arm fully repaired, he raised his hand again, wiggling his fingers.

Her heart skipped a beat, and the word *demon* rang in her head again.

"That really hurt." His eyes, now the color of blood, met hers.

Her mind screamed, *Not human!*

He unleashed a low growl that trembled over her skin, and she became keenly aware of each of her breaths.

He lunged for her. Instantly, she brought her knee up and into his chest, redirecting his momentum into the cabinets next to the kitchen counter. Wood splintered with the impact.

He started to stand, but she kicked him in the head. Her boot shattered his nose, spraying blood on the kitchen tile. He fell back holding his face.

"Ursula," he purred, slowly getting to his feet. His eyes wild, he unleashed a wicked set of claws from his fingertips, and Ursula's mind screamed with panic. He pressed the end of the pen, and a thin blade protruded from one end. "You should have signed."

He moved so fast she didn't have time to react before he'd pinned her against the wall, gripping her wrists in one hand. The tips of his claws tore her skin, and a low growl escaped his throat, rumbling through her core.

His teeth—his fangs—lengthened, and he pressed in closer, leaving no room for her to kick him. Cold fear stole her breath as she struggled to free her wrists, but this freak was terrifyingly strong. *What is he?*

He leaned in closer, his breath warming her skin. His eyes roamed down her body, and candlelight flickered off his pen's sharp blade. "It's a shame you're going to make me do this. There's something about you I like."

She tried to yank her wrists free. "You don't have to do anything. You can just leave me alone." She could hardly breathe. This was it—the last few moments of her life. *What do I say about a sad life like mine?* She was nothing—a complete loser. No family, no job, no money, no future. Her whole life was just a name, a date, and a piece of paper...

A trial.

Ursula, you idiot.

"I request a trial," she breathed into his neck.

Surprise flickered across his beautiful features, and his fangs retracted. "What did you say?"

"A trial," she said more firmly.

Still pinning her to the wall, he clenched his jaw. "You've *got* to be kidding me." His eyes returned to their emerald green color, and he began muttering in that strange language again. His words transfixed her, soothing her racing heart. A strange sense of calm flooded her body, until her world began to dim.

CHAPTER 4

A humming noise woke Ursula, and she cracked open her eyes. The sound grew louder as she pulled herself out of the dense fog of sleep. Her head throbbed, dulling her senses, but there was movement around her—flashes of blue and white in the darkness. For a moment, she wondered if this was the road to the afterlife, but the shooting pain behind her eyes suggested she hadn't yet shuffled off this mortal coil.

When her pupils focused, she saw Kester sitting next to her, his face now clear of blood and his nose unbroken. His hands gripped a steering wheel. *Shit shit shit.*

The only possible explanation for his rapid healing was that... she hesitated to even think it. Could it be that the words he'd whispered had repaired his arm, fixed his broken nose? Could it have been magic?

If that were the case—if he could cast spells—she didn't even want to think about what else he could do. She clamped her eyes shut again, trying to regain control. *No. Magic isn't real.* She'd had a fever tonight, and a psycho had kidnapped her.

Unfortunately, that thought wasn't reassuring either.

Kester focused on the road ahead. The radio blared pop music, and the sound rattled through her throbbing skull. Blue road signs flashed by on the shoulder. *The M4.*

On the plus side, she was alive. On the down side, she'd been kidnapped by a man who'd tried to claim her soul. She didn't know what that meant, but there was a strong chance it involved murder.

"Where are we going?" she managed.

Lazily, his gaze flicked to hers. "You requested a trial, though I have no idea how you knew to ask for that, since you know literally nothing else."

"It was on a note I'd written to myself." She glanced at her right hand, handcuffed to the passenger door handle. "Where does the trial happen? And what is it, exactly?"

"Outside of London."

"Thanks for narrowing it down." *Okay, so he's not going to be helpful with details. Why would he be, if he's about to murder me?* "My flatmate, Katie, is going to be worried about me. She's going to call the police."

"We'll sort that out later."

She glanced at the handcuff again. It wasn't an ordinary manacle. It almost looked like a golden circle of light trapping her wrist. It almost looked like... *magic.* The thought curdled her stomach.

Kester's glowing eyes, her own fire powers, the mysterious attacks, the healing spell, the handcuffs made of light... It was getting a little harder to convince herself that magic wasn't real, and yet she *really* didn't want to be a part of this madness. She could barely cope with her normal life. *Please let me get back to my poverty and unemployment.*

Even though the handcuff didn't burn her, the circle of light held her wrist in a sort of force field. The unnatural sight of it tightened her chest, filling her with a sense of dread. If things like this existed—along with glowing eyes and flaming hands—what *else* didn't she know about the world? She swallowed hard, still trying to free her wrist. "What the hell is this?"

"I can't have you jumping out the door while I'm driving. You're unpredictable, as you so helpfully informed me earlier."

She felt the now-familiar heat and rage begin to simmer insider her, as if her body knew what it was doing. She wanted to burn this thing off of her.

"You won't be able to melt it." Kester continued, his voice bland. "It's immune to hellfire."

If she had to be manacled to get her to this trial, maybe it wasn't something she really wanted after all. Now that she thought about it, trials weren't generally fun events. The phrase "trial by fire" popped into her mind, and she felt a sudden desperation to rip herself free from the car, to tumble into the road and sprint through the dark fields. Suddenly, the impending homelessness she'd been fretting about earlier no longer seemed as daunting as this nightmare.

She glared at him, her pulse racing faster. "Can you at least tell me if I'll get to keep my soul?"

"Maybe. Maybe not. It depends how you do."

Great. With her heart thrumming, she scanned the car's interior, searching for weapons. It was upholstered in deep red leather, intermixed with chrome and instruments the color of gunmetal. The GPS was off, but Ursula could see that the speedometer read 160 kilometers per hour. They were flying down the M4. Even if she managed to free herself, her body would shatter when she flung herself from the car.

"Aren't you going a bit fast?" she asked, her mouth dry.

"We're in a hurry. Besides this is a Lotus. It's not made for driving slow."

Another pop song blared on the radio—Hugo Modes, warbling in a falsetto... The sound grated, the banality of the music such a sharp contrast to her rising fear. The band crooned on, and she could hardly think straight.

But maybe a sense of normalcy could save her right now. Maybe if she got Kester to see her as a person instead of just his victim, he'd empathize with her. Wasn't that what they told the parents of children who'd been kidnapped? Show the human side, tug on the heart strings.

She had the strangest feeling that Kester didn't *have* a human side, but it was worth a shot. She'd only just turned eighteen, and she wasn't ready to die before she'd had the chance to do anything with her life. She took a steadying breath. "Hugo Modes. What's his band called? The Four Points?" She nodded at the radio, trying to keep her voice steady. "I suppose you like boy bands."

"I wouldn't call them a boy band," he snapped. "They play their own instruments."

She tightened her fists so hard her nails pierced her flesh. *This isn't going to work. I can't make small talk about boy bands when I'm about to be murdered.* She seethed with hot anger. She didn't give a shit about the Four Points. What she cared about was that she'd been kidnapped against her will, and she wanted to smash Kester's stupid rich-boy face into the pavement. So maybe her life was pathetic, but she wasn't ready to give up on it. "What the fuck am I doing here?" she shouted in desperation.

Kester let out a low whistle. "You're not really a people person, are you?"

"I'm handcuffed to the door of a car," she snapped. "Don't expect me to be cheerful about it. You broke into my house in the middle of my dinner, attacked me, and abducted me." She gave the manacle one last tug, but it wouldn't budge.

"That was seriously your birthday dinner? Eating bread and butter in a hovel?" He arched a sympathetic eyebrow. "That's just sad. Frankly, I'm doing you a favor. Assuming you survive."

She clenched her jaw, trying to calm herself, and turned to look out the window. *Don't lose your head, Ursula.*

The landscape flew by—a blur of grey branches and patches of snow. Her breath frosted against the window.

A part of her was terrified, but another part knew she'd make it out of this. Her will to survive was too strong. Less than three years had passed since the firefighters had discovered her in the church. That meant she had less than three years of memories—and the most vivid in her mind right now was Rufus, telling her she would never make anything of her life. She couldn't die before she proved him wrong.

CHAPTER 5

*A*fter turning off the M4, they barreled down an empty one-lane road lined with hedgerows. At last, the car slowed, and they turned into a small driveway. A gate stood before them, flanked by stone columns. To the right, tufts of frozen vegetation dotted brown fields stretching out into the darkness.

Isolated, secluded, and alone with a complete nutter. Former Ursula—or F.U., as Ursula was now thinking of her prior self—had a lot to answer for.

She glanced out the driver's window at a small hill with a flattened top. Bare trees protruded from it, like skeletal hands clawing out of graves. She stiffened. The look of this place turned her blood to ice.

Kester turned off the ignition and stepped out of the car, walking around to the back. Ursula watched him, her pulse racing as he rummaged through the boot. Panic rising, she yanked on the manacle, but her hand remained stuck. *He's going to pull out a gun and blow my head off.*

After yanking out a dark grey jacket, he crossed toward Ursula's door, pulling it open. A blast of icy air flooded the cabin, and Ursula's mouth went dry as she looked up at him. She swallowed hard, not yet willing to move. Whatever the trial was, her best chance of survival was probably to get the hell out of here.

He held out his hand. "I'll need your phone."

Still manacled, she jammed her free hand into her back pocket and pulled out her phone with a shaking hand. She passed it to him, watching as he slipped it into his coat. Dread welled in her chest. He was enormous and strong, and she didn't think she could outrun him. She'd have to fight him, though her chances weren't good there, either.

"Wear this." Kester handed Ursula the jacket, then leaned over her, unlocking the handcuff with a gold key. "Don't try anything stupid. You won't outrun me."

Christ. Can he read my thoughts? Stepping out of the car, she slipped into the grey parka, welcoming its warmth. If she was going to fight him in remote fields, she didn't need the added disadvantage of hypothermia. She pulled up the hood, eyeing him cautiously. You didn't give a jacket to someone you wanted to murder, did you? Then again, he was obviously stark raving mad.

A beep sounded as he locked the doors with the key fob. "I'm going to make sure that we're alone. Stay here." Clouds of breath bloomed around his face.

Like hell I'm going to stay here. If she strained her eyes, she could see lights shining on the other side of the fields. There was a faint smell of wood smoke in the air. As soon as he was gone she'd jump the fence, sprint across the field, and run to the nearest house to dial 999. The next time she'd see Kester's pretty face would be on the evening news.

He turned away from her, then glanced back with a wolfish grin. "You should know that if you decide to run, I'll sniff you out before you can get 100 meters. It's only fair to warn you."

Sniff me out? Creep. She shivered, trying not to picture a madman sniffing around her ankles.

Kester faced the berm, tilting back his head. He began to mutter.

What happened next went beyond creepy and right into the realm of pure terror.

As he spoke, his body began to tremble. Panic spread through Ursula as she watched the side of his face transform. His nose protruded, and his clothes disappeared into dark fur. With a sharp crack, his spine lurched forward, bones snapping as they repositioned. Where Kester had been only moments before, now there stood an enormous black hound.

When it turned to Ursula, the beast's eyes glowed green.

Ursula's heart stopped.

She stumbled back toward the car, gaping. *Kester isn't human. It's real. Witches, magic—the fire goddess, my condemned soul.* Her world tilted.

The beast prowled toward her, sniffing the air before emitting a growl than rumbled through her bones.

She tried to steady the shaking in her hands, balling her fingers into fists. *I'm losing my mind.*

Then the hound turned, bounded up the berm, and disappeared into the darkness.

* * *

ALONE BY THE LOTUS, Ursula felt a cold wind bite through her clothes. Kester's transformation from man to hound had shattered her very understanding of reality, and her blood roared in her ears. For a moment, she wondered if she'd hallucinated the whole scene.

Maybe she'd stolen this car, dreamt up a beautiful dog-man, and convinced herself that her life had a purpose—that she wasn't just a screwed-up, unemployed loser, but was part of a new magical reality.

Or maybe Madeleine was right. Witches were real, and Kester was one of them—just like the monsters who had terrorized Boston.

She watched the snow drifting to the ground, trying to root herself in reality. A sudden ability to conjure fire with her thoughts wasn't exactly normal. Still, she'd assumed there was a scientific explanation she just didn't know about. It wasn't like she'd spent a lot of time in biology classrooms, so maybe she'd missed something.

But magic and werewolves were the stuff of fairy stories. And she didn't want to believe in them, because if magic was real then maybe the gaping-eyed monsters of her nightmares were real, too. A gut-churning image flickered in her memory—a beautiful man with midnight eyes, and a smile cold as death… She shook her head, pushing the image beneath the surface.

Her breath came thick and ragged. *Focus, Ursula. Did I really just see a man transform into a hound? Or have I lost my mind?* The most likely explanation was that she was a mental case—a newly unemployed mental case

—with imaginary magical powers. Perhaps she had only just now come to her senses, alone in a field with a stolen car. But mental cases didn't really come to their senses so suddenly, did they?

So what the hell do I do now? Do I run, or will that beast hunt me down and tear the flesh from my bones?

A distant shriek pierced the frozen night, and a moment later the hound bounded down the slope. Blood dripped from its jaws. Her stomach flipped, and panic threatened to overwhelm her. She stepped back again, her calves thudding against the Lotus's fender.

Panting, the beast retracted its claws, and its snout shortened. As Kester's spine straightened, clothing spread over his body and the fur disappeared, revealing the smooth skin of a movie star.

Her breath came in short, sharp bursts. No, she hadn't finally cracked. People didn't assess their own sanity while they were hallucinating, which meant that Kester was telling the truth. Apparently, Ursula's soul belonged to a fire goddess.

Bloody hell. What the hell had F.U. been doing with her life?

Kester wiped a hand across his mouth. "Looks like we're alone." He followed Ursula's eyes to the blood staining the snow. "Sorry about that. I was hungry."

Her fists clenched tighter, her nails digging into her palms. Who did he just kill? "Did you—" she stammered, "just eat someone?"

Kester smiled wolfishly. "Not a person. What sort of monster do you think I am? Just an old ewe I found on my way back here. Put her out of her misery to be perfectly honest." He scratched his cheek. "She shouldn't have been outside in this weather."

Ursula exhaled. *A sheep. It was only a sheep.*

Kester glanced at her. "We can't talk all night. We have business to attend to, since you wanted the damn trial."

"I have no idea what's going on. F.U. wanted it."

"I beg your pardon?"

"Former Ursula. It's what I call the version of myself I can't remember."

He glared at her like she was the mad one—as if he hadn't just eaten a raw sheep—then crossed toward the car, clicking open the boot. The car lights shone on his dark hair while he rummaged around.

Straightening, he pulled out a long object wrapped in black leather. With a flick of his wrist he yanked the sheath away, revealing an ancient sword. Strange patterns wove and writhed along its iron blade as though it were alive, and the air left her lungs.

Okay. Now I know how he intends to kill me.

CHAPTER 6

$\mathcal{U}$rsula's chest unclenched a little when Kester shoved the sword back into its sheath. He slammed the boot shut, turning to climb the slope. "Come, my dear. You've got work to do up the hill."

He trudged toward the bank, and she was left with only the sound of the wind rushing across the snow. She glanced one last time at the distant lights twinkling in the night. If she ran in an all-out sprint, she could be sitting before a fireplace in five minutes. But she'd never make it. Kester would hunt her down like the ewe he'd so casually disemboweled.

Dread wrapped its fingers around her heart as she climbed up the slope. *I have to get out of here.* Her best bet would be to convince Kester she was stupid, and then disarm him when he least expected it. In fact, given his condescending tone, there was a good chance he already thought she was an idiot.

If she could get the sword from him, she stood a chance. She was skilled with a sword, even if she had no idea how she'd learned. When she'd been discovered in the church, she had no memories beyond her name. But even though she had no idea *who* she was, the doctors who'd treated her had explained that she still had something called "procedural memory." She remembered how to walk, cut up her food, and speak English. She couldn't type, which meant she'd never learned, but as soon as she saw a piano, she'd been struck by a certainty that she knew what sounds her fingers would make on its keys. She just had no memory of how she'd learned to play in the first place.

When she thought of sword fighting, it was the same. She could imagine herself wielding a blade with precision, each thrust and parry as familiar to her as the movements of walking. As she envisioned herself fighting, a little of the terror seeped out of her chest, and she smiled to herself. In all likelihood, Kester was not counting on her expertise in this area. At least F.U. had done something right for her.

The berm was more slippery than she'd expected, and near the apex she had to scramble on her hands and knees so as not to slide down its side. On the flattened hilltop, she straightened, shielding her eyes as a strong gust of wind whipped snow into her face.

When she'd wiped the snow from her eyes, she found herself standing beside an enormous grey rock, its rough-hewn surface crusted with ice. Two more stones rose from the ground on either side, and if she strained her eyes, she could see the dim edges of more boulders curving off into the darkness.

Kester gripped his sheathed sword. He nodded at one of the rocks. "What do you think of the ringstones?"

She turned to gape at him. *Is he seriously making small talk?* And what sort of opinion was she supposed to have on rocks?

"They're big." She kept her eyes on the weapon that swung by his hips. "But why are we here?"

"A trial can only be conducted in a place of ancient magic." With the sword tucked under one arm, he led her further into the stone circle. As they walked, another ring of giant stones came into view.

She took a deep breath. How, exactly, was she going to distract him long enough to get that sword? He'd nearly lured her into his trap through the power of suggestion, but that really wasn't part of her skill set. Especially not when she was stuffed into a grey parka, half freezing to death.

Then again, men could be simple-minded creatures.

Kester turned to her. "We need to be within the inner circle."

She shivered, gazing out over the dark and empty fields. If she could move in close enough to kiss him, she could ram her elbow into his Adam's apple. He'd drop the sword immediately. And yet, a voice in the back of her mind urged her to follow him.

Maybe, if she survived whatever the hell was about to happen, she could learn the truth about herself, about where she'd come from. If she killed him, she'd be stuck in the darkness forever. There was also the fact that she didn't particularly want to drive a sword through someone's heart, even if he was a psychopath. She'd have to see how this played out before she did anything drastic.

They reached the second circle of stones. Crusted in ice, the monoliths towered over Ursula. Her heart pounded.

His green eyes flashed like storm clouds in the dark. "Wait here a moment."

Cold fear inched up her spine. A few feet from her, Kester pulled the sword from its sheath. Puffs of frozen breath drifted from his mouth as he whispered over the weapon. When he finished, a glowing orb appeared, hovering above his head and illuminating a small patch of snowy grass in the center of the stones. The word *magic* rang again in her head, and her body thrummed with a dark thrill. *It's real.*

Gripping the sword in both hands, Kester raised it above his head, blade pointing toward the earth.

"O' shadow stalker." His voice was firm. "A thane awaits a trial." He stabbed the frozen earth with the blade.

Ursula's stomach clenched. *What the hell is a shadow stalker? And, is this thane supposed to be me?*

The wind died, and a deathly, unnatural silence enveloped them. The orb's flickering glow revealed nothing beyond the stones. In the icy air, each intake of breath froze Ursula's throat.

A snowflake fell on her eyelash and she blinked. Had something shifted in the darkness just beyond the inner stones? The hair rose on the nape of her neck.

She whipped her head around, sensing an unseen danger. "Kester, what—"

He lifted a silencing finger, still holding the sword's hilt. As he raised his eyes, he seemed to search the stones. "Moor fiend, reveal yourself." His grip tightened on the pommel of the sword.

Her heart hammered against her ribs, and time seemed to stretch out as she waited.

Between the stones, she could make out a faint outline—tall and hunched, and nearly as large as the rocks themselves. Her breath caught in her throat. *What is that?*

Kester beckoned Ursula to come closer. "Shadow stalker, I have brought you a thane to battle."

Her mouth went dry, her spine stiff with fear, but she stepped toward Kester. *I can do this—whatever* this *is. I know how to use a sword.*

He looked at her, one hand still on his sword. "You wouldn't sign the pact," he said in his velvety voice. "This is the third option. If you defeat the wight, you'll become a servant of Emerazel, like I am. You can repay your debt that way."

She took a deep, steadying breath. "I don't really want to do that either. Can't I just go back to my flat—"

"Ursula," he interrupted. "You must decide now. Either sign the contract or defeat the monster. Otherwise, I'll be forced to reap your soul. I don't particularly want to do that. It means you'll die now."

From just beyond the stones, a guttural growl rumbled. A shiver snaked up Ursula's spine. She had a feeling that whatever was out there wanted her soul, too. She gritted her teeth, nodding. *Shadow stalker it is.*

With his eyes locked on hers, Kester released the sword, stepping away. Ursula tried to steady her breathing, stepping toward it.

She inhaled deeply, yanking the sword from the frozen earth. *Lighter than I thought.*

Kester stepped away. "The wight will enter the circle when the light dims. You must defeat him."

As she gripped the sword in both hands, she took a tentative swing. The blade moved easily through the air, and she nearly smiled at the sensation, relief flooding her for the first time tonight. Somehow the sword felt like an extension of her body, like one of her own limbs. F.U. must have swung a sword a thousand times before.

Kester chanted a spell, and as the air crackled with electricity, fur sprouted from his body. He lurched over, bones cracking; with a deep growl, he transformed into a hound. For a moment, he studied her, green eyes flashing, before bounding from the circle.

Above her, the orb began to dim.

CHAPTER 7

*D*espite the cold, sweat dampened her brow, and she gripped the sword hard. This blade would be her savior.

She strained to see in the dark, but she could no longer make out the monster's hunched form. The wind picked up again, spraying snow between gaps in the ringstones.

She lifted her weapon, trying to keep the fear at bay. *I'm a sitting duck here.* Her mind raced. She was at a serious disadvantage, since she had no idea where or what this *shadow stalker* was. At least a stone could guard her back. She backed into the shelter of the nearest one.

To her right, something scratched at one of the stones, and she spun to face it. She held the sword in front of her, her breathing ragged. Ice flaked off the boulder, drifting to the ground, and fear stole her breath. Snow crunched behind her, and she whirled again. More fragments, crumbled off the stones. Where was this monster? A low growl spread through the circle, rumbling through her gut, followed by a sharp, scraping sound.

The fiend is sharpening its claws.

Without the orb, darkness enshrouded her. She pressed her back against the basalt rock, her sword wavering as she peered into the darkened center of the circle. How did one see something made of shadows?

In the center of the stones, something whirled—tendrils of black on a phantom wind, deeper and darker than the night sky. *Please let me get through this.*

From two feet above her head, yellow eyes flickered into existence, as large as dinner plates. Panic inched up her spine. The fiend was at least eight feet tall. Following the eyes, its body shimmered into view, shoulders as broad as a ringstone.

A wave of fear slammed into her. Sure, she knew how to swing a blade, but did she know how to fight a giant?

She clutched the sword, pulse racing as the fiend lurched forward. It balanced on the knuckles of a long arm, like a monstrous gorilla. She readied herself for its attack.

It lunged, swiping at her with a clawed hand. She dove to the side, slashing upward, but the blade cut only air. Scrambling to her feet, she searched frantically for the monster, but it was gone.

Bollocks bollocks bollocks. It had only feinted to draw her away from the safety of the stone. She whipped her head around, searching for her opponent—but not fast enough. The creature's arm flew from the darkness behind her, slamming into her side like a cudgel.

The sound of her arm and ribs snapping cracked through the air, and she was lifted off her feet. She slammed into the frozen earth next to one of the blue stones, and pain shot through her like a white-hot knife. She screamed.

A wet, guttural sound drowned out her cries. *Laughter.*

Agony pulled her apart. *I can't die here. I can't die alone, not knowing who I really am.* She gritted her teeth and pulled herself to her feet, lifting her sword. The monster had smashed her left arm, and something warm and metallic dripped from her mouth. *Blood.*

She turned her head toward a movement. The fiend was creeping into the circle again, eyes blazing yellow.

She glared back, her jaw set tight. *If I'm going to die tonight, it's going to be on my terms.* She slashed at its ribs, but despite its enormous size the shadow stalker dodged easily. Fighting this thing was like trying to grip a plume of smoke.

A third option, Kester had called it, but this trial was just a slow and terrifying execution. The moor fiend was toying with her. Kester was probably enjoying every minute of it. He'd sacrificed her to this monster, before she'd even come to grips with the existence of magic.

She tried to block out the pain coursing through her shattered side. *Hell of a birthday.* She'd been fired, stalked, assaulted, kidnapped, and now she'd be mauled to death by a creature made of smoke and wrath.

I didn't even get a chance at life. Rage roiled inside her, simmering away her fear.

"It's my bloody eighteenth birthday!" she shrieked.

As far as she knew, no one had ever baked her a cake. That somehow seemed like the worst offense of all, and anger simmered. *Three years. I only had three years.* As her right hand grew hot, heat burned through her veins. From her palm, fire surged into the sword and flames licked along the blade.

The fiend shrank back, and Ursula stepped forward, emboldened by the flaming sword. *I am an angel of death,* her mind whispered.

The pain in her side threatened to rip her apart, but she held the blade before her like a priest holding a cross to ward off evil. Fire engulfed the whole blade. The few snowflakes that drifted onto the metal sputtered and popped in the heat. *I am wrath.*

The fiend took another step away, pressing its back against a stone. Despite the glow of the fire, the beast's edges were still difficult to make out—a mass of dark hair, muscle, and sinew surrounded by shadows. Its yellow eyes blazed, but no longer just with hunger. She saw fear there, too.

The fiend's shoulders straightened almost imperceptibly, then it leapt. She thrust the sword up just in time to shield herself as the wight grabbed for her. She was ready for it this time, and her blade sliced into its forearm.

Grunting, the fiend slammed its arm into her, sending the sword skittering across the circle. She turned to run for the weapon, but a strong hand grabbed her ponytail and flung her to the ground.

She landed on her broken ribs, and agony fractured her body. *I'm broken.* Gasping for breath, she tried to roll onto her front, desperate to stand, but the fiend leapt on top of her, crushing her lungs and shattered ribs into the icy soil. Long, clawed fingers reached for her throat, and Ursula gasped for breath.

In desperation, she kicked her feet, struggling to free herself, but the fiend slipped its fingers around her throat. It squeezed, like a snake constricting its prey.

Inching toward her face, its golden eyes stared at her with a primitive intelligence. *This is the face of my executioner: bestial and merciless.* Slowly, it opened its mouth, revealing jagged rows of nubby teeth. She braced herself for the bite, until she realized this repugnant display was a smile.

It squeezed harder. Ursula's windpipe flattened with a soft popping noise, and pain splintered her mind.

They say that in your final moments, your life flashes before your eyes—a series of still images projected from your subconscious to your dying mind. For Ursula, it began at fifteen: the firefighter pulling her from the rubble of St. Ethelburga's Church, the flashbulbs as she left the court-house with her first foster family. The next few scenes were a blur, one family after another, accompanied by a soundtrack of tutting, screaming, and finally shrieks of "I can't take this girl anymore!"

When her lungs were close to bursting, the filmstrip slowed. Her tiny apartment in Bow flickered past. Those two arsehole students fighting in the club. Last of all, Rufus's words reverberated through her skull: "You're a sad cow who won't make anything of your life."

He's right. Because now her shitty life was over in a flash of shattered bones and burning lungs. *Burning.*

A final burst of rage inflamed her—rage at the unfairness and the futility of it all. She hadn't asked for any of this—to be a mystery girl with no family and an infernal fire inside her. Anger flowed, a hot magma in her veins. It erupted from her, broiling and volcanic. She pressed her blazing hands into the wight's shining eyes.

Its hands wrenched off her throat, and she heard her own scream.

CHAPTER 8

$\mathcal{H}$ot blood gurgled from Ursula's throat, bubbling into her lungs. Drowning in her own fluid, she was kept conscious only by the agony wracking her body. Then her vision blurred, and she no longer cared about the injustice of her short life. She just wanted to sleep, to rest peacefully in silence, free of this mind-shattering agony.

But instead of silence, a melodious sound drifted into her ears. Kester, speaking in Angelic again—but she understood the words, something about healing waters and leaching out the pain. Her sight began to clear. She caught a flash of green eyes above her. Kester kneeled over her, changing, his brow furrowed with concern.

As he spoke, she could feel her bones shift and slide into place, the pain slowly dulling. Gently, she touched her neck. It still throbbed, but the skin was smooth, healed over. She rolled over, hacking a crimson spatter of blood onto the blackened earth.

Still crouching, Kester quirked a smile. "I imagine this hasn't been the best birthday celebration you've ever had. But you made it."

He'd called up a demonic and lethal creature without warning her, and now he was smiling about it. "Wanker." She choked out the word, her voice box still raw.

"Is that any way to talk to the man who just saved your life?"

Ursula rose to her knees, gasping. Though her ribs and left arm were

healed, they still throbbed with pain. "That wasn't a trial. That thing almost killed me." She was fresh out of patience.

"I told you. I'm not in control of these things; Emerazel is. I'm not actually a god, even if I look like one."

Arrogant wanker. She wanted answers. Now. Another foxfire orb burned above them, illuminating the scorched and charred earth around her. At the edge of its glow, something glinted in the shadows. *The sword.* She rushed toward it, plucking it from the frozen earth before whirling to point it at Kester.

"You need to tell me what is going on, or I will slice you in half."

Kester tilted his head thoughtfully. "Fine. I brought you to the Avebury Henge for a trial. To become a hellhound, you must defeat a demon."

She stalked closer, still pointing the sword. Had he said *hellhound*? "I thought fighting the demon—shadow stalker, whatever you call it—I thought that would resolve my debt."

Kester shook his head. "The trial merely gave you the *opportunity* to repay your debt. Your soul still belongs to Emerazel until you pay it off."

The frigid air stung her cheeks and fingers. "So I'm not free?"

"Not free." The tip of his nose had grown pink in the cold. "But on the bright side, you're employed, so that's a step up from a few hours ago. Your new job is to collect either souls or signatures from those who owe a debt to Emerazel. Plus, you're alive, and to be honest my money was on the shadow stalker."

Finally having got an answer, she lowered the sword. "Why didn't you just reap my soul, like you threatened?"

"A request for trial is always honored." His breath clouded around his head. "And now, we need to go. Sunrise is in an hour, and I don't want to have to explain to a warden of the National Trust why you desecrated a Neolithic monument."

"We're going back to London?" Ursula turned to walk back to the car, but Kester's voice stopped her.

"Not the car, Ursula. We'll be traveling by Emerazel's sigil." He strode toward her and gently pulled the sword from her grasp. Gripping it in both hands, he pointed the tip toward the scorched earth. "And no. Not London."

Ursula jammed her hands in her pockets, trying to warm them. "I don't suppose you're going to tell me where we're going." Apparently that fire had burned the fever right out of her, because her hands were freezing now. Shivering, she watched as Kester carved a triangle in a circle in the snow and soil—the same symbol that marked her shoulder.

Kester slid the sword into its sheath, and reached into an inner pocket of his jacket. With a half-smile, he pulled out a silver flask.

He unscrewed the cap and took a slug, then offered it to her. "Want a sip? It's Glenfiddich, 1937."

Ursula shook her head. "No thanks." She swiped a hand below her eyes. Her eye makeup must be halfway down her face at this point. At best, she probably looked like a drunken KISS fan, but at least she was alive.

"Suit yourself." He poured the contents of the flask into the furrows he'd scratched in the soil. He knelt for a moment, his hand glowing white hot, then flames snaked along the lines in the dirt.

As he straightened, his gaze lingered on Ursula. "You will need to stand right in front of me."

Shoulders hunched in the cold, she edged closer to him. She tensed as he reached for her, pulling her into a tight hug. He smelled faintly of cedar wood—and somehow, the warmth of his body was oddly comforting.

"You'll want to hold your breath," he whispered into her ear.

He chanted an Angelic spell softly, and she listened to the words, understanding each one. He spoke of a portal of fire, and Emerazel's eternal grace. Now, she knew something else about F.U.—she'd apparently been some sort of witch.

As he finished the short spell, the flames blazed high above them. For a moment, her skin seared in an exquisite agony, then she crumbled to ash.

CHAPTER 9

With the crackling of a thousand cinders uniting, she reconstituted in the center of a circular room, atoms and molecules joining together again with the force of an exploding star. She rested her hands on her knees, her body shaking as she retched. Whatever the fuck she'd just done, she was pretty sure human bodies were not meant to do it.

Her skin crackled with electrical power, and an odd buzzing noise sounded in her head. Each one of her nerve endings blazed in rebellion.

Kester glanced at her. "Are you all right?"

As she straightened, she looked around at the circular room in which they stood. A wrought-iron chandelier, blazing with candles, hung from a towering brick ceiling.

She glanced down. At her feet, a few tongues of flame licked at the edges of an encircled triangle carved into the floor.

Bits of hot ash burned her throat like she'd just pulled too strongly on an unfiltered cigarette. "Bloody hell." She coughed. "What was that?"

"That was sigil travel. You can travel between Emerazel's symbols by knowing the right spell, and envisioning where you want to go, but it's not the most comfortable method of transportation. I recommend actually holding your breath next time."

She rubbed her eyes, still trying to get her bearings. Between three tall windows, the walls were painted with strange frescos of dancing nymphs, satyrs, and occult symbols. On one part of the curving wall stood a mahogany door carved with stars and flames.

Ursula wondered if they might be in some sort of antechamber to the underworld, until the windows caught her eye. Distant lights twinkled through the glass. On the other side of a park, a cityscape glimmered. Entranced, Ursula stepped toward the glass, watching the falling snow that blanketed the treetops and distant buildings. *Where am I?*

She searched for the usual London landmarks: the London Eye, the Thames, or the pointed tip of the Gherkin.

But this wasn't her city. The buildings lining the park were far too tall for London's skyline.

Dizzy, she stepped back from the window. "Where are we?"

"New York City."

She shook her head, trying to clear the confusion. It didn't seem possible—then again, she'd just defeated a demon and travelled through a blaze of fire and ash. Clearly, she needed to rethink what was possible. "So, so…" she stammered. "I'm looking at Central Park."

"Yes." Kester traced a gloved finger over the glass. "It's dark now, but on a clear day you can see the roof of the Metropolitan Museum of Art, and beyond that, Harlem."

She gaped at him, wondering if this was all some kind of dream. "The fire you lit transported us here. With magic." She felt stupid saying the words out loud.

He pulled off his gloves, turning to the sigil. "Precisely. I can call on Emerazel's power with her symbol. With the right spell, it is possible to travel between them."

"I need to let Katie know I'm okay."

"No. There is no Katie anymore. You need to leave your old life behind. I'll take care of the explanations to anyone who knew you."

She eyed him. "You've got to be joking. I can't contact my best friend?"

"You don't want to test me on this. There are worse things than death, and they'll be waiting for you if you defy that order." His voice sent a shiver over her skin, putting an end to that conversation.

Her skin felt hot, and she pulled off the coat Kester had given her, trying to think of what to say next. *I was burnt to ash, and then I traveled to New York through a flaming sigil. Magic, demons, hellhounds...* Her mind raced in a jumble of confused words that she couldn't process. *F.U., you were a raging lunatic.* "Where are we standing right now?"

"This room has been properly prepared to receive those who travel by Emerazel's fire," he said, pointing at the markings on the walls. "It's on the top floor of the Plaza hotel."

"The Plaza Hotel. Right. And witches and demons are real, and you eat raw sheep and steal souls."

"We don't say 'witch' in our world. 'Philosopher' or 'mage' are the preferred terms. And I am your new mentor, so you'll need to watch that unpredictable attitude, or you'll find yourself on the wrong side of my wrath. Are we clear?"

She choked back a retort, forcing a smile. "Clear as day."

"Good. Come with me." He pulled off his jacket, tucking it under his arm as he walked through the door. "I think you'll find this place an improvement over your usual haunts."

She followed Kester down the hallway and into a cavernous main hall. *Bloody hell.* She let out a low whistle. The place looked like some sort of medieval castle. *Is this where he lives?*

High above, the ceiling's arches gave the room an almost cathedral-like quality. Persian rugs carpeted the floor, and rich taupe velvets upholstered the sofas. A baby grand piano stood in a far corner. Above the fireplace hung an antique portrait of a beautiful ivory-skinned woman, her raven hair threaded with wildflowers. On a small plaque pinned to the bottom of the gilt frame was the name *Louisa.*

Fancy as it was, a musty smell hung in the air. Dust coated the floor, and flowers in a vase had dried into drooping husks. This place had clearly been unused for quite some time. *What a waste.*

Kester waved a hand. "The living room."

"Who lives here?"

"We'll get to that."

"It looks… fancy." She glanced around furtively, feeling like an intruder in a rich person's home. "But how do you get out of here?" Admittedly, escape routes were a bit of a preoccupation, but since she'd been attacked by two different creatures tonight, she thought she could be forgiven for a little neurosis.

He pointed to a doorway. "The elevator is through there, but the

Plaza's security is excellent. No one is coming in here unless you want them to. You're perfectly safe. Come with me."

Ursula followed him down a hallway, gaping at the vibrant paintings of pale, ecstatic women dressed in gold and crimson gowns. The place was decadent, but intensely beautiful.

He stopped by an open door, flicking on a light switch. "This is the library."

Ursula peered inside. Distant streetlights flickered through a single window at the opposite end, and a comfortable window seat nestled under it. A small table stood in the center, and dark bookcases lined the walls, their shelves filled with leather-bound volumes. She had a sudden desire to lock herself in the room and page through each book for the next month. "I love this room," she breathed. Maybe she wasn't much of an intellectual, but the room's coziness called to her.

"You'll have time to look around later. There's more to see," said Kester. He strode to the end of the hall, and she followed. Through another door, he pointed out an enormous kitchen with marble countertops.

This was a kitchen made for something a little more delectable than buttered bread. Her stomach rumbled, but Kester had already moved on.

Down the hall, he flicked on a light through a doorway. "The armory."

Ursula's pulse quickened. *Weapons.* She'd grown quite fond of that sword tonight.

She peeked inside. The armory was as large as the main hall. A mirror lined one wall, and beige tatami mats covered the floor. A wooden sparring dummy stood in a corner. Across from her, a magnificent collection of daggers, swords, and spears hung on wooden racks. Grinning, Ursula hurried across the room to inspect them.

"Take your time," said Kester. "I'm going to see about some food. I can hear your stomach rumbling from here."

Ursula's eyes went wide at the gleaming collection. There was a Viking sword like the one she'd so recently used to fight the shadow stalker, pointed blades for puncturing hearts and lungs, stubby Roman swords, and even a Scottish claymore. But it was the rack of Asian weapons that most drew her eye: a sword for chopping the legs off of charging horses, a pair of daggers, two long spears, and a wicked-looking katana. She had no idea why, but these swords called to her.

She bit her lip, fighting the urge to steal a few daggers. She didn't know where she'd be resting her head tonight, but sleeping with a cold blade by her side might not be a bad idea. Especially since her new mentor had the disturbing tendency to grow claws and fangs. Maybe he was being civil to her now, but he was clearly dodgy as hell.

She reached for the katana. Black silk wrapped the hilt, and the guard was forged in the shape of a dragon. The blade shone like a viper's tooth.

It was perfectly weighted. She hurried to the center of the room and sliced the blade through the air in a practice swing, thrilling at the feel of the steel. She swung again, and the muscles in her shoulders loosened. *Home. This feels like home.* Her arm still throbbed where the shadow stalker had broken it, but with the sword in her hand, the dull ache began to ease.

Turning toward the mirror, she caught a glimpse of herself and winced. Her auburn hair lay matted to her head. Blood and dirt stained her shirt and jeans, and her black eye makeup formed two dark semicircles below her hazel eyes. *I look like a goth clown—definitely worse than a drunken KISS fan.*

At least the sword was beautiful. With a faint smile, she raised it above her head. She sliced downward with a yell, halting when the blade was parallel to the floor. As she lifted her arms to take another swing, Kester's voice interrupted.

"I see you're making yourself at home." He leaned against the door frame, staring at her. "I would ask how you learned to wield a sword like that, but I'd wager you have no idea."

"You'd wager right." She turned and pointed the sword at him. He stood ten feet away, and she could be there in two steps. Before he'd have a chance to blink, she could bury the sword in his chest. After stopping his heart, she'd just take the elevator to the ground floor and disappear into the New York City night. Would it be so hard to start over as a waitress in New York?

But something stopped her. It wasn't just his pretty face. As insane as he sounded, Kester had actually been telling the truth. *Magic is real.* She'd seen him transform into a hound, summon a shadow stalker, and whisk them to New York through a flaming sigil. She felt it when she lifted the sword, and what was more, some sort of magical fire now flowed in her veins. And if Kester was telling the truth, that meant there was no escape from Emerazel and her infernal flames.

She lowered the blade, wiping the makeup below her eyes on the back of her other wrist.

If Kester suspected that she'd just run through the pros and cons of stabbing him to death, his face didn't show it.

He nodded at the sword. "I see you've acquainted yourself with my friend Honjo Masamune. I know he's quite charming, but he can wait until morning. Dinner is served."

With a heavy sigh, Ursula crossed to the racks, placing the katana in the empty spot. *Until we meet again, my friend.*

CHAPTER 10

*K*ester led her down the hall, past the sigil room, and pulled open the door to a dining room. A domed ceiling arched impossibly high above them, painted with a fresco of dryads and centaurs. Mahogany cabinets displayed antique porcelain and crystal glassware. In the center of the room, a silver candelabra cast warm light over the rich wood of a banquet table. Two place settings lay in one corner, along with a pair of domed silver trays.

Ursula's back stiffened. *I'll just have to pretend that I don't normally eat a dinner of beans and toast in front of a TV.*

Kester crossed to the head of the table. "Have a seat."

Instead of sitting in front of the tray, she pulled out a chair on the opposite side, giving herself a clear view of the door. She needed to know if anyone else was going to slip in here.

He arched an eyebrow. "A little nervous, are we?"

Reaching across the table, she dragged over the other place setting. "I like a view of the door."

"In case an intruder comes in?"

"Wouldn't be the first time tonight."

"What is *that?*" He nodded at her hand.

She hadn't even realized that she'd pulled out her white stone and was rubbing it between her thumb and forefinger. "It's my good luck charm."

"What is the point?"

"There's no point. I'm just attached to it." It was the one constant thing in her life.

"Good luck charms are for the desperate."

"I'd say that describes me perfectly."

"May I?" He asked, holding out a hand.

Reluctantly, she handed it over. "I suppose you're going to tell me it's something magical."

He sighed, rolling it around in his fingers. "No. It's ordinary hecatolite. Completely uninteresting."

"It has sentimental value." Though what it tied her to, she had no idea.

He eyed her. "I thought you had no memory."

"I don't, but I always assumed F.U.'s life was better than mine."

"You're a very strange person, you know that?"

"I saw you turn into a dog and eat a live sheep," she sputtered. "I'm not sure you have a great handle on normal behavior."

"You still seem cranky. Have some dinner." He pulled the dome off her tray, revealing a beautifully plated steak, a bowl of cauliflower soup, and a small watercress salad.

Her mouth watered at the rich aromas. "Where did this all come from?"

"Room service here is fast and Michelin rated." He filled her wine glass. "Hopefully, some filet mignon and red wine will placate you."

She picked up her knife and fork to cut the steak and took a bite; it was as soft as butter. For the time being, she could almost forgive Kester for kidnapping her in the middle of her slice of bread.

"I hope you like it here," he said.

"It's… fancy. Empty, but very grand."

"You don't find it comfortable?"

She cut another piece of rich meat. "It's not what I'm used to. It's amazing, but I was about two days away from being homeless, and it just seems like it's a waste for a place like this to lie empty when there are probably families freezing outside." She frowned at him. "You're not eating?"

"I filled up on lamb."

It took Ursula a moment to realize that he was talking about the ewe he'd devoured. "Right." The image of his gore-covered teeth almost put her off her food. "What exactly are you? Some sort of werewolf? Am I going to turn into a wolf now that I work for Emerazel?"

"A hound. I'm a hellhound, and so are you. But you won't transform for a number of years."

"Are we..." She struggled to get the word out. "Witches—I mean, mages? Like people are talking about? The terrorists who slaughtered people in Boston?"

Kester shook his head. "We are mortal demons, compelled by our marks to work for the fire goddess. I know magic as well, but you needn't learn it. I just need you to learn to fight and to collect souls."

She nearly choked on her wine. "I'm sorry—did you say I'm a demon?"

"I did." His tone was matter-of-fact. "And your job is to find those in Emerazel's debt. Force them to sign the contract, by whatever means required."

She took a deep breath, trying to process the word *demon*. "I'm having a hard time with the demon concept. Surely demons are scaly creatures with pointy tails and claws." She stopped herself. "I mean, you have claws, but no scales." She shook her head. She was babbling like a loon now. "Demons are monsters. I don't look like a demon, do I?" She gripped her knife so tight she thought the silver might bend.

"Right now you do."

"It just sounds like madness." She sucked in a deep breath. "I'm not sure when you last spent time around normal people, but normal people don't talk about demons. They don't fight monsters in ringstones, or eat live sheep, or travel across continents by incinerating themselves."

Kester leaned back in his chair. "But you're not normal. Normal people don't have severe retrograde amnesia, and they can't light things on fire with their hands. Given the rest of your life, the fact that you're a demon shouldn't be much of a surprise." His green eyes gleamed. "What exactly was your explanation for your powers?"

"Genetics," she blurted. "A mutation. I have no clue. I've hardly taken any science classes. And anyway, it just happened for the first time tonight so it's not like I've had time to think about it."

"You think a random mutation in your DNA could allow you to do this?" He held up his silver fork. For an instant his hand glowed incredibly hot, like he'd pulled the door to a furnace. Then the fork collapsed on the table in a molten lump.

She felt dizzy, overwhelmed by a strange sense of vertigo. "I have no idea. I don't understand any of this." Maybe he was right, though. Only the supernatural could explain everything she'd seen. "I need to know more specifics about this new job."

"You track down people who've struck a bargain with Emerazel, people who've traded their soul for fame and wealth. You need them to sign the contract to bind their soul to the goddess when they die. Very rarely, you might meet another such as yourself who has carved Emerazel's mark in their body. But there aren't many around with these." He unbuttoned his shirt collar, and her eyes landed on the familiar scar in the center of his athletic chest. "Emerazel's strength can only be granted through one of her blades, and there aren't many in the world." He buttoned his shirt again, and she tried not to think about his body.

"I don't even know how I got my scar," she said.

"You really have no idea?"

"Nope." She swirled the wine in her glass. "What happens when someone signs their soul away?"

"Each god has their own hell. Emerazel's is the inferno. The debtor's soul will go there once they die."

Suddenly, she was no longer hungry. "And the soul burns forever? Does it hurt?"

"I assume so. That's why I've been keen to avoid it."

She stared down at the lump of meat on her plate, fighting a growing sense of nausea. "I can't do that to people. I can't send them to hell."

"My darling, you don't have a choice. It's you or them. You won't win in a fight against Emerazel. You'll come to understand that over time. Anyway, the debtors agreed to the bargain. It was their choice."

She rubbed a knot in her forehead. "How do I know where to find them?"

"Emerazel will tell you." He leaned closer. "You know the symbol we travel through?"

"It's familiar, yes, since it burned me to a crisp a half hour ago."

Kester ran his fingers over the rim of his wine glass. "A sigil of fire can also be used to contain demons. Even gods. We can summon Emerazel within it."

"I light the symbol, and Emerazel appears with instructions?"

"Precisely."

Whatever Emerazel was like, it couldn't be much worse than working for Rufus. "And I suppose I need to find a new flat?"

"This apartment is your new home."

Her jaw dropped. "There's no possible way I could afford to live here."

He shook his head. "This apartment is paid for. You don't have to worry about rent. And of course Emerazel pays an annual stipend of ten ingots of gold."

She stared at him. "Gold what?"

"Gold ingots are 400 ounces each, and the price of gold is about $1,500 an ounce." He looked at the ceiling, muttering calculations. "That's six million dollars a year, or about four million pounds. Give or take." He dabbed the corner of his mouth with a napkin.

She gaped at him. *This must be a dream.* There was no way she could be making that much money. "Six million dollars a year," she repeated. The amount was so far out of her frame of reference that it almost had no meaning. "What would I do with six million dollars a year?"

His cheek dimpled as he flashed a smile. "Oh, I'm sure you could find a worthy anti-gentrification cause to fund."

"Uh-huh." *Definitely better than working for Rufus.* She took a long sip of her red wine. She had no idea what kind it was, since Rufus's club never got any more specific than *red* or *white.* "So why was this place empty? Who used to live here?"

"Another hellhound. But he's moved on to other things."

"And he has a scar. Just like ours?"

"Exactly."

"How did you get yours?"

He reached down, twisting a silver cufflink. For the first time she saw a hint of vulnerability, when he didn't meet her eyes. She liked this side of him better. He swallowed, still examining his cufflinks. "Everyone has their stories."

Wow. That was amazingly...vague. "Right, but what is your—"

"Oh, I almost forgot." Reaching under the table, he lifted up a silver bucket that held champagne and crystal flutes. He looked at her again. "It is your eighteenth birthday."

CHAPTER 11

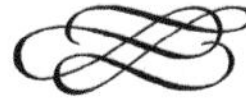

*S*he sniffed the champagne, waiting until Kester took a sip of his before she put the glass to her lips, just in case it was poisoned. It tasted fruity and crisp, like fall apples.

"This is delicious," she said.

"It's a 1928 Krug. One of my favorite vintages. I keep a few bottles around for special occasions."

"Champagne from the '20s. This glass probably cost more than my annual wages," she mused.

"Things have changed for you." He stood, a champagne flute in one hand and the bottle in the other. "Shall we see the rest of the apartment?"

"There's more?"

"There's the second floor." He stepped out the door.

She rose, gripping her champagne as she followed him into a large foyer with a marble staircase. He pointed to a set of double doors. "The elevator, which should satisfy your paranoid tendencies in case you need to make a fast escape." He flicked a wall switch. Above, a chandelier sparkled with a hundred tiny lights. "The bedrooms are on the upper level."

As she climbed the stairs with him, her shoulders tensed. Maybe magic was real, but that didn't mean he wasn't a pervert.

She glanced at him. If he attacked her in some way, she could smash the champagne flute and stab him with the stem. "Before you try anything funny, you should know that I'm pretty good at brawling."

He shot her a sharp look. "Charming. First, you will not beat me in a fight. Not ever. And second, I promise you there's no need for me to force myself on unenthusiastic women when there are many willing participants to choose from."

"Is that so?" It was the only retort she could come up with.

"Do I need to remind you again that I'm your mentor?" That cold, commanding tone had entered his voice again. Gone was the whole soothing charade he'd plied her with earlier in the dining room. Obviously, persuasion was part of his hellhound skill set.

She loosed a sigh. "You don't need to remind me." As she climbed up the stairs after him, she ran her fingers over the brass railing. "This is all part of the hotel?"

"The upper floors of the Plaza are all private residences. A former hellhound purchased this apartment in the twenties for a pittance. The Plaza tried to reacquire it in the thirties but… well, let's say we have our ways of getting what we want."

They reached the landing at the top of the stairs, and a hallway stretched out in either direction. Kester crossed to a door, pushing it open and flicking on a light. "Bedroom one. The greenery room."

Ursula peered inside. This bedroom appeared to double as a botanical conservatory. A wrought-iron scaffold supported glass panes, enclosing half the room. A small day bed stood in one corner. It was pretty in a way, but rotting orchids and cacti lined shelves, and a smell of decay filled the air.

She stepped out. "Interesting. Maybe I'll get into gardening."

"I'll have the cleaning staff come through in the morning," said Kester, closing the door.

He continued down the hall, gesturing through a doorway. She stuck her head into a grey-tiled bathroom. An enormous claw-foot bathtub stood in the center, with a shower in the corner. *Beautiful.* She'd never had a proper shower before, just grimy tubs with handheld sprayers that emitted a sad trickle of water. "I'm really going to enjoy that shower."

"I thought you'd like it. Come. There's more." Kester led her to another room. When he entered, he muttered in that strange language, and candles blazed all over the room. Shadows danced over high, arched ceilings and stained glass windows. In the center stood a four-poster bed with a black canopy. Shelves lined the walls, filled with jars of potions and animal skulls. "The master bedroom."

Stunning—but creepy. Not unlike my new mentor. "Great. Maybe I'll sleep here."

There was no way she was sleeping with the skulls. She'd sleep in the living room.

"There's one more." He walked to the end of the hall.

She stepped inside. This room was smaller than the others. A twin bed with a cream coverlet nestled below a window, and an antique dresser stood in the corner. Kester muttered the spell again and the lantern that sat on the bedside table flickered to life, bathing the room in warm light. On the ceiling, someone had painted the zodiac—gold on midnight blue. It was perfect. It just needed a few finishing touches, maybe a bit of color, to make her feel at home.

"I love it." If Ursula had brought a bag she would have tossed it on the bed to claim it as her own.

"There's one more thing you need to know." He stepped back into the hall, pointing to a door across from hers. She couldn't believe she hadn't noticed it before.

Made of rough oak studded with iron nails, it could only be described one way: *creepy as hell.* It looked like something you'd find in Vlad the Impaler's castle. A pale yellow glow surrounded its frame, the exact color of the shackles Kester had clamped on her wrist in the Lotus.

"In case the spikes didn't make it clear enough, that room is off limits."

Suddenly chilled, she hugged herself. "What's in it?"

Kester glared at her. "You don't need to know that. And now, I'll leave you to that shower. Alone, of course."

He turned to leave, but she touched his arm. "Kester. What happened to the last hellhound? What did he move on to?"

He stared her down. "That's not for you to worry about, Ursula. You have enough to take care of. Get some sleep."

His response didn't do anything to put her mind at ease.

* * *

KESTER LET HIMSELF OUT, leaving Ursula to rifle through the drawers and cupboards on her own. After a glorious hot shower to wash off the remnants of the Muppet's stale beer, she picked through the apartment again, one room at a time.

In the kitchen, she discovered a chrome espresso machine and coffee grinder stowed in a closet. She dusted them off, moving them to one of the marble countertops. *I love coffee. I belong in America. Would it be strange to pay for coffee beans with gold ingots?*

Returning to the library, she read the spines of every book in the room. There were first editions of all the modern classics: Melville, Poe, Dickens, and Brontë. She even found older works by Chaucer, Dante, and Shakespeare—many of them written on parchment and beautifully illustrated in the margins.

Strangely, a lower shelf seemed to be protected by the same golden glow that blazed from the door upstairs. When she reached for the books, her hand was repelled by an invisible force. So of course, those were the ones she most wanted to read. Gold lettering looped up their faded blue and maroon spines: *Fasciculus Chemicus, Iconologia,* and *Picatrix.* She had no clue what any of that meant, just a strong desire to do whatever she wasn't supposed to do.

After giving up on the enchanted books, she rose to take one last peek in the armory. When she stepped into the room, she caught a glimpse of the clock mounted above the mirror. It was past midnight. That was, what, five or six a.m. in the UK? She really needed to get some rest.

She trudged up the stairs to her new bedroom and crawled under the coverlet. As she lay in the darkness, she closed her eyes, trying to calm the thoughts blazing through her mind.

Muppet's singed shirt, Kester's fiery eyes and clawed fingers, the moor fiend's leering grin.

She'd never fall asleep with these thoughts whirling in her skull. She imagined one of her favorite places: a ruined church near the tower of London, its crumbling stone walls covered in ivy. But even with that serene image in her mind, Kester's words rang in her head: *You're a demon.*

The concept was horrifying. She'd always known she was different, but... a demon? A mortal one, no less. You'd think that one of the benefits of demonhood would be immortality, but no. Not only was she an abomination and a bringer of death, but she had to die, just like everyone else.

She rubbed her white stone between her fingers, but it wasn't giving her comfort tonight.

She pulled her bedsheets tighter. She hadn't asked for any of this. At least, she didn't *think* she had. As long as she could remember, the strange scar had marred her shoulder. Who knew how she got it? She was a Mystery Girl all right—a Mystery Girl who'd made a terrible decision she couldn't even remember. And now she was stuck in a foreign country, permanently cut off from her best friend.

That was the thing that really bothered her. More than anything, she wanted to find a way to phone Katie, just to hear a friendly voice again. But she really didn't want to find out what Kester's threat meant. And what could she even say to Katie without sounding like a complete and utter lunatic? Heat rose in her chest, and sweat beaded on her face.

She rolled onto her back, staring up at the blue ceiling flecked with gold stars. There was something oddly comforting about the night sky. At times like this, when the world seemed to suffocate her, she felt like she wanted to throw herself into the freezing night air, to drift along in the wind, riding a night storm...

Basically, she was a lunatic, trapped with her own thoughts.

And as if they weren't enough to keep her awake, a glowing, spiked door lurked just outside her room.

She threw off her covers and rose from the bed. Shivering, she returned downstairs and snatched a dagger to slip beneath her pillow.

CHAPTER 12

As her nails dug into her palms, Ursula stood by the empty reception desk of Ostema, a hair salon near the Plaza Hotel. Around the room, tall mirrors gleamed over bamboo countertops. The air had a faint citrus sent. The place was designed to lull customers into a sense of peace, but Ursula's head was a war zone. Her mind burned with everything that had happened in the past twenty-four hours: her newfound wealth, Kester's hound form, a soul that was no longer quite her own.

And her new, icy companion wasn't doing anything to calm her nerves.

That morning, Kester had brought with him a slender young woman named Zemfira. With platinum-blond hair cut in a chic bob, and a patterned mini dress, she looked like some sort of retro supermodel. Ursula, on the other hand, wore the same black clothes from the day before, her red hair pulled into a messy ponytail. She'd been too overwhelmed to care how she looked this morning.

Before Kester had left, he'd explained that Zemfira—or Zee, as she called herself—would be getting Ursula settled. And, at Zemfira's insistence, their first *crucial* stop was a hair salon.

"Try to look cool," said the girl, her accent faintly Russian.

"I don't even know what that means." *Be nice, Ursula.* This girl was frosty, but if Ursula could get on her good side, maybe Zee would be a little more forthcoming than Kester. Like, about what had happened to the last guy who had Ursula's job.

Working at Rufus's bar, Ursula had met glamorous girls like Zee before. They *loved* to gossip.

Zee leveled cobalt blue eyes at her. "I don't enjoy being seen around the city with someone who looks like she drank twenty wine coolers at a skanky art student party last night."

Or maybe not. For some reason, Zee had decided she hated Ursula. Something had obviously struck a nerve, and Ursula needed to figure out what it was. "That's how you'd describe me? A drunk art skank?"

"I suppose." Zemfira's eyes flicked to her steel-grey nails, as though they were the most fascinating things in the room. "But Luis is a master with hair. He'll be able to help you with… the thing you've got going on with your head. Is it a British thing?"

"Is *what* a British thing?" Ursula asked, no longer trying to hide the irritation in her voice. Zee was a nightmare.

"Having your hair plastered flat to your head like that. Like it wants to escape its miserable existence on your head, and you won't let it."

Ursula gritted her teeth. She would find a way to be nice to Zee, even if it killed her. She could do this. "I don't know, but your hair is pretty." She'd been trying for a compliment, but with her jaw clenched like that, it had somehow come out sounding like a threat. Like she'd just proposed scalping Zee and wearing her platinum hair as a wig.

"It is pretty," Zee agreed cautiously.

"Absolutely. Very… straight. And blond."

"At least you noticed. Kester did not."

Aha. "Oh. Is he your boyfriend?"

Zee cut her a cold look. "He is not. He likes to pick up strays. Women who are beneath him." Her narrowed eyes implied that this included Ursula.

And I've just found the raw nerve. "I hope you don't think *I'm* one of his strays. We've only just met, and he's my mentor. I work with him, as of last night, but our relationship is purely professional. In fact, I'm fairly certain he doesn't like me." That was certainly true.

"Right. Like he 'worked' with that orange-skinned girl from Hoboken he met at Tatty O'Rourke's. And yet he doesn't seem interested in 'working' with me. Because he likes *skanks*." She picked up a magazine, flipping a page with a ferocity that suggested she had a vendetta against paper. "He likes slumming it."

"I wasn't using 'working' as a euphemism. I mean actual *work*." Sure, it involved reaping souls and traveling through a fire portal, but it was work all the same. "Do you know what we do for work, by any chance?"

"Of course I do." Zee arched a thin eyebrow and snapped her magazine shut. "Ah. Here is Luis."

A dark-haired young man approached them, his crisp white shirt vibrant against his bronze skin. He was nearly as big as Kester, and he'd accessorized beautifully with a gold watch and chunky glasses. He peered over them, staring at Ursula's hair. "Hello, gorgeous."

Ursula straightened. *Odd behavior for a hairdresser, but okay.*

"Keep your hands to yourself, Luis," said Zee. "She works for Kester."

"I'll behave." He smiled at Zee. "So glad you could bring in this beauty. I love redheads."

"Beauty?" Zee glared at Ursula. "Her head is an aesthetic crime scene. I was hoping you could clean it up. I told her you were the best. And very discreet, of course."

Luis brightened and waggled a finger. "I never tell Emerazel's secrets."

Ursula raised an eyebrow. *Does everyone know about Emerazel but me?*

"Of course you don't tell our secrets. You wouldn't want to land on the Headsman's bad side."

The Headsman. A shiver crawled up Ursula's spine. She didn't like the sound of that. Of course, life among the demons was bound to be unnerving.

Luis pursed his lips, studying Ursula. "The cut is all wrong, but her auburn hair is simply delicious." He reached out, wrapping a tendril of her hair around his fingers. He stared at it, licking his lips in a way she could only describe as lascivious, as a glazed look overtook his eyes. *What the hell?* He took a shuddering breath before dropping the lock of her hair, his eyes becoming alert again. "A treatment with my Brazilian conditioner will really bring out the color." He beckoned her to a room in the back, his gaze still lingering on her hair.

He seated Ursula in a soft leather chair, easing her head into a shampoo sink. Warm water trickled through her hair, and his fingers lathered her scalp with sensual swirls. "Red hair is my favorite."

Ursula almost thought she heard Luis moan, but she shut out that disturbing thought.

Zee plopped into the chair next to her. "Oh, Luis. You and your redheads. As if you don't get enough of them at Oberon's."

Ursula had no clue what they were talking about, but she breathed in the calming aroma of the pineapple-scented shampoo. Maybe she could get used to this life if she absolutely had to. As soon as she left the salon, she was going to buy paints to brighten up her new bedroom. She'd paint bluebells and aster, to make herself feel at home again.

Then again, there was that whole *Headsman* thing. Whoever that was, he sounded terrifying.

She opened her eyes, glancing at Zee. "Zee. Did you say something about a *Headsman?*"

Luis stopped lathering her hair.

Zee let out a long sigh. "Oh. That's Kester's nickname."

Goose bumps raised over Ursula's skin. "Why the Headsman?"

"It means *executioner.* He's Emerazel's most senior hellhound. Kester gets the most difficult cases, and his numbers are unparalleled. He has sent more souls into Emerazel's flames than you can imagine. He's lethal, and practically like a god himself."

And she'd fought him last night. She was lucky to have survived her eighteenth birthday at all. No wonder he'd warned her that she wouldn't win in a fight against him.

Luis's fingers resumed their massage.

At least I got Zee talking. What she was hearing was terrifying, but at least she was hearing something. "So what you're saying is that I'm in good hands?"

"As long as you stay on his good side. You'll need his protection, you know." Zee sighed loudly. "All this effort to make you look presentable, and you'll probably just be shredded anyway."

Ursula's pulse raced. *This is getting worse.* "What do you mean, *shredded?*"

Zee straightened, peering over at Ursula's face. "You mean Kester didn't tell you why there was an opening in New York?"

Her stomach clenched. "No, he was a little quiet on that point."

"Ugh, it was ghastly. Someone gutted the last guy, and strung his entrails over the trees in Central Park. They looked like Christmas tree ornaments, only made of flesh." Zee smiled sweetly. "And now you have his job."

Bloody hell. Pictures of bluebells and asters won't be nearly enough to help me sleep soundly tonight.

CHAPTER 13

*I*n the armory, Ursula faced herself in mirror, staring at her glossy locks. Luis hadn't cut off much—just enough that her hair now fell above her shoulders. He'd been a little creepy—in fact, he'd pressed his cell phone number into her palm and demanded that she call him for a scalp massage—but at least he'd done a wonderful job with the cut.

She was already feeling much better about her insane new life. After she'd returned that afternoon, she'd finished painting a small mural of wildflowers on her bedroom wall, making it feel a little more like home. And when she'd strode downstairs, covered in smudges of periwinkle and honey-hued paints, she'd found bags of clothes waiting for her on the living room floor.

Inside one of the bags, there was a handwritten note from Kester explaining that she'd need the clothes for work. Whoever had bought them had exquisite taste. Apart from some gorgeous dresses, they were, unfortunately, all black—not exactly her thing. But still, she wasn't going to complain about Louboutin boots and Burberry trousers.

If only she could have ignored the whole *eternal torment* thing—not to mention the *shredded hellhounds* thing—she'd be having a wonderful time in New York.

As she gripped Honjo in front of her, she pointed the blade straight at the mirror, her feet planted in a fighting stance. She now wore a new pair of black trousers—real leather this time—and a black tank top. She looked like some sort of American action hero.

She sliced the katana to the side, eviscerating an imaginary assailant. She resumed the ready position with the blade parallel to the floor. As she watched her form for precision and balance, she slowly raised the sword above her head. She slashed it down. *Thanks ever so much for the work clothes, Kester, but did you forget to mention that bit about the entrails in the park trees?*

Beyond the evisceration and public display of intestines, Zee had known no more about who or what had killed the last hellhound. She didn't know if the murderer was still a threat, or if he was likely to come for Ursula.

The steel glinted in Ursula's hands. If someone was after her, she'd be prepared.

Footsteps echoed behind her, and she turned to find Kester standing in the doorway, dressed in a fitted black suit.

She gripped the sword's hilt. "When were you planning on telling me the last fellow was gutted in Central Park?"

A muscle worked in his jaw. "Zee has a little problem with discretion. And tact." His green eyes lingered on her a little too long; something feral flickered in them. "You clean up nicely. Black suits you."

"It does not suit me." At the carnal look in his eyes, heat burned her cheeks. "I'm more of a spring colors girl."

"You're not a 'spring colors girl.' You're a god-damned demon. Do you understand that? You're going to have to kill people."

Dread tightened her chest. She hadn't really thought about that. "Speaking of killing people..." She strode across the room and pointed the blade at his chest. "I want to know what's going on. Why was the last hellhound murdered?"

He didn't flinch. Apparently, even when she was armed with a katana, he didn't view her as dangerous. His eyes flashed with anger. "I don't know why he was murdered. You're here to help me find out, once you've calmed down a bit."

"I'm perfectly—"

In a fraction of a second, he'd moved behind her, swift as the wind—one powerful arm wrapped tightly around her, and the other hand gripping her sword arm. Heat from his body warmed her. He squeezed her wrist, and she gasped at the pain, dropping the sword. "Don't take on an opponent you have no chance of beating, Ursula," he whispered in her ear. "Not unless you have a really good plan."

Her frustration lent her boldness. "Oh, right. I hear you're 'the Headsman.' Quite the nickname you have." Her heart raced. She shouldn't be prodding this beast, but she wasn't so sure she could cope with being a hellhound. What did she really have to lose at this point? "Your colleague was gutted, his intestines strewn about like holiday decorations, and you have no idea why?"

He loosened his grip on her, slipping away. "It could have been any number of things. Some demons enjoy dispatching their prey with a dramatic flair. Sometimes a curse can rebound, injuring the caster. A lot of things could have led to Henry's demise."

Demons. Curses. All in a day's work around here. "Hellhounds use curses, too?"

"We do what Emerazel tells us. Usually it's signing pacts and reaping souls, but sometimes she has more specific requests."

"Such as?"

"When you get one, you'll know." Something wicked glinted in his eyes. "And if you must know, I really don't mourn Henry's loss. He was something of a psychopath."

She narrowed her eyes. "Speaking of psychopaths, Headsman, why are you in my apartment?"

He flashed her a wolfish smile. "I couldn't resist your warm and inviting company."

She crossed her arms, eyeing the sword on the ground. "Seriously. What did you come for?"

"I left a box of gold ingots on your kitchen table—your annual stipend—and I'm here to teach you how to summon Emerazel." He turned toward the hallway. "Follow me."

She snatched Honjo from the ground, returning it to the rack, and stalked after Kester.

He spoke over his shoulder. "When you meet the goddess of passion and wrath, please don't mouth off. She can compel you to do whatever she wants, including throwing yourself through a window, so I'd advise you to be pleasant and charming." He slid a cold gaze her way. "In other words, don't be yourself."

"I'm perfectly charming to people who haven't abducted me and threatened my life," she shot back.

"You asked for this." They stopped at the door to the sigil room, and Kester continued. "Summoning her is simple. You just need three ingredients. The first is her symbol."

"The encircled triangle. I've got that one memorized." She followed him into the sigil room, glancing out the windows at the snow-covered city. She was about to meet an immortal goddess of fire, yet her blood had turned to ice. She hugged herself tight.

Kester pulled the rug aside to reveal the symbol on the floor. "The second ingredient is fire." He produced a box of matches and the small silver flask from inside his jacket.

He unscrewed the top, taking a swig. "Glorious." After pouring a few ounces of scotch on the sigil, he struck a match and dropped it. His voice took on a professorial tone. "If you're using alcohol, be sure that it's high enough proof to take a flame. You don't want to be caught with your hand on a pact and a sigil that won't light."

"High proof. Got it." It didn't have to be expensive, just alcoholic.

"Lastly, you need to intone the summoning spell." Kester reached into his pocket and produced a small scrap of parchment. "I've memorized it, but here's a copy so you can follow along. You'll need to repeat after me."

Ursula looked at the paper. Spidery letters crowded its surface. Kester started to speak, and though she didn't know the name of the language, she found she could read it phonetically. F.U. was just full of surprises.

As they worked their way through the spell, the words began to roll off her tongue.

When they finished the final line, fire blazed like an erupting volcano, and Ursula shielded her face from the heat. The flame died abruptly, revealing a dark, smoky form crouched in the sigil's center.

A feminine figure rose. Dark tendrils of smoke curled off her, and her eyes burned like supernovas. Wincing, Ursula looked away before her retinas burned out.

A raspy voice, crackling with fire, spoke. "Is this the girl you told me about?"

"This is Ursula."

Ursula shielded her eyes, but Emerazel's heat filled the room. Plumes of smoke wafted through the air like tentacles, encircling the two hellhounds. Outside, Ursula thought she caught a glimpse of Central Park now blazing with spewing lava and ash. *That isn't real, is it?*

She couldn't breathe. What had happened to the air? She wanted to get the hell out of here. Ash seemed to fill her lungs. It was too hot.

"Interesting," whispered the goddess. "Very interesting. I see something in her."

"She is… feisty," said Kester.

"There's something else. Something I didn't notice before, the day she carved herself."

The day I carved myself. Does she know me? Nausea welled in Ursula's gut. Something felt wrong. It was too hot in here—too bright. She needed the cool night air, needed to slip into the shadows, to ride the dark wind into cool, quiet space. Her body trembled, and she clamped her eyes shut. She wasn't sure she could speak, even if she wanted to.

"You remember her?" asked Kester. "She doesn't know where she came from."

"That's for the best," Emerazel spat. "I want to see her kneel before me."

The words rang in Ursula's head, and without thinking, she fell, her knees cracking against the floor. Her body trembled. Emerazel had complete control over her, just as Kester had told her she would.

"A loyal subject to do with as I please. How delicious." The goddess's voice hissed like water on a hot stone.

Ursula had no reply, couldn't meet the goddess's eyes. Nausea and dread wound through her, curling around her thoughts. *I don't belong here.*

"Tell me you're my subject," whispered Emerazel.

Ursula felt her mouth moving. "I am your loyal subject," she intoned. "I am yours."

A deep laugh rumbled through the room, shaking the floor. "You burn for me."

With a great force of will, Ursula dared to raise her eyes, though not high enough to meet the goddess's shining gaze. She stared instead at Emerazel's lips, cracked into a cinder-flecked smile. *She knows something about me.* If Ursula had had any control over her own body, she'd have asked what it was.

"Do you remember when she carved herself?" Kester pressed.

"I remember the day, though I didn't know who she was then. So many souls came to me that day. It was glorious." An ashy smile played about the goddess's lips. "That's all you need to know. I have an assignment for my sniveling little subject."

Ursula fought against the urge to scream. Her skin was on fire, and she was in the center of a volcano. Pain ripped her mind apart. Why didn't Kester mind the heat? How could he stand this?

Emerazel's smile widened. "The target is a particularly delectable soul. He allied himself with me a few months ago. You might have heard of him —Hugo Modes. You're to collect his soul for me. Do not disappoint me. Kester, give her a ledger. One thousand pages. One page for each task, until the book is full."

Ursula's body trembled. *Did she say a thousand pages?*

Kester nodded. "She's had no training, so I will go with her on her first assignment."

"No," Emerazel bellowed. "I want to see what she can do on her own. And, Kester, when you train her, make sure she remains submissive. Do not go gentle on her. I want this one to obey."

"Of course," he said, his tone flat.

"If she needs to die," Emerazel mused. "Be sure you bring her to me first. I will dispose of her myself. In fact, I rather look forward to it." Emerazel's lips began to crumble, and her body collapsed into a pile of ash.

Ursula gasped as cool air filled the room, and the icy winter day returned through the windows. Shaking, she hunched over on her hands and knees, fighting the urge to vomit. Her body twitched uncontrollably. A strong taste of creosote filled her mouth, and sandpaper seemed to line her eyelids. Coughing and gagging, she blinked, trying to force some moisture from her tear ducts.

"That was awful. You didn't tell me it would be that awful." She hated the way her voice broke. She didn't want Kester to see her weakened like this. He already had far too much control over her life.

"Gods below," said Kester, his voice low. "Your first lesson is never to look directly at her."

He held out a hand, lifting her up. "Are you all right?"

Too tired to care about her pride, she leaned into him. "I won't make that mistake again," she managed. She needed a cool bath, and a long sleep.

Kester slipped an arm around her waist, holding her up, and studied her. "I didn't know that would happen," he said quietly. "I've never seen her act that way before. And her flames shouldn't burn one with the mark. I don't feel her heat when she appears. You were in agony."

"I thought I was dying."

"You've certainly earned that *Mystery Girl* nickname."

She straightened, pulling away from him as the nausea subsided. "I don't suppose I can convince Emerazel to tell me what she knows about me."

"She clearly hates you for some reason, so no."

Trapped in the constant desperation of trying to pay her rent and buy food, she'd ignored the most fundamental question for so long: *Who am I?* And now it blazed in her mind like Emerazel's terrifying eyes. "Why would she hate me? What did I do?"

Kester's gaze bored into her. "I can tell you that your Angelic incantation was very clear. In fact, your accent is perfect. You were a scholar, once. How can you remember Angelic if you can't remember anything about yourself?"

"Same reason I can speak English and know how to use a knife and fork. It's a different type of memory." She frowned. *Scholar* was not a word she'd ever associated with herself. "But an Angelic scholar? Where would I have learned it?"

"No idea. I guess that's what makes you the Mystery Girl."

She swallowed hard. "What did she mean by a ledger?"

"Every hellhound has a book—a ledger to track your progress. One page per task. When it is full, your soul is free. I'll have one ready for you when you return from your assignment. I haven't even begun training you, and I honestly have no idea why Emerazel has given you an assignment already. You're not ready for it. But she has it in for you, so you'd better get it right, because it seemed like she wanted to kill you."

Cold dread bloomed in her mind. *My assignment. Right.* "I was in too much pain to focus when she was talking. I almost thought she was talking about Hugo Modes—the lead singer of Four Points. But that can't be right."

Kester quirked an eyebrow. "She was. You'd best pick out one of those dresses I bought you. Charm is one of the best weapons we have, though I don't get the impression it comes naturally to you."

CHAPTER 14

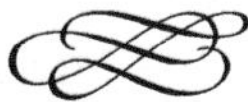

$\mathcal{U}$rsula sat in the back seat of a Bentley, staring out the window at a line of shivering club-goers. She wore a silky cocktail dress that felt gorgeous against her skin. Black—of course, since Kester had picked it out. With her nerves frayed beyond recognition, she'd arrived at her first assignment twenty minutes early.

Outside, snowflakes drifted through the air. A few had melted on the car's warm windows where they reflected the neon lights of Brooklyn like tiny jewels. In the front seat, the driver hummed tunelessly to the radio, a Mets cap on his head.

"You think the Mets will be any good this season," she asked. She wasn't even sure what sort of sports she was talking about, but she needed a distraction, some sense of normalcy.

"Yeah," he said.

So much for small talk.

She drummed her manicured fingernails over her bare thighs. *Hugo Modes.* She was supposed to claim the soul of Hugo Modes. Could she really send his soul to a fiery afterlife? And what, exactly, did Emerazel plan to do with it down there?

Honestly, if his music was anything to go by, he didn't have much of a soul. His songs were the melodic equivalent of a white-bread and margarine sandwich. In fact, if she were ever tasked with designing her own personal hell, it would involve listening to The Four Points song "Girl, You Got a Magic Body" on a loop.

Still, it wasn't like she wanted to murder him for it.

And yet, there were only two options: get the contract signed, or reap his soul. "Just stab him right in the heart with the blade of the pen," Kester had explained, like it was nothing.

Soul-reaping didn't seem to bother him. Of course, someone with the nickname *the Headsman* probably didn't have normal, human emotions. Over a glass of wine, he'd casually declared, "By the way, you can't contact any old friends, since you're officially dead. The police notified them yesterday. I say 'friends'—really it was just the flatmate and an ex-boyfriend. Kind of a sad life you left behind. Anyway, the papers have already reported the Mystery Girl's overdose. Heroin and crack. Naughty girl."

Just like that, Kester had told her only friend of her demise.

Three years was the sad sum of her life, according to the tabloids. Found in a church, couldn't handle the fame, shifted from one foster home to the next. "Unstable," her former boss Rufus had reported. "Couldn't be trusted around customers. I had to fire her after she attacked someone."

The British tabloids now speculated that she'd started the St. Ethelburga fire herself. Though, now that she knew about her fiery hands, that might not be a million miles from the truth.

Bloody Kester. He couldn't have orchestrated some kind of heroic death.

She tightened her fists. Two minutes before her first mission was no time to get emotional. She needed to keep a clear head. She had a soul to collect, and she wasn't going to screw it up, because it sort of seemed like the fire goddess really wanted to slaughter her.

She pulled out the new mobile Kester had given her, and flicked open a web browser, searching for "Hugo Modes" to get a refresher on his face. He grinned at the camera, all white teeth, pink lips, and large brown eyes —virtually indistinguishable from the three other mop-haired boys in his band.

Kester had been clear on the plan. She and Zee were supposed to approach Hugo together. Keep a low profile, and stay in the shadows. That part was easy enough. She liked shadows. It was just the whole *killing* thing that made her uneasy. Hopefully it wouldn't come down to that. She might be a mortal demon, but she wasn't a murderer.

Someone rapped on the window, and Ursula jumped. It was Zee, clad in a belted white coat, her breath clouding around her face. Ursula opened the door, stepping into icy air that nipped at her bare legs.

"Zee." Ursula shut the door behind her. "Thanks for meeting me here."

The Russian stepped back, surveying Ursula's black coat and tan heels. "You don't look as gross as you did before."

"Thanks." She hugged herself. "What do you do for Kester, anyway? Are you his employee?" *Or do you just do what he says because you fancy him?*

"I have certain skills for which Kester pays me. That's all you need to know. For one thing, I can get us in anywhere." Her eye makeup shone gold in the tungsten streetlights. "This place is like my second home." Behind her, gold-plated lettering read *Club Lalique.*

Ursula's teeth chattered. "I'm freezing. Shall we get in line?" She stuffed her phone into a small clutch the color of smoke. *Wyrm skin,* Kester had said. Dragon hide was invisible to normal humans, which made the clutch perfect for what she had to carry into the club.

"Come with me." Zee looped her arm through Ursula's, leading her to the front of the line.

"Are we just going to jump the queue?" Ursula whispered. She felt like a tit cutting in front of everyone, and she could feel their angry stares burning into her.

"Of course."

A ruddy-faced bouncer in a long heavy coat stood behind a red rope. "Good evening, Zemfira."

Zee smiled. "Just my friend and me tonight."

The bouncer lifted the rope, then pulled open a black door. It led into a short hallway lined with pale marble tiles, and once she was inside its warmth Ursula's stiff shoulders began to relax. They walked through a narrow hall to a set of gold-plated doors.

Zee pushed a button, and the doors opened to reveal an elevator's mirrored interior. They both stepped inside.

Ursula took a deep breath. *Calm down. All you need to do is give Hugo the parchment, and ask him to sign. He should be perfectly reasonable about it.* What Emerazel wanted with his soul was a mystery, but she supposed Kester would probably just tell her it was none of her concern.

As the elevator silently climbed fifteen stories, she glanced at a CCTV camera in the corner. This place was probably littered with cameras. A bit tricky to stay in the shadows.

At the top floor, the doors opened to reveal a vast room dripping with opulence: platinum, muted gold, and vibrant amber. It was like something out of a Russian palace before the revolution. No wonder Zee liked it here.

A few patrons clustered around a circular bar, while others lounged in cream leather booths. Above the bar, a gold column branched out like a metal tree, and crystal lights sparkled among its boughs. But the most eye-catching aspect of the room was the view: across the East River, Manhattan's buildings jutted into the sky, a glittering, steel forest. This place was so far from Rufus's club that it might as well have been on another planet. *You've come a long way, Ursula.*

A grey-haired man in a black sweater approached them. "May I take your coats?"

"Yes, please," said Zee.

Zee wriggled out of her white coat, revealing a pale cocktail dress that hugged her delicate curves. A pearl necklace draped around her neck, and she gripped a small, indigo clutch that matched her shoes.

The man turned to Ursula. "Miss?"

Ursula slipped out of her coat. The black Prada dress hugged her body perfectly. Short and A-line—good for running if she needed to slip away fast. She handed over her coat.

Zee appraised her outfit. "Black. Sophisticated. Very nice."

You're not the only one out here who can pick out a dress. "Thanks."

"I don't know about you," Zee continued, "but I'm dying for a cocktail." She headed to the bar, nabbing the last gold-cushioned seat. Ursula had to stand awkwardly behind her.

Within moments, a blond bartender leaned across the wooden bar. "The usual, Miss Zemfira?"

"Yes, but make it two." She turned to Ursula. "You like champagne cocktails." It was less a question than a directive. *Drink it or else.*

"Sure. Whatever." With her nerves blazing, Ursula wasn't really in the mood for drinking, but it would help her blend in. Champagne wasn't so alcoholic as to get her drunk, and she could slowly nurse it.

"Great." Zee smiled. "Save my spot. I have to pee."

After Zee hurried off, Ursula slipped into her seat, watching as the bartender put together their drinks. After dropping two sugar cubes into a pair of champagne flutes, he retrieved a bottle of Angostura. He dropped the bitters onto the cubes—deep red drops, like blood on snow. As he filled the glasses with champagne, Ursula shivered for a moment, thinking of the last hellhound, and the entrails that had decorated a tree.

The bartender slid the glasses across the rich wood.

"Thank you." When she took a sip, the bubbles tickled her nose.

A thin hand snapped up the other drink. "Just in time," said Zee.

"When do you think Hugo will get here?" Ursula whispered.

"Soon, I suppose. He's a regular here." Zee leaned in close. "I can't believe he's your first target."

"How is it that you know all about this? About what I do?"

Zee's blue eyes sparkled. "I take it Kester hasn't told you very much about me."

Of course not. He hadn't told her very much about anything. Before Ursula could asked her what she meant, Zee shushed her. "Hugo's here."

"Where?"

"In the corner booth. Three o'clock. No wait. Nine o'clock? Whatever. To your left."

Ursula shifted in her seat.

"Don't look. He's seen me. Did you see him? Don't look!" Zee paused for what seem like a minute, but was probably only a few seconds. "Ok, you can look now, but don't be obvious. He's with a brunette. A lingerie model. I recognize her." Zee took a sip of her champagne. "Shall we chat with him?"

Zee's onslaught of directions had left Ursula confused. "Now? I was planning on cornering him here at the bar."

"He has bottle service. He won't leave his table." Zee slipped off her stool and started toward Hugo's booth. After smoothing down her hair, Ursula followed. Apparently, they were just going to walk up and introduce themselves to the superstar.

Hugo slouched into the pale leather of a large U-shaped booth. A bottle of champagne sat in an ice bucket shaped like a golden egg. Just to the side of the table hovered an enormous bald bodyguard, with a face the color of raw meat. A snake tattoo curled around his scalp. Even with fire magic on her side, Ursula didn't want to learn how she'd do in a fight against him. She'd have to find a way to leave the hulk behind, and get Hugo on his own.

She stopped just next to Zee at the edge of the table, clutching her champagne. She tried to loosen her shoulders so she didn't look quite so much like a grim reaper on a death hunt. *Except that's pretty much what I am.*

Zee plonked her champagne on the table, flashing the group a dazzling smile. The model grinned, throwing her hands in the air and trilling in a French accent, "Zee! I'm so glad you're here. You look amazing, as usual." She wore a tiny, beaded white dress, so delicate that it reminded Ursula of dew drops on a spider web. The woman draped a thin, tan arm over Hugo's shoulders.

She knows Zee. Zee didn't mention that.

The bodyguard turned his head. "Good to see you again, Zee. I was hoping we'd see you tonight."

And the bodyguard, too? Ursula frowned, staring at her companion. If Zee was a regular here, maybe she'd know the doorman, the coat man, and the bartender. But what were the chances she would happen to be close friends with a French lingerie model and Hugo Mode's bouncer?

Is this magic, too?

CHAPTER 15

Only Hugo seemed immune to Zee's spell. Over a pale green cocktail, he narrowed his eyes. Up close, his features were less plastic than they appeared in the music videos, and his dark blue irises glittered in the dim club's lights.

The model twirled the stem of her Manhattan glass. "Please. Join us, Zemfira."

Zee scooted in next to the model, while Ursula took a spot next to Hugo. Yanking a thin straw from his drink, he flicked tiny droplets over the table. "I was in the middle of a story."

Zee took a sip of her cocktail. "Don't let us stop you, Hugo."

Hugo shifted in his seat, looking around the table. "I was explaining why I had to dump Madison. I'm sure you saw it in the papers." He raked his fingers through his hair. "So my PR guy sent me Virginie here. We're supposed to go to the opera tomorrow. Like, to be seen together."

Virginie smiled.

"Oh?" Zee cocked her head, feigning sympathy. "What happened with Madison?"

Hugo frowned. "She bought a one-piece for our vacation in Saint Kitts. And there were going to be paparazzi there, obviously." His clipped accent and soft Rs suggested he had some history in a British boarding school, but also that he'd lived in the US long enough to give his voice a

85

nasal quality. He sounded a bit like a 1920s radio announcer. Hugo turned to Ursula, dark eyebrows raised. "Do I look like the kind of guy who would date a girl with a one-piece?"

"I don't even know what that means."

"A one-piece bathing suit. A swimming costume." He spoke slowly, like she might have a head injury. "Like, not a bikini."

"Yeah, I get the bathing suit concept. I just didn't know there was a recognizable type of man whose girlfriend—"

Zee kicked her hard under the table and Hugo glared at her. *Shit. I'm supposed to be charming.*

She smiled, widening her eyes. "But of course I never wear swimming costumes—I mean bathing suits."

"You don't swim?

She licked her lips in what she hoped was a seductive gesture. "I only swim *au naturel.*"

Hugo shifted toward her, suddenly interested. "What else do you do *au naturel?*" His gaze rested firmly on her breasts before moving to her face.

"Oh, you know. *Things.*" She said it softly, gently placing a hand on Hugo's knee where Virginie couldn't see. Hopefully the knee-touching would distract him from the fact that she'd just tried to say "things" seductively.

Hugo stared into her eyes, and little smirk played around the corner of his mouth, before he abruptly looked away, slapping his hands on the table. "I need to go for a slash."

He pushed his leg against Ursula's, indicating that he wanted to get up from the table. Ursula scooted out, watching as Hugo and the bodyguard disappeared into the crowd. She took a sip of her champagne cocktail. *Charm him and isolate him. One point for Ursula.*

Her cell phone vibrated in her purse and she pulled it out. Zee's name popped up.

"r u going to follow him????"
"should I?"
"He wants u 2. Now is ur chance."

Virginie was gushing to Zee about her upcoming opera date—as if the

Russian ice princess were the warmest, friendliest person in the world. *Definitely magic of some sort.* Ursula would have to ask Zee about that later.

Straightening her short dress, Ursula stood and strode toward the bathrooms. She'd read somewhere that British soldiers were given a rum ration before they went over the trenches. She downed the rest of her cocktail. In Club Lalique, champagne would have to do.

She glanced down at the wyrm-skin purse tucked under her arm. It held a credit card, 250 American dollars, a tube of red lipstick, her lucky stone, and her cellphone. But most importantly, it contained a small parchment pact and a bone-colored pen with a razor-sharp nib. All she had to do was remind Hugo of his contract, jab his palm, and get him to sign in his blood. *Simple.*

The dance floor had begun to fill, and Ursula wove her way through the crowd of lithe, glittering women and besuited men. She tried not to think about the pen's second function. Kester had shown her a button hidden in its side that, when clicked, extended the nib into a small blade. That was the soul-reaping blade.

But she wasn't going to use that. Even by the Headsman's standards, that was a worst-case scenario. No one would agree to these bargains if word got round that Emerazel's hellhounds murdered everyone on their eighteenth birthdays. In order for the system to work, they needed signatures, not corpses.

In one of the corners, a gold-plated letter *M* hung above a dark alcove. Hugo's bodyguard stood just next to the entrance. As Ursula approached, the bodyguard gave her a wink. *Good. Hugo's definitely expecting me.*

She pushed open the door and slipped inside. There was a short, curly-haired man by the sinks with a white towel in his hand. A silver tray of cologne, Club Lalique matchbooks, and breath mints were arranged on the counter behind him. "Miss, this is the men's—" he started to say, but he fell silent when he glimpsed the one-hundred-dollar bill in Ursula's outstretched hand.

"Can you give us a few minutes?" she whispered.

He nodded silently, pointing to the end of a row of black stall doors.

Ursula's heels clacked over the tiles. Steel urinals lined the left wall under tall windows that granted a view of Manhattan. Any man taking a piss in Club Lalique could imagine that he was urinating on all the poor sods below. *Ugh. If the revolution came, I'd be on the wrong side of the palace walls.*

As she took a deep breath, she tapped the last door. "Hugo?" *Seductive. Sound seductive.* "It's Ursula," she breathed.

He cracked the door open, and she slipped inside, gripping her purse in anticipation. A window filled one entire wall, with only a thin black curtain covering the lower half for discretion. She could only hope no one was spending their evening scanning the Lalique bathrooms with a pair of binoculars.

Hugo pressed himself flat against the window, loosening his shirt collar. "Who are you?"

Ursula tried tossing her hair, but with the awkward jerk of her head it probably came off more like an involuntary twitch. "I'm Ursula. Zee's friend."

A cold sweat beaded on his forehead. "But I don't know who Zee is, or why my date seemed to know her. When I asked my bodyguard, he couldn't remember where he knew her from either."

Zee had *definitely* used some sort of spell on them. Time to dispense with the pleasantries. "You've just turned eighteen. I'm here about your pact with Emerazel."

He wiped a hand across his mouth, staring into her eyes. Emerazel's fire now blazed behind his indigo irises. "No one came on my birthday. I thought I'd gotten away with it."

She exhaled. So he knew the drill and this wasn't too much of a shock. "Sorry, no. You didn't get away. And now it's time to sign the papers." She stepped closer, pulling the pen from her bag and popping off the cap.

"And after I sign… I'm just a little fuzzy on what I'm agreeing to."

"When you die, Emerazel will take your soul to burn in the inferno for eternity." *Bollocks. I might need to work on my pitch a little.*

Hugo's blue eyes bulged. "I don't want to do it anymore."

"Of course you don't. It's awful—" Ursula sputtered. "—Not ideal, but you don't have a choice. The deal was, you gave your soul in exchange for —" She pulled the parchment out of her purse. "What was it you asked for? Fame?"

He swallowed hard, eyes open wide. "For people to hear my music and think it's amazing."

She thrust the contract toward him. "Hmmm… Well I guess it only works on a portion of the population. Anyway, you made the deal verbally. And now you get all the French models, Grammys, and green cocktails you can consume until you die. Considering most of the world has to live on $6 a day, you're getting quite lot. I mean sure, the eternal torment—"

"It's the soul part that concerns me." The pink had vanished from his cheeks. "It was just a lark with my mates. I thought it was a fairy story."

Was she going to have to act as a therapist with all the supplicants? She wasn't very good at this hand-holding stuff. How was she supposed to convince him this was a good idea? This was an *awful* idea. And even if he was a knob, she didn't want him to burn until the end of time. Bloody hell, she wasn't a psychopath—she definitely wasn't cut out for this gig. Still, she'd have to put forth the effort if she didn't want to face slaughter at Emerazel's hands—or perhaps Kester's.

She squared her shoulders. "Well, chin up, and all that. Here's the pen." She forced a smile onto her face. "Please sign, and everything will be fine… for a while." She couldn't bring herself to outright lie about it. She was a terrible liar.

"I'll have to spend eternity burning in the inferno," he sputtered.

This tidbit would likely be a bit of a sticking point in these negotiations. "From what I understand, the other option is starting your sentence now, and I'm sure you can see that's worse. You're young. Death is a long way off. Unless you refuse to sign, and then it's a very short way off."

Hugo's shoulders hunched. "What do you mean?"

Ursula gazed into his indigo eyes, trying to convey the gravity of the situation. "If you don't sign, I have to reap your soul now, and then it's straight to the fires. The torment can start now, or later." *God I don't want to be doing this.*

Hugo swallowed hard, his body trembling.

She depressed the button on the knife and the blade popped out with a snapping noise. She pressed the button again, retracting the blade. Hugo's eyes bulged.

"Of course, Emerazel doesn't want me to reap your soul now. It's bad for business if you guys don't get anything in return for eternity. She needs to keep the bargains coming, you know?"

Hugo tightened his lips, reaching for the pen with a resigned look on his face. But just as he was about to take it, he swung an elbow at her head.

90

CHAPTER 16

Ursula dodged, but not before Hugo's elbow grazed her cheekbone. She stumbled into the side of the stall. He followed his elbow with a wild haymaker, but she saw it coming. As she ducked, she struck upward with the sharp nib of the pen, slicing into his forearm.

Hugo let out a shrill scream, gripping his wrist. "You cut me."

"You're lucky I haven't killed you yet." She thrust the bloody pen toward him. "Sign. Now."

She was losing control of this situation. Kester had told her not to call attention to herself, that she was supposed to work in the shadows, but she had a hysterical pop star on her hands. Just as she thrust the parchment at him, Hugo lowered his shoulder and charged.

She tried to sidestep, but the stall was too narrow. He knocked her backward through the door and onto the marble tiles. Her head smacked against the floor, and pain exploded in her skull.

Clutching his arm, blood dripping between his fingers, he stood looking down at her. "Unbelievable," he said, then sprinted from the bathroom.

Ursula clenched her teeth, forcing herself to stand. Little flecks of light sparked in the periphery of her vision, and she held onto the edge of the sink for support. She rubbed the back of her throbbing head. *I can't let*

Hugo get away. She had royally cocked this up, but at least the bathroom was still empty.

Outside the door she could hear Hugo shrieking, "A crazy woman cut me! Call the police!"

Shit. How was she supposed to get out quietly now? This place was littered with CCTV cameras, and everyone would be looking for her. If she screwed this up, Emerazel was going to take pleasure in personally executing her, for reasons Ursula did not even understand.

Think, Ursula. If she ran through the door, she could make it past Hugo's guard, but some well-meaning club patron would surely tackle her before she made it across the room. What about a diversion? If she used Emerazel's fire, she could set off the sprinklers and the fire alarm. In the ensuing chaos, she might make it to the elevator, but likely not much further before a bouncer caught her. She tightened her fists. *F.U., you bloody maniac, you dragged me into a hellish world I don't even understand.*

She needed to escape now—before anyone came in.

Outside the door someone shouted, "She's still in there, right?"

Sodding hell. So much for working in the shadows. In a few moments, Hugo's bodyguard and the bouncers would be in here. Her heart raced, heat blazing from her hand. If she didn't control herself, she'd be lighting something on fire. Or worse—she'd be lighting *someone* on fire. She glanced down at her hands, at the black smoke curling from her fingertips.

Then it came to her. She rushed to the door, gripping the doorknob. She closed her eyes, willing the heat from her hand into the metal. It was just enough to warp the latch shut.

Someone banged on the door, shouting and trying to turn the knob, but it wouldn't open.

Okay. I've locked myself in. But how was she supposed to get out? There were windows over the urinals, but they were sealed shut. And even if she could break one, she was fifteen stories up. She hadn't exactly brought a parachute. *Magic. I need to use magic.*

She grabbed a bottle of cologne and a matchbook from the attendant's tray. Gripping the bottle, she smashed off the top on the steel edge of the sink before pouring it on the floor in the shape of Emerazel's sigil. She struck a match and dropped it. Flames blazed around her.

What was that transportation spell Kester had chanted? He hadn't taught it to her. *Bollocks bollocks bollocks.*

An authoritative voice boomed through the door. "Is she still in there?"

She closed her eyes. *It's in my brain, somewhere.* In her mind's eye, she was back in the stone circle. Kester held her against his chest. She could almost feel his heartbeat next to her cheek. He'd intoned the strange magical words about a portal of fire, and Emerazel's grace. She repeated after him, and the spell slipped from her tongue, as though she'd known it all her life—which, perhaps, she had.

The bodyguard pounded on the door, shouting. But the fire was raging all around her, and she dissolved into ash.

CHAPTER 17

Ursula blazed into the sigil room before doubling over with a coughing fit. Hot soot seared her lungs, and her body burned with preternatural pain. *I really need to remember to hold my damn breath.* At least she'd escaped the club in one piece. Granted, she didn't have Hugo's signature on the pact, and she'd left Zee behind, but neither was she in handcuffs in the back of a police cruiser.

Footsteps sounded in the hall, and Kester appeared at the doorway. "What happened? How did you get here?" He paused, sniffing. "Did you douse yourself in cologne?"

She'd never thought the sight of his strange green eyes would be a relief. "Sigil spell. Forgot to hold my breath." She wiped tears from her smoke-stung eyes. "And I had to use Giorgio Armani as the accelerant."

"You look gorgeous." Candlelight danced in his eyes, and his gaze trailed over her short dress. "But I still don't understand how you got here. I never taught you that spell."

"I remembered what you said."

He stepped closer, narrowing his eyes. "Impressive as that is, I'm a little alarmed that you felt the need to use it. You collected Hugo's signature, right?"

Ursula brushed ash off her dress. "Things got messy. Hugo made a scene."

A muscle clenched in his jaw. "You didn't get his signature? Then why are you here?"

"I had to escape." *How do I explain this?* "Hugo ran away and started shrieking that I wanted to stab him." *The truth again, I guess.*

Kester moved closer, irises burning. Had she really found his face a welcome sight? He looked—terrifying. "We're supposed to work in the shadows. If your face becomes known, Emerazel will destroy you. If you fail to get a target's signature, as you have, Emerazel will destroy you. She hates you, for reasons I don't understand, and she seemed very eager to reap your soul. I told you the importance of getting this right."

Oh, God. I can't escape the lectures about my own failure, even among the hellhounds. "You told me the importance, but that doesn't make me any more experienced. You and I both agreed it was insane that Emerazel wanted to send me off without training. I don't know why you're suddenly surprised that it didn't turn out well. And you know what? I still don't understand what she wants with everyone's souls. What does she do with them?"

"It's the stakes that mattered. You couldn't afford to fail." Ignoring her question, he rooted her in place with his gaze, and stepped closer. "I don't know why you didn't just sign the pact like I told you to in the first place. Then neither of us would have to worry about this mess."

She crossed her arms, taking a step back, until she was backed up against the wall. "I don't know—why didn't I sign that pact?" She touched her finger to her lips. "Oh yeah, I guess I was a bit put off by the 'burning in eternity' thing. It sounded unpleasant—which, by the way, is why I'm not going to be a great salesman for this deal, because only a psychopath would want someone to burn forever. Hugo gets some cash in exchange for everlasting torture? And I'm supposed to convince him that's a good deal? It's insane. I'm not a monster, Kester."

"Oh, but you are," he snarled. "And so am I." He pressed his palms to the wall on either side of her head, boxing her in.

Adrenaline surged. "I never wanted this."

"You and I don't get the luxury of morality and soul-searching. You asked to be just like me when you wanted a trial, and now you're one of the demons. And I notice you quite happily accept the lodging and the payment for your work."

White-hot anger burned her cheeks. "All I wanted from life was a normal job, enough for food and rent, and a couple of normal friends. I was happy in my hovel of an apartment. It was my home, before you told everyone I overdosed. I don't need three bedrooms in a mansion, or a four-hundred-dollar haircut. And I don't need gold ingots. For fuck's sake."

His eyes bored into her, and for a second, she thought he might tear into her neck like he'd slaughtered the ewe. "Has it occurred to you that there might be worse monsters out there than hellhounds like me?"

Her fingernails dug into her palms. "Worse than agents of perpetual agony? Is that so?"

"There are monsters who would torture you without your consent, who prey on the innocent—unlike hellhounds, who approach only those who've agreed to the bargain. Whether you remember it or not, you agreed to serve Emerazel, and so did Hugo. So did I. Now we all reap the consequences. That's life."

"And you're fine with that?"

A low growl escaped him, and she caught a glimpse of lengthening fangs. He was going to murder her. "Don't you get it? It doesn't matter if I'm fine with it. You can't fight it. Emerazel is as old, as powerful, and as immovable as the stars. If we don't reap the souls, she's more than capable of taking them herself. Hugo's soul will be collected whether you do it or not. But if you defy the goddess, you will join him in the inferno. In fact, Emerazel will want your soul now for your mistake."

A hollow opened in the pit of Ursula's stomach. "For one cock-up?"

Kester's face was stony. "Hugo is internationally famous. Your image will be plastered across the news. If I don't tell Emerazel about your failure, she'll slaughter me along with you."

Ursula fought the urge to vomit. *Of course.* There had been CCTV cameras all over the club, recording her image. She could already imagine the headline: *Insane Mystery Girl Fakes Death, Attacks Hugo Modes.*

"Maybe no one remembers me," she said, her voice breaking.

An eternity in the inferno. Kester was going to give her up to Emerazel. Her heart pounded. She needed to get out of here. Glancing around for an escape route, her eyes landed on the chandelier. She could leap up, kick Kester in the face, and bolt into the elevator. But it wouldn't be on her floor, and she'd have to stand there waiting for it to arrive while Kester summoned the goddess of fire and brimstone. *Bollocks, Ursula.*

Could she make it out a window? Did windows in penthouses even open? Even if she did escape, the goddess had total control over her mind and body. There was no way to run from her.

Raw panic flooded her body, and she began pacing like a caged animal.

Kester's phone buzzed, and he stepped away from her, yanking it from his pocket. After a moment, he exhaled, his shoulders visibly relaxing. "You are *very* lucky Zee was there."

"Why? What happened?" Hope bloomed in her chest.

He shoved the phone in his pocket. "Zee was able to glamour everyone at the club. They won't remember you."

"How?"

"Zee's a fae. That's one of the reasons I sent her along."

"Fae? I don't even know what that is." She was still vibrating with panic; her statement came out as an angry shout.

"The fae can influence people's thoughts. Luckily for you, she convinced the security guards to hand over the tapes of your panicking face."

Ursula loosed a long breath, steadying her nerves. She slid her face into her hands, trying not to imagine Hugo burning in hellfire. "A relief from my death sentence. I could kiss Zee. And now I just need to find Hugo. I heard him saying he was going to the opera tomorrow night."

Kester smirked. "You see? The prospect of your own torment clarifies your thinking, doesn't it?"

She glowered at him. "I don't need you to gloat about it."

"Obviously, you need training. I can give you until tomorrow night to collect Hugo's soul, but beyond that I'll have to report to Emerazel. Even this amount of leniency is risking my own skin." His glacial voice chilled her blood. "And do not create a scene again, or we'll both end up in flames. You have one thousand pages in your ledger—a thousand souls you must collect. Don't give Emerazel the pleasure of reaping your soul before you get through them."

He pivoted, stalking out of the room, and Ursula was left on her own to stare at the cold vastness of New York.

Ursula hugged herself and crossed into the cavernous living room. The apartment felt noticeably colder without Kester in it.

On an oak coffee table, an uncorked champagne bottle rested in a bucket of ice, two empty glasses next to it. She sighed. Kester had obviously been planning a little celebration, assuming she'd somehow succeed.

Instead, she was left on her own. Again.

Her sense of loneliness threatened to crush the breath out of her. She had no one—not in a world where people kept their secrets closely guarded, disclosing only the tiniest glimmers of truth.

She poured herself a glass and collapsed onto the stiff crimson settee. Might as well make use of this.

She tried to ignore the ache of isolation gnawing at her chest, and flipped open her phone, scanning the news. A story about a crazed fan at Club Lalique was the top story. Fortunately, Zee had apparently glamoured everyone into believing the assailant was a blue-haired man with a tattoo of a spider on his cheek. It was a bizarre enough description that it wouldn't lead to any false arrests. Only Hugo would still remember the truth.

Kester was right. She needed to find him as soon as she could, or the truth would get out.

And yet, Kester's secrecy made her blood boil. The man was full of mysteries: the death of Henry, the truth about Zee, his own mysterious past, the locked library books—even the forbidden room upstairs.

At this point, she was entirely dependent on him to tell her about this bizarre new world, yet the guy clearly wasn't trustworthy. He was *the Headsman*, for crying out loud. He'd even referred to *himself* as a monster. How could she trust anything he said? What if all of this was a lie, and there was another way out?

Moreover—what was it he was so desperate to keep from her, that stood locked in her own apartment? He'd said this was her place, but he sure didn't act that way. There were rooms she couldn't enter, while Kester was free to swan in and out whenever he pleased. She drained another glass of champagne. She was going to start finding out secrets on her own.

She refilled her champagne flute and rose. Clutching the glass, she hurried upstairs into the hallway. As the bubbly took hold of her mind, her mood brightened. *I'm not a screw-up. I just have a normal aversion to sending people to hell.*

At the end of the dark corridor, the forbidden oak door shone with an otherworldly light.

Slowly, she approached the door, its surface punctuated by iron spikes. It certainly didn't look inviting, but maybe some kind of answers lay inside. She was done with secrets. She gripped the doorknob, cursing when it wouldn't twist open. Kester hadn't lied when he said it was locked. She'd need to find another way in.

She stalked down the hall to the botanical room, which stood adjacent to the locked door. She inhaled deeply. *Oranges, rosemary, and marigolds.* Kester hadn't just had the place cleaned—he'd had the whole greenroom replanted.

She stepped inside, shutting the door behind her. In the frost-covered panes, Manhattan's lights appeared hazy and distorted.

She gazed down at the yellow taxis and the few pedestrians foolhardy enough to brave the winter night. What were they doing, with their normal human lives? Hurrying to their parents, their spouses, their lovers? Maybe just slipping down the block for last call at the bar?

Still agitated, she took a long slug of her champagne. She'd grown sick of all secrets and mystery. She didn't want to be the bloody Mystery Girl. She wanted to know where she came from, who her parents were, and how she'd ended up with Emerazel's mark carved in her shoulder. But short of that information, she at least wanted to know what lurked in the locked room in her own apartment. *Is that too much to ask?*

She glanced at the windowsill. A little brass handle protruded from the iron rail, and she pulled at it, cracking it open. *I guess that answers my question about penthouse windows.*

If she was going to break into the locked room, her only hope was to climb along the outside wall and through one of its windows. She drained the last drops of her champagne. She'd need a little Dutch courage for this.

A hard push was enough to open the window wide. A frigid breeze blew into the room. Ursula held tight to the sill, leaning out, and peered to her left, at the windows of the locked room just eight feet away.

A small stone ledge jutted from the wall a few feet below, barely large enough for her to stand on. A giddy thrill bubbled through her—one which turned terrifying when she looked past the ledge at the streets below. She was at least fifteen stories up.

She edged back into the safety of the conservatory. She needed a plan. One slip on the ledge would send her plunging to her death. Crawling would be safest. On her hands and knees she'd be more stable.

Still, she would need a way to pry open the window of the locked room. A crowbar would be ideal, but it was too late for a trip to the hardware store. A small blade might work, and that was something she had.

She hurried to her bedroom, snatching the dagger from under her pillow.

Her pulse raced as she returned to the conservatory. The window was still open. She held her breath and crawled through it and onto the ledge, keeping the knife clenched between her teeth.

A thick layer of crusted snow covered the ledge. A strong gust of wind blew up her skirt, pushing it up over her waist and exposing her tiny thong. If any eagle-eyed New Yorkers were watching from below, they'd catch a wondrous view of her arse. *Why didn't I change into trousers first?* Her bare knees were freezing against the ice. She'd been too charged up to think this through, as usual.

Another gust of wind blew her hair into her eyes. She wanted to brush it away, but she couldn't lift a hand from the ledge without slipping.

Her heart hammered against her ribs. As she inched toward the window, she did her best to ignore the auburn tresses slapping her cheeks. She crawled forward, and the ice on the ledge thickened. She glanced down at the street fifteen stories below. The falling snow obscured most of the details, and it looked as though she was peering into a bottomless void. *What the hell was I thinking? This is insane.* She started to edge backward, but her knee slipped from the ledge, and she scrambled to press herself close against the building.

She gasped, and the knife almost slipped from her teeth. She didn't want to move forward or backward at this point, but she obviously couldn't stay here. *I really am a first-class idiot.* She'd failed at holding down a job, keeping a boyfriend, achieving any sort of education or achievement. Tonight she'd screwed up her hellhound job, and now she was stuck on an icy ledge fifteen stories above Manhattan's streets. No one would really care if she lived or died. Her only contribution to the world so far was her ability to light things on fire.

Although… A thought sparked in her mind. Maybe she could channel Emerazel's fire and melt some of the ice.

But how to do it? Before when she'd used the fire, she hadn't uttered any Angelic to call up the fire. Neither, as far as she could tell, had Kester. It had just sort of been there when she needed it, burning her veins and channeling into her fingers until they glowed, white-hot. Maybe she just needed to envision it.

She imagined her palms burning, her fingertips blazing like candles.

She glanced at her hands. *Nothing.*

As she closed her eyes, she envisioned a raging forest fire. She peeked at her fingertips, frozen to the ledge. A frigid gust of wind blew up her skirt again. How did you explain to a hospital how you'd got frostbite on your arse?

Bollocks. Imagining fire couldn't be it. And when she thought about it, she hadn't even known she had this ability when she'd burned Muppet in Rufus's club.

Another snow squall whipped by her ears. Her hands were freezing against the stone. Damn it, this had been a terrible idea.

And then she felt it: a distant trickle of heat. Almost as soon as it was there, it flickered away again.

Ok, what did I just do? The wind blew, I looked at my freezing fingers, I swore. That had to be it. The fire came from anger. She could do anger.

Ursula closed her eyes, imagining Rufus and Madeleine cuddling on his sofa, surrounded by empty wine bottles and expensive cheese. The familiar warmth flowed in her veins. This was a start, but it wasn't going to clear a path anytime soon. She didn't really give a fuck about Madeleine. She needed more heat.

In her mind's eye, Rufus leaned over his desk. "The problem, Urse, is that you have no goals—no vision," he whinged.

The heat poured out of Ursula like liquid metal from a crucible. The ice in front of her melted with a hiss and a burst of steam.

Rufus continued to play his part in her imagination. "You're just a sad cow who will never make anything of your life."

Flames burst from her palms pouring along the ledge. Sparks fell toward the street below in a waterfall of hellfire. Ursula watched the fire, entranced by its beauty, until a great gust of freezing wind snapped her out of her reverie. *Get a grip.*

One the plus side, the ice had fully melted. Ursula inched forward over the stone. When she reached the forbidden room's windows, she pressed her face against the glass, but all she could see were heavy curtains. She wouldn't learn any secrets unless she actually broke into the room.

She kneeled flat against the wall, the dagger still clenched between her teeth. Gingerly, she released it into her hand, careful not to slice herself with the sharp edge. Holding it firmly, she slipped the blade into the crack between the window and the sill. A twist of the dagger's hilt ratcheted the window open.

Slipping her fingers into the gap, she pulled it open further. Crouched on the ledge, she didn't have the leverage to open it all the way without leaning dangerously close to death. She would have to clamber in as best she could.

CHAPTER 19

Teeth chattering, she squeezed through on her stomach, tumbling onto the floor of a pitch-black room. She crouched, clutching the dagger, and listened. All she could hear was a soft hiss of air from the window behind her head. Otherwise, the room lay silent as a tomb.

She rose to her feet, holding the dagger defensively. She still shivered, and it shook in her hand. When nothing leapt at her from the darkness, she pulled open the curtains, letting light fall on the room.

She almost dropped her knife when she saw what lay before her.

The interior looked like some sort of alchemical laboratory, with a rib-vaulted ceiling that arched high above. A small forge stood in a hearth, and shelves of strange glassware lined the walls: rows of delicate Alembic flasks, Dimroth condensers, Thiele tubes, and Thistle funnels.

How in God's name do I even know these words?

Tentatively, she crossed the room to the shelves, reading the hand-written labels on the flasks. They bore names like *nigredo, aqua regia, dragon's blood,* and *philosophic mercury.* She sniffed the air. *Stale creosote.* This laboratory hadn't been used in a long time.

She turned, surveying the rest of the room. The walls were painted a deep indigo blue, patterned with golden astrological symbols and strange alchemical glyphs that twinkled and drifted like stars in the sky.

Ursula crossed back to the window, pulling it closed. If she left it open, Kester would know she'd been in here. With no breeze, an eerie silence descended and the tension returned to her shoulders. Ursula let out a slow breath. She could hear her heart thrumming in her chest. *Why am I so nervous? There's no one here.*

Slipping the dagger into her belt, she crossed to another rack of shelves. A thin layer of dust covered the flasks. She slid her fingers around one of the containers, picking it up. As she blew off the dust, she held it in the pale of light of the window. Her face reflected in its surface, and behind her the laboratory. Even an old bed, tucked into the shadows.

A cold chill slithered up her spine. In the glass's reflection, it almost looked like a dark shape lay on the bed. *A body.*

Ursula hardly dared to breathe. She turned, placing the flask back on its shelf as quietly as she could. Slowly, she drew the dagger from her belt again.

She approached the bed, gripping her weapon. An enormous, muscled man lay atop a deep crimson bedspread. He was huge. *Bloody hell, is he even human?*

"Hey?" she called out in a low whisper.

He didn't move.

"Hey!" She said it louder this time, but he remained motionless.

She moved closer, hardly daring to breathe. The dagger trembled violently in her fist.

His eyes were closed and raven black hair framed his face—his perfect, sublimely beautiful face. He had the most stunning features Ursula had ever seen: sharp cheekbones, a strong jaw, and perfect, kissable lips. His body was strong and muscled, and his skin had a deep Mediterranean tan, rich and warm, even in the faint light. Her dagger stopped its frantic shaking.

He must be asleep, right? Surely I don't fancy a corpse. At least, his warm olive color suggested that he lived.

"Hello?" She shouldn't be here. She should turn around, wrench open the door, and never come back into the forbidden chamber again. But something drew her toward him. Maybe it was his thrilling masculine allure, or maybe it was simple compassion. What if he needed her help?

She stared at the stranger's chest. It neither rose nor fell, and the only sounds of breathing were her own anxious breaths. "Who are you?" she whispered, more to herself than to him.

Muscular arms lay crossed on his chest, and his feet were bare. He looked like an effigy carved on a medieval tomb. He wore dark jeans and a grey t-shirt. Thin iron chains snaked around his body. When she looked closer, she could see tendrils of dark air curling off him, like black smoke.

What the hell is that?

If he was dangerous, at least he was bound, but she still clutched the dagger in case he sprang to life, desperate for her blood.

Slowly, she reached for his wrist, tracing her fingers over his warm skin. As soon as she touched him, something sparked like an electrical charge. It coursed through her body—a thrilling vibration of dark and ancient power.

She exhaled, trying to focus. *Definitely a magical creature.* She touched his wrist again, trying to ignore that rush of magical energy. The man had no *actual* pulse.

You don't feel dead, but you don't breathe, and your heart doesn't beat.

Her mind turned over the possibilities. He could be a fresh corpse that Kester had stored after a recent kill—but the warmth of his skin and that energy that radiated from him seemed so alive. Plus, there was a certain tautness to his muscles, a look of composure in his perfect face.

Perhaps he was a vampire? Heartless, strong, and gorgeous. With the way things were going, vampirism didn't seem like such a stretch, but it was the middle of the night, and weren't vampires nocturnal? Maybe he'd been subdued with some sort of sleeping spell, and he wouldn't awake until the right person kissed him. Tempting, but if the corpse scenario turned out to be accurate, there wouldn't be enough soap in the world to clean off her mouth.

She took another step closer, studying the man. With a burst of horror, she realized the crimson wasn't the color of the bedspread beneath him. Her heart threatened to gallop out of her chest.

It was blood. Gallons of dried blood.

Ursula leapt back from the bed, almost tripping on the rug. The blood stained the sheets in a crimson halo. She scanned the body for wounds, but whatever had injured him had left no visible mark. Something very bad had happened to the stranger, but she didn't know what. Maybe the Headsman had murdered him.

A terrifying reality settled over her like a burial shroud: she was in way over her head.

Gripping the dagger, she moved to the door. She could see no sign of the magical lock and she desperately hoped that meant it would open from the inside. She twisted the handle and relief washed over her when it turned in her grasp. A gentle push cracked the door open and she slipped out, shutting it behind her.

She crouched in the doorway of her bedroom, watching the door. Her eyes were beginning to water, but she didn't blink. The dagger remained ready at her side.

Even though his chest didn't rise and he had no pulse, the beautiful man had felt alive when she'd touched him. His warm skin had seemed to exude a powerful, shadowy magic. If he was alive, then she had to consider the possibility that she might have disturbed his slumber. What sort of a creature could lose that much blood and live? She'd actually been able to *feel* the intensity of his power. Hadn't Kester said something like "there might be worse monsters than hellhounds?" She had a bad feeling that she might now know what he was talking about.

The stranger could burst through the door at any moment and rip her to shreds. In fact, maybe he was the monster who had slaughtered the last hellhound. Then again, if he was such a threat, Kester would have locked the door from the inside too. Her pulse began to slow. She was probably safe for now.

Ursula slid the dagger into her belt before she got up from her crouch and walked to the conservatory. Her hands were still shaking as she shut the window and collected her empty champagne flute. She couldn't have Kester discovering her unsanctioned nocturnal activity, or he'd send her straight to Emerazel.

She closed her eyes, and for a moment, her mind flashed with an image of her body burning in hellfire, her skin blistering and blackening. She shuddered, shoving her fingers into her hair. *I'm going to lose my mind.*

Maybe Kester was right about her. Maybe she'd quickly shove her moral qualms aside to do what she needed to save herself. After all, she only had herself to rely on in this world.

She tightened her fists, sighing. Tomorrow, she would hunt down Hugo Modes at the opera, even if it meant she'd become a monster herself.

CHAPTER 20

$\mathcal{U}$rsula poured herself a cup of coffee, her mind rejoicing in the rich aroma. An old rock song played on the radio—Iggy Pop, *The Passenger*. She loved this song, and even through the fog of exhaustion, part of her wanted to dance, just to feel human again. Clearly, she was running on some kind of insane adrenaline at this point, trying to drown out all thoughts of the man or demon upstairs.

She'd gotten a few hours of sleep—if fitfully rolling around, trying not to think about impending doom, was considered sleeping. There'd been just one period of rest between two and six a.m., until the sound of her dagger falling to the floor woke her with a shout.

Morning's arrival had been a blessing, restoring some sense of normalcy. After she'd climbed from her sheets, she'd slipped into a pair of thin grey trousers, her thigh-high boots, and a bright blue top—one of the few bright things Kester had bought her. She'd pulled up her hair into a high ponytail, and carefully applied her eyeliner. Monsters be damned, she would wrench back some sense of control and normalcy over her own life.

She took a long sip of coffee and cast an approving glance at her reflection in the chrome coffee maker. *So maybe I live in a hellish new world of monsters and headsmen because F.U. sent me here. I'm not going to let myself fall completely to pieces.*

The caffeine rejuvenated her. With the radio on, she almost felt like herself again, and she let her hips sway to the music, dancing along as Iggy Pop sang about stars coming out in the night sky. She loved that part...

Footsteps clacked over the floor, and she whirled, nearly spitting out her coffee.

Kester stood in the doorway, wearing a black T-shirt and dark jeans. It would have been a perfectly sensible ensemble, if it weren't for the sheathed sword at his waist, and the strange alchemical tattoos covering his forearms. "I like the way you move."

She narrowed her eyes. "You can't just stride in here whenever you want."

"What are your plans to find Hugo?" he demanded.

"Is there any way you can start knocking, or at least calling first?" What she really wanted to ask, but resisted, was *Hey, can you tell me about that gorgeous and terrifying man upstairs?* The Headsman clearly wasn't in a mood for insubordination from a novice hellhound today.

"What is your plan?" he repeated.

"I'm pouring you some coffee first. You seem cranky." She grabbed a ceramic mug from one of the cabinets, filling it with coffee. "I'll approach Hugo at the Metropolitan Opera this evening. He's going with some French model. I'll get his soul." She slid the coffee across the table.

"And you think he'll be more agreeable tonight?" His gaze roamed over her fitted blue top.

Is he checking me out? "My plan is to do whatever it takes so I don't have to burn for eternity." She hated what she was becoming, but self-preservation came first. She'd have to sort through the ethics later. "And I was hoping Zee could come again and use her fairy magic."

"Of course." Kester arched an eyebrow, pulling out his cell phone. "God knows you'll need some help." He tapped on his phone, then took a sip of his coffee.

"Seriously, though. You need to knock. I could have been in my underwear."

For the first time in two days, he flashed a smile. "That's hardly going to put me off."

"Do you want me busting into your apartment?"

"Fine. I'll knock next time." His phone buzzed, and he flicked open a text. "Zee says she'd love to go to the opera. She'll meet you at seven p.m." Kester put his phone back in his pocket. "Right. Now that that's settled, I believe we have some training to do."

* * *

BAREFOOT, Kester stood in the armory, inspecting the blades. "Choose your weapon."

She picked up Honjo from the rack. Ursula's gaze flicked to his powerful arms, tattooed with the same glyphs and astrological signs that covered the walls in the sleeper's room. "Why are we training with blades? Am I supposed to force Hugo to sign at knifepoint?"

"If that's what it takes," said Kester. "But this isn't for Hugo. He's not the only thing you need to worry about."

"What do you mean?"

He leveled his green eyes on her. "We're not the only monsters out there, Ursula. There are legions of demons who want us dead, and if they ever scent your fear, they will tear you to shreds. For whatever reason, Emerazel won't allow me to accompany you on your mission, but I'm going to make sure you don't die. And that means you need to know how to protect yourself. Understood?"

Ursula raised her eyebrows. "That sounds comforting and ominous at the same time."

"I'm your mentor. Whatever Emerazel's problem is, you're my responsibility, and I'll keep you alive. I've seen you use a sword, and you look like you've had some serious training already. It's a good place to start."

Maybe he was on her side, even if he was the Headsman. She really had no clue at this point. "When you said there are other monsters out there..." *Do you mean monsters like the bleeding guy across from my room?* She was desperate to ask about the sleeping stranger, but she bit her tongue. "What types of monsters do you mean?"

A muscle tightened in his jaw. "I forget how little you know."

"The only things I know about this world, I've learned from you. Which is basically fuck-all."

"We don't have time to go into the whole history, but I can tell you this. Light demons have been warring with the dark ones for a hundred thousand years. Our gods are in a race to collect souls, and that means you're a prime target for the shadow demons."

A shiver crawled up her spine. *Is that what is sleeping in the room across from mine?* "What makes them dark? Are they more evil?"

"No. It's just how the universe keeps magic in balance, with equal amounts of light and dark magic, like day and night. Only the fae are neutral. What you need to know is that you can kill shadow demons with certain weapons—especially those made with iron. They must be charmed with the right spells."

She suppressed a shudder, thinking of the sleeping man upstairs, and the ancient magic that coiled off him in electrifying midnight tendrils. "And some of these shadow demons might be after me tonight?"

"Perhaps. And that's why you need to learn to fight them." He pulled a small glass jar full of amber liquid from his pocket, then a handkerchief. He poured some of the oil onto the cloth. "I'm going to anoint your sword with Zornhau's oil. It's a salve that protects a blade from damage. Also prevents you from seriously injuring your opponent—limits the chance of an accidental *coup de main* considerably."

He held out his hand for the sword, and Ursula handed him the hilt. Kester rubbed the blade with the cloth, holding Honjo with a casual confidence that told Ursula that he was an experienced swordsman. Once the katana glistened with gold, he handed it back to her. "Just remember to clean the sword thoroughly when we're done. The steel is useless with the oil on it."

Backing into the center of the room, he drew his own sword from the sheath at his waist. It was the same blade Ursula had used at her battle with the Moor fiend, already glistening with amber oil. "Are you ready?"

Ursula gripped the Katana, planting her feet in a fighting stance. "Whenever you are."

Kester lunged, his sword striking hers like the fang of a venomous serpent. Ursula deflected his blade with a deft parry, but he stepped back before she could counter. She danced closer, looking for an opening, but he sidestepped, staying just out of range. Their swords clashed, though Kester didn't break a sweat.

He pushed in, striking. "I spoke with Zee about your encounter with Hugo."

"Oh?" Apparently Kester was planning on incorporating a bit of chit-chat into their bout.

"She told me you argued with him about bathing suits." His tone was somewhere between a joke and an accusation. She slashed at him, but he parried easily. He was trying to throw her off her game by bringing this up now.

"Yes, Hugo was saying that he broke up with his girlfriend because—"

But before she could detail Hugo's misogynistic attitude towards woman's swimwear, Kester cut in. "I don't care what he said. My point is: you need to lure people in. Make them think they can trust you, that they want to please you." He flicked his blade, and she had to leap to the side to avoid being skewered.

"He seemed to like it when I told him I prefer to swim nude."

She caught a flicker of interest in Kester's eyes. *Two can play at the distraction game.* She hadn't failed to notice his eyes lingering on her cleavage whenever he got the chance.

"Nude?" He parried, and a thin sheen of sweat covered his forehead. "Is that so? You like the feel of the water against your bare skin?"

You've got him, Ursula. Keep going. "Yes, and I eat ice cream nude, because I like when it melts and drips down my breasts."

Nope. That was just weird. Really, really weird.

Weird or not, Kester faltered. With him off balance, Ursula stabbed at him. He dodged, but not before the tip of her katana nicked his ribs.

"Touché," Kester swiped the blood from the hole in his shirt and sucked it off his finger. He lifted his sword again. "We're not done."

"You want more of that?"

His sword clashed off Honjo. "You got off on the wrong foot with Hugo." He began to circle her, fire flashing in his eyes.

"Is this some sort of interrogation?"

"Yes."

Kester feinted at her head and then slashed at her knees. Ursula just barely deflected the blow with a downward swipe. He moved out of range before she could counter. She couldn't keep up with him.

His fiery gaze was hypnotic. "To succeed as a hellhound, you need both steel and silk, weapons and charm. You can't always force a signature. Sometimes you must lure in a debtor, convince him it's in his best interest to sign over his soul."

She thrust her sword at him, but he dodged. "You think I can't do that?"

"Zee said you have all the social graces of a water buffalo."

What. A. Bitch. "That's a load of bollocks." Ursula said it confidently, but inwardly she knew he'd touched on something. How many foster families had she been through? Four? Five? She'd lost count. Even the people she'd loved had told her the same thing.

Rufus's voice rang in the hollows of her mind: "The truth is, you're a sad cow who won't make anything of your life." Hollowness welled in her chest. Worst of all was the dawning realization that this character deficit might explain her amnesia. Was she some sort of magical reject? Forced to forget her past and then cast aside because she put everyone off? Was it possible that no one had ever loved her?

She felt tears prick behind her eyelids. *Bloody hell, Ursula. Do not cry. Do not cry.* Not in front of Kester. She needed to prove she had both the skill and character to be a hellhound, or she could forget about that whole "self-preservation" thing.

"So—" Kester held up his hand and then laid his blade on the mat indicating that the sword-play was on hold. "Prove it."

"Prove what?"

Kester stared at her like she was off her meds. "Prove that you know how to charm people. Look approachable."

She scowled. "How am I supposed to prove that?"

"By not making that face, for one thing."

She lowered Honjo and straightened. She pushed out her chest, smiled and cocked her head.

"Much better, but your smile doesn't look genuine. You'll need to soothe him. Keep him from panicking."

Ursula felt a familiar heat rise within in her. First, she had to force people to sign away their souls. On top of that, she had to condemn them with a lullaby, cooing at them as she consigned them to hell? How much would she end up hating herself if this was the person she was to become? But she couldn't say that out loud—not to Kester.

"Put down your sword." Kester stepped closer, his green eyes drinking her in. "Ask me to sign the pact."

She tucked her sword in the corner of the room before straightening her shoulders. She tried to force a pleasant smile onto her face. "You just need to sign here." She pointed to an imaginary pact in her hand, using a firm but gentle voice, like she was a police negotiator convincing a suicidal man to step away from the edge of a bridge.

Kester answered in a perfect impression of Hugo's posh British accent. "No I don't want to sign. This must be some sort of stunt. Are you having me on?"

"This is not a stunt. Hasn't your career taken off since you asked Emerazel for her power?" The content was good, but Ursula stumbled over the last few words.

He continued to ape Hugo's accent. "I'm not doing it. I'm not giving my soul away."

"You have to. You agreed to the bargain."

He shook his head. "Relax your shoulders. You're supposed to look alluring."

"How did you do it, when you broke into my kitchen? I was ready to bash your head in with a frying pan, and then the next thing I knew, I wanted to do whatever you wanted."

"Some of that was my natural charm, but some of it was magic. It's taken me a long time to learn how to bend people's wills, and I've honed the skill well. You were surprisingly resistant to my influence. I don't encounter that often."

"I'd had a very bad day." She eyed him warily. "You can mind-control me?"

"It's not something I use unless I must. In any case, you don't have that skill, so you'll have to rely on your charms." A smile played over his lips.

"And my razor-sharp wit."

"Right. Get on with it."

She closed her eyes, trying to remember how Kester had approached her in her kitchen. His intense eyes had slid all over her body, like he was memorizing each one of her curves. He'd somehow managed to project strength and temptation at the same time. Gazing at him, she stepped closer, letting her eyes trail over his strong arms, and down the front of his shirt for a moment. Just inches from him, she stared up at him, eyes wide and innocent.

He leaned in, whispering in her ear. "Closer."

She pressed forward, relishing the heat that radiated from his body, and his delicious scent—cedar and fresh earth. It wasn't hard to feign attraction.

She stared into his eyes. "If you sign now, you'll get everything you ever wanted. Everything you could desire for the rest of your life." She had no idea what possessed her, but she traced her finger down the front of his chest, feeling the hard body underneath.

His breathing sped up, and he grabbed her hand, his fingers burning. "That's good. But you don't need to touch him. Not if you don't want to. You only need to lure him in."

Her body grew hotter, and she could feel her cheeks flushing. "I guess I've got the silk thing covered."

"Good. Now I want to see how you can use your fire." He stepped away, picking up his sword. This time when he faced her, his smile had turned predatory; hellfire flashed in his eyes. Ursula's stomach lurched.

His blade whipped at her gut in a blur of metal, but she dove out of reach. "Use your fire," he said, his voice husky.

Her sword clashed against his, and her heartbeat raced. He was going to disembowel her. "I don't know how."

His sword flashed again and she was only just able to deflect it above her head. The sound of clashing steel rang in her ears.

"Use your fire," he commanded, louder this time, eyes burning with hellfire.

She tried to envision flames blazing through her body. "I'm trying." She had to leap into the air to avoid losing her legs as his sword passed clean under her.

"Try harder." He struck at her, and she parried. Immediately he struck again. She deflected, gasping for breath. Sweat broke out on her brow. His attacks grew faster, driving her across the room. She had to call up the flames, but she could hardly focus her attention with Kester's sword threatening to rip her to shreds.

She stepped back, banging against the wall. Retreating was no longer an option. Kester struck again, locking his sword with hers, and slowly pushed his blade closer and closer to her face. His breath was warm against her cheek, fueled by Emerazel's flames.

Her arms burned with exhaustion. She hadn't been training, and her muscles weren't ready for this. Kester's blade pushed closer, grazing her cheek. *He's going to cut my face off.* As panic flooded her, an image burst into her mind: a blood-soaked floor, a crumpled body, twitching finger-tips. What *was* that? She didn't recognize the images, but a hollow opened in her chest all the same, a void so deep and cavernous it could never be filled. Her heart ached.

Kester's eyes were incandescent, the heat from his body overwhelming. He was going to kill her. She was certain of it. "Get away from me." Fire kindled in her core, filling the void with a burning sensation. Almost instantly, it turned violently hot, like a dying star. Strength burned through her nerve endings. *I am hellfire, and I will bathe the world in flames.*

Fire blasted out of her body, knocking Kester away.

He dropped his sword, holding out his hands. "Get it under control."

Glorious flames poured from her body in waves. She was no longer standing in the armory. She was in the center of a volcanic maelstrom, blessed with the power of a god.

Distantly she heard a hissing noise. Within moments, the inferno was gone, replaced by snow, and she coughed. But this snow wasn't cold; it was suffocating. She couldn't breathe. She fell to her knees, gasping.

Kester stood above her. "Use Emerazel's fire for strength. Don't burn down your apartment."

"Something snapped in me when you held that blade to my cheek." Whatever spell Kester had used stung like hell, and it tasted awful. The room smelled of burnt straw, and the tatami mats lay scorched. As she turned toward the wall-length mirror, she caught a glimpse of herself covered in white powder.

"I was trying to teach you to use your power. It doesn't burn me, but it will burn the shadow demons."

"It looked like you were about to cut my face off." She rose, shaking off the powder.

"Why would I do that?"

She cocked a hip. *I don't know. Why did you leave a man to bleed out across from my bedroom?* "Maybe you wanted to wear it on your next mission because of my considerable allure."

"I'm pretty enough as it is. And I was trying to teach you how to use your power to fight. Remember, Zornhau's oil won't let me hurt you." He raised his sword, wrapping his fingers around the razor sharp blade. With a grunt of pain, he yanked the sword from his fist. Blood poured from his fingers, and Ursula gasped. But when he opened his hand, the wound had already healed. "It still hurts, but you can't seriously injure yourself. But if you don't learn to channel the hellfire, you'll find yourself trapped in a burning building."

"I think I need a lot of practice." She wiped the white foam off her cheeks. "What kind of spell did you cast on me?"

"Not a spell," he nodded at a fire extinguisher.

"Ugh. I'm going to make use of that shower." She turned to walk out of the room.

"Ursula. You did well, at least until you exploded. Use that charm on Hugo tonight, and everything will be fine. But if anything happens—if you need me, just use that mobile I gave you."

"I thought Emerazel wasn't letting you help me."

"I can help you. I just can't go with you."

"That is good to know." She flashed him a tentative smile.

Even with her aching muscles, as she strode up the stairs to the bathroom, she felt a little better than she had that morning.

CHAPTER 21

Ursula leaned against the balcony's railing and looked down into the crowd, ten minutes before the start of Act One. She wore a long gown, the slate-grey color of a winter sea, which slid silkily against her bare legs. She'd accessorized with a necklace of black pearls, and finished off the ensemble with a spray of lavender perfume. The scent should have encouraged a sense of calm, but it did nothing for her nerves right now.

She closed her eyes, inhaling deeply. Just before she'd left for the opera, Kester had stopped by her apartment again—knocking this time—and had cast a long, approving glance over her outfit, that carnal look sparking in his eyes again. *If only he weren't a psychotic headsman with boundary issues, he'd be my kind of guy.*

She opened her eyes, scanning the lobby. From her perch on the upper level, she had a view of the lower floor and the marble stairs, curving below like the inside of a sea shell. Her hand rested lightly on the wyrm-skin purse, Emerazel's pen and a pact tucked safely inside, along with her white stone and opera glasses. *Not to mention the small dagger.* Silk and steel were her weapons, just as Kester had said.

In theory, she had everything she needed—except Hugo. *And where the hell is Zee?* She'd arrived early with the hope that she might extract Hugo's signature before the opera began, but as the minutes ticked by that became less likely. Closing her eyes, she inhaled deeply, pushing out all thoughts of hellfire and shadow demons. Tonight, she needed to focus, or she'd have to face Emerazel and submit to those horrific flames again. The thought curdled her stomach. Maybe someday she'd figure a way out of this—maybe even a way to save Hugo—but right now, she had more immediate problems. Like avoiding the wrath of a bloodthirsty goddess.

Someone brushed her elbow and she moved to make room.

"Thanks, miss," said a melodious voice.

She glanced at her neighbor, and found herself staring into the face of a gorgeous, man, immaculately dressed in a black tuxedo. Golden skin and pale grey eyes contrasted with his dark hair, and he flashed her an inviting smile. This was the kind of gorgeous man she should be lusting after—a normal, human man who wouldn't attack her with swords and tell her friends she'd overdosed on heroin.

The man adjusted his cufflinks, and the way his eyes raked over her body made her want to blush. "My name is Abe. It's a pleasure to meet you."

"Ursula," she said, trying to keep her eye on the lobby.

"Is this your first time at the opera?"

With a great deal of effort, she pulled her gaze away from his beautiful face. She wasn't here to socialize, and she needed to focus on her target. "First time. Yes." She stared at the lobby, desperate for a sign of the pop star.

"You seem a little overwhelmed."

Act normal, Ursula. "Just excited, and a bit preoccupied by work." *Condemning people to hell isn't a walk in the park, you know.* Her hands tightened around the railing.

He kept his gaze fixed on her. "Well, I think you'll find the opera is the perfect place to set aside life's anxieties and experience something extraordinary."

"That's what I'm hoping for." If only she could set aside her anxieties—her overwhelming fear of Emerazel's flames, the gnawing guilt at her new role. And what *were* those images she'd seen when she thought Kester was going to slaughter her—the crumpled body on the floor, drenched in blood? She shuddered.

Whatever they were, this wasn't the time to delve into it. *Focus, Ursula.*

The crowd below quieted, all turning to look at the entrance. Ursula's heart skipped a beat as she watched the crowd part. Hugo and Virginie stepped into the lobby, flanked by three security guards. Ursula's breath caught. This was her moment to save her own life.

"Ah," said the man by her side, tapping his fingers on the railing. "A celebrity has joined us." The lights above flickered, and the lobby quieted. He turned to her. "I think that's our cue. I do hope you enjoy the show."

But as she thought of what she needed to do tonight, her blood roared in her ears. She'd come to condemn a man to hell.

* * *

URSULA HURRIED through a warren of red carpeted hallways before finding her seat. Enormous chandeliers hung from the gold-leaf ceiling, glimmering like icy fireworks.

Although the opera was sold out, Kester had managed to buy an entire set of box seats on the second level. Since Zee hadn't bothered to show, Ursula had it entirely to herself. She plopped into a seat in the front row.

From here, she had an expansive view of the opera hall. Beneath her, patrons in suits and gowns filled rows of red velvet seats. Ushers directed a few stragglers down the aisles. Next to the stage the orchestra readied itself with trills, scales, and arpeggios.

Ursula dug around in her purse and found the set of opera glasses. The miniature brass binoculars would give her a view of Hugo, and she'd be able to intercept him after the first act. With Zee's help to distract Virginie, Ursula could blink her eyes and lure him into signing.

She took a deep breath, trying to relax. *But where the hell is he sitting? And where is Zee?* She lifted the binoculars to her eyes, scanning the room, but only found row after row of stuffy older couples.

As the chandeliers began to dim, the hall fell silent. In thirty seconds, the entire room would be dark. *Bollocks.* Everyone had stared at Hugo when he'd arrived, but now he'd gone invisible.

She bit her lip. Perhaps they'd still be staring at him.

She glanced at the box to her left. A woman in her fifties, crammed into a red corseted dress, focused her binoculars on an upper balcony.

Ursula followed her gaze. Sure enough, there was Hugo, his cheeks slightly paler than they'd been when she first met him. Maybe he knew what waited for him—that death had come for him at the opera tonight, scented with lavender and dressed in a gown of grey silk.

She loosed a long breath. She'd found her target. Now she just needed to wait for the first act to end, and then she'd sidle up to him and try her whole *silk* routine, all verbal caresses and whispers of eternal happiness.

Only, there weren't many private places for a tête-à-tête in this place. Was she going to have to follow him into the loo again? When Kester had told her she would need to "keep a low profile, and stay in the shadows," she hadn't realized that meant working next to urinals.

The hall was completely dark until, after a few moments, a spotlight beamed onto the orchestra, illuminating a grey-haired conductor. He bowed, and the audience roared with applause. Then, turning to face the orchestra, he raised his hands. With a flick of his wrist, the musicians were off.

As the first notes sounded through the hall, an enormous gold curtain lifted to reveal the set. She'd been expecting something opulent, but saw instead a stage set with a shabby room—a hovel, as Kester would call it.

But the music itself was as lush as the theater, and the violins and trumpets washing over Ursula in a glorious wave. As the music swelled, she leaned forward in her seat. A man with dark hair walked to the center of the stage and began to sing in a rich baritone, full of passion. Another man strode onto the stage, joining him in a clear tenor voice. *If only I knew what they were singing about.*

By their costumes, she could tell the characters were poor, but the way they sang to each other suggested warmth between them. As the music flowed around her, she thought of Katie, and how they'd spent their weekends exploring London's forgotten canals, too broke to do anything else. She'd been happy enough then, right? Perhaps, in her isolation, she was romanticizing, but at least she hadn't had a bounty on her head and a goddess of hellfire who wanted to torture her to death. And, moreover, at least she'd had Katie. Right now, her loneliness threatened to swallow her whole.

On the stage, the tenor was joined by a young woman, wrapped in a woolen shawl and rubbing her arms as he serenaded her. *Amore.* That was a word she recognized: love. The tenor's emotional outpouring held no artifice, no silk or steel—he simply bared his soul. The music built, and Ursula nearly forgot to breathe, her chest aching.

As the aria reached its climax, she couldn't help but imagine someone looking at her the way the tenor looked at his beloved. For just a second, she closed her eyes, and an image rose from the back of her mind—a painfully beautiful man with star-flecked eyes, deep and dark as the night sky.

With a jolt, she realized exactly who she was picturing—the injured demon who lay asleep in her apartment.

What the hell?

CHAPTER 22

$\mathcal{U}$nnerved she glanced around, exhaling slowly as she caught a glimpse of Zee slipping into the row, dressed in a crimson gown. *About time she showed up.*

As Zee took her seat, she studied Ursula with an expression that fell somewhere between annoyance and concern. "Are you having another bad day?"

"What are you talking about?" But even as she said it, Ursula realized that a few tears had slid down her cheek. She started to wipe her eyes, but Zee pulled her hand away. "You'll ruin your makeup," she whispered. "Let me do it."

Zee opened her purse, pulling out a tissue, and she dabbled Ursula's cheeks. "I also cried the first time I saw *La bohème*," she whispered.

"You're an opera fan?"

"I love the romance. Puccini understood how it felt to get swept away by love." There was something wistful about the way she spoke, and her eyes glistened. The ice princess had disappeared for just a moment, until her clear gaze focused again. "But we're not here for the music. Where's the target?"

"Up there." Ursula nodded at the box on the upper level, where Hugo still sat whispering with Virginie. Maybe this was going to be easier than she'd anticipated.

The first act ended, and Ursula sucked in a long breath. *It's now or never.* She turned to Zee. "Can we approach them in the booth? Would you be able to glamour his girlfriend again?"

"Of course."

Zee slipped out of the box, and Ursula followed. In the hall, patrons mingled with glasses of wine. Zee slipped between them, like a deer weaving between trees in a forest, and Ursula hurried along behind her.

"Thank you for helping me, Zee."

"Of course. It's what I'm paid for." She stepped into a curving flight of stairs. "But you must relax. You look nervous."

"I'm not nervous. I'm dreading my part in this."

"Oh. The whole *eternal torture* thing. Well, Hugo asked for it."

"Do you think there's another way out, without me collecting souls?"

Zee shot her a sharp look. "Keep your voice down. And, no. What Kester says is the truth, or he'd have freed himself ages ago. You think he likes it any better than you do?"

"You trust him?" Ursula desperately wanted to ask Zee about the bleeding man in her apartment. What if he needed help—and what if Kester had put him there? She choked down the questions for now.

"Of course I trust Kester. I've known him a very long time." They reached the top of the stairs—Hugo's level. "I don't think he likes collecting souls any more than you do. But there is no other option, believe me."

They strode down the hall toward Hugo's box, and Ursula clutched her wyrm-skin purse. "Do you know why Kester carved his mark?"

"Yes, but it's not for me to tell." Zee paused at a door. "I think this is Hugo's. Do you want me to go in first?"

"I think that's a good idea. It's likely to alarm him when he sees his own damnation coming for him." Plus, Zee could glamour everyone around him. Ursula pulled her pen from her purse, ready to charm the pants off Hugo.

Zee open the door, and Ursula lingered in the doorway, keeping in the shadows—just like a good hellhound.

"Oh hi, Zee!" Virginie trilled, throwing her arms in the air. "I didn't know you were going to be at the Opera tonight."

"Hi, Virginie." Zee's glamour was utterly convincing. Too bad Hugo wasn't there.

Zee's hand flew to her chest. "Where's your gorgeous date?"

"He went to the little boy's room."

Ursula began to slip away. *Of course. That's where I have all my traumatic encounters with pop stars.*

The theater's lights flickered, signaling the end of intermission. *Show time, Ursula.* She turned, hurrying through the hall, the bone-colored pen clutched tight in her fist.

A few stragglers rushed back to their seats in the corridor. At the end of the hall, Ursula spied a door labeled *Men* in gold lettering. *No body-guards—good.* That would simplify things.

Ursula swallowed hard, trying not to think about fire. She glanced behind her to make sure no one was around, then slipped inside.

Gilded moldings and pictures of famous opera singers decorated the walls.

"Hello?" she called out in her most soothing voice. "Hugo, darling?"

Only the sound of dripping water greeted her, and the faint swell of violins from the orchestra. *Shit.*

Ursula's mind raced through the possibilities. If he'd returned to his box, she would have seen him in the corridor. He wouldn't have just left Virginie alone at the opera while he went somewhere else, would he?

Actually, that did seem like something he'd do. This was a guy who'd dumped his girlfriend for wearing the wrong swimsuit.

But, no—his jacket had been hanging on the back of his chair in the box. He *had* to be here.

Maybe he'd gone out for a smoke? She turned, catching a glimpse of herself in the mirror. Her auburn hair was piled on her head in a glamorous up-do, a few tendrils cascading over her pale shoulders. If she couldn't lure Hugo into his own damnation looking like this, she'd never get anyone to sign.

She turned, eyeing the stalls. The doors reached the floor, so she couldn't peer under them. Instead, she began pushing them open, one by one. The doors creaked as she opened them. "Hugo, my love. I've been wanting to see you again." *Creak.* "I thought perhaps I could explain things better." *Creak.* "Maybe over some wine—"

From the furthest stall, a sucking sound interrupted her investigation. *What the hell?*

"Hugo, darling?" she said in her most soothing voice. "Is that you?"

The noise stopped, replaced by the muffled voice of the tenor singing on stage.

"Hello?" She softened her voice into a low caress, walking toward the final stall, heels clacking on the floor. "Are you there? We got off the wrong foot before, I know. I'm here to make everything better."

No response. As she stood before the final stall, the hair rose on her arms. Something felt *wrong*—the air felt a little too cold, almost electrified. Was it just a draft, or was that dark magic crackling in the air around her? She flicked out the blade of the reaping pen. Dread rose up her throat, and she leaned closer, knocking on the door. "Hugo, my darling. It's not as bad as you think." *Lies. Horrible, evil lies, tumbling from perfectly-glossed pink lips. She was a monster now.*

She took a deep breath, waiting for his response, but she heard only shuffling in the stall, and a low moan.

She stepped back. Her heels wouldn't be good for running, but she could still kick down a door. She hiked up her dress and slammed her foot into the wood. Her kick snapped the lock, sending the door smacking open.

A rush of fear ran over her skin. The man she'd met earlier—the one with the pale grey eyes—stood, cradling Hugo in his arms like a baby. As soon as the man's eyes locked on Ursula, he dropped Hugo onto the toilet seat, and the pop star's head smacked hard against the stall's wooden walls. His skin had taken on an unhealthy sheen.

Ursula swallowed hard. *What. The. Fuck.* "What are you?" she breathed.

Abe stepped toward her in a single flowing motion, like smoke rising from the wick of an extinguished candle. The air temperature dropped at least ten degrees. He fixed his otherworldly gaze on her, his eyes gunmetal grey.

He moved closer to her. When he smiled, fear twisted in her gut—but something else, too. She couldn't stop staring at his smooth, golden skin.

"Hello, pretty girl." His voice whispered over her body. When he spoke, it almost felt as though he were touching her with a feather-light stroke. "I was wondering if you'd stop by."

She tore her eyes away from him, glancing at the crumpled pop star on the toilet. Nausea welled in her stomach. This was all wrong. "Did you kill him?"

"I may have been a bit greedy with him. His soul tasted delicious."

"You devoured his soul?" Horror slithered over her skin. She had a dizzying feeling she was facing one of those shadow demons Kester had mentioned. And what would Emerazel do when she learned Hugo's soul had been stolen?

Abe's cheek dimpled as he smiled. "Nyxobas needed more souls. I know you understand." He reached out, stroking her cheek, and his touch sent a thrill racing through her body, pushing out all of her dread. "But of course, you are the real prize this evening. You're the most beautiful woman here, and it's not every day I get to consume a hellhound's soul."

CHAPTER 23

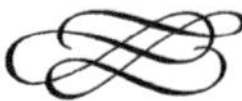

Her body was growing hot, and sweat beaded on her neck. "Look, I don't know who you think you are, but I've become quite attached to my soul, and I plan to hang on to it." His lips looked full and soft, but she forced herself to tear her gaze off them, stepping backward toward the sinks. A strange ache was beginning to fill her body, and she couldn't stop looking at him.

Slowly, he moved closer, his eyes trailing over her shoulders, her cleavage, her hips, as if he could see right through her dress to the lacy pink bra and panties underneath, and the thought sent a strange thrill through her belly. *What is he doing to me?* With a trembling hand, she lifted the blade of the pen toward the center of his chest. "Don't get any closer. I won't hesitate to reap your soul." *I need to burn him, but I can't remember how.*

"You silly little thing." His eyes blazed with desire. "Do you have any idea how powerful I am?"

A battle raged in her head—carnal desires warring against the corner of her mind that wanted to bash his head into the tiles. Some traitorous part of her wanted to rip off her dress right there and invite him closer, while the rest of her knew she should stab him with the pen. *I need to get out of here.*

She could yell for help, but Emerazel would surely slaughter her for calling attention to herself.

Abe prowled closer, licking his perfect lips. Ursula let the silky strap of her gown fall lower. She wanted him to see all of her, wanted his hands on her bare skin.

Just inches from her, he ran a finger over her collarbone, and heat blazed through her. He leaned in, and she arched against him, desperate to feel his lips against hers. "I wish I could take you to Oberon's. It would be so fun to show off a gorgeous human pet like you, with your perfect breasts and ass..."

Fuck. Hadn't Zee and the hairdresser said something about Oberon's? But it hadn't sounded nearly as tempting as when the word rolled off Abe's tongue. Whatever Oberon's was, she wanted to go with him. What *was* she doing here? She was here for him, wasn't she? Here to please this god of a man. She felt her legs opening, and her hand slid up his chest. There was something she was supposed to be doing, but her mind was a blank.

He slipped his hand around the back of her neck, his eyes trailing down her heaving chest. A pleasurable heat radiated from his body, and she could think of nothing but his touch.

He lowered his mouth to hers, and for one glorious instant an inferno of euphoria flared—until it died as quickly as it had arrived, replaced by a gnawing emptiness and overwhelming sense of revulsion.

Abe pulled away from her, his face contorted with disgust—just like Ursula felt. He wiped the back of his hand across his lips, as if trying to wipe away her taste.

"Ugh." Infuriated, he glared at her, gripping her wrist. "What the hell *are* you?"

Rage simmered in her chest. She was getting sick of being treated like a toy for the demons to play with. "I'm a hellhound." Free of his spell, she could feel the fire rising through her arms, hot and molten. Abe jerked away from her, and she threw a hard punch at his pretty face, thrilling at the smack of knuckles against bone.

Abe's head snapped back, and he growled. Faster than a storm wind, his hands were at her throat, and his cold stare hypnotized her. He opened his mouth, sucking in air from her body. As he did, a deep void filled her chest. She kicked his shins, but his eyes remained locked on her, unflinching.

Her blood rushed in her ears, her limbs tingling and weakening. *What is he doing to me?* She was going to die in the men's bathroom at the hands of a pervert she'd just kissed. This was worse than the fake heroin overdose. Abe's fingers dug into her neck, his icy eyes flashing with cold light.

Her vision grew dark, and she could hear her own heartbeat growing weaker as he sucked the life from her. Panic exploded in her skull. *He's killing me.* Lights flashed before her eyes. Her lungs were going to implode, as the fire inside her guttered and dimmed. A tiny lick of flame danced in the recesses of her mind, and as her energy drained from her body, she tried to stoke it to life, but it sputtered and died. Something else was filling her mind now—a memory: a gleaming sword in the sunlight, in a field overgrown with wildflowers, a smaller sword in her own hand. The blade cut through the air, glinting in the sunlight, as she was taught to wield it.

Fight, Ursula.

Someone, long ago, had wanted her to be a warrior.

Fight.

She blinked, trying to refocus her vision, and she made out the blurred outline of her attacker. She needed to—

Thwak! Something hit him in the side of the head, and he released his grip.

Abe let her crumple to the ground, and her head smacked against the floor, the nape of her neck pressing against the bathroom tiles—cold, just like her body. She felt as though a heavy weight pressed on her, crushing the life out of her. Nearby, Abe was fighting with someone—a woman—but Ursula's limbs were frozen, drained.

"Ursula!" they shrieked. *Zee?*

She licked her lips. She needed to warn Zee away—Abe's kiss was death—but she felt herself drifting away, a cold wind whispering over her skin.

I need to help Zee. She willed herself to get up. She would fight him, smash his pretty face into the tiles.

With a great force of will, she forced her eyes open, staring up at the ceiling. Abe had drunk so deeply from her it took virtually all her remaining strength to roll to her side. She blinked, her vision coming into focus. Abe, a few feet from her, stood clutching Zee like a rag doll.

If she'd had any of Emerazel's fire still within her, she would have tried to scorch him, burn him to ashes, but he'd sucked her dry. She needed to hurt him another way.

Her eyes flicked to Emerazel's pen, glinting in the yellow lights just a few feet away. Slowly, like she was moving through quicksand, she reached for it until her knuckles brushed its bony cylinder. She tightened her fingers around it, pulling it into her grasp.

Zee's blond hair hung down as Abe held her in his arms, her black high heels dangling over the floor. Ursula inched closer, shivering at the chill that emanated from him. Had she actually been *attracted* to this monster?

Gritting her teeth, she rolled closer and stabbed the pen's blade into his heel with all the strength she could muster.

He wrenched his foot away with a muffled grunt, then tottered for a moment before crashing to the floor, the knife protruding from his foot. She yanked out the pen, its blade stained with blood.

"Gods below," he sputtered.

A small smile curled her lips. She wasn't going down without a fight.

He rose, lunging for her like a lion attacking its prey. She stabbed him again; she'd aimed for his heart, but the blade lodged in his stomach instead.

On his knees, Abe threw back his head, roaring, the bony pen shaking where it protruded from his gut. He clawed at it, as the wound started to smoke. The smell of burning flesh filled the room. *Emerazel's weapon.*

Abe leapt to his feet in a blur of motion and staggered toward the exit, blood and steam bubbling between his fingers.

She rose on her elbows, trying out one of her new seductive smiles. "For such a little thing, it's got a hell of a bite."

"Bitch," he spat before flinging open the door and disappearing into the hall.

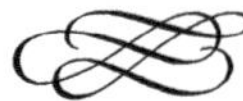

CHAPTER 24

Ursula lay on her back and stared at the eggshell-white ceiling, trying to will herself to move.

But the first step was peeling herself off the bathroom floor. Her legs tingled with pins and needles, and she almost cried with relief when she moved her toes. She pushed herself up, onto her hands and knees. She crawled closer to Zee, panting. Hadn't Abe said the opera was the perfect place to put aside one's anxieties? *Wanker.*

She crouched next to Zee, her heart tightening at the sight of her. The fae girl's chest hardly moved. Blood stained her dress and matted her hair, though Ursula was pretty sure that belonged to Abe.

She reached out, feeling for a pulse on Zee's neck. It was faint, but blood flowed gently beneath her translucent skin. If she could only get her outside, there was a Bentley waiting for them by the Met's entrance.

Thank God Abe hadn't killed her, but she wasn't about to walk out of here. *How the hell do I wake her up?*

Once, she'd seen someone come back from the dead. Braden, a boy in her first foster home, had a nut allergy, and he'd chowed through a packet of almond macaroons without realizing. He'd passed out in less than five minutes, but an EpiPen had completely revived him.

That was what epinephrine did, right? It sent hormones racing through your veins. She just needed to get her hands on one. Her pulse raced. This was *not* a good situation.

She panted, still trying to catch her breath, her knees pressed into the cold tile. Maybe this was a good time to call Kester.

As she glanced around for her purse, she heard the door creak open. She lifted her head, bracing for another fight—not that she *could* fight at this point. A silver-haired opera patron, dressed in a beige suit, stood in the doorframe. Ursula blinked through the fog of exhaustion, trying to make sense of this new player in the game.

Half-conscious, her first thought was *What sort of knob wears a cravat? And her second was He's going to call the police.*

For a moment, his eyes locked on hers, and she recognized the horror in his face. "Good god!" He shouted. "What did you do?"

With a tremendous effort, Ursula sat up. Her eyes flicked to Zee, whose jaw hung open like a corpse's. Of course the man was panicking. He'd just discovered two women on the bathroom floor covered in fresh blood, one of them apparently dead. It was a small mercy he couldn't see Hugo's corpse slumped over the toilet in the stall.

She imagined how the next twenty minutes would go down. First, Silver-Hair would alert security and call the police. They'd find Hugo's carcass. None of the authorities would believe her when she described Abe's death kiss, and as the only conscious person in the room, she could find herself accused of the pop star's murder, as well as some sort of assault on Zee. Her heart thrummed.

"I'll get the police," he stammered. "Security."

So much for staying in the bloody shadows. I'm getting sent straight to the inferno when Emerazel learns of this. In a few minutes the bathroom would be full of security guards. If she'd had any energy, she'd have lit the place on fire to give herself enough time to escape, but she could feel her embers dulled.

"Wait," she said, holding up a hand. She couldn't let him leave.

There were two options: she could create a diversion using hellfire, or she could find some way to attack the man and get out of here with Zee. Only, she couldn't manage either of those things without energy.

Shit. What would a normal woman do in this situation? Probably not thinking about lighting things on fire and stabbing people, for one thing.

A normal person would cry.

"Wait," she repeated. She let her eyes fill with tears, and pouted, choking out a sob. "She wasn't feeling well," she sniffed, letting the strap of her gown drop again. "I told her not to order the salad. She didn't have her EpiPen. Or her inhaler. And I tried to take her to the women's room, but she said she couldn't make it. So we came in here. And then she slipped on the tile and cracked her head. She's my dearest friend. Please help us." She let a tear roll down her cheek. *Please, please, please, convince him.*

"Oh. That's awful." He pulled out his phone. "I'll call an ambulance."

"No!" she shouted, before letting her face soften again. "It will take too long for them to get here. If she doesn't get an EpiPen now, she'll die."

His face blanched. "Where do I get an EpiPen?"

"There are three thousand people in here. One of them is bound to have an allergy."

He cleared his throat. "Shall I… shall I interrupt the performance?"

She let the genuine desperation show on her face. She didn't know how long Zee would have before her heart gave out. "Please hurry, before it's too late."

The man turned, flinging open the door and breaking into a run. As Ursula was left with her own thoughts, she could feel some of her energy returning. She could call Kester now, but she didn't want to bring him into this until she'd already gained control of the situation. She didn't need to call him just to tell him she'd become entangled in another disaster.

She reached down, feeling Zee's pulse again. Still there, but growing fainter. Panic twisted through Ursula. She couldn't let Zee die. Maybe this *was* the time to call Kester. She turned, reaching for her purse that lay on the tiles, when Silver-Hair slammed the door open, a green tube in his hands.

"I've got it!" he said, beaming. He rushed across the tiles and handed it to Ursula.

"Thank you so much. You've saved her life." She popped off the blue cap, sliding the EpiPen out of its tube and scanning the directions.

"We should call an ambulance," said the man.

"Let me concentrate." It came out harsher than she'd meant it. "Please."

She pulled off the blue safety, reared back her arm, and jammed the pen into Zee's leg. She counted to ten, watching as Zee's eyelids fluttered.

"See, she's getting better." She couldn't believe this had worked. "You saved her. You're an amazing, beautiful man." *Too much, Ursula. Rein it in.*

He cleared his throat. "She's not awake yet. I really think we should call that amb—"

Ursula slapped Zee in the face as hard as she could, and when the fae's blue eyes opened, Ursula leaned over. "Zee, you had a reaction to the salad. It was the hidden walnuts."

Zee's gaze met hers, registering understanding.

Ursula leaned in close and whispered: "You need to *tell* this man you're OK." *I really hope she can still glamour them.*

"I—I'm OK." Zee's voice wavered, but Silver-Hair nodded.

Silver-Hair stepped closer, leaning over her. "Let me help you up."

Zee shot up, grabbing the man by his collar. "I'm feeling much better now. You are no longer needed. Get the fuck out, and don't tell anyone about me."

In a daze, he rose and tottered out the door.

"Calm down, Zee." Ursula sat back on the tile, letting out a long breath. "I asked you to glamour him. Not assault him."

Zee's eyes were wild. "What did you do to revive me? I feel like I want to kill something."

"Epinephrine."

Zee shook her head. "What is epinephrine?"

I really have no clue. "I think it's some kind of life-giving hormone. Anyway, it fixed you. Let's get out of here."

Scowling, Zee lifted a hand to her cheek. "Did you slap me?"

Ursula shook her head. "Nope. Just an effect of the epinephrine, I think."

Zee narrowed her eyes before glancing down at her dress. "Whose blood is on my Valentino?"

"Abe. I think he was a shadow demon. He tried to kill us. Look, we need to get out of here. Can you walk?"

Zee slowly stood, smoothing her hair. "I can't believe that prick ruined my dress."

Clutching her wyrm-skin purse, Ursula rose, unsteady on her feet. Zee shot her a sharp look before slipping her arm around Ursula's waist. They staggered into the corridor, and Ursula kept her gaze on the floor, hoping to remain unnoticed. *Nothing to see here, folks. Just two chicks in opera gowns, drenched in demon blood.*

CHAPTER 25

Stepping out of the cold winter air, Ursula folded herself into the soft seat of the Bentley like a bird settling onto its nest, and Zee followed, shutting the car door.

Zee clutched her chest, shrinking into the corner. "I don't feel so good."

Ursula rubbed her arms, trying to warm herself. "Holy fuck. That was a close call."

"My heart is racing," said Zee.

"Are you okay?"

The fae took a deep breath, staring out the window. "I'll be fine. Where are we going?"

Ursula glanced at the driver. "Take us to my place, please. The Plaza Hotel." Just as she was letting out a sigh of relief, she realized she wasn't out of trouble yet. Her target's soul had been claimed by a shadow demon, and that meant Emerazel would murder her slowly. Dread raced up her spine.

The driver turned on the engine and tried to edge into the stalled traffic.

Outside, the wind beat against the sedan's windows. Ursula rubbed her temples. "What the hell kind of demon was that? I think I'm in huge trouble."

Zee didn't answer, instead staring out her window. But something was wrong with the angle of her neck—she wasn't moving. Ursula moved closer, touching Zee's shoulder. The fae's head slumped to the side; her mouth hung open and her eyelids fluttered.

"Zee!" Ursula gripped Zee's shoulders. She slapped her cheek again, but this time Zee didn't wake up—didn't even flinch.

Horror tightened around Ursula's heart. "Driver! We have a situation." She dug around in her purse until she found her mobile. With trembling fingers, she scrolled to Kester's number. He picked up after a few rings.

"Kester?" she shouted, pulse racing.

"Is everything okay?" Apparently the cell phone had no trouble conveying the panic in her voice.

"Zee's unconscious." The words poured out of her. "And I think Hugo's dead. Something called Abe kissed me and he sucked out my fire. And then he kissed Zee, but I stabbed him. I gave her an EpiPen—"

"Slow down. Hugo's dead?"

Ursula took a deep breath, trying to steady herself. "I went to the men's room to talk to Hugo. I didn't think he was there at first, but then I found him in a stall in the back. He's dead. I think. Abe was kissing him, and said he'd drunk too deeply."

"What *exactly* did Abe look like?"

"Tall. Gorgeous. Golden skin. Grey eyes. His touch was like ice cubes. He made me feel—" Her stomach clenched. She wasn't going to go into the whole arousal scenario. "Do vampires exist?"

There was a long pause. "He made you feel *how?*"

Ursula thought she detected a note of anger in his voice. "He made me think I wanted to kiss him." That was both a euphemism and a secret she had no desire to share with Kester, but maybe it would help identify whatever the hell that thing was.

"Not a vampire," he snarled. "Where are you?"

"In the Bentley. Outside the Met. Should I come back to the Plaza?"

"No. Tell Joe to take you to the Elysian. Tell him to floor it." He hung up.

Ursula glanced at Joe. "Elysian. He said to floor it."

Without responding, Joe stepped on the accelerator, cutting into traffic. They raced up 10th Avenue and turned onto West 66th street, weaving between taxis. She clung to Zee, trying to keep her from bouncing all over the car—there hadn't been time to think about seatbelts. For a few moments, a city bus blocked their path, but Joe swerved around it like he was driving a Formula One race car, until—at last—he veered wildly into an empty parking lot by the Hudson River. Frantic thoughts ignited Ursula's mind—Zee's poisoned body, her own skin blackening in a fire.

The car skidded to a halt, and Joe popped the locks on doors.

"Where are we?" Ursula asked, shuddering at the sound of the wind howling and keening against the car windows.

Joe simply tapped his fingers against the steering wheel.

"Thanks, Joe. That's really helpful." She turned to scoop the diminutive fae into her arms, clumsily pulling her closer. As she grasped Zee's waist and shoulders, someone yanked open the door behind her, and an icy wind rushed into the car.

Kester stood in the dim street lights, the wind tearing at him like a wild animal. Despite the cold, he remained perfectly still, oblivious to the frigid air. He stood barefoot, wearing only a pair of boxers, his strong chest covered in menacing tattoos. Wordlessly, Kester gathered Zee into his arms, eyes blazing.

"Will she be okay?" Ursula asked, stepping out of the car into the freezing air.

"Come with me," he said, as Joe drove away.

So he's not going to answer my questions. She was obviously in trouble—big trouble. He'd warned her that if she screwed up, he'd have to send her to Emerazel.

She rubbed her arms, trying to burn some warmth into her skin. "Is she okay?" she repeated, clutching her purse to her chest. *Please wake up, Zee.*

Silently, he pressed on over the icy pavement.

Ursula's heels clacked over the asphalt as she followed him, and her body burned with fatigue. From the river, the wind whipped off the tops of the waves, blowing a freezing spray that coated everything in a thin layer of ice. Ursula hugged herself, shivering in her flimsy dress.

He led her toward a dock that jutted into the water. Despite his bare feet and state of undress, he navigated the slick planking with ease. Swirls of steam rose from the ground as his fiery body melted the icy ground. Ursula trailed behind, clutching a frozen rail.

At the end of the dock, a paint-chipped tugboat floated in the water, tied to a post. Its stern had been painted with gold lettering: *ELYSIAN*. Not exactly what she'd expected of a place with such a poetic name. It looked like a large, shabby version of a child's bathtub toy. *Is this where he lives?*

Kester slipped over a narrow gangplank, disappearing inside. Teeth chattering, she followed, treading carefully to avoid falling into the churning water.

The boat's warmth washed over her as she stepped inside. Although the tug's exterior had suggested a state of total disrepair, the inside was immaculate. Books lined tall wooden shelves between a row of portholes. A wooden table nestled into an alcove, and a fire crackled in an iron stove that stood in the center of the cabin. She eyed a green velvet sofa, fighting the urge to give in to her aching body and rest. The only thing unusual about the place was the dark mark of Emerazel on the floor—another sigil.

Kester held Zee's unconscious body, examining her face. "I won't be able to heal her." His eyes flicked to Ursula's, burning with accusation. "Were you so enthralled by the incubus that you let him feast on Zee, after you failed at your task for a second time?

"Incubus?" He was clearly accusing her of something, and his words stung. "I don't know what an incubus is, but I think you well know that whatever powers he used on me were magical and therefore hard to resist. Abe was attacking me, and Zee came in to stop it. Hugo had been sucked dry before I even got in there."

"Abe." He spat the word like a curse. "You said he had golden skin and grey eyes?"

"Yes. And dark brown hair. He seemed perfectly charming at first."

"Abrax," he choked out the word, laying Zee down on the table. "I can't believe you succumbed to his charm. I want to flay his skin from his body."

Holy hell. "Who is he?"

"He's an incubus. He works for Nyxobas, the god of night." He crossed to her, his body crackling with fiery magic. "There aren't many incubi in the world, and this one is pure evil."

Dread crawled up her spine. "What, exactly, is an incubus? And what makes him so evil?"

"Incubi like him have the power to drain people. They can drain energy, magic, even souls to give to Nyxobas. That's what he did to Zee. And an incubus can inflame sexual energy and take power from that. I'm guessing that's how he transfixed you."

She cleared her throat, listening to the sound of the howling wind batter the side of the boat. God, she was freezing. "There's no point rehashing what already happened. It's over. What do we need to do *now?*"

"It's amazing to me that you dismiss tonight's events so quickly." He stepped closer, boxing her against the wall, his face burning with fury. "You failed to reap Hugo's soul, and you let a shadow demon claim it. You do realize what this means?"

Fear tightened her chest. *He's going to send me to Emerazel.*

CHAPTER 26

$\mathcal{P}$reternatural power flickered in his eyes.

Adrenaline flooded Ursula's veins. *I need a weapon. He's going to kill me.* She still clutched her wyrm-skin purse, but Abe had run off with her blade lodged in his gut.

She scanned the room for something sharp, her eyes landing on an old cutlass that hung above a porthole. But with Kester blocking her path, she wouldn't be able to get to it.

He inched closer. "I should never have let you go on your own."

"Emerazel said you *had* to send me alone, and I know you can't disobey her." Anger tightened her chest.

His eyes flashed. "That's one of the few sensible things you've ever said."

Frantically, Ursula's eyes darted around the room. Since the cutlass was out of reach, she needed to identify an escape route if he was going to sacrifice her. "And she said you need to send me to her if I screwed up again."

He stepped closer, bare feet padding across the deck, until he stood so close she could feel the heat rolling off him, and smell his earthy scent. His eyes trailed over her shivering body, like he was sizing up the value of his sacrificial victim, and her muscles tightened at his gaze.

Her heart thrummed. There was no way she could take on someone with his strength, not when she'd been drained by the incubus. And yet, she had no other choice. An image flashed in her mind—swords shining in the moonlight as someone trained her. *Fight, Ursula.*

Just as he took another step closer, she dropped her purse, throwing a hard punch to his jaw. He flinched, but didn't move. With a racing pulse, she threw another, but her aim was off. He caught her fist in his hand, his grip iron-clad.

Spinning her around, he pulled her arm up behind her back, pushing her up against the wall. The splintered wood pierced her silk dress, and she fought to catch her breath.

"I told you," he purred in her ear, his breath hot on her neck. "You can't fight me. Let me—"

Like hell I can't. She elbowed him hard in the stomach, and he stumbled. She tried to race for the door, but he caught her by the hair, yanking her head back. He slipped his other arm around her body, holding her tight, and growled. "What is wrong with you?"

"I don't want to die. Or burn. I don't want to suffer for something F.U. has done, and I don't want Zee to suffer because of her either. If I could murder anyone, it would be F.U., but that would create a paradox…" She let her thought trail off. She was babbling like a nutter now.

His strong body pressed into her back. "I wasn't going to kill you."

With one of his hands tightly fisted into her hair, and the other grabbing her shoulder, she wasn't going anywhere. His arm heated her skin through her dress, warming her breasts.

"Are you talking about yourself in the third person again? It's really strange."

Relief flooded her. "You said there was no point fighting Emerazel. Just like there's no point in me fighting you."

He loosened his grip on her. "I should kill you. I won't pretend it didn't cross my mind."

She stepped out of his grasp, hugging herself. Away from his warm body, the air chilled her skin. "But you're not going to?"

Golden lantern light bathed his chiseled body. "I should, but no."

"Why?"

He shrugged, confusion and anger warring across his features. "I don't want to kill you."

"I thought you did whatever Emerazel told you to."

"Mostly, yes." He looked away, his face suddenly sad. "But I loathe her."

Ursula shook her head. "I don't understand. I thought you were her Headsman. Why would you do whatever she wanted if you loathe her?"

Flames glinted in his eyes. "I hate that name. And the rest of it isn't for you to worry about now." He clearly wasn't ready to bare his soul.

Shivering, Ursula hugged herself, eyeing the inviting sofa that called to her aching body. "Fine. But what is the point of all of this? Why is she so obsessed with claiming souls anyway?"

"Rest for a minute," he said, nodding at the chair. "Maybe it's time for you to learn something about your world before we hunt down Abrax."

She collapsed into the chair with a sigh, letting the soft cushions embrace her. Her muscles sang with relief.

Kester ran a hand through his hair. "The souls of men are what give gods their power. Emerazel's fire is fueled by the souls of her supplicants. Nyxobas's magic works the same way. The gods are constantly warring over this human currency, and long ago they formed factions of shadow and light to fight against each other. When Abrax drained Hugo, he stopped us from acquiring the soul. He also steals any magic that Emerazel had invested in Hugo." He eyed her with concern. "Like how he drained your fire before Zee stopped him. Honestly, it's a miracle he didn't take your soul."

"It was odd. We became repulsed by each other as soon as his lips touched mine."

He stared at her, surprise flickering across his features. "Really?"

She nodded. "But that means he stole Zee's soul?"

"Half of it, at least."

"Shit." Ursula took a deep breath, trying to push that horrific thought out of her mind. "If incubi work for Nyxobas, what god do the fae work for? Is there a god we can appeal to for help?"

"No. Unlike every other magical creature on earth, they're unaligned. They're descendants of angels who chose to come to earth long ago."

"Why would they want to live on earth instead of in the heavens?" She ached with exhaustion, but this was the first time someone was actually telling her something, and she needed to get as much out of it as she could.

"The fae are simply hedonists. They enjoy earthly pleasures."

Ursula glanced at Zee, whose arm dangled limply over the side of the table. "We can save her if we find Abe."

"Abrax." His eyes blazed. "And maybe we can get Hugo's soul back from him, too, so Emerazel doesn't need to claim your soul. Then I'll crush the life out of him."

"What happens if we don't get the rest of Zee's soul back?"

"She won't live for more than a few days."

Dread snaked up her spine, and she pulled her white stone from her purse, rolling it between her fingers. "She'll die?"

"Yes. Put your charm away. I've got to refill you. You drained the rest of your remaining energy in your foolish attempt at fighting me."

She opened her mouth to protest, but she was too tired for an argument. "How do you refill me?"

He crossed to her, holding out his hand. She grasped it, and he pulled her up. As she stood, dizziness fogged her mind, and he slipped an arm around her back to steady her. "I will imbue you with Emerazel's fire."

She was suddenly acutely aware of his bare skin and the heat radiating from his body. She looked down at the slow rise and fall of his chest, drinking in his delicious, earthy smell. *Oh, God. I don't have the hots for this guy, do I?* "Will that be painful?"

"No." His gaze slid down to her shoulder. "I'm just going to put my hand on your scar. My heat will flow into you."

"Okay." She couldn't take her eyes off his stunning face. *No wonder he's full of himself.*

Kester pulled down the strap of her gown, then her pink bra strap. The cool cabin air tickled her skin. He pressed his palm flat against her shoulder. He closed his eyes, chanting in his strange language. A glorious, tingling heat pulsed from his fingertips over her skin, caressing her neck. The heat moved slowly, whispering around her throat, slipping lower over her breasts before pulsing down her abdomen. Was it her imagination, or was his thumb moving slowly up and down on her lower back, lazily stroking her skin through her silk dress? A hot, euphoric thrill seeped into her body, blazing through her core, and she fought the urge to press herself against his strong body. Molten power ignited her veins, and she felt a smile curl her lips. *I'm back.*

Kester opened his eyes, gazing down at her. "Better?" His thumb still languidly stroked her lower back, and she could feel herself arching into him.

Her eyes lingered on his perfect lips, and for just a moment, she considered kissing him—before she reminded herself that a) he was an entitled wanker most of the time, b) Zee's unconscious body lay just a few feet away, and c) his nickname was "the Headsman." *Probably not a good idea to kiss someone named for an executioner.*

She rolled her neck. "I feel amazing. I'm ready to find this incubus."

CHAPTER 27

Kester crossed his room, pulling open a drawer in a small, wooden dresser. He took out a black sweater, slipped it over his chiseled torso. "There's a little problem with our plan."

"What?"

"I have no idea where to find Abrax. He's an ancient and powerful incubus. He dwells in Nyxobas's Manhattan lair, and I have no idea—"

"I know where he was going."

Pulling on a pair of grey trousers, he shot her a sharp look. "He told you?"

"He mentioned a place called Oberon's. Something about wanting to bring me there as a pet."

Kester curled back his lip in a snarl.

"Do you know what it is?"

"No, I was hoping you might."

"It's a private club for the fae. Unfortunately, they have a strict door policy, enforced by ancient and powerful magic even I can't manipulate. You can only get in if a fairy gives you explicit permission." He nodded at Zee. "And she's the only fae I know. Obviously, Abrax is connected."

Ursula shook her head, the guilt pressing on her chest like a rock. "If Abrax is as elusive as you say, I'm not letting this lead get away." It was her fault Zee's soul was missing. If she hadn't screwed up her first mission

153

with her off-putting personality, none of this would have happened. And, of course, if F.U. hadn't carved the mark in the first place, Zee would be sipping a champagne cocktail in Club Lalique right now. "There must be someone you can bribe."

"The fae aren't interested in money."

"Are you serious? Have you ever been shopping with Zee?"

"She's an exception—she's a solitary fairy. Most of the fae in New York are part of Oberon's court, and have all the wealth they could possibly desire."

"Oberon's court. That's where we're going? Some sort of fairy realm?"

"Yes. And Oberon is their king." He slipped into a pair of shoes. "Maybe we can catch Abrax coming in or out. It's our best chance."

"But he had a huge head start." She closed her eyes, trying to think of all the times she and Katie had sneaked into clubs in London when they couldn't afford the entry fee. They'd usually asked a bartender or waiter they knew to add them to the list. "Are there staff there? A hostess you could charm?"

Kester paced across the floor like a caged animal. "We won't be able to talk to them until we get in. It's in another dimension. The only way in is through magic we can't control."

Another dimension? Bloody hell. "Well, how does Zee's hairstylist get in? Luis? She said something about how he's always there with redheads."

Kester stopped pacing, and his green eyes flicked to hers. "Tell me about him."

She rubbed her forehead. "I don't know much, except that he's slightly creepy and into gingers."

"How big is he?"

"Big. Muscular. About your size."

Kester rubbed a hand over his chin. "He might be fae."

"What would a fae be doing cutting hair, if they're infinitely wealthy?" She touched her lips. "Though you did say they're hedonists—and he was a little too fond of massaging my hair. He leaned down and sniffed it at one point. I did think that was odd."

"Exactly. Fae have their own particular earthly pleasures that excite them. For some it's food, for some it's sex. And for Luis, apparently, it's hair."

"I'll call him."

Kester nodded. "Good. Just don't tell him why we want to go. Oberon's is supposed to be used for pure pleasure only. If he invites any trouble inside, he'll be banned for life."

She bent down, snatching her purse from the floor. "Don't worry. I'll use my silky charm." She pulled out her mobile phone, and dialed Luis's number. He picked up on the third ring. In the background she could hear "Girl, You Got a Magic Body" playing.

"Hi, Luis. This is Ursula. You, um, cut my hair recently."

"Mmm. Ginger. You want a scalp massage?"

"Actually, I was wondering if you're going to Oberon's tonight? I heard you talking about it with Zee when you were doing that amazing thing to my scalp. And, well, I just wanted to try it out. I've heard it's the best place to enjoy yourself."

"I wasn't planning on going. But for you, I could change my plans."

"Ooh, that's wonderful." She let her voice drip with honey. "And Kester will be with me."

"Oh," he said flatly. "They won't want the Headsman inside."

"I'll let you touch my hair," she blurted. "It's important. I mean, it's important that I enjoy myself." *Lure him in, Ursula, like a master.* "And it's important that my hair… enjoys itself… with your fingers on it. You can smell it." *Bollocks.*

"Mmmm." She heard him take a long breath through his nose. "Yes. Let me get dressed. You'll be on the list under Kester's name. Peele. I'll tell them to make an exception for tonight, and the wards will be lifted for both of you. Your hair will get to enjoy itself with my hands all night." He hung up with a click.

She grimaced at what she'd just agreed to.

Kester was staring at her. "That was your silky charm?"

She scowled. "Hey. It worked. I'm getting us into Oberon's, which is more than you could do. Let's go." She was charged up with Emerazel's fire, and her body burned with power.

"Not so fast. We have some preparation to do first." He looked down at her blood-soaked dress. "Staring with getting you out of that gown."

She arched an eyebrow. If Zee's unconscious body weren't a few feet away putting a damper on things, that statement might have made her blush. "And what did you have in mind?"

"Fae fashion is extremely opulent." He walked around her, his gaze sliding down her body. "I think I know just the right look for you."

She crossed her arms. "You're going to dress me?"

Before she'd even got the words out, he was chanting in his magical language, and his magic caressed her skin. Her dress began to transform, the grey silk taking on a stunning grass-green hue. It floated around her legs as if on a vernal wind, the delicate fabric skimming over her thighs. Two long slits inched up the front while her neckline plunged. Gold vines snaked around her waist to just below her breasts, holding the stunning fabric in place. Silver bracelets appeared on her wrists, and a warm, white fur jacket appeared in his hands. With a graceful flourish he placed the jacket on her shoulders.

Staring at his creation, he ran a finger over his lower lip. "Now you look perfect."

She glanced down at her ensemble. "I didn't have you pegged as a clothing designer."

"There's very little I'm not good at."

She nearly pulled a muscle rolling her eyes.

CHAPTER 28

He turned to one of his bookcases and began retrieving magazines from a shelf and tossing them onto the floor. Each featured a boat on the cover, and had titles like *All Things Sailing* and *Anchors Away.*

She narrowed her eyes. "Is there some sort of nautical solution to Zee's missing soul?"

He leaned over, staring into the shelf. "I need to consult my grimoires. We need to conjure a protective ward to prevent the incubus from using his shadow magic on us."

"You know when a magical ward would have been helpful? When I was at the opera." She stepped closer, peering over his shoulder. The magazines had hidden a metal button, and Kester pushed it. Something clicked loudly, and a nearby bookcase swung forward on a hinge, creaking over the floor. On the back of the bookshelf was a small collection of swords and knives, but the real treasure seemed to be a hidden alcove in the wall, that glowed with that magical amber light. As she peered over his shoulder, she saw that the light protected a small collection of books, just like the ones in the Plaza apartment.

"I'm going to need your help in a minute."

That was something she'd never thought she'd hear him say. "What do I need to do?"

He glanced at her. "A ward spell derives its strength from the souls of the people who create it. Magic is always more powerful when there are multiple spell-casters. If we cast one together, it will be doubly strong."

"And we'll be reading from one of those books?"

"Yes." He held his hands over the amber light, closing his eyes. Slowly he intoned a single word, his deep voice a velvet caress over her skin: *Oriel.* As soon as he'd enunciated the final syllable, the glow on the bindings ebbed away.

The driving wind battered the boat, and Kester ran a finger along the spines of the volumes, muttering to himself. "The *Heptameron* is too celestial. The *Liber Juratus* should have it." He pulled it from the shelf and began flipping through the pages, skimming the text. "Ok, here it is. Honorius's Armor—this will repel almost any magic." He pointed to the looping lettering written on the page. "It's Angelic. Do you think you can read it?"

She stepped over to his side, looking down at the yellowed pages. She couldn't quite understand the words, but she knew how to sound them out—just as she had when she'd first summoned Emerazel. Obviously, F.U. had done something useful with her time. "Definitely."

Kester began to read and Ursula joined in. As soon as they began to speak she felt the magic rushing over her skin, like she'd just stepped into a warm bath. As they intoned the spell, her skin grew warmer and the sensation grew more sensual. The words almost seemed to draw her closer to Kester, like a magnetic pull. Underneath his cedar smell was something darker she couldn't identify, something that drew her in. The dull ache of loneliness that always seemed to gnaw at her heart began to soothe.

As they intoned the final stanza, she felt his arm brush against hers, sending a jolt of electricity through her body. But at the final utterance, the spell between them snapped away. Ursula gasped like she'd been dropped into the river outside. For a moment, her skin felt like it was encrusted with ice, then a dull fatigue took over again.

"What was that? I felt something..." She struggled to describe the sensation.

He closed the book, sliding it back onto the shelf. "That was a magical aura, a byproduct of casting a spell. It's strengthened my aura, giving me a sort of magical armor from fae weaponry. On top of that, any spell I cast will be more powerful now."

"Your aura? What about mine? You said the spell would protect *us*."

"It protects me, and I will protect you. There's a good chance we'll need to fight our way out of there."

She fumed. "My role is to be protected? I thought I was supposed to be a demon warrior now."

"Swords are great, but you don't know any magic." He crossed to Zee, scooping her up from the table. "Look, I'm going to tuck Zee into bed and get myself ready. We'll leave in five minutes." He disappeared into one of the rooms in the bow of the boat.

Alone in the main cabin, Ursula had time to look around. The fire crackled invitingly in the stove, while the spray from the river lashed the portholes.

With a groan, she stretched her arms over her head. Her whole body ached like she'd just gotten over the flu. Giving Kester part of her aura was apparently hard on the nervous system—not to mention the rest of the magical shitstorm she'd been through this evening.

She walked to one of the bookshelves. For some bizarre reason, learning that Kester was a voracious reader was the most shocking revelation of all tonight. She scanned the spines—a row of the classics: Shakespeare, Melville, Dante, Dumas.

Ursula pulled out a volume of Homer and flipped it open. The pages were stiff and smelled of fresh ink; he wasn't reading these books. The shelf below held more recent novels: Doyle, Verne, Burroughs, Christie, even Brontë. The spine of Jane Eyre was creased and faded. Flipping through, she noticed some underlined passages. *I am no bird; and no net ensnares me: I am a free human being with an independent will.*

Kester's heels clapped over the boards, and she nearly jumped out of her skin, suddenly overcome by the feeling that she was invading his privacy. She shoved the book back on the shelf before glancing at him.

He now wore a moss-green shirt, open to his stomach to expose his chiseled chest, and leather bands around his wrists. His trousers were midnight blue velvet, and fitted to his body, and boots were laced up to his knees.

Ursula gave a low whistle. "You look amazing."

He frowned. "I look like a knob. But this is how they dress." He picked up the white fur jacket he'd spelled into existence and passed it to her. "Joe will be here any minute. I'll instruct you in the car on the way over. Are you sure you're up for this?"

She shot him a sharp look. Ursula was gradually coming to understand that F.U. hadn't been a girl to be trifled with. "Don't underestimate me, Kester Peele. Let's go." She slipped into the jacket, and strode off his boat into the stormy winter air.

<h1 style="text-align:center">CHAPTER 29</h1>

The Bentley stopped on a deserted New York City block, the street lined with darkened brick buildings. Ursula stepped out of the car, tugging the fur coat tightly around her flowing green dress. A rusty steel door in a brick wall wasn't exactly what she'd expected for a portal to the faerie realm. There was nothing around it but a small buzzer set into the brick, and a camera discreetly positioned above the door. The air smelled of stale piss.

Wrinkling her nose, she clutched her wyrm-skin purse, her good luck charm tucked safely inside. "Are you sure this is the right place?" she asked.

"Yeah, this is it." His green eyes flashed a look that said *don't second guess me*. "Do you remember your instructions?"

"Of course." How could she forget them? He'd made her repeat them to him on the way over in the Bentley. "Don't speak to anyone. Don't eat or drink anything, but somehow manage to convey debauchery while not having any fun whatsoever."

"You'll have to maintain control. You've never been exposed to a legion of fae auras before. Even going in there might make you susceptible to hedonistic impulses."

"And you won't be susceptible to these impulses?"

"Males don't react to the fae aura in the same way. We're more likely</p>

161

to get possessive or territorial. All the more reason for you to stick near me, so I don't have to murder anyone who tries to take advantage of you."

"I feel like we're walking into some kind of caveman era."

"Their culture is different from yours. The women are submissive. They're only around to please the males."

She shuddered. *What did he mean by 'your culture'?* She made a mental note to ask him about that later. "What century are these people from?"

He shrugged. "The king is nearly a hundred thousand years old. So, yes, caveman era."

Her stomach tightened. "Are you serious?"

"I'll need to act as though I've claimed you. An unclaimed women can be taken by the king."

"What does *claiming* me mean?"

"It means it's a good thing you find me attractive."

Her mouth dropped open. "What are you talking about?" she sputtered.

"Don't think I didn't notice." He adjusted his leather wristbands. "Anyway, that's not important. Abrax will probably be swanning around Oberon. We need to get invited into the king's inner circle. You'll have to catch his eye, while making it clear you're with me, or he'll try to drag you away to mate with you. The fae are quite keen on redheads."

"Drag me away to mate? You've got to be kidding me."

"Just let me do the talking. I know you'll hate it, but in the fae world, these matters are only handled by men. They respect physical strength." The frigid wind rippled his dark hair.

"Can we just get this over with? It's no wonder Zee got the hell out of the fae world."

Kester pressed the buzzer. Nothing sounded, but after a few moments, the door cracked open. A young man with long, silver hair peered out, the room behind him obscured in shadows.

"Your names," he prompted. His fingernails were filed into points and painted white.

"We're on the list under Peele," said Kester, wrapping his arm around her waist. "Guests of Luis."

The man's eyes flicked to Ursula's red hair, and she tossed it over her shoulder for emphasis.

"Of course." He shut the door, and they waited. At least a minute passed as Ursula drummed her fingers against her thighs, trying to force images of Emerazel out of her mind. With Zee's soul missing, there hadn't been time to think about her own fate yet. But how long could Kester keep the fire goddess in the dark about her failure tonight?

Kester shot her a sharp look. "Relax. You look like you're on a suicide mission."

"We *are* on suicide mission," she snapped.

At last, the man reopened the door and beckoned them into a high-ceilinged hall, draped on one end with lush green curtains. The walls were bare, seemingly made of tree bark, and dimly lit with honeyed light. At first she thought the light came from candles, but when her eyes adjusted she saw miniature luminescent orbs hanging in the air above them.

The fae's eyes matched his silver hair; she hadn't once seen him blink. It was deeply unnerving. "Welcome to Oberon's." Halfheartedly, he held out a hand. "May I take your coat?"

Ursula pulled off her jacket and handed it over, but the fae simply yelled, "Mavelle!"

A raven-haired female in a transparent red gown hurried through the curtains, grabbing Ursula's fur jacket before disappearing again.

I guess that's the female submission thing. God, she was going to hate this place.

The male fae beckoned them toward the curtains. With a flick of his wrist, he pulled them aside, revealing an enormous pair of wooden doors, ornately carved with oak leaves. A large stag's antler was affixed to each door as a sort of handle. The doors were inscribed with gold letters that seemed to twist and move like living creatures—just like the walls in the locked room she'd broken into.

Without a word, the fae grasped the antlers, pulling open the doors.

Ursula sucked in a breath, gaping at the enormous hall. They walked forward onto a small balcony, and she peered down at a stairwell that curved to a dance floor below. Fae danced and drank over a floor carpeted with wildflowers and grass.

Still, her eye was drawn upward. Great columns of wood, as thick and sturdy as the trunks of redwood trees, supported a ceiling so far above them it disappeared into darkness. Glowing orbs lit the hall, some as small as insects, others as large as horses, swirling and dancing in the air above their heads like sea creatures buffeted by an unseen tide.

"How does this place exist?" Ursula breathed.

Kester slipped a hand around her waist. "Magic," he whispered.

She glanced down at the crowd, at the fae dressed in stunning styles she'd never seen before—flowing silks of sapphire, plum, and fern green; limbs ensconced in curling gold jewelry. One woman sported hair that pulsated blue and green like the lights of a deep-sea fish. Another, dressed only in gossamer film, spun in a circle, sparks of magic streaming from the tips of her fingers like summer fireworks. Around the edges of the hall, leather clad men sat in wooden chairs, watching beautiful women dance in nothing but a few strategically placed seashells and flowers. Deep, resonant music filled the air, vibrating through Ursula's body, and she inhaled the rich scent of moss and lilacs.

Flipping heck. She hadn't even drunk the alcohol, and she was already getting seduced by the atmosphere.

"Stay focused." Kester grabbed her hand, leading her down the stairs. "Abrax will be skulking somewhere near the king."

As she stepped onto the dance floor, fae brushed against her. They moved effortlessly, their bodies swaying in perfect rhythm to the beat that trembled over her skin. There was a charge—an energy—in the air; it intoxicated her, and she had to remind herself why she was here. *I'm here for Zee.*

Kester slid his fingers down her arm, leaving a trail of tingles, and grabbed her hand. "Scan the crowd, but he'll probably be in the king's inner circle. He doesn't trifle with commoners."

"What are you going to do when we find him?"

His jaw suddenly tightened, and a hint of violence glinted in his green eyes. "I'm going to try not to rip him limb from limb, but I make no promises." The terrifying look on his face was enough to shove the lingering waves of pleasure to the back of Ursula's skull, and she let him lead her between the dancers.

They threaded their way through the sea of writhing fae as she scanned for Abrax. They moved deeper into the hall, and the men's clothing changed, becoming more formal—stiff golden brocades and ruffled lace collars. The women, of course, still wore transparent gowns and scraps of lace. As Ursula watched the ladies dance, it was hard not to let her own hips sway, or feel a thrill at Kester's body brushing against hers.

She leaned into him, whispering. "What's with the Elizabethan ruffs?"

"These fae are part of King Oberon's court."

Just as she was going to ask what the king looked like, she glimpsed something between the dancers: surrounded by armed males dressed in golden armor, a tall fae sat enthroned on a low wooden dais. His pale hair shone in the light, his body radiating a shimmering golden glow.

Ursula gaped. "Is that the king?"

Kester stepped in front of her. "Don't look him in the eye yet."

"What's the matter?"

"You're new here. And you stand out. If we want to get into his inner circle, we want him to notice you, but not claim you." He slipped one arm around her back, touching her cheek with his other hand. "I need them to know you're here with me."

With Kester standing so close, it was hard not to breathe in his delicious loamy aroma, and she wanted to wrap her arms around him. The music trembled over her skin in rushes of pleasure. Part of her mind screamed that Kester had an arrogance problem, that she hated guys like him, that she needed to stay focused on... something. Only she couldn't remember what. Her gaze landed on a beautiful blond fae dressed in white lace lingerie, dancing for one of the fae males. *It would be so great if I could just let go...*

The slow, sensual beat reverberated through the hall, hypnotizing her, and her gaze flicked to Kester's stunning mouth. She glanced up at him, licking her lips. God, he was gorgeous, and the carnal glint in his eye was driving her crazy. Her pulse raced.

The music rippled over her body, sending thrills through her as the beat slowed down. With the rhythm pulsing, Ursula let her hips sway against him. She slipped her arms over his shoulders, pressing her body against his solid muscle. Delicious warmth radiated through his clothes.

Slowly, he leaned down, tracing his soft lips over her throat, his thumb lazily stroking her back.

"What are you doing?" she whispered, her pulse racing faster.

"Showing them you're taken," he murmured into her neck. He slid his fingers into her hair and gripped it tight, pulling back her head, then grazed his fangs along her throat. A hot thrill rushed through her belly, all rational thought leaving her mind. Was there some reason they'd come here?

High above them, magical orbs flashed like strobe lights and the bass reverberated through her very core.

"The king's watching," Kester whispered, his breath warming the shell of her ear. "I'll just make sure he understands he can't claim you."

Ursula ran her hand down his strong back, and his eyes took on a glazed look. He leaned closer, pressing his warm mouth against hers. The touch of his soft lips sent fire racing through her veins, and she arched into him, her lips parting. His tongue brushed hers, and she wanted to rip off his clothes and run her hands all over his golden skin. *This* was why they'd come here, right? Heat coursed through her; she wanted him to pull her into a corner and—

From behind, a hand gripped her shoulder, ripping her out of the kiss. With a tremendous effort, she pulled away from Kester, and turned to see two guards in golden armor, their blond hair and pale blue eyes exactly like Zee's. Ursula's stomach tightened, and she forced herself to move away from Kester as she surveyed the men. That kiss had completely knocked her off her feet, and she could hardly think straight. *Focus, Ursula. This is life or death.* The men's breastplates were finely-tooled, with silver stags around an oak leaf—but her gaze darted straight to the sheathed swords, encrusted with glittering pearls. *Always good to know where the weapons are.*

One of the guards spoke. "Oberon has requested an audience."

"We would be honored to speak to the king," said Kester.

The guards pivoted, flanking them. As they were escorted to the dais, the fae stopped dancing, and hundreds of eyes followed them. Ursula swallowed hard as the guards led them right up to the edge of the dais, where the king stood, flanked by soldiers.

CHAPTER 30

$\mathcal{U}$p close, Oberon looked like four hundred pounds of pure muscle. His outfit was formal—regal, even: a yellow robe tied at his waist with a golden belt and a pair of silver pauldrons to protect his shoulders. He held a halberd with a copper-plated point in the shape of stag's antler, and he stared at them with a grim expression. A sword lay strapped across his back. It was a hall of pleasure, but he'd obviously come ready for a fight.

"What brings you to my hall with this beautiful female, *Headsman?*" His voice was melodious and soft, but he still managed to spit the last word like he'd been fed a piece of spoiled meat. When he spoke, long pointed teeth shone in the amber lights.

"We simply wanted to partake in the festivities." Kester's eyes scanned the room, probably looking for Abrax.

Were they getting close to that point where they'd have to fight their way out? Ursula eyed one of the guard's swords. She could draw it from its sheath with a quick yank, and slice through two of them. Unfortunately, she had no idea how to leave the hall, especially with all the guards that would descend upon her. Also, she had no idea what F.U. had been up to in her spare time, but New Ursula didn't quite feel like a murderer. Better to wait and see how things played out, before jumping right in with the stabbing.

"Here for pleasure?" Oberon's gaze raked her up and down, and she had the disconcerting feeling that he could see right through her gown. "She's a beauty. But she belongs to you?" His voice dripped with disappointment.

"She does."

The king sniffed the air, his lip curling. "One of Emerazel's," he hissed. "She must be hard to tame. I like that."

Gross. Ursula felt the fire rising in her chest.

"I'm still working on taming her." Kester gave a low bow, and she resisted elbowing him in the gut.

Oberon let out a snarl. "Since I can't have her, I would like to watch you mate with her."

Ursula's jaw dropped open. *What?*

Kester smiled nonchalantly, as if this were a completely reasonable suggestion. "Of course. But she's a bit shy. We must go somewhere with a smaller crowd."

Her heart raced. That wasn't what he meant by *claiming,* was it? Obviously, Kester was hot, but she wasn't about to put on a public show.

"Fine," said Oberon. "I'll take you to my exclusive suite."

Kester nodded. "She won't disappoint."

Ursula bit down a thousand angry retorts. *What. The. Fuck.* She tried not to scowl, reminding herself that they were here for Zee, and that surely Kester had some plan in mind that didn't involve shagging her in front of the king. Then again, it wasn't like Kester was open about his plans.

One of the guards beckoned them forward, and Kester led her onto the dais, pulling her close. Oberon stamped the butt of the halberd on the wood. With a slight jerk, the whole platform began to rise slowly into the air, until they were thirty feet off the ground.

Kester leaned into her, whispering, "Don't worry."

The dais continued to rise, until they were a hundred feet in the air, the crowd below growing smaller. She tried not to give in to the vertigo, or the disorientation of realizing that the columns were actually enormous tree roots. *Are we in a giant tree?* Dizzy, she stepped back from the edge.

"Magnificent, isn't it?" Oberon intoned from behind her. "I've ruled these fae since we first came from the heavens, and I never grow tired of the view."

She turned, surveying the king. His eyes were clear and his skin unlined. If she'd been asked, Ursula would have guessed he was no older than forty, though with his strange coloring and enormous size, he looked distinctly otherworldly. She wasn't supposed to speak, and this man was creepy enough that she was actually pleased with that particular demand. So she just widened her eyes, trying to look as innocent and stupid as possible.

He moved closer to her, bending over her neck and taking a long sniff. "Ahh. I never get tired of that, either. The scent of a female ready to mate."

Revulsion rose in Ursula's throat. *Get me out of here. I'll take Emerazel's hellfire over this guy.*

The king continued on his monologue. "I was born before the sundering, before the gods were exiled from the heavens, and yet I still thrill at the sight of a young beauty like you." He laced his fingers together. "Out of curiosity, has the Headsman told you how old *he* is?"

"Three hundred ninety-four," said Kester from her side.

Ursula turned, gaping at him. *He's three hundred and ninety-four years old?* That meant he'd been born in the 1620s, back when people thought diseases were caused by an imbalance of the humors, and went to public executions for fun. Did that mean *she* would have to reap souls for four hundred years to pay off her debt to Emerazel? A spark of anger ignited. Kester had been remarkably silent on that point—and what *was* his plan for this mating thing? It wasn't like she really trusted him.

She shuddered. Honestly, she wouldn't make it four hundred years. Not if she continued to fail at reaping souls.

Fire roiled in her blood, and she tried to push her panicked thoughts out of her mind. She needed to focus on getting Zee and Hugo's souls back, and then getting the fuck out.

The dais slowed, pulling up at a wooden balcony that jutted from a tree root.

"Welcome to my private apartment," said Oberon. "Some of my closest friends are here."

A lick of hope sparked. *Does that include Abrax?*

The platform slid neatly against the balcony, and the king's guards ushered them forward into another, smaller hall, its ceiling a network of flowering vines. In the center, vibrantly dressed guests stood around a banquet table, and others lingered around a bar carved from oak, sipping jewel-colored cocktails.

As Oberon led them into the hall, every one of the guests turned to stare at Ursula and Kester. Kester gave a cursory bow, but his eyes never stopped scanning, searching for Abrax.

The crowd parted for Oberon as he walked to the banquet table, laden with a suckling pig and fruit. With a low growl, the king pushed the food off the table. Rage burned in Ursula's chest. *Is he clearing space for us to mate? Am I supposed to replace the suckling pig?* She glanced around the room, searching desperately for Abrax, but she couldn't find the bastard.

Oberon turned, his lips curled back from his sharp teeth. His footsteps echoed through the room as he approached Ursula, and her stomach tightened. He stopped just inches from her, and warm light glinted off his rings as he reached up to touch her cheek.

Okay, this has gone on for long enough.

"Don't touch my mate," said Kester, his voice booming.

"I can see the fire in her eyes," the king snarled, touching her neck. "I want to tame—"

Dropping her wyrm-skin purse, Ursula snatched his hand, molten hellfire inflaming her veins. She was an ancient fury, come to bathe the world in fire. "I'm not fucking around anymore," she shouted. "Give me Abrax or I will burn this place to the ground."

The king's face contorted in agony; smoke curled from his hand. The guards drew their weapons, but Kester was already chanting in Angelic. As he spoke, his words froze the king and his guards. They grimaced with agony, the sound of crunching bones and sinews filled the room as fae bodies twisted, breaking. The king gagged, his eyes bulging.

So that's why he got the creepy nickname.

While Kester crippled Oberon with his magic, she let go of the king's arms, stealing a sword from one of the guards. It felt glorious in her hands, light and swift. "Where is Abrax?" she demanded—louder, so the whole crowd could hear.

Frantically, her eyes scanned the room for any signs of him by the back of the room, but it wasn't until she turned to look back at Kester that she saw the incubus.

Abrax stood right behind Kester, tendrils of inky midnight magic curling off him like smoke.

"Kester!" she shouted.

But it was too late. In a blur of shadowy motion, Abrax snapped Kester's neck. The crack of his spine echoed off the ceiling, and horror blared through Ursula's skull.

CHAPTER 31

As Kester's limp body crashed to the floor, Ursula lifted her sword. His spell no longer held the fae in thrall, and they snarled, eyes flashing at her. She gripped the sword, raw panic tearing her mind apart. *Kester. Kester is dead.* She tried to shove the horror deep into her mental vault. She couldn't let fear overcome her now, not when a pack of furious fae surrounded her, baying for her blood.

But as she stared into the vengeful face of the fae king, something else began to surge, coursing through each of her muscles: a sharp sense of sureness, as if she knew exactly how each of her joints needed to move. Primal wrath hit her like a wave, imbuing her body with a dark power. *I will avenge him.*

Oberon reached behind him and drew a wicked looking sword from the sheath on his back. His eyes locked on hers, his grin a thing of terror.

But hot battle fury overtook Ursula, and she grinned back, cutting her sword through the air in a display of her skill. She was no longer Ursula. She was Vengeance, ancient and primal. When Oberon lunged, she was ready for him. His blade struck hers, and the sound of clanging swords rang out. The king was fast—almost too fast for her—and his sword slashed above her head with a *whoosh*.

I will avenge him.

Wrath flooded her nerve endings. She began to circle Oberon, her movements fast and precise, and she saw a glint of fear in the king's eyes. In a lethal dance, they whirled and ducked, fast as the wind. The air rushed over her body, until the king began to falter. She scented his fear, wanted his blood.

As the king tired, his guards moved in, swords drawn, and she was no longer fighting one fae, but three. She spun, her sword clashing in a blur of steel, slicing into muscle and flesh. Arcs of red blood sprayed through the air, and she no longer knew who she was fighting; she only knew that she wanted to kill.

Another guard swung for her and she ducked, her sword slashing for his legs. But the fae leapt into the air, bringing the pommel of his sword down on the back of her head.

Pain exploded through her skull; she stumbled back, dropping her blade. Her vision darkened and rough hands grabbed her, pulling her to the floor.

When her vision cleared, the king and Abrax stood above her while six fae guards pinned her to the ground.

"You stupid bitch," Oberon spat. "Once I'm done using you for pleasure, I will flay you alive."

Rage stole her breath. *Kester is dead. And they're going to kill me. Bastards.*

Wild with fury, she struggled to free herself, but the grip of the fae's hands were too strong. Abrax bent low, narrowing his eyes. He touched her cheek, purring. "What kind of thing are you?" He ran his fingers over her skin, and bile rose in her throat.

"Strip her," said Oberon.

Fire. In her panic she'd forgotten to use Emerazel's fire. She let the volcanic rage blaze white-hot, and the fae released her.

Just as she was scrambling to her feet, a growl rumbled through the hall. A dark beast crashed into the crowd of fae, green eyes blazing. The female fae screamed, running for the movable dais. As soon as they crowded on, it began to lower.

Kester? The hound circled her, snarling at the fae who surrounded her with swords drawn. He was protecting her.

Relief flooded her. How the hell was he alive?

It struck her like a bolt of lightning. *The spell.* Whatever spell they'd chanted before leaving had actually worked. Not only that, but it must have changed his hound form. He was ten feet tall at least.

She rose, snatching the fallen sword from the ground.

Kester's eyes blazed; blood dripped from his jaw. A guard swung for him, and he roared, picking up the fae in his teeth and flinging him across the room.

The king drew his sword again, his eyes locked on Ursula. "Filthy animals."

Kester snarled at the king, who now stood surrounded by a troop of fae guards.

"Get him to safety," one of them shouted. As they closed in around the king, their bodies shimmered away, leaving behind only a pale, iridescent glimmer. The temperature in the room chilled by ten degrees.

Ursula whirled, gripping her sword and scanning the room for Abrax. The incubus stood near the balcony, gripping the king's halberd. Blood dripped from his fingers—Kester must have bitten him before lunging into the crowd.

Kester's lip curled back from his teeth, and his deep growl resonated through her bones. Abrax swung the halberd in a tight figure eight, his eyes locked on the hound. The incubus's blade began to glow, charging with some kind of magic. When he slashed it, a bolt of blue light shot straight at the hound. But Kester had already leapt away. Snarling, he charged the incubus. Abrax dodged, moving like a cloud of curling black smoke and reappearing a few feet away. Kester skidded to a stop, just missing him.

Just as Abrax swung the halberd's blade, Ursula heard footfalls behind her. Sword ready, she whirled to find one of the king's guards remaining, his platinum hair swirling around his head like a living thing. "The king will enjoy playing with you once I subdue you." His pale eyes flashed, and he slashed his blade, but the battle fury already burned through Ursula, and she parried.

That sense of precision filled her muscles, warming her like a desert wind. *They think I'm an animal.* He was fast, but she was faster. *They want to slaughter me like a pig.* Their swords clanged as she attacked and he parried. She backed him against the bar until he faltered. *Kill.* She drove her sword through his chest.

As she watched blood bubble from his mouth, horror hit her. She'd just *killed* someone. But there wasn't time to think about what she'd done

—not with Kester's growl filling the hall. She spun to find his jaws locked on Abrax's arm, snapping the incubus's bones.

Her hands shaking, Ursula stared down at her crimson blade. *What kind of killer was F.U.?*

The incubus's roar called her attention back to the fight, and she watched as his halberd skittered across the floor. Her heart sped up—they were too close to the edge.

Kester leapt for the incubus's throat, but he curled away in a cloud of black smoke, appearing again at the platform's edge. Kester pounced, and Ursula's world tilted as she watched them both plummet over the edge.

"Kester!" she screamed, running to the ledge. Her blood roaring in her ears, she peered into the abyss. Desperately, she hoped to see Kester clinging by his fingertips to one of the tree roots, but there was no sign of him. Far below she could see the orbs swirling, and the music thumped in the distance. Panic stole her breath, and for just a moment, the steep drop into oblivion called to her, like a magnetic pull.

But oblivion did not await her at the other end of death. Eternal hell-fire awaited her.

All the blood rushed from her head, and she fell to her knees. He'd survived the neck snapping, but surely even magic couldn't save a body from a fall like that. Her chest welled with an aching sadness, before pure terror overcame her. *There's no way out.* She was stuck in a fae's subterranean lair with an army of soldiers who wanted to rape and murder her. Even death wasn't an escape.

There was no air. *I can't breathe.*

Please let this be a terrible nightmare—there was no fight, no fae, no incubus. Kester didn't fall to his death. In a few moments she'd wake up in her East London flat, ready to drink tea on the couch while Katie regaled her with details of all the guys she'd kissed the night before.

Ursula closed her eyes, taking a deep breath. The floor of the hall was still a thousand feet below her, the abyss oddly inviting in her desperation.

She turned back to the balcony. Apart from the crumpled body of the guard she'd slaughtered, it was empty. Blood stained the wood, and the sweet, metallic smell was overwhelming. She scanned the floor for her wyrm-skin purse, but she couldn't see it anywhere. It must have gotten knocked off the ledge in the fight. Her heart hammered against her ribs. *My white stone.* She had nothing now.

She glanced down again at her bloodied hands. She'd killed someone tonight, with a great degree of skill. What the hell kind of monster had F.U. been? A trained killer? An assassin? And what had happened to Kester?

A hollow opened in the pit of her stomach. Kester's fall would have landed him right in a crowd of fae who wanted him dead. And what did that mean for *his* soul? He hadn't paid off his debt yet, even after four hundred years. Tears stung her eyes, but she clenched her jaw, marshaling her resolve. This was not the time to cry.

Distantly she could hear the beat of the music. *Thump. Thump.* She couldn't tell where her pounding heart ended and the music began.

The fae king wanted her dead, and at any moment he and his guards could return to finish the job. Even if she was some sort of master swordsman, she couldn't fend them off forever. But with the dais gone, there was no way out. *Thump. Thump.*

The sigil. If only she could find something flammable.

Her eyes darted to the bar in the back, and she rushed across the blood-slicked floor, stepping over the guard's corpse. Bottles lined the back shelves, and with a shaking hand she snatched a bottle of a dark-looking spirit. She popped the cork and gave the bottle a sniff, then grimaced. It had to be at least a hundred proof.

The bass deepened. *Thump. Thump. Thump.* Distantly, the crowd cheered, the party still raging. Maybe incubi and hellhounds falling to their deaths from the king's balcony was an everyday occurrence here. She wanted out of this awful place.

In the center of the room, she poured the whiskey in the shape of Emerazel's sigil.

Thump. Thump. The bass was so loud it rattled the floor. How could they continue to dance, with the two pulverized bodies in their midst?

The beat was almost deafening. Something was happening in the hall, but just as she started toward the edge, a gust of icy wind rushed over her skin. She stared in horror as enormous wings rose above the balcony. *Thump. Thump. Thump.* She stared into Abrax's cold, beautiful face.

He looked glorious and terrifying at the same time, like a medieval painting of the Angel of Darkness. His body had transformed, and claws and talons had grown from his hands and feet. All around him, black mist twisted and swirled like ink in water. His frigid gaze fixed on hers.

"Did you think I forgot about you?" Gracefully, he landed on the edge of the balcony and stalked closer.

Ice ran up her spine, and she stumbled back. *Where the fuck is that sword?* Her gaze landed on the king's halberd, discarded on the floor. She dove for it just as the incubus swooped in, his talons raking the wood. She slid across the floor, grasping for the weapon, but the incubus caught her leg with one of his talons, yanking her toward him, ripping through her flesh. As the pain pierced her, she unleashed an agonized scream.

Abrax flipped her over, yanking her under him and pinning her to the floor, claws piercing her wrists. He was going to tear all the flesh from her bones, and the agony blinded her. She arched her back, screaming.

"Really, Ursula. That blade wouldn't have stopped me," he growled, his leathery wings spread out above her, and pressed his claws further into her flesh. Pain screamed through her forearms.

Her pulse raced, the pain so intense she couldn't think straight. She wouldn't be able to fight him anymore, not with her muscles torn apart. "What do you want from me?" she managed.

He leaned closer, whispering, "I want to know who you are." His voice was soft, seductive.

She gritted her teeth, trying to think through the agony. "You and me both," she choked out. Fury flooded her, and she let Emerazel's fire blaze, burning like the sun's core, until it seared the incubus's hands, igniting his clothes. He leapt up, his wings beating the air. Embers sparked from his wings, and he swooped over the main hall, circling like a beast of prey. He wasn't finished with her.

Blood poured from her wrists, and flames licked at her body. Emerazel's fire had ignited the whiskey, and the sigil blazed brightly around her.

Her eyes flicked to Abrax, who was diving right for her, his face etched with cold wrath. She closed her eyes and chanted the sigil spell, just before the incubus's powerful body had the chance to slam into her.

CHAPTER 32

Ursula reconstituted on the floor of the sigil room. For once, she'd remembered to hold her breath, but the pain that tore through her arms and legs was far worse than the soot in her lungs. She glanced down at her ravaged forearms, and the gashes in her leg from Abrax's talons. They had ripped right into the muscle, and blood pumped from the wounds. Dizzy, she tried to stand, pain splintering her limbs, and only made it to her knees. Her body shook violently, and nausea overwhelmed her. An image flashed in her mind of the slumped fae corpse—the man she'd so casually killed.

She couldn't give in yet. What if Kester was still in the fae realm, still alive somehow and being tortured to death? Nauseated, she stayed on all fours, watching the blood pour from her wounds.

Kester could have saved his own skin at least once by giving her up to Emerazel after her failure. Was that why he'd been so reckless tonight—because he knew he'd probably die anyway? Her stomach heaved, and she vomited.

Suppressing a scream, she forced herself up, her legs shaking. *How long until Emerazel comes for me?* Her right leg had been shredded by the talons, and she only lasted a few seconds before she was on the floor again, crawling this time. Slowly, each movement torture, she dragged herself into the hall. There was an extra cellphone in her bedroom. It would be agonizing climbing the stairs, but she'd get there eventually. *As long as I don't bleed out first.*

Blood smeared the hall as she crawled. If anyone wanted to fight her now, she'd just roll over and give up. *Just get to the phone, Ursula.* As soon as she dialed 911, help would be on the way. They'd stitch her up in the ER, maybe sew her veins back together. The gashes went straight through to the bone, but it would give her some time.

She paused, gasping for breath. *I'm not going to make it that far...*

What other options did she have? Kester had used a healing spell after the fight with the moor fiend. A healing spell would get her, quite literally, on her feet.

Focus, Ursula. Could she recall the spell, like she had with the sigil spell in Club Lalique? Probably not. She'd been unconscious when he'd chanted it over. She closed her eyes, racking her brain. Maybe it was somewhere in that procedural memory of hers. But, she had nowhere to begin.

The pain drowned out nearly all rational thought. She leaned back against the wall, closing her eyes and taking deep breaths to manage the agony.

She could *read* Angelic, even if she couldn't produce a spell out of thin air. What she needed was a spell book. Her eyes snapped open. *The library.* Those books had to be Henry's collection of grimoires, and she'd seen Kester unlock the books on his shelf. All she had to do was recite the unlocking spell and skim through their pages.

With a shock of pain, she forced herself onto her hands and knees again and crawled down the hall to the library. The hallway had never seemed so long before—but she'd never felt like she had knives piercing her bones before.

Kester. He had some sort of history with Abrax, she was pretty sure. He'd had an intense reaction when she told him about the incubus. He'd already wanted to kill him. Whatever their history, she wanted to hunt down Abrax and finish the job for him. She shuffled forward, groaning as she reached the library.

Almost there.

She dragged her broken body to the locked books. They stood just as she remembered them, lined up on the bottom shelf with that familiar glow emanating from their bindings. Grimacing, she reached for one, but the force field pushed her hand away.

She grunted, trying to think clearly. *How did Kester do it?* He'd simply held his hands out and recited a spell.

Not a spell, she thought. *That word—like a woman's name.* Gasping, she rolled onto her side and held out her shaking hands. She closed her eyes, picturing Kester's mouth as he spoke the word, his deep voice caressing her skin, and she repeated after him. *"Oriel."*

As soon as she finished, a magical aura whispered over her skin, just like it had when she'd chanted the spells with Kester. The glow around the books flickered for a moment but didn't disappear. *Bollocks.*

She slumped back to the floor, the pain in her legs pure agony. Her breath came in short gasps, and the blood continued to pump from her wounds, staining the rug. There wasn't much time left.

She closed her eyes. If Oriel was a name, then maybe each of these locking spells were personalized, like a password on a computer. And if this apartment had belonged to Henry... How the fuck was she supposed to guess Henry's password? She knew nothing about the man apart from the festive state of his organs after his death. Her heart thrummed. Had she seen anything in the apartment, any photographs...?

The painting. There was a painting in the living room of a beautiful woman named Louisa. And if Kester had named his spell after a woman...

She reached out her hands again, choking out the name. *"Louisa."*

For a moment she thought she'd guessed wrong, but then the yellow glow faded. Relief washed over her. *Finally getting somewhere.*

Her eye raced along the titles on the books' spines. There were copies of the *Fasciculus Chemicus* and the *Theatrum Chemicum Britannicum,* an ancient-looking book simply called *DAEMONS,* and an Angelic book that translated to "Lenus's Healing Spells and Poultices." *Bingo.* She pulled it from the shelf with a thud, barely able to lift herself off the floor. She flipped through it, translating the Angelic spell names at the top. God, she was so tired. She needed to sleep...

But if she fell asleep, she'd wake again bathed in flames.

Fear pushing her on, she refocused her attention. Spells for curing rashes, tinctures for alleviating gout, and conjurations by Ashmole, Norton, and Starkey. She flipped through an entire section on bovine maladies and crop sickness, rapidly losing the will to live.

Her hands were beginning to shake uncontrollably, and she glanced back at the shelf. One book was different from the others—smaller and made of leather, with no name on the spine. It looked more like a journal than a spell book. *Henry's ledger.* She pulled it from the shelf and flipped through page after page of Henry's adventures as a hellhound—each soul he'd claimed, rendered in his spindly handwriting. Desperately, her eyes searched for anything about injuries or a healing spell, until at least she neared the end of the book.

"Collected a pact from Gloria Franklin. A beautiful woman, but Emerazel's fire made her quite the diva. She scratched me so deeply that I had to incant Starkey's Conjuration..."

She almost screamed with relief. *Starkey's Conjuration* it was. She'd seen that one. She flipped back through *Lenus's Healing Spells.* Her vision began to narrow, darkening at the edges.

Please, gods, work.

She focused her dimming sight on the page, and read through the Angelic words about healing waves of light. The words rolled off her tongue, and as she got to the final stanza, she nearly smiled—it was the part she'd heard Kester recite over her broken body after she'd fought the moor fiend—the part about healing waters and leaching away pain.

At the final words, the air charged with a crackling electricity that traveled over her body in a rush, washing through her flesh and muscle. When it reached her arms and legs, a tremendous shock ripped through her. Her tunnel vision narrowed all the way down to a point, until nothing remained but Ursula and the darkness.

CHAPTER 33

$\mathcal{U}$rsula opened her eyes, staring at the library ceiling, her head resting on *Lenus's Healing Spells.* Her gaze darted to the window —still dark outside. Wind rattled the pane.

I'm not burning in an inferno. I must be alive.

She sat up, examining her arms and legs. Not a single scar remained, and her muscles felt strong enough to run a mile. If it weren't for the bloodbath around her and the shredded gown, she might have been able to convince herself it had all been a terrible dream.

She rose, surveying the room. *Blood everywhere.* It looked like a crime scene, red spattering the rug and books. Stepping into the hall, she eyed the trail of gore that led back to the sigil room, overcome by a desperate desire to clean it all up. She didn't know what sort of killer F.U. had been, but the sight and smell of it turned her stomach. Worse, the trail of blood in the hallway sparked something in the darkest recesses of her memory, something she didn't want to remember…

Frantically, she rushed to the kitchen, yanking open the closet and grabbing a mop and bucket. Her hands still shaking, she filled the bucket with water from the sink, and a hefty dollop of soap. *I need to get rid of the blood.*

She nearly spilled the bucket in her rush to drag it back into the hall, where she manically pushed the mop over the boards, sopping up vomit and gore. *I need this gone.* She'd killed someone tonight, and she'd seen Kester die. She hadn't known him long and hadn't liked him most of that time, yet she had the strange feeling that she'd miss him terribly if he were truly gone. She could envision his perfect face, his lips as he'd kissed her. *Please, Kester, don't be dead.* Maybe he'd bust through the door unannounced at any minute.

What the hell had happened in the fae realm? She didn't even know what Abrax had been doing there in the first place. Kester had said the fae were unaligned—they had nothing to do with the god of night.

She scrubbed the crimson-stained floor, trying to push out the image in her mind—Kester falling over the ledge—but the horrible vision kept returning to her. Abrax had slaughtered him viciously, without waiting to hear what they'd needed. They hadn't come to the fae realm to hurt anyone, just to get Zee's soul back. And she'd failed—miserably. Again.

Something cold and primal chilled her heart. She wanted revenge.

She'd lost not one but two souls tonight. She glanced down the hall at the sigil room, hoping to see Kester's athletic frame suddenly appear by some magical stroke of luck. But she was an idiot for counting on things like luck to save her—things like her stupid white stone. Luck was for the desperate, not for those with any sense of control over their lives.

A harsh, gnawing emptiness welled in her chest, and she threw down the mop. She needed to get control for once in her life, before Emerazel showed up and dragged her to the underworld. Maybe she could still reclaim Zee's soul. She could at least try. And maybe—with Zee's help—she could find out what happened to Kester. If she was the one missing, Kester wouldn't just sit around mopping floors and crying. He'd do something about it, for fuck's sake.

Adrenaline coursed through her blood. She would be different—a New Ursula, one who took the hand she was given and dealt with it.

First, she needed to get out of her tattered, stained gown. She raced upstairs to the bathroom, stripping off her dress and turning on the shower. She stepped in, letting the hot stream of water wash the blood into the drain. She was already feeling better. After just a minute, she turned it off and toweled dry before crossing to her bedroom.

She rifled through her drawers for some of the black clothes Kester had bought her. *If I'm going to be an assassin, might as well own it.* Kester had been right—she wasn't a "spring colors" girl anymore. She was a demonic killer, and it was time to get used to it. If nothing else, she wanted to hunt down Abrax and rip out his claws, one by one.

She slipped into a pair of black leather pants, her black boots, and a dark top before pulling on a jacket.

She needed to hunt down the incubus. She'd get Zee's soul back, and then she'd slaughter him for what he'd done to Kester. Or, at least, she'd die trying.

Except—hadn't Kester said he'd been searching for Abrax for years with no success, and that tonight had been their only chance? So where the hell was she supposed to start? She didn't know the first thing about demonic lairs.

She crossed through the hall, thundering down the stairs. Whatever the case, she needed to start by reclaiming Zee's unconscious body.

She hurried to the armory, grabbing Honjo from the rack. A sense of strength flooded her as soon as she picked him up.

In a drawer under the rack of weapons, she found the Kevlar sheath that allowed her to attach the sword to her back. As she armored up, she stole a glimpse of herself in the mirror. She looked like an angel of death. *Good.* That was what she was tonight.

On her way to the sigil room, she grabbed a bottle of whiskey from the kitchen, taking a long slug and grimacing as it burned her throat. This would do to light the sigil.

As she poured the whiskey into the furrows of Emerazel's sigil, she chanted the words she'd learned the first night she'd met Kester. At the last word, flames engulfed her, burning her body to cinders.

Moments later, she was hunched over on her hands and knees in Kester's boat, coughing. *Dammit, why can't I remember to hold my breath?*

Only moonlight lit the inside of the boat. The cold stove stood in the center of the room, its fire now dead. As the sigil flames cooled around her, she caught Kester's scent—his warm, cedar smell, and her heart ached.

Her jaw tightened. There was no time for sentiment now. She had a mission to accomplish. But before she could rise, she saw the blade of a sword coming right for her head.

CHAPTER 34

*S*he leapt away, hitting the floor hard and rolling behind the bookshelf they'd moved earlier. Somewhere on the other side of the cabin, her attacker chanted in Angelic—a spell for light—and a luminescent orb appeared in the center of the room. *So much for hiding in shadows.*

Kester had told her not to enter a fight unless she had a good chance of winning, so she wanted to get an idea of exactly who she'd be fighting. From her position, peeking around the bookshelf's edge, she could see his outline glinting in the orb light. *Armor—fae armor.* She'd killed one fae tonight. She'd kill another if she had to.

The fae soldier's heels clacked over the boards, and she reached over her shoulder to unsheathe Honjo, stepping out from behind the bookshelf.

The man had long, honeyed hair, and his handsome face split into a wide grin. His suit of armor was ornate complete with silver vambraces to protect his forearms. "Looking for a fight, little girl?"

"Yes, unless you want to take this opportunity to piss off, which I strongly suggest. For your own benefit," she added, for emphasis. She was going to have to work on her sword fighting smack-talk.

Laughter danced in his eyes, but in the next moment, his face hardened, telegraphing an imminent strike.

Ursula parried gracefully, knocking his sword into one of the wooden bookcases. "I don't want to hurt you. But I already killed one of your brothers tonight. What's one more?"

The guard ignored her, yanking his sword free with a growl.

His movement left an opening, and with a flick of her wrist, she slid her blade between his hand and the vambrace, slicing his skin. He grimaced, and she pulled away her blood-stained sword. "I did warn you."

"My orders are to bring you to Oberon. Dead or alive."

This time, he didn't telegraph his strike, and she had to dodge behind the stove. He stalked after her, armor creaking, backing her into a corner. She sliced Honjo, but the fae parried, sparks showering from their swords. He rounded the edge of the stove, swinging for her face. She ducked, and his blade whistled through the air only inches above her head. She had to do something offensive, but she didn't know how to penetrate that fae armor without room to wind up in the cramped corner.

The image of Kester's falling body blazed through her mind again, and fury flooded her. She lowered her shoulder and charged.

The force felt like tackling a steel beam, but she'd gotten the leverage right. The guard toppled back, hitting the floor with a crash that sent his sword skittering across the room.

Ursula stood over him, pointing Honjo at his throat, piercing the skin just enough to draw a small drop of red blood. "I did warn you."

Fear shone in his eyes, his grin gone. "Have mercy."

"A coup de grâce then?"

"Please don't kill me..."

"What happened to Kester?"

"I don't know..." he stammered.

"Don't lie to me." Her voice came out in a cold roar, almost foreign to her.

"He died," the fae yelled. "He fell to the ground and died. His body was mangled. He's with his beloved fire goddess now, which I'm sure is what the filthy dog always want—"

Ursula stabbed downward, but not into his throat. Instead she drove Honjo into the gap between breast plate and pauldron, her blade tugging on the sinews of his shoulder until it *thunked* against the wooden boards. He screamed piteously, but dark fury filled her. "I didn't like where that sentence was going."

The guard moaned.

"Don't worry. You'll live." She wasn't sure where this cold, icy Ursula had come from.

She crossed to the other end of the boat, pushing open the door to Kester's room. She cast one last glance at the moaning fae. "If I hear any spells or incantations, I'll be back to reap your soul."

Dim light from two portholes illuminated Kester's bedroom. Tucked into his bed, Zee slept, her chest rising and falling slowly.

Ursula scanned the room, her throat tightening. The walls were steel blue and the bed was covered in a grey duvet. The room was tidy, and a small bookshelf hung on the wall above his bed, lined with more old novels. This was Kester's home. He'd been alive for four hundred years, and she'd led him to his death tonight.

Apart from the bed, the room was sparsely furnished with a small reading chair and a dresser. Something glittered on the top of the dresser —Kester's reaping pen. Ursula stuffed it in her pocket before turning to pull the covers off Zee, who still wore her bloodstained opera gown. Ursula slid her hands under the fae girl's petite shoulders, lifting her from the bed. She was lighter than Ursula expected, and she carried Zee back into the the main room, cautiously eyeing the soldier. He was just where she'd left him, pinned to the floor like an enormous entomologist's specimen. "What do you want with that whore?" he spat.

"She's a friend of mine."

"You know she's tainted? King Oberon never lets a fae leave his troop unless they're unclean."

"King Oberon is unclean," she shot back. She didn't know what that meant exactly, but clearly the old fae king was a filthy bugger. She hoisted Zee over her shoulder like a sack of potatoes, and gripped Honjo's hilt. "I'm going to free you now, but only because I want my sword back."

She ripped the blade from the fae's shoulder. He screamed, hands gripping the wound.

She trained the point of the dripping blade at him, backing away. "If you get up, I'll stab you through the other shoulder."

She stopped when she reached Emerazel's sigil. Holding Zee tight, she whispered in Angelic. At the last words, she and Zee disintegrated in a burst of flame.

* * *

Ursula was gasping for breath by the time she reached the gothic bedroom in the Plaza apartment. It wasn't every day that she carried a limp body up a flight of stairs.

She dropped Zee on the black canopy bed, ignoring the animal skulls that lined the walls. She tucked Zee under the blankets and slipped out the door, her body aching.

A tear slid down her cheek, and she wiped it on the back of her hand. She'd retrieved Zee's body, only to learn that Kester had died in the fall— died trying to clean up her mess, in fact. She'd only just been getting to know him, still hadn't gotten the chance to learn his secrets. Who had Oriel been, and what had she meant to him?

No use wondering about it now. She still needed to figure out exactly how to hunt down an incubus lair. Kester would have known what to do. The man had been an experienced hellhound with an encyclopedic knowledge of spells and arcane magic.

Of course, she *did* have a literal encyclopedia of arcane magic in the library below. A lick of hope ignited, and she rose.

CHAPTER 35

The library was just as she'd left it, with blood drying on the rug. She collected the grimoires, organizing them on the table. In one pile, she stacked the volumes that were way off-topic—the farming spells, and curses.

She flipped through the *Picatrix*, but it was a jumble of arcana, astrological facts, and descriptions of heavenly deities. Into the discards it went.

That left only one book: *DAEMONS*. As if its title wasn't forbidding enough, the heavy volume was bound in a black leather that reminded her of Abrax's wings. Dread whispered over her skin as she cracked it open. Someone had rendered a long-toothed demon in excruciating detail, his head capped with a blood-soaked conical cap, a pile of bones laying at his feet. Along the top of the picture were two words: *Red Cap*.

She flipped the page. Amongst a pile of gold and jewels sat a monstrous man with bull horns protruding from his temples. Above his head his name read: *Raum*.

With a shiver, she reminded herself that these were her people now.

At least this book was going in the right direction. It didn't include any words—only pictures—but it appeared to be some sort of demonic guide.

She flipped through from the beginning: *Aamon, Apollyon, Abezethibou, Abrax, Abyzou...* She stopped. Flipped back one page. Even without the name *Abrax* emblazoned on the top, she'd have recognized him: black wings, talons sharp as knives, and the face of an angel. The incubus had his own page, and someone had written in the margin—Henry's spindly scrawl, by the look of it.

Try as I might I haven't been able to learn much about Abrax. He appears to have led the assault on Mount Acidale, but after the battle he disappeared.

Ursula shut the book. To say that he'd reappeared would be a major understatement. *Bloody hell.* The fact that he had his own page suggested she was up against one of Nyxobas's most powerful demons. She gritted her teeth. She still didn't know where to find him.

She glanced at the clock—two a.m. Her body burned with a mixture of adrenaline and exhaustion, and she scanned the shelves again, searching for Henry's ledger again. She'd scanned through it quickly before, but maybe there was something in there about Abrax, considering Henry had been researching him.

She pored through the ledger, filled with page after page of conquests, starting in the 1830s.

Near the end, where he'd written about Starkey's Conjuration, he'd written the name *BAEL.* Below, he'd scrawled:

"I have imprisoned him in my study. Despite my attempts at persuasion, he refuses to reveal the location of the New York lair. When my interrogations rendered him mute, I used Perrault's Enchantment to put him to sleep."

Bael. That was the beautiful man upstairs.

Her heart raced as she reopened *DAEMONS.* With a trembling hand, she thumbed through to the letter *B.* The sleeper's perfect, wrathful face glared at her from the page, his features etched with sublime fury, lip curled back from his teeth. An enormous pair of golden wings jutted from his back. At the bottom of the page, written in Angelic, were the words *Sword of Nyxobas.*

She dropped the book, and the bang of the cover hitting the table shattered the silence.

She'd been calling herself an angel of death tonight, but the real deal lay on a bed just one floor above her.

* * *

URSULA STOOD in front of the iron-studded door, the reaping pen in one hand, and a contract in the other. She wasn't going in there without a plan, and for extra security she'd strapped a kaiken dagger to her belt.

After spending the last three quarters of an hour arguing with herself, she kept returning to the same conclusion: her only option was to wake Bael.

She'd read Henry's journal entries from the beginning, starting from the time he first contacted Bael to the moment he captured him. He was a little sparse on the details, but she'd learned Bael was some sort of high-value prisoner. Henry had planned to use him as leverage in negotiations with the night god.

Even with this sketchy information, it was clear that all roads to Abrax ran through Bael, and the sleeping demon was her only connection to the incubus.

She just had to wake an ancient demon and convince him to tell her where to find the incubus.

Fear slithered over her skin. It wasn't just that she had to wake Bael that turned her stomach—it was *how* she had to wake him.

Her grip tightened on the dagger, and she chanted the word *Louisa*. After the glow around the door dissipated, she pulled it open and stepped inside.

The interior was just as she remembered. Gold astrological symbols glittered against midnight blue wallpaper. Dusty alchemical glassware stood solemnly on the shelves. Yet this time the air held a strange tension, like the room was holding its breath.

She moved toward the bed, gripping the reaping pen. She had a plan to get a little leverage of her own, but the idea of it sent fear racing through her body.

Tendrils of inky magic curled off Bael's body like smoke, and the air around him crackled with a dark power. Her gaze flicked to the crimson gore staining the sheets. She recoiled, bile rising in her throat. He'd had wings in the picture—beautiful, golden wings. Had Henry cut them off during his interrogations?

Her eyes roamed his chiseled features, his face perfect in repose. His arms, even after months asleep, still rippled with muscle. Despite his otherworldly beauty, the sight of him terrified her. Even unconscious and bound in iron chains, he exuded raw, dark power.

Clenching her jaw, she touched his hand, already feeling his dark magic flowing through her like waves of electricity. She slid the reaping pen into his enormous fingers, folding them around the pen until they loosely gripped it. She held the contract up to the pen's nib, and in a haphazard scrawl, she scratched the letters B A E L. *Bingo.*

She had no idea if that counted as a legitimate signature, but it was at least worth a shot. He was immortal, so he shouldn't care too much, but if he was pledged to Nyxobas, he'd surely want to reclaim his soul for his shadow god. And that meant he'd need to do what she wanted if he wanted to retrieve it.

Taking a steadying breath, she folded up the contract and shoved it into her pocket before drawing the kaiken dagger. Dread inched up her spine.

What she had to do next was even more horrifying than touching his hand.

According to the books, there was only one way to wake someone from Perrault's Enchantment.

Tonight, Ursula would have to kiss the Sword of Nyxobas.

She clutched the dagger, her entire body rigid with tension, before exhaling slowly. *I've got this.* Surely demons like him were bestial creatures, and the scent of fear would only stoke his predatory instincts.

She leaned over him, somehow repelled and attracted at the same time to the shadowy tendrils of power coiling off his muscled body.

"Relax," she reassured herself. "He's bound in chains, and I've got his soul." Still, she placed the tip of the dagger against the soft flesh between his ribs. If he attacked, it would take only one thrust to puncture his heart.

She leaned closer. He smelled of sandalwood, a scent both ancient and exotic. His eyelashes twitched. She almost jumped across the room, but then she realized it was her own nervous breath that had made them flutter. She eyed his lips. For a man made of pure muscle, they seemed oddly sensual.

Marshaling her resolve, she closed her eyes, leaning closer. Her heart threatened to gallop out of her chest as she pressed her lips against his warm, soft mouth.

CHAPTER 36

For a moment, nothing happened, then a powerful thrill rippled over her skin, and she jumped away from him.

Bael's eyelids snapped open, and he surveyed her with glacial, pale eyes that sent raw fear snaking in her gut. Her pulse racing, Ursula's grip tightened on the dagger.

His eyes flashed with ancient wrath; his voice rumbled through the room like thunder. "What did you do to me?"

She tried to stop herself from shaking. She couldn't show him her fear or he'd find a way to rip through the chains and pulverize her. "We'll get to that."

"Who are you, little girl?" he barked. "Where is the other hound?"

"I'm Ursula. Henry is indisposed." Probably best not to mention *he's been eviscerated* just yet.

He narrowed his icy eyes, studying her. "Do you know with whom you speak?"

"Bael. Sword of Nyxobas." *Shit. Maybe he hates that name.*

"Good. Now release me," he growled.

"Sure. I can release you."

When she didn't move toward him he added, "Now."

"I'll release you *after* you tell me where I can find Nyxobas's lair."

The tendrils of dark magic swirled around him. "No."

She raised the kaiken. "Abrax stole my friend's soul, and I want it back. And he has another soul that belongs to me."

His smile was a thing of terror. "Do you mean to threaten him with your little dagger, hound?"

"I have a sword."

"Abrax is the Lord of Alnath, the eldest son of the Nyxobas. A little hound like you cannot stand against him."

Holy hell. She'd felt pretty good with the sword tonight, but she was clearly way out of her depth. Still—she had no choice. Finding Abrax was the answer to every one of her problems.

"Henry was able to bind you pretty well." She looked pointedly at the iron chains that wrapped round the demon. "For a mere mortal, he put you in quite the predicament."

Bael yanked on his chains. "Fetch him for me."

"That won't be possible." Her heart still thudded hard, but Bael at least seemed well contained by the chains. "He's dead."

"How?" Bael didn't so much say the word as growl it.

"He was murdered."

He closed his eyes, and took a long breath. For a moment, she almost thought he'd fallen back asleep—until he unleashed a roar that shook the entire building. It was a terrifying, bestial sound that threatened to tear her apart. She fought every instinct screaming at her to flee into the hall and down the elevator. When he glanced at her again, his eyes were black as night. "He was *mine* to kill. Who killed him?"

"I don't know."

"I will find the one who did it and rip his heart from his chest."

Nerves of steel, Ursula. Nerves of steel. "I don't doubt that, but from your current position that may take some time."

Bael studied her, his eyes seeming to peer into her very soul. For a moment she thought he might roar again, but then he gathered himself. "Tell me how he was killed."

"He was found in Central Park. Apparently, his intestines were strung from the trees like Christmas tree ornaments."

Bael strained against the iron shackles, his muscles taut. "Let me out of here," he roared.

"Will you help me find Abrax?"

"I'm going to find Abrax and tear his ribs through his back. Henry stole something from me, and Abrax was the one who murdered him. That means Abrax has my possession. So let me free if you want to find him, little hound, because you don't stand a chance on your own."

She shifted uncomfortably, her pulse racing. She was going to have to tell him about the soul thing. If he didn't know about her leverage, he'd just eviscerate *her*.

"I was a little worried you might be opposed to working with me," she began, "since you're a shadow demon."

"It's true. I feast on Emerazel's creatures."

Her mouth went dry. "Right. So, as leverage, I got your signature." She pulled the contract from her pocket, unfurling it so he could see, and focused on trying to keep her voice steady. "I put the pen in your hand and made you sign. Now, if you want your soul back, you have to do what I say."

For a moment, a deathly silence filled the room, and Ursula could hear only her own heartbeat. Then, Bael's face shifted—eyes darkening and horns growing from his brow. Cold fury glinted from his black eyes, and Ursula stumbled back, hands trembling. Bael threw back his head and roared again, the sound shaking the entire building, rattling the chandeliers and floorboards. Dark magic swirled wildly around him, snaking through her body. Every instinct in her body told her to run.

When his roar quieted, he closed his eyes, his body shaking with fury, and after a moment, his face returned to normal. He glanced at her, eyes a pale, icy grey again. "Unchain me."

Suddenly, she no longer wanted to release him. He was going to slaughter her. She swallowed hard. "I'm not sure you won't kill me."

"I can't kill you, as you so cleverly ensured. You have stolen my soul and given it to that great monstrous whore, Emerazel. You have your leverage. Unchain me, so I can murder Abrax and get my soul back."

Ursula crossed her arms to hide their shaking. She didn't want to anger him, but she had the upper hand now, and she was going to find out what she could. "What did Henry take from you?"

Bael's furious gaze never left her eyes. "Do you see these bloodstains beneath me? He cut off my wings."

"Why would he do that? Part of your interrogation?"

"And because they're incredibly valuable." He studied her carefully. "What sort of a hound are you?

Apparently, she'd asked a stupid question. "I'm new. How did you know I was a hellhound?"

"You smell of Emerazel's fire." There was a hint of distaste in his voice.

She glanced at the stains again. "Why does the blood look fresh?"

"The wounds aren't healed. If they heal, it won't be possible to reattach my wings. Until I find them, I must remain mutilated. Do you have any more questions, girl?"

"Doesn't it hurt?"

Bael glared at her, the *yes* left unsaid.

Ursula paused, considering what to say next. Which, in hindsight, she should probably had been doing all along. "What makes your wings so valuable?"

"They allow me to fly," he snarled. He didn't say *obviously*, but his tone clearly implied it.

She shook her head. "Abrax already has wings, and I saw him fly."

"You saw him in his true form?" Bael interrupted, surprise flickering across his face. "And you survived?"

She wanted to shout *obviously*, but instead she shrugged like it was no big deal. Bael didn't have to know that she'd almost bled to death in the library. "You didn't answer my question about why he'd want the wings."

He clenched his jaw. "They were a gift from Nyxobas himself. I will be condemned for eternity if I don't find them."

"How do you know he hasn't given them to Nyxobas already?"

"Because if he had, I'd be withering in the shadow void, not trapped in a room with one of Emerazel's dogs."

"Why wouldn't he have—"

"Do you always ask so many questions, little girl? I can't give you these answers. Only Abrax knows. If you free me, I will take you to him."

Ursula gazed into his pale eyes. If she could ignore the fact that he was terrifying, he had a certain sublime beauty, his grey eyes such a stark contrast with his golden skin—warm and cold coming together, like storm clouds tinged by a rising sun. He looked like a god himself—hell, he practically *was* one as far as she could tell.

She wasn't convinced he wouldn't murder her when she removed the chains, but what choice did she have? If she didn't get to Abrax, both she and Zee would lose their souls. "I'll release you. If you help me find Abrax without killing me, I'll give you your soul back." She had no idea how to give a soul back, but she wasn't about to mention that now. Anyway, he was immortal, and he'd never need to know.

"If you fail on your promise to return my soul, your fate will be worse than Henry's."

"I don't doubt it."

"Now unchain me," he roared.

She took a deep breath, eyeing the chains. The links were dull grey. Compared to the glowing wards that had guarded the bookcases and the door to Bael's room, the chains appeared positively mundane.

"How do these chains hold you anyway? They don't look magical."

"Henry forged them with magic. You can't see it," said Bael with an audible sigh.

"So is there a lock somewhere?"

"Melt the links with your fire."

She winced. She was liable to set his whole body on fire, and then she had no doubt he'd tear her limb from limb. "I don't, um, exactly have very good control of my fire."

"Of course. I almost forgot that you don't know what you're doing."

Ursula picked up a link of chain, testing the metal with her fingers.

"I only just learned I was a hellhound a few days ago. I have no memory. Kester just showed up in my kitchen—"

"Kester? The Headsman? He *lives?*"

Grief flooded her, and she forced back the tears. "Not anymore. Not since a few hours ago."

Bael growled. "You lie. I killed him at the great battle of Mount Acidale."

"What? No. I've been with him the whole time. Abrax just murdered him."

Bael's eyes blackened again, the horns once again appearing. He thrashed on the bed, the chains around his body smoking. He screamed in frustration, but his face had returned to its beautiful, human form. Against his skin, the iron links sizzled and hissed. The room filled with the smell of burning flesh. Through gritted teeth he spoke. "Release me. Now."

"I'm trying to, but you need to stay still."

The chains were white hot. Whatever spell Henry had worked into the iron, it was fighting back, burning the demon. She paused, her hand inches from the smoking metal.

"It won't burn you. Hellhounds are immune to fire," said Bael. The only clue that he was in agony were a few clipped vowels.

Ursula closed her eyes. She needed to channel her fire. Draw just enough to melt the chain. Her stomach clenched a little. This time, if she lost herself to the flames, Kester wasn't standing by with a fire extinguisher.

She thought of Rufus's smug face—her old standby for calling up the hellfire—and heat began to kindle in her fingers. *It's working.* Her fingers glowed, and a thrill of excitement raced through her.

On the bed, Bael lay perfectly still, probably enduring intense agony as she gathered her flames. He hadn't taken a breath for a minute or two. Was he alive? She glanced at him, at his beautiful face that stared at her with anticipation. It was like she was trying to solve a math problem with the teacher standing just over her shoulder—an exceptionally handsome teacher. The fire in her veins sputtered and died.

"Bollocks." She unsheathed the kaiken dagger. This, at least, she was good at.

"You know you can't kill me with that."

"I'm not going to kill you. I do hope you'll return the favor." She flipped the knife in her hand. With all her strength she stabbed downward, thrusting the tip of the dagger into the gap in one of the links. Then, with a twist, she snapped the chain in two.

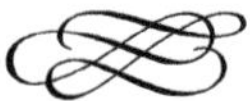

For the briefest of moments Bael stared at her. Was that incredulity she saw in his eyes? Red welts were seared into his arms where the chains had burned his skin. Then, like smoke caught in a breeze, he slipped free. In an instant, he gripped her shoulders, his face taught with fury, and he slammed her into the wall with the speed of a gale-force wind. His strength was terrifying. He slipped a hand around her throat and snarled, "You gave my soul to the fire goddess. You deserve to die a painful death."

Ursula's heart hammered against her ribs. *This is it. I'm going to die.* "You can't kill me," she stammered. "I have your soul."

"You're lucky I'm not at my full power, or I'd compel you to do as I pleased," he growled. He relaxed his grip on her, but his eyes continued to bore into her. "Of course one of Emerazel's dogs would act dishonorably." He stepped away, glaring at her with disgust. "Stay here."

Ursula raised her dagger in a shaking hand. "You need to take me to—"

But he was already gone. Just a rush of air and dark magic, and the sound of the door slamming. She started after him, and something heavy crashed outside the door. He'd locked her in. *The fucker.*

She tested the door anyway, but it wouldn't budge. Muffled noises echoed through the wood—doors opening and shutting and unidentified banging, a demonic rampage through her apartment. As she was deciding whether to try her luck on the ledge, she heard a scraping sound by the door. She whirled, just in time to see the door ripped from its hinges.

Bael stood in silhouette, shadowy magic curling from his enormous body in dark tendrils. Backlit by the crystal chandelier, he filled the door-frame. The man was a mountain of muscle. In one hand he clutched one of the Zhanmadao swords. The blade was close to five feet long, but looked smaller in his grip. In his other hand, he held Honjo.

"The wings aren't here."

Ursula had to fight every instinct to run for the window and throw herself off the ledge. "You said Abrax has them."

"I had to be sure you weren't lying about Henry—that you weren't secretly working for him. I had to be sure that my wings weren't hidden here."

"And now you're *sure* that I'm not working for Henry?"

"Yes. I can hardly smell Henry's stench anymore. He hasn't been in this apartment in months. Kester has been here, though."

Ursula's eyes locked on the sword in Bael's hand. Why had he brought it? She was defenseless with the stupid dagger. He could hack her to pieces in an instant. *Don't antagonize him.* That's what Kester would have told her. *And don't let him see your fear.* "I admire your taste in weaponry."

"I feel more comfortable with a blade in my hand." He tossed Honjo to her, and it spun through the air. She caught the hilt nimbly, and relief flooded her. He wasn't going to murder her. Shockingly, her plan was working for once.

"I smelled you on that one. Please understand that you can't use it against me, or you will die." He spoke matter-of-factly.

"That is fairly obvious." As she followed him out the door, her eyes flicked to her overturned dresser. Apparently, he'd used it to barricade her in.

As they walked through the hall, the sword hanging loosely in his grasp, his eyes followed her every move. She had the distinct impression he was calculating and recalculating how quickly he could decapitate her if Honjo so much as twitched in her grip.

Up close, he was downright terrifying. Where Abrax was all lethal grace, Bael was pure, shadowy power. His arms were massive, knotted with muscle. She was certain he could tear her limb from limb without breaking a sweat. He'd certainly rearranged her entire apartment in only a few minutes.

"How do you move so quickly?"

"Emerazel gives you access to her infernal flame, Nyxobas lets me draw upon his shadows." It wasn't much of an answer, but his expression told her that she wasn't going to get any more than that. He cast her another disgusted look. "Your natural smell is polluted by Emerazel. It sickens me."

"You know, in the human world, it's kind of weird to comment on how people smell."

"You're not human."

As they walked down the stairs, Bael continued to glare at her, but didn't speak. God, he was unnerving.

She cleared her throat, watching as he pushed the elevator button. "How are we getting to this lair?"

"We drive."

Drive? "We're not using some kind of magic method?"

"I can't fly, and without my wings…" As they stepped into the elevator, he studied her carefully, a look of uncertainty on his face. "I don't have all the magic we need, since one of your brethren mutilated me."

"I guess it's a good thing we've got Joe."

His pale eyes slid to her, as if he was staring right through to her soul. "I must warn you that you're in way over your head."

She nodded grimly. That much was clear.

* * *

Ursula and Bael stood on a crumbling pier, completely alone. A row of industrial tanks roughly the size of two story buildings towered over them. The black waters of the East River flowed nearby.

Chilled by the winter winds, she hugged herself. "So this is the lair?"

Bael growled. He hadn't said much in the car, beyond giving basic instructions to the driver—"right," "left," and "next exit" being the entirety of his dialog. Not that Ursula had been in the mood for talking. While the streets had flickered by, cold and desolate in the early morning darkness, she'd rested her head against the window and shut her eyes. She desperately needed sleep at this point.

Now she stamped her feet to stay warm in the cold. Out of habit, she took a mental inventory of the weapons she carried. One, Honjo strapped to her back. Two, Kester's reaping pen stuffed in her pocket. Three, a kaiken dagger hidden in her boot.

Lastly, zipped into her jacket were a flask of scotch and a plastic lighter.

Scanning the buildings, Bael gripped the great Chinese Zhanmadao sword. She suspected he had a bunch of other weapons hidden beneath his coat, pilfered from the armory during his rampage.

"Down here," he said at last, nodding to a stairwell that led to the river.

She followed him down a flight of rickety steps to a rusty old pier. The air bit her skin, and she wished she'd brought a warmer coat.

Bael muttered the spell for light, and a small orb bloomed into existence above his head. He peered around, looking for something, then bent and pulled on a rope that dangled into the water. From the shadows under the pier, the hull of a small rowboat glided into view.

"We're going onto the river in that?"

Bael nodded, then turned the boat over to dump out the water.

Ursula shivered as her toes slowly lost feeling.

"Get in," Bael said at last.

She sat in the front, while the demon took the middle seat, his weight creaking the boat's old wood. He pulled a pair of oars from under the seats. Dipping them into the water, he pushed off, maneuvering them onto the river. As she sat in the bow, her back to the river, she could see the whole of New York City lit up before her. With each stroke of the oars, the gleaming lights seemed to get a little smaller. Had it been only a few days since Kester first brought her here? Her whole world had changed in the blink of an eye.

Bael rowed silently, his oars gliding effortlessly in the water, the river rippling behind them.

Ursula twisted around to see where they were headed. In the gloom, a dark shape loomed. She strained her eyes, just making out the form of a small island.

"Are we going to that island?"

"Yes."

"That's were Nyxobas's New York lair is?"

"In a manner of speaking."

Man of few words. She peered at the island again as they rapidly drew closer. Trees covered the land, but no lights glinted from the forested depths.

They pulled up on a gravelly beach and Bael hopped out into knee-deep water, dragging the boat onto the rocky shore.

Ursula stepped onto the rocks. Ice slicked the stones, but the tread on her boots gripped them tightly. She glanced at Bael, who already stood at the tree line, his pale eyes watching her impatiently as she hurried up the beach.

"You could have waited," she grumbled when she reached him.

"We were exposed on the beach."

Before she could ask where they were headed, he started into the dark forest.

It was slow going as her boots crunched between frozen kudzu vines. She had to shield her eyes from branches that clawed at her face. After a few minutes they broke clear of the underbrush onto a narrow animal track. Bael paused, sniffing the air. A thin dusting of virgin snow covered the ground. No one had been here.

"It looks like we're alone," she said, more to break the tension than anything else.

"That may not be true. Most of Nyxobas's brethren are nocturnal, and most can fly."

In her mind's eye, an image flashed: Abrax standing over her, his great leathery wings beating the air. She reflexively reached to touch Honjo's hilt from where it protruded from the sheath on her back.

With Bael in the lead they moved along the path, deeper into the island, until the dense underbrush cleared. This would have allowed Ursula to see more of the interior, had the canopy not simultaneously thickened.

On her left, a dark form towered above them, but Bael hardly paused as they neared it. Up close, she could see more clearly in the pale moonlight—an abandoned building, completely overgrown with kudzu, as if the vines were trying to suffocate it. The path wound on between more abandoned buildings, totally desolate in the cold light. Ursula had a distinct feeling of déjà vu, like she was again walking between the towering blue stones on her way to her trial with the moor fiend.

At last, the path opened into a clearing. Bael held up a hand, and Ursula stopped behind him.

"What is it?" she whispered.

"We've reached the lair."

CHAPTER 38

An enormous Victorian building towered over the other side of the clearing, its dark windows staring vacantly like empty eyes. A dark wrought-iron gate covered its door, giving the appearance of a row of black teeth. Her mouth went dry. She knew it was stupid, but right about now, she really wanted her lucky stone—her anchor. She had to wonder if all of this would have been an ordinary day in the life of F.U.

She shivered, staring at the building. "What *is* this place?"

"It was once a hospital. The brethren of Nyxobas live here now."

"This is his headquarters?"

"Were you expecting something more grand? You'll find that Nyxobas is less concerned with aesthetics than your monstrous goddess." He sniffed, his back stiffening. Drawing his sword, he stepped into the center of the clearing. Ursula unsheathed Honjo, gripping it like her life depended on it. *Which, come to think of it, it probably does.*

"I am Bael. I wish to speak to Abrax." His voice boomed through the forest, rustling the leaves and sending shivers over her skin. Ursula scanned the building, but saw nothing move.

A voice hissed from the darkness of the ruin, "We were wondering when you would finally deign to visit us." A dark form materialized in the shell of a window on the second floor, face hidden in shadow.

"I seek Abrax," Bael roared.

"Abrax sends his regards, and offers his apologies that he couldn't be here to see you die in person." The silhouette disappeared into the depths of the decaying structure.

Bael spoke softly. "Get ready to fight, Ursula."

Her pulse raced, adrenaline igniting her nerve endings. This did not seem like a good situation, even with the Sword of Nyxobas on her side.

He leaned closer, whispering, "The only way to kill a—"

There was a movement in front of Bael, a blur of shadow so fast she couldn't make it out. Bael's sword flashed in the moonlight, and something thumped on the ground. A severed head rolled before her feet, its mouth lolling open. Ursula suppressed the urge to vomit as the head shriveled and blackened before crumbling into ash. The crunching of bone cut the silence, and she turned to see Bael holding a dripping heart in his hand. "The only way to kill a vampire is to cut off its head and rip out its heart."

She swallowed. "Right."

Footfalls sounded to Ursula's right, and she swung Honjo reflexively, the blade slicing into something soft—a young woman's stomach. Bile rose in her throat as the girl shrieked.

Ursula froze. This was different than the fae—she didn't even know who this woman was yet, or if the woman had meant to kill her. And moreover, her opponent looked like an innocent teenager, her blond hair cascading over a pink, floral dress. Sobbing, the girl at the end of Ursula's sword tried to pull the blade from her gut, and Ursula's stomach turned.

"I'm so sorry—" she stammered.

"Don't apologize," barked Bael. "Cut off her head,"

Ursula yanked out her sword, and the girl lunged at her, fangs bared. She ducked, slicing upward, and Honjo's razor-sharp edge ripped through the girl's jaw. Through her remaining teeth, the girl growled, ready to attack again. The little blonde no longer seemed quite so human.

"The whole head, Ursula," Bael shouted from somewhere in front of her.

"I'm working on it." *Don't you have someone to fight?*

Slowly, the girl circled her, the wound in her gut apparently forgotten.

More footfalls crunched over the snow, moving in a blur of motion to her left. A dark-haired man appeared by her side, fangs bared. They were trying to flank her. Shifting her weight, she slashed toward the man. In one fluid motion, Honjo ripped through his spinal column like a freshly sharpened butcher knife. She arced her sword right, slicing through the neck of the jawless girl. Two heads thumped to the ground.

"Good," said Bael now at her side. He leaned down, punching through the man's chest cavity to rip out his heart. Almost instantly, the body turned to ash, and he moved on the girl. Then he disappeared in a swirl of shadows.

Gripping Honjo, Ursula scanned her surroundings for movement, attuning her ears for footfalls. A clash of steel turned her head, and her gaze landed on Bael, locked into combat with a trio of men before the hospital's gates.

His movements were swift as a storm wind, his sword gleaming like quicksilver. The fighting sped up, so fast she couldn't track their movements. Blades flashed. A head thumped to the ground. Then, with a spinning slash, Bael separated two more heads from their necks.

As the bodies of the men crumbled, Ursula stared at Bael in disbelief. Even without his wings, he moved like a god. What would he be like *with* them?

After ripping out three more hearts, Bael turned to the derelict hospital, and Ursula gaped at the empty windows, trying not to think about what other demonic nightmares might make their homes within the decaying hospital.

"Don't provoke my wrath, Fiore. Your little vamps are outmatched. Besides, I have no quarrel with you. I'm here for Abrax."

"Who's Fiore?" Ursula whispered.

"The leader of this pack of vampires."

The dark form appeared at the window again.

"Abrax has promised me a place in Nyxobas's inner council if I bring him your head." Fiore's voice was faintly accented and cold as tundra.

"You and I both know that's not going to happen," said Bael.

"He showed me your wings. Without them, you're just as mortal as that mongrel you brought with you."

He's mortal? No wonder he was so desperate for his wings back.

Bael growled. "I will get them back. Why don't you come down here and fight me, Fiore? If you win, your reward is the soul of a hellhound."

"What?" Ursula raised her sword.

"He won't win," said Bael simply.

She glared at him. *Pretty confident for a mutilated demon.*

Fiore's silhouette disappeared from the window. A moment later he reappeared by the entrance. Unlike the vampires they'd decapitated, he was a mass of pure muscle—only slightly smaller than Bael. A pair of katanas gleamed in his hands. A smaller vampire with cherubic blond curls stood by his side.

Bael squared his shoulders. "Do you accept my challenge?"

"It really is sad how far you've fallen," said Fiore. "If you'd like me to put you out of your misery, I accept. Emerazel's cur will be your second?"

Bael nodded. "To the death then."

Bloody hell. Ursula's palms sweated on Honjo's hilt.

Bael backed into the clearing, raising his blade—nearly five feet of lethal steel.

Fiore circled, his katanas poised like the fangs of a serpent. There was a flash, followed by a great clash of metal, as they struck in unison.

Through a blur of shadow and steel, Bael spoke. "I will give you a clean death if you tell me where to find Abrax."

"The only death you'll be getting is your own." Fiore's voice gave no hint of exertion.

As their swords engaged, Ursula's eyes began to adjust to the intense speed, tracking their strikes. Fiore slashed; Bael parried. Before Bael could recenter his blade, Fiore's second sword drove at his chest. It was a brutal strike, but Bael managed to leap out of range, rolling across the snowy clearing to rest on his back.

While Bael lay on the snow, Fiore closed on him like a shark sensing blood. The Sword of Nyxobas didn't move. Ursula reached for her sword, but then Bael lashed out with his foot, his toe connecting with the back of Fiore's knee.

The vampire's leg buckled, and he fell to his knees. In a whirl of shadow, Bael sprung up and kicked the katanas out of reach. He lowered his own sword to the vampire's neck, just piercing the skin. "Tell me where to find Abrax."

Fiore's lips pressed together in a thin line. The two demons glared at one another.

"Any last words?" asked Bael.

Fiore's eyes flicked to where the blond vampire stood. From under his coat, the blond vamp drew a small crossbow.

Ursula lifted her sword, but it was too late. The bolt flew through the air, piercing Bael's mortal chest. Ursula's entire body went cold as she watched Bael topple back into the snow.

Fiore scrambled to his feet, snatching up one of his swords to deliver the final death blow. Power flooded Ursula as the night wind rushed over her skin, and she charged across the snow, Honjo ready in her grasp. A bolt whistled by her head, just as she swung for Fiore's blade. She knocked Fiore's strike off course, his blade driving into the dirt only inches from Bael's neck.

Fiore's dark eyes widened as he pulled his sword from the frozen earth. "What *are* you?"

Before he could strike again, she kicked him hard in the groin. He grunted, hunching over, swords falling to the snow.

Ursula pressed Honjo against his throat. Just as she'd seen Bael do, she kicked Fiore's swords out of reach. She scanned the building, looking for Fiore's second, but the smaller vamp had disappeared. She called into the darkness, "If you shoot me, I swear my last act will be to slice Fiore's head from his shoulders."

No one responded, but neither did an arrow come winging at her heart.

She glanced at Fiore, whose face had gone white. "Help me move Bael." He grunted.

"Do it, or I will cut off your head." Ursula pushed Honjo against his throat. A thin line of blood wetted the edge of the blade.

"Okay." Fiore held up his hands, and she eased up on the blade, giving him room to bend over.

Fiore gripped Bael's jacket, and she heard the high demon groan.

Thank God he's not dead. "Drag him into the trees," Ursula commanded, imbuing her voice with as much authority as possible.

Fiore dragged Bael by his shirt, pulling him into the trees, and Ursula followed, her blade never more than an inch from his neck. When he'd pulled Bael out of the clearing, he rose, and Ursula pushed her blade against his throat again. "Where is Abrax?"

Fiore's eyes narrowed, his mouth pressing into a thin line again.

"No one is going to save you this time," said Ursula. "Blondie ran away."

Fiore closed his eyes. "I will die and deliver my soul to Nyxobas."

"Who said your soul was going to Nyxobas?" Still holding Honjo to his throat, Ursula pulled the reaping pen from her pocket. It glinted in the moonlight. "I'm sure my goddess will happily provide you a warm place to live."

His eyes snapped open. "No."

"Then tell me where to find Abrax."

"I don't know where he is." For the first time, his eyes betrayed real fear. "He didn't tell me."

"What *do* you know?"

"He spends all his time at Oberon's. They're working together on something. I don't know what."

"Good. Now you get what Bael promised you."

"What?"

"Your clean death." Ursula swung Honjo, severing his skull from his spine.

CHAPTER 39

The vampire's body crumpled to the ground. *Bloody hell, do I really need to cut out his heart?* Maybe F.U. had been a trained killer, but New Ursula didn't feel like a full-blown psychopath. Just a few days ago, she'd been painting wildflowers on a wall and clothes shopping like a normal person, and now she stood over a vampire's headless body, trying to decide if she should mutilate it further.

So F.U. had been some sort of master swordsman, but organ carving took her into serial-killer territory. How exactly would a vampire's head return to his body, anyway? Surely it would take some effort. Maybe a vampire doctor. Perhaps she didn't really need to *kill* him; maybe it was enough just to keep him out of her way. She ran to grab one of his katanas from the clearing, before running back to stab it hard through his shoulder blade, pinning him to the ground like she'd done with the fae.

She turned to Bael, kneeling by his side. The demon's enormous chest rose and fell slowly, his head resting against the root of a fir. His dark eyelashes lay closed, just as when she'd first seen him in the Plaza Hotel. Around the base of the bolt, his blood bloomed in a crimson circle.

She knelt next to him. "Bael," she whispered. He didn't move. *Dammit, you need to wake up.* If she was going to return to Oberon's, she'd need his help. And more than that, she didn't want to be responsible for sending his soul to Emerazel. *Shit.* Why had she forced him to give up his soul?

"Bael." She said it louder this time, pushing his shoulder. His pale eyes opened, locking on her.

"Get it out of me," he whispered, eyes closing again.

She looked at the bolt. The wood's grain was twisted and coiled. Was it enchanted? Hesitantly, she touched it, but no flash of pain shot up her arm.

Setting down Honjo, she drew the dagger from her boot. Carefully, she cut away Bael's shirt, revealing his muscled chest. Every inch was inscribed with tattoos, astrological and alchemical symbols intermixed with Angelic script. Her eyes flicked to the wound. Blood bubbled from where the bolt had impaled him, just under his collar bone. A few inches to the left, and it would have punctured his heart.

What was her plan? It wasn't like she could call an ambulance. She'd need to heal him with Starkey's Conjuration spell. She just needed to rip this thing out first.

Ursula gripped the blood-soaked bolt. This wasn't going to come out easily. She slid her leg over him, straddling his chest, and closed her eyes. *I'm only pulling a piece of wood from a man's chest. It's not as bad as cutting out someone's heart.* With a jerk, she yanked it free, then tossed it into the woods.

Bael howled, thrashing. Smoke rose from his wound. He arched his back, and she pressed her palms against his shoulders, trying to calm him. "Bael, you need to lie still, so I can heal you."

The demon's eyes had gone black, glinting with primal violence, but his body went still.

She leaned over him, touching his skin lightly with her fingertips. "Relax. I pulled out the bolt." *Like you asked me to.*

At the touch of her fingers, he sat up with a start. He gripped her shoulders so hard she thought they might break, pulling her to him. "You tried to kill me." He spoke quietly, but quiet rage laced his voice.

"I'm trying to help you."

"Abrax, you bastard. You tried to kill me."

Bollocks. He's lost it. "I'm Ursula. Abrax isn't here."

His eyes remained as dark as night, and he growled. "You will never possess the house of Albelda. As the Sword of Nyxobas, I will slay you."

"Bael, relax. I'm going to heal you."

He rose, throwing Ursula off him. "The god of night granted me immortality. I was chosen by him—" He swayed, then fell forward, the ground trembling at the impact. His body twitched, and she looked closer at his back.

She gaped in horror. Through his ripped shirt, she could see that fresh blood covered his back. Between sodden bandages, blood poured from the two huge wounds where his wings had been. The fight with Fiore must have re-injured them. Nauseated, Ursula looked away.

What had Bael told her about the wings? He couldn't be healed, or he'd lose his chance to reattach them. That meant Starkey's Conjuration was out. Still, she needed to do something to staunch the bleeding. It wasn't like she'd ever taken a first aid course, but maybe she could just jam up the wound somehow, stop them from leaking blood everywhere. Whatever he'd done back at the Plaza wasn't working anymore. She took off her jacket. The high-tech fabric didn't look very absorbent, but her shirt was all cotton. She pulled it over her head, as an icy wind whipped at her bare skin.

Drawing the kaiken dagger from her boot, she began cutting the fabric into strips.

As she stuffed the strips of fabric into his wounds, Bael groaned. Ideally, she would have boiled these first to prevent infection, but she didn't exactly have that option right now. The strips were staunching the blood flow, but they wouldn't stay in place on their own. With a bit of effort, she pulled off his belt, and threaded it under him. Then she buckled it into place across his chest.

She sat back, surveying her work. The blood wasn't pouring from the wounds any more. He could still die, but she'd bought them some time. How exactly could she get his soul back to him? She still wasn't clear on that point, but she didn't want him bleeding out before she got the chance.

She glanced up. The rising sun was beginning to stain the sky a dusky rose, chinks of pale light dappling the snow. *Morning already.* She shivered in the brittle air, tugging her jacket tighter around her bare skin. This would be a good time to use Emerazel's fire to heat herself, but she was far too exhausted for any sort of anger. An icy wind rustled the oak leaves above her. They needed to get out of here before they either froze to death or fell victim to a vampire slaughter.

She dug out the flask of scotch, pushing back the tears. This had been the worst night of her life. *Or at least, I think it was. It's not like I know for sure.* She took a swig, the whiskey burning her throat. Then she stood and began to pour it in the shape of Emerazel's sigil.

* * *

URSULA STOOD in the shower's hot water, letting it thaw the tips of her toes and pound against the tired muscles in her shoulders. She squeezed some shampoo into her hand and began to lather her hair. The scent of eucalyptus mixed with the hot steam.

Bael still slept on the floor of the sigil room. She hadn't been able to move his enormous frame.

She rinsed her hair. Her entire body ached like it had been pummeled with tiny fists. After she got out of the shower, she wanted to sleep, just for a few hours, so she didn't completely lose her mind.

She turned off the water, stepping into the bathroom. Her black clothes made a sorry-looking pile on the floor. Of course, she was never putting them on again—they were soaked in Bael's blood. She wrapped herself in a towel and padded back to her room, where she slipped into a cotton t-shirt and knickers.

Too tired to dress further, she crawled under the covers, her entire body burning with fatigue. Pink morning light filtered in through the blinds, warming the room.

When was the last time she'd eaten? She had no idea at this point. She stared at the wildflowers she'd painted on the wall, but they didn't feel like home anymore. How could anything feel like home when you had no idea who you were in the first place? She let her eyes drift closed, feeling a wave of sleep wash over her, soothing her body. Her mind filled with images of fields of aster, bathed in moonlight—

A pair of strong hands gripped her shoulders, and her eyes snapped open.

Bael kneeled over her, the strap of his belt tight across his chest. His cold gaze bored right through her. "Where's Fiore?"

Ursula's heart raced, and she blinked away the sleep. "Fiore?"

His enormous hands tightened on her shoulders. "Why are we here? Why aren't we at the lair?"

She pushed his hands away and sat up, having forgotten what she was wearing—or rather, *not* wearing. For a moment, Bael's eyes flicked down her body before he averted his gaze. She pulled the sheets up around her. "I used Emerazel's fire to bring us here. You were bleeding to death."

Bael looked at the window, unwilling to make eye contact. "Fiore cannot hide from me. I will rip his sinews from his bones until he talks."

"I'm not sure he'll be talking any time soon. I pinned his body to the ground with his own sword before I cut off his head."

Bael head swiveled back to look at her, and his eyes darkened. "You did what? I needed information from him."

"I only cut off his head after he told me me where to find Abrax."

A hint of surprise flickered in Bael's eyes. "Where is the usurper hiding?"

"I'm not sure I entirely trust you yet. You did offer up my soul to Fiore, if I recall."

"That was a tactical decision. Fiore wouldn't have agreed to a duel if there weren't something in it for him."

"What if you'd lost?" She looked him straight in the eyes. "Oh, wait you *did* lose." Bael let out a low growl, but Ursula held his gaze. "If I tell you where Abrax is, you must promise never to sell me out again. One of those promises on the honor of Nyxobas or whatever you said before."

The demon's jaw tightened, but he nodded. Ursula suspected that the nod might have been a tactical decision as well—not nearly as binding as a verbal pledge.

"Fiore said Abrax went back to Oberon's," said Ursula. "Probably should have gone back there to begin with, since that was the last place I saw him."

"What's he doing with the fae?"

"No one seems to know, except that they've formed some sort of alliance."

"The fae don't form alliances with earthly gods."

"Things have changed, I guess. You have no clue what they'd be doing together?"

Bael looked at the window again, considering the question. "If Abrax and the fae were united, they could make a play for Nyxobas's shadow kingdom." He coughed, wincing in pain.

"Are you ok?"

"I'll manage."

She eyed the belt binding his enormous chest. "I'm not sure if it helped, but I bound your wounds."

"Of course you did." His pale eyes threatened to pierce her soul. "You won't stand a chance against Abrax without me."

"I did pretty well against your vampire friend."

Bael's fists clenched so tightly his knuckles whitened. "Fiore was a dead man as soon as his second became involved," he said through clenched teeth.

Obviously, this was a tender subject. She glanced at his shoulder, which seemed to be clotting. "I got out the bolt that they shot you with, but I couldn't do anything for the wound."

"You mean the quarrel?" Bael's fists unclenched a little. "It was carved from a hawthorn tree. Hawthorn wood is an anathema to creatures of the night, especially if it's forged with iron."

Ursula winced inwardly, thinking of how the wound had smoked when she'd pulled the bolt from his chest. "You're better now?"

"Good as new."

She crossed her arms in front of the sheet. "There's one little problem. We can't get into Oberon's without the invitation of a fae."

"Ursula. I am the Sword of Nyxobas. I go where I choose."

"You take that name quite seriously, don't you?"

His eyes lingered over her bare legs for a moment before his jaw tightened. He turned, walking out of the room. "Seven hells, woman. Put on some clothes."

CHAPTER 40

They stood in front of the unassuming grey door—the portal to the fae realm. Bael had ransacked the apartment for a shirt large enough to fit him, though the fabric still strained over his chest, threatening to tear.

"Are you sure this is the place?" he asked, nodding at the rusted door. "It doesn't look fae."

"I guess the fae are less concerned with aesthetics than Nyxobas."

"Nyxobas eschews frivolity. It is a sign of weakness. The fae are the opposite." Bael's eyes narrowed, inspecting the stone. "I imagine they simply have this place glamoured."

Ursula reached to press the buzzer, but he grabbed her hand. "Don't alert your enemy of your presence before you attack." He stepped back from the door and studied it for a moment. Then, in a blur of black wind, he slammed his foot into the door. It splintered with a crack of shearing steel.

She gaped. "That won't alert them?"

"Not as much as a bell," he grumbled. While Ursula pondered this logic, the demon unsheathed his sword and stepped inside. "Come."

"Right."

Ursula followed, gripping Honjo. Bael muttered his orb spell, illuminating the interior with amber light. This time, no doorman waited to collect their jackets.

The enormous wooden doors blocked their path, and their golden Angelic inscriptions glittered ominously in the half light. Ursula's hands sweated on Honjo's hilt, as an uneasy feeling settled over her.

"Last time, we walked through those doors and they took us to Oberon's hall," said Ursula. "I think they're some sort of portal. But we can't get through those doors just by kicking through them. There's some sort of impenetrable fae magic—"

Bael closed his eyes, chanting in Angelic. Dark magic swirled around his body, whispering past her skin in thrilling tendrils of power. He opened his pale eyes again and pulled the handles. Slowly, the doors creaked open. With a final glance behind them, they walked through.

A cold breeze nipped at her ears, and she stiffened as they stepped into a thick fog. Instead of illuminating a wooden balcony, the glow of Bael's orb was quickly swallowed up by a swirling mist. The air smelled of wet wood and fresh pine needles.

"This isn't Oberon's hall. Do you know where we are?" she whispered.

"No," he replied, his tone suggesting he was entirely unconcerned by this turn of events.

Oberon's voice pierced the mist. "I'm so glad you could join us at my high court."

Bael turned, sniffing the air, and the mist swirled faster. "Reveal yourself, Oberon," Bael's voice boomed. "We simply want to parley."

"Will you swear that on the soul of Nyxobas?"

"I will."

The mist thinned, revealing the golden glint of fae armor in silvery moonlight. It was night here—maybe it was always night in the fae realm.

Slowly, the forms of at least a hundred fae soldiers came into view. A chill snaked up Ursula's spine. Each soldier held a pike, aimed at them. They weren't in the hall; they were outside somewhere, on some sort of wooden platform.

She started to raise her sword, but Bael grabbed her wrist, pushing it down. This was not a fight they were going to win.

The mist continued to dissipate. Beyond the soldiers, tips of trees became visible in the clearing air. Where *were* they? Ursula glanced down and her knees almost buckled as a wave of vertigo hit her. Apparently they were standing on a platform of branches woven together like the nest of a giant bird. Through the branches, she could make out the dark form of an enormous tree trunk—and beyond that, nothing. Just darkness. Ursula had a suspicion that Oberon's hall was buried somewhere far, far below them.

The king's voice came from behind them. "What was it you desired to ask me?"

Ursula spun around, her gaze landing on Oberon, who sat on a wooden throne carved into the form of a kneeling stag, its antlers forming his seat. He wore a silver robe, and a small circlet of gold in his pale hair. A golden satchel lay at his feet.

"Is it true that you've struck a deal with a whelp of Nyxobas?" Bael demanded, as if he was in a position to demand things.

"I am a hundred thousand years old, as old as the earthly gods," said Oberon. "I should have the power of a god." He flicked his fingers and the guards moved to flank them, keeping their pikes trained on Bael.

"And you think Abrax will grant you that?" His voice dripped with disdain.

"He's pledged his loyalty to me. We will lead his brethren out of the darkness and into the light. Abrax and I will rule the mortal realm together."

On cue, Abrax stepped from between a pair of soldiers to stand by Oberon's side. Ursula's breath caught, as an icy chill constricted her chest. She remembered how Abrax's claws had carved chunks of flesh from her legs. He'd tried to murder her—twice.

"Give me my wings," Bael roared, and the platform beneath them trembled. Ursula clamped her hands to her ears, the sound sending a rush of pure fear through her bones. God, he was terrifying.

In front of them the pikes of the fae soldiers quivered and shook like reeds in a storm.

"You can scream all you want, but your wings are mine," said Oberon, his eyes sliding to the golden satchel. From within, he drew two pieces of skin.

Ursula grimaced. *What the fuck is wrong with these people?* Blood dripped from between Oberon's fingers. She strained her eyes, just making out a tattooed design on the strips of skin: golden wings. *Those were Bael's wings? Yuck.*

"If you damage my wings, I will tear your spine through your throat." Bael didn't scream this time, but pure venom laced his voice, and somehow, it was worse than his roar.

Oberon ignored Bael, holding the skin higher. "These wings are a direct conduit to the magic of Nyxobas." The soldiers cheered again. "With their power, we will no longer need to conceal ourselves in this realm. With their power, we will rule the mortals."

Abrax stepped forward. "Are you ready to receive them?"

"I am."

"Good. I want Bael to watch."

Ursula wasn't sure what was happening, but her stomach turned.

Oberon let his robe drape off his back, exposing his skin in the moonlight. From behind him, Abrax drew a thin dagger from his jacket. The king bowed his head.

"Get away from my wings." Bael boomed, the timbre of his voice shaking her.

Oberon turned his head to address his soldiers. "If the fallen demon speaks again, incinerate him." The soldiers began to weave the ends of their pikes through the air, magic hissing and sizzling at their tips. Ursula's heart raced. This had not turned out well.

Next to her Bael stood, his entire body rigid with tension. She could tell that it took every ounce of his willpower not to charge forward.

Abrax held the dagger over Oberon's back. "Prepare yourself to join the kingdom of Nyxobas," he solemnly intoned.

"I am ready for the power of the night god."

Abrax's dagger glinted in the moonlight. Then, like a silver meteor, it plunged into the center of Oberon's back.

CHAPTER 41

Oberon threw back his head, screaming in agony. As the king slumped, Abrax grabbed him in his arms. Ursula felt an icy chill ripple through the air as the incubus drained Oberon's soul.

For a moment, the fae soldiers stood transfixed, as if they weren't sure if this was all part of the process, until Oberon's limp body tumbled to the ground.

"Get down," said Bael, pulling Ursula to the floor and shielding her with his arms. Above their heads, the pikes unleashed their magic like a thousand lightning bolts.

For few moments it was eerily silent, until a voice cried out, "The king is dead!"

Ursula lifted her head. Abrax stood by the throne, Bael's "wings" clutched in a bloody hand, the body of the king at his feet. Fae soldiers circled him, their pikes ready.

"Your king was weak. It is better that his soul join Nyxobas in his kingdom of eternal night."

"Avenge the king!" the soldiers shouted, shooting another round of magic. It didn't seem to touch Abrax, who glided closer to the throne. He chanted in Angelic, moving fluidly in a swirl of black tendrils.

Bael rose, pulling Ursula to her feet with an iron grip. "Get your sword ready."

Dark mist rose around them again, churning and twisting like a maelstrom. In the center of the vortex, a small figure appeared. With child-like proportions and an innocent face, it could have been a cherub—a theory that was immediately invalidated when it leapt onto a nearby soldier and began tearing the flesh off his face with sharpened teeth. The vortex whirled faster, and more and more of the horrific cherubs appeared, attacking the soldiers with inhuman speed.

Bael pulled her close, shielding her again. "First we kill the Oneiroi. You must move quickly to defeat them. Then, we get my wings." He released her, and with a bone-trembling battle cry, he charged at Abrax.

Ursula gripped Honjo, her gaze darting around as she tried to figure out what to do. A few feet from her, a soldier writhed on the ground, one of the Oneiroi attached to his head like a leech. Honjo effortlessly sliced the creature from the fae's scalp.

A blur of movement at the edge of her vision warned her that an Oneiroi was coming her way. She ducked, and as the demon passed over her head she cut her sword upward. Hot ichor splashed in her face. It smelled terrible, like sour milk. Gagging, she wiped it from her eyes.

Hopping to her feet, she spied Bael fighting through a group of the demons. She ran to him, cutting through the necks of two more Oneiroi. This time, she managed to avoid drenching herself in their juices.

Bael carved through them with the stunning grace of a seasoned warrior, his sword swirling effortlessly through the dark mist. Each one of his movements was precise, calculated, no energy wasted—and with each stroke he dispatched another Oneiroi, until the last of their bodies lay on the platform. He'd hardly even needed her help. He turned to Ursula, pale eyes focusing over her shoulder. "Duck."

She crouched, glancing up just in time to watch Bael decapitate another Oneiroi above her head. The little demons were fast, but predictable. They went straight for the throat.

She straightened, and Bael lowered his sword. "That's all of them."

She turned to see the once-orderly platform strewn with Oneiroi corpses, and her heart clenched. She knew they were monsters, but dead, they looked like *children.* Among them lay the bodies of dead and injured fae warriors. Other fae scrambled around, shouting confused orders to search for the incubus. Blood soaked the woven branches, giving the platform the appearance of the nest of a bird of prey.

"Where is Abrax?" she asked.

Bael inclined his head, leading her to the throne, and he pointed to the floor. The wood before the throne opened into a stairwell that led down into the tree's trunk. Carved from wood, it was narrow, big enough for only one man at a time. This passage must have been Oberon's private entrance to his high court.

Bael started in and Ursula followed. He had to crouch, his broad shoulders brushing the walls. Ursula had a bit more room, but not enough to hold Honjo unsheathed. With Bael in the lead, she was probably safe, but she kept a hand on her dagger's hilt.

They passed a few corridors that led off into darkness, Bael sniffing at each before continuing downward. Her thighs burning, Ursula lost track of how many flights they descended. As the adrenaline from the fight wore off, the tension returned to her shoulders. They were going straight to Abrax. She'd seen what the incubus could do. Hopefully, Bael had some sort of plan, though she wasn't getting the impression he was particularly cautious.

"This way," he said suddenly, turning into a dark passage. She could just barely make out the shapes of doorways in the dark wood hall. Bael stopped, and Ursula bumped into his back.

"Don't make any noise," he whispered.

"I wasn't—"

Bael's hand covered her mouth, another strong arm wrapped around her stomach. Somehow, he'd slipped behind her in the darkness. That shadowy movement thing he did was *extremely* unnerving.

"He's in there," he whispered into her ear, giving absolutely no indication which door he'd meant. He released her.

Before she could ask him which room he meant, he was in front of her again ripping open the door with a splintering crack. Apparently, his whole plan was to charge in. She followed, drawing Honjo from her sheath.

CHAPTER 42

*A*brax stood in a tall stone hall, resting against an oak table, arms folded. Starlight glittered through arched windows. Wisteria and honeysuckle climbed the stones, their sweet scents filling the air, and grass carpeted the ground. It was a beautiful, idyllic scene—a stark contrast to the slaughter that was probably about to unfold.

Abrax looked at his nails, seemingly bored. "I don't have time for this."

Bael pointed his sword at Abrax, his rage almost palpable. "Where are my wings?"

"Someplace safe."

"Return them to me."

"Mortal," Abrax spat, "you and Nyxobas have no dominion over me. Not anymore."

Bael lunged, his sword on a lethal trajectory. But the incubus slipped away, and the blade cut through the air. Like a toreador dodging a charging bull, Abrax directed Bael's momentum into the table. Bael was an astounding fighter, but weakened without his wings. Ursula's mouth went dry. *We might not make it out of this.*

Bael spun, his sword slashing ferociously, but the incubus slipped away again in a blur of black smoke. He emerged in solid form, hands clamped around Bael's throat. Ursula's heart skipped a beat. *This is it.*

Black smoke swirled off Abrax. "I never understood your allegiance to

Nyxobas. The things he's done to you. To me. He's not a god—he's a tyrant." Something crunched as he squeezed Bael's neck. "A tyrant that understands only strength and power, and depends on you to enforce it. This is why I will bring him your wings." Bones crunched in Bael's neck, and Ursula's stomach swooped. "And your head." Shadows gathered around him, midnight tendrils reaching hungrily around Bael.

Time to get involved. Ursula readied Honjo, but as she stepped forward, Abrax casually flicked a finger at her. Dark filaments raced across the room, tightening around her chest. They squeezed the breath from her lungs. Agony gripped her chest, her body shaking. *Air. I need air.*

Abrax's grey eyes flashed. "I will create a new realm of the night without you."

Air. Please, let me breathe.

Bael clutched Abrax's arm, straining to break the grip, but his eyes were locked on Ursula, almost pleading as the light in them faded. His eyelids closed.

Air before I die... Ursula thrashed against the magical bonds, desperate for release. *I can't die yet, not before I've done something.* Something simmered within her, and the fire began to simmer, her veins blazing. The air around her crackled with infernal magic.

Abrax dropped Bael, spinning to face her. "Don't even think—"

Her scream cut him short, as the fire poured from her like an exploding star, burning through the filaments.

Right now, only one thought screamed in her mind: *kill Abrax.* He'd torn her legs to shreds, stolen Zee's soul. He'd thrown Kester to his death —and right now, it looked like he'd killed Bael.

Ursula lifted her sword, the blade glowing. She pointed it at Abrax. Flames licked along the steel, and she pressed forward. "I don't believe you've met Honjo," she said. She slashed—a short, controlled swing, carving an eight-inch gash across Abrax's chest. The smell of burning flesh filled the air.

The demon bared his teeth. "You honestly think you can defeat me?"

"No," she snarled. "But I can hurt you before I die."

Abrax backed away as she advanced, her blade sparking with heat. She knew it was futile; she'd seen his power. At any moment he'd transform and rip her limb from limb. Still—this time, at least, she'd make him work for it.

Flames twisted and writhed along her blade, and its heat warmed her face. She slashed at him again, but he dodged, and Honjo only cut through wisps of smoke where he'd been standing. He tended to dodge to the right; she could use that.

"Come and get me then," he said, a lascivious grin on his lips. "A little pain just whets my appetite."

She feinted and stabbed to the right, where she knew he'd dodge. Honjo sizzled, the sword's burning tip plunging through his gut.

The smile disappeared from his lips. He started to speak, but she twisted the blade, wrenching it up towards his heart.

Abrax unleashed a chilling scream.

"Got you," she said.

But before she could finish the job, he dissipated again, leaving Honjo stabbing only vapor.

She heard a voice behind her—speaking Angelic—and she whirled. Horror wrapped its cold fingers around her heart as she stared at Abrax in his true form. Black wings beat the air, and the temperature dropped ten degrees. His talons clattered on the floor; the wounds on his chest and stomach were gone, replaced by rippling muscle.

Abrax roared, and the sound sent a chill racing up her spine. He slashed at her with a talon, but she dove under the table. When she rolled to her feet, he was gone. Heart thrumming, she searched the starlit room. *Where was he?*

Agony seared her shoulder as a claw pierced clean through her. With a jerk she was lifted off her feet, skewered like a piece of meat at a slaughterhouse. One of Abrax's arms slipped around her waist, and he breathed into her ear. "Now, *I've* got you."

The pain stole her breath. She needed to call on her fire—to burn him off her, but she couldn't think straight. *My sword... where is my sword?* She glanced down at Honjo on the floor. In the shock of the pain, she'd dropped him.

Abrax tore at her shoulder again, and she let out an agonized scream.

"I have someone you need to meet," he said in his honeyed voice. The talon had punched out under her collar bone, and agony burned through her mind, her vision blurring.

"You've disrupted my plans," he said.

She closed her eyes, trying to manage the pain. She heard Abrax open a door, and then he ripped his talon from her shoulder. When her body hit the floor, her vision went dark for a few moments. When it cleared again, she found herself staring at bare stone walls.

Gasping, she tried to take a deep breath, but her chest ached. Blood bubbled from under her shirt. Abrax must have punctured a lung. At least she knew Starkey's Conjuration spell now.

As she whispered the spell, a soothing magic washed over her, healing her injured shoulder. She gasped with relief, all the pain ebbing from her body. *I will never again take the absence of pain for granted.*

Standing shakily, she surveyed the gloomy cell. Iron bars blocked the windows, and iron plates lined the walls. The door behind her was solid metal. There was even an iron cot in the corner. She looked closer, her blood chilling. A body lay on it.

"Hello?"

No response. Ursula dug out the dagger from her boot. *It's probably a corpse, but better safe than sorry.*

A dirty blanket covered the figure—a man by the shape of him, his head turned to the wall.

"Hello?" She said it louder this time.

Holding the dagger ready, she rolled him onto his back and stifled a scream.

Kester.

CHAPTER 43

The hellhound gaped at her vacantly—the same glazed look she'd seen on Zee's face. Abrax had drunk his soul.

A lump rose in her throat, and her hands trembled. "I thought you were dead." Even if he couldn't feel it, she slipped her arms around his neck, feeling the warmth of his body against hers. She'd *grieved* for him. And, now there was a chance—a very small chance, but one all the same— that she could save them both.

Apart from the fact that I don't stand a chance against the incubus.

She pinched Kester's arm, but his eyes remained shut. He wasn't waking up. The silence of the room was oppressive, broken only by an uneven drip of water.

Sitting on the end of the cot, she ran through her options. She still had the dagger, the reaping pen in her pocket, and a half-consumed flask of scotch. A lesser woman would finish off the rest of the scotch right now. She could get them out of here with Emerazel's sigil, but that would leave Bael behind, and she still wouldn't have anyone's soul. Her friend would die, and Emerazel would send her to the inferno. *Not a great outcome.*

Could she kill Abrax? Maybe stab him with the pen when he returned? Unlikely.

Bollocks. What other options did she have? Abrax wouldn't leave her in the cell forever. He'd be back to suck her soul or slowly torture her to death.

She'd need to stab him with the reaping pen. That was the best bet. If she stood by the door with her back flat against the wall, she might have a chance. She'd slash with the dagger and jam the pen into his chest.

Before she could move to the door, she heard a shuffling on the other side of it, then the iron ripped open with a bang. *There goes my element of surprise.*

The dark silhouette of a man stood in the doorway. Not Abrax. Not Bael. Yet she knew instantly he was one of *them.* Another powerful shadow demon. Darkness emanated from him, and fear slid through her bones. The lights dimmed, and around her, the room seemed to fall away. She now stood on the edge of a precipice, black and bottomless—a void. Her entire body went cold, and for a moment the chasm called to her, beckoning her into its bottomless depths.

The room refocused as the demon studied her, his eyes shining like starlight. Ursula lifted her dagger.

The demon stepped closer. His skin was pale as milk, a stark contrast to his raven-black hair. He wore a black cloak that swirled around him like smoke on the wind. His stunning features looked a lot like Abrax's. "Put the dagger away," he cautioned, his cold voice sliding over her skin.

Ursula clutched the dagger in front of her. As she recognized his face, terror ripped her mind apart. He had the icy eyes of the man in her dreams. "Who are you?" she stammered.

"Most know me as Nyxobas."

A sharp tendril of dread pierced her.

Looking past her at Kester's limp form, the god continued, "Kester and I have met previously. You, however, are new to me." Yet, the way he said it, she could tell he wasn't convinced. "Who are you?"

"Ursula," she stammered.

"Ursula." He closed his eyes, savoring the word like it was a delicious morsel. "Like the constellation?"

"I guess." Why had Abrax wanted her to meet the god of night? "Why are you here?

"Abrax summoned me. It seems that Bael has gotten into some trouble."

"He's alive?"

"What do you care if a demon lives or dies?" Nyxobas's eyes narrowed. "He helped me."

Nyxobas studied her with a keen intelligence. "Interesting." turned, beckoning her to follow. She didn't know where he was taking her, but questioning a god seemed like a bad idea. Ursula stuffed the dagger into her belt and followed Nyxobas into the starlit stone hall.

Bael and Abrax stood a few feet from each other, and Abrax glared.

Nyxobas stalked in front of the incubus, his cloak swirling around him. "Abrax, my oldest son. Why have you carved The Sword's wings from his shoulders?"

Abrax's eyes burned with cold rage. "Bael is weak. The edge of Nyxobas's Sword has grown dull—so dull that he allowed one of Emerazel's hounds to imprison him and torture him. It was that cur who carved the wings from his back. I merely tried to retrieve them for you."

Nyxobas turned to Bael. "Is this true?" The rage in his voice was unmistakable.

"It is." A line of blood dripped from the corner of Bael's mouth, but he didn't wipe it away.

Bloody hell, this isn't going well. She needed to intervene. "Did your son mention that he murdered the fae king?" said Ursula.

The god's eyes bored into her and the edge of his lip twitched. "The fae are worthless, godless creatures."

At his words, she thought she saw a flicker of fury cross Abrax's face.

Nyxobas turned to Bael, his voice steely. "You know the punishment for losing your wings?"

"Yes." His eyes flicked to Ursula's again, but she couldn't read his meaning. He dropped to his knees. The blood roared in Ursula's ears as Nyxobas gripped his sword.

An execution. That was the unspoken punishment. Bael would be sent to the inferno. *I need to do something.*

But what the hell was she supposed to do? Nyxobas was a god. She didn't stand a chance against him.

Nyxobas raised the sword. In moments Bael's head would be rolling to her feet, and his soul—

"Stop!" Ursula shouted. "If you kill him his soul goes to Emerazel."

Nyxobas's eyes flashed to hers. Pure malevolence bored into her, but he stayed his sword. "What?"

"I took his soul for the fire goddess. When he lay asleep, I forced him to sign."

"Is that true?" Nyxobas's voice was pure wrath.

"I felt the change in my soul. It has been tainted," said Bael, and the agonized tone of his voice suggested he'd have preferred death to this admission.

Nyxobas threw the sword to the ground, unleashing a primal roar.

CHAPTER 44

The whole room seemed to vibrate, and Ursula hoped the roar wouldn't fell the entire tree. Shadows whirled, and Nyxobas appeared in front of her, his eyes black and bottomless. Icy darkness washed over her, then she was standing at the edge of the void again, staring into its depths. A few glimmers of memory whispered past her eyes—the fields of wildflowers in the moonlight, someone teaching her to fight—a woman, her hair like fire. But then the images disappeared, drifting away like smoke in the wind.

She stared once again into the darkness, ice gripping her chest.

Nothing.

This was what death looked like: cold and solitary. Everyone died alone, left only with their thoughts and memories, stripped of everything but identity. But she had no identity, hardly had any memories, for her there was only the void.

Her fingers itched to touch her smooth, round rock, but it was lost. She had nothing but the gnawing emptiness, drawing her deeper. Soul-crushing grief pressed on her chest, so cold and harsh she could hardly breathe.

"Release his soul at once." Nyxobas's voice rang into the void.

The desolation was so sharp and oppressive she could barely speak, until at last she choked out the word "No," her body trembling.

"Then I will kill you."

Nyxobas was terrifying, but she had nothing left to lose. As she looked up at him, her vision refocused. She concentrated on her feet, planted firmly on the floor. "Kill me, then. I'm going to die anyway. Abrax stole a soul I was supposed to collect. When Emerazel finds out she'll send me straight to her inferno." Ursula felt the fire begin to burn within her. "So you can kill me now or you can wait for Emerazel to do it for you, but I'm not going to give you Bael's soul." Not to mention, she didn't even know *how* to return a soul.

Nyxobas's eyes darkened. Before she could stop him, he grabbed her arm in an iron grip. She could feel his power race through her, cold and lethal.

The god reached into her jacket, yanking her flask from her pocket. Pushing her away, he began to pour it on the floor. It took her a moment to recognize Emerazel's sigil. He chanted—some sort of spell for fire— and as the flames flickered, he summoned Emerazel.

At his final words, the goddess appeared with a burst of flame. Immediately, the room felt unbearably hot, like Ursula had been shoved in an oven. Across from her, Abrax and Bael writhed in agony.

This time, Ursula knew not to stare her into the goddess's eyes.

"You summoned me, Nyxobas?" the goddess hissed.

"Your cur tricked one of my demons into signing a pact against his will."

Ursula could feel her body burn; Emerazel's burning gaze must have turned to her. "Oh *really?*"

"So I tricked him," shouted Ursula. "Since when are demons supposed to play fair?"

"Let me see the paper," said Emerazel, her voice simmering with rage.

Shaking, Ursula dug in her pockets, but they were empty. "I can't find it. It must be back at the Plaza," she sputtered, like an idiot student who'd forgotten her homework.

"I saw the contract," said Bael, eyes burning with fury. "I felt it. The fire whore has my soul."

Nyxobas's lips peeled back from his teeth. He looked like he might roar again.

"Well, that settles it, then," said Emerazel. "There are no rules about how a pact is signed. His soul will hold a place of honor in my inferno.

He *is* a gorgeous specimen of man, and I'm sure I can make use of his body."

"Perhaps we can make a deal," said Nyxobas, his voice icy.

Ursula's gaze raised just high enough to catch Emerazel's ashy smile. "Oh, I think not. I can tell Bael has a powerful soul."

Nyxobas's cold gaze flicked to his son. "Get the Headsman." Without a word Abrax disappeared into the hall. A few moments later, he returned, dragging Kester's body over the floor.

"What have you done to Kester?" said Emerazel. The room grew hotter, like the inside of a volcano.

Please make it stop.

"I took his soul," said Abrax. "He wasn't very careful."

Heat rolled off Emerazel in waves. Even Nyxobas seemed to be affected, wiping a line of sweat from his brow.

"Fine. A soul for a soul," said Emerazel at last.

Abrax lowered Kester to the ground. For a moment the incubus looked at Ursula, his expression burning with pure hatred, then he knelt. With an unnatural jerk, his back arched and a golden light unspooled from his mouth, curling into Kester's. As the last of Kester's soul passed from between Abrax's lips, the incubus fixed his eyes on her. They were black as pitch, his expression almost feral. There was no doubt in her mind that he desperately wanted to kill her.

Even from where she stood, Ursula could see the color begin to return to Kester's face. His eyelids twitched, and he moaned softly.

She cleared her throat. "What about Zee and Hugo's souls?"

Abrax stared at her, disbelieving. "Those were fairly acquired."

"Hugo agreed to give me his soul." Emerazel's voice sizzled through the room like water on hot iron.

"What will you give me in exchange?" asked Nyxobas.

"What do you want?"

The god of darkness looked at Ursula, a small smile on his lips. Dread tightened Ursula's chest.

"Her?"

"Yes."

Emerazel frowned, considering. Ursula wanted to scream. This couldn't be happening. Just one peek at the void of shadows had been terrifying. Now she might be sent there permanently.

Nyxobas, sensing Emerazel's reluctance, added, "I don't need her entirely. Just a portion of her soul would suffice."

"I'll share Ursula with you. You'll get her skills for half of each year."

Nyxobas grinned. "This is acceptable to me."

"Wait," Ursula sputtered. Emerazel's eyes blazed, and Ursula could feel the goddess begin to control her. There would be no arguing her fate, but maybe she could save another.

"Are you returning Zee's soul too?"

The night god's smile widened. "Whatever you want, my little hound."

Ursula wasn't sure if she wanted to drop to her knees with relief or run screaming through the halls, but at least everyone was going to live.

On the floor, Kester moaned again, and Ursula rushed to him, putting her hand on his chest. His green eyes fluttered open.

"Ursula?" he whispered.

She cupped his cheek. God, she was glad to see him. "Yes, Kester. It's me."

He smiled weakly. Then his body spasmed, eyes rolling back into his head. He'd passed out. Apparently regaining your soul wasn't easy on the nervous system.

The room suddenly went cold, and Ursula looked up. They were alone. Emerazel, Nyxobas, Abrax, and Bael had all disappeared. She gotten everything she'd wanted, but an uneasy feeling still whispered over her skin. *Why* had Emerazel agreed to that deal? Why give up a perfectly good hellhound for half the year, just to get the soul of a pop-star and to save a fae girl she could not care less about? It didn't make any sense.

A rhythmic sound vibrated through the walls—the drumming of hundreds of feet. The fae soldiers must be looking for them. Whatever Emerazel's motives, Ursula didn't have time to unravel them now.

Straining her thigh muscles, she dragged Kester into the center of the sigil Nyxobas had lit on the floor. She held Kester's limp body, intoning the sigil spell, and with a scorching heat they burned into ash.

CHAPTER 45

$\mathcal{U}$rsula hugged her coat around her, stalking over the icy pier to Kester's tugboat. Cold wind nipped at her face as she rapped on his door.

Kester pulled it open and smiled, his cheek dimpling. "Ursula. Did you miss me?"

"Terribly. It's been at least eight hours since I dragged your body from the fae realm."

He arched an eyebrow. "And you've come back for more of my body? In that case, come inside."

She rolled her eyes, stepping onto the boat. Her eyes flicked to the floor, where blood had soaked into the wood. "Sorry about the blood stains on the floor."

"Was that your work? I didn't know you had such a vicious side."

"I *did* let him live, which was more than he was going to do for me." Pulling off her coat, she plopped onto his green sofa. Tonight, she was back in her spring colors—sky blue and amber. She needed a night off from being a lethal, blood-soaked assassin.

Kester collected a bottle of whiskey from one of his bookshelves, and began pouring it into two glasses. "You impress me. Did you come by to celebrate your first victory?"

"I wanted to see how you were doing. Zee has been in my apartment all day pounding champagne and ranting about shadow demons. She seems a little on edge."

He joined her on the sofa, handing her a tumbler. "That's just how she is."

"And I don't understand the deal that Emerazel made with Nyxobas. Why would Emerazel want to give up a hellhound for half the year?"

Kester sighed. "The gods have been warring for a hundred thousand years. They always will. If they strike a deal, it's because they think they can get some advantage over the other. My guess is that they both think they can use you in some way. I imagine Emerazel hopes you're going to spy for her."

"Lovely. So no matter what happens, I'm going to enrage at least one of them, and probably both."

"You'll need to be very careful. You'll need my guidance, of course."

She took a sip of her whiskey, rolling the peaty taste around her tongue. Her muscles still burned, and she still hadn't managed to sleep more than an hour at a time. Every time she'd closed her eyes in her bedroom, a vision of the void had haunted her. Was that where Bael was now? Her chest tightened. Maybe Nyxobas had chosen to spare him. Bael was terrifying, but she didn't want to be responsible for his fiery afterlife.

Her gaze slid to Kester, his skin a beautiful gold in the warm lantern light. "Why would Emerazel want me to be her spy? I don't even know what I'm doing. Isn't that obvious?"

He held her gaze. "You're not a normal hellhound."

"There are normal hellhounds?"

He smiled. "More normal than you. Hellhounds who don't burn when they encounter their goddess. Hellhounds who don't repel incubi, and who have a basic grasp of their own history."

Cold dread prickled over her skin. "I'd seen Nyxobas before. I saw his eyes in my dreams."

Kester eyed her over the rim of his drink. "You've certainly earned your nickname."

"And you yours." The whiskey leant her boldness. She had to know about Kester's past. She took another sip, and it burned her throat as she swallowed. "Who was Oriel?"

Surprise flickered across his features, and he studied her face for a moment, as if deciding whether or not to tell her. At last, he spoke. "My sister."

"Were you close to her?" She must have died centuries ago.

"I was." His eyes glistened with pain. "Until Abrax stole her soul, sent her to the shadow void."

A lump rose in Ursula's throat. "Because you were a hellhound?"

"That's *why* I became a hellhound. I needed power to avenge her. And I still haven't succeeded. Abrax is Nyxobas's son. He's not an easy man to kill. But Emerazel made me a promise: once I'd filled my ledger, she would find a way to reclaim Oriel's soul. I just needed to do everything she told me, to please her in every way. Every soul I reaped, every person I killed—it all had a purpose. It was all in the name of getting Oriel out of hell. Only I've started to wonder if Emerazel has any intention of sticking to her bargain. As I've come close to filling my ledger, she's only added more pages. And yet I keep going, because if I fail, all of it was for nothing."

Ursula swallowed hard, almost wanting to look away from the raw pain etched on his face.

"When my soul was stolen in the fae realm," he continued. "I experienced just a brief glimmer of Oriel's torment. Pure, crushing isolation. Complete abandonment in the void. That is what Oriel has felt for centuries. And it hit me like an arrow to my heart: there is no Oriel anymore. After all that pain, her mind would be completely shattered, lost in the rush of Nyxobas's night winds."

Sorrow tightened Ursula's chest. "I'm so sorry, Kester."

He lifted his glass, his eyes suddenly clearing. "But you got me back from that. I owe you my sad, sorry life."

She touched his arm. "We got through the impossible last night. We reclaimed your soul, and Zee's. And I'm spared from Emerazel's punishment. Maybe we can free ourselves from our debts to the gods."

He shook his head. "You can't fight the gods, Ursula, even if you fought Abrax. And didn't I tell you not to take on fights you couldn't win?"

"It worked last night, didn't it? We got everything we needed."

"But you lost your lucky rock." Mischief glinted in his eyes again.

"I'm not ready to joke about that yet." She scowled, then arched an eyebrow. "Wait. How did you know I lost that? I never told you that."

He reached into the pocket of his grey trousers, pulling out her smooth, white stone.

Her heart sped up. "How did you *get* that?"

"After my body reconstituted on the dance floor, I grabbed this out of your wyrm-skin purse. I would have returned it sooner, but Abrax interrupted me." He folded his fingers around it, curling it to his chest. "And now, I'm afraid I'd become quite attached to it. It's brought me such good luck, you see. You'll have to find your own."

She lunged forward, spilling her whiskey as he held it above his head, out of her reach. She climbed onto his lap, prying it from his fingers.

As she slid the stone into her pocket, he gazed up at her, his face a picture of innocence. "Any excuse to get your hands on me."

She opened her mouth to protest, before closing it again. His hand slid around her back. God, he was beautiful. And right now, she could kiss him, feel his soft lips against hers again. But even with the thrilling sensation of his hand on her back, his thumb moving slowly up and down— something stopped her.

She couldn't unsee the sadness in his eyes. Her own brush with the shadow void had chilled her to the bone, and she couldn't shake her mind of that soul-crushing emptiness. She slipped off Kester's lap, hugging herself. Maybe Bael was in that shadow void now, tormented by complete and utter abandonment.

"Are you all right?" he asked, studying her closely.

She nodded. "My brush with Nyxobas left me a little unnerved."

"The lord of the shadow hell has that effect on people."

She touched his cheek. "I'm glad to have you back. Even if you kidnapped me the first time I met you."

"Sorry about that."

She rose, pulling on her coat. "I'll see you tomorrow. Just remember to knock, like I did."

"I wouldn't dream of barging in."

Smiling, she pulled her coat tight as she stepped out into the icy winter air. She slipped her hand into her pocket, pulling out her white stone to roll between her fingers, its smooth surface comforting her as soon as she touched it.

She had to admit, some things weren't looking good. Emerazel planned to use her as a double agent, Nyxobas had his own devious agenda, and Bael remained a prisoner, possibly dead.

The cold wind rushed off the East River, biting her skin through her coat as she walked to the Bentley. But at least she was alive, and so was Kester. That was certainly a better outcome than she'd expected last night. And maybe it *wasn't* so impossible to fight the gods.

Moreover, with every day she spent among the demons, she was one step closer to learning the truth about herself, to learning the story behind her memories of the flame-haired woman, and the person who'd taught her to fight.

Sometimes, the utterly improbable did happen. After all, if Kester could find a tiny white stone in a sea of angry fae warriors at a dance party—maybe there was a chance to free the hellhounds.

She pulled open the back door of the Bentley, stepping into its warmth. As Joe turned on the engine, she let her eyes drift shut, soothed by the car's soft hum. Before she took on the ancient gods of wrath and death, she'd need at least a few hours of sleep.

C.N. CRAWFORD

SHADOWS
&
FLAME
SERIES

NOCTURNAL MAGIC

A DEMONS OF FIRE AND NIGHT NOVEL

CHAPTER 1

Through the wide bay window, a summer breeze blew in, bringing with it the earthy smell of Central Park. Ursula paced over the hardwood floor, catching a glimpse of her reflection in the glass —her skin ten shades whiter than normal, her curls framing her face in a wild auburn halo. She was on edge tonight, tension tightening each of her muscles, holding her stomach in a vise-like grip.

Zee sat on a nearby sofa, a laptop propped on her knees. "Ursula, you need to relax."

From outside, a car horn blared, and Ursula jumped.

"See?" Zee let her shoe dangle from her foot. "You're all tense."

With a shiver, Ursula glanced through the window at the pearly moon. "What time is it now?"

"Time for you to calm down. No matter what comes next, getting worked up isn't going to help." She turned her laptop to Ursula, show-casing a catwalk model dressed in nothing but lilac ribbons, strategically covering her nipples and crotch. "Come look at Francesco Sforza's fall line. It sort of puts things in perspective, you know? Like, maybe you're going to be forced to stay in the Shadow Realm with some psychotic demons, but at least no one has made you to wear ribbons over your tits." Ursula forced a smile, turning to stalk across the room again. "Thanks for trying to make me feel better. I'm having a hard time putting aside my impending damnation, though."

Zee plucked a glass of chardonnay from the table. "Well, there's nothing you can do to change it. When you made the deal with him, it sealed your fate."

Ursula folded her arms. "Emerazel made the deal after I stole Bael's soul for her." A twinge of guilt pierced her chest. *He got his soul back, but Nyxobas had probably killed him for his failure.* "If it hadn't been the only way to get your soul back, I'd never have agreed to it. Nyxobas literally shows up in all my worst nightmares." A shiver crawled up her spine. "He always has, in fact. Even before I knew who he was."

"Well, he didn't show up tonight."

Ursula turned to scrutinize the elevator once again, but its bronze doors remained tightly shut—just as they had been all day. Did gods arrive in elevators?

Nyxobas was supposed to summon her to the Shadow Realm today. For six months, she'd have to live with him, work for him, do whatever he wanted. Fear snaked up her spine. *And I have no idea what he wants from me.*

She glanced at the bags she'd packed. Honjo rested on top of a black duffel. At least she'd have her trusty katana with her, in case that psychopath Abrax tried anything. The incubus had attempted to drain her soul more than once.

But she wasn't going into this unprepared. In the bag beneath Honjo, she'd packed a collection of daggers and her finest ass-kicking boots. Plus, she had the reaping pen tucked in her pocket.

"Ursula," said Zee, her glass now empty.

"The bottle's in the kitchen," Ursula said absent-mindedly. "If it's empty, you can open a new one."

"Ursula!" Zee snapped, her eyes wide. "There's someone behind you. At the window."

The hair rose on the back of Ursula's neck. Now, the wind on her skin felt positively frigid.

Ursula grabbed Honjo from the duffel and spun, ready to defend herself. A dark form hovered in the window, cloaked in shadow. Dread crawled up her throat. Nyxobas had definitely *not* forgotten about her.

"Ursula?" said the figure, its voice light.

She jumped, her fingers tightening on Honjo's hilt. She'd been expecting Nyxobas's deep voice, but this shadowy form was definitely female.

"That's me," she said, trying to see into the darkness. *Who the hell is this?*

"Wonderful," said the woman as she stepped through the window, hopping onto the rug—not a human, but a small, sharp-toothed demon. The kind with an affinity for human flesh—an oneiroi.

Ursula raised the blade defensively. With her cherubic face, the oneiroi looked harmless enough. Her long, silvery hair hung over a simple dark gown, and something like kindness glimmered in her pale eyes. She was almost matronly. But Ursula had encountered oneiroi in the fae realm. And they'd tried to rip her face off. Matronly or not, if this demon was going to leap for her throat, she'd be ready.

"You're not Nyxobas," she said, gripping her sword. *Way to state the obvious.*

"No, Ursula." The demon's pale brow furrowed. "I was sent to collect you. I am Cera."

"Oh. All right, then." Ursula couldn't think of anything better to say.

Cera's gaze landed on the laptop. "You do have such interesting fashion here. Who is it?"

Zee muttered something that sounded like *Francesco Sforza.*

"Fascinating," said the demon, before turning to Ursula, all business again. "Are you ready to go?"

So this was it—tonight she was leaving for the Kingdom of Shadows.

"I guess I don't have much choice." She shot a panicked look at Zee, who simply shrugged, before she faced Cera again. "How are we getting there? And where do I put my bags?"

"You won't need the suitcases." Cera flashed a lethal smile of razor-sharp teeth. "You'll have anything you could possibly want when we arrive. The lord is very generous, milady. Besides, Sotz won't be able to carry it."

Before she could ask who Sotz was, she caught a glimpse of movement through the window—enormous leathery wings beating the air and shining dark eyes. A chill crawled over her skin. As the creature moved closer, she made out a pair of long diaphanous ears. *Is that a giant bat?* "What the fuck?"

The bat's eyes widened. Did it understand what she was saying?

"Shhh..." said Cera. "Don't upset Sotz. He has very sensitive hearing. The creature squeezed its body onto the windowsill, gripping the stone with fleshy feet. It was enormous—the size of a small horse.

"Don't worry, little buddy," Cera said, scratching the bat's head. "I don't think she's ever met a lunar bat before." Sotz nuzzled the demon and a low rumble filled the room. The creature was *purring.*

Ursula crossed her arms, staring at them. "I'm confused. I thought Nyxobas was coming to get me."

"The god?" Cera laughed. "He's far too busy to come himself. Sotz and I will be taking you to his kingdom." She glanced at the bat. "Sotz, can you turn around?"

The massive bat inched out of the window, flapping his wings twice before backing up into the window. A leather harness and saddle were strapped to his back.

Lifting her skirts, Cera hopped onto Sotz's shoulders, twisting her fingers into his fur. She looked back at Ursula expectantly. "Whenever you're ready, dear."

Ursula turned to Zee who now stood, her empty wine glass forgotten on the coffee table. The fae girl had been keeping her company for the past six months. While Ursula had helped Zee recover from her soul-sucking trauma, Zee had tried to distract Ursula from her terrifying fate in the Shadow Realm. Their tools: champagne, loud music, and trips to Madison Ave—at least, in between all the hellhound work. "Zee, I'm really going to miss you."

Zee's eyes glistened, and she wrapped Ursula in a hug so tight it threatened to crack her ribs. Despite being only a size two, she was surprisingly strong. When she finally released Ursula, a tear was streaking down her cheek.

"Go." Zee gestured at the oneiroi woman. "I'll see you in six months."

Ursula flashed Zee her most stern look. "Make sure you take care of yourself."

Zee straightened, wiping her eyes. "I will. And, I'll even put your stuff away. Though I might borrow that gold Valentino dress I bought for you."

She picked up the duffel and headed toward the hall. Ursula had the feeling she didn't want anyone to see her cry.

By the window Cera cleared her throat, and Ursula's muscles tensed. *Time to go.*

CHAPTER 2

*U*rsula shoved the sword into the Kevlar scabbard and strapped it to her back. She was leaving her clothes behind, but there was no way in hell she'd travel to the Shadow Realm without Honjo.

By the window, Cera turned to her, a wicked glint in her silver eyes. "Are you ready?"

"Not really."

"Have you ever ridden a horse before?"

Ursula shrugged. *Good question.* "I don't think so, but I don't remember anything from before the age of fifteen. For all I know, F.U. may have been a champion rider."

Cera's pale brow crinkled. "F.U.?"

"Former Ursula. My pre-amnesiac self."

Cera flashed her a sympathetic *you-should-probably-take-your-medica-tion* smile.

Ursula forced a smile back. *Right. I sound like a nutter when I talk about the amnesia. Then again, we're about to ride on the back of a giant bat, so a little nuttery is in order.*

"Well," said Cera. "Whatever the case, I'll be guiding Sotz, so you'll just need to hold on." She arched an eyebrow. "I do hope you're not afraid of heights." "Not really." A chill whispered over her skin. *But I'm terrified of Nyxobas.*

255

Her brush with the shadow void still haunted her nightmares—the god of night filled her with a horrifying, gnawing dread. A painful emptiness that still flickered in the hollows of her mind. She tried to push the thoughts away. Her voyage on the bat would be bad enough without dwelling on the void.

"Climb on." Cera nodded at a pair of leather handles on Sotz's saddle. "Grip there. Then step into the stirrups. Just be sure to hold on tight."

Pretty sure I'll be clutching on for dear life. Ursula pulled herself up to the windowsill, then hooked a leg over the saddle. Gripping the handles, she slipped her feet into the stirrups.

As Cera whispered into the Sotz's ear, Ursula's fingers tightened on the leather. It didn't seem like the safest way to travel. Surely, hurtling through the sky on a giant mammal required a seatbelt or helmet.

In the next second, the bat launched from the window. For a moment, Ursula's breath caught as the creature began a stomach-turning plunge, then the bat's wings unfurled. Their path steadied, and they swooped past West 59th Street and over Central Park.

Ursula clutched the harness in a death grip, her pulse racing. Her auburn hair whipped about her face with each beat of the giant wings. Sotz angled his wings, and they turned sharply. The movement cleared the hair from her eyes, and she caught a glimpse of the Plaza Hotel.

"Where are we going?" she shouted over the wind.

"Brooklyn," Cera said, turning in her direction, her sharp teeth glinting in the moonlight as she spoke.

The Shadow Realm is in Brooklyn? She frowned. It was hard to imagine the terrifying incubus Abrax cramming himself into skinny jeans. Maybe extending his talons to spear a vegan burger at a Park Slope diner.

The night wind whipped over her skin, and she shivered, thinking of the high demon. She had no idea if he'd made it out of the fae realm alive.

Sotz soared over the Plaza's white marble crenellations, then higher above the twinkling lights of New York. Distant car horns floated on the wind, and the bat alternated each wing beat with graceful glides.

Her grip on the harness relaxed. The view was extraordinary.

The great avenues of New York carved between the buildings like golden rivers of light. All around her, skyscraper glass gleamed faintly in the moonlight.

As they flew toward the tip of Manhattan, she breathed a sigh of relief at the quiet of the night air. After four years living in London, she'd grown accustomed to the perpetual background hum of busses, traffic jams and people asking for money. Up here, she heard only the distant beat of a helicopter's blades. Somehow, floating through the dark night sky felt like home.

Before she could get too comfortable, a piercing screech sent her heart racing. Cera screamed in an unintelligible language as Sotz folded his wings into his body. Ursula gripped the harness and they plummeted down, dropping out of the sky—but not fast enough.

As the wind whipped Ursula's hair into her face, something large and scaly slammed into her side, nearly tearing her from the harness. The force of the impact sent them careening toward a skyscraper. Gritting her teeth, she clung to the handles with an iron grip.

Cera shrieked hysterically, letting go of the bat's neck.

"Watch out!" Ursula pulled back on the harness. Her heart pounding hard against her ribs. Sotz's wings snapped out, and Ursula jerked the harness away from the skyscraper. Sotz turned, veering away from the building.

F.U. *had* apparently been bit of an equestrian.

A second screech shattered the night, and she glanced to her right, her blood chilling. She caught a glimpse of an enormous, shimmering outline. A translucent creature, at least the size of a bus. And it was heading right for them. *Bollocks. We're fighting something nearly impossible to see.*

"You need to steer!" she shouted at Cera.

Clenching her knees against Sotz's sides, she drew Honjo from his sheath. The long katana glinted in her hands—and not a moment too soon. She twisted in the saddle, slashing at a long, translucent limb. The blade jerked as it cut into solid flesh.

A howl rent the air.

In the next moment, the creature yanked the sword from her grasp.

Her blood turned to ice. Honjo—her only weapon—had just been ripped from her hands.

Sotz folded his wings, diving lower. Wind whistled in her ears as they raced like a falling meteor toward the East River. Just as Ursula resigned herself to a watery death, Sotz unfurled his wings, redirecting them toward the steel cables of the Williamsburg Bridge.

Somewhere behind them, their attacker screeched, a bloodcurdling sound that shriveled her stomach. Adrenaline surged. *Honjo hadn't killed the damned thing, he had only annoyed it.*

The Williamsburg Bridge grew rapidly larger and Ursula's muscles tightened as she braced for impact. At the last second, Sotz turned, diving between the cables, heading for the tunnel's mouth.

Ursula's heart hammered against her ribs. Lights flashed in its entrance, and a rumbling noise echoed off the walls. *A subway car is heading right for us.* She shouted a warning, but with a single flap of his wings, Sotz cleared the train, flying between the car and the ceiling.

The train raced by beneath them, and she let out a long breath when they cleared it.

Only the flashing red signal lights illuminated the tunnel, flashing off the rows of steel beams and girders on the ceiling. They winged down the tracks as a second train rumbled toward them, its lights glowing brighter and brighter. At the last possible moment, Sotz veered left into a dark corridor.

This tunnel was completely dark, and only the sound of the air rushing by her head told her they were still flying. After what felt like an eternity, Sotz slowed the beating of his wings, and glided to a landing.

Ursula slid off the bat, falling to her knees on a dusty floor. Pure adrenaline pumped through her veins. "What was that creature? I couldn't even see the bloody thing."

Cera pulled something from her pocket—a glowing, violet crystal. From the stone, tendrils of magic snaked into the air, creating a sphere of light that illuminated the space.

Ursula surveyed the derelict subway platform, the space around them covered in broken wood and debris. "That creature," Cera smoothed out her dress, trying to regain her composure, "was a dragon."

CHAPTER 3

Ursula stared at Cera. "But I remember learning that dragons were extinct, and that's why their wyrm-skin hides are so valuable. I was told they were all killed in the ninth century."

Cera brushed the dust off her black dress. "Definitely not extinct."

"I don't understand." She hugged herself, her body still buzzing with panic. "Why did it attack?"

Before Cera could answer, a heavy *thud* reverberated from the ceiling, and bits of plaster drifted down like snow.

Thud. "It's followed us." Cera looked up, shielding her eyes from the plaster dust. "We need to leave at once."

Thud.

White dust rained down on Ursula's clothes.

She scanned the platform, instinct kicking in at last. If there was one thing F.U. had seared into the lizard-part her brain, it was how to find the best escape route when danger closed in. In either direction, two tunnels curved off into the darkness. Her odds were fifty-fifty of choosing the best one.

Thud.

Thick chunks of plaster littered the floor, and her pulse sped up. *We're running out of time.*

"Which way—" she started to ask, but the sight of Cera leaping down from the edge of the platform interrupted her. "Cera?"

"We always keep one of these around in case of emergencies," she called out from under the platform's ledge. Slowly, the oneiroi dragged a child's play-pool onto the tracks. Murky water filled the blue plastic, and faded yellow seahorses and scallop shells decorated its sides.

Ursula gaped. "Are you going to bathe the dragon into submission?"

THUD!

This time, a scratching noise followed the impact. It took a moment for her to realize the dragon was digging.

"Look," said Ursula, raising her voice. "We need to run. It's fifty-fifty odds. We just need to choose a direction."

"Be quiet," Cera hissed. "And take your clothes off."

"I beg your pardon?"

"There is nowhere to run. Not in this realm, anyway." The demon fixed silver eyes on her. "If we don't go now, we *will* be eaten."

Before Ursula could protest, Cera stood, holding up her violet crystal. The rippling water in the pool stilled. Black shadow magic curled over a glass-smooth surface.

Cera turned to hear again, her eyes sparking with irritation. "Why are you still wearing your clothes? I told you to strip."

Bloody hell, woman. Another *thud* sounded from above, and chunks of masonry and plaster poured from the ceiling. *Definitely running out of time. Screw it.* She pulled her shirt over her head.

"Hurry!" Cera shouted, giving an unnerving display of her sharp teeth.

Ursula unzipped her jeans. "Will you at least explain the need for nudity?"

"No clothes may contaminate Nyxobas's water."

Ursula unhooked her bra just as a great crack split the air above them. She glanced up at a shimmering claw tearing through the ceiling. She tore off her knickers.

"Jump in!" Cera leapt into the center of the kiddy pool.

Completely nude, Ursula held her breath, and plunged into the black water.

Her feet didn't hit the bottom of the pool—instead, she plummeted deeper into the inky water, sinking below the surface. Instinctively she shut her eyes, her chest clenching as frigid water completely enveloped her naked body.

How deep was this pool? She opened her eyes, searching for a point of reference in the pitch-black water. Fear tightened her chest—the pool's surface was nowhere in sight.

From the depths, a deep voice whispered, "This one has fire in her veins."

She kicked her legs, moving away from the sound. *Who the fuck is that?*

"The shadow god's enemy," murmured a second voice—a gravelly tone.

The water grew colder, freezing her skin, and shivers wracked her body. Her lungs ached for a breath.

"But there is darkness in her, too," said the first voice.

"And pain. She did a terrible thing," hissed the gravelly one.

"What should we do with her?"

She needed to get away, to get to air and out of the water. She kicked her legs frantically, her fingers clawing for a surface that no longer seemed to exist.

I need to breathe.

"She wants to visit the Shadow Realm."

"But her fire is forbidden."

"Then we take it from her."

"Yessss," said another voice. "Her flames will warm us. It is so very cold here."

Her body shook in the frigid water.

Something cold and slimy brushed her cheek, and the words *deadman's fingers* rang in her mind. She thrashed in the darkness as an ice-cold hand grabbed her foot. *What the fuck is happening?*

More hands grasped her limbs, pulling her deeper. Agony inflamed her lungs, as water began to trickle down her throat. She jerked and twitched in the grasp of the fingers. The hands were all over her, clammy fingers pulling her mouth open.

Cold water rushed in, and her lungs spasmed. *I'm dying.* With each spasm, more water filled her lungs, dousing the flames of her magic.

"Remember the darkness. Only the darkness will save you." the voices whispered. The hands released her, and a light appeared above her.

Am I dying? No, she couldn't accept it. She'd hardly begun to live, and she still had no idea who she really was.

The voices were lying—where there was light, there was air. *Life.*

Fighting her body's desire to convulse, she stretched out her arms, kicking her legs to swim upward. The circle of light grew larger. Her lungs burned.

She kicked her legs, reaching for the light. If she weren't drowning, she would have sighed with relief as one of her hands brushed something solid. A final kick and her fingers broke the surface. Pain ripped her mind apart, and it took every last bit of strength to control her body. She clawed, grasping at an edge. With the last of her strength, she heaved herself up.

And then she was gasping. Coughing. Cold water pouring from her mouth, hot tears streaming from her eyes.

CHAPTER 4

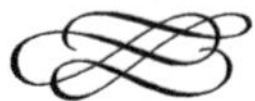

rsula lay on a marble floor in the fetal position, as she coughed up another lungful of water.

Cera wiped the wet hair from her face. "Earthly gods below, what took you so long?"

She sucked in a deep breath, trying to find her voice again. "There were dead things in there, dragging me down."

"Oh, dear. The Forgotten Ones found you?"

Ursula rolled onto her back, staring up at a ceiling painted with constellations. Her teeth chattered, and she hugged her naked body. "The Forgotten Ones? Is that what they are? They took my fire."

Cera sighed. She'd already dressed in a cozy-looking black robe. "There wasn't time to warn you, but at least we've escaped the dragon."

Ursula forced herself up on her elbows, surveying her surroundings. She lay in the center of a round room, her feet dangling in a clear, circular pool no more than six inches deep. Was it really possible that she'd been drowning in this shallow water just moments ago? She'd nearly died.

Around the room, thin columns flanked windows that reached from the floor to ceiling. Through the glass, a gray landscape stretched out under a canopy of gleaming stars. Only a few rocks interrupted the flat horizon—no buildings, nor trees or any sign of life. *Where the hell are we?* Her teeth chattered.

Before she could form one of the million questions on the tip of her tongue, the little demon came up behind her and handed her a velvet robe. "Perhaps you should put this on."

Ursula took it gladly, wrapping it around her freezing shoulders. Instantly, her muscles began to relax.

Enveloped by the robe, she glanced out the window again.

She drew in a slow breath, her gaze drifting upward. Above the stark landscape, the pale wash of the Milky Way splashed across the night sky, more vivid than she'd ever seen. Too vivid. *This is not Earth.*

Her breath caught in her throat. "I guess we're not in Brooklyn."

Cera snorted. "No, we're not in Brooklyn. The Shadow Realm is on the moon."

"The moon," she repeated, turning to gape at Cera.

"Of course. Nyxobas's water carried you here," said Cera, crossing the room to a black door. She cast a critical eye over Ursula's bedraggled hair. "Shall I show you to your quarters? You look half-dead."

"Okay," said Ursula absently. Barefoot, she padded over cold marble as she followed Cera, still trying to process the fact that she'd left the earth. She didn't *feel* any lighter. Shouldn't she be floating around the room?

Cera pushed open the door. "This way."

Ursula followed the oneiroi into the cold air, her heart skipping a beat as she realized they were *outside*.

Outside. On the moon. Without a spacesuit or helmet. They stood on a milky, marble bridge, a thousand feet above a deep, cratered valley. The bridge spanned the space between two round towers.

Ursula paused as a bitterly cold wind ruffled her hair, gripping the marble ledge to peer into the crater. Her pulse raced. In the center of the caldera, a towering spire of purple glass loomed above them. Unlike the sleek lines of New York's skyscrapers, this tower was all jagged edges and sharp angles.

All around them, stark palaces of shining, silver towers jutted from the crater's walls. If she strained her eyes, she could see a faint horizon on the far side of the spire, the gleam of distant buildings.

She gazed down at the vast valley spread out below, filled with stone dwellings. She drew in a slow breath. The human race had managed to send twelve people to the moon, and yet here was a vast kingdom no one had ever noticed.

She searched the skies for the Earth—home, something familiar—but only stars twinkled in the black sky. Out here, the air smelled faintly of creosote, and dizziness overwhelmed her. She glanced at Cera, who moved at a fast clip across the bridge, her silver hair trailing behind her.

"Wait!" Ursula called out. "I don't understand. There's a whole colony on the moon? Why doesn't NASA have pictures? And how can I breathe if there's no atmosphere? And why doesn't the gravity feel any different?" Those were just the first four questions that entered her mind, but she could keep going.

Cera paused near the other end of the bridge before a gray door. She pointed at the sky. "Can you see that glimmer there?"

As Ursula walked, she looked up at the dome of stars. At first she couldn't see what Cera meant, but then she noticed a faint shimmer along the horizon. Like the sheen of gasoline on a puddle.

"A glamour of magic surrounds us," said Cera. "It both hides us from satellites and gives us air to breathe. And it takes care of the gravity problem."

"How?"

"Magic."

"Oh," said Ursula, searching again for signs of the earth. "Are we on the dark side of the moon?"

"Yes. The far side, some call it."

A dry wind toyed with Ursula's hair. Shivering, she pulled the robe tighter around her. When she'd left for the Shadow Realm, she hadn't realized it would be *quite* so far from home.

Cera pulled open the black door. "It's freezing out here. Are you quite finished gaping?"

Not yet. She pointed at the spire. "What is that?"

"It's called Asta. Where the god of night dwells."

Ursula looked back at the building, trying to imagine what the home of a god might look like inside.

"Are you quite ready?" said Cera impatiently. "I prefer to walk around clothed and wearing shoes."

Ursula hurried toward the door, her eyes focused straight ahead. As soon as she glanced at the bridge's ledge, she knew dizziness would overwhelm her.

Through the door, Cera led her into an octagonal hall—half of it black marble. The other half lay completely destroyed, as if a giant fist had smashed through the wall, opening it to the night air. *What happened here?* Hugging herself, she surveyed the space.

The hair rose on the back of Ursula's neck. On the mangled side of the hall, sheared steel beams twisted into the air like gnarled fingers. Wind rushed between them, chilling her skin. Shards of glass glinted in the starlight from the remains of old window frames. On the floor, a tile mosaic of a lion's head lay half smashed. Part of the beast's mane had been scorched and half its face smashed to dust. Opposite where she stood, steps climbed to a small platform with a circular black door. Some sort of crystalline stone—obsidian maybe.

"Okay. What happened here?" she asked aloud this time.

"A battle." Cera's eyes shone in the darkness like starlight. "Our lord is very strong. He protected us." She turned, crossing to a door in one of the remaining marble walls. "This way to your quarters." She yanked open the door.

Carefully, Ursula tiptoed over the shards of smashed glass and tile, following Cera onto another towering bridge. She kept her eyes on the demon, refusing to look over the vertigo-inducing railings as she crossed.

At the far end, Cera pushed open a door into a pitch-black room. As Ursula stepped over the threshold, candles in silver sconces flickered to life, casting warm light over a dark hall.

"I will be back in the morning," said Cera, stepping back to the door. "You'll have everything you need here." She pulled open the door, then stepped out and slammed it shut with a click.

Ursula crossed to the door, tugging on the handle, but it wouldn't budge. *Locked in.*

CHAPTER 5

$\mathcal{U}$rsula surveyed the wide hall. On one side, a spiral stairwell curved upward. The opposite wall abutted a delicate wooden table, adorned with a display of faintly glowing mushrooms.

Beautiful, but slightly unsettling.

Pulling her robe tighter, she followed the hall into a dimly lit, semicircular room.

A great panel of windows curved in the shape of the tower. Through the glass, she had a perfect view of Nyxobas's gleaming spire, jutting from the crater like a jeweled spear. *Guess I won't be walking around here naked.*

A set of marble statues flanked the windows, each at least eight feet tall—nude, athletic men with curly hair and vacant eyes. Ancient Greek, by the look of them.

Arranged about the room, glass cabinets held clay urns and vases, painted with letters from dead languages and geometric designs. Apparently, moon demons had major hard-ons for the Classical era.

Possibly the hots for human men too, given the choice of statues.

She scanned the walls, eyeing the fine glassware. She tried not to stare at the black velvet couches that were nestled into the corner of the room, or she'd give in to temptation and sleep in one for days.

Water portal travel did a number on a person's body.

Her eyes lingered on a silver clock on the wall that looked like an antique ship's clock. It featured a complicated lunar cycle of waxing and waning moons that she couldn't quite figure out.

Before she could move on to another room, her gaze landed on a portrait, framed in silver. The subject—a woman—had gorgeous dark eyes, and long brown hair that curled over a delicate white dress. She wore a solemn, regal expression. Olive skin, sharp cheekbones, full lips. Beautiful as hell. The vulnerability in her eyes seemed remarkably human.

She wasn't exactly an art history expert, but it looked like something from the Renaissance. From one of those painters who depicted gorgeous women—Botticelli, maybe.

So maybe Classical Art Demon was into women, too.

Her rumbling stomach turned her attention away from the beauty. *I'm starving.*

She spotted a small bar tucked in another corner of the room. On it was a platter of cheese, grapes, and a carafe of wine.

Cera might have locked her in here, but at least she'd left something to eat.

As Ursula drew closer to the food, she noticed a beige envelope resting against the carafe. On it was scrawled her name in deep red ink. She popped a grape in her mouth, then snatched up the envelope, tearing it open. She scanned the letter.

I have asked Cera to look after you during your stay. She will be able to provide anything you need. This apartment is yours, and you are free to move about as you wish. For your own safety, I cannot give you free rein of the entire manor at this time. We will speak in the morning.

She crushed another grape between her teeth, letting the sweet juice run down her throat.

Had Nyxobas written this letter? She'd been expecting to meet him here upon her arrival, but now the idea that a god would greet her personally seemed completely stupid.

Then again, she hadn't quite understood Nyxobas's power until she'd come here. Now she could see it, visually represented. Total domination over an entire planetary body, not to mention the demons he controlled on the earth.

Grabbing a chunk of bread, she walked over to the window. Nyxobas's spire glinted in the starlight. She'd been expecting to stay with him, that he had some sort of purpose in mind for her. But clearly, she hadn't been brought to his palace. So what the hell was she doing here?

A hollow opened in the pit of her stomach. She was in some sort of manor, and she had no clue who owned it. And the first name that came to her mind was *Abrax.* The incubus had tried to murder her more than once, and she was pretty sure he was a rapist. He'd pulled some kind of mind-control seduction trick on her. At least, until he'd become disgusted by her and moved on to attempted murder. Clearly, the guy had issues with women.

A chill snaked up her spine. Not only did he hate her, but she had an unsettling feeling she hadn't even begun to witness Abrax's power.

Suddenly, her appetite deserted her. *I want Honjo.*

Her hand was shaking as she placed her bread on the coffee table, and her old, familiar instincts kicked in. If there was one thing that came naturally to Ursula, it was self-preservation.

I need to find a weapon in case Abrax shows up. Her pulse racing, she scanned the room for something that could be used for skull-smashing or organ-puncturing.

Bars had knives sometimes, didn't they?

She hurried across the room and began pulling open the drawers. Coasters, fancy napkins, toothpicks. Bugger all, basically. Not a lot of damage you could do with toothpicks.

She yanked open another drawer. A corkscrew. *Bloody hell. I won't get very far fighting an ancient demon with a corkscrew, but it's better than nothing.*

She shoved the corkscrew into the robe's soft pocket. *Maybe I can find something a bit better.*

She crossed to a door off the living room, pushing through into a bathroom. She scanned the gray tile. The silver, claw-footed bath looked amazing, she had to admit, but she found not a single toilet plunger or towel rack that could be used to smash a head in.

She ran back to the front hallway, her frantic gaze landing on the spiral staircase. She bounded up it, two steps at a time. At the top, more doors lined a long hall. She flung open the first and walked into a luxurious bedroom: floor-to-ceiling windows and a large bed covered with a violet bedspread.

A dresser stood against one wall. Candles and a jewelry box resting on the top, but unfortunately, nothing so handy as a knife. She pulled open the jewelry box, finding only actual jewels. Of course. People didn't tend to keep weapons among their diamonds, but you never knew.

Her pulse racing, she yanked open a drawer, cursing when she found it empty. One drawer after another, each completely weaponless. Not only was this place completely weapon-free, like a psychiatric facility, but she hadn't even been given clothes.

So much for "providing everything you need."

She hurried into the hall, flinging open another door to find another bathroom. An enormous tub stood before the curving windows. *Not a lot of privacy here.*

She crossed to a white porcelain sink, yanking open the cupboard below it. She rifled through a few extra rolls of toilet paper, and some ancient-looking vials of green and blue liquids. Not even a toothbrush she could file down to a point.

Her heart racing, she stood and patted the corkscrew in her pocket. Its thin twist of steel was all she had to protect herself.

Somehow, it did not reassure her.

Ursula trudged down the stairs again. Of course there weren't any real weapons in the apartment. Abrax, Nyxobas—whoever was in charge here—didn't want a hellhound able to defend herself. As a hound of Emerazel's she was simply too dangerous to the night demons.

In the living room, she headed for the bar, then popped the cork off the carafe of wine. She grabbed a wine glass, filling it nearly to the top, then crossed to one of the sofas.

She plopped down onto the rich, velvet fabric and took a long sip. She'd have to keep the glass nearby. In a pinch, she could smash it and stab someone with the shards.

Her stomach tightened. One of these days, she'd like to have a normal Friday night. Though hoping for an ordinary night in the Shadow Realm was probably a bit of a stretch. The alcohol warmed her stomach, soothing the tension from her shoulders.

Abrax or Nyxobas...

Somehow, Nyxobas didn't seem like he'd have a golden lion mosaic in his atrium or a suite of rooms filled with classical art. She shivered. Abrax seemed more like the type to relish intimidation through luxury. He was also the kind of perv who'd put her in a glass cage so he could watch her every move.

She tucked her feet underneath her. If Kester were here, he'd have a clear idea of what she should be doing. He'd stretch out on the sofa, full of confidence. He'd level his green eyes on her and tell her precisely what spells she needed to be practicing and how to evaluate her true threat. Then again, she'd hardly seen him in the past six months. After she'd saved him from Nyxobas, she'd gone to visit him on his tugboat. And that's when she'd learned the truth—that Kester was in this to save his sister's soul. She'd felt so close to him that night, like she'd made a true friend. And yet, since then he'd been a ghost. He'd stopped by the flat once or twice with Zee. He turned on his usual arrogant charm. Flirting, double entendres, references to his prowess with a sword. But when she'd asked what he'd been doing, he'd just shrugged. "On a special assignment given to him by Emerazel," was all he'd said. And then, he'd disappeared again for another month.

When she'd asked Zee about it, the fae girl had shaken her head. "That's Kester for you. Wham, bam, thank you ma'am. It's how he operates."

But that didn't explain it at all. She and Kester had neither whammed nor bammed. Sure, she'd thought about it. How could she not, given his chiseled beauty? But nothing had happened…yet.

And meanwhile, she'd been missing a mentor. Kester was supposed to teach her how to become a hellhound, but there'd been no magic lessons, no practice sessions in the armory to build her skill. In the last six months, she'd learned virtually nothing new about the job.

Sure, she'd kept busy in other ways. There was the mob boss assignment in Hell's Kitchen—a first-rate wanker who'd been forcing his thugs to sign over their souls. Ursula had been tasked with hunting down each of the Mafiosi.

Because they'd signed over their souls involuntarily, her task had been to nullify pacts. She'd thought it'd be easy—who actually wanted to burn in the Emerazel's inferno for eternity? But once the Mafiosi had tasted Emerazel's power, they seemed to stop caring about eternal damnation. She'd been forced to reap more of their souls than she cared to think about. It had been brutal work, but at least she'd filled a good number of pages in her ledger.

And each page was another step toward freedom. Once she managed to fill her ledger, it was *goodbye* to the hellhound life.

She took another sip of wine, pushing her worries about the ledger to the back of her mind. Right now, she had more immediate concerns. After the dragon attack and the near-drowning with the Forgotten Ones, exhaustion burned her muscles. She propped her wine against the base of the sofa, then leaned back into the velvet. She pulled a soft, white blanket over her body, staring through the window at a perfect view of Nyxobas's palace.

The sharp spire glimmered like a shard of glass. And as her eyelids drooped, dark clouds seemed to whirl around its summit.

CHAPTER 6

"Ursula." Someone tapped her shoulder.

"Mmgghhft," Ursula groaned, opening her eyes. Cera stood above her. It was still dark outside. Maybe it was always dark here? She still wasn't quite sure how that worked. She pushed up onto her elbows, blinking to clear her mind. "What's going on?"

"You need to wake up. You're to meet the lord in fifteen minutes."

"I don't understand. What time is it?"

"Almost eight p.m. Earth time. You slept all day. You need to get dressed."

"But I don't have any clothes to wear." Ursula's brain was slowly turning on. "I'm supposed to meet Nyxobas now?" Cera held up a white bag. "I brought you a dress. I'm not entirely familiar with Earthly fashions, but I based it on that gold gown I saw in the picture in your apartment."

She straightened. "The Francesco Sforza dress? With the ribbons?"

"Not quite as revealing as that one, but the same idea. The women in Nyxobas's kingdom don't show off their flesh quite so wantonly as Emerazel's women do." She shook her head. "No respect for yourselves."

Ursula frowned. She hadn't been a fan of the ribbon dress, but there was no need for slut-shaming. "There's nothing wrong with female bodies, you know. Or showing them off."

Cera's silver eyes narrowed. "You'll need to adapt to the culture here. I know incubi and vampires flout Nyxobas's rules on Earth, indulging in all sorts of heresies, but you're in the Shadow Realm now." She thrust the bag at Ursula. "Nyxobas believes in denial of bodily urges in order to reach heavenly perfection."

"Right." Ursula peered inside the bag. A lilac dress nestled next to silver shoes and a bag of toiletries.

She stood, then pulled the dress from the bag—an exquisitely delicate fabric that shimmered in the candlelight. She stood, holding it up. It certainly had more fabric than the Sforza dress. This one reached the floor, but it still featured a plunging neckline and tiny shoulder straps. The fabric was practically sheer, but gathered enough around the skirts that she wouldn't be showing too much off.

"Wow," she breathed. "It's gorgeous. Where did you get it?"

Cera's chest seemed to swell. "I sewed it. There aren't any designer shops here, so if you want a pretty dress, you have to make it yourself. I'm glad you can recognize fine craftsmanship when you see it." She beamed. "There's underwear in the bag. I figured a hellhound would like the skimpy kind." She sniffed.

Ursula peered in the bag at a pale blue thong. "Thanks, Cera." Weird as it was to get thongs from a stranger, it was actually very nice of the oneiroi to try to choose things she thought Ursula would like.

"Perhaps you'd like to go into the bathroom to try it on," prompted Cera.

"Sure." Apparently, Cera was horrified by the idea that Ursula might strip right here, even though the demon had already seen her completely naked.

"And while you're at it," Cera called out, "you may as well bathe and beautify yourself for the lord. It will help him warm to you, I'm sure. There are toiletries in the bag."

Ursula frowned. "When you say 'lord,' are you talking about Nyxobas?"

"Honestly, child." Cera chastised her as though it were the most absurd question in the world. "Clean yourself up. You mustn't displease him."

Sighing, Ursula carried the bag into the bathroom and closed the door behind her. A lantern bathed the bathroom in warm light. So, she had to make herself look good for her lord. Whoever he was, she was apparently at risk of provoking his wrath with her bedraggled appearance. This was just getting weirder by the minute. Still, she wasn't going to argue. Makeup was its own armor, and one that made her feel like herself. A war paint of sorts.

Ursula untied her robe, hanging it from a hook on the back of the door.

She crossed to the claw-foot tub, turning a silver knob and letting the bath fill with water. Stepping into the warm bath, she grabbed a bar of floral soap. Steam curled from the water, filling the room with the scent of lavender and mint. Around the bath's rim, candles flickered, casting dancing light over the gray tile. She lathered under her arms, and ran her fingers over her neck to clean up the grime. The water felt soothing over her skin, and she splashed warm water over her shoulders, rinsing off the soap.

She might not understand why she'd been called to the night realm, but she knew Nyxobas had good reason to hate her. She'd forced the high demon Bael, Nyxobas's general, and his second in command, into signing his soul over to Emerazel. A twinge of guilt pierced her chest. Nyxobas had probably ordered Bael's death since then. She didn't imagine the god of night would forgive a tactical failure of that magnitude.

Her stomach tightened. And if Nyxobas *hadn't* ordered Bael's death, the high demon would probably rip her limb from limb. She'd completely destroyed his plans to take over the Shadow Kingdom.

A knock sounded at the door. "Don't take too long in there," Cera cautioned. "We mustn't keep the lord waiting."

Ursula rolled her eyes. Whoever "the lord" was, he sounded like a real prick.

After a final scrub of her legs, she rose, feeling the soapy water drip off her skin. She unplugged the drain and stepped from the tub, grabbing a towel. Goosebumps rose on her bare skin as she dried off.

Cera banged the door again. "You really don't want to make him angry."

Ursula tried to ignore the demon's frantic knocking. Peering into the bag, she grabbed the tiny blue underwear and slipped into it. Somehow, it fit her perfectly. Probably precisely *because* Cera had seen her totally naked and was able to gauge her exact measurements. *No bra, I see.*

She grabbed the dress from the bag and pulled it over her head. The silky fabric skimmed luxuriously over her breasts, hips, and thighs before reaching the floor.

Her gazed flicked to the mirror, and a smile curled her lips. The neckline plunged to her belly button. Braless and with a daring neckline, she was exposing a little more than she normally would. But she *had* just proclaimed the importance of pride in one's body, and she wasn't going back on it now. Plus, she looked damn good.

She slipped into the silver heels, then turned to study her reflection again. She ran her fingers through her auburn waves, trying to tame them into submission. She had to admit—the red of her hair looked stunning against the cool tones of the dress. Cera might be cranky, but the demon was a genius with a needle and thread.

She leaned over, picking up the makeup page to unzip it. As Cera continued to hammer on the door, she lined her eyes with black, rouged her cheeks, and slicked her lips with a rather stunning shade of cherry red. A dusting of shimmery white powder over her cheekbones was the final touch.

If the lord could be mollified by makeup and dresses, she was certain this ensemble would do the trick.

She pulled open the bathroom door into the living room.

Cera beamed at her. Clearly, the woman was proud of her work. "The lord may have a bit of a shock when he sees you. But dark god above, it is gorgeous."

"Well, I wouldn't want to offend the lord with a poor dress choice."

Cera nodded enthusiastically, apparently missing her sarcasm. "Oh yes. Very true. Now, we must go." She looked at the clock, visibly shuddering. "I don't want to anger him," she muttered, turning to hurry for the door. "Please come with me."

Sharp claws of panic gripped her chest. She'd left her only weapon in the bathroom. "Wait," she said. "I need to wee."

"Not now!" scolded Cera.

Ignoring her, Ursula ran back to the bathroom. She gripped the robe, yanking the corkscrew from its pocket. She swallowed hard. *Where the hell am I supposed to hide it in this outfit?*

She didn't have much of a choice. It was going in her thong or it wasn't coming at all. Suddenly, she was no longer so keen on the dress's sheer fabric. She hoisted up her skirt, tucking the corkscrew into the front of her knickers, pointy side up. She didn't want the sharp bit doing any damage to the most delicate parts of her body.

"Hurry up!" Cera wailed.

Ursula smoothed out her hair, pulling open the bathroom door into the living room. She hoped her facial expression conveyed some sense of normality—as opposed to, "I've just shoved a corkscrew in my knickers, and I'm trying not to hurt myself." Plastering a smile onto her face, she followed Cera through the hall and out the front door, trying not to look over the bridge's railings. She didn't need her stomach turning any more flips than it already was. Plus, vertigo and heels seemed like a bad combination.

This time, when they entered the lion atrium, Cera led her across the tiles. The demon climbed the stairs, pausing at the onyx door.

Ursula frowned. "Is this all part of the same manor?"

"Yes. You're about to meet the lord who owns your apartments. He will have control over every aspect of your life for the next six months. So you understand why this is important to get right."

She hugged herself. *And if it all goes to shit, I'll just fight him with the corkscrew in my knickers. Top planning, Ursula. You've really outdone yourself.*

At the top of the stairs, Cera flicked her fingers. The heavy onyx door creaked open, revealing a tunnel.

Cera held out her hand, gesturing for Ursula to enter. "Go along. The lord is waiting for you."

"You're not coming?" said Ursula, her skin growing cold. With a growing sense of dread, she climbed the steps.

"No. He wants to meet with you alone."

The hair rose on the back of her neck. "Can you at least tell me who I'm meeting? Is it Nyxobas? Or Abrax?"

Cera frowned. "I'm not at liberty to say. He's a *lord*. I'm not allowed to call him by any other name, and I'm certainly not going to defy him. Everyone here knows their place, and if you're smart, you will, too. Your life depends entirely on the lord." The little demon backed down the stairs, her milky skin a shade paler than normal. "You're going to be late. You need to go."

Ursula folded her arms, reluctant to plunge into the dark hall without knowing what she was getting into.

She watched Cera hurry across the tile, turning to Ursula one last time before pulling open the door. "Good luck." She disappeared through the door, leaving Ursula entirely alone.

Cold dread bloomed in Ursula's chest. *Well, it's not like I can run away from whoever this lord is.* She was going to be in the Shadow Realm for six months, living in his house. She was going to meet him one way or another. She turned, taking a tentative step into the tunnel. Candles flickered in sconces, their dim light wavering over rocky walls. The tunnel seemed to be carved from a cliff of the moon crater itself.

Hugging herself, Ursula strained her ears for any sound, but she heard only deathly silence.

She walked further into the hall, trying to soften her footsteps on the smooth stone as much as possible. She considered pulling the corkscrew from her knickers, but decided against it. It was too big to hide in her palm, and clearly showing up armed to meet "the lord" would be a major breach of protocol. Still, the bulky feel of sharp metal in her thong was oddly reassuring—a thought she'd never before imagined would cross her mind.

Of course, she never imagined she'd be going to meet a demon on the moon, before.

Goosebumps rose on her skin, and she made her way deeper into the tunnel. Unlike the hard lines and cold steel of the exterior rooms, this part of the manor seemed ancient. Twisting patterns and faded runes adorned the jagged walls. The light changed subtly as she walked, and she glanced down. The illumination no longer came from candles. Instead, glowing mushrooms grew along the floor's edge, and the tarry creosote smell gave way to something earthy and alive.

Ahead of her, the tunnel opened into a large chamber, and a path curved between gray boulders. As she stepped into the hall, her breath caught in her throat. It wasn't so much a chamber as a vast cavern. Huge stalactites hung from the ceiling, their surfaces encrusted with glowing mushrooms.

The path led through the cavern to a thin, stone bridge suspended between two cliffs. No rails, no sides. Just a narrow strip of stone over a vast chasm. Tentatively, she approached the edge. She stepped onto the bridge, her gaze briefly flicking to the stark blackness, the sheer rocky drop into a bottomless abyss.

Her heart hammered against her ribs. *Maybe this is why Cera wanted to stay behind.*

A cold sweat beaded on her forehead, and she took another step forward in her tall heels. *No turning back now.* A deathly silence hung in the air, broken only by the clacking of her stupid heels over the stone.

If there had ever been a time for running shoes, it was now.

She pulled her gaze away from the abyss, glancing at the ceiling. Bioluminescent mushrooms nestled among glowing indigo crystals. The fungi light refracted through the crystals, bathing the bridge in an other-worldly violet light.

She glanced at the bridge again, so she wouldn't lose her footing, and her gaze trailed to the abyss. The darkness seemed to beckon her forward, luring her off the bridge. Her stomach swooped, and a strange sort of terror bloomed in the back of her mind. She wasn't afraid she would fall.

She was afraid she would jump.

She blinked, clearing the disturbing thought from her head. *I'll face forward then, won't I?* A few more careful steps, staring straight ahead, and she cleared the final bit of the bridge, stepping onto a rocky platform. The temperature in this cavern seemed ten degrees cooler than the rest of the hall. She crossed her arms in front of her. She didn't need "the lord" seeing just how cold she was.

After a few more paces, she paused, her heart skipping a beat.

At the far end sat a figure in a jet-black throne, cloaked in shadows.

Night magic curled in front of the lord's features, moving like seaweed caught in an invisible current. He exuded power. And pure menace. Here, in front of the lord, the void called to her. That vast abyss, just a few steps away, beckoned her closer, tempting her to jump.

This was no simple demon's power. This was a god, ancient and wrathful. *Nyxobas.*

It had been a mistake to come here. As if a corkscrew could protect her from this dark hell.

"Ursula." The lord's rough voice boomed through the hall, echoing off the rock.

Fear twisted her gut. She concentrated on straightening her spine. Kester had taught her not to show fear to a demon or god. It only brought out their primal instincts, and the next thing you knew, they were pinning you to the ground, teeth at your throat.

"Why have you brought me here?" She worked to steady her voice.

"You think I wanted one of Emerazel's dogs here? Like *I* had any choice in the matter?" His rage thinned the air.

Despite everything she'd learned about showing confidence, she took an involuntary step back.

"I don't understand." She was trying to make sense of his words. Nyxobas had struck a deal with Emerazel—he'd been a willing part of the bargain. She was supposed to stay with him for six months of every year. "If you didn't want me, why did you make a deal with Emerazel?"

Silence descended on the cavern. Tendrils of black magic gathered around him, undulating from his powerful body like serpents. "You are mistaken," he said at last, rising from the swirling darkness.

Violet light washed over pale eyes, chiseled features, and a body of pure, thickly corded muscle.

Ursula choked down a scream. *Bael.* So *that* was the lord Cera had been talking about. She'd been scared of Nyxobas, but this might be worse. She'd seen him fight, and right now, she could feel his raw power rippling over her skin. Once a demon like Bael decided you were his enemy, that was it. You were dead.

And the truth was—if anyone had a reason to hate her, it was Bael. She'd forced him to sign over his soul to Emerazel. Nyxobas had been furious—in fact, the damage to his manor was probably the night god's doing. Bael was lucky to be alive at all.

And that had all been Ursula's fault.

Cold fury glinted in his eyes, which darkened from gray to black. *That's not a good sign. When a demon's eyes turned black, it usually meant they were about to rip someone's heart out.*

Her back was to the stone bridge. She stood, trapped between an enraged demon and a bottomless chasm. *So that's why he didn't reveal himself earlier.* He'd wanted to wait until she was most vulnerable.

"You stole a soul from me, Ursula." Venom laced his voice. "And left me to die."

Yeah. She was definitely on his enemy list. And now, as she stood before him in a flimsy dress and heels, without a sword to defend herself, he was going to exact his revenge.

Panic sunk its claws into her chest, and a buried memory flitted through the recesses of her mind. Something about his cold fury was familiar. Had she seen him before? Did F.U. know Bael, and was she warning Ursula away?

Run, Ursula. Run before he rips you to pieces.

She turned to run—one step, two—then her heel caught on the hem of her dress. At the edge of the cliff, her arms windmilled in the air as she teetered at the edge of the abyss.

Time seemed to move in slow motion, and the void pulled her over the edge. How long would she fall before she hit the ground? Two seconds? Five? The impact would knock the organs from her body. A burst of light. Then raging fire as she began to burn in Emerazel's infernos.

Or maybe there *was* no ground, and she'd fall forever, trapped in Nyxobas's hell of unending darkness.

As she plunged over the cliff, powerful magic rushed around her, then strong arms enveloped her, trapping her. *Bael.* He pulled her back from the brink, his eyes still black with fury. On the cliff's edge, he pinned her arms to her sides.

He was going to kill her. He just wanted to do it his way.

She brought up her knee, striking his groin, and his dark eyes widened, his grip loosening just enough that she could slam her fist into his Adam's apple. Stunned, he stepped back.

She yanked up her dress, and ripped the corkscrew from her knickers.

If she thought Bael had been surprised before, he now looked like he was about to pop a vein in his forehead.

"Do you mean to attack me, hellhound?" he snarled.

In a blur of black magic, a tattooed arm gripped her throat, powerful fingers encircling her neck. He was about to choke the life from her.

She jammed the corkscrew into his forearm, and he let out a roar, his fingers tightening.

She ripped the thing from his flesh again, before bringing it down a second time. Bael dropped his hand. But in a movement so swift she nearly missed it, he snatched the corkscrew from her grasp. Growling, he flung it into the chasm.

Her heart thudded. *There goes my only weapon.*

In the next second, his arms were around her again, pinning her in a vise-like grip. "Are you quite done?" A cold fury laced his voice.

Adrenaline blazed through her veins, but as much as she strained, she was stuck fast. She stared up at him. Gods, he was enormous. "You know that Emerazel will send someone to avenge me. If you kill me—"

"I'm *not* trying to kill you."

"You're not?" Some of her panic began to ebb, and she studied him. She hadn't quite noticed before, but with his perfect features, he looked a lot like an angel. An angel of death, perhaps, but an angel nonetheless.

"No." He loosened his arms, but he didn't release her. He smelled like the sea, and faintly, of sandalwood. "You have angered me, but I cannot kill you. Nyxobas has tasked me as your guardian while you are in his realm."

"Why you? Did he return your wings?" With his wings and immortality intact, he'd be a powerful protector. If not...

His arms tightened again, crushing her chest.

Clearly, he didn't want to talk about the wings. So that would be a *no*.

He leaned down, his breath warming the shell of her ear. "It would be an understatement to say your kind isn't liked here. You wouldn't be safe in Asta, Nyxobas's spire. So he has burdened me with you. I suspect this is part of my punishment."

"For the whole soul debacle."

"That isn't quite how I'd describe it."

"If you're tasked with protecting me, does that mean you'll stop crushing me?"

He narrowed his eyes. The gray irises were lined with remarkably thick lashes. "Are you going to continue attacking me?"

"No."

Bael loosened his powerful grasp, and she stepped away from him.

His eyes trailed over her dress for just a moment before he glanced away again. "That isn't how most women dress here."

So he was a bit of a prude. Interesting. "Cera made it for me. She warned me it might be a bit shocking."

A muscle tensed in his jaw. "Not quite as shocking as your choice of holster for your corkscrew."

"Well, a lady can never be too careful."

His gaze met hers again. "You're smart to bring weapons with you. You are not safe in this realm. There are many who would like to kill one of Emerazel's hounds. Or worse." He studied her carefully, his magic licking the air around him. "Is it true what Cera told me, that the Forgotten Ones stole your fire?"

Grimly, Ursula nodded. "Yes. And the bastards nearly drowned me, too."

"It is unfortunate that I could not have come for you myself. I should have told Cera to warn you about them."

"I don't think there was time. It was very chaotic when we were leaving. I'm sure it was an oversight."

Bael nodded. "Without your fire, you don't have much to protect yourself. You must remain in your quarters."

Her shoulders tensed. Her quarters were beautiful—luxurious, even—but they were also incredibly lonely.

Bael turned from her, stalking back to his onyx throne. As he neared the stone dais, shadows rose around him. Without looking back, he disappeared into the coiling tendrils of darkness.

<h1 style="text-align: center;">CHAPTER 7</h1>

For her return trip, Ursula removed the shoes. Much easier to walk over the stone bridge without them.

As she pushed through the front door into her quarters, she found Cera standing in the front hall, chewing a fingernail.

"Oh dear!" Cera cast a critical eye over her tattered dress, the bare feet, and the silver pumps dangling from her hand. "What in the lord's name happened to the dress?"

Ursula glanced down at herself. It was worse than she thought. The hem was torn up to her thigh, the bodice soaked in Bael's blood. She felt pretty bad about ruining the gorgeous gown—Cera's hard work, now ragged and gore-spattered.

She smoothed the front of her dress, as though trying to reclaim her dignity. "Bael was a little confrontational."

Cera's jaw dropped. "Is that blood?" Her brow furrowed. "Whose blood is it?"

"I'm fine."

Cera's body began to shake. "What did you do to the lord?"

"It was just a little misunderstanding. He'll recover quickly, I'm sure, but I will need another corkscrew at some point."

Cera's hands fluttered in the air like frightened birds. "Of course. The corkscrew. When he asked me to remove all the weapons from your quarters, I didn't even think to take the corkscrew."

Frowning, Ursula crossed her arms. "He asked you to remove all the weapons?"

Cera's hand flew to her mouth, making an audible slapping noise. Given her sharp teeth, Ursula would be surprised if she didn't stab herself.

"Please don't mention this to the lord. He specifically told me not to say anything about the weapons. He said you were prone to violence."

Pot. Kettle. Black. "I won't say a word."

"Thank you." The little demon took a deep breath, then crossed into the living room. "I've brought you dinner."

At the mention of the dinner, Ursula's stomach rumbled. She hadn't eaten anything apart from a few grapes since she'd first arrived. As she crossed into the living room, she saw that Cera had arranged a few folded piles of clothes for her on the sofa. As soon as Cera left, she'd change into them. But right now, she just wanted to tear into the sumptuous-smelling meal.

At the bar, Cera had cleared up the wine and cheese from the night before. In their place stood a silver domed place setting. Cera pulled off the lid. Steam curled into the air, and Ursula's mouth watered at the scent of grilled meat. Cera had arranged fingerling potatoes next to a T-bone steak with a small salad. Ursula pulled a chair up to the bar, a grin curling her lips. "This looks amazing. Did you make it?"

Cera beamed. "I did."

"Thank you so much." Ursula popped a potato into her mouth, savoring the buttery flavor. *Amazing.* She glanced at Cera. "Cera, you are indeed multi-talented. Are you going to join me? It's a shame to eat alone."

Cera shook her head. "I've already eaten."

She picked up the knife and fork. "Maybe tomorrow you could join me."

Cera's brow furrowed. "No," she said with some finality. "Fine." Ursula picked up her knife and fork. *Guess I'll eat alone.* Still, she didn't want to be completely isolated. She'd lose her mind in solitary confinement. Maybe she could keep Cera here for conversation. "So how does the food get here? Surely you don't have cows on the moon."

"The salad and the potatoes are grown here. The lunar soil isn't very rich in nutrients, but that's easily remedied with natural compost. But you're right about the beef. It is imported."

"And how does that work?" She shoveled in a forkful of salad. "I had to leave all my clothes behind to travel through Nyxobas's water."

"That's right," said Cera nodding. "Since it's impossible to bring anything through a portal with you, we have the lunar bats fly it in."

"Bats like Sotz?"

"Exactly. They can fly between the Earth and the moon."

"They fly through the vacuum of space? Without air?"

Cera shrugged. "They don't appear to need air. They're Nyxobas's creatures."

"Fascinating," said Ursula, carving off a piece of the steak. Red streaks of blood oozed from the flesh.

"Is it okay? We don't usually cook steak. I hope I didn't overdo it."

After ruining the dress, Ursula didn't want to insult the demon. "It's delicious." She cut off a piece from the edge and popped it into her mouth.

Cera's eyes crinkled at the corners when she smiled. "Well, I should leave you to eat alone."

Ursula turned to Cera. "Sotz flew back on his own?"

"Yes. He's in the rookery now. Well, perhaps I—"

It was a long shot, but she had to ask. "I don't suppose you can tell me what I'll be doing here for the next six months. Am I really supposed to just hang out in my quarters?"

Cera frowned. "No. Of course not. And I completely forgot the wine."

Before Ursula could tell her not to worry, Cera was already behind the bar. She slid a glass over the bar and pulled out a carafe of red wine.

Ursula took a sip, letting the rich flavor roll over her tongue. Delicious. It also helped rinse out the taste of raw meat. "If I'm staying here, how often will you visit me?"

"I'll deliver your meals and clothes," said Cera, eyeing the raw steak hungrily. "That's all I know."

"And you'll never eat with me? Even if the food is delicious?"

"That's not how it works. Everyone has their place here in the Shadow Realm. And my place is not at the table with you."

Ursula forked another potato into her mouth. "I don't understand."

"The lord doesn't allow the oneiroi to eat his food."

"You mean Bael?"

Cera frowned. "Yes. The lord."

"I won't tell. You can have the steak, if you want. I don't eat much meat," she lied.

Cera drummed her fingernails on the marble bar for a moment before snatching the plate. "If you insist."

The demon grabbed a fork, lifting the entire steak to her mouth. She opened her mouth, her sharp teeth glinting in the candlelight. She tore into the meat, ripping off a chunk with her teeth.

As Cera ripped into the meat, Ursula crossed to the other side of the bar and pulled out another wine glass. She slid it over to Cera, then filled it. "The steak goes well with the wine."

"You don't mind?"

"Of course not. I don't want to be stuck here on my own. And will you please sit? Make yourself comfortable."

Cera climbed into a chair and continued working her way through the steak, little grunts of pleasure emitting from her throat.

"So tell me about yourself," said Ursula. "How did you come to work for Bael?"

"My mother was the lord's maidservant. When she grew too old to work, I took over the position."

"You seem afraid of him." Ursula sipped her wine, eyeing her new dinner companion cautiously. Maybe she could learn a bit more about Bael while she was at it. "Is he cruel to you?"

Cera stopped chewing, her eyes widening. "Of course not. He's very good to me, but *all* the lords have dominion over the oneiroi. If an oneiroi steps out of line, we can be brought before the council, and—" She glanced out the window, as if Nyxobas could overhear her. "The council demands obedience. Everyone has their place. The lords serve our god. Shadow demons serve the lords. Women serve their husbands. And oneiroi serve everyone."

Lovely. "Can you tell me what happened to damage the manor?"

Cera swallowed the last of her meat. "When the lord returned, we were very happy. He had been away a long time. Having the lord in the manor makes it feel complete. Like we're protected. But he was hurt. When the other lords learned of his injuries..." Cera swallowed, her pale eyes glistening. "They attacked. Our lord—he bravely fought them. He was able to defend the manor, but many oneiroi died. Only a few of us remain now. And he doesn't come out of his quarters anymore."

"What do you think will happen?"

Terror trembled in Cera's voice when she spoke again. "The other lords will find another way to kill my lord. Among the warrior lords, only the strongest are considered fit to live. The weak are sacrificed to the void."

Ursula swallowed hard. "I don't understand. If Nyxobas wants me protected, why did he put me with a mortal lord everyone wants to murder?"

Cera lifted her tear-streaked face. "No one else knows you're here. My lord is weakened, but Nyxobas trusts him like he trusts no other. When Nyxobas ordered the lord to protect you, he knew he would follow through with every ounce of strength remaining in his body. Even if he doesn't like you."

Gods willing, that will be enough. "I didn't realize I was meant to be a secret here." She nodded at the window. "Can't people see me through the giant windows?"

Cera shook her head. "No. The light reflects off them." Cera rose. "Thank you for the meal. I'll return tomorrow."

"I hope you enjoyed it."

Cera's chin glistened with steak juices. "It was the best thing I've eaten in years."

As Cera left her quarters, Ursula stared out the window at Asta. The protection of the night god was the one thing keeping Bael alive. And here, in the Shadow Realm, Bael was the one person keeping her alive. Terrifying as the god of night was, she needed him on her side.

CHAPTER 8

After Cera left, Ursula tidied away the clothes the little oneroi had left behind. She tucked the knickers into her bureau, then hung the dresses and shawls in her bedroom closet. As she organized, she ran her fingers over the soft fabrics: cotton dresses for home, delicate embroidered tulle for speaking to the lord.

Nothing she could fight in, but apparently that wasn't supposed to be her role here. She just had no idea what her actual role was.

In her bedroom, she pulled off her bloodstained gown and slipped into a black cotton dress that hung to her ankles. And conveniently, the simple dress had pockets by her hips—so she wouldn't need to store anything in her panties.

She glanced around the bedroom—the stark gray walls and clean lines of the violet bedspread weren't exactly inviting. What were the chances Bael would allow her to decorate this place? She needed a reminder of her most calming dreams—of the dusty-blue forget-me-nots and yellow aster, bathed in the amber light. Those beautiful but intangible memories she could never quite grasp... Honeyed sunrise, blue flower petals, tall blades of grass. The warmth of a landscape so different from Nyxobas's Shadow Realm.

With a shawl wrapped around her shoulders, she crossed to the enormous windows. What, exactly, was she supposed to do with her time?

There was no TV in this place, no armory where she could hone her skills, not even a bookshelf with a collection of novels.

She stared out at the vast crater. The opposite side of the rim was so far away, its enormity dizzied her. Even Asta, with the strange, gray clouds that swirled around its violet peak, looked thin and delicate from this vantage point.

Ursula glanced down at the houses that clustered around the valley floor. Could she glean anything about the habitants by looking at their homes? In the darkness, it was difficult to make out much. *What I wouldn't give for a telescope right now.*

Still, if she strained her eyes, she could tell the houses were small and built of stone. Among the sea of darkened windows, a few lights twinkled. Did Cera and other oneiroi live in those humble dwellings? From the crater's valley, they could literally look up to their lords in the imposing lunar palaces.

How long had Bael lived here in the Shadow Realm? At the thought of his otherworldly power, a shiver ran up her spine. Instinctively, she reached for her white moonstone—her lucky charm. Her stomach flipped. Of course, it had been left behind when she'd stripped off in the subway. *Bloody hell.* She'd had that thing for as long as she could remember, not that that was very long, but still it had been the one constant that had travelled from her former life to her new one.

She bit her lip. She'd been stripped of everything on her journey here —her magic, her sword, and her touchstone.

She turned, scanning the room. She'd just have to find a new lucky charm. Her gaze landed on a mahogany jewelry box that rested on the dresser.

She lifted the lid, momentarily dazzled by the small treasure inside. Among the silver and diamonds, she found a beautiful brooch. Inset into the silver setting, a cameo stone depicted a lion's head. She ran her thumb over the surface. Somehow, it didn't feel soothing.

She dropped it back in the pile, and picked her way through rings and necklaces. *Too delicate.* She needed something strong and solid.

As she dug her way to the very bottom, she found a ring of solid silver. The thing was enormous—far too big for her own fingers, but heavy enough to feel like an anchor. More importantly, it fit perfectly into the palm of her hand. She stroked the smooth metal, then slipped it into her pocket.

With the ring tucked safely in her pocket, she returned downstairs. She'd already grown more comfortable in the living room than anywhere else in her living quarters.

On the sofa, she curled up into the corner and pulled a snowy blanket over her body. Before she let her eyes close, she glanced around the room. She could still spruce it up a little, bring a bit of life to the place. Some apricot and bronze paints could go a long way...

She let her eyes close, rubbing the solid ring between her fingers. And when she drifted into the dream world, she visited a man with gray eyes, his body hewn of pure muscle. Around them, a room burned and screams pierced the night air...

It seemed like only few moments had passed when Cera tapped her on the shoulder.

"Ursula."

Ursula blinked, slowly waking. Cera peered down at her. Outside, stars still shone in the dark sky. Bloody hell, this place was disorienting. It felt like she'd only been asleep for a few moments.

She sat up, trying to clear the fog of sleep. "How long, exactly, does the night last on the moon?"

"The lunar day lasts twenty-seven Earth days. The sun won't rise for another..." Cera looked at the clock. "The sun will rise in one hundred and eight hours."

Ursula's eyes widened. "It's dark for a month at a time?"

"No, it's only dark for half of that. For just over thirteen days, we see the sun." She gestured at the window. "Lucky for us, the tinted glass blocks out most of the light. Anyway, you need to get dressed. The lord's carriage leaves in thirty minutes. If you want a shower, now is the time to do it."

"The lord's carriage?"

"He has requested your presence. He did not explain why." Cera thrust a silky dress at her.

Of course he didn't. She took the dress from Cera, unfurling it. Deep indigo silk, so dark it almost look black, embroidered with fine silver stitching. This time, a delicate silver bra and panties lay on top of the fabric, plus a pair of indigo flats.

Cera turned her back. "Please hurry."

Ursula stepped out of her clothes, then folded them neatly on the sofa. She slipped into the panties and bra, then plucked the silver ring from her dress pocket, tucking it into the front of her cleavage. "A carriage, you said?"

"Precisely. The lord awaits you. We weren't given much warning."

Ursula stepped into the dress, pulling it up over her hips and sliding the sheer sleeves over her shoulders. From the tops of her thighs down, the dress grew increasingly sheer, sparkling with silver thread. The wide hem gave her more freedom of movement than yesterday's dress. The neckline plunged, giving off a view of her cleavage. Apparently, Cera was enjoying creating fashions for hellhounds with no sense modesty.

She stepped into the shoes. "It's gorgeous."

Cera turned, frowning. "Let me help you." She tugged at Ursula's hair with her fingers, twisting and forcing the waves into submission. When she'd finished, she appraised her work. One of her black eyebrows flew up. "Open your mouth."

Ursula did as instructed, and Cera whipped out a small silver canister, spraying her mouth with a minty liquid. In the next second, Cera was slicking her lips with red gloss. "Perfect. You have everything you need."

"There is one thing this ensemble really needs," said Ursula.

"What?"

"A sword."

Cera snorted. "Fat chance of that. Here, women are meant to please the eye. Not pluck them out with blades. That's men's work. Let's go. The lord awaits you."

Cera turned, hurrying into the hall. Ursula quickened her pace to keep up with Cera as she crossed the bridge, the wind whipping her auburn hair into her face.

When she crossed into the half-shattered atrium, her heart skipped a beat. A metal cage stood in the center, with a hinged door. It looked like something that belonged in a medieval torture chamber. "Um, what is this, exactly?"

Cera yanked open the door. "Don't be afraid. On Earth, I believe you call this an elevator."

Ursula glanced up at the thick steel chain that rose from the cage's ceiling. "Right." As

Cera held the door open, Ursula stepped inside. Without entering, Cera closed the door on Ursula.

"You're not coming?" asked Ursula.

The little demon crossed the smashed tile. "No. The lord only requested your presence."

Ursula wrapped her hands around the elevator's bars, watching as Cera pulled a lever. A great creaking noise pierced the air, and the rattling chain slowly lifted the cage from the ground.

"Good luck!" shouted Cera from below.

CHAPTER 9

The cage rose slowly, swinging gently from side to side with metallic groans. Ursula laced her fingers through the bars to steady herself. A chilly wind rushed over Ursula's skin, raising goosebumps.

On her journey upward, she passed one balcony after another. This place was *enormous*—practically its own city. Except, as she passed each floor, darkness greeted her. No candles lit the rooms, no voices warmed the air. Starlight shone through cracked glass shards of shattered windows. Instead of art, ragged holes interrupted the sleek walls, and burn marks scarred the marble floors.

The only signs of movement were the pale curtains, dancing in the lunar breeze.

Before the attack, this place would have been stunning, and perhaps teaming with life. As the elevator continued to rise, the walls narrowed. The cage slipped through a narrow gap in the roof, and into the night air.

On the slick roof's surface, the icy breeze blew more strongly through the bars, bringing with it a faint smell of creosote.

A dome of stars spread out above, and Bael stepped from the shadows. Starlight caressed the sharp planes of his cheeks, glinting in his eyes. He wore a dark cloak around his broad shoulders, fastened with a silver lion clasp. Another piece of cloth covered one of his arms. From under his hood, his pale eyes pierced the night like stars.

As he opened the elevator door, his expression appeared grim, almost hostile. The door creaked as he opened it. "Tonight, you will do everything I say."

She frowned. She hadn't expected high-fives and cookies, but there was a hint of rage in his voice she hadn't heard before.

Her stomach fluttered. "What's the matter?"

"Who did you tell about your visit to the Shadow Realm?" Vicious shadows whorled in his eyes.

"No one." She eyed his cloak enviously. Too bad Cera hadn't shown up with a jacket. "The only people who know are Emerazel, Zee, and Kester. None of them would tell a soul. And they certainly don't gossip with shadow demons."

Bael cocked his head. He was doing that creepy demon thing—the eerily still body and penetrating eyes that she was certain could read more than she wanted them to.

He took a step closer, his powerful magic rippling over her skin. "Somehow, someone has told Hothgar about you. He's specifically requested that you show fealty to the council," he snarled. "Your presence here was supposed to be a secret."

"I take it Hothgar is one of the lords?"

"A lord without honor."

Whoever Hothgar was, he'd probably put at least some of those holes in the palace. "Abrax knows I'm here. He wants me dead."

"Abrax wants you for himself. It would not be in his interest to inform the council about you. Once they learn of your presence in the Shadow Realm, they will howl for hellhound blood. The location—the very existence of the Shadow Realm—has been protected for millennia. Outsiders within our boundaries have never left the realm alive. And worse, you belong to Emerazel."

Ursula shook her head. "Nyxobas specifically requested my presence."

"He tasked me with protecting you from Abrax. But he won't risk upsetting the cohesion of his council if they all find out. I cannot protect you from the other eleven lords if they want your neck."

The wind picked up her hair. Maybe this was an opportunity. "Maybe

I should return to Earth. You don't want to start a war with Emerazel over me. I'm really not worth the hassle."

"For whatever reason, Nyxobas wants you here. But he's not fully protecting you. If he were, you'd be in Asta or he'd have issued a decree to protect you. He's done neither."

Her forehead crinkled. "So...what's the deal? Surely there are easier ways to kill me than bringing me to the Shadow Realm."

"He hasn't seen fit to fill me in. Whatever he has planned, I view it as my duty to protect you. Tonight, you will come with me to the council." His tone was pure command. "They must understand that you're not here as an enemy, but as a captive. You must convey the message of captivity through acting submissive. It's what they'll understand."

Sounds like a great time. She crossed her arms, shivering. "Can you tell me more about Hothgar?"

"He is the new Sword of Nyxobas." Cold rage laced his voice. "And he belongs in the void."

The cold wind stung her skin and she tightened her fingertips on her forearms. Bael's gaze flicked to her shivering arms. He pulled the dark cloth from his arm, handing it to her. "Put this on."

She took it from him—a black wool cloak, identical to his. She wrapped it around her, savoring its warmth, and fastened it with the silver clasp. A lion, just like Bael's.

"You'll need to cover your head." Bael leaned in closer, pulling up the hood. "It is important you don't draw any unnecessary attention to your-self. And your hair is difficult to ignore." He turned from her, facing the crater, then put his fingers to his lips and whistled sharply.

A shadow crossed over their heads, and Ursula glanced up. Flying above them, a team of lunar bats pulled a black carriage, fastened to the creatures by silver cords. It looked like a gothic chariot from the eigh-teenth century.

I've either wandered into a nightmarish version of Cinderella, *or a hellish Christmas tale, with lunar bats instead of reindeer.*

With the whoosh of beating wings, the bats lowered the carriage to the roof, then landed on the slick marble with an ear-piercing scratching of claws.

A male oneiroi hopped down from the front of the carriage, his black hair slicked back off his pale face. He opened the door to the main compartment, then bowed to Bael.

Bael gestured for Ursula to enter.

She tugged her shawl tighter, her gaze skimming over the magic swirling around the carriage's thin, black wheels. *That's what keeps this thing in the air—shadow magic.*

Inside, the indigo seats faced one another. Ursula nestled into the one that faced the front of the carriage. Shutting the door behind him, Bael climbed in the seat opposite. He kept his gray eyes locked on her, and he rapped on the window glass behind him.

With a lurch, the carriage surged into the sky. Through the window, she had a clear view of Bael's manor. Built against the cliff's side, it loomed above the crater, a shining tower of glass and silver. It looked like a skyscraper from a war zone. Jagged holes marred the walls, and great beams of metal twisted into the darkness like metallic innards. Thick dust covered some of the floors, like funeral ash.

Her heart tightened at the sight of it. She didn't know Bael very well, but the loss of all those people must have been catastrophic.

Bael glared at her from across the carriage, not a single muscle moving. "When we get to Asta, you will stay by my side. Keep the hood over your head to cloak your face in shadow. Speak to no one."

Ursula nodded, half-listening. Asta, with its stunning violet glow, came into view through the window. The enormity of the Shadow Realm astonished her. The crater's rim curved around them, and thousands of buildings filled the vast space.

She pointed to the stone buildings below. "Who lives down there? In those small homes?"

"They are the homes of the brethren, and the oneiroi."

"Who are the brethren?"

"Nyxobas's followers."

She shook her head. "So the oneirei aren't all Nyxobas's followers? How did the oneiroi end up here if only followers of Nyxobas are allowed, on pain of death?"

"Very astute." He arched an eyebrow. "The oneiroi dwell within the crater because they were here first."

"I don't understand."

"Nyxobas was imprisoned here one hundred thousand years ago. The oneiroi were here first."

"Wait, so the oneiroi are—" Ursula struggled to process the implications. "They're extraterrestrials?"

He cocked his head. "They're not native to the Earth, so I suppose they are."

The bats' wings beat the air rhythmically, pulsing like a heartbeat. Outside, Asta shone in the darkness, tinging the gray clouds with purple. There really was something odd about the clouds—the way they twisted and writhed, curling high into the air and then diving down in spinning vortexes. Almost like a living thing.

As they approached, a low humming reverberated through the carriage. Her seat began to vibrate, and she tried to ignore the sensation. Especially since it wasn't exactly a *terrible* sensation, but it's not like she wanted to mention that to Bael. Her cheeks warmed, and she could feel her chest flushing.

She was concentrating on blocking out the faint wave of pleasure pulsing through her body, when something *thunked* against the window. A vicious green smudge streaked the glass.

"Watch that you don't fly too close to the moths," Bael called out to the driver.

"Yes, milord."

Bael gazed at Ursula. "We could blow out windows if we flew through one of the murmurations."

"A what now?"

"The astral moths." He pointed at the clouds outside. "They're attracted to Asta's light."

Thunk. A gray wing the size of a dinner plate stuck to the window a moment before peeling off. Ursula pressed her face to the glass, watching the carriage descend. Clouds of moths swirled above them. It took her a moment to realize the low, vibrating hum came from the beating of a million insect wings. Outside, the moths flew in unison, like a flock of birds.

That's why the clouds moved so strangely.

They *were* alive.

"Why do they group and cluster like that?" asked Ursula.

"The murmuration? For protection." He pointed out the window at a gray form gliding toward one of the clouds. "Look."

As the bat approached, the moths dove in unison—a tight spiral of fluttering wings. The bat twisted and jerked. In a gut churning instant, it crushed a moth's body between its jaws. The circle of life, right here on the moon.

When Ursula turned back to Bael, her heart stopped.

The demon lord pointed a dagger directly at her heart.

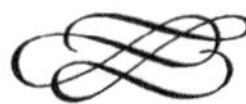

She froze, only her eyes moving to scan the carriage for a weapon. Who was she kidding? Of course he hadn't left weapons lying around. "I thought you were my protector."

His eyes narrowed. "You scare easily. The blade is for your protection." He turned the dagger, offering her the hilt. "Take it."

"Oh, I thought—" Ursula cut herself off. There was no need to belabor his point. The fact was, she *did* scare easily. She constantly searched her surroundings for escape routes or weapons. She had no idea what had happened to F.U., but whatever it had been probably wasn't pleasant. Perhaps that burning room from her dreams had something to do with it.

Taking the blade, she rolled her wrist, inspecting the steel. Perfectly weighted. When she held it to the light, she glimpsed strange angular patterns etched into the metal.

"Be careful with it. The dagger was forged from a meteorite, and it's more powerful than you'd think." He reached into his cloak, pulling out a set of leather straps. "Stick out your leg."

"Why?"

His eyes met hers. "So I can attach the sheath."

"Oh." She didn't need his help getting a sheath on her thigh, but something stopped her from protesting. She rested her foot on his seat by his thigh, feeling the heat radiating from him. She pulled up the hem of her dress.

Bael's gaze trailed up her leg, his eyes darkening from pale gray to a deep black. His jaw tightened, his dark magic swirling from his body. He handed her the sheath. "Perhaps you should do it."

She couldn't suppress a faint smile, and she let her leg rest against Bael's as she strapped the leather around her thigh.

Bael kept his gaze fixed firmly out the window. "If you keep the blade strapped to your thigh, you'll have to be seriously comprised before someone finds it."

Ursula slid the blade into the scabbard. "Let's hope it doesn't come to that."

"If it does, I think you'll find it's considerably more lethal than a corkscrew."

In the darkness of his hood, Ursula couldn't tell if he was joking or not.

Outside, Asta's glow burned brighter, washing the cabin with violet light. They seemed to be on a collision course with the spire, and just when she was sure they would crash into it, the carriage veered to the right. It jerked to a stop so abruptly that Ursula lurched from her seat, tumbling into Bael's lap.

Instantly, his powerful hands were around her waist, steadying her. She breathed in. *Sandalwood and sea air.*

"We're here," he said quietly, his breath warming her throat.

"Right. Sorry." She stood, smoothing out her hair.

Bael leaned over, opening the door. Ursula stepped onto a balcony by the side of the spire, pulling her cloak closer around her. Here, the wind felt ten degrees colder, seeming to cut through even the heavy woolen shawl.

As Bael stepped from the carriage, she surveyed her surroundings, trying not to peer over the side of the balcony. Violet light washed over her, like she was standing in front of an enormous gemstone. On the other side of the balcony, an arched doorway interrupted the smooth crystal. From what she could tell by looking up, they'd landed about midway up the spire. Great walls of purple crystal rose up before her, shimmering in the starlight. Scattered balconies jutted into the air.

When she looked closely, she could see that scars marred the crystal's surface. In other places, great chips had flaked off. When she strained her eyes, she could see a jagged scar that bisected the crystal, as if it had been severed and reattached. What the hell had happened here?

They stepped out and the carriage pulled away from the balcony with the great beating of bat wings. Bael crossed to the opening in the wall. Before following him in, she pulled the hood more tightly over her head.

In the door's opening, he turned to her. "Remember, if you want to live, you must do everything I say. Even if it doesn't make sense to you. Do you understand?"

Do I have a choice? "I've got it."

"Good. Now, your first command is to be silent. Absolutely no talking. Keep your hood over your head. Use the dagger only if your life is at risk."

He turned, striding into a dark hall. She hurried after him, keeping her face downcast. Could he tell where they were going? Surely shadow demons had amazing night vision.

A moment later, his strong hand grabbed hers, drawing her next to him. They'd stopped walking.

A voice boomed from somewhere in front of her. "Was that your carriage, Bael?" The tone changed, growing soft and mocking. "I can't imagine getting dragged around in one of those things. You must miss your wings." A chorus of laughter echoed around them, but there was no mirth in it.

Quiet fury tinged Bael's voice. "Yes, Hothgar. It is I."

The familiar urge to identify an escape route began to take hold, tightening her muscles. The Forgotten Ones may have snuffed out her fire, but apparently they'd left her instincts intact.

Too bad she couldn't see anything. As her eyes adjusted to the darkness, she could make out only the faint sheen of gray marble below her, but she kept her head tucked down, hiding her face.

"Then let us convene this council. Do we have a quorum?" said Hothgar.

Another voice answered. "All twelve lords are here, sir."

A cracking noise like metal against stone made Ursula flinch, the sound echoing through the space. It was only after the third crack that she realized someone was banging a gavel.

Hothgar's voice boomed again. "The quorum is convened. Bael, have you brought the cur?"

"I have," he replied. She heard his footsteps circling behind her, and he ripped the hood from her head. In the next second, he had forced her to her knees.

Her stomach clenched. *He did tell me to be submissive, but this is a bit much.* Still, she forced herself to keep her eyes on the floor.

"Good, I see that she is obedient," said Hothgar.

Fury simmered. *I hate these people.* She let her gaze rise, taking in a granite, semicircular table twenty feet in front of her. Behind it sat eleven demons. And not merely mortal demons, like she was. No—these were high demons, ancient and powerful. The dim light of luminescent mushrooms cast their bestial faces in violet light.

At the center of the table sat the man with the gavel—Hothgar, she presumed. He wore a shirt of thin chainmail. His hoary beard and white eyebrows marked him as older than the rest. From his left, Abrax glared at her, his gray eyes glacially cold.

On Hothgar's right sat a literal giant. Snowy skin, horned temples, flared nostrils. Demon-Bull, she'd call him.

She scanned the other lords, trying not to show her alarm at the array of muscled demons before her. Through eyes the color of obsidian, ice, and starlight, they stared at her with a mixture of disgust and hatred.

Mostly hatred.

Terrifying as they were, they paled in comparison to what perched behind them. An ancient throne, shrouded in shadow magic, so thick it almost looked tangible. An enormous form sat there, cloaked in darkness.

There's Nyxobas, the god of my nightmares.

For just a moment, his magic thinned, and she caught a glimpse of his head lolling to one side. *Is he asleep?* No. Not quite. His eyes were open—not their usual pale gray, but black as obsidian.

Hothgar leaned over the table. "Why are you in the Realm of Shadows, hellhound?"

Her chest tightened. Hadn't Bael told her not to speak? Was she supposed to answer Hothgar's question or not? She didn't feel like she'd been properly prepared for this encounter. A soft nudge of her shins from Bael cleared it up for her.

Kneeling, she said, "Nyxobas struck a deal with Emerazel. I'm to spend six months of every year here."

"If that's a lie," growled Hothgar, "I will tear your guts out myself and use them to decorate my mansion."

Ursula's mouth went dry.

"She speaks the truth," said Bael. "I was there."

"Why should I trust your word, *mortal?*" asked Hothgar.

"You don't have to trust it." His voice boomed. "Abrax can tell you."

Dread filled Ursula's gut. Bael had just put her life in the hands of Abrax—the one demon who most wanted her dead after she'd ruined his plans of world domination.

Abrax spoke so softly, it was almost inaudible. "I can confirm Bael's story."

"So it is true?" asked Hothgar. "Your father summoned her?"

"Yes," said Abrax.

"Why would the god invite one of Emerazel's curs to his Realm?"

Abrax's eyes bored into her. "I don't know."

Hothgar studied her carefully with a look that suggested he was still thinking about decorating his house with her entrails. "Let me see her more closely."

Before Ursula could stand on her own, Bael picked her up by the collar of her cloak and threw her on the granite table. Her head smacked the stone so hard, she saw stars. It took every inch of her mental strength to lay still.

Be submissive, Bael had said. At this point, with the concussion he'd just given her, she didn't have many other options. Her head throbbed. Hothgar leaned over her, stroking the side of her face with a cold finger. "She's a pretty one. Maybe Nyxobas wanted her for himself."

"Gross." Dizzy from the blow to the head, the word was out of Ursula's mouth before she could stop herself.

Bael squeezed her wrist.

Hothgar glared at Bael. "But what I want to know is why he put her in *your* care. You lost your wings. Your house is in ruins." He emphasized the next set of words: "You are unfit to hold a manor of the night."

What the hell? Why don't they just ask Nyxobas, who was sitting about ten feet away? He seemed to be in some sort of catatonic state. Asleep or in a mystical trance.

"Nyxobas chooses his lords," said Bael.

"And yet he hasn't given you a new set of wings." Hothgar leaned back in his chair. "We have decided to give your manor to Abrax."

Bael's eyes darkened, and a cold, dark aura whipped from his body like hurricane winds. "No. Only Nyxobas himself may appoint a lord to a manor."

"The choice was unanimous," said Hothgar.

"It's not your province—" Black tendrils of magic snapped around Bael's throat, cutting him short. Ursula's eyes flicked to Demon-Bull, who chanted in Angelic. He was choking Bael with magic.

"We are tired of listening to a mortal," Hothgar snarled. "Your time as lord has come to an end. Prepare to enter the void."

Around Bael's neck, the filaments began to constrict. His eyes were dark as voids, and his fingers strained at the threads twisting about his neck.

Panic stole Ursula's breath, but she lay flat on the stone, trying to go unnoticed. Whatever she was going to do, she didn't want to telegraph her actions.

Her pulse racing, she glanced at Nyxobas, still wrapped in shadows, unmoving. *Why isn't he doing anything?*

Bael hadn't explicitly told her what constituted "an emergency," but she was pretty sure this was it. While the demons watched Bael suffocate, she slowly drew the dagger from the sheath on her thigh. Just as she managed to extract it, she felt Hothgar's fingers grab the corners of her cloak. In a single motion he picked her up and heaved her across the room. She slammed into a crystal wall with a bone-jarring smack. Her dagger clattered on the floor.

Bollocks.

"The hound had a blade," Hothgar roared.

Demon-Bull flicked his wrist, and black tendrils raced across the room. She ducked, diving for the dagger. Just as she gripped its hilt, dark magic slammed into her chest. She flew back against the wall, grunting from the pain.

Pinned to the wall, shadow magic coiled around her chest. Demon-Bull was crushing her lungs, her blood roaring in her ears. *Air. Please.* How long would it take for her ribs to shatter and pierce her heart? *Please. I can't die here.*

Ten seconds, maybe twenty.

"You have disrespected our hospitality," Hothgar roared. "You tried to assassinate the Sword of Nyxobas."

She opened her mouth to speak, but the pain ripped her mind apart. She doubled over as the magical bonds began to crack her ribs. Across from her, Bael hung limply, suffocating. He dropped to the ground, his large body twitching.

Air.

Her vision darkened, and for just a moment, she caught a glimpse of a woman with vibrant nectarine hair, wielding a sword with expert skill—her face like Ursula's, but her eyes a deep shade of brown...

A voice in the hollows of her mind whispered, *Kill the king.* A clear voice, ringing like a bell, reverberating off her skull. A voice so familiar, it was like a part of her soul. *Kill the king. Kill the king.*

With the last of her strength, she lifted the blade.

Hothgar laughed. "We are immortal—you cannot hurt us with that."

It's not meant for you, fuckwit.

It's for the king.

With the last of her strength, she hurled the dagger at Nyxobas's slumped body.

CHAPTER 11

The blade sank into Nyxobas's chest. The lords froze, staring at the god of night. Time seemed to slow, and the temperature in the room plummeted.

The filaments around Ursula's chest loosened, and she gasped. *Air.*

She sensed the terrifying presence of the void, flickering in the edge of her consciousness. Watching her.

"Who has done this?" Nyxobas's voice boomed through the silence. His eyes had shifted from black to a glacial gray—the icy gaze of her most terrifying nightmares.

Black blood bubbled around the hilt of the dagger in his chest.

Hothgar slowly turned, pointing at Ursula.

"The hound?" Nyxobas roared.

At the sound of his voice, a vast emptiness filled her mind. She stood at the edge of the precipice. Black and bottomless, it drew her closer. She only had to step off the edge, to give herself into eternal descent.

No sound, no light, no sensation. Just Ursula and the unending darkness.

Distantly, she felt the pain of her broken ribs. *I can leave this wrecked body behind, this withering carcass.*

Is this what the Forgotten Ones had meant when they told her the darkness would save her? She could join Nyxobas now. Supplicate herself to him—become one of his brethren. He would give her power she couldn't begin to imagine. She just needed to accept the void, to give up this decaying flesh.

To give up the broken ribs and burning walls, the rapacious hunger that could eat her alive...

Give up the tall grasses, beams of light through yew trees, the salty taste of sea air on her lips...

No, she thought. *I want to live.*

Before her, the darkness thinned. Her heart thrumming, she stared as Nyxobas slowly drew the blade from his chest. He crushed it between his fingers. "Why have you roused me?"

"They were murdering Bael." Her voice was rough and strained. Agony still pierced her chest where the cords bound her.

From the floor, Bael moaned, no longer enshrouded by dark magic.

Still alive.

Nyxobas turned his gaze on Hothgar. "You chose to murder one of my lords?" Ice tinged his voice.

Hothgar straightened. "He has lost his wings. Since we last spoke with you, he has proven himself unable to protect Albelda Manor. The palace has been destroyed, half his men slaughtered. As a mortal, he has been unable to fulfill his duties as lord. Abrax, your son, can hold the manor until another lord is appointed."

Nyxobas's glacial eyes bored into him. "Is this true?"

Bael pushed up onto his elbows, blood dripping from his lips. "The other lords attacked. I defended. Albelda Manor stands, and I live."

Hothgar's eyes flicked to Ursula. "He wasn't able to control his captive very well either. The hound is out of control, as you have seen."

Ursula's mouth went dry. *This is not going well.* "Isn't there a way for Bael to get his wings back? When I became a hound, I was offered a trial—"

"A trial," said Nyxobas, lifting a finger. "The wretched hound has the blood of a warrior."

Hothgar and Abrax both turned to glare at her. *Shit. What did I just suggest?*

Shadows coiled around the god of night. "The code of the warrior has always allowed for a trial. If Bael wishes to keep his manor, he must fight for it. Win, and all is forgiven."

Bael rose to his feet. "I will kill whomever I need to. I may be mortal, but you know my strength."

The god's silver eyes narrowed. "There will be a tournament. The lords may nominate five champions each—their greatest warriors. For the tournament, all demons shed their immortality. And if you, Bael, wish to reclaim your status, you must win the trial."

Bael nodded. He spoke through bloody teeth. "So be it."

"Then it is settled," said Nyxobas. "When the shadows grow long above Lacus Mortis, and the sun sets, we will conduct a melee. Those who survive will join the race. Finally, a duel. The prize is the remnants of Albelda manor, and a position as lord. If Bael wins, I return his wings."

An icy silence fell over the room, then Hothgar slammed his gavel onto the stone. "A trial for all the lords. A just ruling." His voice boomed, echoing off the crystal ceiling. After a moment, the room filled with rumbling cheers.

Hothgar stood. "Before the melee, we will hold a feast. We will present our champions. Then, the bloodletting begins."

* * *

BAEL STARED out the window of the carriage, his jaw set tight. He kept his eyes fixed on the gray horizon. In the distance, his ruined manor glittered faintly.

The bats' wings beat the air, an oddly soothing sound after her close brush with death.

Bael hadn't spoken for the entire carriage ride. He'd regained his regal bearing, and blood no longer dripped from his mouth. But his demonic stillness sent a chill up her spine.

She was quickly learning that the stiller a demon's body, the more unquiet his mind.

"Are you okay?" she asked.

Bael fixed his eyes on her, his irises shading over. "I *told* you to be subservient," he spoke in a guttural growl. "Not to put a dagger in the god of night." Dark magic whorled from his body, skimming her skin like an ice breath of wind.

Anger inflamed her cheeks. "I was about to die. And if you hadn't noticed, I saved you from suffocating to death. If stabbing Nyxobas is what it took to save us both, then so be it. I owe him nothing. He might be your god, but he's not mine."

It took only a second for Bael to cross the carriage in a blur of black smoke. He boxed her in, one hand on either side of her head. "That's right. You worship Emerazel, the wretched beast of hell. You have bathed in the fires of her evil heart."

Anger simmered. She'd never had a choice in aligning with Emerazel —at least, not one she could remember. She lifted her legs, kicking him in the chest. He slammed against the other side of the carriage, emitting a low growl.

Ursula's lips curled. She no longer had Emerazel's fire in her veins, but her own rage blazed through her blood. "I do not worship Emerazel. I'm a pawn in the game of the gods. Like we all are. I don't remember carving the mark in my chest, or why I thought it was a good idea, or anything about my life before three years ago." She pulled down the shoulder of her dress. "The only thing I know is that this stupid scar is the worst mistake I ever made." She yanked it up again. "I'm not Emerazel's worshipper. I'm her slave, and I don't know why. That's the truth."

Shadows still clouded his eyes, and his nostrils flared. His cold magic thrummed over her skin. "You don't belong here. The god of night has asked me to protect you, but I hate this job with every fiber of my being. He's making a mistake. As a fire demon, you're naturally inclined to destroy Nyxobas. To destroy all of us. Tonight proves it. You do not deserve my protection."

The coldness of his words pierced her chest.

Brilliant. Her only true ally here hated her. Tears stung her eyes, and she blinked them away. *I'm not going to cry in front of him.* "I was about to die," she said through clenched teeth, trying to gain mastery over herself.

"You could have thrown the knife at Bileth, the one whose magic assaulted you. But you're Emerazel's hound, and even without her fire, you are destined to fight the darkness. Her flames have tainted your soul."

"It wasn't like that." She swallowed hard. It *wasn't* like that, was it? She'd heard a voice in the back of her mind telling her to "kill the king." Was it simple self-preservation, or the voice of Emerazel?

Flustered, she waved a hand. "I didn't have a lot of time to think about the options. And it was eleven against one. If I weren't a hellhound, you'd be thanking me right now."

"But you are a hellhound. You don't belong here. Every time I look at you, I'm reminded of the hell-beast and the evil that runs through your blood."

"And Nyxobas isn't evil?" Her fingernails dug into her palms. "Are you really that loyal to the god of night, so devoted you think there's a vast difference between the gods of night and fire?"

He cut her a sharp look. "It's not because of my loyalty to Nyxobas that I hate her."

"Then what's your deal?"

"Her mind has been twisted by the flames, and has been since the dawn of civilization. She is an abomination. I owe her vengeance, and I will not rest until I have ripped her heart from her chest." The hatred in his eyes cut Ursula to the bone, warning her not to ask any more.

A pit opened in the hollow of her stomach. He hated Emerazel with a ferocity that literally chilled the air. And here she was—wearing Emerazel's sigil on her skin. A hellhound, loyal to his nemesis. Suddenly, she didn't feel so safe around Bael. He might be mortal, but he could still kill her.

Still, she knew how to handle men with rage problems. A year surrounded by drunks in her London bar had taught her how to manage that.

Stalling and distraction were her greatest assets.

She sighed, schooling her face to serenity, and drummed her fingernails. "So what happens now? What's this trial all about, and the code of the warrior?"

His steely gaze met hers. "You've manage to buy yourself some time. But you should know you've made some dangerous enemies tonight. The pale one, Bileth, is a psychopath. And while Hothgar might look old, he is the most powerful of the lords. You humiliated him in front of Nyxobas. He will want revenge." The ash-gray returned to his eyes.

"I thought you were the most powerful of the lords."

A rueful smile curled his perfect lips. "Before I lost my wings, I was Nyxobas's Sword. The leader of his legions, but now—" He coughed and Ursula saw him wipe blood from his lips. "I am still a warrior, but I am a mortal. A mortal's power is not the same. Still, I will fight in the tournament. And I plan to win."

"You certainly don't lack for confidence." *And I hope to hell you're right.*

"I am the best fighter the world has ever known." His pale eyes slid to the window again, the chiseled lines of his profile showing silver in the starlight.

She crossed her arms, sitting back in her seat. *Biggest ego the world has ever known, too.*

CHAPTER 12

The rest of their journey passed in silence as Bael brooded over whatever nightmares plagued his mind.

After their elevator had touched down, he'd disappeared into the shadows without a goodbye.

When she finally reached her quarters, her ribs were throbbing. Gingerly, she sat on the sofa, staring through the window.

The crater looked the same as it had when she'd left. In this desolate place, loneliness gnawed at her. Bael was right about one thing—she didn't belong here. And now, she'd landed herself in a whole new shitstorm.

Tension turned her stomach. Hothgar, Abrax, and Bileth would want vengeance. Worse, she'd attacked a god. Obviously a major breach of protocol. And what if Bael was right—that Emerazel could still somehow control her? It would make sense. Help explain why Emerazel had been willing to give her up in the first place. Though it didn't explain what Nyxobas wanted from her.

What she needed was a stiff drink. She rose, sucking in a short breath as she was greeted by a jolt of pain in her chest. Her ribs felt like they were on fire where Bileth's black tendrils had crushed them. Wincing, she carefully pulled off her dress, inspecting the damage. Deep bruises encircled her ribs.

Grimacing, she searched her mind for the Angelic spell—Starkey's Conjuration Spell. She remembered how it would feel—the familiar burst of pain as the spell knitted her bones back together, then blessed relief.

Only, she couldn't remember the bloody thing.

What the hell? She'd properly memorized it, having used it dozens of times to heal herself.

In fact, when she closed her eyes, she couldn't bring to mind a single Angelic word, the divine language of magic. Not even the spell for light.

The Forgotten Ones hadn't just stolen her fire magic. They'd ripped all the magical knowledge from her mind.

Dead-fingered bastards.

When she touched her ribs again, pain shot through her chest. She winced. She'd have to find some other way to heal.

A banging noise at the door turned her head, and she practically jumped out of her skin. Rising, she lifted the dress from the couch and slipped it over her head. If Bael were at the door, she didn't need to shock him by the sight of her naked flesh, though something about the idea amused her.

As she crossed the room, a part of her actually *hoped* it was Bael, even if he hated her. Suddenly, she had a deep desire to know why he hated Emerazel so much.

But instead, when she pulled open the front door, she found Cera, dressed in a woolen cardigan and holding a dome-covered tray. The rich smell of meat wafted into the room.

Ursula's mouth watered, and she gripped her chest. "I'm starving."

Cera's pale brow furrowed. "Oh my, what happened to your dress? It's been rumpled and torn."

"Bileth attacked me."

Cera's jaw dropped. "What happened?"

"Hothgar demanded my presence at the meeting of the lords. Bileth attacked Bael—"

"Is the lord okay?" Cera pushed inside. The door slammed behind her.

"I think he's okay. His throat is injured. He nearly died, and so did I. I did end up stabbing Nyxobas, which I realize overstepped a boundary or two. But in my defense, it was an emergency."

The tray in Cera's hands trembled violently. "You did *what?*"

"Did you hear the bit about the emergency?" Ignoring the throbbing pain in her chest, she grabbed the tray from Cera, carrying it to the bar. Her stomach twisted with a mixture of panic and hunger. "Anyway, now, in order for Bael to get his wings back, there's got to be a tournament. When the sun next bleeds into the sky. Bael must fight and win if he wants to live and get his manor back." She dropped the tray on the bar, cautiously eyeing Cera for her reaction.

"This is a disaster." Cera's eyes were wild. "If he was injured tonight, he won't have much time to heal. How will he fight?"

"He can't use magic to heal himself?"

Cera shook her head. "No. He must keep the wounds on his back fresh so he can reattached the wings when he wins them back."

That didn't sound good. "Can't he choose five champions, like everyone else?"

Cera shook her head, her eyes glistening. "Who would he choose? His men have all been killed."

"So each lord gets five champions, and he only has himself? That doesn't seem fair." She cocked her head. "Given those odds, he seemed pretty confident, though." She winced as a sharp spear of pain stabbed her ribs.

Cera studied her. "Are you injured?"

Ursula touched her ribs. "It hurts. I think I may have cracked a rib. Or three. And those Forgotten Arseholes erased all the healing spells I memorized."

Cera hurried to her side, her features pinched with concern. "Let me see. Lift your dress."

Ursula pulled her dress over her head, draping it over a chair.

Cera bent lower, letting out a low whistle at the purple bruises darkening her skin. "A lord did this to you?" Ursula could hear the hatred in Cera's voice.

She nodded, wincing as Cera gently she palpated her chest.

"It doesn't seem like a complete fracture, but I think you're right about it being cracked. I can heal it for you."

"Thank the gods." Ursula exhaled.

Cera reached into her sweater pocket and pulled out a purple crystal. It shimmered in the darkness.

Ursula took a step back as an icy wave of shadow magic washed over her skin. "What are you doing?"

"This is a lunam crystal. I keep it with me at all times in case I need to perform a spell. I can control the shadow magic within it. Even without knowing Angelic."

"You've never learned Angelic?"

"The oneiroi are not allowed. I'm not one of Nyxobas's brethren."

Ursula leaned closer, studying the crystal. It looked exactly like the ones she'd seen on the ceiling in Bael's cave. Shadow magic swirled from the violet rock, buzzing over her skin.

With a faint smile, Cera said, "The lord gave it to me. It's from the druse that grows in his cavern. It contains some of Nyxobas's magic."

She gripped it between her fingers, closing her eyes. Ursula stared as powerful shadow magic wafted from the crystal, curling around her ribs. The magic caressed her body, soothing her and exiting her at the same time. And most importantly, it leached the pain from her body, drawing it out as her bones fused together.

Ursula took a deep breath, sighing as the magic curled back into the crystal.

"Did it work?" asked Cera.

"Beautifully." Ursula grabbed her dress, pulling it back over her head. "Thank you."

Cera smiled. "Excellent."

Ursula pulled the dome off the tray, revealing a steaming meat pie with a side of mashed potatoes. "Will you join me?"

Cera wrung her hands. "I am quite hungry..."

"Please, eat with me."

Cera plopped down on a stool, grabbing a fork to delve into the pie.

Ursula speared a potato and bit into it, letting it melt in her mouth. "I'm confused. Nyxobas said the melee begins when the sun sets over Lacus Mortis. But the sun has already set. It's night."

"Lacus Mortis is on the other side."

"I see. Seems a long way to go."

Instead of answering, Cera shoveled another forkful of meat into her mouth, gnawing away.

She had to wonder who Cera would have shared a meal with before the Abelda Manor massacre. This place was almost entirely deserted now. Ursula couldn't be the only one plagued by loneliness. "How many oneiroi lived here before the attack?"

Cera's face fell for a moment. "Hundreds. Most died. The rest ran away."

"Why didn't you?"

Cera's face contorted with anger. "Serving in a lord's manor is a lifetime appointment. Without loyalty, we have nothing." She shoved a hunk of pork into her mouth.

"I see."

"And besides, if my brother's lord learned I'd failed in my duties as a servant, it would be very bad for my family."

She scooped a piece of buttery, flaky crust into her mouth. *Gods below. This woman can cook.* "You never mentioned you had a brother."

"Yes, it's just me and Massu now. He's a soldier. Even if I wanted to desert the lord, I couldn't, for his sake. I must protect Massu by remaining loyal to my lord." Savagely, she tore into a hunk of meat, swallowing quickly. "Of course, I don't hear much from him these days. I'm not sure that his lord would find out if I ran, but it's better to be safe than sorry. I worry about him terribly."

"Are you close?"

Cera nodded. "We were, before we were split into different manors. He was the sweetest boy. He always wanted to dress up like a lord, and he'd parade around with his little toy sword in secret. And he used to draw little pictures for me, of moths and bats and ships that flew in the air."

Ursula smiled. "He sounds adorable."

"He certainly was. All grown up now, but I'm sure the same sweet boy inside, even if he serves another lord."

So which one of those sadistic arseholes does Massu work for? "Which lord are we talking about?"

Cera shook her head. "I'm not allowed to say the name of any lord."

"Can you write it down?"

Cera shoveled a forkful of potatoes into her mouth. "Why is this so important to you?"

Because I watched Abrax bring an army of oneiroi into the fae realm, and I killed dozens of them. "I just like to know the lay of the land. And I may have seen him in the fae realm."

Cera silently nodded, swallowing her food. She placed her finger on the granite countertop, slowly tracing out letters. Ursula followed along, tracking the movements as Cera spelled out a name:

A...B...R...A...X

Ursula's blood went cold. *Fuck. Fuck. Fuck.* Cera's brother *was* a soldier in Abrax's army. Had Ursula killed him—murdered the brother of the only person she actually liked here? Had Bael killed him?

"You think you saw him in the fae realm?" asked Cera hopefully.

Ursula's chest tightened. *I can't tell her now—not until I know the truth. It would only worry her.* "I can't be sure." Feigning calm, she plucked a fingerling potato from the plate, biting into it. "When was the last time you heard from him?"

"It was before the attack on the manor. He said he was going on a special mission. He wouldn't say where."

Sweet mother of hell. I could have slaughtered Massu, the boy with the spaceship drawings.

Cera cocked her head. "Are you okay? You look ill."

"I'm—I'm okay." Ursula put down her fork, staring at the now empty tray of food. "I'm just feeling a bit queasy from everything that happened today."

"Of course." Cera plopped the dome back on the tray. "I'll let you get some rest."

"Thank you."

"I'll be back later with some food. I must check on the lord now." Tray in hand, Cera slipped out of the room.

But Ursula knew she wouldn't get any rest, not with her thoughts roiling like storm clouds. Bael hated her, the lords wanted her dead, and she may have killed the beloved brother of her only ally.

And what the hell had happened earlier, with that voice in her head? *Kill the king?* It had sounded so familiar, like it was a part of her very being.

Ursula pulled off her dress, dropping it on the floor, then kicked off her shoes. Exhaustion burned through her body, and she longed for sleep. In her underwear, she curled up in the corner of the sofa and pulled a downy white blanket over herself.

Loneliness tightened its fingers around her heart. If she'd been a normal person—one with memories—she'd probably take this opportunity to recall the times that her mother had looked after her, bandaged skinned knees or quieted her fears. Those sort of memories would soothe her soul, she imagined.

Instead, the best she could do was think of Zee, with a champagne cocktail and a fashion magazine. She missed her friend terribly.

In the darkness beyond the windows, Astra glowed faintly, and the clouds still twisted and writhed around it. Now that she'd learned what they were, the clouds no longer seemed quite so beautiful. Each vortex, each tendril, was a flock of moths fleeing in terror from a hungry bat.

She closed her eyes, and in her mind's eye, streams of moths whirled in frantic eddies.

She was one of them now—a moth hunted by Nyxobas's creatures.

CHAPTER 13

Curled up on the sofa, Ursula awoke with a start, adrenaline flooding her veins. What had roused her?

She scanned the room. Nothing seemed amiss—nothing had moved, not a single Grecian urn out of place. And yet, the hair on her neck stood on end.

An uneasy feeling licked at the back of her mind, telling her that someone was *watching* her.

Could someone have entered the room while she'd slept? She lay perfectly still, pretending to sleep, searching the darkness through slitted eyes. Had one of the demon lords come for revenge?

You're just paranoid, Ursula. Probably Emerazel's mind tricks, fucking with you.

Then, she caught a flicker of movement in the darkness outside her window. *Shadow magic.* Her pulse raced.

Not paranoid after all.

She opened her eyes wider, straining to see through the swirls of magic. She pushed up onto her elbows, desperately searching for a plan. Without so much as a corkscrew, what would she use to fight? Urns? Not to mention the fact that she was wearing nothing but lace knickers and a bra under her blanket. *Please don't let it be Nyxobas or any of the other perverts.* As she stared outside, the magic thinned, revealing an enormous lunar bat.

It hovered in front of the window, wings beating silently, blood-red eyes and wings of the color of bone. Something moved on its back—a rider dressed in gray. He straightened, then flung a sticky black substance against the window in front of her. Then, in a single silky motion, he aimed a small crossbow at her.

Panic stole her breath. *What the fuck is going on?*

She threw herself from the sofa.

The black tar exploded, shattering the window in a spray of glass that ripped into her skin.

Curling into a ball, Ursula tried to shield her body from the crossbow. Her stomach clenched as she heard the soft *whirr* of the arrow flying through the air.

Her heart raced. She waited for the thunk of the bolt when it struck her, the searing jolt of pain, the tearing of her flesh.

Instead, she felt only the sharp ringing in her ears from the blast.

When she opened her eyes, the rider had disappeared into the night. She gaped at the remaining shards of glass. The bolt had missed her. Why? It's not like she'd been a moving target.

She rose to her knees and glanced down at her body, at the crimson streaks cutting across her pale flesh. She'd been cut all over by the glass. But at least that was the worst of it.

Still, she couldn't exactly forget about it. The rider had left a gaping hole in the bottom of the window, and anyone could return to finish her off. She slipped into her shoes, then slipped behind the sofa. Blood dripped from her cuts, staining the floor. Injured or not, she had to protect herself. Now.

Using the couch as a shield, she pushed it closer to the window, grunting as she shifted it. *Not only can they enter into my quarters,* she thought, *but they can see me here, too.* Suddenly, she felt very exposed.

When she'd finished pushing the couch, it blocked the bottom of the hole, but she still had more work to do. A thin sheen of sweat rose on her forehead. *A moth hunted by the creatures of Nyxobas.*

With one eye on the window in case the rider returned, she crossed to an armchair on the other side of the room. She pushed it across the floor, straining her muscles. Sweat dripped down her skin, mingling with the blood. A combination of adrenaline and brute strength allowed her to lever it on top of the sofa with a pained groan.

The sofa and chair together covered most of the window, and a second armchair added extra support to the structure. *Not ideal, but better than nothing.*

She stepped back and took a shaky breath. With the adrenaline draining from her system, the cuts in her skin began to burn. She ran a hand over her bare abdomen, smearing blood across her fingers.

What the hell had just happened? The rider had practically been at point-blank range, but still missed. Could this be only the first volley before a second attack?

Or maybe, someone wanted to frighten her, to flush her out of the quarters. Nothing protected the bridge to the lion atrium—an ideal spot for an assassin to hide.

Ursula turned in a slow circle, searching for the bolt. She'd heard it fly from the crossbow. Maybe it would hold some sort of clue.

As she turned toward the portrait of that dark-eyed woman, she froze. There, in the center of the painting, a bolt jutted into the air.

She crept cautiously closer, examining the weapon. It was carved from black wood. Ebony maybe. As she stepped closer, she could see that something had been wrapped around it—parchment.

This hadn't been an attempt on her life. Someone had wanted to deliver a message.

Ignoring the pain that seared her skin, she pulled the bolt from the wall and peeled off the parchment. When she unfurled it, she found a message scrawled in black ink:

YOU ARE NOT WELCOME HERE, HOUND. THIS IS YOUR ONLY WARNING. NEXT TIME, WE WILL NOT MISS.

CHAPTER 14

The door to her quarters flung open with a bang.

Instinctively Ursula dove behind the bar, her knees and palms scraping over glass shards. She groaned in pain.

"What in the seven hells is going on in here?" Bael's voice boomed through the room. Ursula exhaled, rising unsteadily. Maybe Bael hated her for being the enemy, but he viewed it as his job to protect her. She rose unsteadily and crossed in front of the bar.

He stood in the living room, dark magic swirling around him, wearing nothing but a pair of black shorts. He held an enormous broadsword, and the cold battle fury blazing in his eyes made her stomach clench. "Are they gone?"

"Yes. I think so."

His chest was bound in bandages, but it didn't hide his perfect, chiseled body. And peeking out from the bandages, she could see glimpses of his tattoos—a crescent moon, a pointed star, a lightning bolt, sharp as a blade. Terrifying—but magnificent to behold nonetheless.

He gazed at her, some of the fury fading from his eyes. Concern flickered across his features. "You're hurt."

She nodded. As the adrenaline left her body, her teeth began to chatter. "There was a lot of broken glass."

He crossed the room in a blur of shadow, dropping his sword on a chair. In the next second, Bael's strong hands were around her waist.

Surprise flickered through her. Gently, he lifted her onto the top of the bar, careful not to touch her wounds. He examined her skin, pulling out a shard of glass from just below her ribs. She clenched her teeth, trying not to cry out at the pain. A warrior like Bael wouldn't be impressed by a load of whining. For a man with such large hands, she had to marvel at the nimbleness of his fingers as he plucked one tiny shard of glass after another from her skin. A deep concentration furrowed his brow, and he worked silently, like an expert craftsman.

When he'd finished, he gazed into her eyes, resting his hands on the counter on either side of her legs. For the first time, she saw a hint of softness in his glacial eyes. "You're withstanding the pain remarkably well."

She swallowed hard. His otherworldly beauty was distracting, and she could feel the warmth radiating from his body. If she hadn't been covered in blood and cuts, she wasn't sure she would have been able to stop herself from pressing herself against him.

Flustered, she blurted the first thing that came to her mind. "I'm quite badass, actually."

She cringed. *Idiot.*

His brow knitted with confusion. "Right. Well, I'm going to heal you with my magic. When I'm done, I want you to tell me exactly what happened."

She nodded, watching as he traced his fingertips just below some of the cuts in her skin. His magic caressed her skin, soothing her pain. As she closed her eyes, the shadow magic licked at her skin, then seeped deeper into her body. Her heart sped up, and the waves of pleasure dizzied her. An image rose in her mind of a sandstone temple, gleaming in the sun.

Her eyes fluttered open, and before she could think better of it, she touched the palm of her hand to his cheek.

Nearly imperceptibly, he leaned into her. His gray eyes roamed over her bare skin. With a hoarse voice, he asked, "What happened? What did they do to you?"

She dropped her hand. "A bat flew up to the window and threw some sort of bomb against it."

His brow furrowed. "A bat threw a bomb on your window?"

"No... No, I mean." Bael's bare skin and his closeness was distracting. Her pulse raced, and her cheeks flushed. Could a demon tell when you were turned on? *Probably.* "Someone rode it."

"The rider didn't come in to attack you?"

"No. He just sent a bolt through the window with a warning about how I don't belong."

Bael backed away from her, glancing at the punctured portrait. "What happened to your clothes?"

She shrugged. "I was asleep. I wasn't expecting any visitors."

"Are you okay now?"

"Completely knackered, but unharmed. Now that you've healed me."

He turned, studying the broken window. "You made a barricade from the sofa and chairs."

"I was worried they might try to come in, and I didn't want them to see me."

"That was smart." Suddenly shy, he wouldn't meet her gaze. Without the cuts, her nudity seemed to bother him. "Where's the note?"

She slid off the bar, then pointed at the floor where she'd dropped it. "It's right there."

He reached down, snatching it off the floor, along with the bolt. "I hope you didn't touch it. It could be cursed."

"But it's okay for you to hold it?"

Ignoring her, he inspected the wood. "So he blew out the glass and then shot at you with the crossbow."

"Exactly." *Why do I get the feeling that Bael knows more about this particular method of assassination than he's letting on?*

"And he didn't hit you?" Bael scanned the room.

"No."

He shook his head, still searching the floor for something. "That rider is a dead man."

"You're going to kill him for trying to murder me?"

"I don't need to. His lord will." He glanced again at the painting of the dark-eyed beauty.

"For not assassinating me?" Ursula asked. Blood still covered her body, and a chill washed over her skin. Shivering, she crossed her arms.

"It is the law here. Failure to complete a mission is punishable by death." For a second, his gaze flicked to her, then he sucked in a sharp breath, glancing at the painting of the beautiful woman. His pale eyes shined in the dim light of the candle.

"Have you executed any oneiroi because they didn't complete a mission?"

"I follow the law." Slowly, he crossed to the painting. He reached out to touch the canvas, running his fingertips over the tear.

Ursula frowned. "Why are the laws so draconian?"

"Nyxobas provides order in the chaos. Before he arrived here, the oneiroi were lawless. Vengeance and blood feuds ruled the darkness. The god of night has civilized them."

"Yeah, it seems really civilized here, with all the murder and assassinations."

"We have our own code." His fingers traced over the hole in the painting.

"Why can't the oneiroi speak your name? I don't see what that has to do with security."

His gaze slid to Ursula, his eyes so black they might have been direct conduits to Nyxobas's void. "My name was given to me by the god himself. Only the brethren may utter it." Bael crossed his arms over his mammoth chest. "The bolt tore the painting."

"Right. I hope it wasn't valuable."

He fell silent for a moment, his jaw working. "Perhaps you should get dressed."

"You're not dressed, either," she pointed out. She glanced down at herself, at the sticky blood still covering her skin. "I need to bathe before I put anything on. But I still have questions for you. Come with me."

"You want me to bathe with you?"

Her cheeks flushed. "That's not what I meant. I'll leave the door open. You can stand outside."

He nodded curtly. "I'll be staying here tonight. To stand guard."

A wave of relief washed over her. "Perfect. Thank you." She crossed to the bathroom, leaving the door partially open. Bael's presence both unnerved and calmed her at the same time, but she still had a million things to ask him. She leaned over the bath, turning on the water. Steam filled the room, and she unhooked her bra, sticky with blood, then stepped out of her knickers.

As the bath filled with warm water, she stepped in. "I saw your bandages," she said, calling to him. "Are you hurt?"

He paused a moment before answering. "Without my wings, I can't use magic to heal myself."

She grabbed the bar of lavender soap, lathering her arms. Bael's healing magic had left not a single scar on her skin. "I don't understand how you plan to fight the champions with two bloody holes in your back. You know you're not invincible. You could die trying to keep your manor."

"It's not like I have any other choice. If I lose, Hothgar and Abrax will hunt me down. My existence will always be a threat to them."

She splashed the water over her soapy skin, and her blood stained the water pink. Suds dripped off her shoulders and breasts. "Why would your existence be a threat to them?"

"Because Nyxobas chose me to be his Sword. He didn't chose them. And I am the strongest warrior the Shadow Realm has ever known."

"Not really big on humility, are you?" He was silent for a moment. "I'm starting to learn. I'm no longer as strong as I was." He cleared his throat. "I'll return in a moment."

Outside the bathroom, the faint sounds of tinkling glass filtered through the air.

Ursula's mind churned. Bael was obviously trying to fulfill his role as protector—whether he liked her or not, it was his duty. But how much could he really do—especially with this tournament hanging over his head? He might have been the best fighter the shadow world had ever known at one point. But now, he wasn't a match for immortals.

She pushed the thoughts to the back of her skull, and rose from the bath. Water trickled from her skin. She leaned over, unplugging the bath.

As goosebumps rose on her skin, it occurred to her that she'd failed to bring any clothes inside the bathroom. *Idiot.*

She grabbed a towel, drying off. "I don't suppose you could grab me some clothes?"

He cleared his throat. "Right. Clothes."

Clearly, a lord of Nyxobas was unused to fetching women's dresses.

She shivered. If the lords were going to keep coming after her, maybe she'd have to find a new place to live. The manor was huge—surely there were some hidden depths where she could remain unnoticed.

The door creaked open another inch, and Bael thrust a dress through. She grabbed it from him. "Thank you."

She unfurled the dress—black lace with embroidered swirls that climbed up the sheer bodice. Way too fancy for hanging around in a half-demolished house, but she couldn't expect Bael to be an expert on women's clothes. Nor could she have expected him to include knickers and a bra—which he didn't.

She stepped into the living room, eying the floor. He'd cleared up all the glass. Starlight washed his deep golden skin in silver.

For just a moment, Bael's eyes roamed over her body, then he nodded at the remaining sofa. "Get some rest. I'll keep watch to make sure no one returns for you."

"This place is huge. Why don't we go to another part of the building?"

"You're safe as long as I'm here."

"You need to sleep, too."

He cut her a sharp look. "I have lived over twenty-two thousand years. I can survive a night without sleep."

As she crossed to the sofa, he sat in an armchair facing the window, arms folded.

She dropped into the sofa, pulling a soft blanket over her body. "Twenty-two thousand years?" The number made her dizzy. "Where do you come from, anyway?" "Canaan."

Okay. Bael was maybe a few millennia behind the times, but it must be hard to keep up with things when you're twenty-two thousand years old.

Still, despite his staggering age, he wasn't one of the original fallen. They'd arrived on Earth a hundred thousand years ago. "Was your father a high demon? Or your mother?"

"You have a lot of questions for someone who is supposed to be sleeping."

Her muscles ached, and she pulled the blanket tighter over her shoulders. "I can't answer the questions about myself, so I have to satisfy myself with learning about other people. And you have a lot of history to cover."

"We're not going to cover my history," he said tersely.

"Fine."

A silence fell over the room, and she closed her eyes, trying to sleep, but her tense muscles wouldn't relax.

After another moment, Bael spoke again, more softly this time. "What do you remember of your youth?"

She shook her head. "Only brief flickers, like an old film strip. Fields with aster and blue wildflowers. I usually try to paint them in the places where I've lived, to remind me of... wherever I'm from. Must be some rural part of England, because there aren't exactly many fields of wildflowers in London. But the flowers feel like home."

"I saw them in your room. In New York, after you roused me from a very long sleep in your attic."

What she didn't add was that there was another side to her. The flowers were home, but sometimes she longed for the night sky, to feel the cold wind over her skin and to escape into the darkness. To hide from the world.

"Is that all you remember?" he asked softly.

"A few more things. Burning walls. Sometimes I remember a woman who could use a sword, like me. I'm guessing that was my mum."

"A warrior woman."

"Just like me."

"Warrior women are a rarity in the Shadow Realm. Perhaps that's why Nyxobas is so interested in you."

"Maybe. Though I'm not doing much fighting here."

"It seems you have no family now."

"Nope. None that I know of."

He glanced at her. "Sleep. I will watch over you."

Her eyes began to drift closed, and as she fell asleep, she dreamt of soft grasses tickling her ankles, and air thick with humidity.

CHAPTER 15

The clinking of glasses jolted Ursula awake.

In the pale starlight, Cera stood over her. "It's time to get up. I've brought you breakfast."

Ursula rubbed her eyes, trying to bring the room into focus. A familiar, delicious scent wafted through the air.

"Is that...coffee?"

Cera flashed her a toothy smile. "I thought you might like some. The lord said you had a difficult night."

"You're the best." She sat up, stretching her arms above her head. She glanced around the room. Surprise flickered through her. She no longer lay on the sofa in the living room. Someone had brought her up to the bedroom while she'd slept and tucked her under the violet duvet.

"How did I get here?"

Cera dropped a flannel robe next to her on the bed. "How should I know?"

"Did Bael carry me up here? I don't remember it."

"The lord is very strong and swift. I'm sure he could have carried you while you slept." She frowned. "Are you sleeping in one of your finest gowns?"

"Bael chose it."

Smirking, Cera arched an eyebrow. "Did he, now?"

"Just—I needed something to wear. I was in my—never mind." Ursula pushed off her blanket and grabbed a cup of steaming, black coffee. She took a sip of the hot brew, letting it energize her. Beside the carafe of coffee lay a basket of warm bread and butter. Her mouth watered, and she bit into a fresh roll.

"Fill your belly," said Cera. "Then come downstairs when you're dressed in something more appropriate."

Ursula ate her way through several rolls and another cup of coffee, taking care not to get crumbs all over the bed. When she'd had her fill, she pulled off her gown and selected a simpler dress—gray cotton with a deep V neck.

As she made her way downstairs, she combed her fingers through her hair to tidy it.

In the middle of the living room, she found two oneiroi men standing next to Cera. Just outside the window, a third rode on the back of a lunar bat.

Ursula's muscles tensed. "What's going on?"

"It's only Sotz," said Cera. "He's helping with the window replacement."

Ursula nodded, staring as Sotz clutched a rope in his feet. As she moved closer to the window, she saw that a large plate of glass dangled at the other end of the rope.

At the direction of the oneiroi workmen, Sotz flew higher, lifting the glass. With a volley of shouts and frantic gestures, the men were able to maneuver the pane into the room. Ursula watched as the workmen carefully fitted the window into place, Sotz hovering just outside. The rider on Sotz's back slowly adjusted his position in a fascinating display of control.

"Ursula." Cera touched her arm. "I brought you a present."

Ursula smiled. "You did? What for?"

"Not my idea. The lord told me to give it to you. He thought it might keep you busy."

"Right. So I won't stab anyone else, presumably."

"That would be for the best." Cera scurried off toward the hall. When she returned, she carried a shiny black bag.

Ursula's eyebrows rose. *More clothes?*

"The lord said you liked to paint."

A smile curled her lips. "The lord is right."

Cera reached into the bag, pulling out brushes and tubes of paint. Lastly, she pulled out a small canvas stretched over a wooden frame. "He said if you want a larger canvas, you should let him know."

"This is such a lovely present."

"The lord provides," said Cera.

The two oneiroi workmen approached. The smaller of them met Ursula's gaze. "The window is in—airtight. The lord protected all the windows with his magic. Nothing will destroy the glass now. You're safe inside here."

"Thank you so much," she said. *Thank the gods.* She wouldn't have been able to relax in here, knowing that a man on a giant bat could shatter the glass at any moment.

As Sotz flew off outside, the two workmen left the apartment.

Cera turned back to Ursula with a mischievous grin. "The lord spent the night in your quarters."

"Not like that."

Cera's eyes widened. "He hasn't come in here in centuries. I think it's because it pains him to see the portrait."

Ursula frowned, glancing at the spot on the wall where the portrait had hung. Someone had removed it during the night. "Of the woman? Why?"

Cera's hand flew to her mouth. "I should not have spoken."

Well, now I have to know. She touched Cera's arm. "You can tell me. Who else am I going to tell? You're my only friend here."

Cera's eyes shifted frantically from side to side. She was obviously trying to decide how much she was allowed to tell Ursula.

Finally, she whispered, "The lord's wife, gods protect her soul."

Her jaw dropped. "He was married? I had no idea. Did she die in the attack?"

"No. It was long ago, long before my time. I should never have said anything." Cera backed toward the door. "It's not my place to talk about the lord's life."

Her face even paler than usual, Cera hurried out the door, slamming it behind her.

CHAPTER 16

On the day of the Selection of Champions, Ursula's stomach was twisted in knots. She filled the bath with warm, lavender-scented water, trying to soothe away her nerves, but one terrifying thought rang loudly in her skull.

Today, she would find out exactly who Bael had to kill.

If he failed, he'd forfeit his life. Terrifying and gruff as he might be, she didn't want him to die. And moreover, if he lost, she'd be joining him in the afterworld.

Or worse—Abrax would enslave her for an eternity of sadistic torment.

As she soaked her body in the bath, Cera's voice rang out from the living room. "Hello? Ursula?"

"In the bath!" she shouted.

"Good. You've started preparing yourself. I've brought you a new dress for the ceremony. Everything must be perfect!" she shouted. "We must help the lord by making everything perfect!"

Ursula winced at the shrill tone. *Apparently, I'm not the only one plagued by nerves.* She rose from the bath, grabbing a towel. She wrapped it around herself and then stepped into the living room.

Wearing the gray coat, Cera stood in the center of the room, her knuckles white as she clutched a box. A bag hung over one of her arms. "I have pressed the lord's clothes to perfection. He will have not a wrinkle on him before the other lords. Mortal or not, they will know his glory through his divine beauty." Her eyes were wide, slightly frantic.

Ursula held up the towel with one hand, taking the box from Cera with the other. She flashed a placating smile. The little oneiroi was losing it.

Still, Cera wasn't kidding about Bael's divine beauty, though Ursula wasn't going to admit it.

She dropped the box on a chair. "Why doesn't Bael look like a demon, like the other lords? They all have horns and creepy eyes."

"Nothing creepy about silver eyes," snapped Cera. "But as for how the lord looks, you'd do best to mind your own business. Open the box."

With one hand, Ursula pried off the top of the box. Tucked neatly inside were tiny silver knickers, and a dress of a gorgeous midnight blue, the fabric so thin and sheer it almost seemed enchanted.

"Wow," said Ursula. "This looks amazing."

She saw the beaming smile on Cera's face before the oneiroi turned around to give her privacy. "All the great ladies will be dressed in their finest clothes. I wouldn't want Abelda House to fall short."

Ursula pulled off her towel, then stepped into the lacy silver underwear. When she picked up the dress, she gasped. It was stunning—a delicate gown, dappled with silver gems around the belted waist. She pulled it over her head, and the silky fabric brushed over her thighs. Like the dress she'd worn before, a V neck plunged down to her belly button. The sheer fabric gathered at the waist, providing just enough coverage for her lower half. But if she extended a leg, she saw that the dress had a slit all the way up to the top of her thigh.

"Gorgeous," she said.

Cera turned, grinning. "I knew it would be perfect. It's skimpier than the ladies of the Shadow Realm wear, but you're a hellhound. Everyone will expect you to be a harlot anyway," she chirped, rifling around in her bag.

Before Ursula could come up with a retort, Cera was standing before her, wielding eyeliner. "Sit."

Ursula did as instructed, and Cera spent the next two minutes attacking her face with eye makeup, blush, and a berry lipstick. When she'd finished, she packed away the makeup, and pulled out a pair of black heels and a new cloak made of dark silver feathers that shimmered as it moved. Ursula pulled the cloak around her shoulders. She plucked the silver ring off the bar, shoving it into the cloak's pocket.

"What was that?" Cera asked suspiciously.

"Just my lucky charm. I think I might need it tonight." Her eyes flicked to the window, searching for signs of the rising sun. Dread welled in her chest.

When the sun sets over Lacus Mortis... For the finishing touch, Cera slid a sparkling silver headband onto Ursula's head. "Splendid," she purred, stepping back to admire her work.

Ursula slipped into the heels. Somehow, she felt at home in these clothes.

Cera arched a cautionary eyebrow. "My only request is that you don't destroy the clothes through bloodshed and mayhem."

Ursula grinned. "I'll do my best."

Cera scowled. "Please try to behave appropriately when you meet the lords' wives."

Cera tilted her head. "Do they all have wives apart from Bael?"

"Most do. It can get pretty lonely on the crater's rim."

"I've noticed, I was going to ask if there were any books I could read. I don't think I can make a shank from the pages of a novel."

Cera frowned. "A what?"

"A shank, you know, like what prisoners make to stab—" *Abort, Ursula. Abort!* "I mean, since Bael said to remove anything I could use as a weapon. Surely books are harmless."

Cera nodded slowly. "There's a library I can take you to tomorrow, if you like." She glanced at the clock. "It's time for us to leave. You can eat at the ceremony."

Ursula's stomach rumbled. The last thing she'd eaten was a soup made from those strange, glowing mushrooms.

Cera crossed over to the door, flinging it open. "Come along!"

Ursula hurried to keep up with Cera as she made her way across the windswept bridge and into the atrium. There, the elevator waited for them.

Cera gave a little bow outside the elevator. "Good luck."

Ursula pulled open the door, stepping inside. The door clicked shut. "Thank you, Cera."

As the cage rose slowly on its chain, her chest clenched. Tonight, she'd be facing all the lords again, and getting an eyeful of the champions. She didn't know what to expect, but she imagined they'd be terrifying.

She shoved her hand into the cloak's pocket, running her fingertips over the smooth silver ring. It seemed to center her.

The elevator creaked up past one flight after another of shattered glass, twisted steel beams, and layers of gray ash.

Bael was an ancient, stunningly powerful demon. And maybe he was mortal right now, but he had enough magic and brute strength on his side to fix this place up. Still, he'd chosen to leave the damage untouched.

Perhaps he wanted to leave it as a testament to his rage, fuel for his fury.

Ursula could only hope that was enough for him to win in a battle against the champions.

* * *

THE ELEVATOR LIFTED onto the roof. Bael stood before her, the cold wind feathering a few strands of hair across his face. He pulled open the elevator door, and she stepped out.

He wore fitted black clothes with a high mandarin collar. A dark cloak —feather at the shoulders—was held together over his enormous chest with silver chains and a lion insignia.

Starlight glinted in his pale eyes.

He looked every inch the military leader. At the sight of him, hope sparked in her mind. *He looks like he can actually win this thing.*

As she stepped onto the roof, a frigid wind toyed with the hem of her dress, lifting it into the air. The delicate fabric floated in the breeze.

"You look..." he said, his gaze trailing down to her leg, exposed in the breeze. "Exactly as you should."

That... might be a compliment. "And how is it that I should look?"

"Stunning."

A blush warmed her cheeks. "Thank you. It's nice to see you in some clothes, after you were traipsing around in your smalls all night."

Bael's mouth twitched with the hint of a smile before he lifted his fingers to whistle for the carriage.

The faintest hint of purple stained the sky, and she shuddered, watching as the team of bats whisked the carriage before the moon.

Ursula bit her lip. "So am I to be subservient again, or do I get to act on my own volition this evening?"

With a gentle scraping noise, the carriage landed on the rooftop.

Bael's jaw tensed. "You must act subservient. All the women are, and you mustn't draw attention to yourself."

Of course they are. She heaved a deep sigh, fighting the urge to ask him about his wife. Even in the painting, the determined look in the woman's eye told Ursula she had never been subservient.

Bael pulled open the carriage door, and she stepped inside.

"Can you tell me what to expect tonight?" she asked.

Bael climbed in, sitting across from her. "As you wish. We're going to the hall of lords. There will be a feast. The lords will choose their champions, apart from me, of course. Hothgar will announce the rules of the melee. Then we will leave. Hopefully alive."

Well, that inspires confidence.

"Do I get a dagger again?"

One of Bael's eyebrows rose. "After last time? No. Absolutely not."

She rubbed the solid ring in her pocket. "You're going to leave me entirely unprotected, then. And if Abrax decides he wants to get me alone—"

"I'll protect you."

"You said I don't deserve your protection."

He winced. "I will protect you," he said again.

She leaned forward, studying him. "Why don't you choose me as your champion?"

Surprise flickered across his features, his eyes widening. "Why in the name of the dark god would I do that?"

"The other lords have better odds with five champions each. You've only got one. If I fight with you, it doubles our chances of winning, right?"

He shook his head. "You misunderstand. There will only be one left alive at the end," he said. "None of the other champions will be left alive by the end of the tournament. I would have to kill you."

She swallowed hard. "You're injured. I could take your place, then. I may have a better chance than you."

His eyes bored into her. "Don't be absurd."

Maybe he has a point. She might be pretty good with a sword, but she was no match for someone who'd been fighting for twenty-two thousand years. And moreover, she lacked a weapon and her firepower.

His eyes darkened. "Tell me you won't call attention to yourself this evening. That you won't attack anyone."

"I can see you're still upset about the kerfuffle with Nyxobas."

"Tell me."

"Fine. I'll do what you say." *Within reason.*

CHAPTER 17

*T*he carriage plunged lower and lower through the air, and Ursula gripped the seat to steady herself. They were descending all the way to where Asta met the crater floor.

With a lurch, the carriage touched down on a rocky avenue.

She peered out the window at a long line of carriages. As the bats inched forward slowly on their claws, Ursula gazed out at the desolate lunar landscape. Apart from Asta's violet light, darkness shrouded the land. Deep fissures cut into the stone around the base of the spire.

Their carriage slowly pulled forward to a covered entrance, and two footmen in gray jackets hurried out to open their door.

Bael stepped out, holding open the door for her. He offered her his hand as she stepped out.

Ever the gentleman.

This close to the ground, Asta's crystal was a deep mulberry, the color of a bruise. Above them, gray clouds of moths swirled and danced, blotting out the stars.

"This way," said Bael.

A walkway, lit by glowing mushrooms, led to the arched entrance. Ursula walked by Bael's side, rubbing the silver ring between her fingers.

Through the doorway, she stepped into an enormous hall, carved from the purple crystal. The walls arched at least two hundred feet above them, and great clusters of glowing mushrooms hung from the ceiling like chandeliers. Long, onyx tables, populated by demons filled much of the hall. An open space had been left in the center, like a dance floor. By Bael's side, she walked further into the center of the hall.

At the far end of the massive room, a single table stood on a dais. Eleven lords sat at the table, proudly enthroned in silver chairs. Abrax glared at her, licking his lips, and a shudder ran up her spine. No one here seemed to know or care that he'd tried to overthrow the entire Shadow Realm. Apparently, losing your wings was unforgivable, but a full-fledged divine coup was okay, assuming you were a demigod.

In the center of the table, in the largest chair, sat Hothgar. A gavel lay on the table before him.

Ursula frowned. *That should be Bael's spot.* Until Abrax had stolen his wings, Bael was Nyxobas's Sword, the most senior of all the lords.

Ursula looked at the whorls of shadow magic behind the table. *Nyxobas.* Behind the powerful clouds of magic, she'd nearly missed him. He sat in a silver throne, half-shrouded by writhing shadows. As a swirl of magic cleared, his eyes—two dark abysses—seemed to stare right at her. At the sight of him, dread tightened its grip on her heart.

A small oneiroi hurried up to them.

"Milord," she said with a deep bow to Bael before turning to Ursula. Her eyes trailed down to Ursula's dress, and the shockingly sheer fabric that hung below her cloak. The oneiroi scowled, then plastered a smile on her face once again. "Please follow me, milady. The lord will be seated at the table of nobles."

Ursula looked to Bael for help, but he was already moving toward the dais, leaving her behind.

"Right this way," the oneiroi chirped, beckoning her forward.

Ursula took a deep breath. *Let's do this.*

She quickened her pace to keep up with the oneiroi, who navigated between the sea of demons, seated at the tables. Some appeared entirely human—and shockingly beautiful. Others sported more demonic features: horns, talons, or even eyes the color of blood. And yet they were beautiful in their own ways, too. Men with chiseled features, women in glittering gowns, their bodies lithe and delicate. Since arriving here not long ago and spending time with Cera, her definition of beauty seemed to be expanding.

She surveyed the guests—gowns of dusky purple, midnight blue, or shimmering black seemed to be the favored colors. Some women had jewels threaded into their hair, and many of the men wore dark suits with silver accents.

And each one of the demons stared at Ursula as she passed their tables.

Obviously, word had spread about her presence. The hellhound harlot. *Wait till they see the whole dress.*

Avoiding their stares, Ursula followed the oneiroi deeper into the hall, closer to the platform. Finally the oneiroi stopped, and gestured to an empty chair at a long table, filled with female demons sporting totally demonic features: horns, talons, white eyes, sharp teeth. All beautiful. All dripping with diamonds. And all staring right at her.

The oneiroi pulled out a chair by a striking woman whose jet-black hair tumbled over a white gown.

"Your seat, milady." The oneiroi held out a hand. "May I take your cloak?"

Ursula unclasped the cloak, pulling it off. Before she handed it to the oneiroi, she snatched the silver ring from her pocket.

As the other women took in Ursula's daring gown, they gasped audibly.

Ursula's shoulders tensed. *That's me. The hellhound harlot.* She rubbed the ring between her fingers.

She tried to force what she imagined was a pleasant expression onto her face and sat down next to the raven-haired woman. Immediately to the right of her sat a striking woman with flowing black hair. Her skin was so pale, it could have been carved from marble or alabaster. Ursula almost mistook her for human until she glimpsed a flash of sharp fangs. *A goth princess.*

To Ursula's left sat a woman in a dark blue dress. Two long blond braids draped over her formidable bosom—appropriately covered in opaque fabric. *Unlike my gown.* But what most drew Ursula's eye were the delicately curled horns growing from the woman's forehead. Their tips had been capped with gold. Overall, she looked like some kind of terrifying Viking.

As Ursula sat, the women turned away from her. Her eyes flicked up to the dais, and she watched Bael take his seat at the end of the nobles' table. It must really irk him to watch Hothgar steal his role as Sword.

The goth princess raised a delicate white arm. "So who will be joining the pool?"

Around the table, the demonesses began plucking off their jewelry, tossing them onto a plate in the center of the table—enormous diamonds, black opals, and deep violet gemstones so rare, Ursula didn't even know what to call them.

Her eyes widened. There, on a silver plate in the center of the table, lay a pile of carelessly discarded jewels that were probably worth more than the GDP of a small nation.

Goth Princess rubbed her hands together. "Is everyone clear on the rules?"

The Viking raised a hand. "The one who picks the winner gets the whole pot. Yes?"

Goth Princes sighed. "No, a quarter of the pot goes to whomever chooses the most finalists in the melee, a quarter goes to the one who picks the winner of the race, and the remaining half goes to whomever picks the winner of the duels."

The Viking grinned. "This is going to be so exciting. We haven't had a proper tournament in ages."

A woman whose silver hair tumbled over a black gown narrowed her eyes at Ursula. She drummed long, pearly talons on the table. "Did you want to join the pool, hellhound?" The woman's eyes were nearly as pale as her skin, framed by black lashes. "You'll have to contribute if you want to join."

Ursula tried to flash a friendly smile. She knew how rich, glamorous chicks worked. They were perfectly happy to be your best friend, as long as you never threatened to outshine them. *Best to be humble in this crowd.* "I'm afraid I have nothing of value to offer."

Talons nodded approvingly.

The Viking's brow furrowed. "So what do we do about Bael?"

"What about him?" asked Goth Princess.

Viking cocked her head. "He's already won a tournament before. He's older than the rest. I don't think it's fair to pick him for the final winner."

The princess nodded. "Excellent point. Can we all agree to leave the Lord of Albelda off the ballot, mortal as he might be?"

Around the table, the women nodded. No one wanted to annoy Goth Princess.

Viking flicked one of her braids behind her shoulders. "I still can't believe that he lost his house. Such a shame. From what I understand, he was the only one of the lords who actually knew how to pleasure a woman."

"Not that his skill in bed made a difference." Talons sighed, eying Ursula. "He was never going to marry again. I believe he never quite got over Elissa."

Viking's eyes widened. "I heard one of Borgerith's ogres ripped his wings out. Two millennia, and he was felled by an idiot ogre."

Ursula's chest clenched. *It was Abrax, you twats. Abrax ruined him.*

Goth Princess took a sip of champagne. "I'm not sure it was a wise decision for Nyxobas to appoint him Sword in the first place. You all know his background, I'm sure." She let her dark eyes wander to Ursula. "He was bound to snap at some point."

Ursula's face heated. *This arsehole knows he hasn't told me about his background. She is throwing some serious demon shade.*

The princess cocked her head, staring right at Ursula. "Bael might be a legendary warrior, but he's broken inside. Always has been."

They all nodded, then clinked their glasses in some kind of fucked-up toast.

Please get me out of here. She was quickly getting the impression that it was going to be *very* difficult to get through the night without hurting someone. For Bael's sake, she kept her mouth shut.

Viking stroked one of her braids. "Worst of all, my husband lost a third of his legion trying to drive Bael from his manor."

Goth Princess twirled the delicate stem of her glass between her fingers. "A travesty we weren't successful. Bael should have been sent to the void months ago—"

A loud banging from the dais interrupted her. All heads turned as Hothgar slammed his hammer down again, his eyes flicking to the Viking for just a moment.

"Tonight, the lords select their champions to determine who is worthy of Abelda mansion," he roared. "But now, it is time to feast!"

CHAPTER 18

A crew of oneiroi waiters bustled into the hall, carrying silver platters laden with food. A waiter pushed one of the trays between Ursula and Goth Princess, and her gaze slid to the roasted meat, seasoned with rosemary and garlic. *At least they know how to eat here.*

Her mouth watered at the sight of meat and potatoes—and the bowls of luminescent mushroom soup.

The waiter placed a bowl in front of Ursula, and she breathed in the rich, earthy scent. It looked terrifying, but smelled amazing, and her mouth was already watering. As he dropped a bowl before Goth Princess, he leaned in to ask, "Would you like bottle of wine for the table?"

Goth Princess's lip curled back from her fangs, and she snarled, "Would you like a bottle of wine for the table, *milady*."

The waiter nodded frantically, avoiding eye contact. "Milady, I'm sorry—"

"Stop talking and fill my glass," she snapped.

"Of course, milady."

Ursula glared at her. *Wanker.* Too bad there would be no tournament between the women of this table.

Ursula focused all her energy on keeping her mouth shut. A waiter bustled around the table, slicing up the meat and serving it on plates. Ursula waited until Goth Princess began cutting into her food and then

353

followed suit. The meat tasted as delicious as it smelled. Roast beef maybe? It wasn't ham, she was certain.

Viking raised her hand, snapping her fingers at one of the waiters. She pointed to her plate. "Is it from Nyxobas's stables?"

The waiter bowed. "Yes, milady. Strictly moth-fed around Asta, no supplements or additives."

Ursula stopped mid-chew, her stomach turning. "What kind of meat is this?"

The waiter bowed again. "Milady, it's bat-shoulder. Just slaughtered this afternoon." He flashed a proud smile.

She swallowed the lump of flesh in her mouth. *Maybe I'll just stick to the mushroom soup.*

She lifted a spoonful into her mouth, savoring the woodsy, garlicky flavor. *Perfect.*

She tried not to stare at Viking, who ripped through the bat-shoulder with the terrifying ferocity of a pit bull. *Maybe it's for the best we're not part of a tournament.*

Talons leaned across the table, her eyes locked on Goth Princess. "How was your vacation on Earth?"

"Glorious. We rented a little cottage on a private atoll in the Maldives. The water was amazing—beautiful night swimming. The locals were delicious."

"I'm so jealous," Viking cut in. "Hothgar's idea of romance is drinking five pints of blood and asking me to watch him rut with a human in a hayloft. He likes to control their minds, you know. Make them supplicate themselves before him. He makes them call him Nyxobas and praise his lunar staff."

"We know," said Talons. "The entire Shadow Realm knows."

Goth Princess shrugged. "Abrax does that, too. It's just what demon males do. Especially incubi, of course. He can't get enough of his little human playthings."

"I hate Hothgar," muttered Viking. "The last time he showed me any affection was our claiming ceremony. But it isn't a woman's place to complain to a husband. At least, not to his face."

"All demons want to dominate humans," said Goth Princess. She turned to Ursula. "You're basically human. I mean, you're a mortal demon. You have no powers here in the Shadow Realm."

Ursula paused, mid-spoonful. "What, now?"

"We know you're here to be someone's whore." Talons poked a finger in her face. "Is it Bael? Are you his consolation prize for the loss of his wings and his manor?"

Ursula cringed. "Can we go back to when you were ignoring me?"

Goth Princess narrowed her eyes. "What depraved things has he been making you do in that ruined manor of his?" She licked her fangs. "He is quite gorgeous, so I'm not sure that I'd mind if I were you."

Talons licked the soup off one of her curled claws. "He is reputed to be an amazing lover, you know. Not like Hogarth. Long ago, he was worshipped as a god in his home country. It could be worse for you."

Ursula frowned, and she glanced at Bael on the dais, sitting silently by the other lords. "I have no idea what you're talking about. He's a perfect gentleman."

Viking snorted. "You're an idiot. They don't exist."

Talons raised her champagne flute, smiling. "Demon males view all women as their property and playthings. And when it comes to weak little human women, that goes double. You're here as a harlot, my dear. We all know that."

Ursula could feel her face heating from anger. Just as she was about to indulge in a tirade, Hothgar banged his gavel from the dais.

"It is time to begin the Selection of the Champions. We will start with the most junior lords." He turned to the lord furthest from him, a cloaked man with milky-white skin and eyes like black pearls.

Hothgar raised his gavel. "Lord Vepar. you may nominate your five."

Vepar stood and spoke in a firm voice. "I nominate Inth from my legion."

A lanky demon in a full suit of silver armor entered from a side entrance, gripping a long spear. He strode into the empty space in the center of the hall, then bowed deeply toward the dais.

"Inth of the Vepar Legion. May Nyxobas grant you the grace of a shadow and the strength of a warrior."

As Inth finished bowing, inky tendrils of magic lifted from his body, curling toward Nyxobas.

"What is that?" asked Ursula.

"His immortality," said Talons. "It's not much of a fight to the death if no one can die."

"He'll get it back if he wins," said the Viking. "Except, he won't win."

His voice booming through the hall, Lord Vepar nominated the rest of his champions—all enormous men, shielded in silver armor.

Without seeing them fight, she couldn't quite gauge their prowess. Somehow, none of them seemed quite as formidable as Bael, but you couldn't always tell just by looking at someone. Some skinny men were just psychotic enough to put up a terrifying fight. In London, she'd once seen a slender Millwall F.C. fan bite the ear off a man in a Chelsea Football Club shirt.

Hothgar called upon one lord after another to nominate their five, and Ursula stared at the stream of muscled champions filling the center of the hall with a growing sense of dread. *Bael must kill all of them. He must cut through each warrior, and he's not even at full strength.*

Her panic only worsened as Hothgar called on the senior champions, whose warriors grew in stature. One—a near giant—sent trembles over the floor as he walked.

When Hothgar reached Bileth—the Demon-Bull— he paused for just a moment. "Lord Bileth. Are you prepared to nominate a champion?"

"I am," said Bileth, his deep voice filling the room. "I nominate my son, Sallos."

An enormous beast of a demon strode into the center of the room. Like his father, his white skin had an almost bluish tinge. He wore only a white fur kilt about his waist, revealing a muscled torso. In one hand, he gripped a massive axe. Ursula's stomach flipped. His weapon was as least five feet long, with a head of blue steel. She'd never seen Bael wield a weapon like that.

"Congratulations, Sallos. May Nyxobas—"

A door slammed open at the other end of the hall, cutting off Hothgar. Completely dressed in gray cloth, a stranger strode through the hall. A scarf covered most of his face, apart from a thin slit for his eyes. The entire hall stared.

"What is this interruption?" Hothgar bellowed.

He strode into the center of the hall, taking his place among the champions. "I wish to compete in the tournament." His scarf slightly muffled his voice, but his words were clear nonetheless.

"Who are you and on what grounds do you claim the chance to compete for Bael's manor?" roared Hothgar, rising from his chair. His cheeks had reddened, and fury sparked in his eyes. "This tournament is only open to the champions of the lords of Nyxobas."

"I am not a member of a lord's legion," said the intruder. "But by the law of the warrior, I request the chance to challenge a champion. I will take another's position." He turned to Sallos. "If there are any here brave enough to take on this challenge."

Before Hothgar could respond, Sallos raised his axe. "I accept."

Sallos circled the stranger, swinging the massive axe around his head like a drum major's baton. Ursula held her breath. The intruder didn't even have a weapon. What was he thinking? As Sallos neared striking range, the stranger dodged back. Sallos lifted his axe to strike, but the stranger dodged again.

"Fight me, you coward," Sallos shouted.

The stranger remained silent.

Sallos continued circling, thrusting, striking—while his opponent weaved and dodged, just out of reach.

Fascinated, Ursula stared. She had a perfect view of the fight from here. She could see the sheen of sweat on Sallos's forehead, but he continued to press his advantage.

From the lords' table, Hothgar called out, "You won't win by the grace of your dancing. A challenge can only be settled with blood."

A few of the lords chuckled. Apparently that comment passed for a joke in the Shadow Realm.

Dodging another strike, the intruder leapt backwards in a perfect backflip. When he landed, he'd deftly produced two daggers, one in each hand.

Ursula's throat tightened. *Bloody hell. He may be small, but he's agile as a gymnast.*

Sallos didn't seem to understand the threat. He threw back his head, laughing. "You think you're going to hurt me with those children's toys?"

The stranger merely stared at him, gripping his daggers.

Sallos advanced again, swinging the ax in great curving arcs. As he closed in on the intruder, he drove him closer to Ursula's table—so close, she could actually hear the whoosh of Sallos's blade as it sliced the air. She turned in her chair, her eyes locked on the fight.

When the stranger stood only a few feet away, he dodged toward Ursula. His foot caught on the fabric of her dress, tearing it. Her heart jumped into her throat as she watched the intruder fall to the floor. *Please don't die because of my dress.*

Instantly, Sallos charged, thundering at the fallen man like a bull at a toreador. Lifting the axe above his head, he prepared to strike the coup de grâce. But as the axe descended, the stranger rolled away.

He dodged the swing. Then, with a perfectly timed stroke, he slashed at Sallos's foot.

Sallos's face reddened, and he bellowed in pain. He spun to face his assailant, but the stranger was already on his feet, already out of reach.

Sallos charged forward, but stumbled as his foot gave way. His axe flailed wildly.

The stranger circled behind him, then dove for the floor, slashing at Sallos's other foot with his blade. Ursula cringed at the audible snap of a severed a tendon.

The stranger had crippled him.

Sallos fell to his knees with a bellow of pain. He gripped his battle axe, glaring at the stranger, eyes red with rage. "Come fight me like a man," he bellowed.

Ursula knew the fight was over, even if Sallos didn't.

The stranger circled him slowly. Sallos tried to lunge for him, but the stranger merely sidestepped behind him. In a flash of steel, the stranger's blade severed the sinews in the back of the Sallos's knee. The demon howled, fear and rage tearing from his throat. He twisted his body, trying to keep the stranger in front of him, but the stranger was faster. With a lightning-fast strike, the intruder slashed through the other knee.

Sallos fell forward, crashing on his face with a boom that shook the hall.

Around Ursula, the demons in the hall sucked in a collective gasp. Sallos rolled on the ground, trying to get away—but the stranger was too fast. In one strike, he carved a gash across Sallos's chest. With another, he severed the ligaments in the demon's wrist. He worked his way around the demon, hacking through tendons, until Sallos lay immobile and trembling on the floor.

Defeated and bloody, Sallos opened his mouth and howled.

The stranger straightened, bowing to Hothgar. "I have defeated him."

Hothgar rose. "And yet he lives."

The stranger shrugged. "He is immobilized."

Bileth's nostrils flared, and angry black magic sliced the air around him. With a deafening roar, the lord leapt over the table and charged. For a moment, Ursula expected him to attack the stranger.

Instead, he snatched his son's battled axe.

Ursula watched in horror as he raised the axe above his head. He brought it down in a ferocious strike, crushing his son's skull with a sickening crunch of bone.

CHAPTER 19

Bileth lifted the axe from the brain-spattered floor, his face contorted with rage. Turning to face the stranger, he spoke through gritted teeth. "I will have my vengeance."

Lord Bileth turned, striding out of the room.

Ursula was just about ready to vomit her mushroom soup all over the table. *Maybe I'm not really cut out to be a warrior.* She didn't want to live in a world where fathers smashed in their sons' skulls.

Trying to calm herself, she rubbed the silver ring between her fingers.

After a long pause, the hall erupted with thunderous applause. The stranger bowed deeply.

And when the hall quieted again, Hothgar spoke. "Congratulations. May you fight well in the melee."

The stranger in gray nodded. Without saying another word, he turned and left. As he disappeared through the doors, the hall erupted into a chorus of chatter.

Next to her, Ursula heard Viking say, "I'd like to change my bid—"

At the table of the lords, Hothgar banged his gavel. Around him, the demon lords called for order. Hothgar stood until it was quiet enough to speak.

"I'm glad you all enjoyed the unexpected show, but we have more champions to present. Who will be the champion for the Legion of Abrax?"

Abrax rose. His icy gaze flicked to Ursula for a moment before he spoke. "I nominate Massu from my legion."

Ursula's throat went dry. *Massu. Cera's brother. The little boy with the spaceship drawings, who always wanted to be a lord.*

On the plus side, she hadn't killed him.

On the downside, one of these champions certainly would.

As the hall waited, a tiny oneiroi man entered the hall. Dressed in tight leather armor, he carried no weapon. As he walked, he drew his lips back in a snarl, revealing his razor-sharp teeth. His whole body twitched with nervous energy.

Hothgar pointed. "What in the seven hells is that?"

Abrax folded his hands behind his head. "My champion."

"He's an oneiroi," shouted Hothgar. "He cannot be a lord."

Abrax shrugged. "That is not an actual law, I think you'll find. Merely tradition. And you know how I feel about tradition." He leaned forward, his glacial gaze on the oneiroi. "Show them what you can do, Massu."

Massu leapt on Sallos's body. With a quick flip of his head, he ripped the skin from the Sallos's chest.

Around Ursula, the women gasped.

"Oh my," said Goth Princess.

Massu held the flesh between his teeth, bowing deeply.

Bile climbed up Ursula's throat. *So much for the sweet little boy.*

"So be it," said Hothgar. He stared at the oneiroi soldier. "Congratulations, Massu. May Nyxobas grant you strength."

Hothgar had begun to lift his gavel when Bael rose.

"I would like to present a champion," said Bael, his voice booming off the ceiling.

Ursula took in his massive form, his perfect, chiseled features. He was powerful. She knew that. But she didn't want him anywhere near these maniacs.

"Right, I almost forgot." Contempt laced Hothgar's voice. "Who will fight for the house of Albelda?"

Bael looked out at the crowd. "I will defend Albelda myself. And I will win."

"Congratulations, Bael." Hothgar waved a dismissive hand. "May Nyxobas grant you the strength of a warrior." He mumbled the last part.

"He already has." Bael returned to his seat.

Ursula sipped her champagne, and Hothgar called upon one lord after another to nominate their second set of champions. By the time the lords had moved on to the fifth round of selections, Ursula had a pretty good buzz going.

Finally, Hothgar banged his gavel to signal the end of the ceremony. His voice boomed, "The champions have been chosen. There will be three trials: a melee, a race, and the duels. The melee begins when the sun sets at the Lacus Mortis, in nine hours. The challengers will fight until half remain."

Bloody hell.

Around Ursula, the women clapped, and cheers filled the hall. The lords rose, smiling and clapping one another on the back. Except for Bael, who stood to the side, his expression grim. Ursula shivered. *My fate is now truly in his hands.*

She rubbed her arms. Even with a buzz from the champagne, the hall was freezing—shadow demons didn't seem to care for heat.

Just as she was about to rise, she noticed that the hall had quieted again, and the air around her thinned. She glanced at the women, who all stared straight at the dais. At Nyxobas. Suddenly, she felt completely sober.

The chill in the room deepened. Shadow magic whorled from the god, and a hollow ache rose in Ursula's chest.

Slowly, the god opened his eyes. They shone a bright silver now. As Ursula stared at him, she could feel the void calling to her. She felt as if she was standing at the edge of a precipice, gazing into a dark abyss.

She closed her eyes for a moment, and a vision rose in her mind. She stood at the edge of the void, her body trembling with fear. But what scared her wasn't that she was going to fall in.

What scared her was that she wanted to jump.

Her eyes snapped open again, and she stared into the icy silver of Nyxobas's eyes. She'd seen those eyes in her dreams, even before she'd met him. *Why?*

"I will also be nominating a champion," he intoned. His voice sent a shudder of dread up her spine.

Hothgar bowed deeply. "Of course."

Nyxobas's eyes locked on Ursula, and cold dread spread through her chest. That piercing gaze, the face of her nightmares. And suddenly, she knew what was coming. *Nyxobas will be my death.* As he stared at her, terror stole her breath.

"No," she whispered.

His pale gaze locked on her, and he boomed, "The hound will be my champion."

"What will be her reward?" asked Hothgar. "A hound of Emerazel cannot be a lord."

"If she wins, I will release her from my service."

"And if she loses?" asked Hothgar.

"She will share the same fate as all defeated. She will join me in the void."

CHAPTER 20

Ursula traced her fingertips over the ring in her cloak pocket, staring out the carriage window. They flew over the barren landscape—small oneiroi houses mixed with the remains of meteor impacts. Asta's glow cast them in violet light, while above, clouds of moths swirled and danced. If she looked carefully, she could occasionally see the black form of a bat winging among them.

A bat among the moths.

On the other side of the carriage, Bael sat mute, his face fixed with a stony expression. She couldn't tell what he was thinking, but she could guess. Since he was a gentleman—despite what the other women said—he was probably considering the most painless way to kill her in the melee. A quick slash of his sword through her neck, perhaps.

Her chest tightened. *What I need is a plan. An escape route. A way to survive.*

And if not, I need to know exactly what I'm up against.

"So how did you win it?" she asked.

Bael's sapphire gaze slid to her. "Win what?"

"The tournament. When you became a lord, how did you do it?" *Give me a bloody clue, at least.*

A perplexed line appeared between his eyebrows. "I won by being the best fighter. And the strongest."

Well, that's unhelpful. "Can you, you know, provide some specifics? How did you survive the melee?"

"I killed any man who came near me." His eyes were cold as glacier water. "The same way I will survive this one."

"So you think you can kill him?"

"Him?"

"The man in gray. The one who killed Sallos."

"Sallos was weak, and a fool. The stranger will be no match for me."

She arched an eyebrow. "Even with your injuries?"

A muscle worked in his jaw. Even obliquely mentioning his lost wings seemed to set him off.

Time to change the subject. "Has anyone else ever survived? I mean, has there been more than one left alive at the end of a tournament?"

"You ask me if anyone has violated Nyxobas's edict? No, the penalty of defying the god's orders is death."

"Hothgar set the rules."

"Hothgar speaks for Nyxobas. It is the same punishment." He turned back to the window, lost in his own thoughts.

She bit her lip. Hadn't the wives said that Bael could use mind control on humans? And if so—did she count as a human? She didn't have her demon magic here. If that were the case, he could just compel her to stab herself. The fight would be over.

"I guess the other women know I'm not here as your harlot now," she muttered.

"What?" he snapped, suddenly alert.

"The lords' wives believed that's why I was here. A consolation prize for you. Apparently their husbands have some kinky desire to mind control human women. They were certain you were the same."

He stared at her, his expression unreadable.

"Could you, if you wanted? Use mind control on me?"

"I won't."

She let out a long breath. "Okay, so that's one of my fears allayed. But there's the matter of me not having a weapon."

Bael leaned forward in his chair and looked her straight in the face.

"I won't control your mind. But it won't matter. You are not going to survive this tournament, whether or not you have a sword." His words slid through her bones. "If one of the other champions doesn't kill you, I will." He looked out the window again, his jaw clenched tight.

* * *

DESCENDING in the elevator should have come as a relief as Ursula neared the comfort of her quarters. But instead, with each passing level, it was as if an increasingly heavy weight pressed on her chest.

The full implications of her new role as Nyxobas's champion were awful to contemplate. A fight to the death—one she had no chance of winning. In order to survive, she'd have to slaughter Cera's brother, the stranger in gray, and a horde of lethal demons. If, by some miracle, none of them killed her, she'd have to face Bael, a twenty-two thousand-year-old demon.

Panic tightened its grip on her heart. *I'm going to die in this barren place, my soul sent to the crushing isolation of Nyxobas's void. For the rest of eternity.* A painful ache gnawed at her chest.

When the elevator finally opened, she turned, heading away from her quarters. Clutching the silver ring in her pocket, she strode toward the water portal, where she'd first arrived. *It's time I get the fuck out of here.* If Nyxobas wanted to kill her, he could do it in New York.

She pushed through the black door into the semicircular portal room, hurrying over to the portal. Starlight reflected off the water's surface. She pulled off her cloak, dropping it on the floor. In the next second, she'd pulled off the dress and slipped off her knickers. The cold air in the portal room raised goosebumps on her skin, and her teeth chattered.

She kicked off her shoes. In a few moments, she'd be back in her flat. She'd call Zee and tell her the whole story over a bottle of wine. Then she'd call up Emerazel and explain the situation. The goddess would quickly realize that Nyxobas had been breaking their terms, and all would be settled. Emerazel hadn't sent her here to die.

She dipped a toe into the frigid water, hugging herself for warmth. *I just need the spell that Cera used...*

Her stomach swooped. *The Forgotten Arsholes ripped all the magical knowledge from my brain.*

She clamped her eyes shut, trying to remember a single Angelic word. Nothing.

She kicked the water in frustration, splashing the marble.

Behind her, a deep voice echoed off the ceiling. "What are you doing?"

Dread coiled around her. *So much for my plan.*

She looked over her shoulder. Bael stood in the doorway, completely avoiding looking at her.

"I was trying to escape. I'm sure you understand why, what with the certain death you promised me."

"It won't work."

"I know. Those stupid Forgotten Twats stole all my magical knowledge."

"It wouldn't matter if you remembered the spell. The spell requires Nyxobas's permission. No one enters or leaves the Shadow Realm without his approval."

She took a deep breath, teeth chattering. *Bollocks. No escape.* Grief welled in her chest, and she choked down a sob. Maybe all the lords' wives thought she was a whore, but she had some dignity. She wasn't going stand here naked and sobbing in front of Bael.

She would stand there naked and sniffling though, apparently. "Why has everything been forgiven with Abrax? He tried to overthrow the entire Shadow Realm. He's the whole reason you're in this predicament."

"He is Nyxobas's son. And the god respects brutality. Abrax demonstrated plenty of that when he tried to overthrow the kingdom."

"So that's it? It was violent enough that Nyxobas isn't mad anymore?"

She heard a long exhale from Bael. "That, and I think Nyxobas feels guilty for what he did to his son."

A shiver made its way up her spine. "What did he do?"

"It's not important right now. I can hear your teeth chattering."

"I'm going to put on my dress."

"That's for the best."

She leaned over, snatching the dress from the ground. "I suppose you still won't tell me anything about the opponents we must face, because my death is certain anyway."

"The man in gray," he said. "He may be someone known as the Gray Ghost."

"Gray Ghost?"

"No one knows who he is. Only that he rides a white bat."

Still shivering, she turned to face Bael. "The man who broke the window. He was riding a white bat." She bit her lip. "Pretty sure he was wearing gray, too."

He stared at her. "Why didn't you say so?"

"I didn't know it was important."

"Every detail is important."

She glanced down at her dress, torn at the hem by the Gray Ghost. She'd ruined every dress Cera had given her.

At the thought of Cera, a lump rose in her throat. "We need to tell Cera about Massu."

"I was on my way to tell her when I saw you."

"Sorry about the...the nudity." She had no idea why she felt the need to apologize.

Bael slipped back into the shadows. "Return to your quarters at once. You'll be warm and safe there. At least, until the melee."

CHAPTER 21

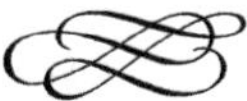

*B*ack in her quarters, Ursula curled up in her usual spot on the sofa. With the slowly rising sun staining the sky a bright purple, fear tightened its grip on her heart. She had about five hours until someone bashed her skull in.

She'd spent her last five hours staring at Asta, the palace of nightmares. The view of the crater no longer seemed so starkly beautiful. Now Asta's shimmering spire and the clouds of moths only reminded her of the danger the day held for her. In eight hours, when red tinged the sky, she would be in a fight for her life, thousands of miles from home.

She curled up, pulling her blanket tightly around her shoulder. And when she slept, she dreamt of Bael, standing over her with a silver sword, ready to strike.

It must have been only a few hours when Cera tapped her on the shoulder. "Ursula?"

"Mmmmghh." Ursula started her morning eye rubbing routine, but stopped when she saw Cera's face. The oneiroi's eyes were raw, her hair looked like a bird's nest.

"I guess Bael spoke to you."

"The lord told me about Massu. And you. I couldn't sleep."

Ursula sat up, the memories of the ceremony crashing down on her. Tears stung her eyes. "There must be some way for us to get through this.

Cera shook her head. "No one violates Nyxobas's edicts." She lifted a shopping bag from the floor, her jaw fixed with resolve. "Still. I won't have you appear in front of the melee looking a mess."

Ursula frowned. "This hardly seems like the time to bring me a dress."

"It's not a dress. I'm tired of you destroying my outfits. Besides, a dress wouldn't be appropriate for the melee." She tossed the bag to Ursula. "Try it on."

Ursula peered inside at the folded pile of midnight-black leather.

"What did you make me?" Ursula stood, pulling out a pair of black leather trousers, a leather corset—reinforced with steel. A leather jacket—also reinforced. And to top it off, thigh-high boots, stitched with a dozen knife-sheaths.

Despite everything she was about to face, a smile curled Ursula's lips. "This is amazing."

"I thought you'd like it."

It took only a few minutes for Ursula to zip up in the figure-hugging black leather. It fit her like a glove, and had pockets—where she could store her new lucky charm. That little ring she'd pilfered from Bael. And more importantly, she felt like she could fight in this. "You're amazing, Cera." She leaned down, hugging the oneiroi.

"You'd better not hurt Massu," Cera cautioned. "Or I'm taking it all back." Cera wrung her hands. Confusion clouded her features. "I mean, I know both of you can't live, and the lord... I just don't want to see you all hurt each other. And maybe you're right. Maybe if you live long enough, there will be some way out of this. Just make it through the melee alive, okay?"

Ursula clamped a hand on her shoulder. "I will. And we will figure something out. Maybe a loophole..." Her voice trailed off. Nyxobas probably didn't give a fuck about loopholes. "Anyway, thank you so much for making this outfit. I'll try really hard not to trash it."

Cera folded her arms. "Even you couldn't trash it. The leather stitching is triply reinforced, and the leather lined with a thin sheet of steel. And that reminds me." She snatched the bag off the floor, plucking out a knife. "It's not much, but I wanted to give you this."

Ursula took it from her, a smile brightening her face. "Finally. A real weapon."

"I believe it's what you call a shiv," added Cera.

Ursula held it up to the light. The blade, black as the void, had been carved from stone. She let out a low whistle. *Gorgeous.*

She examined the lethal tip. "What's it made of?"

"Obsidian. Be careful with it. It's very sharp."

Ursula rubbed her thumb over the hilt. It was perfectly weighted. "Did you make it?"

Cera shook her head. "No. It's been in the family for generations. When Nyxobas and his henchmen first arrived one hundred millennia ago, his demons confiscated all the onerois' metal weapons. Fortunately, their spells can't distinguish between your average moon rock and a knapped blade."

Ursula slid the dagger into one of the sheaths in her boots. Straightening, she felt a certain confidence return. *At least I have a weapon, tiny as it might be.*

Already, her nerves were buzzing with adrenaline. She shot a panicked glance at the window. When the sun began to rise here, it would be setting on the other side of the moon. "Is it time?"

"Yes. I'll be taking you to Lacus Mortis."

"I'm not going in the carriage?"

"No. The lord is taking the carriage. We will be traveling by bat. Sotz is waiting outside. It is time."

"Right." Her stomach fluttering, she glanced at the sky again, certain it was brightening.

Never before had the concept of sunrise seemed so soul-crushingly terrifying.

* * *

Sotz was waiting for them on the bridge, his feet clutching the railing. His beady eyes blinked as they approached.

"Turn around," Cera commanded.

Slowly, Sotz rotated his body until his rear faced them. As she had in New York, Cera mounted his saddle at the shoulders, and Ursula clambered on the back.

Cera turned to face her. "Take this," she said, passing Ursula a black ribbon. "Tie it around your mane of hair to keep it out of your face."

"Thanks." *What I wouldn't do for a helmet right now.* As instructed, she fastened her hair in a ponytail behind her head.

"Are you ready?" Cera asked.

Ursula swallowed hard, trying to steel her nerves. This was it. Once in the air, there would be no turning back. They were heading right for the *Lacus Mortis.* And while her Latin knowledge wasn't spectacular, she had a feeling that name translated to, "the place where you're about to die."

"I guess I'm ready."

Cera whispered in Sotz's ear, and the bat climbed over the railing. "Hold on tight," Cera shouted.

An instant later, the cold lunar wind whipped over Ursula's skin, and they were diving toward the valley floor. With her hair fastened behind her head, the improved view proved so terrifying that she shut her eyes anyway. She opened them only when Sotz leveled off.

"Are you okay?" Cera shouted above the wind.

"Yeah." *And by "yeah," I mean I'm so terrified I might puke into the wind.* "Is it strictly necessary for Sotz to dive like a maniac every time we take off?"

"It's the easiest way for him to build up enough speed to sustain flight. A bat's not really built to take two riders."

Her stomach twisted. *Brilliant. Perfectly reassuring.*

Sotz flew in a lazy curve until they faced the wall of the crater. The frigid air bit at her skin, even through her leather. Still, now that they weren't hurtling at the ground, her muscles began to relax.

Sotz slowly beat the air with his wings a few times. Then he dove toward the side of the crater. They were heading for a sheer cliff of lunar rock at a terrifying speed.

Ursula gripped onto the saddle so tightly she was about to rip the handles off. "What are you doing?" she shouted. "We're about to crash into the side of the crater!"

A moment later, in conjunction with Ursula's terrified screams, they plunged into a narrow crack in the side of the cliff. Sotz had taken them into complete darkness.

Ursula strained to see anything, total darkness enshrouded them. Unlike the subway, no lights hung to illuminate their flight. If she'd had the nerve to release her grip for a second, she wouldn't have been able to see her own hand in front of her face.

"Where are we going?" she shouted.

"Can you be quiet?" Cera barked. "All your shouting will interfere with Sotz's echolocation."

Right. Best not deafen the bat. Ursula tried to peer into the darkness for a few more moments, but she kept imagining stalactites dangling from the ceiling and smacking her in the face. So she shut her eyes and buried her face in Cera's back.

The air rushed around her, but the sensation of Cera's soft sweater against her cheek made her feel secure. After a while, the air around her seemed to warm.

Ursula lifted her head, opening her eyes. A dim, indigo light shone through the crack. Sotz's wings beat steadily. The light slowly grew brighter.

Suddenly, the tunnel widened and they burst into an enormous cavern. A tremendous cacophony of chirping and squeaking assaulted her ears, echoing off the cavern walls. It sounded like a tropical rainforest amplified through a speaker. Down here, the humid air warmed her skin. She breathed in, taking in the sharp, almost chemical scent. It took her a moment to identify it—ammonia.

A luminous glow rose from beneath them. Ursula leaned just far enough to the side to peer over Sotz's side. She gasped. They were flying over a great forest of glowing mushrooms. Enormous fungi, the size of trees, grew from the surface. Each glowed with a blinding cornflower-blue light. And between the fungi, something slithered.

Her stomach fluttered as she realized what they were. Monstrous caterpillars, the size of buses.

"What is this place?" she whispered.

"This is the rookery, for the bats." Cera pointed above. "Look. You can see them up there."

Ursula craned her neck, peering into the darkness. On the ceiling hundreds of feet above, furry bat bodies squirmed like a brown fungus.

Suddenly, Sotz jerked to the side. Out of the corner of her eye, Ursula saw a blur of brown plunge from the ceiling. It struck a mushroom with an audible splat.

"What was that?"

"Guano," said Cera. "The bats aren't exactly polite."

Ursula's stomach turned. *Lovely.*

As they continued through the cavern, Sotz continued to dodge falling guano.

"This is gross," Ursula muttered.

"The guano feeds the mushrooms," said Cera. "It's a well-functioning ecosystem."

Eventually the walls narrowed, and the ceiling sloped lower. As the sounds of the bats faded, the cavern grew dark again.

Sotz flew through the darkness for what seemed like hours. Ursula rested her head against Cera's back, breathing in the smell of garlic and bread that still hung on her clothes from the last time she'd cooked. Apart from the flapping of wings and the rush of air around them, the only sound Ursula could hear was Cera's drumming heart through her back.

Without warning, they burst free of the crevice. Ursula blinked, trying to focus her eyes. When she tried to ask Cera what was going on, her breath caught in her throat. There was no air, the sun hadn't yet risen on this part of the moon. Brutal cold bit at her skin. They were floating in the vacuum of space.

Cera pulled a purple crystal from her sweater. Her mouth moved but there was no sound. Suddenly, dark magic flashed around them. This time, when Ursula gasped, air filled her lungs.

"I'm so sorry, milady," said Cera. "I forgot that you wouldn't be able to breathe." Ursula coughed uncontrollably, wiping frozen tears from her eyes. Dark magic swirled around them, keeping the vacuum at bay.

"You don't need air to breathe?" asked Ursula.

"Some air. But oneiroi can hold our breath for a long time. It's one of the ways we are able to live on the moon." Cera pointed up. "Have you seen the Earth yet?"

Suspended above them, the earth filled the sky, a crescent of emerald and blue. Gleaming like a shadowed gem. She hadn't realized until now that from the moon, the Earth had phases, too—waxing and waning. She blinked, trying to process the rich colors.

"It's beautiful, isn't it?" said Cera. "Before Nyxobas came, the oneiroi worshiped the Earth as a god."

"I'd seen the pictures from NASA, but in person—" She spotted the outline of Europe, and felt a lump rise in her throat. "I didn't realize quite how far away it was."

Cera whispered in Sotz's ear. The bat adjusted his course, bringing them lower—closer to the barren lunar surface. They streaked over a great field of stones and boulders. Only the intermittent pockmarks of ancient meteor strikes interrupted the flat landscape.

She glanced at the sun over the horizon. *Not long, now.* "Where are we?" Ursula asked.

"The Lacus Mortis."

"What does that mean, anyway?"

Cera cleared her throat. "Just... Just *Lake of Death.*"

Yep. Just like I thought.

Ursula studied the barren plain. "This is it?" Why had Hothgar ordered the melee be held here? "There's bugger-all here!"

"The Lacus Mortis is what remains of an old lava flow," said Cera. "It's where Nyxobas built his great amphitheater."

Here, on the opposite side of the moon, the sun still hung in the sky. But it didn't look like daylight on Earth. The sun hung in a black sky, bathing the moon in pure, white light.

Ursula scanned the landscape, but she could see nothing. Not a single hovel, much less an amphitheater. She was about to ask what was going on, when she spotted the rim of a particularly large crater. A dome of silver covered the crater, so thin it was hardly visible. Sunlight streamed through the dome.

Sotz carved a tight turn as they soared through the dome of silver magic, and Ursula let out a low whistle. Just below the dome, demons filled the crater, and they sat in seats carved from the inner walls of the caldera. White sunlight shone over an enormous circular pit in the center, flat and sandy on the bottom. It looked exactly like the interior of a Roman Coliseum.

Panic raked its claws into her chest. *They've all come to watch me die. And I have nothing but a stone dagger to defend myself.*

CHAPTER 22

$\mathcal{A}$ cold fear gripped Ursula as Sotz skidded to a stop in the center of the arena. She could feel the eyes on her. *The hellhound harlot, here to perform for your enjoyment.*

She climbed out of the saddle, wincing. Fatigue burned through her thighs from the flight. *Haven't even started yet, and I'm already knackered.*

From Sotz's saddle, Cera gripped her hand. "Good luck."

"Thank you." She glanced around at the empty arena. She was the only one here. "You're not leaving now, are you? There's no one else here."

"They'll be here, Ursula," said Cera. "I must go."

Before Ursula could say another word, Sotz and the oneiroi launched into the air, the wind whipping through Cera's hair as she flew away.

Okay. So I'll just stand here in the center of the arena, with an entire planet's eyes on me. Her heart squeezed in her chest as she stood below the black dome of sky, washed in milky light.

As she stood on the dusty floor, a wave of terror washed over her. Great walls of stone, at least twenty feet high, surrounded her. Every few yards, grated doors interrupted them. And above the doors, Nyxobas's brethren sat in rows, studying her with a mixture of excitement and fear.

A great clash reverberated through the stadium, and she turned with a start. On a platform at the edge of the arena stood Hothgar, dressed in furs and a silver breastplate. A great silver gong hung beside him, and his

379

Viking wife sat behind him, wearing a shimmering gown the color of starlight. Twelve oneiroi stood before him, each bearing a torch. The torch flames danced in the wind.

And at the back of the platform, a giant stone statue of Nyxobas loomed over the arena. Starlight seemed to shine from the statue's eyes. Ursula shuddered.

She turned, surveying the crowd again. She squinted in the setting sun.

A pig-faced man pointed at her. "Ready to die, whore?"

She swallowed hard. *Now I'll survive just to spite you.*

Glass shattered a few feet behind her, and she whirled. Someone had thrown a glass wine bottle at her. Lucky for her, the tosser had terrible aim.

She moved further into the center of the arena, out of range, inwardly cursing Cera's punctuality. *Why did she need to get us here early?*

Hothgar's enormous form cast a long shadow over the center of the crater. *When the shadows grow long...*

He slammed his wooden mallet into the center of the gong. A silence fell over the crowd, and he stared at Ursula. "I'm so glad you could finally join us, dog. You weren't too busy rutting in the streets like a bitch in heat?"

The crowd laughed, and Ursula felt a flush rise in her cheeks. Anger simmered. "I'm sorry." Her tone dripped with sarcasm. "If you want me to call you 'Nyxobas' and worship your lunar staff, you'll have to control my mind, like you do the other human women who won't have you otherwise."

Hothgar paled, but she caught sight of the slight smile that ghosted across Viking's lips.

Hothgar's nostrils flared. "Are you prepared to join the melee?"

Definitely not. "I am." She projected her voice with as much confidence as she could.

"Good," said Hothgar. "I will enjoy watching you get torn apart."

A pit opened in her stomach. She couldn't come up with much of a comeback to that particular jab. She *was* probably going to die here, and the terror of that thought ripped her mind apart. The Sword of Nyxobas lifted his large wooden mallet. With a brutal strike, he sounded the gong again. Around the arena, the doors opened with a rumbling groan.

Ursula's blood ran cold as she beheld the champions, striding through the doors. Silver tridents, lethal spears, full suits of armor. All manner of nasty-looking swords, battle-axes, and spears. Their weapons' shadows crept over the dirt like long fingers.

Most of the men were probably triple her weight. *Not feeling too stellar about my rock-knife and my fancy boots right now.*

Her heart pounded like a war drum. She searched the champions' faces, but couldn't find Bael among them. She shot a frantic look at the setting sun, drifting dangerously close to the horizon.

Hothgar raised his hands. "Champions! Welcome to the melee." He paused for effect, then boomed, "Are you ready to fight?"

Around her, the champions shouted, lifting their weapons into the air and roaring with cheers. *Didn't they realize they were about to die?*

Ursula half-heartedly raised her knife to the darkening sky, forcing herself to emit a sad cheer. "Wahey!" The sun had begun to slip below the crater's rim.

"Excellent," said Hothgar. "Now, while I am sure most of you know the rules of the melee, we have some outsiders here." He looked at Ursula pointedly. "Fortunately, they are very simple, so even a dog could understand. There are fifty-six of you. When twenty-three of you are dead, the melee ends. Only blades may be used. No magic or ranged weapons, or you will be executed. Begin when I next sound the gong."

Ursula clutched her knife, a cold sweat breaking out on her forehead. As she surveyed her opponents, panic tightened her lungs. Frantically, she searched the crowd for Bael. Rays of sunlight blinded her as the last of the sun dipped below the crater's rim. She didn't know why she was even looking for the lord. Clearly, he wasn't her protector anymore. In fact, he'd said flat out that he would kill her. Maybe she just needed to see a familiar face.

Darkness fell over the crater. Now, only the starlight, the gleaming Earth, and the amber light of the torches lit the arena.

Before she had a chance to find Bael, Hothgar raised his mallet again. He slammed it into the gong.

The sound reverberated through Ursula's gut, and adrenaline blazed through her nerve endings. Her legs started to shake, and everything seemed to move in slow motion.

The crowd rose to cheer, the champions dropped into fighting stances.

She widened her stance, circling to search the throng for danger.

She didn't have to look long.

A champion charged for her, starlight glinting off his silver helm, carved with the face of a lion.

She had no question that behind the visor, she'd find Bael's beautiful face, eyes blazing with wrath.

My angel of death, come for my soul at last.

CHAPTER 23

She gripped the dagger and dove out of his swing. When she looked up, Bael stood over her, his eyes flashing in his helmet.

She slashed for one of his ankles, but he deftly stepped aside.

She leapt to her feet. *I really don't want to hurt him. But if I don't, he'll kill me.*

Still, she couldn't bring herself to stab him yet. Despite what he'd said —the part about how he'd kill her—she sort of *liked* the guy.

She wouldn't be able to draw blood until he'd made the first strike. Then, self-preservation would kick in. Instead of stabbing him, she wound up for a hard left hook. But as she swung for him, Bael caught her fist in a powerful hand.

Hungry for blood, the crowd chanted: "Bael! Bael! Bael!"

"You can't fight me, Ursula," he growled.

What's he doing? Drawing it out to please the crowd?

Her heart hammered against her ribs. Of course he'd gone for the easy target first. The girl with the rock for protection.

"I can fight you," she shot back. "Maybe I can't win. But I can fight." Without waiting for a response, she kicked him in the chin.

His neck snapped back, his helmet flying from his head. When he looked back at her, his pale eyes had turned into black voids, sending ice through her veins.

Her victory didn't last long. In a blur of dark magic, he gripped her arms, pulling her to him. He towered over her, all muscle.

He leaned in close, his body warm against hers. He was pure power, and terror ran up her spine.

Bael whispered, "What are you doing?"

"Trying to fight."

"You don't have a real weapon." He dropped her wrists, and in the next second, he drew his katana.

Brilliant. A sword against a rock. This is bloody pointless.

At the sight of his icy eyes that had seen millennia of combat, her blood roared in her ears.

Run. Maybe I need to run. From his platform, she could hear Hothgar announcing *first blood,* but her eyes were locked on Bael.

Her mind raced. If she was going to get away, she'd need a diversion. The obsidian blade glinted in her hand, and she threw it at his shoulder. Effortlessly, he snatched it from the air.

Bollocks. She'd just thrown away her only weapon, but it had bought her time. She turned, scanning the arena for an escape route. Carnage assaulted her eyes—demons tearing into each other, hacking through limbs, half of them using their teeth. Two giant twins, dressed in wolf furs and metal armor, swung claymores at their opponents. *Where the fuck do I run to? Romulus and Remus over there don't look like a good bet.*

Before she could pick an escape route, Bael slid a powerful arm around her waist, pulling her close to him.

"You're unarmed," he said. "If you run, you're going to die."

He pointed to a demon with blood-red eyes stalking toward them. The creature held a nasty looking broadsword. In a moment, the only possible escape path would put her within range of him.

The rabid-eyed demon grinned. He had replaced his teeth with steel spikes. Already, blood dripped from them into the sand.

Fear coiled around Ursula's heart. It was Steel Jaws or Bael. She swallowed hard, her nails digging into Bael's arm. She had nothing left to fight with.

From behind her, the sound of metal against metal pierced her ears. *He's drawing another weapon.* She braced herself for the final blow.

Instead, Bael stabbed a katana into the sand by her feet.

Hope sparked in her chest. "What are you doing?"

"Take the blade," he said. "I was trying to give it to you."

"I thought you were trying to kill me."

"Do you think I have no honor?" he growled.

"When we were in the carriage, you literally said, 'I'm going to kill you.'"

"You deserve a fair fight. Take the blade." He loosened his grip on her, and Ursula pulled the blade from the dirt.

With the katana in her hand, she felt like herself again, like the metal was an extension of her body.

Bael pointed to the right. "That half of the arena is yours," he commanded. "If anyone gets close, kill them."

He turned his back to her, facing his side of the arena. They stood, back-to-back, so close she could feel the warmth coming off his body, could smell the faint scent of sea air that wafted from his skin.

Apparently, Bael wanted her to fight defensively. It made sense. Might as well let the others take the risk while trying to go unnoticed.

Except she wasn't really going unnoticed. Jaws raised his broadsword, grinning at her. Katana or not, she still looked like easy prey.

A few meters away, just out of range of his steel, the Gray Ghost slipped over the dirt like a phantom. As before, he'd concealed his face with a head scarf, and he gripped a dagger in each hand.

Her mouth went dry. She couldn't tell if he was heading for Jaws, or for her.

Either way, I need to be ready. She took a step away from Bael, gripping the katana's hilt. A part of her wanted to throw herself into the fray, to feel her blade cut through the air. Maybe that was Emerazel.

Jaws was coming right for her, raising his broadsword now. But before he could get to her, the Gray Ghost leapt for him, daggers flashing like a serpent's fangs. The blades cut into Jaws's back, soaking his clothes in blood.

Jaws's scream curdled her stomach. He fell to the ground, and Gray Ghost ended his torment with a quick slash to his throat.

Her eyes scanned for the next threat, and she stared at a trident-wielding demon, his skin elephant-gray. In a blur of black leather and teeth, Massu launched himself into the air. Screaming like a banshee, he attached himself to the demon's head. Ursula could distinctly hear the crunch of bone as he began to chew through the demon's face. *Fuck me sideways. I do not want to fight an oneiroi.*

She took a step closer to Bael.

Bael touched her arm, and she jumped. "Come with me."

She turned, keeping her back to the wall as they moved.

They moved back-to-back, swords drawn, but they might as well have kept them sheathed. The other demons ignored them. Instead, like sharks scenting blood, they charged toward the skirmish in the center of the arena.

"Five, six, seven deaths," Hothgar's voice boomed, his glee audible. "Only nineteen more will die today."

The demons swarmed the center of the arena like piranhas fighting over a corpse. Between shouts of pain, blood sprayed in the sand. From the melee, the sound of clashing steel rung through the air. Around them, the bodies of the fallen champions twitched.

"Eight... nine deaths," Hothgar shouted. "Prepare to light bitumen sands." His voice boomed over the arena like a death knell.

Cold fear washed over Ursula. *The bitumen sands?* The oneiroi, holding torches, ran to the edges of the arena.

"On my command," boomed Hothgar.

"Get your blade ready," Bael growled. "We need to move." He stalked toward the bloodbath in the center of the arena.

As she hurried after Bael, her eyes flicked to the oneiroi, who stood at the arena's edges with their torches.

"Now," said Bael.

There wasn't time to ask what was going on—she just had to decide to trust him. At least for now. Ursula's heart thundered in her chest, and she broke into an all-out sprint, heading for the melee. She no longer had any choice but to fight.

Around the perimeter, they dropped their torches. A ring of fire burst to life, encircling the entire arena. From the edges, the flames spread inward, searing the darkness. Hothgar was forcing them into the melee. As she entered the fray, she tried not to stare at the carnage—at the demon slicing through another's neck with a scimitar, at the blood spurting from his stump like a geyser. If she stared too long, she'd completely shut down mentally.

Still sticking by Bael's side, she looked to the right, at a demon who loomed over her with a broadsword. Blood dripped down his black beard, and he glared at her through milky eyes. "Are you ready to die, hound?"

"Can you handle him?" asked Bael.

Before she could actually answer Bael's question, Blackbeard lunged, swinging for her head. She parried, grunting as his sword slammed against hers. She dodged out of reach.

He swung again, but this time she was able to duck the blow entirely. With a savage thrust, she stabbed at his chest. Growling, he jumped back. The tip of her blade sliced the skin over his ribs. Blood sprayed her face.

"Bitch," he said through gritted teeth. "I will rape you to death."

A hot flood of anger blazed through her nerves. If she'd had Emerazel's power in her veins, she would have immolated him. Instead, raw fury burned away her fear, and she narrowed her eyes. "I'm going to enjoy killing you."

She lunged, thrusting. This time, the blade slid deep between his ribs. With a twisting motion, she directed it upward to where his heart should be. The demon's milky eyes widened with shock. A fat drop of blood rolled from his chin. Groaning, he slumped to the ground, and she pulled out her sword.

"Fifteen deaths!" roared Hothgar to the cheers of the crowd. Their cries had grown increasingly bloodthirsty as the last of the sunlight seeped from the sky.

Behind her, she heard the clash of steel. She stole a glance over her shoulder. Bael was locked in combat with the two enormous demons—Romulus and Remus.

"Can you handle them?" she shouted.

Bael swung for Romulus, grunting.

Was that a yes or a no?

Bael's sword was parried in a clash of steel. Romulus twisted his wrist, catching Bael's blade. He drove Bael's katana into the earth with a *thud.*

Instantly, Remus lunged for Bael's chest, but Bael slipped away, moving like the wind.

He'd dodged the strike, but a third opponent came up behind him—a winged man who slashed at Bael with his talons.

Ursula gritted her teeth. *Time to jump in.*

The three demons boxed Bael in. He fought in a blur of clashing steel, whirling and ducking with astounding grace. *No wonder he's so confident.*

He parried the blows that assaulted him from both sides. So fast—she could hardly see what was happening—he sliced through the neck of the winged man.

"Sixteen deaths!" Hothgar boomed.

Still, Romulus and Remus pressed their assault. *Two against one isn't exactly a fair fight.* "Hey!" she shouted. "Wolf-boy. Right here."

Remus turned, snarling. "You disgust me, dog. I will eat your flesh off your bones."

She tried to ignore her body's trembling. He was maybe four times her size. Speed was her greatest asset here.

He swung for her, and she ducked. They circled each other, swords glinting in the starlight. Remus lunged for her, and she dodged back, but not fast enough. His blade ripped through her shoulder. The blazing pain threw her off balance, and she faltered.

Fight, Ursula.

As Remus prepared to strike again, she steadied herself, blocking his attack. Somehow, the surge of adrenaline flooding her system washed the pain away. The air filled with the sound of her sword clashing against Remus's. The bastard had the advantage of a much longer reach, and her muscles burned as she struggled to keep up with the fight.

And yet, as she fought him, a strange surety filled her. It was almost as though liquid shadow flowed through her muscles, making her movements fluid. Time seemed to slow down. And if she concentrated, she could predict what his next moves would be, could easily block them. *Strike from the left. Dodge. Thrust.*

If she moved in closer to him, he wouldn't be able to strike her with accuracy—not with his giant arms. In fact, he wasn't used to fighting someone her size.

He swung for her in a giant arc, and she ducked. He'd been pressing her and would expect her to dodge back. Instead, she leapt in closer. Unable to strike her with his sword, he slammed a meaty fist into her head. Her vision went dark.

Only the darkness will save you.

Yet even as her vision darkened, some ancient part of her brain took over, fighting for survival. She swung her sword, somehow certain of her mark.

And when her vision cleared again, she stared at her blade, plunged clean through Remus's neck. She gripped her sword, kicking him in the chest to pull her blade out.

Hothgar shouted, "Nineteen!"

Three kills left.

Before she could catch a glimpse of Bael, a sharp blast of pain ripped through her shoulders, knocking her off balance. She landed hard on the arena floor, bits of gravel biting into her palms. If Cera hadn't made her the reinforced leather jacket, she'd be dead by now. Even so, if they kept striking at her shoulders, she wouldn't be able to hold a weapon.

Her heart thundering, she grasped for her sword. Her fingers gripped the hilt, and she immediately swung from the ground at her attacker. Her sword found its mark in a leg, cutting into flesh and bone. Her opponent, wielding a giant scythe, screamed. He swung for her with his blade, she rolled out of range, but not before the tip of his blade carved a furrow in her back.

In an instant, she was on her feet, staring at the reaper. *I have you.* She swung her katana in a wide arc, her steel cutting through the flesh and bone in his neck. The reaper's head rolled over the crater's floor, and his body toppled to the ground. A strange thrill rippled through her body. *Victory.*

"Twenty-one!" boomed Hothgar.

Her eyes flicked to Bael. He was still fighting. In hand-to-hand combat with Romulus.

The giant roared, "My brother has been slain!" Bael had dropped his sword. In its stead, he used the obsidian blade. *My blade.* Bael's movements were so fast, she could hardly track them. Starlight shone off the black rock, flashing in his hand. Even without the use of his magic, Bael's skill was breathtaking.

With a vicious strike, he ducked and stabbed Romulus in the groin. The demon shrieked. When Romulus doubled over, Bael slashed open his throat with a casual flick of his wrist, then rose.

"Twenty-two deaths!" shouted Hothgar.

Ursula's heart raced. *One more.*

She turned slowly, gripping her blood-stained sword, ready to slay. A bestial shriek curdled her stomach, and she turned to find Massu, burying his teeth into the back of a demon's neck. With an audible crunch, he snapped the demon's spine.

Hothgar's voice sounded like a thunderclap. "Twenty-three. The melee has ended!"

Ursula's entire body shook, and she let out a long, slow breath. Nausea welled in her stomach, and she hunched over, trying not to vomit. *I can't believe I made it.* Her body shrieked in agony where the blades had ripped her shoulders.

Soaked in blood, Bael crossed to her, his expression grim. He held the blood-soaked dagger before him. "Where did you get this?" he asked.

She tightened her lips. She was pretty sure a demon like him could tell when you were lying, but she wasn't about to get Cera in trouble, either. "I'm not answering that. I'm pleading the sixth...eighth...whatever Americans call it."

He rolled the hilt in his hands, inspecting it, before fixing her with one of his piercing glares. "The oneiroi are not your friends." A hint of steel laced his voice. "I hope, after what you just saw, you understand that."

CHAPTER 24

Ursula stood in the middle of the arena, next to the remaining demons. Strewn with gore, the dirt floor looked like a butcher shop. She shoved her hand in her pocket, gripping on to the reassuringly solid contours of the silver ring.

She wasn't going to argue with Bael about Cera—not now. In fact, she couldn't get her mind off the carnage she'd just witnessed, the images replaying in her skull. She clamped her eyes shut, willing her mind to fill with darkness.

It didn't work.

She turned to Bael, letting her eyes run over his battle-stained clothes. "Are you injured?"

He sheathed his katana. "No. But you are."

Not a question, but she answered anyway. "It hurts like hell."

From his platform, Hothgar raised his arms to the dark sky. "Let us congratulate the champions for a well-fought battle."

Around them, the crowd stood and roared their approval from their seats.

For just a moment, a thrill flickered through Ursula. And then, the images burned in her mind again: the severed tendons, the sprays of blood. The reaper's head. Her own blade, buried in the giant's chest.

They'd fought each other like rabid beasts. And Ursula had been right there, in the thick of it, slashing away to the dark cheers of the onlookers. Something had taken over her body, and she'd joined in the grim symphony of slaughter.

She closed her eyes again, trying to cleanse her mind of the blood. A part of her yearned for the cleanliness of the void. The words of the Forgotten Ones whispered in the back of her skull. *Only the darkness will save you.*

Maybe this was Nyxobas's plan, to give her the choice between turning into a monster and joining him in the void. Or if not, surely this was his punishment for stabbing him with the dagger.

She glanced at the statue of Nyxobas that loomed over the amphitheater, its eyes blazing. She couldn't understand any of his actions. Why did he summon her here in the first place? Why did his own son, Abrax, hate him so deeply that he had tried to overthrow the kingdom? And above all, what made him think Abrax was no longer a threat?

Maybe the will of gods wasn't really meant to be understood. In all likelihood, they were completely mental from all the time they spent in hell.

By her side, Bael stood perfectly still, his eyes closed. His chest rose and fell in an even rhythm. Entirely unperturbed by everything he'd just seen. *Just another day in the Shadow Realm.*

Hothgar banged the gong, and the noise of the crowd died.

"Of the fifty-six champions who joined the melee, twenty-three remain in his mortal realm. In glorious battle, twenty-three more have joined the void to live for eternity."

As Hothgar spoke, black-cloaked oneiroi jogged silently into the arena. Remembering Massu's ferocity, she shuddered. But these oneiroi weren't here to fight. They were here to clean up the corpses. Silently, the oneiroi dragged them from the arena. The bodies left red smears over the dirt.

Hothgar thrust his hand into the air. "Massu, can you step forward?"

Cera's brother stepped forward, his mouth dripping with fresh blood.

Ursula heard the pause, the sharp intake of breath before Hothgar spoke again. And when he did, he spoke through clenched teeth. "This has been the first melee to include an oneiroi," said Hothgar. "Despite his inferior status, he killed five demons, the most of any champion. As ordained in the warrior code, this accomplishment grants him pole position for the race."

Massu bowed deeply.

Hothgar continued, "The race will be held at Asta. We will commence when the sun reaches its peak above the spire."

Lifting his hammer, the Sword Of Nyxobas smashed the gong a final time.

The demons around her turned to leave, and Ursula bit her lip to stop the tears welling in her eyes. She turned away from Bael so he couldn't see her face.

Sure, she could use a sword. She could fight if she had to. But this had been a complete nightmare. A savage display of bloodlust, for absolutely no purpose.

And the scariest part was that she'd fit right in.

Blinking away the tears, she searched the sky for a sign of Cera. Maybe Bael thought they couldn't be friends, but whether he liked it or not, Cera was her ride home.

"Ursula?" Bael touched her arm, and she turned back to him.

He leveled his intense gaze on her. Apart from the blood spattering his cheeks, he looked perfect. Like a god himself—golden skin, thick lashes framing violet eyes, and full lips.

"You should come with me," he said quietly. "I'll heal you, but not here."

"Where's Cera?"

"She had to return to my manor." He turned to walk for one of the open archways, expecting her to follow.

She quickened her pace to catch up with him. "You didn't let her stay to see her brother fight?"

"No."

"Why? I'm sure she wanted to be here." Ursula's stomach clenched. *She must be out of her mind with worry.*

"What if he'd died? Do you think she'd have wanted to be there for that? Do you think she'd want it to plague her nightmares for the rest of her life?"

Ursula shook her head. "I'm sure she could decide for herself, if you hadn't decided for her."

"She doesn't yet know what it's like to watch..." He cut his own sentence short. "Don't question me."

Clearly, there was a story there. But she already knew if she probed further, he'd rebuff her.

Bael led her through the archway into a stone tunnel, their footsteps echoing off the ceiling. She tried to block out the pain lancing her shoulders—every step was an agony, and she could hardly keep pace with Bael.

He turned to look at her, then spoke a few words in Angelic. A glowing orb appeared in front of them, casting a dull light on the rough stone walls.

She swallowed hard. "I'm confused why you'd care about protecting Cera's feelings. You said the oneiroi are not our friends."

Pearly light shone at the end of the tunnel.

"No. They're not, but that doesn't mean we must be cruel to them." He stole a glance at her. "You fought well today."

"I don't feel great about everything I saw today."

"It's not your first battle. You fought the oneiroi in the fae realm."

She bit her lip. "Yes, but they seemed so vicious then. So inhuman. Now that I know Massu drew spaceships as a little boy, it will be hard to cut his head off. Plus, this battle served no purpose except to entertain people I hate. They could have just given you your manor back and saved us all the carnage. But where would the fun be in that, for people like Hothgar?"

At the end of the tunnel, they stepped out into the cold night air. On the barren, gray land, lines of carriages wound over the landscape. Bael turned, walking a few paces to his black and silver carriage.

He pulled open the door, motioning for her to enter.

She sat, laying the sword across her lap, and he climbed in next to her, closing the door.

"Take off your jacket," he said.

She did as instructed, peeling off the black leather jacket. Blood poured from her shoulder, and she tried not to look at the deep gash that had ripped through tendons and muscle.

Bael's jaw tightened at the sight of it. Remus's blade had found its way past her jacket's collar, straight into her flesh.

He touched her skin, just on the edges of her wound, and closed his eyes. Shadow magic swirled from his body, rushing over her injury in a soothing wave. She could feel the pain leaving her shoulder, replaced by a soft tingling sensation, a powerful caress.

Warmth radiated from his fingertips. Were these gentle hands the same ones that had just slaughtered four demons?

She gazed into his eyes, and her pulse raced. Maybe it was the trauma of the fight, but with him so close to her, with his powerful hands on her body, she couldn't think straight.

"Where else are you injured?" he asked softly.

It took her a moment to remember how to speak. "My back."

He glanced away. "You'll need to take off the corset, and face the other way."

Her pulse raced faster, and she turned away from him. She slowly began unbuttoning the front of her corset, then pulled it off. Her nipples hardened in the cold air.

She felt Bael's warm fingertips trace just over the wound. "You were protected by two layers of Cera's armor, I see. What weapon cut through to your flesh?"

"A scythe."

"Did you kill the reaper?"

"Yes."

She felt his magic washing over her skin, soothing the pain and warming her body at the same time. When she could no longer feel the pain from the cut, Bael's fingertips grazed lower over her back, and heat shot through her body. Despite the cold, a blush rose on her chest.

She tensed. *Ursula, you sick bastard.* Why was she thinking about sex now? She'd just taken part in a massacre.

Bael pulled his hand away. "You can dress again.

She pulled the corset around herself, buttoning it up again. She was certain her cheeks were flushed, and that Bael would notice the blush on her body, the dilated pupils. What would he think of her getting turned on by his touch after everything that had just happened?

Then again, she was pretty sure she'd read once that sex and death went hand-in-hand. During the bubonic plague, people reacted one of two ways: they walked through the streets, whipping themselves in penitence. Or they shagged strangers in the woods.

Apparently, she was the stranger-shagging type. If she had to guess, Bael was probably more likely the self-flagellating kind.

She fastened the button on the top of her corset. "Are we going?"

"You must return to the manor, but I'm not joining you."

"Why not?"

"I must attend to business with the lords." She glanced at him, certain her cheeks still glowed from the intense pleasure of his touch. "I forgot to thank you for the sword."

"You deserved a fair fight. But don't forget that in the end, only one of us can live."

His words sent a chill through her. "I know." *And there's not much of a chance it will be me.*

He started to shut the door, but turned back to her. With a furrowed brow, he leaned in to the carriage and met her eyes. "When you get back, pour a lavender bath. It will help with the nightmares."

He leaned out again, closing the door with a final click.

CHAPTER 25

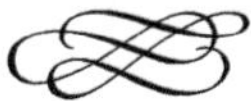

Cera jumped to her feet the moment Ursula opened the door to her quarters. The oneiroi's eyes were frantic, her question unspoken. Faint sunlight streamed through the darkened windows.

Ursula held up a hand. "He's fine. Massu is fine. And so is Bael. We all made it."

Cera dropped to her knees, clasping her hands together. "Thank the gods. I knew it would be okay, just for today." She rose, her eyes wide. "Massu is entirely unharmed?"

"Not only unharmed, but he won the tournament. He killed five demons."

Cera's hand flew to her mouth. "Don't lie to me."

"I would never lie to you. He slew five with his bare hands." *With his teeth, really.*

"Oh my gods. Oh my gods," said Cera softly, kneading her hands. She paused, her eyes widening even further. "Bael fought well, too?"

"Yes, he's fine," said Ursula with a sigh. "Not a scratch on him. He moves like the wind."

Cera dropped her face into her hands. With her face hidden, she could easily be mistaken for a child.

"What's the matter?"

"I didn't know who was going to open the door: you, milord, or someone else. If it had been another—"

Ursula's throat tightened. *Any other demon would have killed you, wouldn't he?* Despite Bael's warning, she couldn't reconcile this sweet woman with the savagery she'd seen from Massu. Could Cera fight that way? It was hard to believe this little seamstress with her cardigans could eat a man's flesh off his skull.

"Cera?" she asked tentatively. "Do all oneiroi fight with their teeth instead of weapons?"

"What?" Cera wiped a tear from her eye.

"Do oneiroi ever use swords or daggers?"

Cera's brow furrowed. "Of course oneiroi use swords. Why would you ask that?"

"Your brother—" *And frankly, all the other oneiroi I've ever battled.* "Massu didn't use his a sword. He used his teeth."

"No." Cera shook her head. "No. Don't tell me that."

Ursula's blood chilled. "What's wrong?"

"That way of fighting is forbidden. Those who taste the forbidden flesh turn into beasts. They become the Corrupted!"

Ursula's mouth went dry. *Abrax has apparently screwed up a whole lot of oneiroi.*

Frantic, Cera gripped her hair. "Once an oneiroi starts, he can't stop. The call of blood is too strong. Before Nyxobas arrived, the Corrupted were ostracized—sent to wander the wastes, where they fed upon each other like wild beasts."

"What is the forbidden flesh?"

"Any raw meat. It only applies to oneiroi. It's something in our nature. Eat too much meat, it changes us. Stokes a different kind of hunger. We become stronger, faster, and angrier, but at the cost of our minds." Her lip curled back from her teeth. "I would murder Massu if he weren't certain to die in the melee. He should have never allowed himself to become Corrupted."

Given the ferocious look on Cera's face, Ursula didn't fancy Massu's chances in a fight against his sister. Even if he'd won the tournament.

A knocking at the door interrupted them, and Cera hurried over to it. "Who is it?"

"Bael." His voice boomed through the door.

Cera flung it open. Bael stood in the doorway in clean clothes that fit his muscular body perfectly. The lunar wind blew a tendril of hair in front of his eyes.

"Milord." Cera bowed. "I'm so relieved you are unharmed."

He nodded at her. "Thank you. I wish to speak to Ursula. Alone."

"Yes, of course, milord." Cera hurried from her quarters, and Bael shut the door behind her. He narrowed his eyes, studying her as he walked closer. "How does your shoulder feel?"

"Fine." She crossed her arms. She couldn't stop thinking about the feel of his fingertips on her bare skin. Just looking at him, she could feel a blush creeping into her cheeks. Bael hadn't actually shown any interest in her, and anyway they were supposed to kill each other. So what the hell was she thinking about his hands for?

She needed to change the subject. "Did you know that Abrax has been feeding oneiroi raw meat?" she blurted.

"Yes. It turns them into savage fighters—brings out the beast within them."

"Right." She swallowed hard. "Thank you for healing me."

His brow furrowed, and he looked at the ground. She had the impression he wanted to ask her something, but he couldn't quite get the words out.

"Did you want something?" she prompted.

"I thought perhaps you wouldn't like to eat alone. I was hoping you might join me for dinner."

Now that was unexpected. She glanced down at her leather outfit covered in sand and dried blood. "I'll need time to change."

"Of course. I'll return in an hour." He turned, departing as suddenly as he'd come.

* * *

As she filled the bath, Ursula peeled off the blood-stained leather trousers and corset.

Cera had been right about the strength of the material. A few slashes had pierced through the reinforced leather, but it still hung together. Still, something would have to be done about the grit that seemed to permeate every crease and fold. If she wore it again, she'd get a rash.

She stepped into the bath, letting the warm water soothe her burning muscles.

She closed her eyes, but the images from the fight flooded her mind: Remus, impaled on her sword. The reaper's head, detaching from his body, the hot spray of crimson blood. Her eyes snapped open again.

She reached for the soap—lavender-scented. Bael had said it would chase the nightmares away. She rubbed it over her skin, working up a pale blue lather, washing away the blood and grit. When she inhaled deeply, some of the images faded from her mind.

Still, a voice nagged in the back of her mind. Fighting—viciously—had come so easily to her. So who was F.U.? What had she done that slicing through a man's neck came as naturally as breathing? Ursula swallowed hard. She couldn't help but wonder if F.U. had been something of a monster.

And she had the strange feeling that Nyxobas knew all about F.U.'s monstrosity. Still, Ursula couldn't remember a damn thing.

She stepped out of the bath, toweling off. As she examined her skin in the mirror, she could find not a single scar marring her pale skin. Bael's magic had worked remarkably well. In fact, as she gazed at herself in the mirror, she couldn't stop thinking about the feel of his powerful magic, kissing her body. What would his lips feel like on her bare skin? The lords' wives had said he was an amazing lover.

She gritted her teeth. *Stop it, Ursula.* It was ridiculous. He was going to kill her—he had no *choice* but to kill her. Unless, by some miracle, she managed to slaughter him first. And here she was, wondering what his lips would feel like on her bare skin.

"There is something really wrong with you, you know that?" she said to her reflection.

Wrapped in a towel, she climbed the stairs to the bedroom she never used. Cera had left some dresses in there.

She opened a drawer, plucking out a pair of purple knickers. She slid them on over her hips, then crossed to the closet. She pulled out a dress— a stunning indigo. She stepped into it, pulling it up over her shoulders. Her milky-white legs shone through the sheer fabric. Delicate, glimmering stitching wound up the front of the dress. *Cera is an absolute genius.*

She slipped into a pair of deep-blue heels.

Cera had left a makeup kit on the dresser, and she rubbed blush into her cheeks.

She felt like she was preparing for a date, which was completely insane. She was meeting another warrior, for a post-slaughter feast, before they jumped into the fray again.

Still, after everything she'd seen, it was a relief to do something normal. The mundane tasks of lining her eyes with black, slicking lip-gloss over her lips—a rich red, the color of—

She slammed the lipstick on the top of her dresser. *That's enough of that.* She wasn't going to think about death right now. She pulled a soft, white cloak from the closet, and wrapped it around her shoulders. Before leaving the bedroom, she shoved the silver ring into her pocket.

A knock sounded from downstairs. *He's already here.*

She hurried down the stairs and pulled open the door.

Bael stood in the doorway, dressed in a midnight-blue cloak, with a deep gray suit underneath. "Ursula. Thank you for joining me. Cera arranged dinner in my hall."

Her stomach rumbled as she stepped outside. "I'm actually starving."

They walked across the bridge, the lunar wind nipping at her skin.

"I thought you might be hungry," he said. "Battle either turns your stomach or leaves you ravenous."

She frowned as they hurried over the bridge. "F.U. seems to have a brutal side."

"F.U.?"

"Former Ursula. Me, before I lost my memory."

He arched an eyebrow. "Right. Her brutal side may have saved your life."

He led her into the lion atrium, where milky sunlight streamed through the shattered wall. On the dark side of the room, candlelight danced over the smashed tile, and her heels crushed the fragments of the floor. "Why don't you repair this place? It didn't seem to take you long to repair the broken window in my quarters."

"I want to remember." He pulled open an onyx door, revealing the tunnel illuminated by glowing mushrooms.

She rubbed the ring between her fingers. "And how long will you leave it that way as a reminder?"

"Until I make things right again."

She took a deep breath. Making things right again meant reclaiming his manor. And that meant she had to die. Dread coiled around her heart. "Will you make sure I have a quick death, if it comes to it?"

His icy gaze slid to her, and his jaw tightened. "Of course. And I'd ask that you do the same for me."

"Do you really think I'd stand a chance against you?"

"Like you said, F.U. knew how to fight. You move like a phantom."

"Too bad I have no idea why."

"That's a mercy."

Surprise flickered through her. "You think severe retrograde amnesia is a mercy?"

"Believe me. There are far worse things than forgetting." Ice laced his tone.

Okay. So that's an awkward topic.

As they walked, Ursula ran her fingers along the rough walls. "Did the oneiroi carve this?"

"No, it was here when I won the manor."

She frowned. "So the previous lord made it?"

Bael paused, reaching out to touch one of the glyphs in the stone, his powerful body just inches from hers. She could feel the heat coming off him, and his delicious smell distracted her. Maybe her attraction to Bael wasn't totally crazy after all. If she was going to die soon, at least she could enjoy her final days.

"No one knows what the symbols mean," he said. "Not even the oneiroi. These tunnels have been here for as long as anyone can remember—even before Nyxobas arrived."

He turned, walking again, his heels echoing off the tunnel ceiling.

Ursula picked up her pace to keep up with him. "I don't understand. Why would anyone take the trouble to burrow through one hundred feet of solid rock?" *And more importantly, is there a way I can use this as an escape route?* Though it was pretty difficult to escape an entire moon. *Perhaps I can hide down here for decades like a mole person, living on mushrooms.*

"I'm not entirely sure why it's here," said Bael as he reached the end of the passage. "But I think it's on account of those." He pointed to the giant indigo crystals on the cavern's ceiling. Together with the luminescent mushrooms that clustered around them, they bathed the cavern in a pale violet light.

Ursula stiffened as a subtle vibration began to hum inside her belly, tugging her closer to the source of the magic, as if on an invisible thread. "What are they?"

"The light of the crystals amplifies magic," Bael continued. "I think whoever carved the tunnel wanted to be closer to them."

They crossed to the narrow stone bridge that hung between the stalactites. Following Bael, she took a tentative step onto the bridge. Her stomach swooped. On either side of the stone strip, the cavern floor dropped away. She shuddered. "It looks like Nyxobas's void."

He turned, violet light sparking in his eyes. "You've seen the void?"

Her heart raced. "Can we have this conversation on the other side of the bridge?"

"Of course."

He moved swiftly to the other side of the bridge, turning to offer his hand. "Is everything okay?"

"Just a little vertigo."

"As long as you don't try to stab me with a corkscrew again."

"Was that supposed to be a joke?"

"I have been known to tell a joke in my twenty-two thousand years."

"And are they the best jokes the world has ever known?"

He shot her a sharp look. Apparently, her jokes weren't funny.

When they reached the central platform, Ursula saw a small, black marble table standing in the center, with two chairs on either side. Two silver domed trays lay on the table, along with a bottle of chilled champagne and glasses. Bael gestured for her to sit.

She pulled off her cloak, wrapping it over the back of her chair. Bael's eyes slowly slid up and down her body, and he took a deep breath.

She sat across from Bael. His gaze locked on hers. "The clothing you wear distracts me."

A blush warmed her chest. "Is that a bad thing?"

"No. Yes. It's hard for me to think straight when I can see your skin through your dresses. Or when I see you standing naked in the portal room. Or that corset—"

"Is this why you asked me to dinner? To lecture me about nudity?"

"No."

"I thought you were supposed to be a legendary lover, not a major prude."

A smile curled his lips. "Is that what you've heard?"

Blushing, she drummed her fingernails on the tablecloth. "That's what the lords' wives say."

Suddenly serious, he frowned. "But you understand that we're not lovers, nor will we ever be. One of us will die soon, and I could never be with a hound of Emerazel in that way."

Angry heat warmed her cheeks. *Well, now I feel like a total idiot.* "Of course I know that. That's not what I meant. And anyway, I'd never want to be with a...an ancient shadow warrior..." she spluttered. She was pretty sure her cheeks were a fetching shade of crimson right now.

"Of course."

"Are we going to eat?" Avoiding eye contact, she pulled the dome off her tray. She wasn't sure what had just happened, but it stung like hell.

Neatly arranged on a plate lay a roast chicken and a watercress salad. *Most awkward non-date in the history of non-dates.* Why had he asked her here?

I'll just eat in silence. She picked up her knife and fork, cutting into the chicken.

Bael pulled the dome off his tray, and steam curled into the air. "The next trial is a race. You will need training."

"I'll be fine. I'm good at running."

"We won't be running. We'll be riding bats. You will need to learn how to fly one."

"Great. And you're going to train me?"

"Yes."

She swallowed a bite of her salad. "Why, exactly, are you so eager to help a hound of Emerazel?"

"I told Nyxobas I would protect you."

"That was before he threw me into the melee," she pointed out.

He took a deep breath. "I don't know why I want to help you." He frowned. "I suppose it's an unfair disadvantage that you're not native to the Shadow Realm. Like I said, you deserve a fair chance."

She cut into her chicken. "So you're just big on fairness?"

His gaze roamed down her body, then up again. "If someone is offering you help to save your life, you'd do best not to question it."

"Fair enough." She sipped her champagne. "I'd just like to note your inconsistencies."

"Noted."

"Is that all you wanted to talk to me about? I mean, that and how we're not going to be lovers?" *Whoops. That sounded bitter.*

"I wanted to talk to you about Cera," he said.

Oh. So that's why I'm here. "You already told me. The oneiroi are not my friends." She obviously wasn't going to change his mind. No point in arguing.

"It's more than that." He reached into his pocket, pulling out the obsidian knife. "This weapon. It could have cost Cera her life if anyone had learned where it had come from. Her desire to protect you puts her in danger."

Guilt pressed on her chest. "I hadn't thought of that." She frowned. "Really though, if you'd given me the katana before the melee, it wouldn't have been an issue."

His jaw tightened. "That was a last-minute decision."

She swallowed a bite of chicken. "So a part of you thought, 'maybe I'll just kill the hound.'"

His eyes pierced her. "A part of me thought a quick death at my hands would serve you best."

"What made you change your mind?"

He shrugged. "What if I'd been wrong? What if you're stronger than I'd thought? I don't know you. You don't even know you. You deserved a chance." He speared his chicken.

She took a swig of her champagne. "Thank you for the chance."

Her mind flooded again with a vision of the gore-strewn crater. Anger simmered, and the sting of Bael's rejection only worsened her mood. "I just—I don't understand this world. It's savage. Nyxobas is savage. He'll kill an oneiroi just for having a rock-knife. He forces his subjects to slaughter each other to prove themselves. Father and son hate each other. No one is actually happy here."

Dark magic whorled off his body, angrily slashing the air. "As if your goddess is any better."

Ursula slammed a hand on the table. "How many times do I have to tell you? She is not my goddess. I don't remember what F.U. did."

"That's right." His voice dripped with sarcasm. "She's F.U.'s goddess."

"Exactly."

"And F.U. was perfectly innocent, I'm sure. A pure follower of Emerazel, who knew how to wield a sword like the most savage assassin. Who Nyxobas has chosen as his champion. Who can't seem to control her fire, and who felt the need to wipe her memories clean to wash away the horror of what she'd done. A coward's way out."

His words slid through her bones, and an image of a burning house rose in her mind. What *had* she done? "You don't know that F.U. was a monster."

His powerful magic slashed the air around him. "When you threw the dagger at Nyxobas, what exactly was going through your head?"

She shook her head. *I don't want to get into that.*

Bael leaned in closer, his eyes piercing. "I can see that you're hiding something. Tell me what you were thinking?"

Tears moistened her eyes. She swallowed hard. "The voice said, *kill the king.*"

He leaned back. "And yet, you're not a savage at all. Not like the shadow demons."

"I don't know where the voice came from."

"Easy to be blameless when you have no memories though, isn't it? When you divorce yourself so thoroughly from your former life that you think of yourself as two people. You're not a killer... F.U. is. How convenient for you."

"It's a little hard for me to defend these accusations when I have no memory. Forget the katana. *This* isn't a fair fight."

"Don't you get it, Ursula?" Venom laced his voice. "Having no memory is a blessing. Stop feeling sorry for yourself and count yourself lucky."

She gripped her knife, tears stinging her eyes. "And what did you do, Bael, to end up here in this wasteland below your manor?" She gestured at the empty cavern. "What guilt eats at you, that you've created your own little void? No messy emotions. No one close, no one to hurt you. Pretty safe here, among the mushrooms and the rocks, isn't it? Tell me, Bael. When was the last time you loved anyone but yourself?"

His eyes shaded to a deep black. "That is none of your concern, hound."

"The lords' wives told me you were an amazing lover. But it doesn't seem you kept any women around for long. No wonder you adore Nyxobas. You're just like him. Lost in the void. Talk about a coward's way out."

She stood, her legs shaking, and crossed back to the stone bridge. As she crossed, she peered over at the sheer drop into darkness.

And the darkness called to her.

CHAPTER 26

Ursula stopped when she reached the atrium. When she'd come through here with Bael, the candles in the sconces had been lit, and sunlight had streamed through the hole in the wall. Now, darkness shrouded the entire space, as if it were night. The hair rose on the back of her neck. Something was wrong.

"Cera?" she called out, her voice echoing off the ceiling.

Maybe I'd do best not to call attention to myself.

She edged back to the tunnel, and then a cloaked figure stepped from the shadows. A cold chill struck her like a slap in the face.

"Ursula," he cooed. Abrax's voice was unmistakable. A soft rasp, simultaneously terrifying and hypnotic. "I was hoping I might run into you."

He pushed back his hood, revealing his perfect porcelain skin and glacial gray eyes. Black magic twisted around him. Not angry and savage like Bael's, but cautious—almost tentative. Little tendrils that searched the darkness, probing for answers. One snaked by her throat, cold as a corpse's fingers.

He stepped toward her and she shrunk back toward the tunnel. That was her only chance of escape, even if it meant a humiliating retreat to Bael after their argument.

But Abrax wasn't a demon she could fight. He wasn't even a demon.

He was a demigod. And without Emerazel's magic flowing in her veins, she didn't stand a chance.

If she let him get too close, he'd lure her in with his seductive spell. He'd drain her soul and send it to Nyxobas's void. She took another step back toward the tunnel. A few more steps and she'd be within the relative safety of its walls.

"Ursula," he purred. "Don't be afraid. I'm not here to hurt you."

You must think I'm a total mug.

Just as she began to turn, Bael appeared in a blur of night magic. "What are you doing in my manor, incubus?"

"Oh, did I interrupt something? A lover's quarrel?" Abrax smirked, his magic retreating. "You know that Nyxobas strictly forbids liaisons between hounds and his demons. But, of course, I'll overlook it. I am sympathetic to perverted urges, secret passions... a bit of unnatural fornication between the godlike and the beasts."

Ursula gagged. *Did he just say unnatural fornication?*

Bael's eyes burned with black fury. "What are you doing here?"

"I wanted to congratulate you two on your performance in the melee. Fighting side by side as you did. It was like watching a ballet performed by trained serpents."

"That's not why you're here," said Bael, his voice cold as ice.

Abrax flashed a brilliant, white smile. Everything about him was repulsive—apart from how he looked. "Correct. I wish to parley."

From what Ursula knew, "parley" was some kind of medieval English way of saying, "I'm going to talk a lot and then screw you over."

Abrax took a step closer to the pair. "You saw how well Massu performed today."

From the shadows behind Abrax, a pair of oneiroi stepped into the light. Ursula hadn't even noticed them before—truly, the oneiroi were creatures of shadow.

They stood to Abrax's right—one tall and one short. An iron muzzle covered the shorter man's mouth, and when he lifted his face to the light, she recognized Massu's eyes.

The larger oneiroi held an iron chain leashed around Massu's neck. Massu glared at Ursula and started for her, but the other oneiroi yanked him back.

"I brought him along to say hello," said Abrax.

Massu growled, jerking at his chain like an enraged pit bull.

"I hope you understand that I will win the tournament with Massu as my champion." He glared at Bael. "Do you still have your wife's portrait hanging in that room? I hope you'll leave it up. I'd like to gaze at her face while I fuck my courtesans in your manor. Sorry, *my* manor."

Bael's magic whipped the air around him. She could feel the fury rolling off his body. He was exercising all of his strength not to rip Abrax's head right off his body.

On a balcony two levels above, a flicker of movement caught her eye. A small figure peered over the rail.

"Massu will not win," Bael growled. "And when my wings are returned to me, I will take my place as Nyxobas's Sword once again. You may be his son. But he will never deem you worthy."

The night magic began to swirl around Abrax again, and the temperature dropped. Ursula's breath clouded around her head.

Cloaked in shadows, Abrax disappeared—only to appear again directly behind her. With a single, powerful hand, he pinned both of her arms behind her back.

"She's very interesting, don't you think?" Slowly, he ran a cold finger along her cheek, sending an icy shiver through her body. "I should have been her guardian. I don't know what she is. Not a normal human. Not a normal demon. She repulses and attracts me at the same time, and that is an intoxicating combination."

With her arms pinned behind her back, she struggled to free herself. Abrax's grip was ironclad.

Slowly, Bael stepped closer. "Get away from her, incubus."

Abrax gripped her by the back of her hair, pulling back her neck. The timbre of his voice changed becoming stronger. "Give her to me, and I will see that you keep your manor."

"No." Bael's razor-sharp voice cut through the air.

"You'll give up your manor for this dog? What is she to you?"

Snarling, Bael began to charge for Abrax—but a burst of magic from Abrax sent dark filaments of night magic racing across the room, wrapping around Bael's chest and mouth.

Abrax's grip on Ursula's arms was surely crushing her bones. "Abrax," she spat. "Do you think your daddy will be pleased that you're assaulting his champion?"

"Shut your filthy mouth, you abomination," said Abrax. "If I can't have you, no one will."

Ursula's heart skipped a beat. *Think, Ursula. Think.*

She slid her leg between Abrax's, and he pressed against her, moaning into her ear. "Have you changed your mind, little dog?" Gritting her teeth, she kicked upward, into his groin.

Abrax grunted, releasing her arms. Then, he pushed her onto the floor. "Massu. Get your dinner."

The taller oneiroi ripped the mask off Massu's face. With a shrill scream, Cera's brother leapt for her throat. She rolled to the side, and Massu landed softly on the tile, like a cat. She clambered to her feet, as Massu leapt again.

She blocked his attack with her arm. A white-hot jolt of pain seared through her as Massu buried his teeth in her forearm. She screamed.

He clawed at her, pulling her hair, exposing the soft skin of her throat.

"Massu!" Cera's clear voice pierced the darkness. "Stop this right now, or I will give you a hiding!"

Massu loosened his grip on Ursula's arm, his silver eyes wide.

"Destroy her," said Abrax.

Massu's gaze turned back to Ursula. Hungrily, he licked his teeth. Ursula's gaze flicked to Bael. Out of the corner of her eye, she glimpsed him slowly working his way out of the bonds. *Come on, Bael.*

"Massu!" Cera shouted. "What did I tell you? Don't make me come down there."

Massu's head swiveled between Abrax and his sister. His arms trembled with indecision.

Cera called out again. "Massu, you let her go. You are not meant to be the Corrupted." "What is wrong with you?" Abrax roared. "I gave you a command."

Massu's turned back to her, baring his teeth, and she glanced at Bael again. In the shadows, he'd ripped away the filaments.

He roared, a sound of pure masculinity, a primal challenge.

His eyes wild, Massu leapt for Bael's throat, a blur of black and silver. A ravenous missile bent on the destruction of Bael's perfect face.

But he never made it that far. A sleek black blade glinted in Bael's hands, and Ursula watched as Bael plunged it into Massu's chest.

Cera's agonized wails echoed off the atrium walls, and bile rose in Ursula's throat.

Bael lifted his knife to Abrax. "You may be the son of Nyxobas, but I will kill you to protect my manor."

Night magic gathered around Abrax once again. The inky tendrils waved furiously about his head. "You killed my champion."

Starlight glistened in Bael's darkened eyes. "You violated the rules of the tournament."

Ursula took a step closer to Abrax. "Your father must be pretty cross about that whole army you raised against him. And here you are, breaking his rules again. How does he punish you? I imagine it's unpleasant."

Abrax's eyes blazed like starlight and his jaw dropped, like he'd been slapped in the face. Slowly, he turned and began to stride toward the hole in the wall at the far side of the atrium.

When Abrax reached the gap in the wall, he turned to face them, the tall oneiroi at his side. His gaze slid to Ursula. "When I capture you and force you into submission, the memories of today will only intensify my pleasure."

A shiver inched up her spine.

Shadows curled around Abrax and his oneiroi, completely enveloping them until they disappeared. Cera's cries still echoed through the atrium.

Bael turned to her, his face stony. "I must go to Cera. Show me your arm, first."

She lifted her arm, wincing at the vicious teeth-marks puncturing her skin. Bael let his powerful magic caress her skin, but this time, she took no pleasure in it. Her eyes slid to Massu's lifeless corpse, and nausea welled in her gut.

She hardly noticed Bael leaving.

She stood alone in the atrium, listening to the sound of Cera's cries. A deep, gnawing loneliness pressed on her chest.

Suddenly, it hit her. She was going to die here in the Shadow Realm, among a legion of demons who hated her.

CHAPTER 27

Ursula hurried into her quarters, pulling open her door. Once inside, she shut the it behind her listening for the familiar click of the lock. For the first time in her visit to the Shadow Realm, she actually appreciated the sound.

She ran for the bathroom, kneeling in front of the toilet, then heaved up her dinner. As she wiped a shaking hand across her mouth, she tried not to think about Abrax.

He'd corrupted the oneiroi. And she didn't know what he wanted to do to her—only that everything about him horrified her. What did he mean—she's not a normal demon, nor a normal human?

She peeled off her blood-soaked dress, letting it drop to the floor. He sensed something about her, something that stoked his perverse desires. What sort of an abomination *was* she?

She grabbed a cloth, running warm water over it, and washed herself off. In a daze, she snatched a fresh nightgown from upstairs, and slipped into it. Half of her wanted to go to Cera, but Bael was already with her. He'd slaughtered her brother, yes. But he still viewed himself as her protector.

Sunlight streamed in through the window, but tired as she was, she'd be able to sleep through it. She curled up onto the sofa and let her eyes drift shut.

She slept fitfully, dreaming of the reaper she'd slaughtered today. Remus chased her through a forest of bones, and Massu waited for her in a desolate wasteland. Each dream ended as they pulled her down and into the unending abyss of Nyxobas's void.

"Ursula?" A female voice jolted her from her sleep.

Ursula rubbed her eyes, blinking at Cera, her eyes red-rimmed.

An image flashed in her mind—Bael's knife slashing through Massu's throat.

"Cera?" She sat up, throwing her arms around Cera. "I'm so sorry about Massu."

"Abrax killed him," said Cera softly.

"What do you mean?" she loosened her grasp.

"The lord... Abrax killed his soul when he fed him raw meat."

Ursula nodded. "I hope to kill Abrax some day."

"Another thing we have in common," said Cera grimly.

The rich scent of food wafted past Ursula's nostrils.

Ursula frowned. "Please tell me you didn't cook. You should be mourning, not making me breakfast."

"I didn't cook. The lord instructed another of his servants to cook for us."

Ursula arched an eyebrow. "He's okay with us eating together? He said it was dangerous for us to be friends."

Cera shrugged. "I think he figures we're in danger no matter what. Might as well not be alone for it." Cera beckoned her to the bar. "Come. Join me."

Ursula stood, crossing to the bar. Since she'd puked up her dinner last night, her stomach was completely empty. Her mouth watered at the sight of orange juice, fresh fruit, toast, eggs, and a carafe of coffee. Cera had already set out two plates.

Ursula took a seat next to Cera and scooped eggs and fruit onto a plate. Ravenous, she dug in, working her way through the eggs and toast. She took a sip of coffee, then glanced at Cera.

The oneiroi pushed her food around on her plate.

"Not hungry?" asked Ursula.

"Not today."

"It will take time, I imagine," said Ursula.

"I hadn't seen him in decades. I guess in some ways, I'd mourned him already. But I didn't need to watch him die."

Ursula nodded. "Bael said to use lavender for the nightmares."

Cera grinned. "He is wise. And what does he have planned for you today?"

"I'm not entirely sure. He said he was going to train me to ride one of the bats, but then we had a big argument, and he said I was a monster, and I said he lived in a void like Nyxobas because he was scared of emotions."

Cera stared at her.

Ursula sipped her coffee. "So anyway, I'm not sure if he's still going to help me."

"Well, if he does plan to train you, the main thing is to hold on tight. It's really not that difficult if you remember to respect the bat."

"How do you do that?" Ursula asked.

"You talk to them. They'll respond to your instructions."

"They know English?"

"No, but they understand tone and inflection."

A knock sounded on the door, and Ursula jumped up. *Guess we're still on, then.* "I'll get it." She hurried across the floor, flinging open the front door.

With the sunlight streaming behind him, Bael stood in the doorway, dressed in black riding leathers. His gaze trailed over her nightgown.

Of course, she hadn't bothered to get dressed before she flung open the door. But then—after their conversation yesterday—she had the strongest urge to distract him out of spite.

"Hello, Bael. Come on in." She turned, knowing that he'd get a full view of the nightgown's plunging backline.

"Do you plan to wear clothes to this training?"

"Thinking about it," she said, turning back to him. She let the sleeve of her nightgown fall down, exposing her shoulder, but not so far that he could see her breast.

His gray eyes pierced right through her. "Are you doing this on purpose?"

Cera cleared her throat. "I feel it's time for me to leave."

"Not yet," said Bael, his eyes still locked on Ursula. "Please help Ursula find some clothes."

Cera let out an exasperated sigh. "Honestly, I don't know what's going on with you two."

As Cera hurried toward the stairwell, Ursula called out, "Make sure it's not too distracting for Bael! He gets distracted easily."

His jaw tightened.

She crossed her arms. "Wouldn't want you falling off your bat."

Bael's features softened, and he glanced away. "Is Cera okay?"

"As good as can be expected. She wants to murder Abrax, but that is perfectly reasonable."

Bael stared at the floor. "I had to kill Massu. Abrax had driven him insane. Once corrupted, there is no returning from the madness."

Ursula nodded. "I know. Plus, he was about to mess up your pretty face."

Bael glared at her. "Pretty?" He spat the word like an insult.

Cera's footsteps thundered down the stairs, and she bustled into the room with a bundle of clothes in her arms.

"That was fast," said Bael.

Cera nodded at the pile. "These should be appropriate for training."

"Thank you, Cera."

Bael nodded, his gaze landing on the top of the pile—on the lacy black knickers and bra.

He turned to walk for the door. "I'll meet you on the roof." When he was halfway to the door, he turned to face Cera, nodding so deeply it was almost a bow. "I'm sorry for your loss."

CHAPTER 28

Ursula stepped out of the elevator and onto the roof, shielding her eyes from the bright sunlight. On the sleek black roof, Bael crouched next to the bulk of an enormous black bat. As she approached, her heels clacking over the marble, Bael turned to look at her.

She wore thick woolen leggings, a leather jacket with a fur collar, and black riding boots that almost reached her knees. To complete the getup, she wore a large leather-covered helmet. She'd asked Cera if the helmet was strictly necessary, but the oneiroi had insisted.

Bael's lips curled in a smile. "Nice helmet."

She frowned. *I knew the helmet was a bad idea.* "Cera said it would protect my head."

Snorting, the bat shifted. It was monstrous, at least twice the size of Sotz.

She pointed. "Am I riding that?"

Bael patted the bat's back. "Vesperella? No, she's *my* baby girl." He put his fingers to his lips and whistled. A flapping of wings beat the air, and a moment later, Sotz landed next to her.

"I think you'll find it's easier to learn on a bat you're already familiar with."

She nodded at Sotz. "We've been getting to know each other."

"Can you steer?" he asked.

"Not really." *Not at all.*

Bael nodded. "You'll need to learn how to do it yourself if you want to have any hope of surviving the race."

"So how does it work? There was a harness that I held onto before." Ursula tried to remember how she'd seen Cera steer, but her vision had been blocked by Cera's back.

"You need to learn to ride bareback." Bael climbed onto Vesperella, demonstrating as he spoke. "You can hold onto the loose skin just behind the ears. Then just direct the bat's head the way you want it to fly." He tugged Vesperella's head to the right.

Ursula took a deep breath, glancing at Sotz. He narrowed his eyes. As she moved in closer, a low rumble rose in his chest and he bared his teeth.

"Easy, Sotz," said Bael. "Just step over his shoulders. You'll need to crouch a little bit."

"His shoulders?"

"Where the bat's wings connect to his chest," said Bael. "You'll want to sit right up against them. When he's flying, grip onto his chest with your calves." His gaze slid down to her legs. "You'll need to use your thigh muscles to hold on."

Ursula stepped over Sotz's neck and eased herself down. The moment her bum touched his back, he clambered forward toward the edge of the roof.

"Slow down," she shouted, tightening her thighs around his body. She gripped the loose skin behind his ears.

An instant later they were streaking down the roof and into the air. She glanced down at the crater, hundreds of feet below, and her breath caught. When Sotz curved wildly to the right, she lost her grip on his skin. Her heart thrummed wildly.

Panic blazed through her body, and she reached again for a grip, but Sotz twisted away from her. The motion sent her sliding to the side and she grabbed blindly, her fingers wrapping around the soft skin of one of his ears.

Sotz let out an ear-piercing shriek, bucking and jerking his body. She tried to hold on, but he threw her into the air.

Her heart stopped, and everything seemed to slow down. For a brief moment, her momentum keep her on an upward trajectory, and the whole valley of the crater spread out before her. She could see the houses of the oneiroi, Asta's purple spire, even the faint shimmer of magic along the rim of the crater, magic that—unfortunately for her—created gravity. She hurtled toward the ground, terror screaming through her mind. A scream tore from her throat.

As the wind ripped through her hair, something jerked the back of her jacket, halting her descent. In the next moment, Bael was pulling her on to Vesperella.

"Hang on to me!" he shouted over the wind.

Instinctually, she wrapped her arms around his neck, her face pressing into his chest. The bat was too large for her to get a grip on with her legs. Instead, she wrapped them around Bael's waist. He leaned in, steering the bat through the air. His heart pounded hard through his shirt.

She clung to him as he guided Vesperella out of a deep dive. The g-forces pressed her against his warm body, and she breathed in the scent of sandalwood by the sea. His sweet breath warmed the side of her face.

"Don't worry," he said. "The first time you fall from a bat is always the scariest."

The first time?

She could feel his muscles shifting as he expertly controlled the bat. With the wind rushing over their bodies, Bael directed Vesperella back to the rooftop in a great lazy arc.

"When you fly again," he said, "don't grip too tightly. It will spook him. You must be gentle with the bat. As I'm steering her now, even a slight twitch of my fingers is enough to make her respond the way I want."

Ursula swallowed hard. *Talk about distracting.*

Bael guided Vesperella into a soft landing on the roof, and Ursula unclenched her legs from Bael's waist. She stepped off, fighting dizziness.

He smirked. "Given the grip you had on me, I know you're strong enough to hang on."

"Thank you for not letting me die."

"I had a feeling you might need some assistance on your first flight. I almost smashed into those rocks over there on my race to get you." He pointed to a particularly sharp looking crag. "But, the main thing is to never grab a bat by its ears. They're very sensitive. I'll call Sotz and you can try again. "

Before Ursula could protest, Bael was whistling for the bat. This time,

Sotz landed next to Bael, his beady eyes trained on her. Ursula was relieved to see that his ear appeared undamaged.

Bael reached down and scratched Sotz's head. "It's okay, little guy. She's just a little clumsy."

"Well, there's no need to rub it in."

"Let's try it again," said Bael.

This time when she sat on Sotz's shoulders, she didn't lower her full weight. Instead she crouched down and whispered into the bat's ear.

"I'm sorry, Sotz. I didn't mean to hurt you."

She nuzzled her head against his. Sotz's fur was soft as velvet, and while he didn't purr like a cat, he didn't growl either.

"You're a good bat. A *good* bat," she repeated. She scratched behind his ears as she had seen Bael do with Vesperella. Then she gingerly lowered her full weight.

This time when Sotz launched, she already had a firm but gentle grip on the skin behind his ears. They hurtled toward the ground, and her stomach dropped. Gently, she pulled back on Sotz's neck and he leveled off. They flew above the crater's floor, barely one hundred feet above the ground, racing over the little stone houses and narrow alleys of the Shadow Kingdom.

"Good boy," she whispered in his ear.

The sound of beating wings made her turn her head. Bael flew twenty feet away, the lunar wind ruffling his dark hair.

"That's better," he shouted over the wind.

"Thanks."

"Lean forward, and allow your weight to shift with each beat of his wings."

Ursula leaned forward until her chest was inches from Sotz's neck. The position felt a bit more unstable. But when she began to shift her weight with each beat of Sotz's wings, she saw that Bael was right. The ride smoothed out into a smooth glide.

"That's it," said Bael. He and Vesperella swooped under her and Sotz. With two great beats of Vesperella's wings, he took the lead. "Follow me!"

Ursula marveled at his change in demeanor. He seemed so comfortable on the bat, like he actually enjoyed life. It was hard to believe this was the same man who'd slit Massu's throat just hours ago.

Bael led her and Sotz in a great curving turn back toward the rooftop.

When they were a hundred feet away, Bael and Vesperella dove for the roof at a terrifying speed. At the last instant, Vesperella spread her wings, landing gracefully on the marble.

Now he's just showing off. She leaned forward to whisper in Sotz's ear. "We got this, big guy." She tried to bring the bat in slowly, but as the roof rose to meet them, she instinctively leaned back. Sotz tensed as he tried to decide whether to land or to pull back up into the air. He chose landing, but they hit the roof with a jerk that knocked her straight from his back. She slammed against the marble, rolling a few times before coming to rest on her back.

When she opened her eyes, Bael stood over her, a look of concern on his face. "Are you all right?"

"I'm fine." Still lying flat on her back, Ursula brushed the dust from her jacket.

"Good, because you must be in one piece for this evening. We have been invited to dinner at Asta with the lords and their wives."

CHAPTER 29

A few hours later, Ursula and Bael stepped down from his carriage and onto the marble, on the very top level of the crystal spire. The sun burned bright in a black sky—thankfully, not at its zenith, yet.

She wore a gown of shimmering white silk, with a plunging backline, now covered by a pale blue cloak.

She stole a quick glance at Bael. "Remind me again why we're here?"

"As lord, I'm required to attend dinners at the spire."

She arched an eyebrow. "And remind me why I needed to come?"

"Because your presence will distract everyone enough that I won't need to speak to anyone."

She cocked her head, the wind whipping through her hair. "I'm not sure that I distract everyone. I think that's just you."

He shook his head slowly. "Everyone watches you."

That's disturbing. Steeling her nerves, she glanced out at the dancing swarms of lunar moths. Asta's purple light shone through their wings, as they wove and dodged silently around the spire. For some bizarre reason, she felt strangely at home here. At peace.

She reached into her cloak pocket, rolling the silver ring around in the palm of her hand.

"We should enter," said Bael.

She turned to see him pulling open a black door that led into a dark hall. She stepped inside, walking at Bael's side. Some insane impulse overtook her, and she slid her arm through his.

She felt his muscle tense as she touched his elbow, but he kept silent.

The hallway opened into an enormous rectangular hall, the walls painted silver. A spray of ravens had been painted over one of the walls. Black chandeliers, lit with candles, hung from ceiling above two long, onyx tables.

The lords sat in silver chairs around the table—apart from Hothgar, who sat in an enormous, throne-like chair at the head. The wives sat at the other table.

A small oneiroi servant bustled up to Ursula, beckoning her forward. "This way, milady."

The servant led her to an open seat at the wives' table, then held out her hand for Ursula's cloak.

Ursula pulled it off. "I'll keep it with me, thank you." She wanted to keep the silver ring as close as possible. She'd need her little good luck charm to get through tonight.

As she draped her cloak over the chair, a hush fell over the group. Eleven pairs of eyes locked directly on her, taking in her pearly gown. And as before, she was seated near Viking, Goth Princess, and Talons.

She glanced at Viking, dressed in a sea-green gown. A deep purple bruise discolored her chin. She nodded to Ursula.

The other women weren't quite so friendly. Goth Princess turned away, showing Ursula her pale back, clad in black lace.

Talons scowled at Ursula, tapping a long red claw on her silver goblet. Talons's silver hair tumbled over a violet gown. "Who invited the dog?"

Ursula narrowed her eyes. "The name is Ursula."

Viking twirled her champagne flute, shooting a sharp look to Talons. "Easy, Budsturga. We're not supposed to make a scene."

So that was Talons's name—*Budsturga.*

Goth Princess shot her a dark look. "It upsets the balance to have a human in here. And the smell is unbearable."

Ursula cocked her head. *You want to do catty? I know how to do catty.* "That's funny. Your husband Abrax doesn't think I'm human. Apparently, that's what he likes about me."

Princess glared. "He has a perverse fascination with freaks."

Ursula plucked her glass from the table. "Doesn't speak well of you, does it?"

Viking slapped the table. "I said, we're not to make a scene. Honestly, ladies. Who is the real enemy, here?"

Budsturga's face was incredulous. "What in the heavens are you talking about? The oneiroi?"

Viking leaned in, whispering, "When was the last time you saw a woman fight? Our husbands say we must do as they say because women are weak." She gazed right at Ursula. "But Ursula is proving them wrong. If they are wrong about Ursula, maybe they're wrong about all of us."

Goth Princess crossed her arms, practically pouting. "What makes you hate your husband so much, anyway?"

Viking shrugged. "I hate yours, too. He is a monster. But Hothgar is the one I have to live with. You see this?" She pointed to the purple bruise on her chin. "That was because I lost a bet on the melee."

Budsturga stabbed her talon into a canapé. "Men are brutal, yes. Best avoided."

Viking turned to Ursula. "Surely Bael is different. He's unmarried. But I'm told he does like women. Is it true what they say about him as a lover?"

Ursula cleared her throat. "I wouldn't know. We train together. That's it."

The furrow in Viking's brow suggested she didn't believe this. "Of course, ladies of the Shadow Realm would never bed a man before marriage. But I assumed a woman such as yourself..." Her sentence trailed off.

Ursula's eyebrows shot up. "I didn't realize demons had rules about sex before marriage."

"Not all demons," said Goth Princess. "Only the nobles of the Shadow Realm."

Ursula nodded. "And let me guess. It only applies to female nobles."

"Of course," said Budsturga.

Viking leaned in close. "It really doesn't seem fair. We should get to try them out before committing. The first time I kissed Hothgar was at our claiming ceremony. It was a horrific disappointment, but by then it was too late."

Ursula took a sip of wine, nearly too engrossed in the conversation to notice the waiters bringing bowls of steaming mushroom soup. "What's a claiming ceremony?"

Viking slurped her soup. "It's the ceremony when a husband claims his wife. It is the one tradition the warriors of Nyxobas adopted from the oneiroi. And because it comes from the beasts, it's positively savage."

Ursula shook her head. "But what is it?"

Budsturga stabbed another crudite with her talons. She'd have a hell of a time eating soup. "When a warrior claims a woman, they exchange rings. Then, the contract is sealed with a public display of lust. Nothing too far, Nyxobas wouldn't allow that. But the warrior must show sexual domination over his woman."

"As you can imagine," the Princess sighed, "Abrax took things a bit far."

"It's a marriage ceremony?" asked Ursula.

"More like an engagement," said Budsturga.

Viking's cheeks reddened. "Hothgar proposed in Asta's spire, then forced his tongue down my throat in front of the other lords. He ripped off my top. Frankly, that was the last time he showed any interest in me, and that was over a thousand years ago."

Goth Princess shrugged. "Men only want what they can't have." Her dark eyes slid to Ursula. "The forbidden flesh. And yet you're telling us Bael has no interest in you?"

Ursula's cheeks warmed. "Apparently not."

Viking wiped the soup off her chin, staring at Goth Princess. "Asharoth. Why does your husband hate Bael so much?"

Asharoth—apparently, that was her name—cocked her head. "He is the son of a god. He demands worship. And Bael has never been sufficiently submissive. His role as Sword of Nyxobas always rankled Abrax."

Viking threw back a long gulp of wine. "Hothgar isn't even a demigod, and he demands worship. You should see the inside of his temple."

Ursula ate a spoonful of her soup. *This sounds good.* "And what would I find in the inside of his temple?"

Viking giggled. "We can't always get humans here in the Shadow Realm. They simply die so easily. But when we run low on human slaves, Hothgar has his dolls."

Ursula leaned in over her soup. "What does he do with his dolls?"

Viking held her hand to her face, whispering. "He gets drunk on vodka, and uses his magic to animate them. He has them bend down to worship him, calling him Nyxobas. One or two he declares to be heathens, and he crushes them beneath his feet."

"And the whole time," added Budsturga with a wicked smile. "He has his lunar staff out."

"And I thought my husband was perverse," said Asharoth.

Ursula's lip curled. "And you're not allowed to have any fun with other men while your husbands do whatever they want?"

Asharoth's jaw dropped. "Of course not."

Ursula sipped her wine. "You ladies are getting a raw deal."

Asharoth shrugged. "It's not all horrible. As soon as a man claims you, you are protected. No man may touch another man's wife. No one may harm us. And men are forbidden from killing the women they've claimed."

Ursula stared. "That's it? They can't kill you? Like I said, you're getting a raw deal."

Before anyone could respond, a commotion erupted at the lord's table.

Bael stood. His dark magic whipped the air around him. "Abrax attacked me in my manor. He crossed my threshold uninvited."

Hothgar held out his hands, a placating gesture. "I know you're angry—"

"I'm not angry." And yet, icy wrath laced his voice. "But I want the fealty to which I am entitled."

Hothgar waved a dismissive hand. "As I said already, you killed his champion."

"His champion attacked me like a wild animal. If Abrax hadn't invaded my house, his champion would still be alive. I'm owed a fealty."

Hothgar rose. "And as I said, your killing of his champion is fealty enough."

"I know you two are colluding. A lord's manor is sacrosanct. A real Sword of Nyxobas would never allow this transgression."

Abrax leaned back in his chair, studying his nails. "Maybe you should have been more careful and not lost your wings." His gaze flicked to Bael.

"If you weren't Nyxobas's son, I would have slaughtered you months ago," Bael snarled. He turned, walking from the table and out of the hall.

Abrax's gaze slid to hers, and Ursula's stomach turned. *Time to get out of here.*

Budsturga leaned in to her, whispering, "I think you should follow him."

Ursula rose, yanking her cloak off the back of the chair. *You don't have to tell me twice.*

CHAPTER 30

*B*ael waited for her in the carriage, and she ran across the onyx platform. She yanked open the door, clambering inside.

She took her seat across from Bael, trying to catch his eye. As the team of bats pulled the carriage into the air, he studied the window intently.

She shoved her hand in her pocket, toying with the silver ring. "The lords' wives really aren't that bad."

He cut her a sharp look before fixing his gaze out the window again. Clearly, he wasn't in the mood for conversation.

She closed her eyes, trying to rid her mind of the image of Hothgar parading before a congregation of animated dolls, stroking his lunar staff. Despite herself, laughter escaped, and she covered her mouth.

"What in the gods' name is funny at this moment?" asked Bael.

"Did you know that Hothgar animates dolls to worship his knob?"

Bael's eyes widened. Slowly, a smile curled his lips. "I did not. Perhaps I could have lived without that knowledge." He kept his eyes on her, studying her intently. All traces of tension had left his face. "Would you like to go riding when we return to the manor?" he asked quietly.

"On bats, I assume?"

Bael nodded.

"I'm not really dressed for it." Ursula glanced down at her evening gown. "I suppose, with the enormous slits Cera cut up the front, I could get my legs around a bat."

Bael cleared his throat. "The cloak will keep you warm. It's beautiful, hunting in the daylight, the way the sun catches the moths' wings."

How could she say no to that? "I suppose I could really use the practice."

"Good." He leaned back in his seat.

Pale sunlight streamed through the window, sparking off his icy eyes and illuminating the perfect contours of his face. She had the strongest impulse to reach out and touch him, but he'd already told her how he felt about "hounds." And if she thought about it, the rebuke still stung. Obviously, he didn't like hellhounds. So what kind of women *did* he like?

She bit her lip. There was no reason she should care. They were going to fight to the death in less than a week, if she even made it that far. Clearly, the wine and the altitude had already gone to her head, muddling her thoughts.

What she needed was to focus on the race that lay ahead of her.

She drummed her fingertips on the seat. "For this race coming up, is there anything else I need to know besides flying?"

He shook his head. "You'll only need to follow behind me, and try to stay on the bat."

"Where does the race take place?"

"Around Asta's spire. We race in three loops."

She nodded slowly. "And the winners are the fastest?" She frowned. "I really do need the extra practice. I can't imagine anyone there will be slower than me."

"Just try to keep up with me."

She felt the carriage touch down on the roof, sliding over the marble, and she grasped a handle to steady herself.

Bael opened the door, and she stepped out onto the gleaming roof. Bael stared up at the black sky, and he put his fingers in his mouth to whistle for the two bats.

As the carriage lifted into the air, she hugged her cloak tightly around herself. "Did you say something about hunting?"

"Yes. Hunting for moths."

She scrunched her nose. "Do we have to kill them?"

His brow rose. "Are you suddenly wary of drawing blood? That's not the warrior I saw slaughtering demons twice her size in the melee."

She shrugged. "I have a strange affinity for the moths." *Because they're prey, and so am I.*

"We needn't kill them, if you don't want to."

She shielded her eyes, catching a flicker of movement in the dark sky.

Gracefully, the two bats glided onto the roof, just a few feet away.

Bael mounted Vesperella, gripping his neck while Ursula climbed onto Sotz's shoulders. She wrapped her legs around Sotz, and the fabric of her dress fell away from her thighs. *I'm going to have a bit of wind burn by the end of this journey.* Bael stared at her for a moment longer than necessary before lifting into the air.

By the time she and Sotz found their way to the roof's edge, Bael was already circling in a wide arc above her.

She tightened her thighs around Sotz, leaning forward to whisper into his ear. "Follow Vesperella."

Sotz beat his wings, taking flight off the roof's edge. He climbed higher, until he flew just beside Bael and Vesperalla.

"Nice work!" Bael shouted over the wind.

"Soon, it'll be second nature."

Bael's flight climbed higher in the sky, rising above the crater's rim, and Ursula followed a few yards behind, moving in time with the beating of Sotz's wings.

"See if you can keep up," Bael yelled. He leaned down, increasing his speed.

Ursula leaned low over Sotz's neck. Simply adjusting her weight was all the encouragement he needed. His wings beat more strongly as they raced around the crater's edge in the pearly sunlight. Ursula's hair blew wildly about her head, but she could still see a stunning view of the crater.

Ahead of her, Bael and Vesperella charged forward, extending their lead and climbing higher into the sky.

Ursula crouched even closer to Sotz. "Can you catch them?"

Sotz's wings whooshed thorough the air and they sped up. Ursula's pulse raced as the wind whipped over her skin.

Despite the icy cold that bit into her exposed knees, a strange feeling rippled over her body, almost as if she *belonged* here, up in the air under a clean, black sky.

She pulled alongside Bael, thrilling at the speed of the flight. They'd climbed higher than she'd ever flown in the carriage, swooping up above Asta's spire. A frothing sea of moths rose up before them.

With a whoop, Bael directed Vesperella straight at the moths. Sotz plunged after them so fast, Ursula almost lost her grip. She tightened her grasp on the bat just as they hit the edge of the cloud.

The moths parted as they entered, both encircling them at a safe distance. Sotz's ears perked up, and a low growl rose from his chest. A rich sound vibrated through her gut—the deep thrumming of the moths' beating wings.

Sotz winged forward, deeper into the cloud.

Ursula leaned into him. "We're not killing today, Sotz. Just riding."

Another growl rose from his throat. She had the feeling he wasn't thrilled about that idea.

Beating his enormous wings, Sotz rose again, climbing out of the cloud of moths until she could see the black sky once again.

From here, Bael led her and Sotz around the edge of the cloud. The writhing mass extended high into the dark sky. From there, the light of Asta reflected off of the moth's wings, washing them in flashes of purple and violet. There was something almost hypnotic in the way they undulated around the spire.

One hundred feet above her, a bat burst from the cloud, a bleeding moth in its jaws. Another followed. She could hear the beating of their wings as they passed over her. Sunlight highlighted their forms in the dark sky, beautiful and terrifying at the same time.

Far above her, another bat burst from the cloud. Ursula gasped. The pale form was unmistakable—the white bat of the Gray Ghost.

"Bael!" she shouted.

He turned to look at her, but when she tried to point, the white bat had disappeared.

"What was it?" he asked, circling back.

She followed his path, the wind whipping through her hair. "The bat of the Gray Ghost."

"Did you see where it went?"

"No!" *Bloody thing disappeared. Much like a ghost.*

Leaning down close to Vesperella, Bael began curving back to the manor. Ursula leaned closer to Sotz, picking up speed to keep pace with

Bael. Her pulse raced with a sharp thrill as they swooped lower over the city. *I actually think I can do this. I can keep pace with Bael just as well as anyone.*

She might have frostbite on her legs at this point, but the clean feel of the lunar air called to her. Somehow, she felt she was meant to fly.

And clearly, so was Bael.

Vesperella dove sharply for the roof of Abelda, and Ursula followed close behind. As the black marble drew nearer, Sotz beat his wings, slowing his descent. He glided gracefully to a landing by Vesperella's side. Bael was already dismounting.

She stepped off Sotz. The inside of her thighs burned from exhaustion, and the outside from the freezing wind.

She straightened, glancing at him. "I take it you miss your wings."

"It's hard to get used to being grounded after twenty-two millennia of flight."

She smiled. "The lords' wives said you were worshipped as a god in the old days."

"The lords' wives have a lot to say about me."

"And yet you're still a total mystery."

He eyed her cautiously. "What do you need to know?"

A chilly lunar wind toyed with her hair. "You said you were from Canaan. Where's the rest of your family?"

"Dead," he said flatly.

Shit. She shouldn't have brought that up. She already knew his wife had died. She swallowed hard. "I meant your parents."

"Dead. A long time ago." He climbed back on to Vesperella's back. "You should get inside. You're going to freeze."

Before she could respond, Bael leaned forward on Vesperalla's shoulders and whispered in her ear. Vesperella's wings stroked the air, and Bael surged upward into the black sky.

CHAPTER 31

$\mathcal{U}$rsula sat on the sofa, rubbing a salve into her palms. She eyed the sun, edging dangerously close to its zenith, and her pulse sped up. *Not long now.*

She'd been practicing on Sotz for several days, building up her speed and control. And now, the day before the race, her muscles burned with a deep fatigue.

She pulled up her dress, wincing at the sight of her inner thighs, rubbed raw from spending hours each day winging around the crater with Sotz.

She dabbed the salve onto her thighs, working it into her skin until some of the red faded to a pale pink.

F.U. may not have ridden a bat before, but she seemed to understand the principles of controlling a beast, making it conform to her will with subtle shifts in muscle, little twitches of her hands. Feeling every movement of Sotz's muscles and sinews. Directing him as though he were an extension of herself. She wasn't as skilled as Bael, of course, but she was getting there.

At Cera's insistence, she'd even dipped her toe into the art of clasping her arms around Sotz's neck to ride upside down, her hair dangling toward the moon's surface. That particular move still made her heart leap into her throat, but she'd attempted it, nonetheless.

She slid her hand into her pocket, glancing at the door. The one thing that had been conspicuously absent over the past few days was Bael. He'd completely disappeared after their conversation about his dead family. *Nice one, Ursula.*

Instead of training her, like he'd said he would, he'd just disappeared into his manor. She wasn't even sure anymore if he still planned to help her in the race, or if he planned to knock her out of the sky. Apparently, stabbing someone with a corkscrew was a forgivable offense. But ask someone a personal question, and you've taken things too far.

She rose, crossing to the bar. Cera had left a neatly folded pile of riding clothes—her racing outfit for tomorrow. Cera had fashioned a leather outfit of a shimmering black—so she could blend into the sky. Ursula ran her fingers over the soft leather, frowning.

Why, in particular, was it important that she blend in to the sky? If they were only racing, she didn't need to disguise herself.

Unless, of course, there was more to it.

A little knock sounded at her door—Cera's knock, and she hurried across the room. Her stomach rumbled. All this riding had given her an uncontrollable appetite, and with any luck, Cera had brought her dinner.

But when she opened the door, she found Cera standing with a bag of clothing instead of a tray of food. Clear sunlight streamed through her hair, and she lifted the bag. "A new dress."

Ursula pulled open the door, motioning for her to enter. "And why, exactly, do I need a new dress right now?"

"The lord has requested your presence at dinner." She thrust the bag at Ursula. "I've made the dress distracting. I have a feeling the lord needs a bit of distraction."

"Where has he been for the past several days?"

Cera shrugged. "How should I know? He doesn't run his schedule by me."

Ursula frowned. "Cera, can you give me more specifics about this race? Why, exactly, would I need to be camouflaged."

Cera's silver eyes widened. "I'm not supposed to tell you."

Ursula's stomach dropped. "Tell me, Cera."

"I believe the lord is going to fill you in over dinner. Now get dressed, and go meet him in his quarters."

* * *

URSULA STARED at her reflection in the mirror. She'd piled her hair on her head in a messy up-do, and she wore a silk-wrap dress—with an appropriately plunging neckline. She ran her hands over the smooth silk, the same pale gray as the clouds of moths. The skirts seemed to float around her legs.

A black-jeweled necklace completed the ensemble—the same color as her knickers. Not that Bael would ever know that.

As she put on her eyeliner, she hummed to herself—David Bowie's "Major Tom." A terrible dance remix of that song had always played in District 5, but suddenly the lyrics seemed much more meaningful to her.

What she wouldn't give right now for a normal night. Cheap wine from the Crobar, loud music, maybe a greasy burger before a night bus home. Granted, her life before Kester burst into her kitchen had been pretty shit. Unemployed, single, and completely broke. But at least she hadn't been surrounded by psychotic demons hell-bent on destroying her.

As she stood back to admire her reflection, a loud bang came from her door. *Bael's knock.*

On her way to the door, she pulled on a black cloak, shoving her hand into her pocket to feel the reassuring smoothness of the silver ring. She pulled open the front door to find Bael standing in the gleaming sunlight in a fitted gray suit.

"Ursula."

She crossed her arms. "There you are. I was beginning to wonder if you'd fallen into the chasm."

"I had matters to attend to over the past few days." He turned to cross the bridge, clearly expecting her to follow.

Outside, an icy breeze rippled over her skin. "So you weren't avoiding me?"

"Why would I do that?"

They crossed into the atrium, and she shrugged. "I don't know. It's just that you said you'd train me to ride, and then you disappeared into your man cave for days. Coincidentally, it was directly after I asked you a personal question."

He turned to her just long enough to arch an eyebrow. "As I said, I had matters to attend to. And I understand Cera was able to train you. She tells me you've been improving remarkably well."

In the narrow tunnel, her heels echoed off the ceiling. "Speaking of the race. Can you tell me why Cera made me a black suit for the competition?"

"I would imagine she thought it contrasted rather fetchingly with your fiery hair."

"Is that another one of your jokes?" She nudged him with her elbow. "I meant, why did she mention it was important for me to blend into the dark sky? Why would I need to go unnoticed, if we're only racing?"

Bael cleared his throat as they crossed into the cavern. "She should not have mentioned that."

Hot anger ignited. "I knew you were hiding something from me!"

"We will discuss it over dinner." He pointed to the narrow stone bridge. "I don't want you losing your footing again as we cross the bridge. There are only so many times I can catch you mid-air."

"Right," she said through clenched teeth.

She trod carefully over the stone bridge, trying not to stare too deeply into the abysses on either side. If she lost this race, she'd find herself permanently trapped in the void, in complete isolation for the rest of eternity. Just the thought of it made her stomach tighten with dread.

She stared at Bael's back as he gracefully crossed over the bridge, his movements fluid. *At least one of us is going to end up in the void.* A lump rose in her throat.

Bael crossed to a black marble table laid out with a domed platter and two glasses of wine. She pulled off her cloak, then took a seat across from him.

His gaze flitted over her neckline, and she heard the sharp intake of breath.

His brow creased. "I thought we'd talked about your dresses distracting me."

"We did. I decided that I definitely do not care. Now will you tell me what's going on with the race?"

Sighing, he pulled the lid off the platter, revealing a roast ham with glazed carrots on the sides. Her mouth watered. Apparently, Bael knew exactly how to distract her, too.

Greedily, she pulled two slices of ham onto her plate and cut into them.

"During the race, you must stay as close to me as possible." He served himself a slice of ham.

"You said to follow you. I don't really understand why. I can't exactly beat you if I'm stuck behind you."

"If you're going to survive, you'll need to stay near me."

She stopped eating, her stomach clenching. "Why?"

"So no one slaughters you while you're riding."

She stared at him. "You told me it was just a race. You never said I needed to practice with a sword. This is a major disadvantage."

"Learning to ride a bat is complicated enough. If we'd added a sword into the mix, you wouldn't have survived the training."

Her fingers tightened around her fork. "You didn't even give me a chance," she spluttered. "Tell me everything I need to know. Now. Don't spare any more details."

He sipped his wine. "Like I said, the race is around Asta's spire. There are two groups. We start at the same place, but fly in opposite directions."

"The groups pass each other at the opposite side of the spire?"

"Exactly. The goal is to make three passes between the points. Or we stop when twelve have died."

"Three passes?"

He shrugged. "They've never gone further than two."

Her mouth went dry. "What kind of weapons are used?"

"The same as the melee. Nothing ranged or magically enhanced. The best riders always win. A good rider can evade even those armed with lances."

"Right. Sounds wonderful. I'm bringing my katana."

"You have a better chance of survival if you stick near me."

She nodded slowly. "And I'm just supposed to trust your judgment. You've withheld crucial information about the race until I no longer had the chance to practice. Plus, every now and then you point out that you will kill me."

Gold candlelight danced over the fine planes of his face. "I *will* have to kill you. Just not tomorrow."

Something cold gnawed at her chest. "And you're okay with that?"

His jaw tightened. "It doesn't matter if I'm okay with that. We don't choose the rules. The gods do, and they do not care for our lives. You must choose if you are predator or prey. There is no in-between. And while I'm pretty sure that F.U. was a predator, I'm not sure you're quite the same." He leaned in closer. "If you don't even have the stomach to kill a moth, how do you expect to survive a brutal sword fight while flying on Sotz? You're better off hiding behind me."

She shook her head, panic rising in her chest. "This whole thing is insane. I don't understand how I'm supposed to depend on you one day and then wait for you to kill me the next. And what if I don't want to play by Nyxobas's rules? There's got to be another way out of this tournament that doesn't involve us killing each other."

"There is no way out," his voice boomed, reverberating through her gut. "Just because you've found a way to forget all the horrible things that have ever happened in your life does not mean that everyone gets a happy ending. And just because I've trained you out of some misguided sense of duty does not mean that I'm your friend. I must either kill or die, and the same is true of you. You mean nothing to me, hound."

His words hit her like a punch to the gut, and she dropped her fork on the table. "You're a predator, so you say. I mean nothing to you. And you're determined to kill me." Humiliatingly, she could feel the tears welling in her eyes. "And yet here you are, asking me to trust you. Asking me to leave my sword behind while you protect me."

He leaned back in his chair, studying her. "I feel obligated to give you a fair fight."

"Before you kill me?" Angry heat flooded her cheeks. "Bollocks. If I'm destined to die—if I'm prey—then what's the point of going through all this effort? Why go through the trouble of training me at all?"

He simply stared at her, the candlelight flickering in his eyes.

She stood and grabbed a handful of ham to eat alone in her quarters. As she turned to leave, she shot him a final glare. "I'm bringing my katana tomorrow."

CHAPTER 32

Ursula and Cera stood on the roof of the manor, looking out over the crater. From the black sky, the pale light of the sun shimmered over Asta's spire, and warmed her skin through her clothes.

She shielded her eyes with her hand, glancing at Cera. "Thank you for teaching me to ride Sotz."

Cera shot her a stern look. "You'd better not die today."

Icy dread flooded her body. "I'll do my best."

Cera leaned closer, giving her hand a squeeze. "If you don't go now, Ursula, you'll be late."

Ursula put her fingers to her lips, whistling for Sotz. After a few moments, a shadow passed over their heads, and Sotz landed on the rooftop, just by the building's edge.

Her stomach turning, Ursula crossed to the bat. Her fingers grazed her katana's hilt. A part of her wondered if Bael had been right. Maybe she should have listened and left the katana at home. But she couldn't exactly rely on someone who kept saying he planned to kill her.

Taking a deep breath, she settled herself on Sotz's shoulders, gripping tightly with her thighs. Sotz clambered to the building's edge, then took flight over the crater.

As Sotz winged toward the spire, she rehearsed her plan: stay alive. She'd try to stay out of the fight and engage only if attacked.

She soared over the crater, thrilling at the feel of the wind in her hair. As Sotz drew closer to Asta, she tightened her grip on his fur. Around Asta's peak, workers had erected a great wooden platform that ringed around the spire. And from the platform, a long wooden dock jutted out into the lunar winds, like a wharf.

Ursula circled closer. In the center of the platform, Hothgar stood, flanked between his wife and his giant gong. The other lords mulled around, sipping from silver goblets. *How fun to drink cocktails while watching death rain down on the city with a perfect, panoramic view.*

The other riders already soared through the air, showing off by turning flips and racing around the peak. Bael flew in a lazy circle around the perimeter, apparently unconcerned with showboating.

Arcing closer, Ursula glanced down at the crater. A vast sea of Brethren swarmed around the spire's base. Unlike the arena at Lacus Mortis, this venue stood right in the center of the Shadow Realm. Anyone in the entire kingdom could get there—and it appeared the entire kingdom had, in fact, showed up to watch the champions die.

A loud crash rang through the air, reverberating through her gut. Hothgar's gong. *Things are about to get started.*

Hothgar raised his hands to the sky, his dark magic swirling around his body. As he spoke, his voice boomed over the crater. "The sun has nearly reached its zenith. The riders must approach the dock."

Ursula's heart was beating so hard, it threatened to break her ribs, but she gently guided Sotz lower, joining the line of riders on the dock. As she flew closer, she could see that the starting positions on the dock alternated directions—some facing clockwise, and some counterclockwise. Apparently, these would be the two groups.

She picked out Bael's muscled form at the end of the dock, facing clockwise. Her pulse racing, she angled Sotz lower to the dock. As she approached, her pulse racing, she was gripped by the terrifying fear that she'd overshoot the bloody thing entirely.

At the last moment, Sotz skidded to a halt, clinging on to the dock's edge. At his clumsy landing, she lurched forward, grunting, before regaining her balance. Sotz inched back, and Ursula took a deep breath, surveying her competition.

She'd landed between a lanky demon with a narrow mustache, and a noseless creature with skin the color of ice. The iceman turned to glare at her, growling.

Leaning forward, she glanced down the row again at Bael. They faced the same direction. In theory, she could follow behind him—assuming he really meant to help her.

At the end of the dock, Hothgar stalked closer, his dark eyes gleaming in the sunlight like black pearls. "Ah, Emerazel's dog. I realize a bitch like you is used to riding your way to the top, but you won't be doing it by opening your legs today."

She snarled at him. "Don't you have some unfortunate dolls you need to seduce in your temple?"

Hothgar's eyes flashed with rage. The lanky man to her right barked a laugh. Ursula shot a quick glance at Viking, who laughed behind her hand. Suddenly, she was glad she'd brought the katana. She wanted to show the city what a woman could do—that they didn't need to submit to their men because they were weak.

As her muscles tensed, ready for battle, Ursula tried to flash her bravest smile at Hothgar's wife.

Above the spire, the sun blazed bright—right above the peak. A cold sweat broke out on her brow. She swallowed hard, tightening her grip on Sotz, feeling his heart thumping through his fur. As she leaned forward, she surveyed the riders once more. Each demon dressed in muted shades of gray, blue, and black—some in furs and armor. Only one rider stood out—the Gray Ghost, draped in white, his face covered by a scarf.

At the end of the line, Bael wore his black fighting gear, his lion pendant glinting in the sun. He faced forward, his grip tight on a long lance.

In a race like this, a long weapon like a lance was a huge advantage. *Might have been nice to train with one.*

Hothgar's voice boomed, "The race will commence when I sound the gong, at the sun's zenith."

Ursula's blood roared in her ears. Her palms were sweating so much, she wasn't sure she could keep hold of Sotz's fur. Her eyes wandered to the crater's floor, hundreds of feet below. What would a body look like if it fell from this height?

The pause that followed seemed to stretch for eternity, and Ursula closed her eyes, trying to marshal control over herself, trying not to picture the explosion of guts from a person's mouth.

At last, the gong crashed, reverberating around the crater. She tightened her thighs on Sotz.

Sotz launched into the air.

Around her, the riders soared, the wings of their bat beating the air. Ursula leaned down, urging Sotz forward. As they arced around the spire, she fell slightly behind the rest of the pack, and she stared at the back of Flesh Scales. There was no shame in hanging behind the others. If this was a fight to the death, might as well let the front of the pack take the brunt of the attack.

The crowd below cheered, and her heart pumped harder. *The other half of the champions must be close.*

They burst into view, weapons glinting in the sun.

Ahead of her, Bael and the other riders spurred their bats to a faster pace, and the two camps collided in clashes of steel. From the corner of her eye, she glimpsed Bael's lance punching straight through a demon's chest.

Keeping out of weapons' range, Ursula watched two bodies fall to the crater's floor, leaving puffs of smoke just like little meteorites.

"Two kills!" the announcer shouted. "Ten remain!"

Arcing behind the main fray, she looked up.

Her stomach leapt into her throat. The Gray Ghost was flying directly for her, his face covered with his scarf. He pointed an enormous ash lance directly at her chest.

Ursula gripped Sotz's fur tighter. She couldn't fight a lance with a sword—the lance would knock her off Sotz before she got within striking distance. But hadn't Bael said a good rider could avoid a lance with the right moves?

She clung tightly to Sotz, arcing away from the attack. Then, she clung to Sotz's neck, and let her body slide down, so that her legs dangled beneath him. The lance grazed Sotz's shoulder.

As she flew hanging from Sotz, adrenaline burned through her nerve-endings. In the distance, she heard the announcer calling out two more deaths. The lunar wind whipped through her hair, and she gently urged Sotz upright again. When she righted her bat, the Gray Ghost had disappeared. The other riders surged forward, already moving on to begin another circle around the spire.

Ursula leaned down, trying to keep pace with the three riders winging ahead of her. Bael's silver lion insignia flashed in the sunlight.

She urged Sotz forward as they arced around the edge of the spire, the violet crystal gleaming in the sunlight. If she weren't moments away from possible death, it might have been exhilarating.

As soon as they slammed into the riders a second time, her hackles were raised. Three riders were already charging for Bael. She arced closer to him, watching as his lance rammed into the chest of the lead rider. The horned demon shrieked, falling from the sky.

Still, two other riders pressed on Bael—and one of them slammed a lance right into Vesperella, goring the bat. Blood sprayed in the air, and Vesperella's wings folded together.

To Ursula, it was like watching in slow motion, even though it happened in an instant. Panic ripped its claws through her heart, and she watched as Bael released Vesperella's neck. He stood on her back for a moment. Then, a thousand feet in the air, Bael leapt towards the rider who'd just killed his mount, grasping at his feet. Vesperella tumbled, blood spraying from her hide as she grew smaller in the sky. Bael's lance sparked in the sun as it fell.

Bael hung by one hand, dangling from the bat's foot, and two other riders moved closer. Vultures, waiting for their chance to finish him off. One moved a little too close, and in a gravity-defying move, Bael swung his body into the air. He landed on the rider's back. It took only an instant for him to fling the rider off.

The remaining rider began to close in on Bael. With Bael unarmed and on an unfamiliar mount, the ice-skinned demon saw a chance for easy prey. He unsheathed a cutlass.

Clenching her jaw, she raced lower toward Bael, the glacial lunar wind whipping over her skin. Saving Bael wasn't part of the plan, but she wasn't ready to watch him die. She ripped her katana from its sheath, charging for the ice-demon. Her body moved fluidly with Sotz's, as if she'd been doing this all her life, and her gaze locked intently on one thing. Her prey.

No one expected death to come from the woman. From the bitch. No one expected *her* sword to find its way clean through their neck.

Crimson blood sprayed through the air as she cut through the demon's head.

The demon's body slumped, then rolled off his bat.

"Twelve down!" Hothgar's voice boomed.

As Ursula glanced down at her blood-soaked sword, a chill spread through her veins. *Predator. It seems, the answer is predator.*

CHAPTER 33

$\mathcal{U}$rsula stared at the thick blood dripping from her sword, then sheathed her weapon. Eyeing her, Bael nodded mutely, then began winging back to the dock. She swooped behind him, still catching her breath. Despite the cold lunar air, sweat matted Sotz's fur and dampened her clothes. Every one of her thigh muscles burned. She wanted to soak in a warm bath for days.

As she closed in on the dock, she maneuvered Sotz to land a little more gracefully this time. He touched down between Bael and a lanky demon in a black doublet. He turned to her, giving a little bow.

She leaned into Sotz, whispering, "That was some good flying." The bat looked up at her with his beady eyes in an expression that could have been mistaken for relief.

"Nice swordsmanship," Bael said, studying her. "A natural assassin."

"It was an easy kill." *Okay. I sound a little like a sociopath.*

An image burned in her mind—her sword slashing through the ice-demon's neck. It *had* come naturally to her.

Wherever she'd come from, F.U. had been a formidable predator. Ursula swallowed hard, eyeing Bael, the sunlight sparking in his eyes, a pale blue-gray, the color of ice floes.

If she needed to kill this man, she'd need F.U. to come out and finish the job. Ursula just wasn't quite psycho enough.

Hothgar stalked toward them, his black cape floating on the wind. "The remaining champions must now choose their opponents for the duel. Of the fifty-seven original champions, eight remain. And what an interesting lot you are." He smirked. "Bael the Fallen of Albelda, Zoth of the giant of Pleion, Inth of Alboth, Bernajoux of Zobrach, Valac of Phragol Mocaden, Chax of Azimeth, and our phantom rider, who could be absolutely anyone." His nostrils flared. "And how could I forget Emerazel's filthy bitch."

Ursula's fingers tightened on her sword's hilt. "Why do I have the disturbing feeling that you'll be animating a ginger-haired doll when you get home tonight?"

"Silence!" Hothgar roared, his cheeks reddening. When he'd regained his composure, he smoothed the front of his shirt. "You must now choose your opponents. With eleven kills, Bael is our leading Champion. He will choose first."

Ursula swallowed, as dread filled her veins. He had been promising to kill her. So did he want to get it over with or delay the inevitable? An icy wind toyed with her hair, rippling over her skin.

Bael shot her a quick glance, and for a moment, her stomach clenched. "I will fight Zonth of Pleion," he announced, his voice booming.

A giant man, dressed in furs and silver, snarled, revealing a row of jagged teeth. Apparently, that was Zonth.

Hothgar raised a hand. "After Bael's eleven kills, the second choice goes to the man all the commoners are calling the Gray Ghost."

From behind his scarf, the Gray Ghost shouted, "Chax of Azimeth."

Hothgar nodded. "Next to choose—my champion, Bernajoux." Hothgar flashed a mirthless smile. "As lord of the Pleion, I will select Bernajoux's champion for him. He leads my legion. He slaughtered twenty-seven men at the battle of Mt. Acidale."

The lanky man in the doublet bowed his head. With his delicate mustache and thin hands, he didn't look like a formidable opponent.

Of course, looks could be deceiving. Hothgar glared at her. "Bernajoux will slaughter the dog. I have so wanted to see what her insides look like."

A chill washed over Ursula's skin, and Bernajoux bowed deeply.

Urusla straightened on her mount. *Okay. That was creepy, but my opponent could have been worse. At least I'm not stuck with Zoth. Or worse—Bael.*

"That leaves Valac of Phragol Mocaden vs. Inth of Alboth," continued

Hothgar. He raised his hands to the pale sun. "The duels will be held at the Lacus Mortis in two days." As he spoke, his voice seemed to boom over the entire crater, rumbling through her bones.

Below, the bloodthirsty crowd erupted with cheers.

* * *

CERA WAITED for her on the roof, her white skirts billowing around her.

When Ursula landed, Cera rushed over to her. "What happened?" she asked, her silver eyes frantic. "Where is the lord?"

Ursula's muscles groaned as she stepped off her mount. "He's fine. He's on his way." She stumbled as she stepped off Sotz.

Cera steadied her, squeezing her arm. "What else? Who do you have to fight at the duel?"

Ursula's muscles still shook from the adrenaline rush. "I need to fight a demon named Bernajoux. He didn't look quite as intimidating as the rest, to be honest. But Hothgar really wants his own champion to slaughter me."

She glanced out at the crater, catching a glimpse of Bael soaring through the sky.

Cera squeezed Ursula's arm again. "He really is magnificent."

"Too bad we have to slaughter each other," Ursula muttered.

Cera's eyes glistened. "The lord will give you a quick death. He is merciful."

"Wonderful."

Bael arced over their heads, then landed on the roof. He stepped off his mount. In the sunlight, blood and gore glistened off his black clothes.

Cera frowned at his mount. "Where is Vesperella?"

"Dead."

"I'm sorry, milord," said Cera. She looked him up and down, taking in the bloodstains that soaked his clothes. "I will lay out fresh clothes for you." She hurried off, leaving Ursula alone with Bael.

Suddenly cold from the damp sweat soaking her clothes, she shivered.

Bael studied Ursula. "Ursula. You will join me in my chambers in three hours."

The way he barked orders set her teeth on edge. She crossed her arms. "I guess that since you've been ordering people around for twenty millennia, you forget how to make a request," she grumbled, before realizing she'd said it out loud.

The corner of his mouth twitched in what almost looked like a smile. "Will you join me in my chambers in three hours?"

She nodded. "Why not? If we're going to fight to the death in a few days, I might as well learn everything I can about you."

"I like the way you think," he said.

"And is there a purpose to this visit?" When she thought of what he'd said to her before the race, his words still felt like a slap in the face. As she stared at his ruthlessly beautiful features, hollow loneliness ate at her. "You've already made it clear that we're not friends and you don't care for me at all, so I'm wondering what the point is."

"You must learn to use shadow magic." He took a step closer, his large form looming over her. "Bernajoux will cut you down if you do not allow me to train you."

She nodded. "And you want the chance to kill me yourself?"

He now stood so close she could feel the warmth emanating from his body. "I will make it painless," he said softly. For just a moment, he let his fingertips brush down her shoulder. "Bernajoux will not."

She looked up at him. He stood over a foot taller than her. "Bernajoux didn't look that scary."

"Bernajoux is powerful and sadistic. There is a reason Hothgar likes him."

CHAPTER 34

Balancing carefully, she walked across the stone bridge. This time, she'd come barefoot and wearing her simple black gown. She didn't need to risk plunging off the side of the bridge because she'd stumbled in her heels.

In her pocket, she gripped the silver ring, feeling its reassuring familiarity between her fingers. For just a moment, her gaze flicked to the abyss, and a shiver crawled up her spine. The darkness called to her.

"Ursula," Bael's voice rose from the shadows, smooth as velvet.

As she crossed into the main cavern, she caught the outline of Bael's enormous form, sitting in his onyx throne. Candlelight sparked in his eyes, and wisps of night magic flickered around him. Raw, dark power roiled around him.

"Come closer," he said.

She padded across the cold stone floor, gazing up at him. Seated in his throne, he towered above her. When she stood only a few feet from him, she could see his piercing eyes, so cold against the warmth of his golden skin.

Suddenly, she felt completely unsure of herself. "What do I need to do?" she asked, rolling the ring in her fingers.

"I need you to feel the magic." His cold aura snaked over her skin, caressing her body.

Powerful shadow magic thrummed along her ribs, skimming her breasts. It encircled her neck. Instinctively, her head tilted back, exposing her throat. As Bael's magic wrapped around her body, it seemed to thrill her at the same time as it filled her with dread. A chill spread over her skin, goosebumps rising on her arms. When she exhaled, her breath clouded around her face. Under her cotton dress, her nipples hardened. She hugged herself, and her teeth began to chatter.

His gaze slid down her body and up again. "You can feel the magic? That is good."

"It's freezing." She clenched her jaw to keep her teeth from chattering.

"Yes. Shadow magic comes from the void." Bael's voice sounded distant, like he was speaking from a thousand miles away. "It is the cold of the depths of space, the endless nothingness between stars. As you learn to channel it, your other senses will learn to feel it, too."

Standing before Bael, she continued to shiver. She wasn't entirely clear why she had to stand below him like one of his subjects while he loomed over her in his throne. "So how do I learn to channel it?"

"It won't be easy. But you're off to an impressive start. When I was first learning, it took me weeks before I could sense the magic. Perhaps F.U. already had some practice."

As Bael's magic slid over her body, she was pretty sure her lips were turning blue. "I don't think I understand the concept of channeling shadow magic. What does it mean?"

His enormous hands enveloped the ends of the throne's arms. "Besides Nyxobas, only certain immortal beings can channel shadow magic directly. It's called gods-magic. Demigods can use it. Nyxobas grants his power to his Sword, so Hothgar has it, as did I before I lost my wings. Abrax has it by virtue of being his son. Now, I can no longer create night magic on my own. Neither can you. You have to learn to absorb it from another source, to take it into your body for later use. That is called channeling."

With all this shadow magic in the air, she really should have worn a cloak. "Right. And how do I channel it?"

Leaning forward, he held out a hand. "Come to me."

Her eyebrows shot up. "What now?"

"I'll act as your conduit. You will draw power from the throne. Magic flows into the onyx from the crystals that form this cave. But if you're subjected to it directly, the power might flood you."

She wasn't entirely sure she understood where he wanted her, but her cheeks were warming already. "So...you want me to sit on your lap."

He loosed a sigh, as though he were losing patience. "Yes. It's the only way you can learn."

"Okay." Her pulse began to race. Something about the thought of being so close to Bael's powerful body sent a strange thrill through her. She tugged up the hem of her skirt, climbing the three steps to Bael's throne.

Turning her face to hide the embarrassing blush in her cheeks, she sat in his lap. He slid a powerful hand around her waist.

Despite the icy magic whirling around him, his muscled body began to warm her.

"I'm going to allow the magic to flow through you, okay?" His breath warmed the side of her face.

She had the strongest impulse to reach back and touch his face, but she resisted. He had said she meant nothing to him, that he felt bound to help her out of some misguided sense of duty. It was humiliating that she even had to rely on him for help. Still, she supposed she had to take help where she could get it.

She straightened. "I'm ready."

Icy magic wrapped around her ribs, kissing the bare skin at her throat —a dizzying, electrical charge of power. As her back began to arch, her legs fell to either side of his. His arm tightened around her waist. Then, from all around her, the shadow magic flowed into her chest, freezing her from the inside out.

A painful, hollow dread bloomed in her chest, a ravenous hunger. The world around her seemed to fragment and collapse, and darkness clouded her vision. She could no longer tell where she was—couldn't feel Bael's body beneath hers, couldn't tell up from down.

From the depths of the void, an image burst into her view: Bael, pressing a dagger to her chest. In shockingly swift movement, he shoved it under her ribs, stopping her heart.

There, she saw herself lying in the dirt, her skin gray, her jaw slackened, lips blue. Red hair spread limply on the bloodstained ground. Dull green eyes, full of mute horror. And in their lifeless reflection—flames. A burning room. The fire that would eat her alive.

As quickly as it had arrived, the image was snuffed out again, and she stood at the edge of an abyss. She just needed to take one more step, to plunge into an isolation so complete it would gnaw the flesh from her bones. An uncontrollable urge pulled her into the void. *I don't exist. I never did. I never will.*

"Ursula!" A deep voice boomed through the void.

She could feel something again—a warm hand on her body. She shivered uncontrollably, her teeth chattering.

"Ursula!" Bael's voice called to her. He pulled her closer to his warm body. She'd changed position, her legs now sideways on his lap. The magic had seeped from the air, but she still shivered. The chill spread through her chest.

Bael's arms enveloped her. "I'm not sure what happened. I was modulating the power. It shouldn't have overwhelmed you like that."

She glanced up into his eyes, that icy gray...

Once more, her vision went dark, and she found herself standing on a dark cliff. There was something she needed to get to—a woman with red hair like hers, and fierce brown eyes. An old man, his hands spotted with age. A wall of darkness slammed against her.

You don't want to remember those things.

She felt a sharp tug from the center of her chest, drawing her to the edge. And when she glanced into the void, its vibrations sang her name. A dark lullaby...this was her mother, her father, her home.

"Ursula!" Bael's voice called her back.

Freezing cold, a violent convulsion overtook her body. Aching sadness pierced her chest.

Bael pulled her in closer, his powerful arms surrounding her. "Ursula. Stay with me. Remember who you are."

Her arms were around his neck, as if she was clinging to him for dear life.

"Use your own memories to warm your body. Think of your life. Use your memories to fill the void."

Hollow agony filled her ribs. "I don't have any memories."

"Right. Maybe that's the problem."

He slid his hand up her chest, pressing it onto her heart. At the touch of his hand between her breasts, her skin began to warm. A dark heat whispered up her spine, curling her back. She swallowed hard. "What are you doing with your hand?"

"I'm drawing the magic out of you." His perfect lips were mere inches from hers.

She could feel a hot blush rising to her cheeks, her body responding to his touch, whether she wanted it to or not. She was sure he could see her pupils dilating, the sheen of sweat rising on her skin.

How easy would it be to just lean in? She knew how he felt—that he didn't care for her at all. But right now, with her body curled into his, with the warmth shooting through her core, she could hardly think straight.

"Tell me what you saw?"

Her pulse raced, and she tried to clear her head. "I saw myself dead. On the dirt of the Lacus Mortis, I think. A burning room. A woman with red hair and an old man. It was like a part of me wanted to remember, but another part of me forbade it. But mostly. I saw the void. And I wanted to jump in."

She was warm now, and sweat beaded on her face. She licked her upper lip, tasting the salt.

Bael's keen gaze seemed to take in the movement, his fingers tightening on her waist nearly imperceptibly. She didn't need him to keep drawing the magic out. *So why am I not telling him to stop?*

His eyes lowered to where his hand pressed between her breasts, and he sucked in a deep breath. "I don't know why or how you pulled that much power at once, or why you're so drawn to the void. We need to find a way for your body to handle shadow magic without becoming overwhelmed. I've always done that by remembering my life. My early life. We'll have to find another way for you."

What were Bael's memories, the ones he rolled over in his mind when the void beckoned? Suddenly, she had a burning desire to know everything about him. She glanced at the black cord around his neck, and she tugged it from his shirt. A thin silver ring—the female twin of the one in her pocket, hung from the end of the cord.

Bael's hands flew to her fingers, tightening around them.

Oops.

She heard his sharp intake of breath, then he pushed the ring back under his collar.

Swallowing hard, she rose. *What the hell am I doing?* "Sorry. I really don't know why I did that."

"It's fine."

He released her fingers, and she dropped her hand. "I saw one more thing."

"What?"

"You. Shoving a blade into my heart at the arena."

A muscle tensed in his jaw, and his expression darkened. "I think that's enough for today. Get some rest."

Shadows gathered around him, and her skin grew positively frigid once more.

CHAPTER 35

Ursula stood by the window. In the distance, the sunlight glinted off of Asta's spire. Despite the pearly rays of sunlight, dark thoughts clouded her mind.

Sitting on the onyx throne, she'd completely lost control, flooded by shadow magic. She'd seen horrifying glimpses of her past, little fragments that lacerated her with horror. And perhaps, she'd seen a glimpse of her future.

Unable to warm herself, she pulled a blanket around her shoulders. Something about her disjointed memories filled her with a deep chill.

Bael had said she'd probably blocked her own memories to forget the horrible things she'd done. And the closer she got to remembering her past, the more she feared he was right. Whenever she thought of the burning room—the red-haired woman, the words *kill the king*—guilt pressed on her ribs like a hundred rocks.

Somewhere, deep under the fog of her forgotten memories, lurked a wild animal.

And if she didn't want to succumb to Bael's blade, maybe it was time for her to unleash the beast. After all, if she couldn't even kill a moth, how could she drive a weapon into Bael?

The odds against her were hard enough without hesitation. If she faltered, she'd be dead. Jaw slackened, red hair stamped into the dirt. The void had been trying to tell her something.

Throwing her cloak around her shoulders, she ran out the door into the sunlight. She hurried over the bridge into the atrium, where the lion's mosaic seemed to leer at her from the floor. She pulled the lever in the wall. After a moment, the lift clanked down in the middle of the room. She stepped inside the iron lift, trying to clear her mind. The elevator creaked upward past the manor's empty floors.

On the roof, the lunar wind nipped at her through the wool of her cloak, and she stepped out onto the marble. Shielding the sun from her eyes, she whistled for Sotz. It took only a few moments for his shadow to pass overhead, and he glided to a landing on the roof's edge.

Carefully, she climbed onto his back, gripping his fur. She squeezed her thighs, sending him soaring over the roof's edge. The wind whipped over her skin, pure and clean. As she leaned into Sotz, she asked, "Want to hunt?"

Immediately, Sotz swooped toward Asta, beating his wings harder. As they soared for the writhing cloud of moths, the sound of beating wings filled the air. A deep humming that vibrated her very core.

When they reached the cloud, the moths parted, fluttering around them, just out of reach. In the cocoon of moths, the sunlight dimmed, like they were walking in a deep forest.

Just as Sotz arced around the spire, an enormous moth shot in front of them—gray wings with faint purple spots. Sotz dove for it, and Ursula gripped tighter. *Time to unleash the beast.*

As Sotz neared, the moth folded its wings and dove. Sotz pursued, his wings pumping. Like a meteorite, they hurtled for the lunar floor, wind racing over her skin. Her pulse raced, a dark thrill rippling through her.

The moth burst out of the cloud, fleeing for his life. Ursula pressed herself tight against Sotz's back. The moth twisted and spun, but inch by inch, they gained on it. The ground neared, and Ursula started to direct Sotz out of the dive, but the moth was only a few feet from his nose. With a final burst of speed, he hammered his wings, snatching it from the air. Only a few hundred feet above the ground, she tugged Sotz's fur to pull him up again before they smashed into the lunar floor.

Sotz chewed happily on the moth as they carved a slow circle around the base of the spire. Now, she could feel the night magic emanating from the tower. It washed over her skin in waves, but it didn't seem to chill her as it had before. Her heart raced with the thrill of the hunt, her body energized.

After she caught her breath, they climbed back into the cloud. Sotz beat his wings, taking her higher and higher, above Asta's spire. He raced upward, until they nearly reached the edge of the magical dome.

The moths thinned, and the crater spread out before them—a great caldera, full of Nyxobas's brethren. And beyond, more craters, ancient lava fields. A great expanse of barren land.

Ursula shivered. Suddenly Sotz tensed. A flicker of movement above caught her eye. Her gaze landed on the great white bat. The Gray Ghost's steed.

"Can you follow it?" Ursula asked.

Sotz beat his wings, rising higher behind the albino bat. The creature flew with powerful beats of its wings and they raced to keep up with it. It moved swift as the night wind, its downy fur stark against the dark sky. They winged upward, skimming the edge of the dome.

But when the bat reached the shimmer of shadow magic, it simply passing into the shadow beyond.

Ursula swallowed hard. *How can it fly in a vacuum, with no air?*

Ursula directed Sotz right up to the edge, until the magic shimmered only inches from the tips of his outstretched wings.

She peered into the darkness beyond. The bat was gone.

CHAPTER 36

Ursula arrived a few minutes late for their second magic training session, and she hurried across the stone floor. This time, she'd worn a soft velvet cape to keep her warm. As before, Bael sat in his onyx throne, cloaked in shadows. Bael gazed down at her, his pale eyes piercing the shadows. "You're late. Take off the cloak."

"Why?"

"I need to see how your body uses the magic."

She swallowed hard, untying the cape and letting it fall to the floor. She wore another of Cera's creations—a purple silk gown, with slits cut all the way up to her thighs.

She cocked her head. "Would you like me completely naked, or is this good enough?"

A low growl rose from his throat, and for just a moment, his eyes darkened before returning to gray. "That will be fine. We'll start with you standing there. I'm going to let the shadow magic wash over you once again. See if you can root your body to the ground. Use the basalt at your feet as an anchor. Feel it beneath your toes, and let the night magic inch slowly up your legs, up to your hips, and don't let it fill your chest until you're in control."

She nodded. She wasn't entirely sure she knew what he was talking about, but she'd give it a shot.

"Close your eyes," he said.

She did as instructed, and in the next moment, she felt a wave of powerful night magic wash over her, spilling through her body like ink. An image rose like the flames—the old man, his wrinkled hands handing her an athame. Bael, pressing a knife into her heart.

The wall of blackness slammed into her, knocking the life from her chest. Darkness threatened to consume her from the inside out.

"Ursula!" Bael called to her.

Shivering, she opened her eyes. Bael had pulled her into his lap, wrapping his arms around her. His warmth enveloped her, and she could feel his heart beating hard against her body. Once again, he pressed his hand between her breasts, drawing out some of the magic.

"That didn't go well," she said through chattering teeth.

He shook his head. "You let it happen too quickly. The magic completely overtook you, like it was drawn to you. Whatever you are, Ursula, the darkness wants you."

"Aren't I the lucky girl?"

"I'm going to try it one more time, allowing through only the smallest amount of magic. I'm going to see if I can help your body control it."

As his body warmed hers, her pulse began to speed up.

"I could see your muscles tensing when you stood there, like you were scared of it. Maybe if you don't resist so much, you'll have greater control. Are you ready?" His breath warmed the shell of her ear.

She nodded, straightening.

Bael allowed the tiniest wisps of magic to curl from him. With his arm wrapped around her back, his fingers rested on the hollows of her hip. Her back arched.

A soft, electrical buzz kissed her ankles, moving up her leg. A delicious vibration—cold, but thrilling at the same time.

"Where do you feel it?" he asked.

Without realizing what she was doing, her legs parted slightly. Her bare skin peaked out of the slit in her dress. "It's moving up my legs."

"Good." Bael's hand hovered just over her leg, not touching her, but guiding the magic. Under her dress, the magic caressed her bare skin.

"Let the magic move slowly," he said. "Take control of it."

As his hand moved in the air above her legs, silky shadows worked higher up her thigh, and she felt her knees falling away just a little more.

She turned to him, her eyes on his perfect lips. Gods, she wanted to press her mouth against his.

His thrilling magic had moved all the way up her inner thigh, and her breath came fast. *If he keeps going, I will lose my mind. If he doesn't keep going, I will also lose my mind.* She was supposed to be focused on the magic, but all she could think of was that hand hovering just over her thighs. How she wanted him to touch her skin, to slide those powerful fingers under her silky underwear. Her breath hitched.

"Do you have control?" he asked.

"Not even close," she breathed, her chest flushing. *What the hell is wrong with me?*

His gaze met hers, and he leaned in, his mouth just inches from hers.

In the next instant, his muscles tensed. "I'm sorry," he said.

Ursula's jaw dropped. She couldn't quite remember how to put a sentence together. "It's fine." Her cheeks burned. *What just happened?* She wasn't entirely clear why he'd apologized.

A look of confusion—one she'd never seen on Bael's face before—had overtaken his features. "This isn't working. Maybe me acting as a conduit is interfering with your ability to feel the magic. Maybe you should try it on your own. If I see you losing control again, I'll stop it."

She nodded. "Of course. I think I'm ready. That all...totally made sense," she blustered.

She jumped off the throne, mortified that her flushed chest gave her away. *Stupid pale skin.*

Bael rose, walking down the steps. "The second I see you losing control, I'll pull you off."

She nodded, still lost in a daze, then sat in the throne.

As soon as she sat, cold magic thrummed over her legs. As Bael had instructed, she concentrated on moving it slowly up her body, inching it up her legs. Inky shadows flickered over her skin, seeping into her pores, climbing from her calves upward. Magic thrummed up her thighs, her hips, filling her body with raw power. As it raced into her chest, filling her ribs, a wave of blackness slammed into her. For just a moment, she stood in a burning room, and an ancient hand passed her a knife. *I need to think of a happier time.* The walls of her apartment in New York came to her—a field of blue and gold wildflowers under an azure sky. *Home.*

Her eyes snapped open again. Bael had been reaching for her, but the look in her eyes seemed to stop him.

She looked out on the world through new eyes, her senses sharpened. As she gazed around the cavern, she could see shadows flickering in the crystals, could smell the warm earthy scent of the mushrooms. And the sound of Bael's beating heart filled her ears.

"Now," she commanded from the throne, her voice resonating off the rock. "Teach me to move the way you do."

CHAPTER 37

*B*ael stood across from her in the cavern. "I can see the magic curling off your skin. It suits you. But you won't be able to move the way I do."

Her body buzzed with dark magic. She tried not to think about Bael's hand, running up her thigh. Had he seen the blush creeping up her chest? "Why not?"

"It takes months to learn."

"I want to try it anyway."

He sighed. "There's no harm in trying."

She crossed her arms. "How long does this magical charge last, anyway?"

"Until you use it up."

She cocked her head. Power charged her muscles, and she had a burning desire to use it. "So tell me. How do you move that way? If I remember from New York, you can disappear. Like smoke."

"Shadow running. It's quite useful in a fight, as you could imagine."

"And how does it work?"

"Once you're charged with night magic, you can move from place to place just by thinking." A cloud of smoke curled around Bael. He flickered out of sight, reappearing twenty feet away.

"You just think of where you want to go?"

"You concentrate, and the magic takes you there. But you must get a feel for shadow magic first. Let it become one with your body."

"I'm going to try it."

She closed her eyes, picturing Bael—his golden skin, the smell of his body—like Mediterranean air. The feel of his beating heart against her ribs.

In the next moment, she was pressed against his powerful body. He looked down at her, surprise flickering across his beautiful features.

"Sorry." She backed away from him. "I didn't mean to get that close."

His brow furrowed. "How did you do that?"

"You told me how to do it."

He shook his head slowly. "No one learns it right away. Maybe F.U. learned it, but...there aren't many lumen crystals on Earth."

"I want to keep practicing."

He drew a deep breath. "Fine. But not here. Come with me to the atrium."

"Why not here?"

"Because one misstep, and you will plunge into the abyss."

"Good point."

She plucked her cloak off the floor, but with the night magic rushing through her veins, she hardly needed it. Now she understood why a demon like Bael felt invulnerable to the cold.

She followed behind him over the narrow bridge—so like her visions of the void. But she no longer felt a strong desire to throw herself in.

As the got to the other side of the bridge, she walked by Bael's side, her arm brushing against his. Every time she thought of his magic skimming up her thigh, a dangerous heat burned through her body. But what did that even mean?

She'd become dangerously aroused, and then he'd jerked away, like he was on fire. Had he realized—was he disgusted by it? The very thought of his revulsion made her want to curl up in the void and never come out again.

You mean nothing to me, he'd said. Ursula had always been of the opinion that you should take someone at their word. Occam's razor and all that. Plus, it was impossible to guess what another person was thinking, so all you had to rely on was their words.

She stole a quick look at Bael, who faced straight ahead. He probably wasn't thinking about the feel of his hand on her thigh. And neither should she, considering they were both facing death in a few days. *Get it together, Ursula.*

The Black Death was parading through the city streets, and there she was, dreaming about shagging.

The tunnel opened up in the atrium, and Bael stopped, eyeing her. "I don't know how, but you've already worked out how to move. You concentrate on where you want to go and your body moves there. But you must use this power sparingly. If you shadow run, you use up your magical reserves. During the duel, you won't have a way to recharge. You must be judicious."

"I understand."

He pointed to a spot on the mosaic floor. "Can you shadow run from where you are now to the lion's mane?

Ursula concentrated, feeling the shadow magic ripple through her body, rushing over her skin like a night wind. In a blur of black, she reappeared on the mane. The shattered tile bit into her bare feet.

She folded her arms. "Easy peasy."

"Don't get cocky." He pointed to a place behind him, close to the wall. "Now try here."

Ursula stared at the spot, in the half of the room where the mosaic tile lay intact. She breathed in, letting the shadow magic wash through her body. As she flitted through the air, Bael reached out, letting his fingers brush over her arm.

She leaned against the wall, catching her breath. "I felt you touch me." She could still feel the warmth of his fingers on her forearm.

"Yes. I wanted you to know that just because you're shadow walking doesn't mean you're invulnerable. Someone with a blade could still do damage if you're in the wrong place."

"Noted."

"One more task." He pointed at the door of her apartment. "Shadow run to your door."

"That's it?"

Bael nodded.

Fatigue began to burn through her body, but Ursula channeled the shadow magic once more. It rippled through her chest, energizing her body. She concentrated on the sleek black door to her quarters. But when she tried to flicker to the spot, she found herself ten feet short of her destination.

Confused, she turned to Bael. "What happened?"

He stepped over the shattered tile. "Another important part of our lesson. You can only shadow run for a limited distance. About ten yards." He studied her. "How do you feel?"

Her entire body ached as though she'd run a marathon. Her hips and thighs screamed with exhaustion. "Completely knackered."

"Good. That's the final caveat—shadow magic is fatiguing. If you use it too much, you'll be too tired to fight."

She wiped a hand across her brow. "I need a nap."

"I will have some lumen crystals brought into the atrium. If you hold them close, you should be able to absorb their shadow magic, just like you did on the onyx throne. You can practice shadow running."

"I take it you don't want me to use the throne."

"Perhaps we should keep our distance until the duel." Shadows seemed to gather around him, and he wouldn't meet her eyes. She had an over-whelming sense that he was hiding something from her.

"Of course," she said.

He turned, disappearing into his hall.

Ursula swallowed. A wisp of the hollow void flickered in her chest.

CHAPTER 38

$\mathcal{U}$rsula stood in the center of the lion mosaic, a lunem crystal in each hand. Tendrils of shadow trickled from her fingers, gathering on the floor in a black mist. Dark magic thrummed through her bones, chilling her skin. Her breath misted around her head.

Bael was most certainly hiding something from her. Something about the way he wouldn't look at her when they'd said goodbye made her muscles clench.

She waved a hand through the air, watching the shadows flicker around it. *I just need to make sure I'm strong enough to fight him when I need to.*

Magic pooled in her body, flooding her muscles with power and demanding to be used. She lowered the crystals to the floor, and focused on a spot across the room.

Shadows rushed over her skin, through her gut, and her stomach flipped as she felt herself brushing the void. She reappeared ten feet away. *I've got this. I'm a natural.*

She straightened her back, then concentrated on a place near the lion's mane. Almost instantly, she flitted across the room in a cloud of black smoke. Wisps of magic curled around her fingers, tingling along her skin.

Most of the raw power had seeped from her body, but some of the magic still buzzed up her spine. *Let's see what I can do when the power is fading.*

She glanced at a spot near the onyx door, letting the shadows carry her through the air. But this time, she appeared a few feet short. Her toes throbbed as warmth returned to them. The magic was almost gone. *A good reminder to conserve magic in the duels.*

Bael's onyx door stood only a few feet away, cold and black as the void. She crossed to it, running her fingers over the smooth, cold surface. Wisps of shadows trailed from her fingers into the stone. The onyx seemed to absorb her magic, thirsty for shadow power.

Bael had warned her away from his quarters, and that only made her more desperate to find out what he was hiding.

Her mind churning, she turned to walk back into her own quarters. As she took a step, a scraping sound echoed off the atrium walls, and she whirled.

The stone had rolled to the side.

* * *

URSULA STARED at the open door. Apparently, the magic from her fingers had acted as a sort of key, unlocking Bael's chambers.

And of course, under no circumstances should she go inside. It would be an intrusion, and a dangerous one at that. She didn't need to provoke Bael's wrath *before* the duel.

Then again...

If he was hiding something from her, it was better to know what it was.

She swallowed hard, taking a tentative step into the tunnel, but the interior was too dimly lit for her to see anything.

Nothing moved in the tunnel, but distant voices echoed off the cavern walls. Male voices. Who did he have in his quarters? The man seemed to live in total isolation, and suddenly he was holding a party.

She crept further down the hallway, and the darkness gave way to the purple glow of mushroom light. She hugged the walls, trying to stay in the shadows. As she walked, the voices grew louder, but she couldn't hear what they were saying.

She pressed on, her pulse speeding up. At the end of the tunnel, she hesitated. As soon as she stepped out onto the stone bridge, Bael would see her. She crouched, straining her ears. The voices grew softer, until they faded away entirely. Slowly, she rose. Silence had fallen over the cave.

She waited another minute, then crept from the tunnel. She tiptoed over the stone bridge, cringing with each scuff of her shoe.

As she entered his cavern, she surveyed the space: his marble table, the violet crystals, and his forbidding throne overlooking it all. Nothing out of place.

Ursula shivered, looking at the yawning blackness of the abyss around her. Who, or what, had been talking in here—and where the hell had they gone?

Depleted of magic after her shadow running, her muscles ached.

Bael's throne seemed to call to her, luring her forward with its promise of thrilling power. If she sat in it, shadow magic would flood her body, filling her limbs with strength. A part of her wanted to give in to its lure entirely. Relinquishing her humanity, letting the void take her soul, becoming one with the god of night.

She brushed a fingers along the throne's arm, only to pull her hand away with a jerk when the image of an endless chasm filled her mind.

What am I thinking? An eternity of nothingness would drive her insane.

She surveyed the platform again. *I know I heard voices in here.* She took a tentative step around the throne, expecting the stony floor to continue on, but she gasped as she found herself on a cliff's edge. A deep chasm yawned behind the throne—too dark to investigate.

She ran back into the cavern and yanked out a small, glowing mushroom that grew near the wall. She held it like a candle, and it cast a cold light over the floor.

She crossed back to the cliff's edge behind the throne, and held the mushroom over the side. A pair of metal pitons jutted from the stone, with thick rope wrapped around either end. The top of a rope ladder— that's where the men had disappeared to.

CHAPTER 39

*I*f one thing was clear at this point, it was that she should turn around and scurry back to her quarters. She could still pretend that she hadn't snuck into Bael's chambers uninvited, when he'd explicitly told her to stay away. *We should keep our distance,* he'd said.

But she knew he was hiding something from her. She was a warrior now, and she'd do whatever it took to learn about her opponent.

Why, exactly, was she worried about protecting his feelings and his request for privacy, when in a couple of days he'd be ramming a knife into her heart, ushering her into the void with a violent death?

If she wanted any hope of walking out of that arena alive, she'd better learn everything she could about her greatest adversary.

She rested the mushroom on the stone behind the throne, and it cast a dim violet light on the rope ladder until it dwindled into darkness.

She climbed over the cliff's side, gripping tightly to the rope. Once she had both feet firmly on the rungs, she retrieved the glowing mushroom, clinging to its stem as she slowly climbed down. With each step down, the shadows seemed to close in, darkening the mushroom's light.

A cold sweat beaded on her forehead. *I can't tell if I'm brilliant or a complete moron.* That would all depend on the outcome of this particular excursion.

The ladder swung as she moved, but it seemed to be anchored at the bottom. She peered down at the heavy darkness. Her pulse began to race. Was there an end to this descent?

Her breath came faster. She closed her eyes, trying to calm herself. But as soon as her eyes were shut, a vision flashed in her mind: Bael piercing her chest with a dagger.

Bollocks. The vision was becoming so clear, it felt like a premonition more than a nightmare.

Focus on the task at hand, Ursula. She stepped down another rung. *Release foot. Move free hand down a rung. Carefully unclasp the hand with the mushroom. Repeat the entire process again.*

Just when she was certain she'd be climbing for the rest of eternity, her foot brushed against a gravel floor. She tentatively released the rope, shocked to find the solid ground beneath her. Fatigue burned through her muscles, shaking her legs.

The fungus illuminated rocky walls and a rocky room, covered in antiques. *What the hell?*

At one end, the walls narrowed into a tunnel—perhaps where Bael and his friend had gone. And the rest of the space was covered in curiosities: an old ship's clock propped on a dusty table, a stuffed raven in a cage, a horned demon's skull in a bell jar, furniture covered in draped sheets. And propped on a wooden stand, the corkscrew she'd used to stab Bael.

Apparently, this was Bael's storage space.

As she scanned the room, her gaze landed on an overturned picture frame next to the ship's clock. When she flipped it over, her stomach swooped. Bael's beautiful wife stared back at her, her brown eyes sad and serious.

Ursula ran her finger over the hole in the painting. *Why did he put you down here?*

She turned it over on the table again exactly where she'd found it. She could try to work out the Freudian complexities of Bael's psyche another time. Perhaps, if she managed to survive the duel.

Further down the tunnel, a shout echoed off the rock, and her heart began to thump. If she was going to follow the sound of the voices, she needed a weapon.

Her pulse speeding up, she crouched, pulling out a box from below the table. She rummaged through old compasses and tools until she found the obsidian blade—the one Cera had given her. *I do believe this belongs to me.*

Her feet crunched over the gravel as she crossed to the tunnel, gripping the knife in one hand and the mushroom in the other.

As she made her way through the tunnel, the fungus glowed over runes and twisting symbols carved into the walls—the same ones she'd seen in the passage above.

At the end of the tunnel, a pale light glowed. And as she drew nearer to the light, she pressed against the tunnel wall, hoping to remain unnoticed. Here, the air grew thick with humidity. A high-pitched squawk echoed off the walls.

She peered around the corner. Much like the passage to Bael's throne room, this passage also opened into a larger chamber. Among a sea of darkness, luminescent mushrooms lit the air. The warm air had an earthy, fungal aroma, and her skin dampened. She wiped a hand across the back of her forehead.

This must be the rookery she had flown through with Cera on her way to the melee.

A gravel path wound through the forest of mushrooms. She dropped her little toadstool by the entrance to the passage and followed the path.

CHAPTER 40

Up close, the mushrooms were even bigger than she'd realized—the size of elms. They glowed a faint cornflower blue.

Her feet crunched on the gravel path that wove between them until the gravel gave way to a loamy soil. She caught a flicker of movement a hundred feet to her left—a large, furry body that slowly undulated around a mushroom stalk.

Her stomach clenched. One of the caterpillars she had seen from Sotz's back.

Another giant insect slithered to her right, its green body curling up a mushroom. She stared in horrified fasciation as it tore out a chunk of fungal flesh with an enormous pair of incisors.

But as she pressed forward, something else caught her attention—the resonant sound of Bael's voice, chanting in Angelic. *Time to hide.* She slipped off the path, moving from stalk to stalk until she got a clear view of the action. She peered out from behind a mushroom, sweat dampening her clothes.

Turned away from her, Bael stood in the center of a clearing, surrounded by mushroom stumps. He wore his black riding cloak. Around him stood a cluster of demons dressed in gray cloaks, their hoods pulled over their heads. Even without seeing their faces, she could tell by their short stature they were oneiroi.

Bael finished his spell, and the oneiroi began to chant in another language—one she'd never heard before.

A chill deepened around her. Whatever spell they were casting, it channeled shadow magic. The oneiroi hunched closer together, and the temperature plummeted. Their voices rose into the air, and a sharp burst of shadow magic ripped through mushrooms. A silent detonation that slammed Ursula in the chest like a fist. Hollowness pierced her, and she fell to her knees, her body shaking from the blast of power.

The darkness threatened to pull her under, and for just a moment, she saw a flash of Bael, holding the knife to her chest.

Stay grounded, Ursula. She sucked in a breath, feeling the damp earth beneath her knees and hands. The air felt thick and warm again. She opened her eyes, her gaze landing on Bael. He still stood before the oneiroi, completely unperturbed, as if a massive blast of magic hadn't just ripped through the mushroom forest.

Thick shadows coalesced around her, and magic simmered in her chest. The blast had completely recharged her body.

"Did the necromancy work?" asked Bael.

"I don't know," said a hooded oneiroi. "It hasn't moved."

She shifted position, trying to get a glimpse of what they were looking at. They seemed to be staring down at something in the center of the circle, but she couldn't tell what.

"Again," said Bael. "We must chant the channeling spell once more." He pulled his hood over his head, chanting again in Angelic. Shadow magic flickered over Ursula's skin.

Did he say necromancy? What the hell is he up to?

She needed a better vantage point. Her gaze flicked to a short mushroom about fifteen feet away. If she could get to the top of the mushroom, she'd have a clear view. *Good thing I'm charged up with magic, now.* She could shadow run there without a problem.

She stared at the mushroom's cap, then let her body fill with shadow magic. She flitted through the air, reappearing on the mushroom's cap. For a moment, she began to slide, then she dug her fingers into the mushroom's flesh, its luminescent juices staining her hands.

She glanced up at Bael and the oneiroi, and her mouth went dry. They surrounded a prostrate form. Long and lean, he lay stretched out on the ground, his skin gray as a corpse. Had they killed him?

As Bael and the oneiroi chanted, the creature lay still as a grave. A chill of shadow magic raised goosebumps on her arms. Any second now, they were going to blast the air with magic again.

She crawled to the edge of the cap, then let herself drop down to the soft earth. She hurried behind a stalk, just managing to find cover when a second blast rocked the forest. Shadow magic blasted through her bones, and she fell to the ground. Ice seized heart, and the void spread through her veins like poison.

It called to her. *Accept the darkness.*

So easy to fall into the void...

Her fists tightened, and a fire roared in the hollows of her mind, a room in flames. The scent of burning flesh, agonized screams piercing the air. *The best way to fight ice is with fire.*

The ice in her chest thawed, and she crawled to her knees. She felt the warm dirt beneath her hands, pressing into her knees. *I'm here,* she told herself.

She glanced up at the strange coven. In the center of the circle, the corpse now stood.

"What are you?" said Bael.

"You know me as the Gray Ghost," it said in a hollow voice.

CHAPTER 41

Something slithered in the corner of Ursula's vision. A shudder crawled up her spine, and she slowly turned. One of the enormous caterpillars was descending the trunk of mushroom just above her head. Thick as an anaconda, with a head the size of a bowling ball, its mandibles snapped audibly. Fear slithered over her skin.

Bael's voice rumbled through the forest. "Did you hear something?" He sniffed the air. "I smell something, too."

Ursula's stomach clenched. *He can't smell me?*

"I'll go check," said one of the oneiroi.

Fuck. They're coming right for me.

She pressed her back to the stalk, trying to avoid being spotted. Unfortunately, she was now trapped between the giant caterpillar and the approaching oneiroi. Adrenaline burned through her veins.

Frantically, she looked around. A smaller mushroom stood a dozen yards away—further than she'd ever shadow run.

She couldn't see the cap, but she needed to find a way to get there before the sodding caterpillar ripped its fangs into her head.

Swallowing hard, she envisioned the top of the mushroom cap. Shadow magic rushed through her bones, carrying her through the air. An instant later, she smacked into the top of mushroom. Even with the relatively forgiving softness of the mushroom's surface, the landing took the wind out of her.

She dug her fingers into its flesh with her nails.

Still, from here, the oneiroi—or Bael—would be able to spot her if they looked up. She needed to get to the canopy's next level.

She narrowed her eyes, focusing on the mushroom caps that towered over her. In the next instant, her body whispered through the air, and the shadows slammed her onto another mushroom top. She dug in her fingers, anchoring herself to the mushroom.

Below her, she could hear the oneiroi mutter to himself, "I could have told him it was just a caterpillar."

Clinging to the mushroom, Ursula lay perfectly still, listening to footsteps moving closer to her. A cold sweat beaded on her skin. She inched forward, spying the tops of the men's heads. The Gray Ghost walked by Bael's side, his hands cuffed behind his back.

She waited until the footsteps faded before dropping down the lower mushroom, then sliding off to the damp ground.

Her jaw ached from where she'd smacked into the mushroom's flesh, but the caterpillar at least appeared to have retreated. As quietly as she could, she followed the path back to Bael's manor. The last of his oneiroi disappear into his storage space.

What were her options? She could wait, then try to sneak back when they'd all climbed up the ladder.

But in all likelihood, they'd be mulling around his cavern, blocking her exit. In fact, they could be mulling around the old storage space. The Gray Ghost's hands were secured behind his back—he was unlikely to climb anywhere.

Right now, the oneiroi were probably guarding him by the old furniture and compasses.

A lump rose in her throat. *In the brilliant/moron stakes, the needle is swinging wildly toward fuckwit.*

She'd just have to find another way out—one that didn't involve revealing herself to Bael. She turned, walking in the opposite direction from the way she'd come. The forest had succumbed to an eerie silence, and a chill spread through the air. She hugged herself.

As she drew closer to the clearing where Bael's coven had conducted the spell, the soil crunched below her feet—frozen solid from the stunning blast of Bael's shadow magic. She had no idea how Bael and the oneiroi had remained standing for that, when the blast had nearly ripped her skin off.

She peered into the clearing. Where the coven had stood, nothing covered the soil but a layer of ice.

She turned back to the path, walking on, her teeth chattering. Honestly, she had no idea if this direction led to a way out, but it was worth a shot.

The air grew warmer as she moved away from the clearing, following the path deeper into the mushroom forest.

Along the path's edges, the mushroom stalks clustered. The path twisted and wound like a serpent between them. Up ahead, she caught a glimpse of a slithering movement, and goosebumps rose on her skin. She drew Cera's blade from her belt.

In this part of the forest, the mushrooms towered as high as sequoias, and just above their enormous caps, she could hear the echoing shouts of the bats.

Her skin grew cold as she took in the landscape. Here, among the larger mushrooms, the caterpillars were everywhere. A giant insect slithered over every stalk, crunching through fungal flesh.

A scream pierced the silence, and she whirled to find two caterpillars fighting over the carcass of a third.

Her skin crawled, and her fingers tightened around the blade. *Isn't that charming?*

Her throat went dry, and she hurried further along the path. But instead of continuing on through the forest, the path ended abruptly with the edge of a cliff.

She gasped. Spread out below her, a second mushroom forest extended into the distance. Hundreds of feet below, mushroom gaps glowed—sea-green, periwinkle, and cornflower blue. Stunningly beautiful, like the surface of a luminescent sea.

A grunting noise behind her made her turn her head. Two caterpillars crawled toward her, saliva dripping from their mandibles.

Her heart sped up. *Okay. Now, I'm trapped between giant flesh-hungry insects and a cliff.*

A third caterpillar inched down a mushroom stalk to her right, and a fourth flanked her from the left. Her throat tightened. *I'm definitely a fuck-wit. Good to know.* They closed in on her, and she clenched her fingers on the hilt of the obsidian blade.

On the path, one of the caterpillars reared up before her, like a snake ready to strike its prey. Her blood roaring, Ursula slashed at the caterpillar's body. Cera's blade sliced deeply into its flesh.

The caterpillar fell back with a shriek. The other insects stared at it, as if in horror. Then they lunged for it, tearing into its flesh.

She loosed a breath. *Better him than me.*

She scanned the horizon, searching for a place she could shadow run. But the entire path now crawled with caterpillars, a sea of writhing fur. Running was not an option. As soon as they were done feasting on their fallen comrade, they'd come for her. She slashed at another insect, cutting into the flesh below its head. Shrieking, it writhed on the ground. She kicked it backward, toward the oncoming crowd of hungry predators.

Like sharks scenting blood, the caterpillars descended on it ravenously. *How long can I keep this up?* She gasped for breath. Her muscles burned. Something brushed her foot and she looked down to see a caterpillar only inches from her. Instinctively she kicked it over the edge of the cliff. The creature cartwheeled down in a whirl of fur, bouncing off the sides before splattering on a mushroom cap.

If she didn't find a way out of here, she'd be joining the caterpillar corpse on that mushroom cap, her guts splattered over the lower forest.

The sound of bats shrieking echoed off the walls, and a spark of hope lit in her chest. *Is there a chance that Sotz is out there somewhere?*

She whistled sharply, just as a caterpillar lunged for her. She dove to the side, dodging its attack, and her face smacked hard into a rock. Pain shot through her skull. Still, it had worked. The caterpillar's momentum carried it over the side of the cliff.

Around her, the other caterpillars edged closer, ready to finish her off. Panic ripped her mind apart. *How the fuck do I get out of this?*

She gripped the knife, pointing it at the giant larvae. "Back off, you furry fuck-maggots!" she bellowed.

Instantly, the larvae stilled their movements.

She frowned. *Why the hell did that work?*

Behind her, the distant flapping of wings beat the air, and relief washed through her. *Sotz.*

The caterpillars weren't scared of her, but apparently, they were scared of bats. She glanced behind her, thrilling at the sight of Sotz's dark shape descending. She whistled again. *Hurry.*

With nowhere to land, he flew along the edge of the cliff. As he passed under her, she jumped.

CHAPTER 42

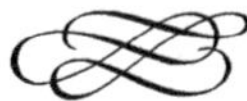

She clung to Sotz, breathing in the familiar smell of his fur, feeling the comforting beating of his heart. She sucked in a shaky breath, her legs trembling. She'd survived, by the skin of her teeth.

All around them, bats shrieked, their voices echoing off the walls. Still, a sense of calm warmed her body. If she could survive an attack by a legion of caterpillars, maybe she had a chance against Bournajoux.

She leaned down, whispering, "Take me home."

Sotz soared through the darkness. As the light dimmed, the cacophony of the rookery dampened. After a few minutes of peaceful darkness, they burst into the light of the crater. Asta's now-familiar spire towered over the ground—an oddly welcome sight at this point.

Sotz curved in a slow arc toward the manor.

Ursula took a deep breath, reveling in the clean air, the feel of the wind and the milky sunlight on her skin. She belonged in the air—not buried in a dark tunnel.

Sotz swooped low toward the manor's roof, then landed gracefully on its slick surface. Ursula caught her breath, her heart still pounding hard.

"Thank you for coming for me, big guy." She rose, her muscles aching. *Not super bright to get into a fight before my actual fight, but too late to fix it now.*

For a moment, Sotz brushed against her leg like a cat, then launched himself off the roof.

As she walked to the lift, she touched her heart, feeling it pounding hard through her shirt. She stepped into the lift, and a stiff lunar breeze rushed over her skin.

The elevator slowly creaked down, past one shattered floor after another, and she wrapped her fingers around the metal bars. She still had no clue what Bael had been doing with the oneiroi. She had no idea he interacted with them at all. How exactly had he ended up with the Gray Ghost in a mushroom forest?

As the lift lowered into the atrium, she glanced at the door to Bael's chambers. She'd left it open, but someone had since closed it. She glanced around furtively, taking care that no one caught her sneaking back into her quarters.

She hurried over the bridge into her living room, then made a beeline for the bath. Blood, mushroom juice, caterpillar fluid, and mud coated every inch of her body, and she stank like the bottom of a grave. She glanced at herself in the mirror. A deep purple bruise had bloomed just below her eye.

As she filled the bath with warm water, she ripped off her clothes. She shoved them under the bathroom sink. *I'll find a better hiding place later.*

She stepped into the bath, relishing the feel of the warm water against her burning muscles. She lowered herself down, letting the water soothe away the aches in her thighs. Still, her face throbbed where she'd smacked it against the rock.

She dunked her hair under the water, then rose again, reveling in the warmth of the bath. It was nearly time for her real battle—the battle against Bernajoux, and whoever else. And she'd need to be clean and rested for the fight.

She grabbed the lavender-scented soap, rubbing it over her skin and working up a frothy lather before washing her hair. When she'd finished soaping up, she dunked under the water again, rinsing off the suds.

From the living room, a heavy pounding punctuated the silence. Her heart sped up. *Definitely Bael's knock.*

As she stepped from the bath, water dripping from her skin, he knocked louder. *And he seems a little cranky.*

He continued to pound on her door, and she yanked a towel off the rack, quickly drying off.

Bael slammed his fist into the door. "Ursula!"

Fucking hell. She wrapped the towel around herself.

"I need to speak to you." His voice boomed through the door, an edge to it that made her spine stiffen.

Why do I have the feeling he knows what I did? "Coming!"

She pulled open the door to find Bael standing in the doorway, his hands clamped tightly on either side of the door frame.

He gazed down at her, a cold fury flashed in his eyes. "Where have you been?"

Ursula's mind raced. How much did he suspect? She could lie completely and say she'd been in her flat all evening, but he must know something.

"I took Sotz for a ride." The best lies always have a hint of truth.

"Did you open the door to my quarters?"

Once you start a lie you cannot budge. "No."

His gaze trailed over her bare shoulders. "I smelled you."

Her cheeks warmed. "What? I don't smell that strongly. And anyway, I wasn't anywhere near you."

Bael studied her for a long moment, then his fingers lifted to her face, cupping her chin. "What happened?"

Ursula brushed her fingertips over her cheek. "I hit a moth when I was flying."

He stared at her for a long moment before grazing his fingertips over the bruise. A rush of shadow magic kissed her cheek, soothing the dull pain below her skin.

He dropped his hand. "Are you hurt anywhere else?"

A million dirty jokes raced through her mind, but she didn't think Bael would react well to them. Instead, she mutely shook her head.

"I believe someone broke into my quarters."

She bit her lip. "That's terrible," she blustered. "Do you think whoever it was is a threat?"

His icy gaze rooted her in place. "No. But when I find the intruder, I will deliver a painful death."

As Bael turned to leave, ice shot through Ursula's veins.

Absolute, complete fuckwit.

CHAPTER 43

Ursula woke on the sofa in her silky nightgown, tangled in the soft blanket. She rose, stretching her arms above her head, and glanced at the clock. She could hardly make sense of the damn thing, but she was pretty sure she only had twelve hours left before the duel began. Her stomach fluttered.

Despite the soothing bath she'd taken after her adventure, her legs still felt like dead weights. The shadow running had sucked the life out of her.

Bael's anger still roiled in her mind. She'd gone from the promise of a swift death to the threat of a painful one, having learned nothing at all from her intrusion into her quarters.

A knock sounded at the door—softer this time. *Cera.*

Barefoot, she padded downstairs and pulled open the door. Cera stood in the doorway holding a silver tray, a bag draped over her arm. "Lunch?"

Ursula nodded. "Is it lunchtime already? I've nearly lost the ability to keep track of time, since the sun never sets."

"Mushroom sandwiches." Cera bustled into the room, heading for the bar. She dropped the bag on the floor. "I let you sleep in. Bael told me you had a late night."

Ursula's stomach rumbled audibly. Even mushroom sandwiches sounded good. "Thank you, Cera."

"The lord said you hurt yourself flying, but I see he healed you."

As she crossed to the bar, Ursula forced a smile. "All better." *Until he severs my head from my body.* No. He wouldn't do that. He'd said a *painful* death, and that wasn't painful enough.

Ursula took a seat at the bar beside Cera and pulled a plate in front of her. She bit into the fresh bread, and the lightly salted mushroom flesh. Her fight against the caterpillars had certainly given her an appetite.

Cera chewed thoughtfully, her eyes glistening. She seemed subdued today. After a few moments, she turned to Ursula. "I don't like the thought of you dueling against the lord. There is no way for this to end well."

A sharp pang pierced Ursula's chest. Cera was right. She shrugged. "At least he said he'd kill me swiftly, if it came down to it."

Unless he figures out I'm his intruder.

Cera nodded.

"Would you describe him as a merciful sort?" asked Ursula. *Like, is he likely to go back on his swift death promise if he gets mad enough? Will he be stabbing me to death with my own ribs.*

Cera tilted her head. "To his enemies? Not particularly."

Wonderful. She took another bite of her sandwich.

Cera frowned at her. "You seem awfully relaxed."

"Why wouldn't I be?"

"The duel is in two hours."

Panic clenched Ursula's heart, and she jumped up. "What? The fight is in two hours?" she practically shouted. "I thought I had twelve hours or something. I can't read the bloody lunar clock."

"Relax," said Cera, nodding at the bag on the floor. "I cleaned and re-stitched your fighting gear."

Ursula's pulse began to race, and she stripped out of her nightgown. It took her only a few minutes to slip into the reinforced leather.

Her hands trembled as she buttoned up the corset. "Thanks, Cera."

Sadness shone in Cera's eyes. "Will you kill the lord?"

A lump rose in Ursula's throat. "If I have to. I know you care for him."

"It's not just that." Cera bit her lip, one of her sharp teeth piercing the skin. "If you kill him. Will you keep me as your servant?"

"Of course!" She touched Cera's shoulder. "Or at least, I'll make sure you're safe. I'll take you with me back to New York."

Cera wrapped her arms around Ursula, squeezing her. "Thank you. Otherwise, the other lords would probably kill me."

Ursula pulled away from Cera, looking her in the eye. "There will always be a home for you in New York. You've seen where I live. If both Bael and I die, take Sotz and fly there. Tell Zee you were my friend. She'll look out for you."

"Thank you." Cera squeezed her hand. "But I'd like you to find a way for neither of you to die."

Ursula's heart ached. She couldn't help but feel that she'd already witnessed her fate—Bael, shoving a blade into her heart. The life leaving her eyes, her jaw slackening, lips turning blue. Red hair stamped into the dirt. Dread coiled around her heart.

Her gaze flicked to the door where she kept her katana, but the sword wasn't there. Her pulse began to race. "Where's my sword?"

"I saw the lord take it," Cera said softly.

A hot tendril of rage coiled through Ursula's body. "I'm going to be in a fight to the death in less than two hours, and Bael has taken my only weapon?" Angry heat warmed her cheeks. "I thought he was trying to help me. He helped me in the melee. He trained me to shadow run."

"Don't get too upset. You'll have to think clearly in the fight."

"What fight?" she shouted. "He just left me without a weapon? What was the point of everything he's done? Why not just kill me in the melee instead of giving me two weeks of false hope? What kind of person does that?"

Of course, he wasn't a person. He was a demon—a predator. He'd told her as much.

Was he even capable of human-like emotions? Love or empathy? Or was he like all the other demon lords deep down—driven by a dark impulse to conquer and dominate? To screw with people's heads for sport?

Surely, if he kept his wife's wedding ring around his neck, he must have loved her. Ursula pointed at the spot on the wall where his wife's portrait had hung. "Cera, you know the portrait of that woman that used to hang there?"

"Elissa, yes. The lord's wife."

"What happened to her?"

Cera's face blanched, and she looked at the floor. "He wouldn't want me to tell you."

"Tell me." Ursula's stomach turned. "I need to know."

Cera's eyes glistened. "She died."

"I know that. But how?"

"Stabbed, I think. With a sword."

A growing sense of dread crept up Ursula's throat. "Who stabbed her?"

Cera spoke so softly, Ursula nearly didn't hear. "The lord."

"Bael?"

Cera nodded mutely, and Ursula's world tilted. Her heart thumped hard, and she ran upstairs, snatching the silver ring from its spot on the dresser. Frantically, she rubbed it between her fingers.

But this time, it brought her no relief.

As Cera called for her, she ran out the door.

CHAPTER 44

*U*rsula gripped Sotz tightly with her thighs, guiding her toward the arena. The icy lunar wind whipped over her skin as she arced lower. Here, on the other side of the moon, no sun burned in the sky. Only the silver glimmer of stars lit her way, and the bright glow of the Earth, hanging in the sky like a vibrant gemstone.

As before, torches burned before the platform, held by oneiroi. The crater's seats crawled with demons and oneiroi. Oneiroi with great hunks of meat walked the aisles, shouting the price of a slice of roast. Oneiroi maidservants held trays laden with steins of beer.

All along the benches, demons waved banners with the insignia of the houses they supported—a lion for Bael, a scorpion for Abrax, a satyr for Bileth...

As she descended over the arena's floor, a great whoop rose from the crowd. To her shock, the crowd began chanting her name. *Apparently, they don't hate the hellhound harlot as much as they once did.*

In fact, maybe someone from the crowd had a weapon they could lend her...

Sotz touched down on the ground and she stepped off, surveying the space. As before, she stood alone in the center. She still wasn't clear where they were supposed to go before the start of the duel, so she might as well start here.

Hothgar stood on the platform, a silver cape billowing in the wind. He stared at her, his eyes completely black.

And by his side, Abrax sat in a dark throne, just below the statue of his father. Abrax's eyes had that same eerie, silver sheen as his father's.

Ursula turned, scanning the crowd, searching for a weapon. Didn't any spectators bring swords to death matches? She couldn't find a single sheathed weapon—not even a dagger. Panic stole her breath.

Before she had the chance to give in to her fears completely, Hothgar sounded the gong. The knell reverberated through her bones, and her pulse began to speed up.

Hothgar's voice boomed across Lacus Mortis. "The dueling commences soon, a fight to the death. Only one man will remain standing."

He didn't even bother to correct himself, to add in the possibility of a woman remaining standing. Anyone watching at this point would realize she didn't have a weapon—that she was basically here to be slaughtered.

Hothgar raised his hands to the night sky. "I call upon Zoth of the giant of Pleion, Inth of Alboth."

As Hothgar called out the names, the fighters strode from a dark tunnel on the side of the arena.

"Bernajoux of Zobrach," Hothgar continued. Ursula glanced at her opponent—her lanky, and apparently sadistic opponent—dressed in a starry doublet. As he took his place, he bowed to Ursula.

"Valac of Phragol Mocaden," Hothgar boomed. "Chax of Azimeth, our Phantom Rider, now known as the Gray Ghost."

Ursula's stomach clenched. *Bael hadn't taken him out of the running? What the hell was his game?*

Hothgar smirked. "Ursula, the Harlot of Hellfire.

"And, our last champion, is the reason we're all here to today. The lord of Abelda, formerly the Sword of Nyxobas, will be fighting to retain his manor. Bael the Fallen." Hothgar solemnly intoned.

Ursula turned, her heart squeezing, and she watched Bael charge from the tunnel like an ox entering a bull-fighting ring. He wore a silver lion helm and a pair of thick leather trousers. No such protection guarded his tattooed chest, however. He strode into the arena shirtless, his godlike physique on full display. He'd left the bandages at home, and she got a full view of his lethal-looking tattoos: stars, lightning, a razor-sharp thunderbolt.

How could someone blessed with such beauty and physical grace be so dead inside? Too much time in the void, obviously. The betrayal felt like a punch to her gut.

But as he moved into the center of the arena, she studied him closer. In one hand, he clasped a silver broadsword, the same color as his helm. But in the other, the katana.

He stopped just by her side, a thin sheen of sweat on his tawny skin, and she looked up at him, her heart slamming against her ribs. Beautiful and terrifying at the same time. A man who looked like a god, but had murdered his own wife.

He held out the sword by the hilt. "Here."

Hope bloomed in her chest. For just a moment, she had the strongest impulse to throw her arms around him, but she remembered what Cera had said about his wife.

She took the sword from him, her eyes moistening with tears of relief. "Why did you take it? I thought you were trying to get me killed."

He shook his head. "You still think I have no honor? I had it cleaned and sharpened."

She stroked her fingers over the hilt. "Thank you. You could have told me, I guess."

"I thought you'd have understood me better by now," he said softly.

"I don't understand you at all." A tear rolled down her cheek, and she turned away to wipe it off her cheek. She did not want the other fighters to see her crying, but her emotions were churning out of control.

Ursula held up the sword, watching it flash wickedly in the starlight. She studied the steel for a moment—it *did* look sharper. She turned back to Bael, but he'd already taken his place at the end of the line of champions, just on the other side of Bernajoux.

Hothgar held out his hands once more. "The eight that remain have proven their skill in battle and air. Today, the duels will test their prowess in single combat."

All around her, the crowd roared, baying for blood.

* * *

"THE CONTEST BEGINS with Bael and Zoth." Hothgar nodded at the two demons. "Proceed to the field of blood."

Ursula's mouth went dry. *Not big on euphemisms here, are they?*

Along with the rest of the champions, Ursula stepped away from the center of the arena. She glanced at Zoth—a massive demon, his arms as thick as tree trunks. Furs and metal breastplates encased his gargantuan chest. In one hand, he held an iron buckler. In the other, a short bastard sword.

He grinned, revealing a ragged row of teeth.

Bael stepped forward, drawing his sword. Although Bael stood at least six and a half feet tall, the behemoth had a good foot on him. Still, Bael didn't appear in the least bothered, despite the monster looming over him.

"When I sound the gong," Hothgar bellowed, "the duel begins."

An icy wind whipped over the arena, and a deathly silence fell. Even though she'd learned that Bael had slaughtered his own wife, she wanted him to survive this. Maybe he wasn't a sociopath. Maybe there was some valid reason, like his wife was a monster who needed to be put down.

But then, why would he keep her painting on his wall? And the wedding ring around his neck?

What possible reason could someone have for slaughtering someone he loved?

So that was the memory he was so desperate to run from, the one that tormented him.

She watched as Hothgar lifted his mallet and slammed it into the brass gong. The crowd roared.

Zoth slammed the flat edge of his sword against his own shield, in an apparent attempt to intimidate Bael. Zoth shifted his weight from one foot to another.

His tactic didn't appear to be working. Bael stood perfectly still. He held his sword loosely, his body perfectly relaxed. Only his eyes betrayed any tension as they carefully tracked the demon's movements. Watching that penetrating alertness in his gray eyes, she began to understand the true meaning of *predator*.

The air seemed too thin around her and then suddenly Zoth charged. Propelled forward by shadow magic, he aimed his sword straight at Bael's heart. At the last possible moment, Bael swiftly stepped aside, like a toreador dodging a charging bull. But his sword remained steady.

In a beautifully savage motion, he ripped it through Zoth's torso. The demon slumped forward, and Bael pulled his sword from the creature. Blood and gore pooled in the dirt.

Zoth mutely opened his mouth to scream, but in a swirl of shadows, Bael was standing over him. His silver sword flashed in the starlight, and he slammed the blade through Zoth's neck.

Ursula's blood ran cold. The whole fight had taken maybe two seconds. Bael displayed a level of skill she wouldn't be able to match if she practiced for a thousand years.

Her knees began to shake. She could only hope her own death would be just as quick.

For a few pregnant moments, the crowd fell completely silent. Then, a chorus of boos filled the air, and a team of oneiroi ran out to clear the body. Zoth's blood left a thick streak of crimson across the crater floor.

The crowd was not happy. They'd wanted a duel. This had been an execution.

Hotghar approached at the front of his stage. "That was—" He paused to think. "Very efficient."

Bael nodded silently, his face perfectly still. For just a moment, his icy glaze flicked to her as he took his place at the end of the line.

Definitely a sociopath. Ursula reached into her pocket, her fingers coiling around the silver ring. She rolled it between her fingers. *What would he do to me if he learned I'd crept into his quarters?*

Hothgar banged his gong again, silencing the crowd.

Of course, no one had bothered to tell them the order of duels, so she had no idea when she'd have to fight Bernajoux. Nervously, she glanced down the line at him. Something about the smug grin he wore infuriated her.

Hothgar's booming voice summoned Valac of Phragol Mocaden and Inth of Alboth to the field of blood. Inth stepped forward, wearing a full suit of armor and carrying a long pole arm. Valac—a muscular demon whose skin had a bluish hue—stood across from him, gripping a battle axe.

The crowd fell silent as the two demons faced each other. Slowly, Inth wove the end of his spear in the air, and a magical charge crackled from the point. Valac growled, a deep sound that seemed to rumble over the dirt.

Deep in her pocket, Ursula rolled the silver ring in the palm of her hand. Even though both men were large, the match was clearly unbalanced—a knight in armor versus an unprotected barbarian. Her fingers tightened around the ring.

A magical charge erupted from the pole arm with a loud crack. Just as the bolt of magic was ready to strike Valac, he twisted sideways, dodging the attack.

Snarling, Inth began recharging the pole arm by swinging it in the air. But before he could strike again, Valac closed the gap between them, stepping safely past the tip of the pole arm. He slammed his axe through the pike, hacking off the tip. The crowd roared.

Inth had just been thoroughly emasculated.

Inth's armor creaked as he drew a sword from its sheath. But Valac slammed his axe into Inth's shoulder, denting the metal. Inth bellowed in pain, but his armor had saved him from losing his arm.

Inth lifted his sword to swing, but his armor slowed him and he was unable to land a blow. Valac's ax slammed against his armor again and again. *Thunk. Thunk. Thunk.*

Inth spun, trying to keep Valac in sight, but he seemed unstable on his feet. Now, Ursula understood the strategy. Less armor meant greater agility.

Just as she thought all was lost for poor Inth, he whirled in a one-eighty. He slammed his metal-encased fist into Valac's head. The crack of skull reverberated across the crater.

How did he manage a blow like that?

A burst of cold air struck Ursula's face. *Ah. He used shadow magic.*

Valac fell to his knees, blood pouring between his fingers. Inth raised his sword and Ursula closed her eyes.

Bile rose in her throat. *I can't say I was ever overcome by the desire to watch someone's head split open.* By the full-throated roar of the crowd, they did not share her sentiment.

When she opened her eyes again, she stared at Valac's limp, blue body on the dirt. The sword had cleaved through his skull.

The field of blood was aptly named.

Hothgar's announced, "Well fought, Inth."

The knight pulled off his helm. Sweat slicked his platinum hair, and blood oozed from the joints of his armor.

"Thank you," he said gruffly. Limping slightly, he returned to his spot at the end of the line.

Ursula's stomach dropped as she stared at Hothgar. The Sword of Nyxobas seemed to stare right at her, his eyes dark as onyx. And above him, Nyxobas's statue stared into the void, eyes gleaming like cold starlight.

Any moment now, it will be my turn.

Hothgar slammed his mallet into his gong. "And now, a fight that should prove extremely satisfying for us all." The wind toyed with his silver cape. "Bernajoux the Unvanquished and Ursula the Whore. Can you please step into the field of blood?"

The crowd's screams pierced her to the bone.

* * *

INSTEAD OF A SUIT OF ARMOR, Bernajoux wore a velvet doublet. He neither looked like a medieval knight, nor an unhinged barbarian giant. He'd slicked back his dark hair, and straightened his thin mustache into a perfect line. He carried a narrow sword at his hip.

Ursula's body hummed with raw nerves. He didn't look like much of a match, but Bael had described him as a sadist. She took her spot, about six feet from him.

As the sound of her heart pounded in her ears, the gong reverberated through the crater.

Bernajoux drew his blade—a rapier. The thing looked flimsy—a long piece of narrow steel, no thicker than a ruler.

Ursula pulled her katana from its sheath, feeling its comforting weight in her hand.

Turning his body sideways, he pointed the blade at her. He arched an eyebrow. "Are you ready?"

"Of course."

Bernajoux's licked his lips. The sight of his long, pointed tongue distracted her.

Bernajoux took the opportunity to strike, springing forward like a venomous serpent. Reflexively, Ursula parried, her sword clanking against his.

"Very nice," said Bernajoux. "I see you've trained in the Shinduro technique."

So that's what it's called. Instead of responding, Ursula kept her full attention on his blade. It glided through the air in a slow serpentine motion, interrupted by an occasional twitch that made her heart jump.

"But have you trained in the style of Calvacabos of Bologna?" he hissed.

She had no idea what he was talking about. But it didn't matter. He was already lunging again. Pain ripped through her thigh as his blade pierced her muscle. She grunted as he ripped the blade out again.

"Did you like that?" asked Bernajoux. "Did you like feeling the tip inside you? Do you want it a bit deeper?"

Bile rose in her throat. *What the fuck?*

Bernajoux darted back, the bloodied tip of his sword dancing before her eyes. *He's toying with me.* Her leg screamed with pain.

Bernajoux attacked again, and she just barely parried it.

"Do you want some more?" he asked. "If only I could take my time with you. Really get to know your body with my blade."

The tip of his sword twitched, and she jumped back. The demon laughed, his tongue flicking between elongated canines.

He pressed in on her, his blade extended. She faltered, stumbling back.

One thing was becoming clearer—her katana was a slashing weapon. It didn't have the reach or precision of his rapier. If she fought on his terms, she'd loose.

The pointed tip of Bernajoux's sword glinted in the pearly light. Still, the sides of the blade were dull.

Adrenaline raced through her body, lighting her muscles on fire. *I need to get out of his reach.* She needed to shadow run. Maybe she could get close enough to slash him with her katana, while avoiding the rapier.

She focused on a spot near him, letting the shadows gather within her. Riding on the wind, she raced forward—right into the tip of the rapier.

It felt like a punch to her stomach, but when she looked down, she saw the blade had pierced clean through her abdomen. Horror ripped her mind apart.

Bernajoux licked his lips. "Does that fill you up nicely? Want a bit more?"

Pain screamed through her gut, stealing her breath. She tried to breathe. *I haven't even managed to attack.* This was a massacre.

She gripped her katana tighter, swinging for Bernajoux. She struck him hard in the side, just below his ribs. He screamed, losing the grip on his sword. He staggered back.

His sword still impaled her stomach, and Bernajoux was muttering in Angelic, trying to staunch the blood flow from his side.

She had to attack while he was still weakened. But first, she needed to get the godforsaken blade out of her gut.

Dropping her katana, she gripped the rapier in two hands, piercing her fingers. Gritting her teeth, she pulled the hilt away from her. Pain splintered through her.

With tears streaming from her eyes, she tugged on it again. With a final, agonized scream, she ripped it free. Just as Bernajoux finished the final words of the healing spell, she flung the sword away. It arced into the air in a whirl of blood and metal.

Too bad he doesn't have a weapon.

"My blade!" Bernajoux screamed.

Hot blood poured from her stomach, but she kept her focus on him.

"Do you like that?" she snarled. "Do you want me to take my time with you?"

Bernajoux's face twisted with rage, and he leapt for her. She jammed her katana up, piercing his throat. The attack speared his brainstem.

Bernajoux the Unvanquished no longer lived up to his name.

His body went limp, spasming as it fell to the ground. She pulled her sword from his neck.

Agony rippled down her body, and she glanced down at the wound in her gut. Staring at the pumping blood, her vision began to darken. The crowd's frantic cheers sounded a million miles away.

A chill seeped into her bones, and it wasn't shadow magic.

She fell back against the cold dirt, staring at the bright blue and green of the Earth. In the next moment, Bael's face appeared, eclipsing the Earth. He lifted her in his arms, and she could smell the scent of sandalwood.

CHAPTER 45

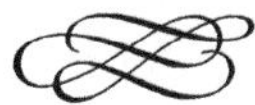

$\mathcal{B}$ael brushed his fingers over her cheek. "Ursula? I need you to wake up."

She opened her eyes, blinking at the starlight. The Earth, nearly full, hung bright in the sky.

Her throat felt dry, her mind foggy. Around her, the crowd roared.

Hothgar's voice cut the braying crowd like a foghorn.

I'm still here. Lacus Mortis.

She licked her lips, then swallowed. *I need water.* "What happened?"

"You slayed Bernajoux, but he injured you terribly. I healed you, but you missed an entire round."

"Who fought?"

"The Gray Ghost and Chax of Azimeth."

She was pretty sure she already knew the answer, but she asked anyway. "Who won?"

"The Gray Ghost." He frowned. "I'll be fighting next. I don't expect it to last long. Will you be ready to fight after?"

No bloody way. "Of course."

"Good. You fight the Gray Ghost—"

Hothgar's voice cut him off, announcing his name. "I must go." His pale gaze pierced her, and she watched as he rose, pulling on his silver helm. "You'll be fine."

She didn't get a chance to ask him what exactly he knew about the Gray Ghost. As she pushed up onto her elbows, he was already walking toward the center of the arena.

Ursula rose unsteadily to watch the fight. She shot a nervous glance at the man next to her. Despite having already fought a battle, the Gray Ghost's clothes still shone a pale gray, like the skin of a corpse.

A shudder crawled up her spine, and she turned her attention back to the duel. Inth—the knight—stood opposite Bael. He held a new, unbroken pole arm. His armor gleamed in the starry light, good as new. *I guess I wasn't the only one who's been healed.*

Hothgar gripped his gong. "For the next battle, Inth of Alboth versus Bael the Fallen." He slammed the mallet into the gong with a thunderous clang.

Immediately, Inth began to charge up his weapon, twisting the spearhead in a complicated pattern. Bael stood opposite him, his body perfectly still, sword held casually.

Inth's pike sparked with dark magic. He swung it in a sharp arc, blasting magic from the tip. But Bael effortlessly sidestepped, holding his sword loosely at his side.

Inth unleashed another bolt. Again, Bael sidestepped. Didn't break a sweat, nor use shadow magic. Didn't even bother to wear armor. *Cocky bastard.* She was beginning to understand why he'd been so confident before the battle.

Worse, a growing certainty bloomed in her mind. The vision of herself lying against the dirt, Bael's knife pressed against her heart.

It wasn't just a fear. It was a premonition.

Inth's pole arm glowed white-hot, and he took a tentative step toward Bael. Meanwhile, Bael stood still as the statue of Nyxobas

Ursula had learned that the stiller Bael's body, the more deadly his thoughts.

When the knight lunged, thrusting his blade at Bael's chest, Bael leapt into the air. Wisps of shadow magic trailed behind him as he cleared the tip of the pole arm. He soared over Inth's head, gripping his sword with the blade's tip pointing down. With a single, vicious thrust, he plunged it through the top of the knight's helm.

Bael landed gracefully on the sand. As Inth crumpled, Bael wrenched his blade from the knight's skull with a sickening crunch of bone.

The oneiroi ran onto the field of blood to drag the body away, and the crowd booed. Another execution.

As with Zoth, the entire fight had lasted only seconds. Bael turned, stalking back to his spot at the edge of the field of blood. Again, his glacial gaze flicked to her for just a moment, his face devoid of emotion.

Her knees were going weak. This was it—she had to defeat two more demons before she could live. The Gray Ghost—a reanimated corpse.

And Bael.

"Congratulations, Bael, on reaching the final duel," said Hothgar, his voice quavering. Was that fear? If Bael were going to resume his position as the Sword of Nyxobas, Hothgar had every reason to be afraid. Bael's vengeance against those who had wronged him would be swift and ruthless.

"Emerazel's whore will now fight the Gray Ghost on the field of blood. The winner of this round will fight Bael the Fallen."

Ursula's heart pounded like a battle drum, her blood pumping hard as she stepped into the center of the arena.

The Gray Ghost prowled forward, taking his spot across from her.

Hothgar sounded the gong, and her nerves blazed with anticipation.

She gripped her katana, keeping her gaze on her opponent. Her stomach throbbed where she'd been stabbed, but otherwise it seemed to be fully healed.

She'd seen the Gray Ghost fight when he'd first announced his participation in the tournament. She'd seen him slay five demons in the melee, and not one of them had touched him.

And yet, she'd also seen Bael revive him in the mushroom forest. So what the hell had happened there?

The wind toyed with the gray scarf wrapped around the Ghost's face and he stood, still as a corpse. Which, perhaps, he was.

When she'd seen him fight before, every movement had been precise, like he was thinking multiple steps ahead of his adversary. Just like Bael, he'd waited for his opponents to attack first, then countered.

Maybe she could throw him off.

Hothgar's voice boomed over the field of blood. "The fight is supposed to begin." He sounded the gong again.

The Gray Ghost raised his blades. Pearly light sparked off them, but he didn't move.

Ursula lifted her katana, her palms sweating. *Any minute now.*

The icy lunar wind rippled over her skin, and she could hear her blood pounding in her ears.

Maybe I can goad him into attacking.

She pointed her blade at his chest, slowly approaching. When she got within striking distance, he stepped back. She followed him, but he stayed just out of range.

She feinted, and he immediately parried—one of his blades flashing up to deflect hers, metal sparking against metal. Her sword vibrated in her grip.

For a corpse, he was strong. Very strong.

She backed away. *Maybe he will come after me now.* Instead, he simply stood there waiting. She feinted again, and he parried, their blades clashing.

"Why won't you fight me?" said Ursula.

The Gray Ghost simply watched her from behind his scarf. She'd seen how he'd baited Vepar into tiring himself out. Only when his opponent was thoroughly exhausted did he attack—diving for the tendons behind his ankles to immobilize him.

A brilliant thought sparked in her mind—what if she faked fatigue?

She feinted again. When he parried, she immediately followed up with another strike. To conserve strength, she didn't attack with full velocity, but with each strike, she allowed herself to be a little wilder.

The brethren loved it, chanting her name: "Ursula! Ursula! Ursula!"

Slowly, she began to drive the Gray Ghost toward the far wall. When they reached it, she pretended to falter at the end of a particularly wild strike.

She'd made herself an inviting target. Would he take the bait?

He dove at the ground, but she'd anticipated his strike, leaping into the air. She swung her katana low, but the Ghost had rolled out of reach.

He crouched, blades drawn, ready to strike.

She began backing away from the wall. "Let's see what you can do."

The Ghost stalked toward her. His daggers didn't have nearly the reach of her katana, but he had two of them, which meant he could throw one. Also, she might need to dodge if he launched a swift counter-strike.

Abruptly, she lunged forward, slashing at his head. He ducked, then dove for her ankles again. She leapt to the side—but not fast enough. One of his blades slashed into her calf, and the pain shrieked up her leg.

Hot blood dripped down her skin inside her trousers.

The Ghost advanced on her. His posture had changed. He leaned forward now, his knives pointed straight at her. He'd wounded her. Like any good predator, he sensed when a kill was imminent.

And maybe she could make him a little more confident then he needed to be...

Grimacing, she forced herself to yelp with pain, hobbling on her leg. Without a moment of hesitation, he dove into his roll—just as she'd expected.

As soon as he was in range, she slashed down, ramming her blade through his throat. And not a single drop of blood spilled from the wound.

Her hand shook as she leaned down and pulled the scarf from his face, and her stomach turned at what she found beneath the cloth.

The thing that looked up from the sand wasn't human, and Ursula was pretty sure it wasn't a demon, either.

So that was why they called him the Gray Ghost. He had no face, just a smooth expanse of gray skin. No eyes. No nose. He had a mouth—now hanging open—but no teeth.

Her blood ran cold.

"A golem!" Hothgar's voice boomed. "Who has entered a golem into the tournament?"

Ursula yanked her sword from the creature's neck. A sticky, gray substance covered the blade.

She glanced at Bael, her next opponent.

She'd seen him raising one of these creatures in the mushroom forest. So what, exactly, did he know about this? From what she could remember of the demon books in her New York library, golems did as their masters commanded.

As she walked across the field of blood, Hothgar's demon guards circled the golem where it lay on the sand.

"Destroy it," Hothgar shouted.

Ursula turned to watch the action.

Around the golem, the guards chanted in Angelic. A chill rippled over the crater as air thickened with shadow magic. When the demons incanted the final words of the spell, the magic condensed into a sphere no larger than a marble.

The sphere hovered above the golem's body. The gray flesh seemed to lift and bend up toward the marble. A crack reverberated over the crater, the golem's body snapped, condensing. The sphere of magic sucked the golem into its darkness. An instant later, nothing remained of the golem but a few lonely pieces of gray cloth fluttering on the sand.

CHAPTER 46

The soldiers cleared the field of the golem's ichor.

It was just her and Bael, and she couldn't bring herself to look at him. Right now, the thought of him terrified her.

Pain splintered up her leg. The cut in her calf wouldn't kill her on its own, but it would slow her down considerably. That in and of itself was probably a death sentence. Especially given her opponent.

She stole a glance at him.

He kept his eyes on the horizon. He didn't want to look at her, either.

Hothgar spoke, "Great men—and a golem—have bled their last on the sand today. Before the final duel begins, let us honor the sacrifice of these champions of Nyxobas."

A great cheer rose from the crowd.

Hothgar continued, "I would have never believed it myself, but the final duel will be between Bael, the Lord of Abelda, and Ursula, the hound of Emerazel."

Finally, at least, he was using respectable names.

"This will be a clash of the fallen versus the filthy..." Hothgar continued.

Anger simmered. *Okay. Fuck this guy.*

"...Of night versus fire." His voice boomed over the crater. "Neither worthy of the House of Abelda." He raised his hands to the sky. "But let us hope that it will be epic!"

Ursula glanced up at the Earth, bathing the crater in a blue light.

From beneath Nyxobas's statue, Hothgar declared, "Step forward onto the field of blood."

Ursula looked down at the blood-streaked sand as she walked, her heart a hunted animal. Only when she'd taken her place in the center of the arena did she look up at Bael. He wasn't even bothering with his helmet for this fight, and she could see his grim expression, his lips pressed tight. She tried to catch his eye, but he looked past her like she wasn't there.

Instinctively, she scanned his weapons a final time. The silver sword, still stained with Inth's blood. Right now, he was probably thinking about how much power he was about to regain. He'd claim back his wings, his manor. His immortality. All he had to do was slaughter her.

And given everything she'd seen tonight, he hardly had to break a sweat.

Dark terror clawed at her ribs, and her legs began to shake. She knew what was coming—Bael's dagger in her chest. The slackened jaw, her skin as gray as the golem's. And then, the void.

Don't give up yet, Ursula.

Her teeth chattered, and she gripped the katana tighter, her palms sweating.

"The final duel." Hothgar gripped his mallet.

Ursula's calculations gave way to raw panic, and her mind raced, desperately searching for an escape. But this place wasn't built for an escape, and it wasn't like she could flee unnoticed with this crowd watching.

The katana shook in her hand. *I need to focus. I need calm so I can think straight again.*

She imagined her fingers wrapping around the silver ring in her pocket, feeling its smooth solidity. Just like her white rock. Her breathing slowed, and her gaze flicked to Hothgar.

He slammed his mallet into the gong with a thunderous crash, and the sound vibrated through her bones.

She kept her eyes locked on Bael—that perfect, godlike face. His chiseled chest. He stood unmoving, shadow magic flickering about him.

And if there was one thing that terrified her about Bael, it was his stillness.

His eyes bored into hers. He wasn't going to move until she attacked. She'd already watched him fight.

The other champions had tried to attack him first, and that had backfired on all of them. Brutally. Like the Gray Ghost, she needed to get him to move.

"Are you going to fight?" she yelled.

He didn't stir. Not a single twitch of a muscle.

She tightened her grip on the sword. "It was me, by the way. I broke into your quarters." A risky move. He might give her a painful death now instead of an easy one, but she wanted to throw him off balance.

The sad truth was—even though she knew he'd come here to kill her, that he'd do whatever he could to reclaim his manor—she still couldn't bring herself to drive her sword through his chest. Not unless he was coming for her, his sword drawn.

She still wasn't thinking like a real predator. And how could she? She'd saved his life—but he'd saved hers countless times. He'd healed her wounds, taught her magic. He'd brought her a sword, freshly sharpened.

So how the fuck am I supposed to muster up any bloodlust?

She swallowed hard. *His wife.* Cera had told her what he'd done—he'd murdered his own wife. There simply wasn't a good explanation for that, no matter how much she wanted to like him.

She let the words play in her head like a mantra... *Wife-killer...wife-killer...wife-killer....*

She needed to shatter that cool, impenetrable exterior. If she wanted any hope of saving her own life, she had to light a fire in him, to see the real Bael.

A chill spread through her body, and she looked him dead in the eyes. "Don't give me any of your false chivalry," she said in a cool, even voice. "The women in the Shadow Realm are just property, isn't that right? Nothing more, nothing less. I thought maybe you were different, but now I know the truth."

A muscle twitched in Bael's jaw, and a deathly silence fell over the arena. Maybe the Brethren knew what she was talking about.

"Nice of you to keep Elissa's portrait up there for a while." A gnawing void seemed to open in her chest as she spoke. This wasn't her—but it was a role she had to play if she wanted to live. She had to let the ice take hold of her heart. "Until you stuffed her back into your storage room."

Across from her, Bael's muscles tightened. The shadow magic flickered around him, thickening into a mist. At that moment, Ursula knew she had him. Her pulse raced hard, and her fingers gripped the hilt so hard her knuckles turned white.

"Because what would you be without your guilt?" she said. "Forget Abelda Manor. Regret is your real home, and you'd be nothing without it."

With a terrifying roar, Bael charged, shadow running right for her. Ice rushed through Ursula's veins. But she was ready. At the last possible instant, she ducked, and brought her katana up, spearing him in the gut. Hot blood pumped onto her hands.

Her eyes flashed to his sword hand, searching for a counter attack.

But he hadn't brought his sword. He'd charged without his weapon.

The world seemed to sway below her feet. *What the fuck have I done?* "I'm sorry," she whispered, tilting her head to look up at him.

He stared at her, his eyes wide.

Her hands shaking, she pulled the blade from his gut. "I'm sorry," she whispered again.

He clutched his stomach, blood pouring between his fingers. But he didn't fall. Instead, he stood, staring at her, his eyes darkening to a wrathful black.

Now, she no longer saw Bael looking back at her. Near death, the primal part of his mind had switched on, and the void itself stared back at her.

CHAPTER 47

The Bael she knew was gone. And now, she'd meet the real predator.

Faster than a heartbeat, one of his hands clamped around her throat. And in the next moment, she fell back, her skull slamming against the ground.

The knock of her head against the sand dizzied her, and she looked up at Bael. He pinned her to the ground, a dagger pressed into her heart.

Despite the damage she'd done to his stomach, he seemed to be at full strength. Obviously, she wasn't a real predator. She'd missed all the organs.

Panic ignited. *This is it. This is what I've known was coming.*

The crowd roared, but Ursula could hardly hear them over her own rushing blood. She wouldn't be able to move an inch without Bael thrusting his dagger into her heart. He had her completely pinned to the ground, under his control.

Her breath came in short, sharp bursts, and she gazed up at him.

The void had left his eyes, and he stared at her instead with his pale gray eyes.

Terror ripped her mind apart.

He said he'd kill me quick.

Longingly, she looked up at the earth, and a deep sadness welled in her chest.

Tears wet her eyes. "I'm sorry about what I said." She had no fucking clue why she was apologizing to a man about to kill her. "About the guilt, and the painting, and that I went into your quarters."

A weariness—a sadness glinted in his eyes. His lips moved. She couldn't hear him over the crowd, but it looked like he breathed the word, *Sorry.* Shadows thickened around him, and his magic whispered over her skin—almost as if he were soothing her before the kill.

This is the end of my life, and no one knows who I am.

With his free hand, he brushed a finger down her cheek.

"Please do it fast." She closed her eyes. She was going to die here, as far from home as it was possible to be, and she still didn't know who she was. She slipped her hand into her pocket, pulling out the ring to feel it one last time between her fingers, rubbing its smooth surface. All she knew was that it reminded her of home, of something solid and constant.

And god, she wanted something constant, tangible. Something she could feel—anything but the void.

She gasped another shaky breath. All around, the crowd screamed for blood.

After a few moments, she forced herself to open her eyes again. But Bael's gaze had landed on the ring.

His ring.

Distantly, she heard Hothgar's voice. "Kill the hound, and take back your wings."

"Just do it," she whispered. "This is agony. Make it quick. Please."

Instead, he pulled the dagger away, snatching the ring from her fingers.

What the hell is going on? He couldn't wait until after he'd killed her to take the ring back?

"Where did you get this?" he growled.

"The ring? I found it in the jewelry box."

Bael grabbed her by the shoulders, pulling her up. She stumbled, nearly falling into him. Her legs shook, and Bael wrapped an arm around her waist to steady her. He stared at her, his piercing eyes burning with ferocity.

Then, he held the ring above his head. "I claim the hound as my wife," he shouted.

Ursula's jaw dropped. *What the fuck?*

Bael yanked the cord from his neck, slipping off the thin silver ring. He grabbed her left hand, holding it up so everyone in the arena could see. Then, he slid the ring onto her finger.

Ursula stared at Bael, realization dawning. Asharoth had told her that a man is forbidden from killing the woman he's claimed. And more than that—no one else may harm her, either.

"No!" Hothgar bellowed. "She is a demon of the infernos. A whore of Emerazel. You cannot claim her!"

"I take what I want," roared Bale. "There is no law forbidding such a wife. A warrior may choose any wife he pleases."

The crowd had fallen completely silent.

Hothgar's black eyes glared at them. "Does the hound consent to the proposal?"

Bael pressed the thick, silver ring into her hand, and he fixed her with a fierce stare.

On the one hand, he killed his last wife. On the other hand, this seems like the best way out of certain death right now. She exhaled, then shouted, "I consent."

Bael cupped the side of her face, seemingly oblivious to the wound in his stomach. He leaned in, his breath warming the shell of her ear. He smelled of sandalwood. "I need to claim you now. Publicly."

She nodded, looking up at him. In the next instant, his fingers tightened around her waist, pulling her closer. Dark tendrils of his magic thrummed over her skin, healing the slash in her leg, snaking up her thighs. It was as if he were doing it on purpose, running his fingers over the most intimate parts of her body.

His body's heat warmed her, and his piercing gaze mesmerized her. He threaded his fingers into her hair, gently pulling back her head. Slowly, he grazed his teeth over her throat, one of his hands lazily stroking her back. Then he kissed her neck softly. Her back arched into him. Heat shot through her belly, and her heartbeat raced.

She slid her arms over his broad shoulders, pressing her body against him. She could feel his heart beating hard under his skin. Bael traced his powerful hands down her back, then slid them under her bottom, lifting her up. She wrapped her legs around his waist. His powerful arms encircled her, his fingertips stroking her thighs. Here, in Bael's arms, she felt safe for the first time in weeks. Years, maybe.

Her pulse raced, and desire burned through her, lighting her on fire. *Kiss me, already.*

As if hearing her thoughts, he pressed his lips against hers. Slowly, his tongue parted her lips, brushing against hers. The kiss grew deeper, sensual. As a wave of pleasure rushed through her body, she lost all sense of time. He tasted of the sea.

The gong clanged again, pulling them out of their kiss, and Bael lowered her to the ground.

All around, the Brethren roared. Bael grabbed Ursula's hand, and turned to address Hothgar. "I have won the duel, but I will not kill my betrothed. Return my wings."

Hothgar's eyes burned with cold fury. "Kill them, Abrax."

CHAPTER 48

*P*anic tore its claws through Ursula's mind.

In a blur of shadows, Abrax leapt onto the sand of the arena. Powerful shadow magic swirled around him—a vortex of night. A black tendril flew over the sand wrapping Bael's chest, and in the next moment, he was on his knees, blood pouring from his wound.

Ursula could hear his ribs crack as Abrax's magic slowly constricted, and she screamed.

Abrax stared at her, a smile curling his lips. "You killed one of my golems, harlot. And your boyfriend destroyed the other. I hope you don't mind if I kill your man."

She glanced around for her sword. How many demons could she fight at once?

Hothgar's eyes were black with rage. "He claimed a hound as his wife. He has desecrated Nyxobas's realm. The god of night could not protect him now."

Ursula could see Bael's muscles straining as he fought against the magical bonds, his face turning blue.

Rage, cold and ancient, burned through her veins. She gathered the last of the shadow magic in her body, concentrating on a spot just next to Abrax. She tore over the sand, slamming into Abrax's side. Knocking him to the ground.

Instantly, his shadow magic lashed at her, wrapping around her chest. Like a giant serpent, it constricted, squeezing the air from her. She could feel her bones flex.

One of her ribs cracked, and she gasped at the pain. Why was Nyxobas never here to oversee his own laws?

Abrax chanted in Angelic, and his magic began to leach into her. She could feel its icy tendrils searching through her veins. The pain was exquisite, like she'd been injected with liquid nitrogen. The magic sucked the warmth from her, wrapping her heart in ice.

Filling with raw panic, she glanced at Bael. He lay on the sand across from her, his eyes open, but unfocused.

There is no loophole, he'd said. *The gods always win.*

Bael had been right.

Slowly, Abrax's magic crept up her neck, stealing her breath. Horror slammed into her as shadow magic slipped into her skull, enveloping her in darkness.

She stood at the edge of the void. Its infinite vastness spread out before her. An endless chasm. A bottomless abyss. If she stepped off the edge, she would fall for eternity. *Only the darkness will save you.*

The lure of the void called to her, a dark lullaby. A siren song. *My mother. My father. My home.*

She took a final step off the edge, and she fell into the abyss. All around her, she sensed Nyxobas's dark power, growing stronger.

"Hello, little one." An ancient voice chilled her to the bone.

"Who are you?" she asked.

"Is it not obvious? I am Lord of the Realm of Shadows, the god of night, king of the void."

A voice rang in her head, clear as a bell, a siren song. *Kill the king. Kill the king.*

"When I look at you, why do I hear the words, 'kill the king?'"

"So you remember."

"Remember what?"

Cold silence greeted her, and dread snaked up her spine. She didn't want to be here. She needed to explain that this was all a mistake. "Abrax and Hothgar have betrayed you." Even as she said the words, they felt meaningless to her—the squabbles of the living seemed inconsequential in the vastness of the void.

"Abrax is foolish and weak," he said.

"He sent me here against my will."

"Then leave."

"How?" she asked.

"The same way you arrived."

"Abrax cast a spell on me."

"Fight back. That's why I brought you here. To see if you are worthy."

"I don't know how to counter his power."

"When you learn to accept the darkness, you will have all the power you could possibly desire."

The icy magic around her grew stronger. Compressing her into a tiny point.

"Don't fight the shadows," he said. "Accept their power."

Shadow magic crawled over her skin, searching for a way into her. She screamed, and inky magic poured down her throat.

Nyxobas was right. The Forgotten Ones were right. And deep down, she knew this was what she wanted. There was no choice but to give in. To accept it. She let the shadows fill her.

"Good, little one. Feel the darkness move within you. The shadows will do your bidding. You just need to ask."

She opened her eyes, blinking at the sudden brightness of the stars in the sky.

Abrax hunched over her. His spell had filled her with shadow magic, and now it hummed in her veins. Power she could use. The bonds that wrapped around her chest melted away.

Abrax jumped back, his pale eyes wide with horror. "Seven hells. What are you?"

"Right now, I'm your angel of death."

Shadows flowed from her, oozing from her pores, pooling on the sand. She bent to pick up her katana.

Abrax charged for her, shadow running at impossible speed. But to her, it looked as though he was moving in slow motion. She side-stepped, just as she had with Bael, then plunged her katana into his chest.

Abrax fell, eyes wide with horror. Ursula pressed down on the hilt of her blade pinning him to the sand.

"I am immortal," he snarled up at her. "You know you cannot kill me."

A strange certainty filled her body, rolled around the inside of her skull. She knew what she had to do. "No, but now I can take your magic."

She leaned down, pressing a hand to his chest. She could feel the shadow magic within him. Cold, ancient, and immensely powerful. Slowly she drew it from his body. Abrax's eyes widened with fear.

"Stop." It was Bael. Blood dripped from his mouth where he crouched on the sand. His skin had paled, and he shook violently. "We need to leave."

"What about your wings?"

"There isn't time to get them." His eyes flicked to something behind her. She glanced behind her at the oneiroi guards now pouring into the arena. Teeth bared, they twitched with the same madness that had possessed Massu. These were Abrax's oneiroi.

Slowly pushing to his feet, Bael whistled, and a dark shaped dove toward them. *Sotz*. The bat flew for them at full speed, but there was only one way to catch him.

She wrapped her arms around Bael's chest. Glancing up at Sotz, she imagined the soft fur on his back, and let the shadow magic coil around her muscles. Clinging tightly to Bael, she jumped into the wind, letting the god of night carry her up to Sotz.

CHAPTER 49

She and Bael landed on Sotz's back—her body facing Bael's. Bael had a good grip on Sotz with his legs, and he leaned in, grasping for a solid handhold. Ursula wrapped her legs around Bael's stomach as he tried to steer the bat, breathing in the scent of sandalwood.

"Can you take us to Bael's carriage?" Ursula shouted. Sotz's wings pumped frantically. Barely keeping them aloft, he strained to lift them above the crater's edge.

Twisting her head, Ursula peered down. Below them, the arena filled with the chaos of fleeing demons and rampaging, flesh-starved oneiroi.

At the crater's rim, they landed with a jolt on the dirt next to the carriage.

"Thank you, Sotz." Slowly, she helped Bael off the bat. He could hardly stand on his own, and he leaned on her for support. His weight nearly crushed her.

The door to Bael's carriage slammed open, and Cera poked her head out. "The lord? What happened? I couldn't watch. How are you both alive?"

"We need to get out of here," said Ursula.

In the distance, the Brethren's screams pierced the air.

"They're coming for us," said Ursula.

Cera ran to the other side of Bael, gamely attempting to support his other arm. From her height, there wasn't much point. Together, they helped him into the carriage, and he lay across one of the seats, closing his eyes.

Cera banged on the wall—the signal for the bats to lift off. As soon as they rose into the air, Ursula let out a long, slow breath.

Cera stared at her. "What happened. Why are you both alive?"

"Bael won the duel." Ursula took a deep breath. "But he didn't kill me like he should have."

Cera's eyes widened. "It was you against the lord in the final round?"

"Yes. And he wouldn't fight me. So I tried to make him angry. I tried to make him lose his temper so I could get the upper hand. He charged me, and I thought he was attacking. But he wasn't. He'd dropped his weapon." It all came out in a frantic rush of words. "And I didn't realize, and I stabbed him. But I think I missed anything important on purpose."

Cera simply stared.

"And then... he was on top of me. He held a knife to my chest. But instead of killing me, he claimed me. He proposed."

Cera's jaw dropped. "He did what?"

Bael's voice rumbled from the bench he lay on. "I claimed her. I gave her Elissa's ring."

Cera looked like she was about to faint. "Does that mean..." She stammered.

"There will be no wedding," said Bael.

Cera's hand flew to her mouth. "So you won't need a dress—"

"No," said Ursula and Bael at the same time.

Cera's brow furrowed. "But what happens now? We can't stay in the Shadow Realm if the lords all mean to kill you."

Ursula took a deep breath. "Now, we go to New York."

Cera frowned. "How do we get there? I thought the lord told you. No one can travel to or from the Shadow Realm without the god's permission."

Ursula's ribs hummed with the void's dark magic, and that strange certainty whispered through the hollows of her mind. "I'm not worried about Nyxobas's permission anymore. He will grant it. I know it."

The carriage soared through the dark sky, and she glanced out the window. Earth blazed bright in the sky, a perfect jewel of green and blue.

Ursula knelt in front of Bael, watching his chest rise and fall slowly.

She scanned his menacing tattoos—the thunderbolt, the crescent moon with its lethally sharp points, the four-pointed star.

Swallowing hard, she looked at the deep wound, just above his hipbone. Guilt pressed on her chest, stealing her breath. How could he heal, if he wouldn't use any healing magic on himself? When they got to New York, maybe she'd have to sew him up. Not like she was a surgeon, but she wasn't entirely sure he'd agree to a hospital visit.

His eyes opened and he fixed his pale gaze on her, studying her.

She bit her lip. "Why did you drop your weapon when you charged?"

He didn't answer. He just let his eyes close.

Her body wracked with fatigue, Ursula leaned against his shoulder, listening to his slow breathing as the carriage carried them back to Abelda Manor. His skin was soft as silk, even if his form was pure muscled steel.

At last, they touched down on solid ground, and she lifted her head from Bael's shoulder. He seemed to be completely passed out, and there was no way she and Cera could carry him.

"Can you wake him?" asked Cera.

Ursula brushed her finger across his cheek. "Bael?"

Slowly, his eyelids opened, and he surveyed her with his icy stare. "Is there a reason you keep talking to me when I'm trying to sleep?"

"We're here. At Abelda. I don't think we can carry you."

He nodded, then pushed up onto his elbows with a grunt. Cera flung open the carriage door and hopped out, holding it open for them. Bael leaned against her as she helped him from the carriage and into the lift. The lunar wind stung her skin through her blood-soaked clothes.

Once inside, Bael leaned against the elevator's bars for support, and the lift creaked down past one deserted floor after another. *It must kill Bael to say goodbye to this place. And all he'd needed to do was push the knife in.*

The lift touched down and she pulled Bael's arm over her shoulder, straining to help him walk from the atrium into the portal room. Once inside, Bael leaned back against a wall, catching his breath.

"We're going to have to take off our clothes," Ursula declared.

Before she'd finished her sentence, Cera had already stripped off and jumped in, clinging on to the side of the portal.

Bael didn't move.

"Do you need help?"

"No," he snarled.

"Fine." As her muscles shook with fatigue, she stripped off her clothes. Her bloodstained trousers, the thick leather corset and boots—acutely aware with every movement that Bael's eyes might be on her body.

Goosebumps rose over her skin, and she folded her arms.

When she looked back at Bael over her shoulder, he was staring at her, but his gaze quickly flicked away.

Her cheeks flushed. "Hurry up."

For a twenty-two thousand-year-old night demon, Bael was shy.

She jumped in, holding on to the portal's side, just like Cera. The icy water chilled her to the bone, and she averted eyes as Bael stripped off his clothes. She felt his silky, muscled body brush against hers as he plunged into the pool. She let herself drift underwater, enveloped by the cold.

She found Bael's powerful hand and slipped her fingers into his.

Nyxobas. She let the thought rise in her mind like a voice. *Grant us permission to leave. To return home, to Earth.*

She felt inky magic spool through her body, coiling through her muscles, dragging her into the water. Deep under the surface, she held her breath, carried by the god of night. And at last—she saw light piercing the water.

Golden light—the honeyed tones of an earthly sunset.

With Bael's hand clasping her own, she swam for the surface. At last, her head breached the water, and she sucked in a deep breath, staring at the warm glow over Central Park.

New York City. *Home.*

C.N. CRAWFORD

PRIMEVAL MAGIC

A DEMONS OF FIRE AND NIGHT NOVEL

CHAPTER 1

Ursula clasped the rough stone of the fountain's lip. She pulled her head from the water, and sucked in a deep breath, gasping after the long journey through the portal. Above, the sun burned hot in the sky, and the humid spring air filled her aching lungs. A faint scent of smoke floated on the breeze. She wasn't in the Shadow Realm anymore.

A stony ground materialized under the water, forcing her upward. She ducked down, crouching behind the fountain's shallow lip to shield her naked body from view. From the stone foundation of the fountain, bits of metal glinted up at her, sparking in the sunlight below the water. Nickels, dimes, and thousands of pennies. The portal had closed.

She whirled, looking for Cera and Bael in the icy water, but she was completely alone, icy water lapping at her bare breasts.

A chill snaked up her spine. What had happened to her friends? Just a few minutes ago, they'd all been jumping naked into the portal from the Shadow Realm. Bael's muscled body had been exhausted, but he'd been conscious when they'd pulled him into the frigid water. On the journey here, she'd tried to keep track of him, but icy currents had ripped them apart.

And now it was just her, stark naked in a fountain in the center of New York City. Had Bael and Cera already climbed out, leaving her behind? Or worse—had they gotten lost in Nyxobas's waters before the portal had closed?

As she huddled out of view, something felt *wrong*. It wasn't just that she was alone, or that the scent of smoke floated on the wind. It was the eerie silence that enshrouded the city. When was it ever silent in New York? She peered over the fountain's edge, her sodden hair dripping onto the weathered stone.

Directly in front of her, a tall building with ostentatious gold-filigreed awnings loomed over an empty street. She was within thirty feet of the Plaza Hotel, her New York home. All she needed to do to get home was dash across the street before someone arrested her for public indecency.

And yet—why would the street be empty outside New York City's Plaza Hotel? She was right next to Central Park. In the middle of the day, there should be honking cars, throngs of tourists, those horse-drawn carriages clopping by. Yet no one was here.

Apart from the flags waving forlornly in the wind, she hardly saw any movement—at least, not until a diminutive form rushed across the street. Her white hair streamed behind her, gleaming in the sunlight, and she wore a black raincoat that came down to her skinny knees. *Cera.* Thank the gods. The little oneiroi hurried toward the fountain, carrying two overcoats.

"Ursula!" Cera chirped, her pale eyes shining.

Still crouching, Ursula peered at Cera over the fountain's edge. "What's going on? Why is it so quiet?"

Cera thrust one of the coats at her. "I haven't got a clue. I'm sure it's nothing to worry about. Perhaps a human plague or something. Surely you're about due for one."

Shadow demons weren't great at reassurance. Ursula rose, water dripping down her body, and grabbed the beige overcoat. Shivering, she pulled it on. Even if the streets were empty, she wasn't comfortable standing here completely starkers in broad daylight.

Tying the belt around the coat, she stepped from the fountain, her bare feet sloshing onto the stony ground. She frowned at the other overcoat. Who was that for? "Where's Bael?"

Cera frowned. "He was with you. You went into the portal together. He *is* your betrothed, if you recall. You're going to need to look after him."

Ursula turned to stare at the fountain, her stomach clenching with dread. What if he was drowning under that closed portal? Without his wings, he was completely mortal.

"Bloody hell. I was holding his hand, but the currents forced us apart. Do you think he could have got out on his own?"

He hadn't been in good shape before they'd plunged into the water. Bael—her betrothed, apparently. The man who'd hastily offered to marry her before a bloodthirsty crowd, just to save her life. He was occasionally brutal and emotionally remote, and he had a dark past she didn't even want to think about. And yet, somehow, the powerful shadow warrior had been growing on her. "What do we do?"

Cera's hand fluttered nervously to her mouth. "We need to open the portal again."

Ursula turned to stare into the fountain. Instead of a stony base covered in coins, the fountain had gone murky and dark. Just then, a bubble popped, followed by another.

Ursula held up a hand. "Wait. I think the portal is opening again."

Something dark lurked under the water's surface—Bael's hair. Frantically reaching into the icy water, Ursula grabbed him under the shoulders and pulled him out, straining at the weight. As she hoisted his torso over the fountain's edge, his head lolled back, eyes open. Bael's eyes, normally a pale gray, had turned completely black.

"Gods below," whispered Cera.

He must weigh three hundred pounds, all of it pure muscle, and Ursula strained to lift him. "Help me get him out of the pool."

Cera grabbed one of Bael's arms, and together they pulled him from the water, until he dropped onto the stony ground with a hard thud. Immediately, he began coughing, and Ursula loosed a long breath. *He can breathe, at least.*

He lay on his back, his powerful body like a fallen Greek sculpture—golden and perfectly proportioned. But in Bael's case, dark tattoos covered his skin. Her heart thrumming, Ursula knelt beside his head. She touched her fingers to his cold throat. A pulse beat faintly beneath the surface of his skin.

"Bael?" She leaned down, whispering in his ear. "Are you all right?"

"Ursula!" Cera pointed to his hip, at an injury from which blood oozed onto the stone, mingling with the water. It was where she'd stabbed him in the lunar arena. Ursula frowned at the wound, her throat tightening. It looked even worse now, as if someone had gnawed at it. He was hemorrhaging blood.

"I don't understand," said Ursula. "It wasn't that bad before we went through the portal."

"I think the Forgotten Ones attacked him."

Bael groaned, shifting on the stone, his eyes now closed.

Ursula touched his shoulder. "Bael, can you move?"

He didn't respond, but his enormous chest slowly rose and fell.

Ursula glanced at the little oneiroi. "We have to get him inside. I just have no idea how we'll lift him." Ursula was unusually strong for someone her size, but even so, carrying Bael was beyond her capabilities.

Cera straightened. "Wait here." Before Ursula could respond, Cera darted back across the street and into the Plaza. After what seemed like an eternity, she reappeared at the entrance pushing a brass luggage cart. The cart creaked and bounced over the empty street as Cera pushed it—jarring sounds in the otherwise silent city.

Smart thinking.

Cera rolled the cart next to Bael, then covered his naked body in the second raincoat. Ursula grabbed Bael's ankles, and Cera grabbed his wrists. Grunting and straining, they hoisted him into the cart. As they lay him down on the cart, his feet dangling over the edge, his eyes fluttered, but they didn't open.

Ursula gripped the brass bars of the cart, wheeling him across the road.

"We need to save the lord," said Cera. "If he is going to marry you—"

"He's not actually my betrothed, you know," Ursula interrupted. "He was just saving my life with that proposal."

"Don't be absurd," snapped Cera.

"You are aware that he killed his last wife?" The wheels of the cart creaked as she pushed it across the empty street.

"I'm sure he had a very good reason."

They approached the desolate Plaza lobby, and Ursula forgot all about their discussion as a sharp tendril of fear coiled through her gut. *Empty.* New York City was entirely empty.

* * *

In the Plaza lobby, only the pale sunlight filtered in through the doors. No light shone from the wall sconces or crystal chandeliers. As the moved further inside, the vast hall was still and dark as a tomb.

"What the bloody hell is going on?" Ursula whispered.

Cera shook her head. "I have no idea. I just grabbed some clothes from a coat rack before I rushed back to the fountain."

Ursula pulled her raincoat closer, wishing desperately for a weapon. The empty shops and corridors in the Plaza lobby deeply unsettled her. As they moved through the interior of the hotel, pushing the luggage cart along in front of them, shudders snaked up her spine. Months ago, not long after Ursula had learned she was a hellhound, demons and mages had attacked the city of Boston. Had something similar happened in New York while she'd been on the moon?

Under the raincoat, Bael's chest slowly rose and fell. At his hip, a growing crimson stain bled into the overcoat, and Ursula's stomach clenched. Once, he'd been immortal, but since he'd lost his wings, that had changed. Bael could be bleeding to death right in front of them, and the thought made Ursula's heart hammer against her ribs.

Cera paused at a junction of pale marble halls, and Ursula pointed down a dimly lit corridor. "The lift to my flat is this way."

As they moved further into the hall, two guards stepped from the shadows, and Ursula's throat tightened. Just thirty feet away, they were dressed in military fatigues, gripping assault rifles. Ursula's heart skipped a beat. Ever since Boston was attacked, humans had been openly hunting demons. Since her fire magic had been stripped from her in the Shadow Realm, she supposed she was an ordinary human now. But Cera sure as hell wasn't, and these humans didn't look particularly demon-friendly.

One of them was pointing the gun directly at her, his brow creased, sweat beading on his skin. His hands were trembling slightly. He looked scared out of his wits. "Identify yourself." His voice echoed off the ceiling.

Ursula's fingers tightened around the brass of the luggage cart, her legs beginning to shake. They were running out of time—fast. Bael was losing blood, and if he didn't get medical attention straight away, he could die. She wasn't going to let that happen. Her first instinct was to get the hell out here and take Bael to a hospital. But first, she needed to know what was going on. Given the desolation of New York's streets, it didn't look like a hospital would be an option.

She considered her options. Option one was easy. They could turn and leave, but that would put them on the sidewalk in what appeared to be a deserted New York City. Bael was apparently bleeding to death, and she didn't think an ambulance would be coming anytime soon to take them to Mount Sinai Hospital.

Option two was more difficult. She could attack them. The problem was, she had no weapon, and she wasn't anywhere near close enough. As she tried to think of a way to close the gap between them, a red dot appeared in the center of her chest—the rifle was fitted with a laser sight.

That left only option three. Talk to them, like a regular person. Just a normal, barefoot woman, naked and soaked under a rain coat, with a bleeding naked man on a luggage cart. Oh, and a tiny white-haired companion. Nothing untoward here. "I live on the nineteenth floor," she said at last. "I think my friend Zee might be up there."

The guard narrowed his eyes at her, studying her as if she looked familiar. "Are you...?" He trailed off, then shook his head. "What are you doing out of your apartment? The city is on lockdown."

I've just transported here from the moon wasn't going to cut it. She needed a lie. A convincing lie. "My friend is hurt." She pointed at Bael. "He called me. He said he'd been attacked..." She allowed the sentence to trail off, unsure if demons were the actual culprit in this lockdown. "Do you know where we can find a doctor?"

The guard shot her an *are you insane* look. "A doctor?"

Ursula cleared her throat. *Wrong question, I guess.* "He's very badly injured." *And you either need to help me or get the hell out of my way.*

"No doctors around here." The guard lowered his gun. "What floor was that again?"

"The nineteenth."

The man spoke quietly into a microphone attached to his lapel, then touched his ear as someone replied. After a few moments, he nodded. "All right. You're cleared to go up."

Ursula pushed the cart toward the guards, with Cera trailing behind, eyes lowered.

As Ursula and Cera moved closer, the guards stepped back from the elevators, keeping their guns trained on them.

Ursula pushed the button, and the soldier's voice echoed off the ceiling again. "What happened to his clothes?"

"He…" Ursula racked her brain for a convincing response. "He's kind of an exhibitionist. I think that's why he was attacked."

From the cart, Bael groaned, his eyes still closed. Maybe he didn't appreciate being slandered.

A ping sounded as the lift arrived, and Ursula loosed a breath. The doors slid open, and she rolled the cart into the elevator. Once they were safely inside, she punched the button marked *19.*

The doors started to close, but then stopped, blocked by one of Bael's legs. She yanked the cart further into the lift, and finally the doors closed.

She fell back against the mirrored wall, heart still racing. "What the hell is going on?"

Cera shook her head. "This is your world. I have no idea. Why didn't you ask the humans?"

Ursula shook her head. "Something told me not to. Not until I have some idea what's going on. What if demons attacked the city, like they did in Boston? I didn't want them sussing out what *we* are. Did you see that soldier's face? He looked really frightened."

The lift pinged as it reached the nineteenth floor, and the doors rolled open to the familiar marble atrium of her apartment. Zee stood directly before them, her eyes open wide.

"Ursula!" She wore a white dress, smudged with soot. "What are you doing here? New York isn't safe for you. You need go back to the Shadow Realm."

CHAPTER 2

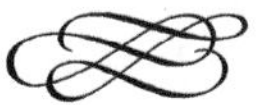

Ursula pushed the luggage cart into the hall, and Cera followed behind her. As they moved into the hall, Zee hurried past them and into the elevator.

"Zee?" said Ursula. "Where are you going? What the bloody hell is going on?"

Zee's blond hair was uncharacteristically messy, and she had dark circles beneath her eyes. "I'll be right back to explain. Did you talk to anyone on your way in here?"

Ursula frowned. "Only the guards at the door to the elevator. The ground floor was empty. What's happening? I need to get Bael medical attention somehow."

The lift door began to close, and Zee slammed her hand on it to stop it. "Did you give the guard your name?" she demanded, ignoring Ursula's questions.

"No, I only told him the apartment number."

"Okay. That's good." The doors closed on Zee.

Ursula's stomach clenched as she crouched next to Bael, feeling for his pulse at his neck. It was there—faintly. "He's losing too much blood. We'll need to stanch the bleeding."

"Get some goldenseal root powder!" Cera barked.

Ursula stood. "What? I don't have that." She bit her lip. "We need to sterilize it, then apply pressure. I think. Can you please fetch the sterile gauze from the bathroom? It's in the medicine cabinet."

Her pulse racing, Ursula dashed into the kitchen. First, she washed her hands, scrubbing them hard to get off any New York grime that could infect Bael. Then, she yanked open a cupboard door.

Saline solution was supposed to be good for cleaning wounds. With shaking hands, she snatched a container of salt from the cupboard, then a glass bowl. She dumped at least a cup of salt into the bowl. *Good thing Bael is unconscious, because I am about to literally pour salt into his wounds.*

This wouldn't help his blood loss—they'd need a transfusion for that—but maybe they could at least clean the wound and stop him from losing more blood.

Ursula rushed back into the hall, and pulled the raincoat off Bael. Dark blood had pooled onto the cart beneath him, dripping onto the marble floors, and she winced at the sight of his ravaged hip. Slowly, she poured the saline solution over his hip, and it trickled into his wound. She had no idea if she was doing it correctly.

Cera's footfalls sounded in the hall, and in the next moment, the little oneiroi was crouching by the cart, frantically ripping through the packages. "No goldenseal root powder," she muttered. "Savages. Absolute savages."

Ursula grabbed the gauze from Cera, then stuffed it into Bael's wounds. "Help me bind this together." She unfurled a long piece of gauze, and tried shoving it under Bael's enormous, muscled form, her hands slick with blood.

Cera reached under him from the other side, pulling the gauze through. Ursula pressed down hard on the bundle of gauze stuffed in his wound, then tied the long strips of gauze together over his hips as tight as she could. Her hands soaked in his blood, she pushed down hard on the gauze, applying pressure.

"Okay," she said. "What next? What do we do about the blood loss?"

Before Cera could respond, the lift pinged, and the brass doors rolled open. Zee stepped out, standing over Ursula. "What are you doing in New York? You were supposed to be in the Shadow Realm. It's not safe for you here."

"Safe?" said Ursula. "Bael and I were instructed to slaughter each other in an arena while thousands of bloodthirsty shadow demons looked on. A demigod and several immortal demons want to slaughter us. I wouldn't call that the safe option. And perhaps you've noticed that Bael is bleeding to death right now. How can we get him a doctor?"

Zee glanced down at the naked body of the shadow demon. One of her eyebrows twitched slightly. "But he's one of Nyxobas's brethren—"

"He is the lord of Abelda manor," Cera interjected.

"And he saved my life in the Shadow Realm," said Ursula. She wasn't going to go into the whole *betrothed* thing. Not now.

Zee shook her head. "Like I said, you aren't safe here. After the dragons attacked, everything went to shit."

"Dragons?" said Ursula and Cera simultaneously.

"A whole clan of them showed up just after you left. Why don't you know this?"

"I've been on the moon."

Zee nodded. "Right. Well, they've razed most of lower Manhattan. Every night they destroy more of the city."

"Bloody hell," said Ursula. "When we were first flying to the Shadow Realm we were attacked by one, but I didn't think they wanted to slaughter the whole city."

"They don't. That part is incidental." Zee looked stricken. "They're hunting for you."

Ursula felt like she'd been kicked in the gut. "What are you taking about? How do they know who I am? *I* don't even know who I am."

"I have no idea, but they definitely want you. Come with me."

Ursula looked down at Bael, the gauze already stained red. "Cera, keep applying pressure to his wound."

Cera nodded.

"Come on, Ursula!" Zee shouted, beckoning her down the hall. "It's nearly noon. The news is coming on, and you need to see this."

"So a doctor is out of the question?" said Ursula as she followed Zee into the living room, practically running to keep up.

When she stepped into the living room, Zee was already pointing a remote at the TV. "Just watch."

The TV screen flickered to life, and a grave-faced news anchor, his black hair perfectly coiffed, spoke in hushed tones. "We can see movement by the door of the pedestal." The screen changed to a view of a granite doorway. A gorgeous blonde woman stepped out. Her makeup was immaculate, and she wore a glimmering golden dress that hugged her figure. She stopped at a low table, and appeared to be speaking, but there was no sound.

"What the hell?" asked Ursula.

Zee held up a hand, and the video changed to what appeared to be a raw internet feed. The woman looked the camera while reading slowly from a piece of paper, her hands shaking uncontrollably.

"Citizens of New York," she stammered. "It has been one hundred twenty-four days and still you have not delivered the woman to us. We will continue to be a scourge upon your island until you return her."

Her eyes terrified, the blonde held up a slightly faded piece of news print. The title of the article read, "Mystery Girl Dead."

Ursula's mouth went dry. An old school picture of her stared out from the page—a photo from when she was fifteen, with frizzy hair and a fuller face. Thank the gods they didn't have a more recent photo, or the guards would have recognized her. *What. The. Fuck.*

The blonde looked down at the note again. "Deliver the girl and we will release the hostages." Trembling, the woman stared into the camera, and then the feed cut. Zee lowered the volume, but images of destruction still flickered over the screen.

Ursula's stomach flipped. "I don't understand. Why would they want me?"

"Every day at noon," said Zee, "the dragons repeat their demands. I don't know why. I don't know what they want with a hellhound who has no magic."

Ursula shook her head, her legacy as the 'Mystery Girl' rearing its ugly head again. "That woman was a hostage, I take it?"

"That was Gabby Rousseau. She's a model," said Zee. "Or she was, before she was abducted by the dragons."

Nausea climbed up Ursula's throat. "Why the hell would dragons want me?"

Zee shrugged. "Honestly, no one knows, but as soon as the dragons took the first hostages, they began demanding that we find you. Every day, they send out a hostage to ask for you." Zee held up a finger. The anchor was speaking with a white-haired man in a dark suit, and Zee turned up the volume again.

"Senator Ranulf," asked the anchor, "has your team had any luck finding the girl?"

The senator frowned. "We are asking the public to be our eyes and ears on the ground. If you see or hear something, call the police. We believe this woman is dangerous. Very, very dangerous to humankind."

"And the reward—"

The senator brightened. "We have raised it to ten million dollars for information on her whereabouts."

Zee turned to her. "That's why I had to run downstairs. If the guards had recognized you, the entire city would drag you from the building. Or at least, what's left of the city. I had to glamour the guards in case they were doing their jobs."

Cera appeared at the door, her hands stained with blood. "Ursula," she said her voice cracking. "It's Bael. I think he's dying."

CHAPTER 3

𝒰rsula's heart climbed into her throat, and she rushed back into the hall. Cera had somehow shifted him, and he now lay on the wood floor, a bloodstained towel over his lower half. Brutal, thorny tattoos snaked over the deep golden skin of his muscled torso. Ursula suspected each one of those dark slashes told a story, and she couldn't let him die before she knew what they were.

She knelt by his side, touching his neck, and his chest spasmed as he gasped for air. His pulse drummed lightly against the tips of her fingers, his skin velvety smooth.

"Why don't you heal him with magic?" asked Zee.

"I can't. They stripped me of magic when I went into the Shadow Realm. Right now, I'm just an ordinary human. And, even if I had it, healing him would prevent him from ever reattaching his wings. He'd be devastated." A pit opened in her stomach. "We need an ambulance."

"There are no ambulances," said Zee. "Hang on. Who exactly is he? If he's a demon from the Shadow Realm, aren't you supposed to be trying to kill him and stuff?"

"Actually, a lot—"

Cera interrupted. "He claimed her! He is a lord of the Shadow Realm, and Ursula is his betrothed."

Zee's mouth fell open. "What?"

"No, it's not like that," said Ursula. "Look, it doesn't matter right now. How do we heal him?"

Zee rubbed her forehead. "I don't know. Healing is not in my skill set. I mostly just manipulate people."

Ursula looked down at Bael, her breath catching in her throat at his beauty: the straight, dark eyebrows, the thick sweep of his black eyelashes formed into wet peaks, his strong jaw, the droplets of water resting on his flawless golden skin. Even half-dead, his beauty was godlike. If she managed to heal him and coaxed him to open his eyes again, she'd be greeted by the most stunning gray—the color of the stormy Mediterranean sky.

Ursula put her hand back to his neck, feeling for his pulse again, fainter now. She had an overwhelming desire to see him open his eyes. "His pulse is fading. We need to do *something*."

Zee cocked her head. "If he's really your Shadow Lord boyfriend, and if you're really human, I suppose there is always the old way. I mean, sharing bodily fluids is a little gross, but if you're banging him anyway—"

"No!" said Cera sharply. "That way is forbidden."

Zee scowled at Cera. "Who are you? Who are these people you've brought home?"

Ursula pointed. "That's Cera. Oneiroi. Friend. This is Bael. Lord of Abelda. Now tell me what you said again. What's the old way?"

Cera shook her head. "No, Ursula, we cannot do what your friend is suggesting. It is an abomination. I forbid it."

Surely Cera would do anything to save Bael's life. What was so terrible that she'd let him die? Ursula rose, her throat tightening. Bael had saved her life in the Shadow Realm, and she wasn't going to let him bleed out on the floor, far from his home. "Explain to me what you're both talking about. I will decide. He is, after all, my fiancé."

Zee narrowed her eyes at Bael, studying him closely. "I can see why you'd be desperate to save this one. He's *gorgeous*. Have you tried him out?"

"Zee!" Ursula shouted. "Focus."

Zee snapped to attention. "Right. All of Nyxobas's brethren can feed on the blood of humans. It strengthens them, gives them power. But it also kinda makes them insane and full of sadistic bloodlust, blah blah. I'm sure it'll be fine though."

Cera shook her head. "For ancient demons such as Bael, it completely robs them of their senses. He would never agree to it. It is *ikkibu*—completely forbidden. He would revert to a primal form, devoid of all humanity, driven by nothing but the lust for human blood."

"But like, he'd get better," said Zee.

Ursula's fingers tightened into fists. Maybe this was *ikkibu* in the Shadow Realm, but what else could they do? They'd run out of time. And at least he'd be alive. They'd just have to fix the whole sanity thing later. Living and breathing was surely better than death, even if he was devoid of humanity. "So I just have to give Bael some blood? Like a vampire?"

"Exactly," said Zee. "Vampires are undead. For them, blood is their only source of nourishment. It must sustain all their bodily functions. But for an ancient demon, already corrupted by thousands of years of Nyxobas's magic, the power of the blood can be all-consuming. On the other hand, he won't die."

Cera gripped Ursula's arm. "Don't do this, Ursula. He will become a monster. There must be another way. A doctor, like you said."

Zee cocked a hip. "I already told you. There are no doctors anywhere near us. People have been literally dying in the streets, and no one gives a shit. Right now, this extremely hot man is about to draw his last breath. If you don't want him to give up the ghost forever, we have to fix this here."

Ursula stared at Cera. "Have you seen this happen before?"

Cera's eyes glistened. "Do you remember my brother?"

An image of Cera's brother flashed in Ursula's mind: wild-eyed, lunging for Bael's throat. How could she forget?

"It's like that," said Cera. "Only a thousand times worse. He would become uncontrollable, driven only by an obsessive desire to consume more blood. He'd slaughter all of us. And if he recovers, he would hate himself forever. He's been burdened with enough self-loathing, don't you think?"

Zee shrugged. "Okay, that's obviously the worst-case scenario. If you only let him feed enough to strengthen himself, he'll just be a little aggressive for a few days. We can lock him in a room. It'll wear off. Not a big deal."

Ursula didn't have a ton of options, and she'd just have to trust Zee. "I'll just give him a tiny bit to see what happens." But Ursula paused.

There had been something in the way Zee said 'the old way' that raised the hair on the back of her neck. "Why do they call it the old way?"

Zee blinked. "Because before Nyxobas called his lords to the Shadow Realm, his brethren lived by the blood. They were a scourge upon the earth, and they nearly destroyed the entire human race before they were banished to the Shadow Realm."

An icy shiver snaked up Ursula's spine. "Oh. Right. Well, let's see how it goes."

* * *

Ursula knelt by Bael again, her chest aching for him. He had quieted now, no longer fighting the inevitable, his breath coming in short, sharp gasps. Around him, dark blood spread across the floor.

"Cera," she said quietly. "We have no other options."

When Cera didn't respond, Ursula took that as silent assent. Even if it meant doing something forbidden, Cera would do anything to save Bael's life.

Ursula turned her palm over and stared at the veins in her wrist. All she had to do was slice one open, and let a little blood drip into Bael's mouth. Bael gasped and his entire body arched against the wood. He was dying. There was no more time for dillydallying.

She jumped up and raced down the hall into the large wood-walled arsenal and yanked a dagger from the weapon rack. As she rushed back to the atrium, her bare feet pounding the floor, she was already drawing the blade across her forearm, blocking out the sharp pain.

Kneeling again, she pressed her wrist to Bael's mouth. For a moment, she just knelt there, her heart thrumming, blood dripping over his lips. Nothing happened. Then his tongue brushed against the wound, flicking over it. A strange wave of pleasure rippled through her body, from her wrist up into her arm. Bael's eyes fluttered, and he grazed his teeth over her skin. Ursula stared at the pulse in his neck, now throbbing faster, his body almost glowing with a pale light. His eyes snapped open, dark as caves. They were locked on her, and yet she knew he wasn't *seeing* her, that some primal part of his mind had taken over completely. Then, he opened his mouth wider, teeth flashing, and his canines pierced her skin —hard.

548

Pain mingled with pleasure, the sensation overwhelming. Dizzy, Ursula clamped her eyes shut. And when she opened them again, she found she was no longer in her apartment, and the pain in her wrist had dissipated. Now she stood in a field of golden-flowered shrubs spreading out over a vast landscape of tawny, rocky earth. She stood below a stormy gray sky—the color of Bael's eyes. Here, the air was dry and clean, and the honeyed rays of the morning sun pierced a cloud, gilding the earth around her. To her right, rolling hills curved around the field, covered in juniper trees and grapevines. To her left, a vast city of ruddy stone towered over the fields.

What the fuck?

She sniffed the air. Whispering over the hills, the breeze carried a rich, briny scent, and traces of sandalwood—*Bael.* She couldn't see the ocean from where she stood, but it was near. Just on the other side of the hills, she thought, so close she could almost hear the waves. She tried to walk, but her body wouldn't move. Her pulse raced.

What had happened to New York? Where was Bael?

In the distance, a rooster crowed. At the sound, her body began to move, but not at her command. Her eyes were locked on a thin plume of smoke rising from behind the city walls, her feet pounding the ruddy fields.

A sword's scabbard bounced at her hip, and when she glanced down, she caught a glimpse of leather sandals, a short tunic, and powerful golden legs—a *man's* legs. From behind the city walls, a scream rent the air, and she sped up, kicking up dust as she ran, until she arrived at the towering city gate, its imposing columns capped by lion carvings, sunlight gleaming off the buildings. She sprinted onto a stone road and as she moved further into the city, people were fleeing past her, screaming, eyes wild with fear.

The narrow road curved up a hill, lined on either side with stone buildings. Smoke wound through the street, curling into her nostrils, and her lungs burned.

She wanted to stop, to catch her breath, but her legs kept pushing, moving toward the smoke. Something was terribly wrong.

* * *

DISTANT SHOUTS PULLED her away from the vision.

"Get him away from her!" A frantic voice pierced the air.

Slowly, Ursula opened her eyes. Her vision swam as someone pulled at her, yanking her onto the cold, marble floor. "What's going—" She tried to speak, but her tongue was heavy in her mouth, her words slurring. Someone was tugging at her legs, and her mind whirled with visions of juniper trees and ruddy stone, a marine breeze caressing her skin. But she wasn't there anymore, in the field and the ancient, burning city. Above her, warm lights were flickering. The chandelier. She was back in New York.

"I'm trying!" Zee's voiced echoed in the hall.

Slowly, the lights of the chandelier receded as someone pulled her away. "Where are you taking me?" she managed.

"I told you what would happen if you gave him your blood," said Cera.

It came back to her in a flash. Bael had been feeding from her—Bael, who smelled of sandalwood and the ocean. Had she been in his mind? Her mouth was dry, and she tried to lick her lips. "How is Bael?"

"He's alive," said Cera in a voice tinged with fear, dragging Ursula down the hall.

Ursula tried to stand, but vertigo over took her.

"Don't move," said Cera as she dragged Ursula into the library, closing the door behind her. "You lost a lot of blood."

Ursula swallowed hard. "He was only supposed to drink a little bit."

"We tried to pull you away, but he is too strong. He would have drained you if Zee hadn't glamoured him."

Down the hall, Zee was shouting in Russian. A bellowing roar answered her.

Ursula blinked. "Is Zee okay?"

"I think so," said Cera. "She manacled him in some sort of golden handcuffs."

As Cera pulled Ursula into the living room, an enormous crash echoed down the hall. "Stop."

Ursula pushed up to her elbows, then tried to stand again, but her head swam as soon as she lifted it from the floor. Cera was right. Bael had drank a *lot* of blood.

"Wait there," Cera barked, as if Ursula had any other option. "I must go check on the lord."

Before Ursula could respond, Cera slipped back into the hallway. Ursula's eyes drifted closed again, her mind echoing with those terrible screams from that sun-kissed city.

* * *

WHEN URSULA OPENED her eyes again, Zee and Cera were standing in the doorway. Zee looked exhausted, her blond hair disheveled, a red welt bulging on the side of her face. Cera stood next to her, staring at the floor.

"How is Bael?" asked Ursula.

"He's fine," said Zee. "He's a real prick when he's blood-drunk, but we've got him confined in his old bedroom upstairs."

"How did you get him up there?"

Zee quirked a smile. "I have my ways of convincing people." She knelt down and slipped her arm under Ursula's back. "Can you sit up?"

Slowly, Ursula sat up. She still felt woozy, but the vertigo had abated.

"So it worked," said Ursula.

Zee took a deep breath. "Technically, yes. But Bael... he's definitely doing the monster thing. Black eyes, bloodlust, rage. Primal growls. That sort of thing."

"But that's what we expected, right?" Ursula rubbed her eyes. "I mean, you warned me that he'd turn into a monster. 'Not a big deal.'"

"I'd just never seen it *quite* like that before, or with someone quite that powerful," said Zee. "I thought you said he was mortal without his wings? He's strong as an ox. If I hadn't glamoured him, we'd all be dead."

"Told you it was a terrible idea," said Cera. "Things are *ikkibu* for a reason."

From the floor above, a deep, guttural bellow pierced the walls, and the bestial sound slid through Ursula's bones.

"He's overcome with bloodlust," said Cera. "He can still smell you, and he's desperate to drink from your veins again. You're not safe here. Right now, he can't think about anything else but draining you."

Ursula blinked. "But you've got manacles on him, right?"

"Yes," said Zee. "But given his strength, they won't last forever. What we really need is someone strong enough to fight him if he escapes, but I'm not sure if any such person exists."

"What about Kester?"

Zee shook her head. "He disappeared from the city right around the time the dragons showed up. He told me he thought he'd figured out why the dragons were after you. He said he knew how to fix it, but didn't give me any details. Then, POOF. Gone. I've been searching the entire city for him, and I'm about to lose my mind."

So Kester was out. That left—Ursula shuddered—the goddess of fire. "Maybe we need to summon Emerazel to grant my fire magic back."

Zee scrunched her pale forehead. "First of all, you can't summon her without your magic. Second of all, I don't think you want to have to explain a bloodthirsty Shadow Lord from Nyxobas's court."

Right. Bollocks. Ursula tried to stand, but her legs buckled, and she dropped down again. "We need to find Kester. He can help me get my magic back, and Zee said he knows why the dragons are after me, right? That he knows how to stop them?"

"Not now," said Cera sharply. "First, you rest. The manacles should hold for a while longer."

Already, Ursula could feel her eyes drifting closed, and she felt a dry, marine wind rush over her skin, bringing with it the scent of death.

CHAPTER 4

*U*rsula spent the night dreaming of gray skies and fields of coppery earth dappled with yellow wildflowers: sandalwood, salty air, and a longing so deep it hurt.

When she woke on the sofa, buttery sunlight streamed in through the living room windows, melting away her dreams. As the visions faded from her mind, their loss gnawed at her chest. She had a sudden desire to run up to her bedroom and paint the dreams over the walls.

But she'd have to save that for later. Right now, the sunlight was hurting her eyes, and her mouth felt like cotton. She was still stark naked apart from the raincoat and the blanket someone had thrown over her. On the coffee table next to her, someone had laid out a fresh change of clothes for her—black jeans, a striped T-shirt, and even a set of black underwear.

She squinted in the sunlight, rubbing her eyes. Her stomach rumbled. When had she last eaten? *The gods only know.* Inhaling deeply, she scented the rich, salty aroma of bacon wafting through the air, and her mouth began to water. She rose on shaky legs and pulled off the raincoat, letting it drop to the sofa. Slowly, she pulled on the underwear, dressing her trembling body.

When she'd finished, she stumbled toward the kitchen, her hunger compelling her toward the scent of breakfast. Still lightheaded, she leaned against the hallway wall as she walked.

In the kitchen, Cera stood over a sizzling pan. Steam from the bacon curled into the air, catching the sunlight.

Zee leaned against the counter, her hands wrapped around a steaming mug of coffee. "Hungry? This is some of the last bacon left in New York City."

"We'll just have to get more pigs," Cera chirped. She looked up at Ursula. "How do you feel?"

Ursula shook her head slowly. "Like I've caught the bubonic plague."

Zee nodded. "Bael had a really good hold of you."

Cera pointed a bony finger at the fae's blonde head. "*She* kicked him in the head."

"I had to gain control of the situation." Zee picked up a plate and fork, eyeing the bacon. "He was going to drain Ursula. And everything is fine now, right? She's alive. He's alive. Everyone wins. Apart from the fact that Bael might slaughter us all." She plucked a strip of bacon from the pan, dropping it onto the plate. "But until then, we have perfectly crispy bacon." She handed the plate to Ursula. "First bite goes to the blood-loss victim."

Her mouth watering, Ursula grabbed the plate. "Thanks." She bit into the bacon, watching as Cera retrieved a tray of pancakes from the oven and began piling a big helping onto a plate.

"Are we supposed to eat all this?"

Cera dropped the tray on the stovetop next to the frying pan. "The pancakes are for the lord."

"You really think he'll settle for pancakes when what he wants is human blood?" asked Zee.

As if on cue, a primal roar ripped through the house, rattling the glassware in the kitchen. Bael sounded a lot like he had when she'd first released him from those bonds, and yet this was somehow more terrifying—the dark, bestial undertone, a preternatural message: *Run.*

Cera piled pancakes onto a plate, fixing Ursula with a hard stare. "I'm bringing him his breakfast. You need to get out of here. As long as he smells your blood, bloodlust will cloud his mind."

Ursula's mouth had gone dry. "Right. Of course." She snatched a coffee cup, inhaling the aroma as she poured it. She still felt half-dead. "My head is a little foggy, but just so I have this clear, I need to leave here before Bael kills me, and walk out into a post-apocalyptic nightmare of a city where everyone wants to turn me over to dragons to end the deaths."

A bestial roar from Bael rumbled through her gut, and Ursula tightened her grip on her coffee.

Zee took a bite of bacon. "I think you've got the gist of it. Why not visit Kester's tugboat? If we can figure out where he went, we can figure out why the dragons are after you. And he's got a billion magical books. Maybe we can find how to handle Ol' Yeller up there. Cera can stay here and look after him."

"Any ideas what Kester was talking about? Why they're after me?" asked Ursula.

"Nope."

"Any ideas how to fix it?"

Zee bit her lip. "I have no idea, Ursula. How hard do you think it is to kill an army of dragons?"

* * *

Zee sat in the driver's seat of the Bentley as they sped through Times Square. She'd glamoured herself to look like a large, balding man, and the sight startled Ursula every time she looked over at her.

Zee pressed her foot on the gas pedal, speeding past the desolate square, the electric lights flickering, the streets eerily silent. Trash blew through the street. Some of the buildings still stood, while others had become blackened, twisted skeletons, steel beams jutting from the ground at odd angles. An ad for watches was plastered on the side of a burnt-out bus, and for just a moment, Ursula recognized the model—the woman who'd been held hostage by the dragons. Apart from the wrecked cars every quarter mile or so, the roads were empty. The dragons had completely transformed New York, and the sight filled Ursula with a quiet dread.

Goosebumps rose over her skin as they rolled past the ravaged square. Instinctively, she ran her fingers over the hilt of her sword, ready to fight. "The dragons did all this?"

Zee nodded. "Yeah. It's been chaos. They hunt day and night."

Ursula swallowed hard. "Are we safe in the car?"

"Probably not, but we don't have much of a choice. Kester is the only one who can call on Emerazel to get your fire back. If a dragon attacks, we'll just have to get the hell out of here. Fast."

Ursula glanced at her reflection in the mirror, momentarily startled. Zee had glamoured her to look like an elderly woman, her skin deeply lined and hair in tight, white curls. "Is there a reason I had to look elderly?"

"Yes. The dragons seem to have a second sense for finding beautiful women. We're safer this way."

"Right. Like the model."

Zee turned left, heading for lower Manhattan. The gray Hudson River rolled just across the wide thoroughfare to their right. A charred, smoking shell of an enormous ship loomed in the river—an aircraft carrier, she thought.

"What is that?" asked Ursula.

"I'm pretty sure that's the remains of the *USS Harry S. Truman.*"

"The dragons did that?"

Zee nodded, keeping her eyes on the road. "When the President first declared martial law, he sent in the Navy to attack the dragon nest on Liberty Island. The dragons destroyed half the fleet before the Navy managed to retreat. Some of Times Square was destroyed in the process. Sending a message, I think."

Ursula studied the ship as Zee drove south toward the tip of Manhattan—its buckled and warped deck and the blackened sides.

When she glanced to the left, she saw what remained of Midtown—husks of buildings resembling carved-out tombstones, ravaged metal facades revealing charred interiors. Debris littered the road, and the acrid smell of smoke hung in the air. The smell, the charred buildings… it reminded her of something—a long-buried memory, elusive as smoke between her fingers.

Ursula's stomach turned at the sight of the destruction. "Any idea about the casualties?"

"Most of the residents had already evacuated. Others were able to escape. FEMA has resettled most of them in Hoboken," said the balding man with Zee's voice. "But since this all started? Hundreds have died."

Zee slowed, turning off the main road. She rolled the Bentley to a stop on the marina. The remains of One World Trade Center loomed above them, the upper third of the building sheared off. Ursula suppressed a shudder.

She stepped out of the car, following Zee onto the docks. The last time she had been here, it had been in the middle of a January night. At this point, nothing looked particularly familiar. Ahead of her Zee stopped, scratching her bald head. "This is Kester's slip." A large catamaran bobbed in the water where Kester's boat had been. "No idea where his boat went."

A silhouette flashed in the catamaran, and Ursula reached for her sword. When a human man walked out—stark naked—Ursula relaxed.

"Hi there," he said in a casual Southern California drawl, apparently oblivious to his nudity. "I'm Hubert."

Though she had to admit he was quite fit, Ursula stared only long enough to confirm that he was unarmed. She didn't imagine Hubert wanted to be ogled by a geriatric woman and her balding companion.

"Hubert," she repeated.

"That's what they call me."

"You're not wearing any clothes," Zee said, her Russian accent thicker than usual, voice strangely high-pitched for a portly gentleman.

"Oh, right. Totally. My bad." He scratched his tanned abs. "I was just catching some rays."

Ursula looked up at the clouds that covered the sky. When her eyes returned to Hubert, he'd retrieved a very small beach towel from the deck and wrapped it around himself.

"So what brings you to the marina?" He squinted in the sunlight. "Not many people around here anymore. Kinda nice. I mean, apart from all the fire and death."

"We were looking for my friend." Ursula frowned. "Were you really sunbathing?"

He smiled, revealing a row of impossibly white teeth. "As soon as the dragons leave I'm sailing to Cuba. I need to keep up my tan."

"Have you seen a tugboat that's usually in this slip?" It took Ursula a moment to come up with the name. "It's called the *Elysium*."

Hubert nodded. "Totally. It's right over there." He pointed to a boat moored a few hundred feet off shore. With its rustic exterior, it certainly looked like Kester's tug.

Zee turned to Ursula, adjusting her trousers below her giant potbelly. "How are we going to get out there?"

"You want a lift?" asked Hubert.

His towel had slipped to the side, and Ursula looked him straight in the eye. "Yes, that would be lovely. Do you want to maybe… put on some clothes first? At my age, I can't deal with too much excitement."

"Sure. Sure," said Hubert, then he frowned again, staring at Ursula's waist. "Hey, is that a sword?"

She swallowed hard. "Yep. That's a sword."

"Cool, man. Okay." He turned to cross into his boat. After a minute, he popped back out wearing a black speedo that did little to cover his modesty. He pointed to a small motorboat next to the catamaran. "My launch is right over here."

Ursula and Zee followed him down the dock, then all three of them clambered into the small boat. As Ursula took a seat by Zee, Hubert started the engine, pulling out into the waves. Seawater sprayed over them, and Ursula licked the salt from her lips. Gods, it felt good to be back on earth again, even if they'd walked into a war zone.

The wind whipped over Ursula's skin, and she shielded her eyes from the sunlight.

"How do you know Kester?" Hubert shouted over the wind.

Ursula raised her eyebrows, surprised that Hubert knew him by name.

"How do *you* know Kester?" asked Zee.

"My bro Kester is like family," said Hubert. "He and I cruise over to Tatty O'Rourke's on the weekends." The way he said 'cruise' suggested it might have a double meaning. "Of course, since the dragons arrived I haven't seen much of him."

"So you don't think he's on the *Elysium*?" Ursula could hear the disappointment in her voice.

"No idea. I haven't seen him in weeks."

Hubert cut the motor as they neared Kester's tug. "We need to keep a low profile," he said, turning to nod at the *Harry S. Truman's* burnt-out hull in the middle of the river. "The dragons attack any boat that goes into the main channel."

Hubert slowed the engine as they approached the tugboat, his motorboat bouncing on the waves. A moment later, he had hopped out of the launch and onto the stern of the *Elysium*. There was a rope on the bow of his launch, which he casually wrapped around a cleat, before turning back to Zee and Ursula.

"Welcome aboard!" he said smiling.

Zee hauled herself over the railing, ungracefully crawling onto Kester's boat in her old-man body. Ursula followed, almost losing a shoe in the water.

Hubert hadn't done much to help the two pensioners, but Zee thanked him anyway, her jowls wobbling. Then she crossed the deck to Kester's door, pulling a key from her pocket. She slid it into the lock, and clicked it open.

Ursula followed closely behind, straining her eyes in the dark until Zee flicked on a light. The cabin air smelled stale, but otherwise everything was just as Ursula remembered: the cast-iron stove, the comfy-looking reading chair, and shelves crammed with books.

"Kester?" Ursula called out, unnerved by the shroud of silence.

As Zee hurried to check his bedroom, Ursula searched the cabin for clues. As far as she could tell, everything was in the right place—an electric light casting a warm glow over wooden tables, the books in neat rows. The sigil for fire travel was carved into his floor.

As she searched the space, Hubert strolled into the cabin. "So how exactly do you know Kester? You related or something?"

"He's my nephew," she replied.

Hubert smiled. "Right. Cool. Do you mind if I smoke?"

"Not as long as you do it outside."

"Totally." Hubert disappeared out the door. If he'd found the sight of a magical sigil on the floor strange, he didn't let on. A few moments later, the sharp scent of marijuana wafted into the cabin.

Zee strode back into the room, rubbing her bald head. "He's not here." She sniffed the air. "Is that pot?"

"That would be Hubert."

Zee nodded. "Righto. So, no Kester. No magic. On to plan B. The grimoires. Do you know—" She paused, narrowing her eyes at Kester's living room table, built of thick oak planks. "Ursula," she said quietly. "There's something here."

Ursula had already looked it over and found it completely bare. Nothing rested on its surface. "I don't see anything."

"He's hidden it. Glamoured." Zee's wrinkled forehead creased even more. "Gimme a sec."

Holding her hands above the table, she closed her eyes. The air above the table shimmered, tinged with gold. Then, a pile of books and papers appeared. Ursula picked up the top book, a maroon leather tome. Emblazoned on its cover was a faded gold title: *Historia Brittonum.* Under it was a brown book entitled *Annales Cambriae.*

Ursula frowned. "Old British history books. Why would he glamour them?"

"I don't know." She turned the large tome over in her hands. "But he used a powerful glamour. There must be something important here."

What the hell?

Footfalls turned Ursula's head, and the look on Hubert's face made her stomach flip.

He pointed outside, his face pale. "There's a dragon."

CHAPTER 5

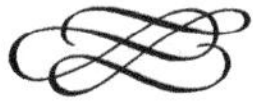

Ursula snatched the leather bag from Kester's bed and quickly shoved the history books into it. "I'm taking these." Then she felt for the hilt of her sword at her hip and rushed for the door.

Zee was scrambling around, searching for something, while Ursula peered out the door. Gray clouds covered the sky. In the distance, the broken stump of One World Trade Center leaned ominously. But she could see no sign of a dragon in the darkening sky.

"Where is it?" asked Ursula.

"Shhh…" hissed Hubert, pulling her back from the door, his eyes now bloodshot. He was stoned as hell. "The dragons are invisible. That's one of their powers. But we can hear them."

Ursula swallowed hard, straining to hear, until a terrible screech rent the air, sending a shiver up her spine. She narrowed her eyes at the skies, still seeing nothing.

Zee crossed to the doorway, clutching a dagger, while Hubert continued to squint at the sky, searching for signs of the dragon's location.

"Is it gone?" asked Zee.

"Hard to say." Hubert shook his head, his knuckles whitening against his tan arms. "But I don't think so. That was some sort of hunting cry," he said. "When they battled the ships in the river, that was the noise they made before they attacked. We just don't know where he's gonna attack."

The hair rose on the back of Ursula's neck, and she flicked off the light in the tugboat, stepping back into the shadows.

Hubert stepped back with her. "I shouldn't have come out here," he muttered. "It's not safe this close to the channel." His eyes widened, and he gripped his hair. "Do you guys think the dragons can read our thoughts?"

"Be quiet," Zee hissed.

Hubert shook his head, staring at the floor. "This was a terrible idea. If you'd seen what I saw during the last attack..." His cheeks were reddening, his voice rising as he met Ursula's eyes. "You seem like nice old people but I never should have taken you out here. I'm too young to die. I was going to sail to the Florida Keys and drink margaritas with Estelle."

"Hubert," Ursula said sharply. "Calm down. It's going to be fine. Just don't make any noise." She dropped her voice to a whisper. "You can see Estelle if you keep quiet. We just need to hide in here. Quietly."

"I'm pretty sure they can hear our thoughts," said Hubert. "We need to get out of here!" He started for the door, and Ursula grabbed him, pulling him back into the shadows.

Hubert looked at her, his eyes wide. Then the tugboat jerked hard to the side, and Ursula slammed into a bookshelf, her head smacking against the wood.

Hubert shouted, but the words were drowned out by the sound of splintering wood. Before Ursula could scramble to her feet, flame exploded through the cabin as the fuel tank exploded. Ursula screamed, shielding her face until the flames receded again.

Squinting through the smoke, Ursula caught a glimpse of a terrifying form—a clear space, outlined by smoke. Through the doorway, she spied the silhouette of an enormous dragon framed by smoke, its wings as wide as a house. The dragon's outline threw back its head, screeching to the skies, and the sound ignited the ancient part of Ursula's brain, directing her to flee. The acrid scent of smoke curled into the air. In the next moment, the transparent silhouette had disappeared again, its clear edges blurred by smoke.

"I think he's coming for us!" Hubert yelled. "We have to get out of here!"

"No!" Zee shouted from the corner. A red streak of blood trickled down her bald forehead.

In the next moment, Hubert was racing for the hatch, onto the deck. Ursula crawled through the doorframe, carefully peering over the edge of the tugboat. Crouching behind the side of the hull, she watched Hubert plunge into the Hudson. In the puffs of smoke over the slate-gray water, Ursula thought she caught a glimpse of a dragon, cutting lazy arcs over the river, biding its time. For just a moment, everything was quiet.

As soon as Hubert's head breached the surface, an invisible claw lifted him from the water. Almost immediately, the front half of his body disappeared with a horrendous crunching noise, and a thick spray of blood arced through the air. Hubert was being eaten.

Ursula's mouth went dry, her body shaking. Slowly, she crawled back toward Zee, whose labored breathing echoed through the damaged cabin.

When she'd slipped back into the cabin, she slowly turned to Zee, who was crouched in the shadows, holding a finger to her lips, her eyes wide. She lowered her finger, then mouthed, *I don't think it knows we're in here.*

Ursula huddled behind the doorframe, listening intently for the sound of screeching—the dragon's hunting cry. A cold sweat beaded over her skin. What exactly would the dragons do with her if they found her? Why the hell was she so important? Apparently, the dragons knew more about her than she did herself.

Of course they did, considering she didn't know a damn thing.

"Ursula," Zee whispered, beckoning her closer. "Come here."

Crawling slowly, Ursula crept to where Zee crouched next to the table.

Zee whispered, "Do you remember the spell for traveling through the sigil?"

"Yes, but I don't have any fire in me anymore."

Zee arched an eyebrow, her glamour fading. She was looking more like her cute blonde self. "Kester didn't show you his laboratory, did he?"

Keeping low to the ground, Zee crept to one of the bookshelves. She tugged on a dusty moss-green tome, and the shelf pulled forward, revealing a small room. Zee slipped in, and Ursula followed close behind, marveling that Kester had managed to hide a room on a boat this size.

The room smelled of bergamot and rue, and a strange power thrummed over her skin. An iron brazier took up most of the room.

Shelves lined the walls, each one crammed with vials and flasks of herbs and colored liquids. They had labels like *bismuth, aqua regia, dragon's blood,* and *Dutch wine*. As Ursula moved in closer, she spied a large basin resting in the center of the brazier.

"Wow," whispered Ursula. "What are we doing in here?"

"We're going to make some liquid hellfire."

"Without my fire magic, the fire will burn both of us."

"Only for a second, my dear. We'll just have to hope it transports us both fast enough that our skin remains intact."

"Wonderful."

Zee knelt, muttering to herself. "I need some of the aqua regia, a pinch of glauber's salt…" She cocked her head. "And the hair of a hellhound." She picked up a faintly glowing yellow ampule and cracked it into the brass basin. The solution quivered at the bottom of the bowl as though it were alive. Then, she held out her hand.

"Right." Ursula plucked a few hairs from her head, and dropped them into the beaker. The glowing liquid hissed and bubbled.

"Now I just have to find where Kester put the quicklime." Ursula's eyes flicked to the open hatch, while Zee continued to study the contents of the shelves. Here in the hidden lab, the dragon would never be able to see them.

"There it is." Zee carefully retrieved a small wax-paper envelope from the corner of a shelf.

She lay the envelope on the floor, then handed Ursula an empty glass beaker. "Hold this."

Ursula took it from her as Zee slowly emptied the contents of the envelope into the brass dish. A blinding light flashed through the room, and Ursula shielded her eyes.

Zee swore softly. "*Suka!* I forgot about the Carnot reaction. I haven't mixed a potion in ages." She carefully poured the liquid into a beaker. It had transformed from pale yellow into a deep cherry red, boiling with an intense heat.

"There," said Zee. "It's ready for you. Don't spill it."

Just as Ursula was reaching for it, an enormous crash slammed the boat to one side, knocking bottles and vials to the floor. As liquids sizzled over the wood, Ursula tumbled into a bookshelf, nearly spilling the liquid hellfire.

"Shit," said Zee. "The dragon must have seen the light."

A terrible screeching, groaning noise pierced the air as the dragon's talons raked the roof of the boat.

"Let's hope this works, then," said Ursula.

The boat jerked viciously to the side, throwing Ursula from the alcove. She clutched the hellfire to her chest as she slammed into the side of the cast iron stove.

A hot light flashed through the cabin. Then, darkness. For just a moment, visions danced in her mind, the field dappled with golden flowers...

Zee was gripping Ursula's shoulders, her voice tinged with panic. "Ursula!"

"Yes?" Ursula blinked, her vision blurry. She felt as if the dragon had ignited the inside of her skull with hellfire. A thick smell of smoke hung in the air, and for just a moment, Bael's memories—the woman screaming, the buildings burning—whispered in the hollows of her skull.

Zee held Ursula's face in her hands. "Ursula. I need you to focus. Incant the spell." As Ursula's eyes focused, she saw Zee crouched before her. Her glamour had completely faded, and her eyes blazed with raw fear.

A ringing noise echoed in Ursula's mind, and she clamped her eyes shut. *The spell...*

"Ursula!" Zee's voice was frantic now. "I know you're hurt, but if you don't get it together, we're going to die."

That shocked Ursula into alertness. As she opened her eyes, the floor seemed to sway under her. "I can do it."

"Good. Because we're not on the water anymore. The dragon..." Zee pointed to the hatch. Light flashed outside the window, and Ursula caught a glimpse of the truncated remains of One World Trade Center gleaming in the sunlight. "The dragon is carrying us."

They must be thirty stories above the earth, dragon wings beating the air above them like a war drum.

Panic tightened its bony fingers around Ursula's heart. "Give me the hellfire."

"You're still holding it. Good job, by the way."

Ursula glanced down at herself. Slowly, taking care not to spill any more hellfire than she already had, she stood, her mind reeling. Pain splintered the back of her skull, and she suppressed the urge to vomit. Slowly, Zee helped her over to Kester's sigil.

"Don't forget to hold your breath," said Ursula. Struggling to keep her balance as the tugboat swayed, Ursula began chanting the transportation spell, staring into Zee's terrified eyes. Neither of them knew what would happen if they transported through a fire sigil without a functioning hellhound to guide them.

As Ursula uttered the final word, she poured the hellfire onto the symbol. It sputtered and flared up when it hit the wood.

For a brief instant, flames blazed to the ceiling, and fire scorched her skin.

* * *

It took a few moments for the intense pain of the flames to subside as Ursula and Zee reconstituted in the sigil room, a tower room surrounded by glass windows overlooking the city. The smell of burnt hair wafted through the room. Dizzy, Ursula glanced at Zee, who coughed and spluttered, her clothing covered in ash.

Pain seared Ursula's feet where the fire had burned the hottest, and she dropped down to her backside, pulling off her shoes. Blisters spread over her toes, the pain excruciating.

She winced. "Bloody hell." Her vision was blurred as she tried to look at Zee. "Are you okay?"

"No. My fucking feet are destroyed. And half my hair is burned off."

Zee's voice sounded distant, and Ursula's vision was darkening.

"Oh my god, Ursula," said Zee from a million miles away. "Your head!"

A fresh burst of pain in Ursula's skull threatened to shatter her consciousness, and she touched the back of her head, wincing at the pain. She glanced down at her hands, catching a glimpse of bright crimson slicking her palms.

A bellow from above rumbled through the building, and her heart skipped a beat. Distantly, she knew it was Bael, demanding her blood, and the sound smashed into her skull like a white-hot poker thrust between her eyes. Ursula covered her ears with her hands.

As she cowered on the floor, another voice entered the fray, this one higher-pitched. "What happened?" Cera asked.

Ursula tried to focus on Cera's face, but the little oneiroi seemed to wobble.

"We failed to find Kester," said Zee. "But we did encounter a dragon, who picked up the tugboat, with us in it. Ursula smashed her head."

"I'll be fine." Ursula tried to stand, but her feet were blistered and her legs felt like jelly. She fell back onto her bum.

"Don't overexert yourself," said Cera. "You've got blood pouring from your scalp."

A sharp blast of pain fragmented Ursula's skull, knocking the breath out of her. Almost as bad, the skin around her feet and legs had been seared by the sigil spell. She could barely breathe for the pain. What was that healing spell she'd learned? The Angelic words had become jumbled in her mind.

"Move Ursula back from the sigil," commanded Zee. "I'm going to get us help."

Vaguely, though a haze of pain, Ursula felt Cera's bony hands grip her around her ribs, pulling her away from the sigil. She stared, her vision wavering as Zee poured the last of the hellfire into the grooves on the floor.

"I don't understand," Ursula slurred.

Flames rose from the sigil as Zee turned to face Ursula. "I need you to summon Emerazel. Can you remember how?"

Ursula nodded. That particular spell had been seared into her memory from repeated use. She swallowed hard, muttering the spell, tripping over her words as she spoke. After a few tries, wincing with pain as she enunciated each Angelic word, she managed to get through it correctly. When she finished the final word, fire spewed from the floor like a volcano, and Ursula shielded her face with her hands. The heat of Emerazel's inferno roasted her skin, practically blinding her. She instantly regretted chanting the spell. Her gaze flicked to Zee and Cera, who cowered at the edge of the room, hugging each other.

The goddess loomed over Ursula, her ashy skin cracking to reveal molten fire beneath her charcoal exterior. Her eyes, two glowing embers, burned into Ursula. Through the windows around the sigil room, flames and magma blazed over the fiery landscape. "You have summoned me?"

"I... I need your help," Ursula stammered.

"Why should I help you?"

The room was so hot Ursula could barely breathe, much less speak. "Because Kester is missing. I've lost my fire magic, and someone needs to find him."

Emerazel's eyes flashed. "Kester's business is not your concern." The goddess leaned closer. The heat was unbearable. "You will not survive that injury. Your brain is bleeding. Your soul is almost mine—"

Ursula swallowed hard, trying to block out the pain, the heat that would roast her alive. "Your headsman is missing. Don't you care?"

Before the goddess could reply, a terrifying roar slid through Ursula's bones. Bael stood at the threshold of the sigil room. His eyes were the color of blood, and he wore only a pair of black trousers, his savage tattoos snaking over his chest. His arms, thickly corded with muscle, were rigid with tension. Tendrils of dark magic curled off his body, and he stared at the goddess with a menacing ferocity that stole Ursula's breath. Right now, she wasn't sure who scared her more—the goddess of fire, or the Lord of Abelda.

The remains of a golden shackle hung from Bael's wrist, and behind him rose the shadows of enormous wings, a lethal caress of midnight. He glared at Emerazel as a low growl rose from his throat, the sound raising the hair on the back of Ursula's neck.

A flash of heat seared the room. "Bael. It's been years since we've spoke. How I've missed you," she hissed. "Aww... Those aren't your real wings. How sad. I imagine you would break quite easily now."

She knows him?

"If I were at my full power," said Bael, "I'd be tearing you apart, piece by piece, and sending your fetid embers into the void."

An ashy smile cracked Emerazel's lips. "But you're not at your full power, are you?"

"I have claimed Ursula," he snarled. "And she consented. If she dies, it is my right to decide the fate of her soul."

Another flash of heat seared the room, scorching Ursula's skin, and the skin on her arms blistered. The pain was unbearable. She tried to scream but fire filled her lungs.

"What have you done, hound?" Emerazel's voice seemed to ring in the hollows of her mind.

Ursula couldn't explain, not with the molten lava igniting her body.

Emerazel's deep voice sounded in her mind. "The hound's soul is mine —you had no right to consent to this union."

"Don't touch her," Bael commanded, his voice booming through the room.

Another flash of hellfire, and Ursula could feel her flesh charring as pain ripped her body apart. This was it. She was going to join Emerazel in the infernos. Then, as suddenly as the flames had started, they cooled. Ursula blinked, staring at her skin—completely unblemished again. Only the memory of agony whispered through her mind. Outside, the vision of Emerazel's hellscape had thinned, the buildings and parks of New York City slowly returning.

Emerazel stared at Ursula with eyes the color of smoldering embers. "The wife-killer doesn't lie. Your soul is his. If I kill you now, your soul goes to Nyxobas." The goddess reached out to touch her forehead. Her fingertips were warm, but this time the heat soothed Ursula's skin, and the goddess's magic caressed her skull. Terror and comfort, pain and pleasure, wrath and love—the finely honed tools used by gods to reap devotion from their followers.

Smoke curled around the goddess, and she narrowed her flaming eyes at Ursula. "You will live—for now. My fire has healed your injuries." Her blazing eyes landed on Bael. "But the demon... He dies. Like I said, without your wings, I can you break quite easily." Fire blazed from Emerazel's fingers, catching Bael in the chest.

"Stop!" Ursula screamed, jumping to her feet.

In a fraction of a second, Emerazel lifted Bael's enormous body into the air, and flung him through one of the sigil room's windows. Shards of glass shattered around the room, melting into glowing droplets when they made contact with Emerazel's flames.

Ursula's world tilted. Without his wings, Bael was mortal. Ursula ran to the shattered window, and the city wind whipped at her hair. Frantically, she searched the streets for Bael's body. Behind her, Emerazel was saying something about Kester, about London, but Ursula wasn't listening. She only wanted to find the shadow demon, the Lord of Abelda with eyes the color of stormy Mediterranean skies.

CHAPTER 6

$\mathcal{U}$rsula swallowed hard, staring out the shattered window. *There*—under the shadows of the elms lining the park, Ursula caught a glimpse of his golden body, marked by dark tattoos. Bael walked barefoot, a dark sweep of phantom wings down his back. The muscled planes of his body appeared rigid with tension, his fists clenched.

"How the hell did he survive that?" Ursula breathed. "Where did those wings come from?"

"They're not his proper wings," said Cera. "But that blood you gave him to drink has restored some of his immortality, strengthening his shadow magic. It won't last. But for now, he has regained a portion of his former power. He's not as weak as Emerazel thought."

Ursula rubbed the soot from her eyes, loosing a breath. Gently, she traced her fingertips over the back of her head where she'd hit it. Her hair was still matted with blood, but she no longer felt the gash in her scalp. And, moreover, an ancient power flowed through her veins now. Emerazel's fire magic had returned.

Zee touched Ursula's arm, studying her closely. "How's your head? That looked *bad.*"

Ursula stepped away from the window, trying to avoid the broken glass. "I'm fine. Emerazel restored my fire and healed me. How are your burnt feet?"

Zee shrugged. "Fae heal quickly."

Cera was still staring out the broken window. "What happened to the lord?"

Ursula's chest tightened. "I have a terrible feeling he's about to go on a blood-drinking binge."

"I must go search for him," said Cera. "He could be hurt."

"You're not worried about the humans he's about to devour, I see," muttered Zee.

Cera hurried to the door, her white hair streaming behind her. "I'll be back as soon as I know Bael is safe." A moment later, the elevator door pinged.

Ursula sucked in a breath. "Humans are at war with demons. Will Cera be safe out there?"

Zee frowned. "Most humans still have no idea what demons really look like, and whatever New Yorkers are remaining in this city won't look twice at a tiny white-haired lady. She's far less scary than the dragons." She studied Ursula, and the breeze toyed with her platinum bob. "So you feel normal now?"

A dull ache throbbed in Ursula's temples. "It just feels like a mild hangover now."

"Right. I know how to cure a hangover. Let's go into the kitchen."

Fatigue sapped Ursula's energy, but she followed Zee into the kitchen anyway. Sunlight streamed through the windows, igniting dust motes in the air. Ursula leaned against a countertop, watching as Zee pulled out some American cheese, a bottle of Cholula sauce, and some baby carrots. "So, now we just need to get you out of New York." She unwrapped the cheese slices, folding them around the baby carrots. "Emerazel said Kester is on a mission in London, though it would have been nice if he'd told me where he was going before he left. He's not always considerate." She drizzled hot sauce over the little blanketed carrots, and handed the monstrosity to Ursula.

Dutifully, Ursula took a bite of carrot with hot sauce and cheese, gagging as she forced herself to swallow. "This is supposed to cure hangovers?"

Zee shrugged. "Well, not specifically. But it's just the only food we have left. The stores have all closed, and that little white-haired lady used up the rest of our food on your psycho boyfriend. Also, I really have no idea how to cook."

Ursula dropped the plate on the countertop. "About the 'boyfriend' thing. We only got engaged so he wouldn't have to kill me in a duel. It's some ancient Shadow Demon law. No killing your spouses."

Zee frowned. "So what was that whole thing about how he killed his wife?"

"Oh. That. Well…" Ursula blinked. "Actually, I have no idea. I think it was a very long time ago. He hasn't told me about it himself. He's a bit of a mystery, to be honest."

"Well, he seems protective of you. Even through his blood fury he was willing to protect you from the fire goddess." She crossed her arms, leaning against the opposite counter. "If Kester is in London, I think you should go after him there."

"To find out answers?"

"That, and because there are dragons after you in New York. And I think you need to stay away from your boyfriend until he stops trying to drink your blood."

Ursula nodded. "Okay. Any idea where Kester's London apartment is?"

Zee flicked on her phone, frowning at it. "Yeah, looks like it's on Fournier Street in London. Do you know where that is?"

"I think that's near Brick Lane, the street with those super-posh Georgian houses."

Zee bit into a carrot stick. "Time to pack your bags."

Ursula's stomach rumbled. She was completely knackered, but at least in London she could get a good sandwich to fill her belly. "I'm on it. Why don't you come with me? There's no food here, and Manhattan's a bit post-apocalyptic right now."

"I think your little white-haired demon friend will need help with the giant psycho Shadow Lord. Don't you?"

"Well, I appreciate your help. They're good demons. I think." Still barefoot from the blisters incident, Ursula padded over the hardwood floor and climbed the gently curving stairs, trailing her fingertips over the rail. She could only hope that a fae and a tiny oneiroi would be able to contain Bael's bloodlust long enough for it to wear off, and that he wouldn't slaughter any humans between now and then.

As she crossed to her bedroom, she tried not to think about the dragons. Whatever it was they knew about her, whatever secret they held, Ursula didn't want to know. She couldn't explain why, but she didn't want to know about her past. If she couldn't remember her own past, maybe there was a good reason. Maybe she didn't *want* to remember.

Sometimes, the past came to her in faded flickers. There were the beautiful memories—the fields of wildflowers, the clouds rolling through a blue sky. A woman, her hair as red as Ursula's. An old man's hands, turning the pages of a book as she sat on his lap.

But then there were the flashes of nightmare: the flames, the screams. The smell of burning flesh. A golden-skinned man towering over her, with eyes the color of the Mediterranean skies... She blinked, confused. Her thoughts had become all jumbled since she'd hit her head.

Right?

At the end of the hall, splinters of oak and iron littered the floor. The fact that Bael had been able to tear straight through the door highlighted his staggering power.

She turned, opening the door to her own room. She pulled out a large rucksack from under her bed. She fought the overwhelming urge to crawl up in her bed, to sleep for hours beneath the spray of blue and yellow wildflowers she'd painted on her wall. Turning to her dresser, she began collecting clothes—trousers, shirts, a dress, and enough underwear for a week. She pulled off her own fire-singed clothes, slipping into a fresh set of blue knickers and a bra, her leather leggings, and a black T-shirt. She tied her scabbard around her hips.

As she hurried back down the stairs, she felt the fire magic blazing through her veins. She had to admit, it felt good to have it back.

When she got to the bottom of the stairs, Zee was waiting for her, holding one of her own katanas from the armory. "You'll want to bring this, I imagine."

Ursula grabbed the hilt, examining the blade. It wasn't Honjo, but it would do. Ursula slid it into her scabbard.

"Thanks, Zee."

Zee leaned over to give her a hug. "Please bring back food for me. And champagne. Mostly champagne."

"I'll try. Look after Cera and Bael. They're a little out of place outside the Shadow Realm."

Ursula crossed toward the sigil room, and Zee followed behind her. Zee had already prepared the sigil, and it blazed with fire. Zee leaned against the doorframe, folding her arms and watching Ursula.

"The name of the flat is the Knight's Terrace on Fournier Street. Kester should have a sigil there. Wait!" Zee began frantically digging into her pocket. "You'll need this too." She pulled out a keychain and tossed it to Ursula. "It's the key to Kester's apartment."

Ursula began to incant the spell, her lips pronouncing the Angelic words as if she'd known them all her life, and she asked the sigil to direct her to the Knight's Terrace. She clutched tightly to the straps of her rucksack as Emerazel's flames blazed all around her. And this time, as she bathed in hellfire, her skin didn't burn.

* * *

Ursula sizzled into a new room, smoke rising from her body. The dying flames at her feet cast a dancing light over a tower room with a brick ceiling. Through the floor-to-ceiling windows that encircled the room, she had a view of Fournier Street. Here, several time zones away, night had already fallen. Warm lights glowed through the windows of the three-story Georgian houses, framed by antique wood-shuttered windows. People strolled along the streets below, dressed in trendy clothes, some already drunk. Ursula felt a surge of warmth. At last, she'd come home.

In this glass-walled tower, she'd be completely visible, so she could only assume that Kester had glamoured it somehow. Gripping her rucksack on her shoulders, she crossed into a hall. She moved quietly, unsure what she was walking into, and kept the lights turned off. Light from the streets filtered in through the windows, and Ursula let her eyes adjust as she tiptoed through the halls. Here the walls were a deep cream, and portraits of idyllic scenes hung on the walls—cherry orchards, a lake in autumn.

To her left was a dark stairwell, to her right, a living room. She peered into the dark room. The décor was more modern here: furniture upholstered in dark navy fabrics, the glint of stainless steel railings, and glass table tops. Kester had forgone the cozy feel of his tugboat for a modernist vibe in this part of the house.

She felt a pang of remorse for the demise of that tugboat. Kester loved that old thing, and there was no way it had survived the fall. It was probably at the bottom of the Hudson River.

As she moved quietly through the house, she realized something wasn't right in here. It didn't smell like Kester—the air had the lightning-seared-air scent of shadow magic. And when she saw what had been painted on the walls, her heart skipped a beat.

Along the hallway walls, someone had painted silver crescent moons, and the three-pronged sigil of Nyxobas.

It might have been Kester's house, but shadow demons had made this place their home. So where the hell was he?

She jumped as she heard muffled voices coming from the floor below. Slowly, she crept over to the stairwell, listening.

"Do you smell smoke?" It was a man's voice—his accent old-fashioned, posh as hell—but not Kester's.

Footsteps moved over the floor, the hardwood creaking. "I do, actually," said a second man. Also not Kester. "Now that you mention it." His voice was moving closer, now at the base of the stairwell.

Ursula's pulse raced, and she slipped back into the shadows. She strained her eyes to see in the dark, watching as two men moved up the stairwell, crossing toward the sigil room—one with long platinum hair, the other tall with close-cropped hair. The hair rose on the back of her neck as she watched them moving with a strange, preternatural grace. She'd seen creatures that moved like that in New York. Vampires—demons of the night who never mixed with hellhounds like her and Kester. In fact, they were natural enemies.

"There's fresh ash on the floor," said the close-cropped one in the sigil room.

Ursula pulled the sword from her scabbard. Moving quietly closer, she watched as the tall one pulled a small pistol from his pocket, while Blondie flicked on a light switch. Ursula blinked at the sudden glare. Just then, the floor creaked under her feet.

The two vamps whirled, staring at her, dark eyes glinting.

The vamp pointed the gun at her. "Put down the sword." He wore a dark nylon jacket. With his closely-shorn hair, he looked ex-military. Next to him, Blondie pulled out his own pistol, narrowing his eyes. "You wouldn't happen to be a hellhound, would you?"

Ursula gripped her sword, as power filled her limbs. In theory, vamps were easy to kill. All she had to do was decapitate them with her katana. But their guns made the situation a little more difficult.

"I said put down the blade!" shouted the soldier.

Her heart thudding, Ursula carefully placed the blade on the floor. Even without her blade, she still had Emerazel's magic. She summoned her fire, and it began blazing through her veins, her body heating.

"Stop that!" Blondie shouted. Just as flames began to lick at her fingertips, two gunshots rang out, the bullets penetrating the floor by her feet.

Okay. So maybe her fire magic wouldn't work against the bullets either. Slowly, she raised her hands. "What the hell happened to Kester?"

Soldier-vamp spoke first, his fangs flashing. "Lie on the floor and place your hands on top of your head."

Glaring at them, Ursula lay down. Best not get shot immediately upon arriving in London if she could help it.

"Don't move," said one of the vamps. The sound of a pistol cocking echoed through the room.

"A hound of the goddess," muttered the other.

"The king will know what to do with her."

A fresh burst of pain ripped through her skull as a boot met her temple, and then, darkness.

* * *

Ursula awoke in darkness, the floor below her trembling. A rumbling sound filled the air, the sound of tires on pavement, the distant hum of a radio. When she stretched out her legs, they immediately hit a barrier. *Bollocks. I'm in the boot of a car.*

Tight manacles bound her wrists behind her back. She might be able to melt them off, but perhaps lighting a fire while locked in the trunk of a car wasn't the best of ideas.

The car hit a bump and a fresh jolt of pain radiated from her temple as her head smacked against the floor. She could only hope the damn healing spells were fixing her brain, or she'd be losing *all* her memories sometime soon.

Quietly, she whispered Starkey's Conjuration Spell—the spell for healing—and the pain ebbed from her temples.

She could hear the engine slowing, the soft jolt of the car stopping. The engine cut, and two doors creaked open. A moment later the trunk swung open, and she stared up at Soldier-vamp, blinking her eyes. He was already pointing his pistol at her chest.

"You slept a long time, my darling," he purred.

Her mouth felt dry, and she swallowed hard. How long had she been out? Hours?

"Get out," said the vamp.

Slowly, Ursula crawled to her knees. When she glanced behind her shoulder, she could see the amber glow of Kester's glowing manacles—the kind that withstood Emerazel's fire. "Where is Kester?" she pressed.

"Save your questions for the king," the vamp snapped. "Get out."

Ursula slowly climbed out of the trunk, awkwardly throwing one leg over at a time, her bound hands making the movement difficult.

As she fumbled her way out of the car and dropped onto her feet, she surveyed her surroundings. They stood in a tiny car park, a patch of green grass to her right and towering brick buildings to her left, like old warehouses. When she looked up, she saw the word *OXO* on the side of the brick. They were at the Oxo Tower—one of London's most popular restaurants, right by the Thames. And if it was this quiet here, she'd been unconscious for several hours at least. The closest streetlight flickered a hundred yards away. Ursula shivered. At this time of night, the only people who'd hear her scream would be three sheets to the wind.

"Follow me." Soldier-vamp jerked his head, leading her onto a dark street along a park. The other took up position behind her, moving soundlessly over the pavement. When they moved onto the South Bank, the wide pedestrianized path by the river, the vamps kept her close to the Victorian brick buildings, moving in the shadows. Across the way, a man in a stained T-shirt stumbled by the railing, not making eye contact.

"Where are you taking me?" she asked.

"You'll see soon enough," said the vamp.

Even with the gun trained on her, she could probably just about get away with killing these two vamps if she summoned her magic fast enough. But that would leave her with two problems: one, she wanted to keep them alive long enough to find out what they knew. And two, the damn manacles. Even if she managed to somehow escape, she couldn't exactly go to the London police and ask them to help unlock the manacles that bound her wrists. They'd ask questions, maybe hand her over to the US demon-hunters desperate to end New York's dragon siege. She needed to find a way to persuade the vamps to free her hands.

The soldier looked furtively around him, and they crossed the darkened river-walkway toward the railway that overlooked the water. He stopped at a gate, and swung it open with a creak. From there, a concrete stairwell led down to the rocky shore of the Thames, which was at low tide.

Ursula arched an eyebrow. "The king lives on the riverbank?"

Soldier-vamp didn't answer her, just jerked his head to indicate she should follow him down the stairs.

A cool breeze rippled over the water, and a briny scent caressed her. Ursula shivered, wishing she'd worn something warmer. At the water's edge, Soldier-vamp turned to face her, his dark eyes glinting in the moonlight. He pointed his gun at her head. "Kneel. And take off your bag. Drop it on the rocks."

Her stomach swooped. *Bloody hell. There is no king. This is an execution.* She grimaced, summoning her fire power. Even if it meant losing a lead on Kester, she'd have to take them out before they shot her. She let Emerazel's magic pool in her core.

"Stop that!" shouted Soldier-vamp, cocking his gun.

The fire blazed through her body, ready to explode. She'd blow these bastards up—

A new, unfamiliar voice spoke from behind her, deeper and more regal. "Is this the hound you found in the Headsman's apartment?"

Ursula turned her head, her body blazing with heat. A man stood at the top of the steps—another vampire, this one with a faint crown of moonlight blazing from his fair hair. Maybe they weren't lying about a king, and maybe His Royal Majesty knew where Kester was. The fire in her veins began to dissipate.

He was taller and older than the other two vamps. He wore a crimson cloak around his shoulders cinched with a golden clasp shaped like an apple, but it was his hair that drew her eye. A blond so pale it was nearly silver, hanging sleekly to his shoulders. His ancient power whispered over her skin, singing of oak groves and dark magic. He looked a lot like the blond vamp standing to her right, only far more powerful. Almost beautiful.

"Yes father," said Blondie. "This is the hound."

The vamp king arched a black eyebrow. "You can quench your fire, hound. My sons will not kill you."

A million questions ran through her mind. "Who are you? What were you doing in Kester's apartment? Where is Kester? And why am I here?"

The two younger vamps now flanked the king.

"I am Mordred, and these are my sons," said the king vamp.

Ursula sucked in a sharp breath. "Mordred. From the King Arthur legends?"

Blondie grimaced at the mention of King Arthur. "My father is the *true* king of Britain."

Mordred cocked his head. "Relax. The hound has no way of knowing that the throne was stolen from me."

The three vampires studied her carefully as the Thames washed over the rocky shore. Cold mist rolled off the river bank.

It was time to get some answers. "And what does this have to do with Kester?"

Mordred's tongue flicked over his lips. "We believe Kester may have found the way to Avalon. You will help us find him."

Ursula shook her head. "Why should I help you with that?"

Mordred's sons aimed their guns at her chest. "Helping us is your only option if you want to live."

"I hate to disappoint the true king, but I don't know anything about the location of Avalon, or where Kester is. I came to London to find him. And I was frankly hoping you might know where he was."

"Is that right?" Mordred's dark eyes bored into her, the air around him darkening with whorls of black. "Well, we'll see what Agnes has to say about that."

Mordred turned to the river, holding out his hands toward the water as he began incanting a spell. The dark water flowed by, reflecting the city lights, then a pale blue sheen glimmered over the surface. Goosebumps rose on Ursula's arms as the temperature dropped.

The river's gentle ripples intensified into waves, until a dark form rose slowly from the water, half-enshrouded in mist. Ursula's fingers curled into fists behind her back, and she took an involuntary step backward.

Slowly, emerging from the foam, rose a crone. Long black hair covered her face, and her skin glowed like moonlight. She wore a tattered cloak over her shoulders, but it was open in the front, exposing drooping breasts, and her skeletal hands were clasped together.

"You have called upon me, Mordred?" Agnes's voice gurgled as she spoke. "You know the undead cannot answer the three questions."

"I have someone alive who wishes to speak to you."

Agnes sniffed the air, through her curtain of hair. "So you do. I smell one of Emerazel's hounds."

Ursula stared at the crone, half-mesmerized. A chill snaked up her spine at the sight of her. Ursula took another step back until one of Mordred's sons cocked a gun.

Inch by inch, Agnes glided closer through the fog. When she moved out of the dense mists, Ursula could see that the hag's cloak was the color of seaweed. Reaching into the shadows of her cloak, Agnes pulled out a faded gray rag. She kneaded the tattered fabric between her gnarled fingers.

"This blouse belonged to Emmeline. Beaten to death in her kitchen by her lover." Agnes raised her face, peering at Ursula through the hanks of her hair. Now Ursula could see a glimpse of milky white eyes. "What is *your* name, dearie?" Something in her voice compelled Ursula to answer.

"I'm Ursula."

"No surname?"

Ursula shook her head. "That's all I can remember."

Leaning back on her haunches, Agnes wrung the fabric between her hands, and blood dripped from it into the water. Ursula cringed.

Mordred sidled up to Ursula, and she felt him pull the manacles off her. He leaned in, whispering, "Ask her where Kester is."

At last her hands were free—yet she didn't want to run. She wanted to know where Kester was, too. "Where's Kester?"

The crone pushed her hair from her face, and Ursula's mouth went dry. Her face was marred by a dark hole where her nose should have been. Her milky eyes searched Ursula's face, and she lowered herself down to her hands and knees, crawling from the water.

"Kester?" hissed the crone, at the river's edge. She drew another cloth from her bundle and began kneading it over the rocks. "Kester has gone to the Castle in the Sea." She stopped working the cloth, looking up at Ursula. "Why did you forsake your betrothed?"

Ursula shook her head. "I'm going back for him. I can't help him right now."

"He needs you."

"I'm going to return. I just—"

Blondie jabbed Ursula with his elbow. "Ask her if she can be more specific about Kester's whereabouts."

"Where exactly is this Castle in the Sea?" she asked.

"The entrance rises from the sea of the great horn. Dumnonia. Only the pure may enter."

Soldier-vamp stepped forward, holding up a cell phone. His finger brushed the screen. A moment later he announced, "She's referring to Saint Michael's Mount. The entrance is there."

Mordred smiled, his hand going to the gold clasp at his throat. "Now we have everything we need to reclaim my rightful place as King of the Britons."

Something touched Ursula's knee. She looked down to see Agnes's hand, the fingers webbed. "Why did you try to kill your father?"

"I—" It took Ursula a moment to process the implications of the question. Her *father*? She had no idea who her father had been. In the wisps of memories that curled through her brain like smoke, she'd never remembered a father. An old man, yes, but he'd always seemed more like a grandfather. "I don't remember. I don't know why I tried to kill him."

"I can see the stain upon your soul," hissed the crone, rising to her full height. She towered above Ursula, staring down at her through rheumy eyes.

"I don't know..." said Ursula. "I don't remember."

Agnes spoke in a gurgling, sing-song voice.

> *"The end starts, when magic thickens the air,*
> *The lost, as if unburied from the soil*
> *Uncovered from the dankest roots of oaks."*

The strange words rang in Ursula's skull like a curse. Agnes was half-crazy, but maybe she had some answers in all her nonsense. The crone's pointed tongue flicked out, and she licked her lips, then pulled another piece of rag from her cloak—this one dark purple with a gold filigree. She lifted it into the moonlight, squinting at it. "I'd almost forgotten about this one. The betrayed and the betrayer. Met a fate she didn't deserve." She knelt again, rubbing it against the river rocks. "You may ask a final question," she said without looking up.

Ursula's mind raced. There was so much she wanted to know. Why had she lost her memory? Why had she tried to kill her father? Were her parents still alive? Where did she come from? The crone rose, turning to the river.

"Wait!" Ursula almost shouted. Slowly, the crone turned to face her. Ursula drew in a sharp breath. "Where do I come from? What happened to my parents?"

Agnes's black hair draped over her shoulders. "I can only answer one. Mount Acidale is where you took your first breath."

The words nearly knocked the breath out of Ursula. Mount Acidale? The crone began to slip into the fog, wading into the Thames again.

Ursula's heart raced, the floodgates opening. Suddenly she wanted to know everything. She needed the answers, *now*. She ran after Agnes, icy water soaking her boots. "Please. Tell me about my parents. Are they still in Mount Acidale?"

Foam rose around the crone, and she turned to Ursula a final time.

"This was your mother's." She handed the purple and gold rag to Ursula.

Ursula gripped the rag in her shaking hands, hardly aware of Agnes slipping beneath the surface of the river again.

Icy water rushed around her legs as she gaped at the cloth, running her fingers over the fabric, her legs trembling. In the moonlight, she could barely make out the texture of velvet, embroidered with gold-colored thread. Water ran in dark rivulets down between her fingers, and she stiffened when she realized it was blood. Her mother's blood.

Ursula's world tilted, and she stared at the blood on her fingertips. Did this mean her mum was dead? The woman she'd glimpsed in ghostly flashes in her mind, the woman with red hair who wielded a sword like a goddess? Cold sorrow crept over her mind like a dark mist, and yet not a single tear wetted Ursula's eyes. This was an icy, empty sorrow for a woman she couldn't remember, whom she must have loved but didn't know.

She stared at the sorry rag—the last remnants of her mum. This could be her only connection to her parents. Emptiness gnawed at her chest, and she knelt, dipping the cloth in the freezing river water, and gently rinsed the blood from it.

When Ursula rose and faced the shore again, she found that only the stony riverbank awaited her. Mordred and his sons had vanished, taking her things with them.

CHAPTER 7

*S*hivering, Ursula climbed the steps. She crossed the deserted river walkway, gripping the tattered scrap of fabric between her fingers. As she crossed back to the darkened parking lot, a heavy sadness weighed on her chest like a ton of rocks. The parking lot was completely empty, the only noise the wind rustling the leaves.

In a rubbish bin in the corner of the lot, she fished out a plastic bag and stuffed her mother's wet rag inside. Water sloshed between her toes as she walked, and she began to seriously regret her decision to run into the river. She hung a left at the end of the dark parking lot, just as thunder rumbled over the horizon and a few fat drops of rain dropped into her skin.

She turned into a park to her right, not quite sure where she was heading. She had no wallet, no phone—and worst of all, she had no weapons. She'd left her sword back at Kester's flat, and her reaping pen and kaiken dagger had been in her rucksack. Right now, she had nothing but a sad old rag.

Mist pooled in the dark park. Normally it might have been a good spot to find some uni students sharing a bottle of merlot, but at this hour, with the rain, she'd be lucky to find a drunk pissing in the bushes.

Shivering in the rain, she turned onto a road lined with brick buildings. So what had she learned? Kester was possibly in Avalon, and she had no idea how to get there. She'd learned that she had tried to kill her father, a man she couldn't remember at all, and that her mother was dead, leaving behind only a ragged bit of blood-stained cloth. Ursula's breath hitched in her throat.

Dead. The word rolled around her mind like a curse.

Ursula had sometimes wondered what her mother would look like now. Red hair graying at the temples, maybe—an older version of herself. Even if she'd never had a clear picture in her mind of reuniting with her mother, in the back of her mind, possibility had bloomed like a wild-flower. There'd been a *possibility* of reunion.

Death certainly changed that, the certainty of it weighing on her chest like a ton of rocks. She'd never felt more alone. Worse, the knowledge that her mother had died, and that she'd tried to kill her father, only confirmed her gnawing suspicions that she had rid herself of her memo-ries because she couldn't face the truth. What the hell had happened in Mount Acidale—wherever that was? Was it something to do with the dragons hunting her?

The dark thoughts roiled in her mind and she hardly knew where she was going. She wiped away a tear rolling down her cheek. She needed to find somewhere to stay for the night, and she wasn't sure she could check into a hotel at this hour. If she could get to a phone... She climbed the dark steps to the pedestrianized bridge, heading north of the river.

Ursula shivered as she crossed the bridge. Her trousers were sodden and freezing. Summer nights in London were chillier than in New York, and she hadn't dressed for the chill. Fog drifted off the river, the cool air kissing her skin.

As she crossed back toward the Thames she reached into the plastic bag, grasping the fabric again. Under the riverside lights, she examined it. It was part of a blouse, really just a sleeve and a ragged chunk of the bodice, made of purple velvet with gold thread embroidered along the sleeve. Given the quality of the silk, it must have been expensive. A lump rose in her throat as she gently rubbed the fabric between her fingers.

She couldn't remember this fabric. When she thought of her mother, it was only faint, insubstantial flashes—the red hair, a sword glinting in the sunlight. She couldn't remember the fabric of her mother's clothes, or the smell of her skin. Had Ursula once sat on her mother's lap and rested her head against this bit of dress? Had her mother stroked her hair, kissed her forehead, and pulled her against this purple silk when she was upset? Had her mother worn this fabric, bending over Ursula in bed to tell her stories or sing her lullabies before she fell asleep? She didn't know. For just an instant, she felt a sharp pang of longing so intense it nearly toppled her.

Dead. It was the certainty of it that robbed her of her breath.

As she walked across the bridge that spanned the Thames, Ursula wiped her hot tears on the back of her hand. The death of a possibility, pronounced in the crone's gurgling river-water voice.

What else had the woman said? 'Betrayed and betrayer.' Something about 'meeting a fate she didn't deserve.' Dread licked up Ursula's spine. Had her mother been murdered?

As she descended the bridge's steps, Ursula's mind churned. Before the river hag, she'd had nothing to go on. Now, she had a name: *Mount Acidale.* If she wanted answers about herself, her parents—about why the dragons were after her—that was where she needed to go. Her mind whirled as she walked, roiling with the possibilities of discovery.

The rain picked up, dampening her hair, and she walked down the narrow lane at the end of the bridge. Most of the shops and restaurants here were closed, and almost no one was around at this time of night. She shivered as she walked, hugging herself. She'd tried to kill her father? She had no memories of him whatsoever. Not even a faint wisp. Was *he* still alive? And if he was, were they enemies? Maybe she'd fled to London to get away from him.

She hugged herself, her clothing soaked by the rain. So what were her options now? She could sigil back to Kester's house, but it had apparently been taken over by vamps. They didn't take kindly to hellhound intruders. They couldn't move about in the daylight, so she'd have to wait until morning. Maybe she could get her bag then. For now, she had to find a place to sleep for a few hours. Too bad she had nothing—no wallet, and no phone. Just a rag, covered in her mother's blood.

What she needed right now—desperately—was a friend.

At the end of the street, she caught sight of a sign before the door of a stone building: *Studio 67.* Ursula hurried toward it. She practically cried with relief when she saw a few people milling under the awning, smoking on the pavement. She walked up to the crowd, clutching the plastic bag tightly in her hand.

A man in a dark jacket, his hair styled in gelled tufts, took a drag from a rollie.

Ursula nodded at him as she approached, catching his eye. "All right? My phone's dead. Do you mind if I borrow yours?"

"Sure." Puffing on his cigarette, he pulled a phone from his back pocket.

She flicked open the cell phone screen, trying to decide whom to call. There weren't many options. There was her former flatmate, Katie, and her ex-boyfriend, Rufus. Considering she'd rather punch herself in the face than speak to Rufus again, that left Katie. On the third ring, Katie picked up.

"Hello?" Music with a heavy bass pulsed in the background.

"Katie, it's… um… It's…" Ursula paused for a moment. After Ursula had become a hellhound, Emerazel's agents had told Katie she'd died of a drug overdose. How would she break the news to Katie that this wasn't actually the case? "It's Ursula. I'm not dead."

Ursula heard a sharp intake of breath. "Ursula? I've seen you on the news. What's all this about the dragons? I thought you was dead for ages. That's what they told me. I didn't even know demons was real until a few months ago. Then you're on the news with the—seriously, what the fuck is going on?"

"I'm not dead," Ursula reiterated. "It was… well, it was sort of a conspiracy. Look, you can't tell anyone I'm here."

"All those demon-hunters in America are after you. You know that, right?"

"I just learned recently. And right now I'm sort of stranded in London."

"But I don't get it. If you was alive, why did you disappear? Why didn't you ever call me? Seriously, what the fuck, Ursula?"

"I wanted to call, but I couldn't. I—look, it's a long story. Can I meet you somewhere?"

"Where are you?"

"I'm not far from Charing Cross. I've lost my cash and—well, everything, to be honest."

"Can you walk to District 5? I can keep it open a bit later for you."

"You work at Rufus's bar?" Ursula asked.

"Yeah."

"I'll be there. Give me time. I'm walking." She hung up the phone, handing it back to the man in the dark jacket. "Cheers."

He waggled an eyebrow at her. "You need anything else, love?"

Yeah. Just to find my hellhound friend in a mythical city so he can tell me how to defeat an army of dragons. "Nope."

Clutching the plastic bag, she picked up her pace, hurrying through the dark city. The closer she moved to Soho, the more people she passed, stumbling around in groups, trying to find night buses.

Dead. The word rang in her mind like a death knell, and a wave of sadness washed over her, threatening to pull her under. *Met a fate she didn't deserve.* Had her mother tried to protect her daughter, before she fled Mount Acidale? Ursula swallowed hard, determined to find out the answers—someday. First, she needed to survive the bloody dragon apocalypse, and then she'd learn the truth about herself. Or perhaps, those two goals would be one and the same.

Her fingers tightened around the bag. She still needed to find Kester—he alone knew how to stop these dragons, apparently. But before that, she needed to find a warm place to stay until the sun rose.

* * *

As the rain started to let up, Ursula strode down Wardour Street, heading for District 5, the underground bar often full of students and alcoholics from the film industry.

In the shadows of District 5's doorway, Katie's blond hair shone in a streetlight. She was standing by herself, puffing on a cigarette. When she spotted Ursula, she dropped the butt in a puddle, her face lighting up. She ran to Ursula, throwing her arms around her.

Ursula hugged her back. "Good to see you too."

"I thought you was dead. Seriously. That's what they told me."

Ursula pulled away from the hug. "I'm so sorry, Katie. I wanted to call, but Kester said I needed to start a new life."

Katie was a few inches shorter than Ursula, and she wore a red dress that hugged her curves. She pushed a flyaway blond hair from her eyes. "What are you on about? Who's Kester?"

Ursula shivered as a sharp gust of wind plastered her shirt against her back. "He's like my boss. He's the one who faked my death."

589

"He sounds like a knob end, but he can't be worse than Rufus. Rufus makes me look at his workout pictures on his mobile phone. Every bloody day, I have to pretend to be impressed."

"Kester's definitely not that bad. He's missing now." Ursula rubbed her arms for warmth.

"You're freezing. I can get you some dry clothes from the lost and found."

"Are you sure?"

"Of course. No one ever comes to collect that rubbish."

Katie started toward the door of the club.

"Wait," said Ursula. "Is Rufus in there? I really don't want to run into him."

"He's inside, but he's locked himself in his office to count his money. Doubt he'll come out. Why don't I meet you in the ladies' washroom? He'll never go in there."

"All right."

As Katie led Ursula down the stairs, the pounding of bass music reverberated off the walls. Ursula's stomach knotted as the memory of her last time in the club came roaring back. She'd burned a club patron, and Rufus—her ex—had fired her, right before introducing her to his new girlfriend. It was quite possibly the worst birthday of her life, though given her memory problem, she couldn't be entirely sure. As she moved into the club—at this point, populated only by the *very* drunk—she kept her head down and let her wet hair cover her face.

She pulled open the door to the women's room, the blue tiles of the room illuminated by teal lights above the sinks.

Shutting the door behind her, she let out a long sigh. The bathroom was empty. She turned to look at the mirror and pushed her hair from her face.

I look like a drowned rat.

She grabbed a paper towel from the dispenser and dabbed it over her face. The cheap paper scratched her skin, but at least it soaked up some of the rain.

The door creaked open, and Katie slipped into the bathroom clutching a bundle of clothes. "Got you some dry things." She held up a pair of leopard-print leggings and a turquoise halter top. "Sorry, hun. There wasn't much in the way of selection."

"It's fine," said Ursula, already pulling her soaked T-shirt over her head. Shivering, she slipped on the halter top. Although it left her arms and back bare—not to mention her cleavage—at least the dry cotton was a welcome relief.

Katie raised her perfectly tweezed eyebrows. "So are you going to explain the dragon thing, then?"

Ursula pulled off her damp trousers and shoved them into her plastic bag. "I don't honestly understand it any better than you do. I still have no memory. The dragons are after me. And a hag in the Thames just told me my mum was dead."

Katie's hand flew to her mouth. "Oh my God!"

Ursula pulled her boots over her leggings. She looked like a deranged stripper. "It's fine," she lied. "I don't remember her." For now, Ursula would leave out the bit about her trip to the moon. Might be a bit much to explain at three a.m. in the ladies' room of a dodgy club.

Katie's blue eyes widened. "Is it true what Rufus said, that you lit someone on fire here in the club? Like, with your hands?"

Ursula shrugged. "It was an accident. I didn't have control of my magic then."

Katie's jaw dropped. "So you're, like, a witch then? Rufus's girlfriend has a thing about witches."

"No, I'm not a witch. I'm sort of a..." She had no idea how Katie would react to this, but it couldn't be much weirder than what she'd already heard about her in the media. "I'm a hellhound. I can use fire magic."

Katie shook her head, disbelieving. "Since when? Why did you never tell me?"

"I didn't know, not till the night I disappeared." She pointed to the scar on her shoulder, exposed by the halter top. "I wasn't born a hellhound. Sometime before I lost my memory, I carved this. No idea why, but that meant when I turned eighteen, a hellhound came to collect me."

Katie's brow furrowed, and she took a step back. "So you're like... a demon, innit?"

"Look, you were my flatmate for a year. I'm the same person now as I was then." Ursula said it as convincingly as she could, but it rang hollow in her heart. The Ursula who'd worked at District 5 might as well have died the night she'd met Kester.

Katie bit her lip, still looking unsure of herself. "So what brings you back to London then? Escaping the dragons?"

"It's complicated—" Ursula started to reply, but Katie gasped.

"Oh my God! Is that blood?" She pointed to the plastic bag that held Ursula's mother's blouse. Red liquid dripped from the bottom onto the floor.

"I think so. I was trying to figure it out myself. The river hag gave it to me."

Katie's face paled, and she gaped at Ursula.

"I'm serious. It was the river crone. She said it was my mother's."

Katie nodded slowly. "Right. Look, maybe it's best if you get out of here. There's all sorts of people looking for you." Some kind of internal war seemed to be playing out on her features. "Do you have a place to stay?"

Ursula shook her head. With vamps in Kester's flat, she was shit out of luck. "Not exactly."

Katie took a deep breath. "Fine. Stay with me for the night. We'll figure something out, okay?"

Relieved, Ursula loosed a breath. "Thank you, Katie."

"Just try not to light anything on fire, would you? That flat is a death trap as it is."

* * *

When Ursula stepped out of the bathroom, clutching her plastic bag, her stomach flipped. Madeleine, Rufus's girlfriend, leaned against the bar in a tiny black dress with a gold jacket, clutching a glass of champagne. At the sight of Ursula, she slammed her champagne flute on the countertop and whipped out her phone. "Rufus!" She shouted over the thumping bass music. "We've got a situation!"

Ursula tried to shield her face with her hand, hurrying for the door. "I was just leaving." But Madeleine was going to pass on her image to the authorities. All the demon hunters in America were after Ursula. She stopped in her tracks, feeling the fire burn in her veins, and she turned to face Madeleine again.

Madeleine was shoving the phone back in her hand bag, all innocence. "I thought you were leaving."

"Give me your mobile."

"I don't know what you're talking about," said Madeleine, fiddling around in her handbag. In all likelihood, she was trying to upload the video already. "I don't even have my mobile on me." She turned her head back to the office. "Rufus! What the bloody hell are you doing?"

As her head was turned, Ursula snatched Madeleine's Chanel handbag off her shoulder. Quick as lightning, Ursula's fingers were on the phone. She'd burn the bloody thing.

But as the hellfire erupted from her fingers, pain seared her muscles. The flames were actually burning *her*. *What is wrong with my fire?* The screen popped, shattering with the acrid scent of burning plastic.

"Rufus!" shouted Madeleine. "It's Ursula. She's here. She's mugging me!"

By this point, a small crowd had begun forming around them.

Ursula dropped the scorched metal husk back into the Chanel handbag. "Sorry about your phone." She thrust the bag back at Madeleine. "I have a feeling you can afford a new one."

"Rufus!" Madeleine screeched. "The demon is here! A demon!"

Abruptly, the music stopped, and the club lights flicked on. Rufus pushed open his office door, narrowing his eyes at Ursula. "What the hell is going on in here?"

Madeleine pointed, her finger shaking. "That's the woman the dragons are after. I think she might be one of their own."

"Don't be ridiculous," said Katie. "Everyone knows Ursula's in America. This is just someone who looks like Ursula."

A valiant attempt at deflection, but an unconvincing one.

An overweight man stumbled forward, his beer sloshing from his pint glass. "Fuckin' hell, is that really the dragon girl? How much money they offerin' for her?"

Ursula's body tensed. "It's been lovely catching up, but I'm afraid I have to go."

As she headed for the door, the overweight man blocked her path. "Hang on a minute, love."

Before Ursula could push past him, Madeleine was by her side again, clutching a vial of red powder, which she flung into the air. The sensation when it landed on Ursula's skin was unlike anything she had ever felt before. It was pure unrelenting pain, like her skin was being peeled from her muscles. She screamed, falling to the floor.

Madeleine stood over her. "Rufus. You need to take her to the Brotherhood. The iron dust will extinguish her dragon magic. You can handle her."

Rufus scratched his blond stubble, staring down at her. "Take her how?"

"Don't touch her!" shouted Katie. "Your girlfriend's a crazy bint. You know that, right? If you touch her, I will fucking glass you. I'm not messing about."

Rufus held out his hands. "Now that's uncalled for."

Katie leaned down, catching Ursula under the shoulders and pulling her up. "Can you stand?"

With Katie's help, Ursula managed to push her way up to her feet. And as she did, she caught a glimpse of the ring of lit up cell phones around them. *Bollocks.*

Madeleine scowled. "Rufus! You need to stop her!"

"I just feel a bit awkward about it," Rufus whinged.

Leaning against Katie, Ursula stumbled toward the door, desperate to wash her skin of the iron dust. Kester had warned her about this stuff— not only would it singe away her magic, but it would sear her skin in the process. She shuffled to the door, trying to block out the agony.

At last, when she made her way through the door, the cold rain was a blessed relief on her skin. She pulled away from Katie, tilting her face to the sky. She let the raindrops wash the powder from her face, cleaning her. Her muscles relaxed just a little, and she wiped the mixture of dust and rain off her skin.

"Thank you for helping me," she said to Katie.

"No problem. Rufus is a total bell-end, and Madeleine's a stuck-up psycho cow. I'm sure you know that."

"Won't you be fired? He doesn't like people defying him."

"Probably, but I was planning on quitting anyway."

Behind them, the door creaked open, and Rufus stood in the doorway, appraising her with his cool blue eyes.

"I have you on video," he said.

"I don't really give a shit."

"The reward for your return is ten million dollars." He adjusted the cuffs of his crisp white shirt. "The rent in Soho doesn't come cheap, you know."

She crossed her arms. "What do you want?"

"Is it true that a demon pays you? In gold?"

Absolute wanker. He's trying to blackmail me.

As the iron dust washed off her skin Ursula could feel the fires of Emerazel pooling in her body, caressing her ribs. Staring at Rufus, she held up a hand. Raindrops sizzled and popped as flames started to lick along her skin. Fire burned from the tips of her fingertips, and a wicked smile curled her lips. "Do you really think that will happen, Rufus?"

She watched his throat bob as he swallowed. "It was Madeleine's idea."

"The demon hunters she's mixed up with are not a good crowd. Do you understand me?"

His skin had gone pale, and he nodded mutely, seemingly transfixed by the flames that danced along her arms.

"You need to give Katie a raise. If I hear that you've fired her, I will come back and brand my name on your arse. Do you understand?"

Rufus nodded again. "Of course," he stammered.

Ursula held out her hand. "Now I just need the money I was never paid the night you fired me. My last paycheck."

Rufus pulled his wallet from his back pocket, handing it to her. She cracked it open, counting the pound notes.

"Only a hundred and thirty pounds? Business not doing so well?" Pocketing the cash, she turned to Katie. "I'll cover our cab fare home."

CHAPTER 8

The sun was staining the sky with streaks of pumpkin and violet. She'd tucked her mother's blouse, still wrapped in the plastic bag, under her arm.

Here in this kitchen was where it had all begun months ago—where Kester had first arrived and broken the news that she was a hellhound. Back then, her life had been a disaster—but a mundane disaster. No job, no education, no money for rent. Dumped and fired by Rufus in the same week.

Now she had money, but also a whole lot more trouble. She had an army of dragons after her, and the past that she'd tried to escape from was coming back to haunt her. Her mum was dead. She'd tried to murder her own father. What terrible secret would she uncover next?

Ursula glanced at the note she'd left for Katie—just a heartfelt *thank you,* and an explanation that she'd be in touch when she could. It was vague on the details, though Katie might wonder what had happened to her kitchen.

In any case, Ursula needed her sword back from the vamps, and she was pretty sure she knew where to find it. She grabbed Katie's vodka off the counter, pouring it around herself in the shape of a fire sigil. When she'd finished, she picked up Katie's lighter and ignited the sigil, chanting the spell for Kester's apartment. Flames seared the air around her in a rush of fiery power, and her body crumbled to ash.

In the next moment, she found herself standing in Kester's sigil room, the morning sunlight streaming through the windows. Just as she'd thought, the vamps had taken cover from the sunlight, probably in the basement. As quietly as she could, she crept through the hall, frowning at the crescent moons painted over the walls. There on the rich leather of one of the living room sofas was her rucksack. Even better, the katana lay underneath it, resting in its scabbard.

She opened the rucksack up and shoved her mother's blouse inside, then took the opportunity to change into some fresh clothes—black leggings and a matching shirt. Then, she grabbed the bag from the sofa, slung her sword and scabbard around her waist, and crossed to an oak desk that stood in the corner.

She pulled open the little drawers until she found what she was looking for. Cash. Just as she'd expected, Kester's desk was crammed with gold pieces and pound notes. For someone with that much money, he didn't even bother safeguarding it. This was chump change to him. Still, she'd pay him back. She stuffed a few hundred in her rucksack—along with the money from Rufus, this might come in handy if she needed to stay in hotels while in London.

Fully stocked with money, her sword, and her rucksack, she crept down the stairs to the front door. She pulled it open onto the milky morning light, squinting in the sun's rays. She hadn't slept nearly enough last night, but at least she'd gotten a few hours' rest.

Walking around in London with a sword had to be completely illegal. She didn't know of a specific law against sword carrying, since it didn't tend to happen often these days, but you weren't allowed to carry knives, and a sword was a step up from that. Not to mention the fact that she had a kaiken dagger and a reaping pen hidden in her rucksack. Still, she'd just have to count on the fact that Londoners saw enough weird shit around Brick Lane to not blink an eye.

Her stomach rumbling, she crossed toward Brick Lane. At this hour, hardly anyone was out and about on Fournier Street, but she should be able to find an open coffee shop within a few blocks. Her mouth watered at the thought of breakfast.

On the narrow, winding street that was Brick Lane—a relic of an ancient brewery—Ursula picked up her pace, a coffee shop in her sights. On the pavement outside a café—charmingly named Wankoffee—she stepped over a sleeping man in a suit who'd obviously had a bit too much fun last night. Gods, it felt good to be back in London, even if she was in the most ridiculous part of the city.

Inside Wankoffee, a young man with muttonchops, a mesh baseball cap, and an olive green cravat leaned on the countertop, glaring at her from between expensive chrome coffee equipment. Around the room, drawings decorated the walls, along with neon lights and large mirrors.

Ursula eyed the food in the glass countertop, her stomach rumbling. "Can I please have two bagels with cream cheese, a milky coffee, and an orange juice?" She pulled out a twenty-pound note, plopping it on the bar.

The barista glared at her for another, long moment. Then, wordlessly, he began fixing her order. While he did, her gaze flicked to the TV, and her stomach clenched. There on the screen was Ursula, kneeling on the floor of District 5, covered in iron dust, dressed in the turquoise halter. Her heart thrummed in her chest. Apparently, the barista hadn't noticed yet, but he had been awfully busy glaring sullenly.

"I'm getting it to take away, please," she said, her cheeks reddening.

He grunted, snatching a paper cup, and Ursula stared as the news got worse. Already, a dragon had attacked tourists outside of the Tower of London. A helmet-haired news anchor breathlessly reported the international plans to increase the reward for her capture to one hundred million dollars.

As soon as the barista had her order ready, Ursula snatched it up and hurried outside, keeping her face covered by her hair. If only she had a bit of Zee's glamouring ability, she'd be in much better shape. She turned into a narrow alley and pulled her mobile phone from her rucksack. Maybe Zee could help. She flicked open the screen, finding about 3423 missed calls from Zee. She pushed *return call.*

After a few rings, Zee picked up, her voice rough. "What the hell's going on? I've been up all night. Have you seen the news? I've been ringing you and you haven't picked up."

"Sorry. I just got my phone back."

"What the hell did you do, Ursula? You weren't supposed to bring the dragons to London. You were simply supposed to find Kester, and to find out what he knows about the dragons."

"Well, I didn't find Kester. I found a hive of vampires in his flat, who abducted me. I went to a friend for a place to stay, and I got caught on video."

Zee paused. "You were abducted by vampires?"

"Yes, they were waiting in the apartment. They're also searching for Kester. Mordred said—"

"*Mordred?* Like from the Arthurian legends?"

"Yes, apparently he is an ancient vampire."

"Shit," said Zee. "Do you think this has anything to do with the books Kester had hidden on his table? The ones about ancient Britain?"

"Seems that way. Mordred and his sons are looking for the path to Avalon. They believe Kester may have found it. I'm not yet sure if this is connected to the dragons, but apparently that's where Kester went." Ursula sucked in a deep breath. "What happened to Bael?"

"Cera still hasn't returned with him, so I honestly have no idea. I'm going to start searching soon, but I've been preoccupied with your latest chaos."

A tendril of dread curled through Ursula. She could only hope Bael wasn't out there slaughtering people. "Okay. Let me know if you hear anything. But until then, do you know why Kester would be interested in Avalon?"

"No idea," said Zee. "All I know is that it's associated with the sea god Dagon, but I'll poke around in the library and see if I can come up with anything."

"That would be fantastic."

"So what's your plan?" Zee asked. "When are you coming back to New York?"

She bit her lip. "If I want to find out how to defeat the dragons, I think it means a trip to Avalon, if I can get there. The river hag said there's an entrance in St. Michael's Mount in Cornwall."

"How are you getting there without being spotted?" Zee asked.

"I haven't exactly figured that out yet."

"Do you know how to drive?"

"Rufus tried to teach me, but no, not really. Or at all. I could watch a YouTube video."

"You'll be fine. It's easy. Look, Kester parks his cars in a private garage on Cheshire Street, not far from his flat. He keeps a set of keys in a magnetic box under the front right wheel, which I know because he had me glamour it for him. It's invisible, but you can feel it. Take the Lotus."

Ursula swallowed hard. "I'm worried people will recognize my hair. It's long, and rather bright."

"Can you get a pair of scissors and a hat?"

* * *

WITH A SHOWER CAP over her new bob (it was the best she'd been able to do), Ursula whipped down the A30 to the throaty hum of the Lotus's engine. Getting out of London hadn't been too difficult. She'd only stalled the Lotus twice, both times at stoplights. Once she'd merged onto the motorway, the verdant hills of the British countryside had flown past. After an hour of driving, she'd pulled over at a roadside stop to catch a few more hours of sleep before rolling out again. The engine churned as she pressed her foot to the accelerator. Right now, the traffic wasn't too bad.

Her katana lay under her rucksack, next to her on the passenger seat. It felt good to have a proper blade with her, on top of her dagger and her reaping pen.

Out here on the open road, she pulled off her shower cap, grinning at her chic bob. She actually hadn't done a bad job with it, and the red hair framed her face beautifully.

In Cornwall, she pulled off the A30 and into a roundabout. The gray water of the Atlantic glimmered on the horizon, and she caught her first glimpse of St. Michael's Mount. Situated in the center of the bay, a conical island rose majestically from the water, shrouded in mists. At its peak, the St. Aubyn Castle glinted in the afternoon sun. Out here, lush greenery covered the island and the roadsides.

She drove along the winding coastline until she passed a blue sign reading *Marazion—Ancient Market Town and St. Michael's Mount*. Here, the meandering road took her into a town center, the streets lined with shops —squat stone or white-walled buildings. After parking the Lotus outside the tiny, stone house she'd arranged to rent on her way here, she stepped out of her car.

The air smelled of the sea, and for just a moment, she thought of Bael, wanting to smell him, to touch his golden skin. The amber sunlight gave Marazion's rough stone walls a warm, almost Mediterranean appearance.

Perhaps it was time she invested in a proper hat of some kind, but for now, a hoodie would have to do, and she rifled around in her bag until she found one. She zipped it up, pulling up the hood, then grabbed her things, heading for the flat. Just as she'd been told, the key lay tucked under the mat.

The apartment she'd booked online was smaller than it had looked in the pictures, but cozy. The living room walls were painted a clean white, and windows looked out onto the ocean. She dropped her bag on a brown leather sofa, then hid her sword under it.

She plopped onto the sofa and pulled out her mobile phone, hoping for an update about Bael, but there was nothing. She texted Zee.

Any news about Bael?

A minute later, a blue text appeared on her screen. *Nope. Cera fell asleep. I'm out hunting for the bastard.*

Ursula let out a long breath, half-wondering if she should be out hunting for Bael. If he didn't show up soon, she'd return to New York to help find him. Maybe the river hag had been right. Maybe he needed her.

Exhausted, Ursula let her eyes drift closed. She hardly felt herself falling into a deep sleep, dreaming of pale blue eyes, of fields dappled with yellow wildflowers, and the smell of sandalwood.

Her rumbling stomach woke her with a start, just as the setting sun began staining the room crimson. It had been hours since she'd eaten, and she needed to fill her belly.

First food—then Avalon. Except she had no idea how to get there. An entrance, through St. Michael's Mount. And how, exactly, was she supposed to operate that? She didn't suppose the vampires would allow her to tag along.

* * *

In the King's Arms, Ursula sat at the bar over a plate of fish and chips and a pint, still keeping the hood up. In the halter top and leopard print leggings, she'd looked like a crazy stripper in the videos—plus the clips had been dark and fuzzy. The other photo circulating of her was several years old. People didn't have a lot to go on. And yet, with millions of dollars on the line, any ginger chick would be suspect.

Ursula took a bite of her fried fish, savoring the rich, salty taste. She glanced at the TV, the news still dominated by the story about dragons attacking London. And by the time she was halfway through her meal, bloody Rufus was on the telly, trying to look sympathetic and aggrieved.

"I always knew she was barmy," he said into a microphone. "If it hadn't been for Madeleine…" He let his voice break, feigning emotion. "I might no longer be here."

Ursula wanted to reach through the telly and smack him.

"Everything all right, miss?" asked the bartender.

"Everything's great," said Ursula. "Just finishing up."

Grabbing a handful of chips, she hurried out the door into the evening air. Outside, sea air kissed her skin and pale moonlight washed the road in pearly light. At night, she wouldn't have to worry quite so much about being recognized.

Keeping her hood pulled up, she began walking toward the sea. She licked her lips, tasting the faint hint of salt. As she walked along the cobbled sidewalk, the distant lapping of waves filled the air.

Ursula pulled out her phone again to text Zee. This time, she simply wrote, *Anything?*

The reply came a few moments later. *Nope.*

Worry tightened her stomach. *What the hell happened to him?* After she scoped out Avalon, she was heading back to help find him.

At last, at the end of a row of white cottages, St. Michael's Mount came into view, and she sucked in a long breath. It towered over the water like a primordial god of rock and sea. Illuminated by spotlights, its peak glowed amber.

As she breathed in the fresh sea air, the hair on her arms stood on end. The air smelled faintly of shadow magic, and she glanced back down the road behind her, catching a glimpse of three figures. They walked with the unnerving grace of vampires, and the tall one in the center had the long, white-blond hair of Mordred.

Ursula turned, keeping her head down as she walked, skulking through the shadows. She stole a quick glance behind her. Not far behind, practically following in her footsteps, were the three vamps. She pulled her kaiken dagger from the sheath under her sweatshirt, and when she got to a narrow alley between cottages, she slipped into the shadows.

The vampires passed her without so much as a glance in her direction. A few houses down, the vampires cut to the right, moving out of sight. Ursula followed them, keeping to the shadows. When she got to where they had turned, she peered around the edge of the building. They'd taken a path that led down to the water. She couldn't see them on the darkened beach, among the sea grass. Quietly, she snuck down, startling at the sound of an engine starting. As she moved along the sand in the dim light, she spotted a small boat motoring into the bay, heading straight for St. Michael's Mount. Would they know how to get into Avalon, how to find the entrance?

Her heart racing, she ran down to the beach toward the calm sea, but it was at least a quarter mile to the island. Even if she swam, the vamps would be long gone by the time she reached to the rocky shore. Scowling, she turned back to the town. Her trip to the island would have to wait until morning.

CHAPTER 9

*I*n the little rented cottage, hot water poured over Ursula's skin, soothing her body. After washing her new bob and scrubbing down her body, she stepped out into the steamy, white-tiled bathroom. The glass of merlot she'd poured for herself earlier still stood on the tile counter. She dressed in a matching set of pink knickers and a bra, then pulled on a blue T-shirt and dried off her hair. But as she pulled open the door to the living room, she froze. Something felt wrong here, as if a powerful, dark magic was pooled in the room. Ursula flicked on the light in the living room, and her heart skipped a beat.

Bael stood barefoot in the center of the carpet, dressed in a black shirt and trousers far too small for him, his eyes the color of blood. Water drenched his clothing and hair, droplets sliding down his golden skin. Shadow magic whirled from his muscled body, seeming to snake and writhe along the vicious tattoos on his forearms.

Ursula dove for the katana, snatching it from where she had it hidden under the bed. Rolling to her feet. she pointed the blade at his chest. "Just trying to keep you at bay, my dear—"

Bael growled and charged for her in a blur of shadow magic, ripping the sword from her grasp. The next thing she knew, he was pinning her to the wall by the fireplace, his powerful body pressed against hers, clothing dampening hers. He stared down at her, eyes blazing crimson.

"You made me into a monster." he snarled, his hands gripping her wrists possessively. Shadows darkened the air around him, sending icy fear up her spine.

"You were going to die," she said. "It was the only way."

He leaned in, sniffing her throat, his eyes closing. For just a moment, his lips curled back from his teeth, and his mouth moved closer to her neck.

Bollocks. He was in complete control here, and there was not a damn thing she could do about it unless she wanted to burn him. But when his teeth grazed her neck—surprisingly gently—a shiver of pleasure rippled through her body. Strangely enough, she found herself tilting back her head, a silent invitation.

Bael smelled of sandalwood and sea air, and when he lifted his face from her neck, peering down at her, the blood-red seemed to fade. His irises slowly shaded back to pale gray ringed with deep blue, a stunning contrast with his gold skin, his black lashes. A dark heat burned in his eyes, and Ursula was struck once more by his godlike beauty. Slowly, the shadows around him receded, and he released his grip on her. For just a moment, he lifted his hand, rolling the ends of her shorn hair around his fingers. "You cut your hair."

A smile curled her lips. "What do you think?"

"Beautiful."

Heat warmed her core, and she smiled again.

Bael blinked as if waking from a dream and stepped away. For a few moments, they simply stared at each other, and Ursula tried desperately to clear her mind, to forget the feel of his powerful body against hers, or his mouth on her neck.

At last, when she could think straight again, she asked, "What are you doing here?"

"Zee found me. She told me you were headed for Cornwall." He spoke softly now. "I know the dragons are after you, and I thought you could use my help." Shadows slid through his eyes. "Assuming I can control the blood fury. Sorry about…" Trailing off, he gestured at the fireplace.

"It's fine. You seem better than the last time I saw you." She shook her head. "I don't understand. How did you get here so fast? And how did you know where I was? I texted Zee not that long ago."

He arched a dark eyebrow. "You have your ways of traveling, and I have mine."

"Nyxobas's waters, I take it." She frowned. "The Forgotten Ones—"

Bael shrugged. "Were not a problem this time. Zee told me you're looking for Avalon. The location is shrouded in mystery. Have you learned anything?"

"Sort of. I know it's somewhere on St. Michael's Mount."

"How did you find that out?"

"A river hag told me, and Mordred and his sons took a boat there tonight."

Bael shook his head. "Mordred. Of course."

"You know him?"

"He's one of Nyxobas's most powerful vampires. I did business with him a long time ago." Bael turned, walking for the door. When he reached the threshold, he turned back to her, his pale eyes piercing. "Aren't you coming?"

"Where?"

"To St. Michael's Mount."

"We don't have a boat."

"The tide is ebbing. We will be able to walk along the causeway."

* * *

WITH HER SWORD at her hip, Ursula walked by Bael's side along the cobblestone path toward the sea. He kept his distance from her, not uttering a word.

At last they reached the beach, where moonlight bathed the sand in silver. The lights at the castle's peak had been turned off, and St. Michael's Mount loomed dark and mysterious in the middle of the misty bay. Starlight streamed through the fog.

Bael moved swiftly over the sand, and Ursula had to hurry to keep up with him. She got the distinct impression that he wanted to maintain space between them—that if he got too close, he'd find his teeth hovering over her neck again.

"What do you know about Avalon?" she asked.

"Hardly anyone knows anything about Avalon," he said. "Only what you've heard in legends. King Arthur was buried there, and Excalibur beside him."

"Excalibur," she murmured. "It's a magical sword, I suppose?"

"Yes." The sea breeze toyed with a few strands of his black hair. "And it kills dragons."

"Ah. So that's why Kester came here." She frowned. "And why are you helping me?"

"You're in danger. I can help protect you."

"Why do you want to?"

At the sea's edge, he stepped barefoot into the water. She looked him up and down, for the first time realizing why his clothes fit so poorly. He'd come through one of Nyxobas's portals, which meant he'd arrived naked.

"Where did you get your trousers?"

"I borrowed the clothes from a gentleman sleeping on a bench."

"Is he okay?"

"He'd imbibed too much alcohol."

"I see."

Bael took a few more steps into the sea, then stopped and turned back to face Ursula. The waves lapped around him and the hulk of St. Michael's Mount loomed ominously in the distance.

Ursula didn't want to ask about his bloodlust, but she had to know what she was facing if she was going to venture out into the dark waters with him.

Bael turned to look at her, his pale eyes glinting in the silver light. "Are you coming?"

"What stopped you from biting my neck back at the cottage?"

His penetrating gaze rooted her in place. "I only temporarily lost control of the hunger. It won't happen again. I'm nearly rid of it."

"Okay." Ursula sat on a rock and unzipped her boots, pulling them off. "So you really traveled all the way here to help me?"

"That's not the only reason."

She stuffed her boots into her rucksack. "And what's the other?"

"I also have unfinished business with the Queen of Avalon. I haven't been able to find her. The path to the Fortunate Isle has been lost for centuries."

She rose. "Do you suppose we're on the right track?"

"I cannot say. It is said that you must possess a Torc of Malicus to enter. But the path itself has been lost for centuries."

Ursula gripped her rucksack as she waded into the water. She'd expected sand, but instead round cobbles met her feet, like a road beneath the dark water. She followed Bael through the shallow water, the icy waves lapping at her ankles. As she walked, she shivered, wishing she'd worn something heavier.

As they walked through the water, her senses seemed to intensify: the nighttime breeze that caressed her bare arms, the taste of salt on her lips, and the rhythmic lapping of the waves. Bael walked gracefully ahead of her, barely more than a dark shadow. She tried not to think about the bloodlust that had nearly consumed him earlier.

The sea receded as they walked, the tide continuing to ebb. As the water thinned, Ursula looked down at the cobblestone causeway beneath her feet.

When they reached the shore, the path sloped gently upward over rock, the stones now dry under her feet. Ahead of her, at the base of a stone wall, Bael stopped and sniffed the air.

"What are you doing?" asked Ursula.

"I can smell the vampires." Bael stared into the darkness, then whispered, "Get your sword out."

Holding her breath, Ursula unsheathed her katana.

With the vamps scented, Bael picked up the pace, and Ursula had to practically run over the cobblestones to keep up. The path sloped sharply upwards, lined by a rough stone wall on one side eventually giving way to lush greenery and thick woods. Above, the dark castle towered over the island. Ursula's breath burned in her lungs as she jogged along just behind Bael.

Suddenly he stopped, holding up a hand. Up ahead, a shout pierced the air.

"What is going on?" she whispered.

"If we are indeed in the right place, those screams mean someone has woken Cormoran."

Cormoran? Whoever that was. Ursula was beginning to remember Bael's infuriating tendency to leave out key details until they were in the thick of it. Before Ursula could press him on this point, another scream ripped through the quiet night.

A dark form swooped over their heads, followed by a crack behind them as it smacked into the trunk of an oak. Ursula strained her eyes in the dim moonlight, her stomach clenching as she recognized the headless body of one of Mordred's sons. In the next moment, the body turned to ash.

Bael turned to his left, nodding at a rocky hill thickly overgrown with brush. "We keep going."

"Who or what is Cormoran?" she hissed.

Ignoring her question, Bael launched into a sprint, and Ursula chased after him, gripping her sword.

Fast as lightning, he moved up the rocky hillside, and Ursula ran after him, weaving through the shrubs. As they moved, the surroundings seemed to change, growing more thickly forested with oak and hazel.

At last, they burst into a clearing at the top of the mount. Ursula caught her breath, staring up at the dark fortress. The castle stood off to the side on top of a series of battlements. In the dark, she nearly missed the enormous man looming over them, until he stepped into a shaft of moonlight.

Ursula's heart skipped a beat, and she took a step back. The man had to be twenty feet tall, his hair long and greasy, and he wore only a tattered loincloth. In one hand he held a monstrous club. In the other, he gripped Mordred's remaining son. Mordred himself was nowhere to be seen.

"That's Cormoran," said Bael next to her.

The vampire flailed wildly in the giant's grip, his eyes wild with fear. Suddenly, Cormoran threw him high in the air, the vamp's body catching the moonlight. As the vamp fell to earth, the giant swung his club like a baseball bat. With a crack of shattering bone he severed the vamp's head, sending it rocketing into the night sky like a cannonball. Ursula's stomach dropped. *Holy hells.*

With a feral roar Bael charged at the giant. *Maniac. He doesn't even have a weapon.* Cormoran swung for him with his club, but with a burst of shadow magic Bael soared over the swing, clutching onto the beast's shoulder. He pulled himself into position on Cormoran's back and locked his arms around the giant's neck. The giant spun, dropping his club to claw at his back, but he couldn't reach Bael.

Her grip tightening on her sword, Ursula stepped closer, starting to circle the giant, her eyes on Bael. His muscular arms squeezed against the giant's throat like the coils of a snake, and the giant's face reddened, his eyes bulging. The giant stopped swatting at its back, bringing its hands to its throat instead. Slowly it began to peel Bael's arms away, sucking in a ragged breath. Bael needed help.

Ursula lunged, slashing at the giant's leg with her katana, but the blade seemed to bounce off his skin. *No wonder he's not wearing anything.*

Grunting, the giant peeled Bael's other arm from his throat. With a brutal jerk, Cormoran pulled Bael off his back, holding up the Lord of Abelda with one arm. Frantically, her heart beating a wild tattoo, Ursula slashed and jabbed at the giant's legs, but her sword wouldn't penetrate the skin.

"Begone, demon," Cormoran roared, in a voice that sounded as if his vocal cords were made from flayed flesh. He reared back his head and flung Bael into the darkness. Ursula's stomach dropped, as the giant turned to face her. Still, she had to believe Bael was all right, given that he'd survived a fall from the top of the Plaza Hotel.

Cormoran's tongue flicked over his purple lips. "Now, you're a pretty one."

Emerazel's fire stirred within her. It was one thing to be attacked by a giant, but it was quite another to be objectified by one.

She pointed her sword at the giant, knowing it would do fuck-all against him, but bravado was about all she had in her arsenal right now. "Where is Mordred?"

The giant growled, reaching for her with one of his massive hands. She dodged, barely escaping his grasp.

"I won't hurt you, my little lovely," he purred.

Ursula dodged again as he snatched at her. So far, she'd been able to stay out of his reach, but she could also see he was slowly herding her toward the castle battlements behind her, trying to block her in. If she got too close to the walls, there would be no room to dodge. She needed a plan. Perhaps the battlements could actually be useful.

As the giant reached for her, she dove under his grasp, then rolled between his legs. She leapt up and broke into a sprint toward the castle, somehow moving as fast as phantom wind.

The giant picked up his club. "You can run, little thing, but you cannot hide."

Ursula sprinted up the hillside, letting the winds carry her, as

Cormoran lumbered after her, until she reached a small battlement—a six-foot-high stone wall holding back the cliff face. She threw her sword on top of it before pulling herself up after it. Cormoran paused as he reached it.

"Now I've got you," said the giant, placing a hand on a parapet, trying to box her in.

Ursula picked up her katana and ran back a few paces before turning to face the giant again. Then she charged, leaping into the air as Bael had done. However, unlike Bael, she had a weapon, and she used it to stab at Cormoran's face.

She aimed for his eye, but he ducked and she only grazed his forehead. Worse, she had miscalculated the height of the battlement. Between the height of her leap, the height of the wall, and the steeply sloping hillside she was now a good fifteen feet in the air. Tumbling as she hit the slope, she curled into a ball and rolled head over heels. She didn't hear any bones crack, but she lost her grip on her sword. At the bottom of the hill, she crawled to her feet, a little woozy.

An earth-shattering crash rumbled the ground next to her— Cormoran landing on the grass. Before she could dodge, he caught one of her ankles in a vise-like grip.

"Gotcha, little one." He lifted her into the air, dangling her upside-down in front of his face. He stared at her with yellow eyes, his fleshy tongue wetting his lips. His hot breath reeked of rotten meat. "You'll be an obedient little wife, now, won't you?"

Blood trickled from the gash on his forehead. As he pulled her closer to his face, Ursula swung her body closer and punched him hard in the cut.

Cormoran grinned. "Oh, I like when tiny ones put up little fight first."

A feral roar rumbled over the horizon, sending a shiver over Ursula's body. She didn't have to turn her head to know it was Bael.

The giant dropped her and she hit the ground hard, pain splintering her skull. Coughing, she rolled over to see Bael leaping for Cormoran. Everything seemed to move in slow motion, Bael's blood-red eyes flashing in the silvery light.

His fist slammed into Cormoran's face, and the giant went down hard, sending shudders through the earth. His lips sagged, and his eyes rolled back into his head. He was out cold.

Ursula crawled to her knees, rubbing the back of her skull. Her entire head throbbed, and dizziness washed over her. Nausea climbed up her gut. She couldn't quite manage standing yet. Just a few yards away, Bael stood with his back to her, his muscled body rigid with tension.

"Bael?" she asked tentatively.

Next to her, the giant's body twitched.

"Stay away." Dark magic stained the air around him.

One of the giant's fingers moved in the grass.

"Bael, Cormoran is still moving."

When Bael turned to look at her again, his eyes had returned to that beautiful, pale gray, though a dark hunger still burned in them. "We need to hurry. He will revive soon." He crossed to her and offered his hand, helping her to her feet. "Nice work cutting him on his forehead. The blood blinded him."

The giant took a shuddering breath.

Silver light glinted in Bael's eyes. "I think we've come to the right place."

"And what makes you say that?"

"Legend says that a giant named Cormoran guarded the path to Avalon, and that his grave formed the entrance." He closed his eyes, sniffing the air, then pointed to small grove of apple trees at the edge of the clearing. "There."

As they entered the clearing, an enormous, dark hole came into view. Bael led her to its edge.

By his side, she peered into it, straining her eyes in the darkness. "Is this it? The entrance to Avalon?"

Instead of responding, Bael began muttering in Angelic, and a glowing orb appeared above them. With a flick of his wrist, Bael directed it into the hole.

The orb descended, revealing an earthen floor twenty feet below—and from that, a deep tunnel carved into the earth that sloped further downward. Bael jumped down, kicking up a cloud of earth when his feet landed. *Of course. It's not like he's going to bother explaining anything.*

After taking a final glance at the unconscious Cormoran, Ursula hopped into the earthen hole. She hit the ground hard, but the dirt on the floor softened the landing. Already, Bael was walking into the tunnel, his amber orb lighting the way.

Sword in hand, she hurried after him, until she caught up with him. The earthen tunnel walls sloped downward, the high ceilings tall enough for a giant. Up ahead, the earth walls of the tunnel gave way to dark stone before reaching a small rough-stone chamber. Unlike Cormoran's pit, this seemed older, almost prehistoric. Apart from a dusty pile of red cloth, it was completely empty.

Rough Angelic words marked one of the walls, and Ursula translated them in her mind:

The path to Avalon is before you.

A golden apple, an unsullied body

Will reveal the way.

Below the inscription, a small, apple-shaped niche had been carved into the rock.

"Any idea what that means?" asked Ursula.

Bael simply stared at the inscription.

"Mordred had a golden clasp on his cloak," she offered. "But I don't suppose that helps us now."

A loud *thud* rumbled over the earth, dislodging dirt from the earthen ceiling. The giant was stirring, and dread shivered up Ursula's spine. She traced her fingers along the apple carving. There was something familiar about it—something she'd seen before.

"Wait," said Ursula her eyes flicking to the pile of dusty, crimson cloth that lay discarded just below the inscription. Was it a crimson *cloak?* Like the one Mordred had worn? "Those—" She pointed at the clothes. "I think that was Mordred."

Bael reached down and picked up the cloak—the exact same shade as Mordred's. When Bael picked up the garment, Mordred's golden apple clanged onto the stone floor.

Just then, the earth rumbled. Ursula peered down the tunnel, her heart racing as she caught a glimpse of Cormoran's form dropping into the earthen pit behind them.

Bael rolled the golden apple in his fingers. "Something killed Mordred when he tried to use this."

Ursula nodded. "The river hag said only the pure may enter. Any idea what that means?" With any luck, this wasn't a virginity requirement.

Behind her, Cormoran's voice boomed through the tunnel, and dirt rained around them. "I see you've found your way into my little cell, my love cave."

Bael met her gaze. "It's the same to travel through Nyxobas's waters. Clothing makes us impure. We must remove our clothes."

Ursula swallowed hard. "Of course."

I hope to hell this works. As fast as she could, Ursula tore off her clothing, slipping out of her panties and bra. The cool night air kissed her skin. She tried not to stare at Bael's perfect body as he undressed, his back to her. As the giant's footsteps echoed off the tunnel, Bael pressed the pendant into the apple-shaped niche. And when he did, the rock shimmered, thinning before them to a heavy mist. Without looking back, they stepped into it.

CHAPTER 10

Shrouded in mist, Ursula hugged herself, and not just for modesty. A cold breeze whispered over her bare skin, raising goosebumps. A few steps forward, and pearly moonlight diffused through the thick mist. When she turned to look, she was surprised to find herself standing directly in front of a stark cliff that towered high into the air, lost in the darkness and fog above.

She stood on damp stone, and when her eyes adjusted to the dim light, she spotted Bael to her right. Shivering, she tried to make sense of where she was in the darkness. A distant surf roared rhythmically, pounding against rocks, and the air tasted of salt. Through the fog, she could see only the faintest outline of Bael's enormous silhouette. As the mist thinned just a little, a low wall appeared through the fog, about ten feet in front of her.

She glanced at Bael again, her gaze lingering on his broad, muscled back, his body turned away from her. Tattoos covered nearly every inch of his skin. Alchemical symbols, Angelic text, a sun surrounded by a laurel wreath—all faintly glowing with a menacing red light. She'd never seen that on him before, but that must be the effects of 'the old way.' On either side of his spine, red wounds marked his skin where his wings had been carved away. Shadow magic shimmered over them, cauterizing the wounds.

"Are we in Avalon?" Ursula asked.

Bael shook his head without looking at her. "No. I don't think so."

She forced herself to keep her eyes off his naked body as he walked to the wall, and she followed him at enough of a distance that the fog shielded her naked body from him. The old way still thrummed in his veins; no sense in risking setting him off.

When they reached the wall, Ursula peered over the edge at a sheer, rough cliff face, about two hundred feet to the sea. Every few moments, water misted the air when the dark waves crashed against the cliff's base. No way down that way.

Ursula glanced behind her again. With the stone slick from the sea air, climbing up would not be an option, nor would leaving the way they had entered. The portal had disappeared. Yet, as the mist continued to thin, she noticed something in the cliff face that she hadn't spotted before—slate-gray doors carved into the rock.

As the sea air chilled her skin, she crossed back to the cliff face, running her fingers over a silver door handle. "Bael."

She pulled it open, revealing a wardrobe of sorts, lit with a glowing amber light. Inside hung a row of cotton cloaks in a variety of sizes. The cloth was a faded periwinkle that looked as if it may have once been a deep royal blue. Old as they were, they beat the hell out of walking around naked. She slipped one over her shoulders, grimacing at the scent of mildew.

Bael's footfalls sounded behind her, and he sniffed the air. "Kester was here." He pulled a large robe from the wardrobe. "I can smell him."

Ursula turned away as Bael pulled the cloak over his body. "These may help us blend in when we get to Avalon."

After a few moments, Ursula turned to look at Bael. The golden clasp was fastened at his throat, and his pale gaze pierced the fog, the faded blue of the cloak nearly matching his eyes. Somehow, the cloak suited him perfectly, a beautiful contrast against his warm skin. "Are you ready for what comes next?"

Ursula frowned. "How do we get there?"

Bael pointed to a part of the wall about twenty feet away from where they stood. "The path lies here."

As she followed Bael closer to the wall, peering over the side, she saw what he meant. Inset into the cliff's side was a narrow staircase so steep it dizzied her. "Here—the path to the sea."

Ursula's stomach clenched. There was no railing—just damp stone steps, roughly hewn. One slip on the sea-slicked stones would send her plunging into the sea. She started to follow him, but words carved onto the lip of the wall caught her eye.

"Wait. There's an inscription." Angelic words marked the stone, and she translated them as she read. "*Call, and the boatman will come for you.* What does that mean?"

"Of course. You need to announce yourself upon entering a kingdom ruled by another god, as this one is ruled by Dagon. It is the way it has been done for millennia. We must call the boatman." Bael lifted his chin before shouting, "I am Bael, Lord of Albelda, Second in command to Nyxobas! I request passage to Avalon." His gaze landed on Ursula.

"What should I say?"

"Just shout your name and where you are from."

Ursula took a deep breath. "I am Ursula!" After a moment she added, "Ursula of Mount Acidale."

Bael's posture stiffened as though he'd been struck by lightning, and inky shadows darkened the air around him as his magic pooled. Shadows slid through his pale eyes, and the temperature seemed to drop. "Acidale?" he said sharply.

Okay. Something about that *struck a nerve with him.* "Have you been there? The river hag told me I was born there."

A muscle worked in Bael's jaw. "I see. I have been there. In battle."

Her pulse raced, and a memory flickered in the back of her mind. A man with stormy gray eyes, fighting with the fury of a wild beast… but in the next moment, her memory swirled away like the sea mist. "What can you tell me about it?"

"It's complicated." His eyes bored into her. "I don't have time for a history lesson. We should go." Without another word, he started down the steps.

Her heart pounded, and she began to follow after him, no longer thinking of the steep drop to the churning sea below. Of course. Of *course* he'd give her a bullshit answer like that.

"Bael. What do you know of Mount Acidale? What's this battle you were talking about?"

"That is none of your concern."

Emerazel's fire began to flow in her veins. He was obviously keeping things from her—important things, about her own life. "I could see it on your face. Something important happened there. What aren't you telling me?"

Taking the steps two at a time, Bael was practically flying down to the sea. She hurried after him as fast as she could, her fingers slipping on the wet stone. The sea wind whipped her hair around her head, and her bare feet nearly slipped off the wet stone. And yet Ursula thought only of getting answers.

Bael, with all his secrecy, was absolutely infuriating. By the time she reached the bottom, he had already made his way to the end of a stone jetty that jutted into the dark, churning sea. With his dark hair and pale blue cloak, he blended into the landscape. Waves crashed around him, spraying into the air.

Ursula ran to him, nearly slipping over the jetty in her bare feet. When she reached him, she grabbed his hand, pulling him so that he faced her. His eyes had darkened, empty as an abyss.

"Tell me. Tell me what you know," she demanded. "Where is Mount Acidale? Why did you react that way?"

"Forget Mount Acidale. You'll find only suffering and betrayal there." Shadow magic flicked around him like a mirage, and a blood-red fury burned in his eyes. She shrank back as he looked at her with the hunger of the old way, his humanity disappearing by the instant.

Still, she needed answers. "Tell me."

Bael merely glared at her, his gaze as cold and terrifying as a god's. Dark shadows cascaded from his back like giant wings, and Ursula's breath caught in her throat. Something had *really* set him off.

Behind him a light pulsed through the swirling fog, and a voice called from the mist. "Who has requested a passage to Avalon?"

The shadows darkening the air around Bael retreated, and the stormy gray returned to his eyes. He turned back to the sea, the shadowy wings now gone.

"I am Bael. I request passage to Avalon."

Slowly, a dark skiff emerged from the fog, a lantern hanging from its bow. In its center sat a man with his back to them. Soundlessly, he dipped a pair of oars into the churning water.

The boat pulled along the stone jetty and Ursula got her first look at the rower's face under his cloak. He was younger than she had expected, strikingly handsome with green eyes and golden skin.

He flashed her a charming smile. "And you must be Ursula?"

"That's me."

"Do you have the golden apple?" he asked.

Bael held up the pendant. "We do."

As the boatman took the pendant, Ursula spotted a tattoo along the edge of his neck, an octopus tentacle. Of course—they were in the territory of Dagon, the terrifying god of the sea.

The boatman arched an eyebrow. "Everything okay?"

"Everything's fine," she said.

"Climb in then." He beckoned them. "Take care not to fall into the sea. I don't get paid to fish passengers out of the brine."

Bael stepped into the stern, his shifting weight rocked the boat to and fro. As Ursula stepped in, the boatman took her elbow to help her balance, and she took a seat in the bow.

With one oar pointing forward and the other backward, the man deftly turned the boat.

"How far is it?" asked Ursula.

"The Fortunate Isle is just through the mist."

"I'd ask if this was a regular journey for you," Ursula began, "but it doesn't seem as if the cloaks have been used in a while."

From his seat in the stern Bael glared at her. Apparently he was unimpressed with her small talk.

The man took a deep breath. "Only those with golden apples are allowed on the island. I will only take you as far as the shore."

Bael stared into the fog, his expression grim, and the boatman lapsed into silence. As the rough sea jostled them, Ursula twisted around so she could see where the boat was headed.

Slowly, a dark form rose from the mist. As they drew closer to it, a breeze swirled the vapor. Ursula breathed deeply. *Is that the scent of apple blossoms?*

The mist twisted and swirled. Ursula didn't realize how close they were to the shore until they had practically run aground on a beach of black sand.

His oars steadying the skiff in the shallow waters, the boatman nodded. "This is where you get out."

Immediately, Bael hopped into the sea and began striding through the knee-deep water.

Ursula gathered her cloak, lifting it to her knees, and stepped out. She turned to the boatman, whose placid green eyes surveyed her though the moonlit mist.

"To whom do I owe my thanks?"

"The name's Lir," he said. For the briefest of moments his eyes flashed with a pale blue light, like St. Elmo's fire. Then, with a dip of his oars, he disappeared into the fog.

* * *

When she turned back to the island, Bael had vanished into the misty night, and she plodded on through the ice cold water, stepping on sludgy rocks. Where the hell had Bael gone?

Beyond the dark sand stood a forest of trees, their trunks gnarled with age. From their branches bloomed a thousand white flowers—apple blossoms. Breathtakingly beautiful. Ursula walked slowly into the grove, her eyes drawn to the extraordinary spray of blooms, glowing in the pearly light like a sea of stars.

Despite the beauty, the atmosphere was strangely unsettling, and an eerie silence enshrouded the forest. Not a single bird trilled nor insect buzzed among the branches; not even a breath of wind rustled the thorny boughs. When a distant voice pierced the quiet, she practically jumped out of her skin. She moved faster through the trees, hurrying toward the sound.

And there was Bael—standing tall in the center of a clearing, surrounded by five young women. Each woman had long hair that tumbled over a silver-white dress—apart from one, a beauty whose raven hair was threaded with pearls and piled in messy plaits on her head.

The women stood in a small semicircle, staring at Bael, their eyes hungry. Ursula was only ten feet away from them, at the edge of the clearing, and they ignored her. Ursula coughed softly.

The woman with plaited hair glanced at her for just a moment. "Is this the one you spoke of?"

"Yes," said Bael softly.

The dark-haired woman—who seemed to be the leader—beckoned Ursula closer. As Ursula approached, she studied the women. They were *all* beautiful, with hair and skin that shimmered in the light of the moon. They wore no jewelry, adorned only with the delicate gold stitching along the cuffs of their dresses.

"You wish to visit Avalon?" asked the leader.

"I do," said Ursula. There was a solemnity in the way the girl spoke that had Ursula subconsciously modulating her voice to match.

"Why do you wish to visit?"

"I am searching for a friend. His name is Kester."

The woman's porcelain face remained impassive. If she knew Kester, her expression didn't reveal it.

"Are you willing to surrender your weapons? Avalon is a peaceful isle."

Ursula opened her hands. "I don't have any weapons. I had to leave them on the other side of the portal."

"A follower of Emerazel carries hellfire in her veins," she replied. "You cannot enter Avalon with the magic of the fire goddess."

Oh, not this again.

The woman arched an eyebrow, and for the first time, Ursula noticed that her face was faintly tattooed with silver stars. "Do you consent to abandon your fire? We will return it to you when you leave."

"It's all right, Ursula," said Bael. "You can trust them."

Ursula sucked in a long breath. She didn't have much choice, did she? "Fine."

"Kneel, please. Both of you."

Bael knelt and Ursula crossed to him, taking up a spot on the damp earth by his side. She glanced at him, taking in the tension in his jaw, his shoulders. Dark magic whirled around him.

The leader reached into her cloak pockets, and pulled out two apples. She handed one to Bael and one to Ursula. "Do not eat the fruit of the island. Hold them before you."

Ursula studied the apple. Perfectly shaped, its skin was a deep red flecked with green. Even in the hazy light it seemed to sparkle.

Next to her Bael lifted his apple up like an offering and Ursula followed suit.

The maidens resumed their positions in a semicircle. Then in a clear voice, the leader began to sing in Angelic, her voice crisp and clear in the night air.

She sang a verse before the other girls joined in. Their voices intertwined, curling around Ursula and Bael like sensual magic. As the girls sang, a gentle vibration began to grow within Ursula's ribs. Emerazel's fire swirled up from her core and out along her arms. Flames licked along her skin until they quenched themselves within the apple.

The women sang louder, and the fire surged faster from her body, burning her veins. Her gaze flicked to Bael, and she took in the dark shadows snaking down his arms, embedding themselves in his apple.

The girls continued their song, their voices slowly building to a crescendo. As they harmonized on the final note, Ursula felt the last of the fire leave her.

The apple trembled in her fingers, now a deep golden hue and hot to the touch. When she studied it closely, she could see the goddess's flames burning within it. Next to her, Bael's apple had darkened to a sooty black, with shadows moving under its skin.

A girl with hair the color of honey crossed to Ursula, holding out her hands. "I will take your apple. When you leave, you can eat the fruit to regain your magic."

Another girl spoke softly to Bael, pulling the darkened apple from his fingers. He remained kneeling, his shoulders sagging just slightly. Ursula's throat tightened at the sight of the red blotches that bloomed on the back of his cloak. The wounds from his stolen wings had begun bleeding profusely.

"He is injured," said the blonde.

The leader cocked her head. "The queen will be able to help him."

Ursula rose to her feet. "You cannot heal his wounds. He needs to keep them open so that he can reattach his wings."

"Don't worry. You can explain everything to the queen. She is just and wise." The leader gestured to two of the girls. They each slung one of Bael's arms over their shoulders and lifted him into a standing position, and the leader fixed her dark gaze on Ursula. "They'll take care of him. Come with me."

CHAPTER 11

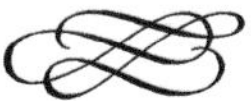

The woman led her from the clearing and into the forest. Here, the canopy of apple blossoms closed in above them, blocking out the moonlight, and Ursula felt a strange comfort in the darkness. "Where are you taking me?"

"To your room in the castle. I will help you get settled for your audience with the queen."

They walked under the apple blossoms in silence, their path lit only by the faint chinks of moonlight that danced on the damp earth beneath their feet. Ursula's bare soles sank into the dirt as she walked.

Ursula strained her eyes in the darkness, trying to see the other woman. "What is your name?" Ursula ventured.

"Elaine."

"Who is the queen you spoke of?"

"Her name is Nimue. She rules over our little isle."

At last they reached the forest's edge, emerging at a narrow ridge that sloped steeply down on either side. On one side, the sea pounded against the dark beach. On the other, a valley stretched out before them, where small farms had been carved from the forest, quiet and dark in the damp night. In the distance, almost entirely shrouded by mist, was the shape of a mountain.

"Are we going down there?" asked Ursula, pointing at the valley.

"No. Nimue's castle is up ahead."

"Who lives down there, then?" asked Ursula.

"That is Camlann Valley. My family's home is on the far side."

It seemed a cozy place—the kind of place it would be nice to raise a family in. "Do your parents still live there?"

"Yes, but I live in the castle now."

"What exactly do you do there in the castle?" She had no idea how castles operated.

"I am one of the queen's ladies."

That didn't exactly clear things up, but Elaine didn't seem particularly eager to chat. In silence, they hiked higher along the ridge, until the castle came into view. Built at the apex of the ridge, its turrets reached into the sky like spindly fingers, and its dark stone glinted in the moonlight. As they drew closer, the path intersected a narrow cobbled road, an icy mist whirling over the stones. Ursula shivered at the chill. The road bent sharply as they approached, curving out toward the cliff's edge. Cold stone bit into Ursula's bare feet as they walked. Ursula peered up at the fortress. The smooth stone castle loomed over them like a spindly crown.

Unlike the carefully restored castle at St. Michael's Mount, Nimue's castle fell somewhere between castle and ruin. Moss and lichen grew over the stone, and in places the tooth-like crenellations along its battlements had collapsed. A dark tongue of wood stuck out from the front of the castle, and it took Ursula a moment to recognize it: a drawbridge spanning a gap in the cliff.

As they drew closer, a sentry appeared at the opposite end of the bridge gripping a long, coppery pike. Iron chains as thick as Ursula's legs held the drawbridge in place.

"She has already relinquished her magic." Elaine projected her voice to the sentry.

"You have followed the ritual of the fruit?"

"We have."

"Welcome to Castle Dahut."

As they walked over the drawbridge, their feet thumped on the oaken boards. When they passed the sentry, Elaine nodded.

"Thank you, Oran."

"You're welcome, my lady. The queen is in the Moon Tower."

Elaine smiled shyly at Oran, and Ursula saw him blush.

Ursula followed her through a stone hall where lantern light danced over the flagstones until it opened into a grassy courtyard. At this hour, few people lingered here. Two soldiers stood at one end, staring at Ursula. A few more soldiers stood in archways, but otherwise the place was empty.

A tall tower loomed over the far end of the courtyard. Elaine strode toward it, and Ursula followed her to a heavy oaken door. Elaine pulled it open, leading Ursula into a narrow stairwell of dark stone, lit by wavering candlelight. A chilly draught curled around her bare feet. She couldn't stop herself from thinking about Bael, and his strange reaction to the words *Mount Acidale*. She had to restrain herself from hunting him down in Avalon and demanding answers from him.

After two floors of stairs, they reached an archway, and Elaine led her to a hall, its arched ceiling sharply peaked. Candles in sconces cast dancing light over the hall. After some twenty feet, Elaine stopped at a door and turned the knob, beckoning Ursula inside.

As soon as she stepped inside, Ursula's body began to relax. In the large, circular room, a fire burned in a large fireplace, and the scent of woodsmoke filled the air. A girl knelt at the fireplace, her hair sandy blonde, a smattering of freckles across her round face. An old halberd hung above the mantle, and Ursula tucked that fact away in her mind for later use. Perhaps it would come in handy.

The girl rose, smiling at Elaine. "You're back already?" She frowned at Ursula, and after a moment, her jaw dropped. Something about Ursula seemed to have unnerved her.

"I'm Ursula."

The girl stared, mouth gaping.

"That's Linnet," said Elaine. "One of our novices." After giving Linnet a sharp look, Elaine pointed at a stairway in the shadows of the room, framed by two tapestries. "Your room is upstairs. Follow me."

Ursula followed Elaine up the stairwell and through another wooden door into a smaller room. Moonlight streamed through a narrow window onto a single bed, and a candle guttered on a simple wooden dresser.

"This is the guest room," said Elaine, turning to the dresser. "Tomorrow, you will meet the queen. She likes to fly Kree from the top of the tower in the afternoon. You will want to wear something warm."

Ursula raised her eyebrows. "Kree?"

"The queen is very keen on hawking. Kree is her favorite gyrfalcon. Tomorrow I will fetch you, and you will join us at the mews."

The mews. Hawking. Handmaidens. What the hell was she doing here? She'd come here for one reason alone—to find out about the dragons. Now she also wanted to find out about Mount Acidale, but instead, she was being sequestered in a room with some sort of hawking plans and a visit with a queen.

"Elaine. It's very important that I find Kester. Can you please tell me what you know?"

Elaine stared at her for a long moment, then turned and crossed to the door. "Goodnight, Ursula, Princess of Darkness."

As Elaine closed the wooden door behind her, a cold shudder snaked up Ursula's spine.

* * *

WHEN SHE'D WOKEN, she'd found a tray of bread and coffee steaming by her bedside. Buttery morning light streamed in through the window. In the light of day, Ursula surveyed her room again, now spotting another door carved into the stone wall.

She rose from her bed, peering out the window at her view of the castle's courtyard and, beyond it, the gray, churning sea. She crossed, and pulled open a drawer. Piles of white dresses lay neatly tucked in the drawer, along with some fresh underwear. She pulled on a pair of knickers and a white cotton dress that felt smooth and clean against her skin, and she caught a glimpse of herself in a small mirror that hung over the dresser. She hardly recognized herself with the short bob, but the full night's sleep had refreshed her, and some pink had returned to her cheeks.

A pair of flat gray shoes lay next to the dresser, and she slipped into them, then plopped down on her bed to devour her breakfast. Her stomach rumbled, and the fresh, buttery bread made her mouth water. When she'd worked her way through three or four rolls, alternating with coffee, her breakfast was interrupted by a knock coming from that stone door carved into the wall. Maybe she'd finally get some answers about Kester.

"Yes?"

The door scraped against the flagstones, and Linnet's freckled face peered through the door. "I'm to take you to the mews," she stammered, her face reddening.

"The mews. Right. The falconry and hawking thing."

Linnet gestured to the door, and Ursula followed her into a hall, their footsteps echoing off an impossibly high ceiling. She still had so many unanswered questions about this place. "How did the other women know where to find us?"

"We are called Nimue's handmaidens," she said shyly.

"All right, how did Nimue's handmaidens know where to find Bael and me? We weren't anywhere near the castle."

"Lir sent us a message when he heard your call." She spoke in a small voice.

"How?"

"There's a spell."

Ursula glanced at Linnet. "I don't suppose you know what 'Princess of Darkness' means, do you?"

Linnet merely furrowed her brow at Ursula, her cheeks a deep shade of red, then she looked away without replying. In the main corridor, with its narrow, pointed windows, a draft caught at Ursula's collar. She hugged herself as Linnet pushed open the door onto the roof of the keep.

Here a briny breeze whipped over Ursula's skin and the keep's roof offered a panoramic view of the kingdom. The valley floor, the slate-gray ocean, the lush apple orchards—and all around, the swirling mist.

The view was so breathtaking, Ursula nearly didn't notice the woman standing by a stack of wooden bird cages. Tall and regal, she was dressed in a cloak of white wool, finely stitched with the outlines of apple blossoms. Ursula supposed that at one time her hair may have been dark, but now gray streaked it at the temples. She looked to be maybe fifty years old. On one arm she wore a heavy leather glove.

"Are you Ursula, the young hound?"

"That's me."

"I am Nimue, the queen of Avalon." With eyes as fierce and cold as the gray ocean, she studied Ursula. "Why have you come to visit me?"

"I am looking for my friend Kester. He has information that I need."

The queen's gaze bored into her. "We know no one of that name." Her attention flicked away from Ursula as a shadow passed rapidly overhead.

The queen held out her arm, and in the next moment, a falcon hand landed on her glove, his wings the color of dawn and starlight. The queen pulled a piece of raw meat from her cloak, and fed it to the falcon.

She knows more than she's letting on. How could she get on the queen's good side? "That's a magnificent bird."

The queen's sharp features softened. "Have you ever seen a gyrfalcon before?"

"No, I don't believe so."

"Come here, then. Kree is very gentle."

As Ursula approached, the falcon gnawed at his meat, completely ignoring her.

"He won't mind if you touch his back," said the queen.

Ursula reached out, stroking the bird's soft feathers. "You haven't had any other visitors? No other hellhounds, or unexpected men?"

"You are the first to visit in a long time." The queen pursed her lips, cooing at Kree.

Ursula couldn't quite let this go. This was the only lead she had—the only clue to figuring out how to defeat the dragons. The river hag had said he'd come here. Unless… unless the old hag had just been full of shit? And then maybe *everything* was a lie—her mother's death, her attempted patricide… How the hell was she supposed to know what was real? "A river hag in the Thames was certain that Kester had come here," she pressed. "Her name was Agnes."

The queen's brow furrowed slightly. "All I can tell you is that I haven't seen him. Do you know why he might have wanted to visit?"

If she wanted the queen to confide in her, maybe she needed to give a little more away. "Yes." She stared into the queen's iron-gray eyes. "Dragons have been attacking New York, and Kester thought the answer to stopping them lay in Avalon."

"*Dragons?*" The queen's brow creased sharply, and she straightened. "Linnet, return Kree to his cage, please."

Linnet stepped forward, now wearing a glove similar to the queen's. While she watched the girl pull Kree from the queen's arm, Ursula's mind raced furiously. She needed them to tell her what they knew. "Dragons have attacked New York and London. Much of New York has been destroyed. It's quite urgent that I find him."

The queen leaned forward, sunlight glinting in her eyes. "Do you know why they have appeared?"

Ursula sucked in a sharp breath. "They're after me, but I don't know why."

"That is most unusual. Dragons don't usually take an interest in the affairs of men. Come closer. Let me have a look at you." The queen pulled off her hawking glove and hooked a finger under Ursula's chin, lifting it to meet her gaze. She studied Ursula for a long moment. Then, releasing Ursula's chin, she continued, "Give me your hand."

Ursula extended her hand, and the queen took it in her long, delicately tapered fingers. She continued to look at Ursula. Then her gray eyes flashed with a pale green light. The queen's hand suddenly felt clammy. Ursula tried to pull away, but the queen held her tightly. A damp magic crept over Ursula's skin. She could taste water on her lips, and the salt of the sea.

The queen's eyes flicked back to their normal gray. Her lips pressed into a thin line, her brow razor sharp. Her fear was almost palpable. "You will leave in the morning," she intoned.

Ursula pulled her hand away. "I don't understand. Why?" Was this to do with the whole 'Princess of Darkness' thing?

"This audience is over," the queen declared. "Linnet will take you to your quarters." She turned to the girl. "She is confined to her room. Do not allow her to leave. Call the boatman tomorrow morning and have him return her to the portal."

Ursula's stomach clenched. Maybe the queen had the answers to her question about the dragons—but like everyone else around her, she wasn't letting on. "What are you talking about? What are you afraid of?"

"A tainted thing," said the queen, her words dripping with disgust. And with that, she turned and strode across the roof. Before she got to the roof's end, her body began constricting with the sound of snapping bones, and feathery wings sprouted from her back until she'd taken on the form of a silver and black falcon. She swooped through the air above Ursula, and then out over the sea.

CHAPTER 12

*L*ocked in her room, Ursula passed the hours staring out the window at the churning waves, trying to picture her mother. But when she thought of Mount Acidale, a man's eyes flickered in her mind—a pale gray, his skin golden—the colors of honeyed light piercing storm clouds.

A shudder crawled over her skin. *Bael?* Had she seen him in Mount Acidale?

It seemed everyone knew more about her than she herself did. Even Bael—supposedly her betrothed—couldn't bring himself to let her in on the secret. And where exactly was he now, as she sat here locked in this room above the sea?

When the setting sun began to stain the sky lurid shades of cherry and lilac, a knock sounded at the door, echoing off the stone walls.

A girl with curly brown hair, tawny skin, and large, mahogany eyes cautiously poked her head in. "Hello. My name is Niniane. I brought you dinner." She carried a tray into the room, and dropped it on the small table by the bed. It held a large hunk of bread and a steaming bowl of stew.

Ursula's stomach rumbled at the rich scent. "Thank you, Niniane," she said. "Can you tell me where Bael is?"

"He's being cared for in the infirmary. He was bleeding badly."

"Can I see him?"

"No."

"Fine." Ursula bit off a hunk of her bread. "But tell them not to heal the wounds on his back, or he won't be able to get his wings back. It's very important to him."

The girl stared at her, eyes wide.

Ursula cocked her head. "Is there a reason everyone here is so scared of me?"

Niniane stared at her with a mixture of fear and fascination. "Is it true that you're a hound of the fire goddess?"

"Yes, I'm a hound of Emerazel's, but they made me give up my fire when I arrived. I don't have any magic. So unless you believe whatever the queen was scared of, you have nothing to worry about."

Niniane visibly relaxed. "I'm only a novice. I don't have any magic either. But Elaine is teaching me."

"What are you learning?" asked Ursula, desperate for conversation at this point.

"Elaine has taught me the song for calling the rain and the verse of light. I've been working on the light spell for ages. Would you like to see it?"

"I'd be honored," said Ursula.

Niniane closed her eyes and spoke slowly in Angelic, carefully enunciating each word. When she finished the spell a small orb appeared in the air. It hovered—a perfect little glowing sphere—for an instant, before bursting into a shower of sparks.

"Oh no!" Niniane's hand flew to her mouth. "I must have forgotten a word."

"I thought it was very good," said Ursula. "I still don't know that one myself."

"You don't?"

"No. I lost my memory when I was a girl. I don't actually know very much about magic."

"Then how did you become a hound?"

"I'm not sure of that either."

"I bet Nimue could help you remember."

"I don't think so," said Ursula. "She saw something in me she didn't like. That's why I'm stuck in here until morning."

"Nimue is a good queen," said Niniane. "There must be a good reason why she asked you to stay in here."

Ursula nodded, but this conversation had revived a cold dread that washed over her skin. What had the queen's magic revealed—what did Nimue know that made her so afraid? The queen, Bael, Emerazel, even Abrax had all sensed it. What was it about her that made them uncomfortable? Bael had practically attacked her when she'd asked him about Mount Acidale.

Ursula bit her lip. "Have you ever heard of Mount Acidale?"

The girl's eyes widened, and she took a step back. "Why do you ask?"

This time I won't make the mistake of mentioning that I was born there. "My friend Kester mentioned it a few times," she lied. "Maybe it has something to do with his disappearance."

Niniane's jaw tightened, and her forehead creased.

"What is it?" asked Ursula. "How come whenever I say *Mount Acidale—*"

"Shhhh." Niniane put a finger to her lips. "We are forbidden to say the name."

"Why?"

Niniane took a deep breath, the ruddy sunlight glinting in her eyes. "A long time ago there were two cities, Avalon and… the other one. Nimue says it was very beautiful. They existed in harmony for centuries. Then, King Vortigern was crowned."

"In Avalon?"

"No, in the other place." Niniane took a deep breath. "He never left the castle. He was obsessed with fire magic. He went insane. Then, the demons of darkness descended, and a terrible battle ensued. We've never heard from them since. No one knows the outcome of the battle."

"No one knows what happened in Mount Acidale?"

Niniane shook her head.

"But the queen must have sent messages."

"Most never return. They say dragons block the roads to… that city."

"Like the dragons that attacked New York?"

Niniane shrugged. "I'm sorry, I have to go."

"I don't understand. Why is everyone here so scared of dragons? Why is it that no one can speak the name of the city?"

Reluctantly, Niniane turned back to her. "It's because of the prophecy."

"What prophecy?"

Niniane's face paled. "I must go. I shouldn't have said anything. I'm sorry."

She hurried out the door, shutting it behind her. Ursula could hear Niniane apologizing again from outside the door—but she also heard the clink of metal as she locked Ursula in.

* * *

URSULA LAY IN BED, staring at the shimmering canopy of stars through her narrow window. As the sun had set, the mist had cleared and a pale moon had risen in the sky. A deathly quiet enshrouded the castle, and she pulled a blanket over her shoulders, shivering as her breath fogged the air.

She sat up in bed, glancing at the empty bowl of stew and the few crumbs of bread. Niniane had returned a few hours later to take her to the lavatory. She shuddered at the thought—calling it a lavatory was generous. A more accurate description would be 'hole in the floor.'

A fluttering noise turned her head, and Ursula stared as a large, tawny-feathered owl landed on the sill. The bird's golden eyes shone brightly in the darkness. *And what do we have here?*

Ursula frowned. "Have you come to keep me company?"

The owl ruffled his feathers. Then, in a thin, slightly nasal voice, he spoke. "No, I have not."

Ursula's mouth fell open. "Are you a shifter, perchance?"

He ruffled his feathers again. "I'm sorry, I should have introduced myself first. I'm Taliesin."

"You can talk?"

"Obviously."

"I've just never seen a talking bird before."

Taliesin blinked. "Are you coming? I really must return."

Ursula rose, rubbing her eyes, and the night breeze kissed her skin. "Coming where?"

"Oh, right. I forgot to give you the invitation."

The owl puffed his feathers, then lifted one of his taloned feet, offering

636

her a tiny, rolled piece of parchment. With a surprisingly dexterous flick of his claw, he tossed the letter toward Ursula.

Ursula unfurled the parchment and read it by the silvery light of the moon.

Dear Ursula,

I would very much like to make your acquaintance. I have been following your exploits with keen interest, and I must say that it is not often that Avalon is visited by someone as distinguished as yourself.

I very much hope that you will take the time to stop by for tea. Taliesin will fill you in on the particulars.

Yours,
Merlin

Of course. Merlin was a real person, and he wanted her to come over for tea. At least he wasn't afraid of her. "Merlin sent you?"

"I run the occasional errand for him."

"And Merlin is a mage, I take it?"

The owl moved in such a way as to appear to be shrugging. "Merlin, High Druidic Mage and Ancient Bard of the Wilds. Are you coming or what?"

"I'd love to chat with the High Druidic Mage, but I'm imprisoned here, and without my magic, I can't travel anywhere."

"Oh, I can fix that."

Before Ursula could ask what 'fixing that' entailed, the owl had launched into an Angelic spell. Warm magic tingled over Ursula's skin, then a flash of sharp pain pierced her muscles as her shoulders hunched together involuntarily. As her bones snapped and popped, feathers sprouted from her skin, and she rapidly shrank. From the cold flagstones, she stared up at Taliesin.

"Okay, enough messing about," said the owl. "Merlin was quite keen on meeting you."

Ursula studied her new body—the beautiful copper plumage, her feet curled into talons. She twisted her head around, eying the sheen of silvery light on her feathers. She couldn't quite tell, but she thought she might be an owl. At least it was a way out of here for now.

"What sort of bird am I?" she tried to say, but instead of words coming from her tongue, she emitted a sound somewhere between a screech and a squawk.

"Well, that settles it." Taliesin turned, and spread his wings. "Follow me."

And with that, Taliesin soared into the glittering night sky.

CHAPTER 13

$\mathcal{U}$rsula stood at the window's ledge, peering down at the rocky landscape below—the jagged black boulders and rugged cliff face leading to the sea. Taliesin had offered her an escape—and perhaps some answers—and she'd be a fool not to take him up on it. Following the owl into the night was her only choice. And yet the thought of plunging into the air made her stomach somersault.

Answers. I may finally get answers. Taking a deep breath, she hopped onto the windowsill, where the night breeze ruffled her feathers. As Taliesin circled in the sky above her, Ursula spread her wings and pushed herself forward, her stomach lurching as she braced for a crash. Immediately she lifted into the air, but she stroked too hard with her wings and veered wildly to the right. She let out a shrill scream, righting herself as she winged into the night. She was flying, the wind whipping at her body, and it felt amazing.

Taliesin swooped back for her. When he reached her side, he said, "Very interesting. I don't think I've ever seen anyone transform into a nighthawk before."

So she wasn't an owl. "How are you able to talk?" Ursula tried to say, but it just came out as a series of screeches.

"Practice. Lots of practice. Just follow me, and you'll be fine." He arced away from her, this time heading back toward the castle. Ursula followed him, soaring higher into the briny air. The wind rushed over her feathers while below the ground peeled away. Exhilarated, she swooped over the castle's turrets and glimpsed its spindly spires gleaming in the moonlight. A circular wall surrounded the keep, and mist whirled over the ground, gathering in leeward eddies between the towers. Faint lights sparkled in the narrow windows. In which of those rooms was Bael, and had he been imprisoned too?

They soared past the castle to the peaked ridge, and over the darkened forest of apple trees. The mix of mist and blossoms was inviting, like a soft white carpet, and Taliesin flew lower, breaching the forest's canopy. Gracefully, he glided between the branches. She chased him, thrilling as her wings caught the night air. They passed the clearing where she'd first met Nimue's handmaidens, then they dove back into the forest of apple trees.

Above them the canopy of blossoms thickened and the tree trunks widened. Between the giant tree trunks, the air stilled. It was deathly quiet, like the entire forest was holding its breath. Taliesin winged forward over the rich soil. Ursula followed close behind, as the trees became denser. Below them the moss of the forest floor gave way to a thick carpet of vines and nettles. It was a strange juxtaposition—delicate clouds of apple blossoms above a wiry sea of thorns. As the forest darkened, a shiver ran over Ursula's feathers.

Suddenly Taliesin swooped up as they approached a giant oak. Burls and the ragged stumps of broken branches gnarled its massive trunk. Taliesin landed on a thick bough, and Ursula alit next to him, her heart racing, wings burning with fatigue.

"Once you've rested a moment, I'll take you inside." But as Ursula caught her breath, Taliesin was already launching off his perch, with a shrill "Follow me." He swooped around the tree's trunk to a narrow hollow. As he dove for it, he folded his wings to fit inside.

Ursula made another circle around the tree before attempting the maneuver, then she folded her wings and slipped into the opening. Inside, she found not a soft nest, but a sort of shoot of slippery wood. She scrambled to balance herself, but only managed to slide down forward on her chest. Like a playground slide, the smooth wood in the oak spiraled downward. She slid down in darkness until light bloomed in front of her, and she skidded onto a dusty stone floor.

Blinking at the glare, she hopped to her feet. Before she could get a good glimpse of her surroundings, Taliesin launched into an Angelic spell, and her wings began to twist and crack. The feathers crawled back into her skin, while her arms and legs regrew. At the last word of the spell, her back spasmed, and she cried out with pain.

"Nice flying," said Taliesin, perched on a twisted root. Ursula straightened, surveying her surroundings.

Ursula frowned. "Next time, please ask permission before transforming me into a bird."

Taliesin cocked his head. "This is where I leave you. Merlin asked to speak to you alone, and I must catch dinner for the missus."

"Where exactly are we?"

Instead of answering, Taliesin flapped his wings and flew through the hole from which they'd entered, leaving Ursula alone in the candlelit room.

She shivered at the cold draft rising from the stone floor. In her human form she was far too big to fit through the hole in the tree that led back to the forest, and she hugged herself, stepping up to the door. It was made of oak planks, the bark rough and untouched. There was no handle. Holding her breath, she raised a hand and knocked.

She heard no reply, just a soft creak as the door slowly opened to reveal a cavernous hall filled with books that reached for the high oak ceiling. It was a chaotic, labyrinthine library of sorts. Lining the walls and in piles all over the floor lay hundreds of dusty tomes. Beeswax candles lit the room, some in brass candleholders, some simply affixed to the top of particularly tall towers of books.

From the shadows between two stacks of books, an old, gray-haired man appeared. Wearing a dark navy cloak, he moved toward her in a quick, twitchy jerks, like a marionette. "Ursula, come in, come in. Welcome to my home. I'm sorry for sending Taliesin, but it's impossible for me to leave the tree. You see, it was imperative that we meet."

"Merlin, I presume."

"The one and only." He grinned, his eyes flashing in the candlelight. "You and I have much to discuss, but first we must get you something to eat. Would you like some rabbit stew? You must be famished. Flying about in the night always whets one's appetite." He spoke quickly in a staccato burst of words. "Taliesin caught the rabbit for us earlier."

Before Ursula could answer, he had turned back into the stacks. She could see now where Taliesin had learned his selective approach to answering questions. A maze of passages and corridors wound between the books, candlelight dancing over their yellowed pages and spines, and the room smelled of rich meats and dusty leather. Merlin moved swiftly, twisting sideways to squeeze through narrow gaps between the volumes.

At last, he stopped at a clearing in the stacks—a sort of rounded room. A wall curved around one side, inlaid with shelves interrupted by a single narrow window. A small fire burned in a cast iron stove, and warm light wavered over a roughly hewn table, strewn with papers.

"Welcome to my home," said Merlin.

"Where exactly are we?"

"This is Avalon's great oak." Merlin walked toward the window, peering thorough it at a lush thicket of vines. As Merlin approached, the vines writhed against their roots, straining toward him as if desperate to touch him.

He stepped away from the window and hurried over to the iron stove, then lifted a lid from a Dutch oven. Sniffing, he declared, "Perfect, if I do say myself."

He muttered something in Angelic, and a small earthenware bowl appeared in his hand. With a practiced flick of his wrist he dipped it into the pot. He turned to Ursula, offering a bowl of steaming stew, then he paused.

"I'm terribly sorry," he muttered. "I forgot you'll need a spoon." With another incantation, a spoon appeared in his hand. Ursula marveled at his Angelic fluency—far superior to her own. Perfect diction, and so fast she could only understand two words in ten.

Merlin smiled. "Now, we just need something for you to sit on."

Three seconds and another spell later, they were seated across from one another at the wooden table. Merlin closed his eyes and leaned back in his chair. "Don't mind me. Eat your stew. We can talk when you've eaten."

"You're not hungry?"

"I had a bowl myself before you arrived. Terribly rude, I know, but I was famished."

Ursula took a bite of the stew, closing her eyes to savor the rich taste— tender pieces of rabbit flavored with thyme, rosemary, and juniper berries. She lost herself in the food, practically slurping down the bowl. Merlin had been right—a spoon hardly seemed necessary.

When she'd finished, she looked up to see Merlin watching her intently. "Did you like it?"

"It was amazing. You must teach me the spell to conjure it."

Merlin grinned, deep lines creasing his face. "No spell. That's my mother's recipe, and a family secret." He laced his fingers together, knitting his extravagant silver eyebrows. "So, how was the queen?"

"The queen?" Ursula stalled. She'd been expecting a question about Kester, or Bael, or the dragons in New York. Certainly not the queen who had pronounced her some sort of abomination.

"She's okay, I guess."

"Still flying her birds?"

"Seemed that way."

"I remember how she loved those little creatures," said Merlin a little wistfully.

"You knew her?"

His eyes flashed. "We were lovers once—it was she who imprisoned me here."

"I thought you were a powerful mage. A high druidic something-or-other. And you're telling me you're a prisoner?"

"Unfortunately, yes. I was fully aware the queen planned to steal my magic and force me into exile, but I loved her. It clouded my judgment." He paused, stroking his beard. "Not that I'd change anything."

Perhaps it was time to gently broach the 'Princess of Darkness' thing. "I don't think she likes me."

Candlelight glinted in Merlin's eyes. "She knows her mind. I have no use for weak women. Which brings me to you. We need to discuss your plans and future. You know winning the sword will be difficult, but if anyone is going to convince the Lady to hand it over..." He trailed off, stroking his beard again.

What was he on about? "The Lady?" Ursula prompted.

Merlin blinked, his eyes refocusing. "If you're to use Excalibur to defeat the dragons, you'll need to convince the Lady to give it to you."

"Right," said Ursula. "My friend Kester supposedly came here to look for Excalibur, though he's gone missing." She leaned back in her chair. "Does this have anything to do with why the queen hates me?"

"The blade was forged with one sole purpose—defeating the dragons."

"Okay. And this is why the queen was so afraid of me? She's worried that I'll steal her sword?"

"Not her sword. The blade belongs to the Lady of the Lake, on the top of the Tor, guarded by the shades of lost souls. Only she may bestow it upon a worthy knight."

"So why is the queen afraid of me?"

Merlin's eyes narrowed. "You don't know the prophecy, do you?"

"I have no bloody clue what you're talking about." Ursula clenched her fingers. "I'm seriously getting tired of not understanding what's going on."

Merlin closed his eyes and spoke slowly.

"The end starts when magic thickens the air,
The lost, as if unburied from the soil
Uncovered from the dankest roots of oaks.

Darkling, remember. Will you ring death knells
for Mount Acidale, kingdom of fire?"

Ursula straightened, leaning forward in her chair. Agnes had repeated part of the poem on the bank of the Thames. "What is that supposed to mean?"

Merlin's bony shoulders lifted up. "No one knows. Some think it's gibberish, a bit of doggerel written by a man half out of his mind. But I think it references the prophecy. One day, the Darkling will come to our shores, seeking the sword Excalibur. And if we allow him to unite with it, the depths of his dark magic will know no bounds, and he will become like a god who rules us all. Perhaps the queen believes you're the Darkling. Of course, you're not. Anyone can see that. A hellhound's power is intriguing, but you're no Darkling."

"Who wrote the poem?

"I did."

"And you're still not sure how to interpret it?" Merlin really was beginning to remind her of the sort of daft pensioner you'd meet on a bus sipping from a paper bag.

"It's a bit perplexing. I had been experimenting with one of the recipes in Rose's Mycological Manual. When I awoke I found the verse written on my napkin."

"Mycologic—are you saying you wrote this high on hallucinogenic mushrooms?"

Merlin shrugged. "I cannot know exactly what brought about the divination, but the first part of the prophecy has already come true. Magic is returning from where it had been hidden for millennia."

"I don't understand. Why do you and the queen think it's to do with me?" she asked. "Nowhere does it say anything about a hellhound named Ursula."

Merlin closed his eyes and repeated the first line of the poem: "*When magic thickens the air...*" He lay back in his chair for a long moment before opening his eyes. "Would you consider yourself to be lost but now uncovered?" His eyes seemed to pierce her very soul.

"I suppose. I don't know who I am."

With a sudden movement Merlin hopped up from his chair. The way he vacillated from lethargy to bursts of manic energy disconcerted Ursula.

He held out a bony hand. "Give me your hand."

Ursula did as instructed, and Merlin wrapped his thin, strong fingers around hers. He stared deeply into her eyes. His hand tightened, and she felt a sensation of water on her skin, and smelled the briny scent of sea air.

"Oh." His eyes widened, and he dropped her hand, almost pushing it away.

"What?"

"I didn't foresee that."

"What? What are you talking about?"

Without answering her, he chanted a word in Angelic, and she fell to the floor with the snapping and popping of muscles and bones as feathers sprouted from her arms.

Merlin stared down at her as she transformed. "Return to the Castle. You must leave Avalon at once."

"Why?" gasped Ursula as her mouth began to transform into a beak.

"I was wrong. Terribly, terribly wrong. I feel the darkness within you. You will bring ruin upon us all."

Ursula flapped her wings, rising into the air. She tried to speak, but only managed a few squawks. Merlin pulled open the window, and incanted another spell as she soared into the air. All around her, thorns writhed like a sea of snakes.

* * *

As she flew, a thorn lashed out at her, but she dove under it. Dodging another, she flapped her wings as hard as she could, the beats carrying her above the seething briar.

Okay. Now I'm really starting to think there could be something wrong with me. Apparently, every magical creature with insider knowledge thought she was some sort of monster. Even Bael did, it seemed.

She swooped around the oak, but the hollow she'd flown into had disappeared. There was also no sign of Taliesin. She was on her own.

She flew higher until she soared above the blanket of apple blossoms. The castle's turrets and tower glinted faintly in the distance, and mist whirled around its base. In the other direction, fog blanketed the iron-gray sea. She circled in the chilly air. Merlin had told her to leave immediately, and somewhere through that fog she could find the portal back to St. Michael's Mount. She had come to find Kester, and Kester clearly wasn't here. Unfortunately, she had no idea how to get through the portal from this side, and she didn't feel great about leaving Bael behind, even if he now found her presence disturbing since having learned of her origins.

Her other option was to return to the tower. The queen had said she'd be leaving in the morning, so she'd only be in Avalon for a few more hours anyway—plus, now that she thought about it, she needed to eat that apple to get her magic back. She didn't relish explaining to Emerazel that she'd lost it yet again. Angling her wings, she turned toward the castle.

Here, above the tranquil sea of apple blossoms, Ursula *almost* felt at peace. Nothing more than the sound of the wind against her feathers— and yet she couldn't hold back the rising waves of dread that churned beneath the surface of her mind. What exactly had Merlin told her? Something about a prophecy, and the awakening of magic. Did that explain the fear in Merlin's eyes, and the queen's? She didn't have the foggiest notion what they were scared of, or why Mount Acidale was important.

Niniane had told her it was the sister city to Avalon. As she soared, the night wind ruffling her feathers, she tried to remember what she'd read about Mount Acidale in the library in New York—hadn't there been a battle? And she remembered Bael mentioning it. Her brain hurt as she tried to recall what had been said. Bael had been upset when he'd learned Kester still lived. That was it. He had believed that he'd killed Kester at Mount Acidale.

Fuck. Her stomach dropped at the thought. Both Bael and Kester had been at this battle—and based on Bael's reaction on the jetty, she had a feeling he would never tell her anything about Mount Acidale. Still, Kester might. All the more reason she needed to speak to him.

She flew over the rocky ridge, which unfolded below her like the vertebrae of a sleeping beast. She looped around the keep and searched for Bael in its windows, soaring past one room after another, but she found him nowhere. Finally, she returned to her own tower room, exhaling a sigh of relief when she found her window still open. This time she was able to avoid any painful collisions when she flew through. She landed on her bed, her talons scrambling for purchase on the sheets.

She looked around the room, puffing her wings. She hadn't learned the spell to transform yet—and in any case, she couldn't speak. How was she supposed to shift back to her human form? When she tried to speak, her words came out as a series of guttural chirps. *Bloody hell.* Before she could fly out again to search for Taliesin, the owl's form appeared through her window, and he spread his wings to land on her sill.

"Sorry for the delay," he said. "Dinner ran late." He began to speak in Angelic, and Ursula felt her bones lengthen and snap, a painful elongation. As before, the feathers retracted into her skin. Her intestines shifted into place with a sickening lurch, and she doubled over. When she straightened again, Taliesin was already gone.

She sat at the edge of her bed, staring out the window. The whole thing felt like a terrible dream. If her bones didn't ache and her skin feel like it had been pierced with a thousand needles, she might have been tempted to believe it was just that.

Slipping under the covers, she closed her eyes. She knew she needed sleep, but as she was drifting off, her mind roiled. Niniane had said the king of Mount Acidale had been obsessed with fire magic. And Merlin had called it the kingdom of fire. Maybe that's why Kester had gone there —to claim the king's soul. But moreover, maybe this explained how she'd become a hellhound.

CHAPTER 14

Ursula awoke with a start. She could have sworn a loud noise had awakened her, but now, complete silence enshrouded the room. Sitting up in the morning light, she pulled up the shoulder of her silky nightgown.

Pale amber light streamed through the window, illuminating her sparsely furnished room. Her muscles burned, and her head felt like it was full of stuffing. Apparently, transforming into a nighthawk was a bit of a shock to the nervous system. Her head throbbing, she rose from bed and crossed the room to test the door. It was still locked. She hoped Linnet or Niniane would come soon. She really needed to pee.

A distant cry pierced the silence, the sound sending a shiver down her spine. It had been faint, but she recognized it nonetheless. She would never forget the scream of a dragon.

Her heart raced, and she crossed to the other door—the one with the stairwell that connected to the room with the fireplace. Wouldn't someone be in there? "Let me out!" she shouted. "There's a dragon."

The only response was the primal screech of the dragon behind her, its scream echoing through the open window, now louder, closer. Her heart hammering, she turned back to the window—nothing but clear blue sky. Of course, she had no idea what she'd been hoping to see, since dragons were invisible. She turned to bang on the door again, until at last the lock turned.

Niniane pulled open the door, staring at Ursula from below her wild mop of dark curls. A linen bag hung over her shoulder.

Ursula grabbed her arm. "There's a dragon. I need to get out of here."

Niniane's voice cracked when she spoke. "We need to go to the cellar. Elaine said to take you there. It's the safest place."

Ursula snatched her boots from the floor, slipping into them. "I can help fight if someone gives me my magic back."

"No." Niniane shook her head, turning to lead Ursula down the stairs. "We're to go to the cellar."

In the main chamber, Ursula's gaze flicked to the halberd above the fireplace. It looked rusty and dull, but it was better than nothing. If the dragon was able to find her in the cellar, maybe it would come in useful. But before she could pull it from the wall, the dragon's screech rent the air again, so loud that it rumbled through her gut. She ran to the arrow slit overlooking the courtyard.

Nimue and her maidens stood in the center. Dressed in white, the women formed a small semi-circle around the queen. She could hear them singing in Angelic.

Ursula's breath caught as terror chilled her blood. Across from them, a dragon crouched. It was enormous—at least the size of a city bus. Fiery red scales glinted in the sunlight. As the girls sang louder, the scales seemed to deepen in color. The spell they were casting had made it visible. And it clearly wasn't happy.

The dragon extended its neck toward the women and shrieked. The sound was deafening. Instinctively Ursula clapped her hands to her ears. Elaine and the maidens continued to sing.

The dragon stalked toward the queen. "Give me the girl," it said in a voice that was something between a growl and a roar.

"No. I will not allow the prophecy to unfold!" Nimue boomed.

"Where is she?" The dragon paused, sniffing the air. "I can smell her. She is near." Its head swiveled to look at the keep. Despite the narrowness of the embrasure, it fixed its yellow gaze on Ursula. She froze, her heart skipping a beat as the ancient part of her brain screamed at her to *run*. And yet, her body wouldn't obey.

Niniane tugged at her arm. "Let's go. Now."

Ursula turned, sputtering, her legs like jelly. She'd never felt such raw terror before, and her mind whirled as Niniane led her by the hand through the corridor.

Niniane pulled on her hand, urging her to run faster. "Hasn't anyone ever told you not to look a dragon in the eye?"

Footfalls boomed over the earth. As she ran, she glanced at the windows, her world tilting as she caught another glimpse of the dragon. His shriek rumbled the castle walls as he hurled his body toward the keep, shaking the walls with an ear-shattering crash. With the next slam of its body, Ursula fell to the floor. Glass shattered around her as a taloned foot punched through a glass window, grasping for her body. Nearby, Niniane screamed. Ursula scrambled to her feet, lunging away from the talons, and she managed to dodge it. A single claw caught her dress, tearing it, but Ursula was already breaking into a sprint.

With Niniane close behind, she headed for the stairwell, legs shaking. *Boom.* The castle walls trembled as the dragon threw its body at the keep again. It felt like being in the epicenter of an earthquake.

"How far to the cellar?" she gasped.

"Just a few more floors." Niniane took the lead, descending deeper into the bowels of the structure. Down here, the light dimmed and the air grew colder. Candles in sconces lit the way, but their flames burned dully. There was a damp, musty smell, like an ancient cave.

A few more turns down the spiraling staircase and they stepped into a low cellar. Niniane held her hand up and incanted a spell for light, calling forth a glowing orb that cast a golden light over dusty barrels and casks lining the walls. A wine cellar, by the look of it. A crash shook the room, and dusty debris rained down on them.

Niniane's entire body was trembling as she stared at Ursula. "Are you all right? The dragon nearly had you."

"Yes. It only managed to rip my dress."

Boom. Another crash shook the walls, and more dust puffed from cracks in the ceiling.

"Niniane," said Ursula. "I don't think we're safe down here. The dragon will dig until it finds us. When I was in New York, a dragon clawed through the street and into the subway just to attack—" Ursula stopped short when she saw the incomprehension in Niniane's eyes. *Of course. You have no idea what a subway is.* "Anyway, it dug into the ground."

Instead of responding, Niniane turned and ran, her linen bag bouncing off her hip. She stopped at a particularly large barrel of wine propped against a wall. "Help me." She leaned over, resting her hands on the barrel's sides. "We need to move it out of the way."

Boom. The room trembled around her and Ursula stumbled, almost falling as she hurried to the girl's side. She had no idea what Niniane was planning, but she'd come to trust Nimue's handmaidens—even if they'd imprisoned her.

"We need to push," Niniane explained. "There's a tunnel."

Ursula stood by Niniane's side, and together they rolled the barrel out of the way. Although it appeared to be made of solid oak it rolled with surprising ease, revealing the mouth of a dark tunnel, about three feet high.

"This way." Niniane dropped to her hands and knees, crawling through the gap.

Ursula paused at the entrance. What was Bael doing right now? She didn't like the idea of leaving him behind. But then again, even without his magic, the man knew how to fight. He was an ancient warrior demon of the Shadow Realm, and he probably didn't need her help.

She dropped to her knees and crawled into the tunnel.

* * *

ONCE INSIDE THE TUNNEL, the ceiling opened up slightly and she could get off her hands and knees, but she still had to crouch to fit in it. The spongy floor smelled of mildew, and as she walked, she felt as if the walls and ceiling were closing in on her. In the dim light, she could have sworn she saw a rat scurry across the floor. *Boom.* Water droplets fell from the ceiling like rain.

As debris and water rained around them, they scrambled through the tunnel, following the golden light of Niniane's orb. They fell into a plodding rhythm, one foot in front of another, soft mud squishing under their knees. At last, the dragon's booms went quiet, and Ursula's stomach unclenched. Down here in the dim light, she felt oddly comforted, hidden from sight.

"I think we're near the end," said Niniane, just at the point where the muddy floor gave way to dark stone. "There seem to be steps here."

Through the dim light, Ursula stumbled forward to a rough stone staircase. She straightened, peering up into the darkness. Niniane sent her orb higher, illuminating the dank interior of a narrow shaft. On one wall, iron bars had been hammered into the stone forming a sort of ladder.

"Up this way," said Niniane.

Ursula gripped the iron, climbing higher behind Niniane. "Where is this tunnel taking us, exactly?"

"Outside of the keep. You mustn't tell anyone. The secret of the cellar tunnel is known only to the queen's handmaidens."

"And she sent you to save me?" asked Ursula.

"No. That was my idea. I couldn't leave you in there, could I?" she said defensively.

"Thank you." Ursula wished she could give the girl a hug.

After a few more feet, Niniane stopped. The orb cast a golden light on a rough trap door, and Niniane pushed on it. More light streamed into the shaft. Above them Ursula could see the gauzy fluttering of apple blossoms. Niniane shoved the round trap door aside, and crawled out.

Ursula pulled herself out onto the mossy earth, then leaned against the trunk of an apple tree. Honeyed rays pierced the boughs, dappling the earth with flecks of gold. Carefully, Niniane slid the wooden cover back over the hole. The side facing up was covered in moss and dirt, and as it closed, Ursula was amazed to see how perfectly it matched the forest floor. When Niniane kicked a few leaves on top, it practically disappeared.

Ursula took a deep breath. "We're out of the castle now, but I don't believe we've rid ourselves of the dragon problem."

As if to illustrate her point, a dragon's screech pierced the air, and Ursula's stomach dropped.

* * *

Ursula followed Niniane through the woods, the sky obscured by the vast canopy of apple blossoms. She hadn't had time to put on a bra before leaving, so she hugged her arms under her breasts for support. "Where are we going?"

"I know someone who can help us." She peered at Ursula. "Do you have a lover?"

Ursula's brow rose. Niniane wasn't anywhere near old enough for this conversation, unless this was one those places where people married at the age of thirteen. "Why are you asking about that?"

"The dragons are coming for you. You shouldn't die without finding true love."

"Mmm. Good point."

Up ahead, the sound of rushing water interrupted the forest's quiet. Niniane's pace quickened until the trees began to thin giving way to the rocky bank of a mountain stream that rushed down a rocky mountainside, spilling between jagged boulders. Niniane hurried toward the nearest boulder, pulling off her linen bag and dropping it on the rock. Then, she pulled her dress over her head.

"I need an explanation at this point," said Ursula.

Niniane splashed the stream water on her body. "We must clean ourselves."

Ursula looked down at her mud spattered nightgown. "Our clothing is covered in muck. I don't think it'll make much difference unless you have a washer and dryer nearby."

Niniane smiled, pointing to her linen bag. "I brought us dresses." Then she jumped into the air, her dark curls trailing behind her, and leapt into the pool.

Ursula peeled off her nightgown, then leaned over to pull off her boots. In just her knickers, she followed Niniane into the pool. The water closed over her head with an icy splash until she surfaced, sputtering. "It's bloody freezing," she muttered.

"Rinse your hair quickly," said Niniane.

Ursula did as instructed—after all, the girl had got her this far alive. Maybe she knew what she was doing. As fast as she could, she rinsed the tunnel-muck from her ginger bob.

When she'd finished, she pulled herself onto the boulder again, and Niniane passed her a blue dress.

"Thanks." Braless, Ursula pulled the silky dress over her head, dismayed to find that it was the perfect size for Niniane—and several sizes too small for her. It hugged her body, and her breasts stretched the bodice fabric. The cleavage situation was out of control. At least the tight bodice would afford her some support.

"You're welcome," said Niniane. She studied Ursula for a while. "I can take you to the ferryman now."

Ursula sucked in a deep breath. "I didn't realize there was a ferry involved. Look, I don't know what happened to the person I came here with."

"I'm sure your friend is fine. As soon as the dragon screamed, everyone ran for the forest. No doubt he fled like the rest."

Ursula's throat tightened as she pulled her boots back on. *That doesn't sound at all like Bael.* "I'm sure he *is* fine, but he would never run from a fight. In any case, I came to Avalon with him, and I'm not leaving without him."

"Seems to me like you don't have much choice."

Ursula shook her head. "I came here for answers, too. I've got to leave with something. I need some way to fight the dragons." What she needed most of all was the gods-damned sword to fight the dragon. She hugged herself, weighing her options. Option one was following Niniane to the ferryman—the easy way out. Option two was going back in search of Bael, but she'd be defenseless against the dragon and could put Bael at risk if he felt the need to save her. Or, option three, she could go back armed. She could wrestle control over this situation once and for all— maybe *she* could get this sword to fight the dragons.

Ursula crossed her arms. "I need you to take me to the Lady of the Lake." What if she *was* some sort of Darkling? With the sword, she'd be able to take on an entire army of dragons. And even if she weren't, the sword was supposed to be the only weapon capable of piercing a dragon's flesh.

Niniane's eyes widened, and she shook her head. "I can't do that. You shouldn't even ask. People might think... people might think you're someone that you're not."

The Darkling thing again. "Okay. Don't take me. Just point me in the general direction. I believe she has a sword I need."

Niniane backed away, nearly falling into the stream. "No. Please stop asking. Don't you know the prophecy? The Darkling will arrive on our shores, searching for the sword?" She seemed seriously spooked. "Look, maybe I should get back to the queen. The ferryman is just over there." She pointed to a grove of trees just on the other side of the stream. "You can go on your own. But you must leave. I shouldn't have taken you this far."

Ursula glanced at the grove of trees. When she turned back to Niniane, the girl had already leapt off the rock, and she was sprinting for the forest in a blur.

"Why are you so scared?" Ursula called.

But Niniane didn't answer, her form seeming to shimmer away as she ran.

Darkling. The word echoed in Ursula's skull. She'd terrified everyone by asking for the sword in the first place, and then something about her had unnerved both the queen and Merlin. Still—if the sword would give her power, that's what she needed right now to end this dragon apocalypse.

Ursula ran after Niniane, but the girl had disappeared like a deer in the underbrush. Ursula called her name, weaving through the apple trees, but after twenty minutes of searching, Ursula only succeeded in finding her way back to the stream. The nighthawk spell would come in handy about now, but she hadn't managed to memorize it. Still, she needed to find a way to survey the landscape.

By the edge of the stream, she surveyed her surroundings. She stood on the side of a ridge, the stream cascading down the mountainside, rushing between rocks. Hadn't Merlin said the Lady of the Lake lived at the peak of the Tor? She didn't know what *Tor* meant, but if it had a peak, it had to be a hill of some sort, and if nothing else, climbing higher up the mountain would give her a better vantage point.

She began trudging up the slopes, her mind echoing with the word *Darkling.* If it was her destiny, there was no point in fighting it.

CHAPTER 15

*A*fter a half hour of hiking, Ursula reached the ridge's peak, completely winded, her legs aching. But she'd been right about the view—she could see clear down the side of the mountain, along its gentle slope that led to the apple blossom forests, and on to the mist-shrouded castle. A black column of smoke rose from the turrets. The dragon was wreaking some serious damage, and she needed to put a stop to it.

Above her was the great ring of basalt that marked the rim of the Tor. Sunlight glinted off dark, volcanic rock—pumice and obsidian. *Okay, so it's not just a hill. It's a bloody volcano.*

If there was ever a good time to have her fire magic, it would be now, but she'd have to do without it.

* * *

SHE'D BEEN HIKING for at least an hour when she came upon the trail that wound between the rocks—a narrow path barely more than a game trail. She would have mistaken it for exactly that had there not been a pile of stones twenty meters up the mountainside. A cairn—a landmark of rocks. Mountain goats didn't build cairns.

Moving as swiftly as she could, she hiked up the treeless trail, bathed in sunlight. Here, a few forlorn tufts of grass grew from the gravel and scree. She was probably imagining it, but she had the sense that the grass seemed to bend away from her as she walked, as if she terrified even the plants. Could they sense her Darkling powers? Up here, a cold wind whipped over her skin, and the temperature dropped, but the hiking kept her warm. A bead of sweat trickled down her forehead. She squinted in the sunlight, looking out for the next cairn when she felt a familiar prickle up her spine. Someone was watching her.

Up here, she had nowhere to hide. She was totally exposed on the mountainside. *Why couldn't Niniane have grabbed a blade?* Even a kitchen knife would have been better than nothing.

Footfalls crunched over the gravel path. Ursula whirled, ready to fight with her hands if she had to. And there was Bael, the sunlight gilding his powerful body. She took in his beauty—the perfect sweep of dark hair, the golden skin and gray eyes, the combination of colors like sunlight piercing storm clouds. Finally, he'd found clothes that fit him—black, as usual, with short sleeves that showed off his thickly corded arms, inked with vicious tattoos. A sword hung from his hip, and he carried a jacket under one arm.

She put her hands on her hips. "Fancy meeting you here. Were you looking for me?"

Bael shook his head. "You shouldn't be up here."

"And yet I am." She wasn't about to tell him about the Darkling prophecy. She'd already seen how he reacted to the fact that she was from Mount Acidale, and she didn't need to make matters worse.

He stopped a few feet in front of her, and she breathed in his seductive sandalwood scent. "Why are you here, Ursula?"

"I'm after the sword, obviously. You said it was the only thing that can kill the dragons." Ursula eyed him suspiciously. *What is he doing up here on the mountain?* "I thought you were in the infirmary."

"I was. They stitched me up, and when the dragons attacked, I started searching for the sword."

"What about your wings?"

"They put Vesalius Ointment in the wounds before they closed them. They won't fully heal, but they no longer require magic to keep me from bleeding to death."

"You still don't have your shadow magic?"

Bael shook his head. "The queen and the maidens hid the apples."

Ursula studied him closely. If he was after the sword, too, maybe *he* was the Darkling. After all, he was the one with dark, shadow magic—not her. Perhaps her betrothal to him had been enough to set off Merlin's and the queen's senses.

"Isn't the sword supposed to be nearly impossible to pull from the rock?"

Bael shrugged. "I've done many things that are supposed to be impossible." There was something about Bael's casualness that almost seemed feigned. What wasn't he telling her?

"We'll find it together, then."

They walked in silence along the path, toward a towering wall of basalt. It was awe-inspiring—extending at least a thousand feet in the air, and perfectly sheer. She didn't think she'd be able to climb it without her hellhound strength.

At the wall's base, the fields of scree transformed into boulders, splintered and chipped. Stopping by Bael's side, Ursula glanced up at the cliff nervously. At some point, the boulders had been ejected from the volcano's mouth. Ursula stared up at the sheer, gleaming, gray rock face. It didn't exactly look easy to climb.

As she surveyed the rock, a carved inscription caught her eye. Written in Angelic was the phrase, *A Knight bears a token of the Lady's Favor.* Next to the inscription, a shape had been carved into the rock—an arch, like a door.

Already, Bael was inspecting it, running his fingers over the carving. "This is the entrance."

"What does the text mean?"

"There are supposed to be a series of challenges to get to the Lady of the Lake. I suppose this is our first one."

Ursula walked up to the cliff, her shoulder brushing against Bael's forearm. At the brief contact of his skin against hers, a wave of heat surged through her, and she forced herself to focus on the rock. Like Bael, she brushed her fingers against the stone, finding the gray basalt cold and a little rough. The groove in the rock was maybe as deep as her fingertip. It didn't seem to extend into the rock any farther. "It feels solid."

Bael frowned. "I don't sense any magic."

"You can normally feel it?"

"Yes. Move away."

As Ursula retreated, Bael took a step back, then charged at the stone with a lowered shoulder. A crack echoed through the air, and Bael stepped back, rubbing his deltoid.

"A noble effort," said Ursula. "But I imagine we need to do what the inscription says. A token of some kind. What's a Lady's Favor?"

Bael scrubbed a hand over his chin. "Ladies used to give knights little trinkets to show their support. Hairpins, handkerchiefs." He glanced at her, and for the briefest of moments, his eyes slid down her body. "A bit of bodice lace if you were lucky."

"Bodice lace?" At the look Bael had given her, Ursula suddenly felt very aware of just how much flesh she was exposing in her tiny dress.

"A piece of cloth torn from the neck of her dress." His gaze flicked to her dress again. "Where did you get that dress?"

When he met her gaze again, his eyes half-entranced her. A pure gray, with faint flecks of blue, framed by black. There was always something so sad in his expression, and right now, she had the strongest urge to reach up and stroke the beautiful planes of his face—but they were here for a reason. "From one of the girls. It doesn't quite fit, I know."

A spark of heat flashed in his eyes as he stared down at her. "It looks perfect on you."

"Right," said Ursula, not trying to hide her skepticism. "So we need a favor for the Lady to open the door? What should I give her? Do you want to help me tear off a bit of my bodice?"

For just a moment, a wicked smile curled Bael's lips—and then, so fast she wondered if it had been there at all, it disappeared again, replaced by his usual stony expression. "Whether I do or not, your bodice won't help us. The inscription says a token *of* the Lady. We need a token *from* the Lady of the Lake. Not for her."

"Right. But that makes no sense. We need a token from her in order to get access to her." She bit her lip. "Maybe it's a metaphor." Then, the answer struck her like a bolt of lightning. "Do you have Mordred's pendant?"

Bael's eyes widened with understanding, and he pulled the golden apple from his pocket. Sunlight glinted off it, nearly blinding Ursula, and immediately the surface of the rock began to move. A pale light raced along the deep, rocky groove. Then a loud bang echoed through the air, like the report of a gun. Slowly, the stone swung open.

CHAPTER 16

At Bael's side, she stepped into a dim interior, and Bael called forth a glowing orb to light their way. It cast a dull, amber light over a rocky alcove that led straight into a twisting rock stairwell. Bael pulled his sword from its sheath as he moved up the stairs, and he directed the orb to float just above them. Quickly, their steps fell into a rhythm, her shoulder sometimes brushing against Bael's warm skin, as they wound round and round. As they climbed higher, her lungs burned and her thighs felt like Emerazel had set them on fire, but Bael hadn't broken a sweat.

By her side, Bael climbed like a god—graceful and smooth. Slow, even breaths. Dark shadows moved around him. Even without his magic, he exuded pure power. Truly, if either of them were the Darkling, it was him.

As they walked, the stone around the stairwell lightened to a pale cream color. Ursula's tongue was dry against the roof of her mouth, and the dip in the icy mountain stream seemed like something from a past life. Speaking of which, it seemed like nearly a lifetime since she'd eaten. In fact, she hadn't eaten since Merlin's. She tried not to think about it, but her mind wandered straight to the rabbit stew he'd served her. The rich flavors had melted in her mouth, a dish Kester would spend fifty dollars on at one of those fancy farm-to-table restaurants in New York.

Thinking of the stew, her stomach rumbled loudly. *Gah, what I wouldn't do for a proper meal.*

Bael stopped sharply and turned to look at her. "You're hungry."

She gripped her stomach. "Yeah. I didn't get to eat yet today."

A line appeared between his eyebrows. "When we leave here, we're getting you food. You need to eat."

"No arguments here."

Bael turned his head, putting his finger to his lips. After a moment, he whispered, "We're near the top."

Faint light shone in the stairwell. Up here, the air smelled different—faintly of smoke and charred wood. "We've reached the top."

Bael moved forward slowly, holding his sword ready. They rounded the final turn of the staircase and stepped out onto the top of the cliff.

A cold wind kissed her damp skin, and Ursula shivered. A whirling mist surrounded them, and the wind whistled faintly in their ears. Around them were the dark outlines of stone buildings, their surfaces covered in lichen and moss. Maybe it was the mist, but somehow the buildings' outlines looked indistinct, like they'd been plucked from an impressionist painting. Ursula studied the closest one. Broken windows interrupted the pale stone, and rotting wood formed the roof.

"What is this place?" she asked

"I'm not sure." Bael's feet crunched over a gravel path that wound into the mist. "Come with me."

Ursula followed close behind him. Unlike Bael, she didn't have a weapon, so she kept alert for any signs of movement in case she had to run.

As they walked further, a conical shape became clearer though the mist, close to the path's edge. Ursula frowned at it, taking in the irregular shapes—a pile of stone rocks. "There's a cairn. We're going the right way."

Their footsteps crunched over the gravel as they moved further along the path, until another building came into view, this one in better condition than the others. Built of pale stone and with towering spires, it looked like a cathedral.

Ursula stared at it, her skin growing cold in the misty mountain air. "What is that?"

Bael paused, studying it through the fog. "I think I know where we are. This is Camelot."

Shivering, Ursula crossed her arms. "I didn't realize Camelot and Avalon were so closely connected. I thought Camelot was somewhere on the mainland, in Cornwall or something."

"It was, but when Arthur left, the kingdom disappeared. And apparently, this is where it went."

"And it's been in ruins ever since?"

"So it seems."

Ursula looked up again at the ancient church, its pale stone crumbling. *Is this what will come of New York one day?*

As Ursula stepped closer the building, it became clear that calling it a cathedral had been generous. One of its steeples had crumbled entirely, and the other looked like it might collapse at any moment. An ancient iron fence surrounded the small yard in front. In its center stood the remains of an elm, half decayed. Bael paused, his gaze fixed on the trunk. She followed his line of vision to the trunk's base, where two stones lay, carved with ancient-looking words. Ursula strained her eyes, trying to read them, surprised to find they'd been engraved not with Angelic, but in Latin.

A shiver licked up her spine. "*Rex Arthurus. Regina Gwenevere.* The graves of King Arthur and Guinevere."

"Arthur was a great man." Bael looked serious, almost solemn.

"You knew him?"

"Only by reputation. Nyxobas tried to bring him onto the council, but he refused." Bael paused, the shadows around him thickening in the air, staining the mist with black. "Never refuse the demands of a god. It tends to end badly."

She had a feeling he was talking about himself, but he wouldn't be ready to explain. "It ended badly for Arthur, I suppose?"

A muscle worked in his jaw. "Could have been worse." He turned, starting down the path again. Suddenly, the air had iced.

Ursula followed "So—what, Nyxobas invited Arthur to join him on the Council, Arthur refused, and Nyxobas killed him?"

"It serves no one to speak ill of the dead." There was a note of tension in Bael's voice. He kept his eyes fixed straight ahead, lengthening his stride, until a towering wall became visible through the mist, looming above them. Made of dark stone, it stretched into the fog in either direction. Inset into the wall was a tall door of dark granite, above it more Angelic text: *A Knight is Honorable.*

Bael was already striding up to the door. When he pushed on it, it swung open with a groan. He turned, fixing Ursula with his pale eyes. "The second trial is through here."

CHAPTER 17

They crossed through the doorway and into a courtyard of tall grass. A small stone hut stood at the far end, and a large oak stump jutted from the center of the yard, its surface deeply scratched. It looked like what a woodsman might use for chopping firewood—except that a deep red blotch stained the surface. The hair rose on the back of Ursula's neck.

Bael stiffened as a man stepped from the door of the hut, stopping immediately outside the rickety building. At the sight of him, an icy jolt of fear raced down Ursula's spine. He wore pitch-black armor and gripped a massive battle-axe. The knight stood ramrod straight—didn't so much as twitch. If Ursula hadn't just seen him step out of the hut, she might have mistaken him for a statue.

Bael unsheathed his sword, stepping forward. "I am Bael, Lord of Albelda."

Almost imperceptibly, the knight nodded. With a creak of iron, his helm turned to Ursula.

She took a deep breath, "I am Ursula. Hound of Emerazel."

The knight nodded. He spoke, his voice dry and raspy, like his larynx was made of sandpaper. "Two contestants, unusual. I am Balach, protector of Camelot."

Ursula jumped when he walked swiftly toward the oak stump, moving faster than should have been possible in the heavy armor. Rearing back his arm, he slammed the head of the axe into the wood, the crack echoing across the courtyard. "Only those who accept my challenge may proceed to the chasm."

Bael raised his face. "What is your challenge, Knight?"

"I won't tell you that until you accept."

This isn't good. Ursula touched Bael's arm. "Don't do it."

Bael bowed his head slightly. "I accept."

Oh, for fuck's sake.

Balach stood stiffly, hands tight on his battle-axe. Ursula could feel the fear prickling along her limbs. *Run away,* it seemed to be telling her.

Whatever was about to happen, it wouldn't be good. Maybe she could stall long enough for Bael to reconsider.

She raised a hand. "Before you start, I have a question. Has a man named Kester been here, by any chance?"

"The names of the challengers are not important to me. Either accept, or leave."

Bael glared at her, gray eyes burning. He obviously wanted her to accept, yet there was something about the knight that warned her away. He moved too little, then too fast. Then there was his broken voice. *Why do I feel like I'm signing my own death warrant?*

And yet—she trusted Bael. She didn't know why—he told her nothing, and maybe he was the Darkling himself. But she trusted him with her life.

She took a deep breath. "I accept."

With a jerk, Balach pulled the axe from the stump. He flipped it around, so the handle faced them.

"Excellent," he said, his voice pure gravel. "The task is simple. I will choose one of you to take this axe and strike a blow. A strike of the axe, through another person's neck." He pointed to the blood-stained stump. "There. When the first person has finished, the other will strike the last person standing." Balach paused to let his words to sink in. "Are you ready?"

"Yes," said Bael.

Ursula was trying to work out the logistics in her mind, but she was pretty sure there was no way she and Bael were both getting out alive if they truly agreed to the terms.

Balach nodded. "The lady goes first."

Before Ursula could protest, Balach moved swiftly forward, thrusting the axe handle into her hands. She examined the blade—it was razor sharp, but poorly weighted. Ursula had a sinking feel that 'former Ursula'—the Ursula she had been before she lost her memory—had never wielded an axe.

"You must choose," said the knight. "Choose who you want to strike."

Darkling or not, she wasn't going to strike Bael with an axe. What the hell was he playing at? Once she struck clear through Balach's neck, they'd simply move on. Right? She pointed the axe at Balach. "I choose you."

The knight nodded, then knelt in the grass with a great groan of iron. Slowly he lowered his head until it rested on the surface of the stump. *Bloody hell. He's serious about this.*

She gripped the axe's handle. "Do you really want me to do this?"

The knight simply lay there, his head on the stump.

"You must strike a blow," said Bael.

This is super fucked up. She slowly raised the axe above her head, her arms straining at the weight. The axe hung heavy in her hands, and her heart raced.

"Do it," Bael urged.

Her heart thudded in her skull, booming like the beats of a war drum. *Thud. Thud. Thud.* A cold sweat broke out over her skin as she lifted the axe high above her head, then brought it down hard, striking the knight in the back of his neck. The steel blade tore through his armor, flesh, and bone, and buried itself in the wood. A spray of blood arced into the air, and in what seemed like slow motion, the knight's head rolled to the side and onto the ground. Blood pumped from his severed neck, and his body jerked and twitched on the ground.

Ursula's stomach lurched. "Gods below." Dropping the bloodied axe, she bent over on her hands, dry-heaving. This hadn't been like killing one of Hothgar's demons in close combat. The demons had been actively trying to kill her in battle. It had felt natural. This had been entirely different—an execution. She gagged again, her stomach rebelling.

Bael peered down at her. "Are you quite done?"

Ursula rose on unsteady legs, wiping her mouth with the back of her hand. "I'm sorry. I've never executed someone. At least, not that I can remember." Blood stained her dress. "So, what? Do we go now?"

Bael picked up the axe from the ground. "Go?"

Ursula's pulse raced. "Why are you picking that up? He's dead. Let's get out of here."

Bael gripped the axe, a glacial look in his gray eyes. Dark shadows whorled off his body, and he looked every inch an angel of death—a dark demon of the night realm. The Darkling, perhaps. What did he have in mind?

Ursula swallowed hard. "I mean, the knight is dead. We can go now."

"No," said Bael with brutal finality. "You gave your word. We must pass this task to go on to the Lady of the Lake."

He took a step closer, jaw clenching.

Her pulse racing, Ursula scanned the yard. She needed a weapon ASAP. Bael's bastard sword lay on the stones by his feet. Apparently sensing her interest in the weapon, he kicked it across the yard. *Fuck.*

Bael's expression softened, and he put down the axe. "Trust me. I won't hurt you. I thought you'd know that by now."

Her heart pounded against her ribs. "Really? Because it sort of seems like you intend to hack off my head."

"I'm not going to kill you. I claimed you by the Lacus Mortis," he said fiercely, "and I'm pledged to protect you."

Did he really take all that seriously? He couldn't think they were engaged. They hardly knew each other. "You agreed to cut off the head off whomever survived, and you appear to be holding an axe."

"You need to trust me. It may sting a little, but I won't kill you." He crossed to her, grabbing her around the waist, and pulled her to him, gazing down into her eyes. He cupped the small of her back, letting his thumb stroke lazily up and down her back, soothing her. At the same time, the feel of his powerful body against hers electrified her, and her breasts seemed to strain against her tight bodice. She slid her arms around his neck, pressing herself against him.

His sandalwood scent curling seductively around her, he leaned down, pressing a kiss to her lips. This wasn't like when he'd attacked her in Marazion—when he'd been drunk on the taste of her blood. This felt slow and sensual, his lips moving gently against hers, sending heat racing through her core. Gently, his tongue brushed against hers, and his fingers tightened on her back, possessive now. The kiss deepened, his powerful arms wrapped around her. When, at last, she broke away from him, his eyes were closed as if he were replaying the kiss in his mind.

When he opened his eyes again, he was studying her closely, as if trying to memorize every detail of her face. Once again, his thumb traced lazy strokes up and down her back. She couldn't help but think of the time she'd sat on his lap on his onyx throne and he'd imbued her with magic, his hands hovering just above her thighs, but never touching her. She'd been desperate to feel his powerful hands on her bare skin, and that same, molten heat surged through her body now—until, with a jolt, she remembered the headless corpse lying at their feet.

Her body tensed again. *Sort of a mood killer.*

He leaned down, his breath warming the shell of her ear as he whispered, "I would not kill the one I claimed." A heavy emotion tinged his voice. "As Lord of Albelda, you have my word. Please. Kneel."

She'd already decided she trusted him, didn't she? "Are you sure you can control that axe?"

"Trust me."

Slowly, she knelt before the stump, resting her cheek on the bloody surface. She grimaced when her face pressed against the knight's blood.

Bael's footfalls sounded behind her. "It's very important that you don't move. Do not flinch."

That's reassuring. One little twitch, and she'd find herself decapitated. Closing her eyes, Ursula focused on keeping her body perfectly still, her muscles completely rigid. Her heart slammed against her ribs.

The sound of whooshing air punctuated the quiet, and a flash of pain seared the back of her neck. Ursula's whole body tensed—and then it was over, the pain already subsiding. She opened her eyes. Blood dripped into her dress, but she seemed to be alive. She took a deep, shaky breath, lifting her head from the stump. "That hurt." She touched the back of her neck, and a smear of blood came away on her hand.

"Only for a moment, though," said Bael. "And we've completed the task. The knight never specified that the blow must be fatal."

"Correct," the black knight rasped. Ursula jumped as Balach climbed to his feet, holding his head, still encased in the iron helm. "You have both kept your word and proven honorable. You may continue on to the chasm." Cupping his head under one arm, he extended his other. "My axe."

Still shaking, Ursula remained on her knees, watching as Bael passed the axe to Balach. "Thank you for the challenge, Sir Balach."

Without another word, the headless knight turned and walked back to his hut, his armor groaning and creaking.

Bael caught Ursula by the elbow, pulling her to her feet. "That was very brave of you."

"I believed you when you said you wouldn't hurt me." She took a deep breath, searching his pale eyes. "When you said you were pledged to protect me by the Lacus Mortis, I thought it was only for show. I mean, we're not really engaged, surely—we don't even know each other. Right?"

For just a moment, she thought she saw a flicker of pain flash in his eyes—and then it was gone. Standing this close to him she could sense the heat of his body. Instead of answering her question, he frowned at her neck, gently pulling her hair aside to examine it. "How does it feel?"

"It stings a little, but I'll be okay."

"Good." Bael stepped away from her and picked up the bastard sword, striding to an arched doorway at the far end of the courtyard. "I believe we have another challenge awaiting us."

CHAPTER 18

They passed through the doorway and onto a flat plateau. Here, large volcanic boulders—nearly as tall as houses—covered the mossy ground. The boulders were inscribed with strange hollows and gashes—rough marks, as if they'd been gouged by the claws of a giant beast. A thick mist wound between the boulders, and the vapor crept up the hem of Ursula's dress and condensed on her skin. Goosebumps puckered her flesh.

Her teeth chattered as she kept pace just behind Bael. Just as he seemed to have barely exerted any effort climbing the stairs to Camelot, the chill hardly seemed to affect him. Even without his magic, the man was clearly not human.

They followed the path through the mist as the sky began to darken above them. Ursula kept her arms wrapped tightly around her, in what was proving to be a futile effort to stay warm.

By the set of his shoulders, Ursula could tell that something was weighing on Bael's mind. As usual, he didn't seem to want to talk, and they walked in silence on a gravel path that curved and twisted between boulders.

After about a half hour, her stomach rumbled, and Bael turned to give her a sharp look. "You're starving." He said it almost as if it were an accusation. "There's no food here. I can't catch anything for you."

She raised her eyebrows. "Catch something for me? What, like—if rabbits were lurking around the boulders, you'd kill one for me, and roast it over a fire?"

"Of course."

She bit her lip. "That's oddly sweet." Her stomach rumbled again, louder this time.

His shoulders visibly tensed, and he halted his walk. "You should have brought food with you. A human like you fatigues easily."

"I was a little busy trying to get away from the dragon who wanted to slay me. Why does it bother you so much if I'm hungry?"

He met her gaze, his expression solemn. "*You* may not take it seriously, but I'm pledged to protect you and provide for you." Without another word, he turned and strode off again.

Okay, so she'd hurt his feelings when she'd brushed off their betrothal. But really—he couldn't be taking it seriously.

She folded her arms across her chest, hurrying to keep up with him. "I just meant that we don't know each other. In this day and age, you don't agree to marry someone unless you know them. You've hardly told me anything about yourself. You said you were from Canaan, and that you were ten thousand years old. I know you were married once. That's all I know."

"You don't know about yourself, either," he pointed out. "You have no memory. But it doesn't matter to me. I know everything I need to know, everything that's important."

"What do you mean?"

He stopped again, fixing her with a fierce gaze. "I know that you're brave and honest, and loyal, and that I can trust you with my life. That's all I need to know." He strode on again.

A lump rose in her throat. *Well, now I feel bad.* She hadn't even told him everything yet, either. Specifically, she'd failed to mention the fact that everyone believed her to be an evil entity known as the Darkling. "I know those things about you too. I just don't know anything *else* about you. You're silent most of the time. You're not really a big communicator, you know. I know you spent a lot of time alone in Abelda Manor, but most people get to know each other by talking to each other. Telling stories about their lives." She'd seen a glimpse of his life—the ruddy, flower-dappled fields in her vision—and she wanted to know more. "You've hardly told me a single thing about yourself."

"My job is to provide you with what you need. And if you want to know about me, I will tell you. Ask me your questions."

She thought back to the few tidbits he'd told her about himself. "You're nearly ten thousand years old, which means you're pretty much from the earliest civilizations known to man. You obviously have stories to tell. You said you were from Canaan. So—where is that now, exactly?"

"The place I'm from is now called Byblos, in Lebanon."

"By the Mediterranean?" she ventured. It must have been the city she'd seen in her vision.

"Yes."

"What about your parents?"

Contemplatively, he stroked his jawline. "They died. Nearly ten thousand years ago. I still remember them vividly. My father was a soldier. My mother's beauty was legendary, and she shone like the North Star. The gods fought over her, but she chose my father instead. Both my parents died young, of a plague."

Ursula frowned. "How? They must have been immortal. Like you."

He shook his head. "I was born human. Nyxobas made me into an immortal, a high demon."

"How? Why?"

"After my parents died, I traveled around the Mediterranean. I was known for my strength and skill with a sword. I worked for the gods, collecting treasures they wanted, killing their enemies. And over time, Nyxobas and Emerazel wanted me to join their courts, to make me immortal. I accepted Nyxobas's offer."

And refused Emerazel's. Ursula was reminded of what he'd said of Arthur. *Never refuse the demands of a god. It tends to end badly.* But there were some things she'd have to broach gently. Namely, what Emerazel had done to punish him, and why, exactly, he'd killed his wife. "And after you accepted Nyxobas's offer, you joined him in the Shadow Realm?"

"No. For thousands of years, Nyxobas appointed me as his representative in Canaan. Over time, the people there confused me with a god. They built temples in my name, and forgot about Nyxobas. You can imagine how much he appreciated that."

"So he called you to his lunar realm."

"Precisely."

"And are you happy there?"

He shot her a perplexed look, as if the concept of happiness had never occurred to him. But there was something else in his eyes—a fierce hunger. "I have felt more alive recently." He peered at her closely.

She felt herself blushing, then quickly reminded herself she still didn't know why he'd slaughtered his own wife. Best not get too big of a crush on him. In any case, she had to ask him about it. Bracing herself, she cleared her throat. "And your wife? The woman whose portrait I saw in Abelda Manor."

Immediately, his eyes darkened, muscles tensing. The damp air iced around them, chilling with frost. "There's water up ahead. A stream." He glanced at her, studying her closely. "Do you want my jacket? It will get cold up ahead."

She shook her head. "You keep it. I'll let you know if I need it."

Bael slipped into his jacket, marching on.

Ursula exhaled, listening to the sound of rushing water. Through the fog, she couldn't see its source. As they moved closer, Bael unsheathed his sword. They rounded a boulder, and Bael stopped abruptly and thrust out his hand to stop Ursula. When she peered down, she saw that the ground dropped away sharply. A deep, wide gorge sliced through the mountain, and a hundred feet below, a torrent of water thundered over massive volcanic boulders. A thick spray rose off the water, mixing with the mountain mist and obscuring the cliff face on the other side.

A narrow suspension bridge hung just to their right. Built of wooden planks, it creaked in the wind, swinging from a pair of thick ropes. Bael crossed to the bridge, pointing at a boulder at its base, inscribed in Angelic.

Ursula stood by his side, mentally translating. "A Knight knows no fear. What do you think that means? We just cross the bridge?"

"I think that's the start, at least." Already, he was stepping on the bridge, placing one of his hands on each of the ropes. He moved gracefully but deliberately, one foot at a time over the boards.

"Just go slowly," he called over his shoulder as he disappeared into the spray.

Following Bael's example, she grasped one of the ropes in each hand. They hummed against her hands. *Must be the wind.*

Warily, she made her way onto the bridge, the wind whipping at her hair, her dress. The boards seemed sturdy, and the spray and mist were so thick she couldn't see the water below—a blessing, really. As she moved forward the world seemed to drop away. The roar of the water and the pervasive fog seemed to disconnect her from reality.

She focused on placing one foot in front of another, but soon the mist was too thick to even see her feet. It closed in around her, enveloping her body like a death shroud. Desperate for a sense of solidity, she tightened her grip on the ropes. Her fingers moved along the cold, wet cords, but she couldn't see her own hands—not even her shoulders.

The wind tore at her hair, whistling in her ears.

"Ursula," a woman's voice whispered, seemingly from within her own skull. "Ursula. I've been waiting for you." Ursula felt a powerful tug at her gut, luring her off the bridge's edge. "Will you join me in the mists?"

"Go away. I'm trying to concentrate."

"Ursula," the voice cooed, soft and maternal. "Where have you been? Why did you leave Acidale? Come, step off the bridge and see me."

"Acidale? Who are you, and how do you know who I am?"

"Of course I know who you are," the voice purred. "Don't you remember your own mother?"

Hope washed over her. Was this her mother, a shade in the mist?

"No," stammered Ursula, gripping tightly to the ropes. "I can't remember anything."

"You were such a beautiful girl. You had nightmares about wolves, and I'd soothe you with lullabies in your bed. In the day, you played in the wildflower meadows in the fields of Fraelissa. You sparred with your grandfather, moving like the night wind."

"In Mount Acidale?" Ursula stopped, her fingers forming a death grip on the ropes.

"Yes. Every summer we would visit Britomart Lake, and your father—" Delicate fingers brushed against her cheek. Then just as suddenly, they were gone. "Oh... I didn't know." There was a sense of urgency, almost fear in her mother's voice.

"What?"

The timbre of the voice changed, no longer feminine as it rushed past her like the wind. "The lost, as if unburied from the soil. Uncovered from the dankest roots of oaks..."

Ursula sucked in a sharp breath. "What do you know of the prophecy?"

But the voice was gone, and she stood alone on the misty bridge, the icy wind chilling her skin. She shivered involuntarily, and after a moment, she began moving forward again.

Was that really my mother? A lump rose in Ursula's throat. Merlin had spoken of the shades of lost souls on the Tor—perhaps it *had* been her mother.

Ahead of her, a shout pierced the quiet—Bael's deep voice. "No! No. No..." A deep, gut-wrenching despair laced his voice.

Her pulse racing, Ursula hurried forward along the bridge as fast as she could. The wind ripped at her hair and clothes, stinging her cheeks and flinging her red hair into her eyes.

Ahead of her a dark shape slowly materialized. Bael seemed to lean over the rope bridge—dangerously precarious. Thick fog swirled around his face, twisting and turning like it was a living thing.

"I'm sorry," he muttered. "I'm so sorry, Elissa."

"Bael!" Ursula yelled, but he didn't answer. Clutching the rope bridge, she made her way toward him, her heart in her throat. "Bael! Stay with me." *Elissa.* Was that his wife?

"You're right," he said softly into the fog. "You're right." He leaned forward, about to topple over the edge, when Ursula lunged, grabbing his shoulder.

He turned to look at her, the shadows in his eyes suddenly clearing.

"Bael," she said. "The mist is lying. It's not Elissa. It's a trick. I'm here now, and I need you here with me."

His eyes shone like starlight through the fog, and he reached for her face, but even as she did, a sharp gust of wind rocked the bridge. It only took a moment for Bael to slip. Ursula lunged, grabbing one of his hands before he completely fell. His legs dangled off the suspension bridge, and with her free hand, she clutched the rope for dear life, her arms burning with the exertion.

Ursula's arms strained at the weight as Bael's torso slid along the wet boards and toward the chasm. If his entire body fell off the bridge, she wouldn't be able to hold him.

One of Bael's massive hands seized the cord above his head. "I've got it. I'm okay." Slowly, he hoisted himself back onto the bridge.

Ursula fell to her knees, her body shaking. The ligaments in her arms felt like rubber.

"How did you know it wasn't real?" asked Bael.

"I heard my mother's voice. She tried to lure me off the bridge. Even though I can't remember her, I'm certain that she loved me. She wouldn't want me dead."

"Thank you." He leaned forward, kissing her on the forehead, then continued on into the mist. As the air began to clear, the other side of the chasm came into view—a sheer cliff face towering above them.

CHAPTER 19

The cliff loomed over them, a hundred feet in the air. Unlike the sheer basalt cliff at the base of the summit, curves undulated across this cliff. A path wound around the curved wall—a narrow ledge that led downward into the ravine.

As they moved closer, stepping from the bridge onto the ledge, it became clear that the ledge was manmade, the rock below their feet chipped and uneven, not smooth like the cliff wall above them.

Mist and spray slicked the rock from the torrent below. Fortunately whoever carved the path had had the foresight to include a length of chain attached to pitons, hammered into the cliff face. Ursula could move carefully along the ledge with one hand holding tight to the chain at all times. The eerie sound of the torrent echoing off the walls sent a shiver up her neck.

They moved slowly, clinging to the thin chain as they walked. Spray saturated their clothes, but at least no one was trying to lure them to watery deaths at this point. The sound of the rushing river grew louder, almost deafening, a constant roar that made conversation impossible. Eventually the path made a tight curve away from the water, snaking around a rocky ravine. Deep in the center of a crater, a small pond glimmered in the sunlight.

Underfoot, the slick rock gave way to dark red sand and chocolate colored stones. Around them, massive cliffs curved like a crater on the moon. Dark basalt rose hundreds of feet into the air above the pond.

Ursula took a deep breath. "Where are we?"

"Inside the volcano's caldera. It doesn't look active. And I believe this is the lake we've been seeking."

Ursula took a deep breath. *I will not imagine this place erupting.* Without her fire magic, she and Bael would be incinerated.

While the enormous walls of stone lent a claustrophobic feeling to the surroundings, they did at least block the wind. Here, at the bottom of the caldera, the pond water lay perfectly still, smooth as glass. A dark shape protruded from the water, and as they moved closer, she could see that it was a large volcanic boulder. From its center, the pommel of a great sword glinted in the sunlight.

The path led further downward, to the very shore of the pond, the water a deep steel gray. Trees and shrubs lined one side of the lake, and between the trees lay two smaller pools of water. Above the pond, wisps of mist twisted and turned in the air. Its stark, otherworldly beauty made the hair rise on the back of Ursula's arms.

When they reached the pond's shore, Bael stood at the edge, looking out at the boulder.

"I think we've found Excalibur," said Ursula.

Bael was already pulling off his shoes.

She frowned. "What are you doing?"

"What I came here to do. I'm going to get the blade."

"You think you should just pull it from the rock?"

He scratched the stubble on his chin. "The instructions are a little unclear."

"Instructions?" Even as she said the word, she caught a glimpse of the Angelic text carved into a nearby bolder. *"A knight has faith."*

Bael stepped into the water. Immediately, he grunted in pain.

"What is it?"

"Gods below. The water is hot."

The lake looked still as glass, the air cool and misty. "It doesn't look hot."

As he stepped out, Bael lifted his foot so she could see the bright red skin.

"Yikes."

He hopped over to one of the smaller pools of water. Carefully, he dipped a toe in, then the rest of his feet, exhaling deeply. He sat at the side of the pool, washing his feet. Gently he prodded his foot with a finger. Ursula grimaced. Bael shook his head. "I think there's something in the larger pond. A poison, perhaps." He nodded at the other tiny pool. "You can get yourself something to drink in the other one. It smells of fresh rainwater."

Ursula's throat was parched, and she crossed to the other tiny pool, kneeling beside it. She cupped her hands in the water, drinking from them thirstily. It tasted cool and clean.

When she turned back to Bael, he was crossing barefoot to the cluster of trees that rimmed the pond. "I'm getting you something to eat."

She smiled, sitting down to lean against a tree trunk. First, she'd eat. Then she'd figure out what to do about the sword. She never could think straight on an empty stomach. As Bael plucked fruit and nuts from the trees, Ursula stared at the lake, now reflecting a darkening sky. Beyond the tall cliffs, the sun had begun to set. Ursula shivered. Her clothes were still damp from the gorge, and the temperature was rapidly dropping.

Bael returned to her, his large hands full of pistachios and the crook of his elbow crammed with apples. Already, her mouth was watering.

He sat by her side, handing her the handfuls of food, and she tucked them into the hollow of her skirt, using it as a bowl. She unshelled the pistachios, popping them in her mouth. She swallowed hard. "The queen and Merlin think I'm some sort of evil Darkling meant to bring about the end of the world."

Bael stopped eating, staring at her. "You met the great druidic mage?"

"I had a midnight visitor. An owl. His name was Taliesin, and he transformed me into a bird. He took me to see Merlin in an old oak. And there's this prophecy about a lost one who will be found, something about an oak."

"What else did he say?"

"He told me about Excalibur. That the Darkling would come for it. He told me the whole prophecy."

Shadows slid through Bael's eyes. "And what is it, exactly?"

Ursula took a deep breath, reciting the poem:

"The end starts when magic thickens the air,

The lost, as if unburied from the soil
Uncovered from the dankest roots of oaks.

Darkling, remember. Will you ring death knells
for Mount Acidale, kingdom of fire?"

Bael looked at her a long time before speaking. "Mount Acidale."

"Do you have any idea what it means? What's the deal with Mount Acidale?"

He dropped her gaze, and the air iced around them. "I don't know exactly what the poem means. I only know that a battle was fought in Mount Acidale, and I was there. Terrible atrocities were committed and few lived." He met her gaze again. "The city nearly burned to ash."

"Maybe that's how my mother died."

Bael nodded solemnly. "But you're not the Darkling. The Darkling is evil incarnate. A creature so vile and so cruel he will destroy humanity as we know it if he gains too much power."

"And how do you know that's not me?"

"I've seen the face of evil. And you're not it. Like I said, I already know what I need to know about you."

She loosed a long breath. "So you've heard of this Darkling before?"

"The legend of the Darkling has been around as long as I can remember. He has many names—Abaddon, Bast, Fenriz, Moloch, even Lucifer. If the Darkling is allowed to return, chaos will claim the world. The Darkling has an allegiance to no god, wants to overthrow them all. Demons, humans, all living creatures on earth would suffer. It would be the end of days."

Granted, Ursula had a memory problem, but that really didn't sound like her. "Is there a way to stop it?"

Bael shook his head. "I don't know." He tossed his apple core into the water of the lake. It landed with a splash, water popping and bubbling around it. They both looked at the spot.

"Seems like some sort of acid," said Ursula.

Bael nodded. "It must be coming from the volcano."

Ursula grimaced. "I think I read about something like this in Yellowstone. People fall in and dissolve. Their bodies are never found."

Bael didn't answer, instead picking up a fist-sized chunk of granite. He hurled it into the lake, and it splashed distantly.

Ursula stood next to him. Together they waited for a few minutes to see if something would happen, but the lake remained still. In its center, the pommel of the sword still jutted from the boulder, tantalizingly close.

Bael cupped his hands around his mouth. "I am Bael, Lord of Abelda, here to seek the Lady of the Lake."

Ursula followed suit. "Ursula. Hound of Emerazel. Here for the same thing."

Silence greeted them. Ursula hugged herself, trying to get warm, while Bael picked up one stone after another, throwing them into the pond.

Ursula began to pace back and forth. "We should do something productive."

Bael hurled another stone. "I am."

"You're just throwing rocks."

"I'm extending the path."

"You are?"

He hurled another large stone. "You can help if you like."

His plan would take ages. "I'm going to walk around the lake. Maybe there's something we missed."

"Do you want to borrow my sword?"

"I'll be all right," said Ursula. "This place is completely deserted."

"As you wish," said Bael.

Ursula began following the shoreline. She scanned the ground, finding nothing but coarse red sand and dark brown boulders. At least there wasn't a shortage of material for path-building.

When she'd come round to the other side of the pond, she spotted an odd shape that broke the monotony of sand and boulders. Burnt in the center of a larger patch of sand was Emerazel's sigil, stained deep amber in the setting sun. Ursula studied it, her mind churning as a shadow crept over the caldera.

"Bael," she called out, projecting her voice as far as she could. "There's a sigil here. I think this must be where Kester left Avalon."

Instead of answering, Bael simply pointed at the sky behind her. Ursula turned slowly, momentarily terrified that the dragon had found her. But when she looked up into the sky, she saw something else instead —gathering storm clouds, blotting out the setting sun.

"Get over here!" called Bael.

Thunder rumbled over the distance, then a spear of lightning flashed in the sky. The sky flashed again, and lightning struck the top of one of the crater walls. A deafening crack of thunder boomed over the caldera. *Bloody hell, that was close.* And she was standing totally exposed, an open beacon for a lightning bolt. She turned, running for Bael and the grove of trees. As she ran, the iron-gray clouds unleashed a punishing torrent of rain, soaking her dress.

Just as she reached the trees, lightning touched down again, striking the sword's pommel. Thunder boomed off the rock.

Bael grabbed her hand, pulling her down. "We should get away from the trees. We can shelter next to a large boulder." Gripping her hand, he guided her to an enormous volcanic boulder that leaned over the earth, sheltering a small dry patch.

"Lean against the stone," he said.

Ursula slid down the rough stone to the ground. From here, they had a perfect view of the lake.

In a surprisingly graceful move, Bael pulled off his jacket. "Put this over your head for now."

She held it aloft like some sort of tarp while Bael dashed over to the trees. Rain hammered her legs and feet, but in another minute, Bael had returned with four sturdy sticks that he jammed into the ground around her. He pulled the jacket from her and secured it over the sticks like a sort of tent, then slid his sword under the makeshift tarp. He sat next to her, both of them with a view of the misty lake, its surface hammered by the rain.

"You'll want to pull your legs in from the rain," he said.

Ursula tucked her knees to her chest, her gaze roaming over his chiseled arms. "Where did you get the sword from, anyway?"

"From the armory, of course."

"And how did you find the armory?"

Bael leaned back by her side, his profile a dark silhouette. "Did the queen give *you* a tour of the palace?"

"No, she just showed me her falcon. Did she really give you a tour?"

Bael laughed softly, and she could feel his bare shoulder move next to hers, his heat radiating into her body. "I did my own exploring last night.

It's a beautiful place. I can see myself living on earth again, in a place like that."

"You snuck out of the infirmary and stole a sword?"

"Well, yes. A warrior needs a sword."

This close to Bael, she could feel his every movement, and smell his now-familiar sandalwood scent wrapping around her like a caress.

Bael studied her closely. "How's your neck?"

She reached up to touch the wound. "It doesn't hurt."

"Let me see."

She turned and felt his breath warming the nape of her neck. "It's fine. Not deep at all. It'll heal up in a few days," said Bael. "I'm sorry about hurting you, but it was the only way."

"I know. We had to do it to get here."

Bael's body warmed hers, but the temperature kept dropping. As the storm abated, mountain mist began to creep over the sides of the cliff and pour into the crater. Ursula shivered, and Bael slid an arm around her, pulling her in close.

Under their makeshift tent, they watched the mist drift down the cliff faces like slow-motion waterfalls, beautiful and hypnotizing at the same time. She could feel each rise of his chest. She closed her eyes for a moment, listening to the rhythmic beating of his heart.

* * *

She awoke with a start in the quiet night, finding that the mist had cleared. A vault of stars blazed above the caldera, brighter than she'd ever seen. She'd been sleeping on Bael's chest, his powerful arms wrapped around her. He breathed deeply, softly.

Despite the warmth of Bael's body, goosebumps prickled along her arms. The mist on the water swirled. Rhythmically—too rhythmically.

She nudged Bael. "Something is happening," she whispered.

He opened his eyes slowly.

"Look, the mist on the water."

He drew in a slow breath. "The Lady of the Lake," he murmured.

The mist moved over the water as if alive, but there was no breeze. It seemed to be gathering in the center of the water, pooling around the sword. It swirled faster and faster—until suddenly everything went still.

A figure stepped from the fog, draped in a long white gown that glided over the water's surface, as if she were floating above it. Her skin was pale as milk, and somehow hard to focus on, as if she were made out the mist itself. Only her eyes were clear: two blazing, golden orbs.

She stared at them, slowly extending a pale arm to beckon them closer.

"What are we supposed to do?" Ursula whispered. "We can't go in that acid bath."

Bael pulled off the makeshift tent and stood, then began to walk toward the water. Ursula rose and hurried after him.

Mist rolled toward them, skimming over the surface of the lake. It stopped when it reached the shore, piling up like seafoam.

Bael stood at the edge of the water, staring at the Lady of the Lake, and Ursula stopped by his side. The way the mist spread out and pooled at the lake's edge entranced Ursula. It had a strange texture, almost like it was a thickening into a path.

"The mist leads the way," murmured Bael.

Ursula bent over and touched the gathering fog as it smoothed over. Instead of condensation, she felt a spongy but solid mass—just a few inches thick above the acid. She glanced at the boulder. *A knight has faith.*

"I think she wants us to walk along the path."

Tentatively, Ursula stepped forward, her feet landing on the soft mist that hovered merely inches above the acid. She tried not to think of Bael's burned foot or the hiss when the apple core had hit the water.

Careful to stay on the path, she placed each foot in front of the other, her pulse racing as she moved closer to the Lady of the Lake.

Around her, little puffs of vapor flitted over the water, keeping pace with her. When she reached the midway point she stopped, turning back to look at Bael. He was following on the path, his movements graceful and smooth. The Lady's golden eyes burned intently into her.

As she neared the center of the lake the vapor thickened, stabilizing.

The Lady held out a graceful, misty arm. "Ursula of Acidale. What brings you to the Lake of Tears?"

"I have come for the sword."

"You wish to wield Excalibur? The sword of kings? You are only a girl."

"That's not what the queen thinks."

A fluttering noise rose from the Lady's throat, and it took a moment for Ursula to realize it was laughter. "Is that so? And what would you do with such a weapon?"

"I would fight the dragons who want to kill me."

The apparition's eyes blazed. "The wyrms have crossed our borders?"

"Yes. One attacked the castle this morning."

She felt Bael's warmth behind her, and the Lady's eyes landed on him. "Bael, *Lord* of Albelda?"

The way the Lady pronounced 'lord' suggested she wasn't entirely convinced about Bael's title.

"At your service." He bowed his head.

"Are you also interested in the acquiring the sword?"

Ursula looked at him, waiting to hear what he would say.

He shook his head. "No. I am here to help Ursula."

"You're a little old to be a squire."

Bael flinched, but he didn't say anything. The lady turned back to Ursula.

The lady floated closer, wisps of mist curling from her ivory face. "Tell me more about why you want the sword."

"Dragons have attacked New York and now Avalon. It seems like the only way to defend myself."

"What do I care of the mortal realm?"

"I don't know. Why do you protect the blade?"

A smiled shimmered on the lady's lips. "Excalibur may not be able to slice me in two, but in the right hands it can change the course of history. Even destiny." The Lady extended a long, graceful arm, reaching for Ursula, brushing ice-cold fingers along her cheek.

Ursula pulled away reflexively.

"Don't worry," the Lady whispered, "I won't hurt you."

Before Ursula could pull away, the lady's hands shot out, grabbing her face with fingers so glacially cold they seemed to sear her skin. Ursula tried to pull away, but her vision darkened, until she was no longer floating above the lake.

Now, she was running through a dark forest, gripping a heavy sword. Faint streams of moonlight pierced the trees' canopies, and the damp air smelled of pine and blood. Dry branches clawed at her, catching at her hair and scratching her arms. Her lungs burned, and adrenaline surged through her body. As she ran, she lifted the sword, slicing at the branches.

The scent of evergreens enveloped her and her legs propelled her forward, even if she didn't know why she was running.

She continued pushing through the trees until she reached a cliff's edge—only the barest sliver of wet stone between her and a thousand-foot drop. Nearly slipping off the precipice, she grasped for a tree branch. Far below, dark, glassy water filled the bottom of a ravine, glinting in the moonlight.

She desperately grasped the pine needles with one hand, her sword in the other. It was then that she realized it wasn't her own hand—she was in the body of another, reliving her memory.

A voice echoed through the forest, sending a sharp stab of fear through her gut.

Ursula could feel her body tighten with terror at the sound of the man's voice.

"Lady Viviane?" The voice called again, closer now, thick with rage.

Someone was trying to kill her—to slaughter Lady Viviane.

Steadying herself on the cliff's edge, she gripped her sword, lifting up the blade with two hands. When Ursula glanced at it, she recognized the pommel. Excalibur.

"Lady Viviane!" The booming voice sounded closer now, and she had to remain completely silent.

Slowly she lifted the blade so that moonlight sparked off the steel. Carved into the blade were three words: *Cast me away.*

The sword shook in the woman's hands, and she turned back to the water in the ravine. Anything was better than letting him catch her…

She leapt, falling soundlessly through the air, the wind whipping at her hair. She didn't make a noise as she fell to the water, nor when the impact tore her consciousness away with an agonizing burst of pain.

Her legs went limp and she drifted under the surface. As she sank into the icy water, a presence rose up from the depths to greet her.

"Lady Viviane?" a gentle voice whispered. "What have you brought me?"

With a sharp crack, the vision disappeared, and the phantom Lady stared, her golden eyes wide, her mouth slightly open. "So you're the one," she said softly.

Ursula shook her head. "What one?" This wasn't still the Darkling business, was it? Because Ursula had no intention of causing the apocalypse.

"The one who's been foretold. The one I've been waiting for." She leaned close, her icy breath against Ursula's ear.

"The end starts when magic thickens the air,
The lost, as if unburied from the soil
Uncovered from the dankest roots of oaks.

Darkling, remember. Will you ring death knells
for Mount Acidale, kingdom of fire?"

Ursula's heart skipped a beat. "No!"

The mist thinned in front of her, the pommel of the great sword protruding from it.

"Take it," said the Lady. "Wield the blade of kings. Kill the dragons if you desire. Or remake the world..."

As if drawn by a magnetic pull, Ursula reached for the sword. She grabbed the handle, slowly drawing it forth. Four feet of steel, perfectly weighted and lethally sharp, with words etched on the blade: *Cast me away.*

CHAPTER 20

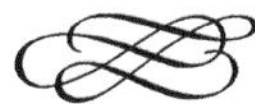

*B*ael had already stepped off the path by the time Ursula turned around, sword in her hand. It felt *right* in her fingers, as if it were a piece of her she'd never known she was missing. Slowly, she walked along the path of fog, the word *Darkling* rolling around in her skull like a curse. She swallowed hard. Was it true?

Her body was trembling when she reached solid ground. Bael's words echoed in her mind. *The Darkling has many names—Abaddon, Bast, Fenriz, Moloch, even Lucifer. If the Darkling is allowed to return, chaos will claim the world.*

And yet this sword felt so right in her hands. Trembling, she stared at the ground, hardly aware of the world around her, until she felt Bael's warm hand on her shoulder.

"What's wrong?" he asked.

"Didn't you hear what she said? I'm the Darkling."

"She's wrong."

"What makes you so certain?"

"I wouldn't have claimed you if you were the Darkling." Bael eyed the sword. "She's beautiful."

She offered him the pommel. "Do you want to hold it?"

He lifted his eyebrows. "Are you sure?"

"Go for it."

Bael took the sword, stepping away from her. He sliced it through the air, but the movement seemed strangely awkward for Bael, the strike veering off course. He tried it again, the blade wavering as he swung it.

Ursula frowned. "What are you doing?"

Bael shook his head with frustration. "I thought this sword was supposed to be perfection, but it's not. It's heavy and poorly weighted. Feels like it weighs a thousand pounds. How are you going to fight with it?"

"What are you talking about?" Ursula thrust out her hand. "Give it to me."

Bael passed it to her and she took a few practice strokes. The blade carved through the air like a peregrine falcon, the blade nearly an extension of her body.

Bael's brow furrowed. "Apparently it's meant for you."

"And you still don't believe I'm the Darkling."

"No." He snatched his jacket off the ground, then his sword. Already, the rising sun was staining the sky a deep crimson. "We should get moving. Let the rays of the rising sun warm our backs. I've already gathered some food for us."

Ursula gripped Excalibur. By Bael's side, she began to walk up the path toward the gorge, her mind drifting back to the memories of that frantic escape through the woods. She felt certain she'd seen the Lady of the Lake's memory—how she had come to live as a phantom in the lake. She just had no idea whom Viviane had been running from, or why she'd been willing to give her own life to keep the sword from him.

When they reached the gorge, the rising sun tinged the mist with deep shades of marigold and coral. This time, as they crossed the bridge, no mist wraiths assailed them. Through the boulder field, and past the Black Knight's courtyard, Ursula nibbled on pistachios and apples. Bael kept a brisk pace, pausing only to pay his respects to King Arthur again.

When they stepped from the forest, the sun had risen higher in the sky, and Castle Dahut came into view. Ursula's breath caught in her throat at the sight of it. If it had been practically a ruin before, it certainly was one now. Where the keep had stood a day before was only a thick column of smoke twisting into the sky.

Bael unsheathed his sword. "We get the apples with our magic. Then we leave."

"And how, exactly, do we get our apples?"

"I know where they're being kept."

Ursula smiled. "Your little tour last night was fruitful." She bit her lip. "So to speak. Anyway, when we get the apples, how will we call the boatman?"

"We don't. He would betray us immediately. Can you travel by Emerazel's sigil?"

Ursula nodded. "As long as we find those apples and I can get my magic back."

"Good. Stay low, run fast. The dragon is bound to be around here, waiting for you."

Without another word, Bael charged forward, running as fast as a storm wind across the grass. Ursula sprinted after him, trying to keep up, but she was no match for his speed. As she ran, she strained her ears for anything that sounded like beating wings, or claws on stone. A hundred feet ahead, Bael reached the moat's edge. He was waiting for Ursula by an enormous pile of rocks.

"You need to run faster," he said.

She pumped her arms faster, sword swinging as she ran. Her lungs burned. At last she reached the stones, nearly slamming into Bael from the velocity of her sprint. For a moment, she caught her breath, until Bael nodded at the pile of fallen stones and rubble. It had once been the draw-bridge, and now the rubble filled the moat, forming a path. Bael led the way, and she clambered over the stones, taking in the ruins of Castle Dahut.

The passage through the wall remained mostly intact, and their foot-falls echoed off its arched ceiling. But she sucked in a breath as they crossed into what remained of the courtyard. The grass was littered with stone fragments—and among the rubble, bodies lay bleeding into the earth, their blue dresses stained red. Nimue's handmaidens. Nausea welled in Ursula's gut, but she tried not to let the carnage distract her.

Smoke curled into the air, and an inferno blazed in what remained of the keep. Bael picked his way through the rubble, his sword ready, and Ursula moved behind him. As they moved deeper into the courtyard, she realized with a sickening jolt that many of the bodies had been mutilated, their dresses torn, their skin carved with claw marks. Battle fury ripped through her nerve endings, and she gripped her sword tighter. She wanted to drive this blade right into that dragon's heart. Maybe she *was* the Darkling, and if she was, the first thing she'd do would be to hack the entire dragon army to pieces. Excalibur seemed to hum in her hands, glowing with a pale light.

"Ursula!" a voice pierced the quiet.

Ursula whirled to find Niniane lying in the rubble, her dressed spattered with blood and mud, dark curls wild around her head. She looked like a broken doll among the carnage.

Her heart slamming against her ribs, Ursula ran to Niniane. When she reached her, she dropped Excalibur on the grass and fell to her knees.

"You came back." The girl's voice was barely a whisper, and a trickle of blood ran from her lips.

Ursula pulled the girl's head into her lap. "I needed the sword to fight the dragons. I got it. Can you sit up?"

Niniane swallowed hard, shaking her head. "I came to assist the queen, but I was too late."

Ursula took the girl's hand in hers. "We need to take you to help. Where's the infirmary?"

Niniane pointed at a burnt-out husk of a tower on the opposite side of the courtyard. Completely destroyed.

"What about your parents?" asked Ursula.

Niniane's eyes began to close.

Bael stood over them, looking down at the girl. "We need to get the apples."

Anger sparked. "We need to help her, not worry about the apples."

"With my magic, I can heal her."

Niniane's eyes opened, her gaze unfocused. "They moved the apples to the chapel."

Without another word, Bael ran across the courtyard.

Niniane blinked. "Is he your lover?"

"Who? Bael? No, not really."

"Then maybe he'll be mine," she rasped. "He's very handsome."

"Don't try to talk, Niniane. Just wait until Bael returns."

Already, Niniane's eyes were closing. "The dragon looked like fire—" She let out a long, raspy breath, and another trickle of blood escaped her lips.

"Niniane." Ursula squeezed the girl's hand. "Niniane." But the girl didn't move, and her chest had stopped rising and falling. Ursula stroked the girl's curls. "Wake up, Niniane." Gently, she lay Niniane's head on the ground, then straddled her skinny body, pushing on her chest to try to jump-start her heart. Niniane's head lolled, but Ursula tried to keep her focus, counting and pressing harder, desperate to revive her.

After what seemed an eternity, Bael's firm hand clasped Ursula's shoulder. "It's too late," he said softly. The scent of sandalwood enveloped her with a comforting, familiar darkness.

Ursula leaned back, a tear streaking her face. Rising, she wiped it off on the back of her hand.

"We need to leave," said Bael firmly. He thrust a shiny, red apple at her. It was warm, almost hot. "Take it. We need your magic to return to New York. I'll draw the sigil."

She bit into the apple, and the flesh of the fruit burned her lips, tasting of ash and creosote. As she swallowed each bite she could feel Emerazel's fire course through her, filling her veins with magic. When her body blazed once more with hellfire, she looked at Bael, his body exuding pure power. He stood in the center of a sigil scratched into the earth, and he gripped a dark bottle. "Calvados. I found it in the rectory. Priests always have the good stuff around somewhere."

He began to pour the brandy onto the sigil.

"Wait. You forgot a line." She traced it in the dirt with her fingertip, then turned to pick up Excalibur from the blood-soaked ground. Just as her fingers tightened around the hilt, a terrifying, inhuman scream ripped through the air. The dragon was returning. Hot, fiery battle rage surged through Ursula's body, and she lifted her sword. "I could fight it."

Bael shook his head. "There's nothing to defend here anymore. The castle is destroyed. And what's more, you don't know how to use this sword yet."

"I'm good with a sword."

"Even if you were brilliant with it, you've got no armor."

The dragon's blood-chilling scream tore through the air, closer this time. Battle fury and a need for vengeance burned through Ursula's body like an inferno, so hot and powerful her body shook, and the sword seemed to hum in her hand. She needed blood—dragon's blood.

"Ursula!" said Bael sharply. "I know what you're thinking, and it's not a good idea. There's nothing left to fight for here."

Another shriek from the dragon ripped through the air, so close now she thought she could feel the flames from its mouth. The thick black smoke billowing above the keep whooshed to the side as an enormous form passed through it. Ursula couldn't burn anymore—but Bael could. He was right. Best to get out of here.

She took a step closer to Bael, into the sigil, her body pressing against his.

"Now." Bael pulled her closer to him.

There was a thunderous slam, and the earth shook. The air simmered and the dragon appeared in the courtyard. At the sight of his yellow, reptilian eyes, his shimmering blood-red body, fear slammed into Ursula like a fist. Her breath left her lungs.

"Now," Bael whispered into her ear.

The dragon crouched, ready to attack, and Ursula summoned her fire magic. Her pulse racing, she recited the sigil spell as quickly as she could. At the final word, the dragon lunged, but before its teeth could close around them, an inferno of fire blazed around Ursula and Bael.

CHAPTER 21

They coalesced in the sigil room, surrounded by smoke and ash. Bael coughed by her side. Since she'd last been here, someone had tidied up. Cardboard and duct tape now covered the shattered window, and the broken glass had been swept from the floor. Ursula's legs still trembled—a relic of looking into the dragon's eyes—and her palms felt sweaty on the sword's hilt.

She stepped into the hall. "Hello? Anyone home?"

Footsteps sounded further down the hall. In another moment, Zee and Cera poked their heads from the kitchen doorway.

Cera ran to Bael, her eyes wide. "Lord. What happened to you?" Her gaze darted between Ursula and the shadow demon. "You're not trying to drink her blood anymore?"

"No. I went to help Ursula retrieve the sword." He coughed as he spoke. "The handmaidens in Avalon took my magic, and with it, the blood hunger." He coughed again.

Cera's eyes widened with concern. "Are you all right, my lord?"

"I'm fine," said Bael with a shrug. "Just a bit of ash in my lungs."

"Sorry, I didn't have time to warn you about that," said Ursula.

"What happened?" asked Cera.

"Another dragon," said Bael. "We had to leave in a hurry. Ursula and I haven't eaten much in the last couple of days."

"Follow me," said Zee. Ursula followed her to the kitchen, her mouth watering. When she'd left New York, the pantry and fridge had been completely bare. Now, food covered every surface—cans of soup, bags of potatoes and rice, even a bowl of fresh fruit.

Ursula's jaw dropped, and she rested her sword on the wooden table. "Where did all this come from?"

"London," said Zee matter-of-factly, grabbing a can of soup.

"London?"

"Kester used the sigil. Brought back loads of groceries."

"Kester?" Ursula had so many questions to ask him. Namely, what the hell was the Darkling? "Is he here?"

"No, you just missed him." Zee began rummaging in the fridge. Over Zee's shoulder Ursula saw containers of eggs, orange juice, and butter. Zee handed Ursula a small parcel wrapped in brown paper.

Ursula smiled wanly at the packaging: Paxton & Whitfield. Pulling open the package, she found a blue-and-white marbled wedge of cheese, and she inhaled the sharp scent of Stilton, her heart still heavy.

Zee crossed her arms, studying Ursula's expression. "I thought you'd be a little more excited. You seem like you've just come back from a funeral."

Ursula loosed a sigh, sorrow weighing hard on her chest. "A dragon attacked Avalon. It was a bloodbath."

"Shit, Ursula."

"I need to stop the dragons."

"First, eat." She thrust a chunk of baguette at Ursula.

Ursula spread some of the cheese on the bread and bit into it hungrily.

Across from her, Bael was eating chili straight from a can, but only managed a bite or two before Cera snatched it from him and dumped it in a pot. Bael sighed, but didn't say anything.

Zee worked on uncorking a bottle of wine. "So what's the plan?"

"We're going to fight the dragons," said Ursula through a mouthful of cheese.

Cera turned on the flame on the stovetop. "How, exactly?"

Ursula nodded at the sword on the counter. "With Excalibur."

"Oh." Zee's eyes widened. "*That's* Excalibur."

Cera's brow furrowed as she stirred the chili. "So... how does it work? Now that you have the sword you can just magically kill all the dragons?"

"No," said Bael with finality. "She'll need to train to use the sword first. Have you ever fought a dragon? It requires certain skills."

Ursula arched an eyebrow. "You've fought a dragon?"

Bael shrugged. "It was a long time ago. I was victorious."

Ursula's stomach tightened. "I now know that I need to avoid eye contact with the beasts. That last glimpse into the dragon's eyes in Avalon nearly had me pissing myself. But how long do you think it will take to train me with the sword?"

Bael stared into the distance. "Dragons are ancient creatures. Like the fae, they existed before the gods were banished to their separate hells. Their skin is virtually impervious to conventional weapons. Apart from Excalibur."

Zee spoke up. "The legend is, that blade was forged by Oberon, the first king of the fae. With it he struck down the Great Wyrm of Avalon. The sword passed down from king to king, until it was stolen by Queen Viviane and given to Dagon, god of the sea."

"Viviane," Ursula breathed. "I saw a vision from her memory. She's the Lady of the Lake."

Bael nodded. "Dagon kept the blade for himself."

Ursula pointed to the Angelic lettering along the edge of the sword. "Cast me away," she said out loud. "What does it mean?"

"Show me the other side," said Zee.

Ursula turned the blade over. There was more Angelic script: *Take me up.*

Zee let out low whistle. "So the stories are true."

"What do you mean?"

"When King Oberon forged the blade, it is said that he cursed it."

The sword seemed to call to Ursula, that strange magnetic pull, but she forced herself to step away from it.

Zee traced her fingertips over the hilt. "The ancient fae king was worried that he'd made it too lethal… too powerful. So as protection, he cursed it to discourage people from using it unless it was absolutely necessary."

Ursula sucked in a deep breath. "What does the curse do?"

Zee shook her head. "I don't know. The blade was forged eons ago. The stories mentioned that King Oberon left a warning on the blade, but no one remembers what he was warning anyone about. That's generally how fae legends go. You get a little bit of the story but nothing particularly helpful."

Ursula nodded. "So it can cut dragon hide, but it might be cursed. Anything else I need to know?"

Zee shook her head. "Not that I know of."

Cera turned from the steaming chili and squinted at Bael, as if scrutinizing him. "What happened to your magic? I cannot sense it."

"As I said, the maidens of Avalon took it from me."

Ursula stared at him. "But we got it back. I have my fire magic back. I thought you had yours, too."

He shook his head. "Mine could not be restored."

She dropped her bread on the counter, no longer hungry. "You didn't get your apple?"

"No."

Her stomach sank. "I'd sort of been hoping you could help me fight the dragons."

Bael crossed his arms over his chest. "I'm strong even without my magic. It's why the gods were fighting over me in the first place."

Ursula cocked her head. *He certainly doesn't lack confidence.* "Right, but if we're going to fight the dragons, we need all the extra help we can get."

Swift as a night wind, Bael deftly grabbed her around the waist and lifted her into the air as if she weighed little more than a piece of lint. "Do you doubt my strength? I was chosen to be Sword of Nyxobas because of my battle prowess." Gently, he lowered her until her face was mere inches from his.

She stared into his fathomless gray eyes, so stark and cold against his inviting golden skin. Her pulse began to race, and she had the strongest urge to lean in and kiss him on his perfect lips, that surprisingly sensual mouth. "I believe you."

Bael lowered her to her to the ground.

Zee coughed. "Are you two quite done, or do you need us to leave?"

Bael snatched the soup simmering on the stove. "Tomorrow I will train you to fight a dragon." He stalked out of the room.

Zee arched an eyebrow. "A little tetchy?"

"My lord was hungry," said Cera defensively.

Ursula rubbed her eyes. "Any idea where exactly Kester went?"

"Yes." Zee popped a grape into her mouth. "He went to speak to the dragons."

703

CHAPTER 22

As they walked through New York's deserted streets, Ursula kept her head down under her wide-brimmed cowboy hat. By Bael's side, she slunk through the shadows into a desolate subway station, the lights flickering on and off. She'd worn a black tank top with a swingy skirt—perfect for mobility. And also, if she was honest, she liked the way Bael looked at her legs. Her sword hung at her hip, her fingers desperate to grasp its hilt again, to feel the perfect surety that imbued her limbs when she gripped it.

Bael's gaze slid to her. "Your posture has changed. With the sword by your side, you're walking straighter."

The air felt humid and sticky, and sweat beaded on the back of Ursula's neck. "It feels right with me. Like it's always belonged with me." Did that make her the Darkling? She wasn't sure she wanted to know. From the little glimpses she had into her own past—her mother's bloodied shirt, the revelation that she'd tried to kill her own father—she was increasingly certain that she'd erased her own memory on purpose. That it had been an escape from her tormented thoughts.

She swallowed hard. "Maybe it doesn't matter who I once was. Maybe the present and the future are the only things that matter."

Bael shot her a dark look. "You can't escape your past, Ursula. Believe me."

His words sent a chill over her skin, and the image from his past flickered through her mind—the ruddy field, the smoke rising from the nearby city. Someday she would ask him again what had happened with his wife, but right now, she was still terrified to hear his answer.

Bael led her down a flight of tiled steps and onto the platform of the Fifth Avenue subway station. A few flickering fluorescent lights lit the platform. Not that there was much to see—trash was strewn everywhere, and there were scorch marks in the middle of the floor, like someone had once lit a small fire. *Grim.*

Months ago, this place would have been packed. Now, only dirty sleeping bags littered the ground, and empty bottles of water. Since the dragons had attacked, it appeared that people had taken up shelter here, though none lingered right now. Ursula had suggested training in the armory, but apparently they needed a large amount of room to maneuver. So a dank, trash-strewn subway station it was.

Bael pushed a pile of rubbish to the side, clearing a place for them to fight, then he unsheathed his sword—another one of the massive Zhanmadao blades from the apartment's armory.

For just a moment, Bael's gaze slid slowly up and down her body like a caress. "Are you ready?"

"To fight you? Aren't we going to use some sort of protection on the blades? When I did it with Kester we applied Zornhau's oil."

"Perhaps Kester isn't as skilled as I am. I won't hurt you." As if to prove his point, he lunged, the tip of his sword swiping the front of her tank top.

There was no time to parry. Instinctively, she dove to the right, landing hard on the ground, then kicked at his legs. Bael deftly leapt over her kick.

Ursula crawled to her knees. "You know you do the same thing every time."

Bael shook his head. "That may be, but at least I'm not spilling my entrails all over the floor." He pointed at her shirt. Where the fabric stretched over her stomach there was a narrow slice that exposed her midriff. "*You* always dodge to the right. And you should have used your sword, not your foot."

Ursula gripped Excalibur tightly, her knuckles whitening. "Fine. Let's do it again."

This time Bael didn't immediately charge. Instead he circled her, the fluorescent lights flickering over the muscled planes of his arms. A half-smile played on his lips—he was enjoying this. Somehow, he managed to look both predatory and playful at the same time. Ursula kept her blade trained on him, following his every movement—the graceful flex of his muscles, the sensual curve of his mouth as he stared at her, like a beast ready to strike at his prey.

"You're a warrior," said Bael. "Be more aggressive. Don't always counter. Attack me."

Ursula lunged, slashing for him. A normal man would have been gutted on the spot, but Bael's blade flashed up effortlessly. The sound of clashing steel rang through the station as their swords came together. Ursula's fingers tingled from the strike.

Excalibur moved in a silver blur, a perfect extension of her own body. This, at last, was her destiny. She only knew she needed to sink her blade into dragon flesh, to slice through one corrupted wyrm after another until the entire legion lay dead. After a life of being a nobody, a mystery girl, this was her chance to matter—to *make* her own identity. She moved around Bael like a phantom wind, her sword slicing through the air in a dazzling display, and a strange euphoria licked at her ribs.

"Better," said Bael.

Ursula struck again, and despite her thrill at using Excalibur, once again it was like parrying an iron bar. Bael's grip on his sword was rock solid, his power immense. Ursula stepped out of range, lowering her blade and rolling her shoulders to release the tension. Bael was toying with her, and he knew he was completely in control.

With her gaze locked on him, she raised Excalibur again, circling him while he remained still. Apparently he was now imitating her earlier strategy of defensively parrying her blows. She studied him. The solid jaw, sweep of dark hair, sun-kissed skin. He looked perfect. Her fingers tightened again. His beauty was distracting—another obviously unfair advantage.

But just as she was staring at him, he was letting his eyes roam over her body, taking in her bare legs, her cleavage. Her eyes narrowed. *Maybe I can use that.*

Lowering her guard, she stepped back again. She placed a hand on her stomach where his blade had sliced the fabric.

"Are you all right?" asked Bael.

"I'm fine." She reached down to the hem of her shirt and pulled it off. "Just worried the loose fabric could get caught on Excalibur's hilt."

Bael's eyes widened at the sight of her lacy black bra—a perfect chance to strike. Excalibur connected with soft flesh just above his hip. Blood wet the tip of her blade.

"Gotcha," she said grinning.

Shadows slid through Bael's eyes, and she had the feeling that the drawing of blood had ignited his primal instincts. Whatever else, Bael was an ancient demon, inexorably driven by urges to kill and dominate. The air seemed to ice around him. Raising his blade, slowly he began to circle her. The playful predator was gone now; only a feral beast stared back at her.

"That distraction was clever," Bael snarled. "Without my shadow magic, my human flaws are more easily engaged." His blade swished through the air in a complex pattern, in a breathtaking fighting style she had never seen.

She made a tentative strike, but he instantly glided out of reach.

"The trick," Bael continued, "is to learn your opponent's weakness and use it against them. Have you fought in the style of the Sfet?"

He slashed at her chest, but with an unexpected twisting motion directed the blade to the right at the last possible moment—directly at the spot she would normally have dodged to. Fortunately, she had chosen to dive left.

"Very good." His gray eyes bored into her. "You're learning, I see."

Ursula shook her head without answering. It required her full attention to track the movement of his sword.

Bael's blade hammered against hers. "The trick with fighting a dragon is the same as fighting a man. You must learn their weakness. Every dragon has an Achilles heel that can be exploited. Excalibur is merely the tool you'll use to finish the job. Your primary weapon will be your wits."

"So you brought me all the way down here to tell me to be clever? How do you think I've survived this long?"

Bael raised his sword again, attacking with a flurry of slashes and thrusts. Ursula parried them, but he drove her back. He hammered at her with his blade, like a blacksmith trying to forge Excalibur anew. Sparks flew in the air.

"Your weakness is that I'm stronger and faster than you," he said, slashing at her so hard she almost lost her balance. "Do you yield?"

"No," she gasped, trying to counter, but his sword was a blur of steel slamming into Excalibur again and again.

He moved around her like a whirlwind, so fast she couldn't keep up. In the next moment, he'd spun her around, pinning her arms to her body with his sword arm.

He leaned down, his breath warming the shell of her ear. "Do you yield?"

From here, with both her arms pinned down, she couldn't strike at him. And in any case, the heat radiating from his powerful body muddied her thoughts. With his free hand, he stroked the waistband of her skirt, just above her hipbone, and molten heat surged through her veins. Without thinking about it, she moved her hips against him, and a soft growl rose from his throat. His fingertips traced lower, just inside the top of her skirt, sending her pulse racing. Her back arched, her head tilting back against him. She wanted to feel that beautiful mouth of his on her neck.

Another stroke of his fingertips, lower this time, and her breath hitched in her throat.

"Do you yield?" he asked softly.

A little of her fire cooled. *So he's still playing to win.* "I thought we were supposed to be training."

His muscles tensed, fingers curling. "Right."

She forced her mind to clear, desperate to prove to Bael that she was capable of fighting just as he could. Granted, maybe Bael had superior strength and speed—and seduction, apparently—but she still had something he didn't.

She summoned her magic, gritting her teeth as Emerazel's fire raced down her arm. Hellfire ran into the blade, and flames licked the surface of the steel, and she felt Bael's muscles tense. *Let's see how you like my fire magic.*

She'd only intended to light the blade on fire, but Excalibur's steel was like a sponge drawing in her magic. The sword began to glow, growing hotter and hotter. Bael dropped his grip on her, stepping away.

Bael circled around her, staring at the blazing blade. Fire flowed out of the pommel of the sword, surrounding her, burning hotter, brighter, blazing like a dying star. Flames surged around her, so powerful she couldn't control it. "Bael, I can't stop it—"

"Ursula," he said.

She stepped away from him, feeling the fire lick up and down her body. But something was happening to it—it seemed to be solidifying, condensing around her, molding itself to her limbs. Plates and joints of platinum flame began to form along her surface. A crack echoed off the walls, and a stream of fire shot from the tip of her sword. It sprayed across the room, but instead of hitting the wall it stopped at some invisible barrier.

When she flicked her blade, the fire moved with it, as if she were holding a blade of pure fire ten feet long and two feet wide. Slowly she turned the blade so that it aligned with Bael's heart. "I may be physically weaker than you, but you don't have a sword that does this."

She stalked toward him, the glowing armor following each movement of her limbs.

Bael slashed at her with his blade, but a single parry sliced it in two, leaving him with only a melted stump of a sword.

"Do *you* yield?" Ursula asked.

With his eyes locked on hers—fierce, vicious—Bael took a step back. She slashed the flaming blade from side to side. Each swipe left an incandescent stream of sparks in the air. Bael backed up to the tiled subway wall. Slowly, his eyes blazing, he lowered the remains of his sword. He lifted an eyebrow, a ghost of a smile on his lips. "I yield."

Ursula lowered the burning blade, letting the hellfire cool in her blood. As the fire left her veins, the armor around her slowly faded, the flames waning from her blade.

Bael inhaled a deep breath, staring at her, before he finally spoke. "How did you do that?"

"I just summoned my fire magic, and Excalibur seemed to draw it in from my body. I don't know how the rest of it worked."

Bael studied her sword. "May I see it?"

Ursula handed it to him—already, it was cool to the touch.

He turned it over, as if entranced. "I've never seen magic like this. It looks like King Oberon forged the spell directly into the steel, and it amplifies your magic." He handed the sword back to Ursula, a faint smile curling his lips. "I think you're ready."

* * *

THE ELEVATOR DOOR ROLLED OPEN, and she and Bael stepped into the brightly lit foyer. A rich smell of roasting meat hung in the air. Before leaving the subway station, she'd pulled her tattered tank top back on.

Ursula crossed the kitchen, finding Zee standing over a large bowl of steaming mashed potatoes, smelling of garlic and butter. She was eating directly from the bowl.

"That was fast. You're done training already?"

Bael slipped into the kitchen, ducking his head under the doorframe. "The sword is more powerful than I thought. The dragons won't be able to hurt her. It's as if the sword was meant for her."

With a spoonful of mashed potatoes hovering in the air, a range of emotions flickered across Zee's face: skepticism mixed with hope that the siege of the city might be over. "Are you sure?"

"I will be there to help."

Cera's voice cut in as she appeared behind Bael. "The roast will be ready in twenty minutes. Don't touch the potatoes!"

Zee scooped out another spoonful. "What do you mean, exactly—that the sword was meant for Ursula?"

Ursula quirked a smile. "Well, for one thing, I was able to finally disarm Bael."

Bael grunted almost imperceptibly.

Zee's eyes widened. "How?"

"It's hard to explain. It amplifies my magic, making it more powerful. It also seems to create a sort of magical armor around me."

Zee whistled softly, lowering her spoon. "Angelic Armor."

"What is that, exactly?"

"You know how the fae are unaligned, right? Unlike your shadowy boyfriend here, we are not allied with the gods of light *or* dark. We're just, like, angels who came to earth to enjoy all the good food and cocktails. Anyway, in the very early days after the fall, we needed protection from all the demons. So the First Fae created a magical ward that made them nearly indestructible. It was called Angelic Armor. I had no clue it would work on a hound of Emerazel. It's supposed to be for godlike creatures. No offense."

"None taken." Ursula sniffed the air, scenting something smoky. "Is the roast burning?"

Cera shoved past Bael and raced across the kitchen, her pale hair flying behind her. "The roast!"

Zee frowned, scooping another spoonful of potatoes into her mouth. "We're trying to have a conversation here." She pointed her spoon at Ursula's ripped tank top. "You look like shit, you know that? Good way to get the dragons to leave you alone."

Ursula crossed her arms. "Right. Perhaps a shower is in order before dinner, then." As she crossed out of the room, a smile curled her lips. *Angelic Armor.* Surely, a creature like the Darkling wouldn't be able to wear the armor of angels, right?

* * *

URSULA'S HAIR was still wet from the shower as she made her way to the dining room, dressed in a yellow sundress. Cera had announced dinner was ready while she was still wrapped in a towel, so there hadn't been any time to dry it.

When she entered, everyone was already seated. Someone, probably Cera, had put a fresh tablecloth down and set the table with expensive-looking china. In the center was a steaming hunk of meat. Despite the smoke and Cera's consternation, it looked perfectly cooked.

There were bowls of mashed potatoes and steamed asparagus, and a large white porcelain vessel full of gravy. The room smelled amazing.

Bael sat by the meat with a large knife in hand. "You want some of the roast?" he asked her. Ursula saw that his hair was wet too—apparently she wasn't the only one who'd opted for a quick shower.

"Thank you, I'd love some."

While Bael carved the meat, she found a seat across from him, next to Zee. Zee was carefully carving her chunk of meat into bite-size pieces.

Across from her, Cera looked on nervously.

"Is it all right? she asked, her voice quavering.

Zee nodded. "It's perfect."

Ursula saw that instead of a piece of meat, Cera had laden her plate with mash, asparagus, and a large roasted portobello mushroom cap. Of course—she couldn't eat meat, unless she wanted to become corrupted and lose her mind.

Bael passed over a plate with a slice of roast, and a large helping of each of the sides. It smelled amazing. Ursula took a bite of the meat. It tasted amazing too.

"The roast is delicious," she said, directing her gaze at Cera. The little oneiroi beamed back at her.

Zee sipped her champagne. "Explain to me specifically how we're going to defeat the dragons. Am I part of this?"

Bael poured himself a glass of wine. "No. Ursula can lead us, of course, but clearly we need an army to fight an entire legion of dragons. I plan to raise one from the fae realm. They owe me some favors, though it will take some time. Months, perhaps."

Ursula's jaw dropped. "We don't *have* time. You saw what they did to Avalon." She tightened her grip on her fork. "You know, you have this habit of withholding crucial information until the last minute."

Bael arched an eyebrow. "You can't seriously expect the two of us to defeat them all, can you?"

How could she tell him she felt it was her destiny? She didn't know why, didn't have a rational explanation for it. She just *felt* it. Niniane's blood-stained face flashed in her mind. Months of delays, and how many more innocents would die? "It's what the sword is for. And the sword has chosen me. I think I'm supposed to do this on my own."

Shadows darkened Bael's eyes. "Don't be absurd. I'm not letting my betrothed into a dragon's lair without an army."

Her cheeks reddened. "I'm not *actually* your betrothed."

His jaw tightened. "I know that. But I still have a duty to protect you."

"I don't know what I did in my past, or who I am. All I know is that it's my fault that the dragons attacked New York. I alone should be the one to fix it. This is my chance to actually do something meaningful for a change. Don't you understand? I've been a nobody ever since I can remember. A fuck-up—no purpose, no identity, the screwed-up mystery girl with no past. And this is my chance to change that. I could be a hero, but I have to accept my fate. The sword has chosen me, and I go alone."

Bael stared at her, the air seeming to frost in the room, but she didn't wait for him to respond. She stood, hurrying from the dining room, desperate to get her fingers on Excalibur again. She needed to sink its metal into a dragon hide like a vampire needed blood. She hurried up the stairs to her room, where Excalibur lay on her bed. Before allowing herself to snatch the sword, she pulled off her dress, then slipped into her fighting gear: leather trousers, an armored corset, and a steel-reinforced leather jacket. Though, given what she'd discovered about the sword, perhaps she wouldn't need all this reinforced leather. A cowboy hat completed the ensemble, just enough brim to keep her face covered from an aerial view.

She zipped up her boots, then finally snatched Excalibur from her bed. The sword glinted in the soft light, and its ancient song of war seemed to sing in her veins.

Reunited with her sword, she moved swiftly through the hall, rushing down the stairs, the blade igniting her body with its power.

As she stood by the lift, waiting for the elevator to arrive, she wondered if someone would try to stop her, but she only heard the faint sound of Zee and Bael arguing in the dining room. Gently, she stroked Excalibur's hilt, and the elevator dinged. At last. *This* was her destiny.

CHAPTER 23

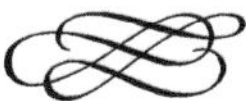

As Ursula walked uptown, she wrapped her fingers around Excalibur's hilt. The buildings loomed above her like dark tombs, the city deathly quiet. She needed a plan—her own plan.

The simplest would be to simply turn around and return to the plaza to wait for Bael's fae army. The guy had a point. It wasn't necessarily a brilliant plan of action to take on an entire dragon legion on your own just because you had a magic sword. And yet... how many people would die before she stopped the dragons? And what if this feeling in her gut was right, the one that said this was her fate? She'd never felt so sure about anything in her life. At least, as far as she could remember.

As she crossed by a broken shop window, a TV flickered. The volume had been turned down, but the screen displayed an announcer, standing with his finger to his ear. In the background, the Statue of Liberty loomed over him.

As Ursula stared at the telly, an inkling of an idea began to spark in her brain, and she leaned in for a better view. They were filming across from the Statue of Liberty itself.

Her pulse quickened, and she picked up her pace, heading for the part of the city that lay broken and burned.

* * *

IT HAD BEEN hours now since she'd left the Plaza, hiking along Fifth Avenue. From under her cowboy hat, sweat trickled down her temples. Power blazed up Excalibur's blade, curling around her body like an embrace, yet the summer heat seemed to steal her breath. She'd kill for a bit of air conditioning right now.

Around her, ruins smoldered. The dragons had decimated Lower Manhattan, demolishing buildings like they were sand castles. Dust and smoke hung thick in the air, burning her lungs. Ahead of her, light broke from between a pair of skyscrapers that leaned against each other. Beyond the buildings was clear air. Energy sparked through her veins. She was almost there.

With her sword by her side, she threaded her way between burnt-out cars and heaps of shattered concrete. As she neared the ocean, the smell of smoke receded, replaced by the briny scent of the sea.

As she walked through Battery Park, she found it surprisingly intact. Dust coated the benches, but apart from that it looked untouched. Sunlight streamed through leafy tree branches, dancing over the grass. Only the absence of people in the park hinted at the dragon apocalypse.

She bit her lip as she walked, trying to figure out where to go next. From what she'd seen on the telly, the news team had a good view of the Statue of Liberty, with the statue framed on the right side of the screen. That meant she needed to turn left.

Just as she veered left by a small stone building, voices echoed off the pavement. Instinctively, she jumped back behind a corner, her pulse racing. She strained to hear, and a few words floated along the sea breeze: "...Phil Rickter reporting live..."

Ursula smiled. She might be exhausted, but she'd found her camera crew. She pulled off her cowboy hat, dropping it onto the sidewalk, before peering around the corner. Sparse trees lined one side of a wide stone walkway, and the ocean lined the other.

The camera crew stood next to a low metal railing, right at the edge of the water. The entire crew consisted of a cameraman and a guy holding a boom mike. The gray-haired newscaster was pointing at the Statue of Liberty as Ursula approached. Her sword sang darkly by her side.

Maybe it was her bobbed hair, or the TV presenter's focus on the statue, but the reporter didn't seem to notice her at all. "—Gabby should be at the doorway at any moment," he said solemnly.

"Hello?" said Ursula raising a hand.

Frowning, the reporter turned in her direction, irritated at the interruption. He looked about sixty, with a serious set of eyebrows.

Ursula spoke more forcefully. "Hello, I'd like to be on the telly please."

The reporter nodded at the boom operator, who began lowering the mike.

Ursula's jaw tightened. "Look, I would like to turn myself in to the dragons. And I don't know any other way to get touch with them."

A whole bunch of things happened at once: The reporter's eyes widened, the cameraman spun to face her, and the boom operator lowered his mike to her face.

"It's her!" he shouted, jabbing the microphone at her forehead.

Ursula took a step back, holding up her hands. "Look, I come in peace. Everyone relax."

The reporter pointed at her, his face reddening. "Grab her before she gets away!"

"Stop," she yelled, but the man was already barreling at her. Ursula dodged. "What is wrong with you?"

Before he could answer, a shadow passed overhead, and Ursula looked at the sky, where a dragon's iridescent, green body materialized in the air, like a chameleon shedding its camouflage. With an ear-splitting scream, it swooped lower. The camera crew ducked, cowering on the grass. Ursula's heart thundered as the dragon circled. Screeching again, it dove for them, landing with a thundering boom that shook the earth, shaking the leaves from the trees. She looked away, trying desperately not to stare into its yellow eyes.

Growling, it stalked toward her, and she tightened her fingers on Excalibur. Maybe this hadn't been such a good idea after all.

"Ursula!" She turned, her heart skipping a beat. Someone was riding a lunar bat—in fact, it was Cera, her white hair streaming behind her, soaring on the back of Sotz. "Jump on! I'll take you to the island."

The dragon screamed again. It didn't look like it planned to allow her to turn herself in. No, it looked like it wanted to eat her. Cera was right, she needed to get to the Statue.

As the sound of dragon footsteps thundered behind her, Ursula ran for the sea railing. She leapt, planted a foot on the edge of the railing, and launched herself into the air.

CHAPTER 24

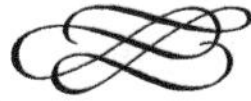

Ursula landed with a thud on Sotz's back, and she grappled for balance, her legs intertwining with Cera's. Sotz soared over the water, and the wind whipped at Ursula's hair.

"How did you find me?" Ursula shouted.

"Bael tracked you."

"Bael?"

"He's right behind us."

Ursula twisted around to see Bael, clutching the fur of his lunar bat. And behind him, clinging to his massive body as if her life depended on it, her face pale as milk, was Zee. Bael's fierce eyes were locked on Ursula's, but the dragon's scream pulled his gaze away.

"To the Statue!" Ursula shouted.

On the back of the lunar bat, they winged over the water. Sunlight dazzled over the waves, and the briny sea breeze kissed her skin. She shot a quick glance at the dragon, who swooped toward them, his green scales shining in the light. Excalibur whispered in the back of her mind, *Fight*, and her pulse raced.

Bael's voice boomed through the air. "Aim for the torch."

Cera pulled up on Sotz's fur, guiding him higher as they raced through the sky. Higher they soared, flying steeply upward, shooting past the soft, pale green contours of Lady Liberty. At last, they arced over the edge of the torch, before veering sharply downward. They landed on the torch's balcony with an ungraceful lurch. Ursula tumbled off, smacking her head into the wall. Dizzy, she refocused her vision just in time to see Bael land gracefully.

Zee leapt off the bat, visibly shaking. "Well? What now?"

Bael crossed to Ursula, holding out a hand. As she grasped it, rising, she glanced out at the water, her heart thundering against her ribs at the sight of the dragon closing in on them. Her legs began to shake—only now, it wasn't fear. It was battle fury that sang in her blood, spurring her on.

Bael crossed to a door on the balcony, but it was locked. He rammed it with his shoulder, and Ursula felt the blow reverberate through the stone —but the door didn't budge.

Excalibur called to her, and she pulled it from its sheath, staring at the dragon as it raced for them, piercing the air with its shrieks. Ursula longed to thrust her blade into its neck, but there wasn't much room on the narrow balcony that wrapped around the torch.

She turned to Bael, who still hammered at the door with his shoulder. She gripped her sword. "Get out of the way."

Bael shifted out of the way, and Ursula swung Excalibur at the locked door. As the steel clashed against the lock, sparks flew into the air. With the second strike, she cut through the lock. Ursula kicked open the door to reveal a dusty shaft. When she peered over the edge, her gaze landed on an iron ladder.

"Go," said Ursula, ushering Cera and Zee in front of her. They clambered down the ladder. The interior of the statue smelled like old pennies.

"Ursula." Bael touched her back. "Go."

She sheathed her sword again, turning around to hurry down the ladder. She'd descended ten feet before she realized Bael wasn't on the ladder. She looked up at his hulking silhouette, still by the doorway. He crouched, his sword drawn.

"What are you doing?" asked Ursula.

"Protecting you."

The walls of the shaft rumbled as something slammed into them, and a dragon claw punctured the copper skin above them. A stream of bright light pierced the dark shaft. With another thundering boom, a scaled, reptilian hand ripped away part of the walls above their heads. Debris rained down on them, and sunlight poured into the shaft.

"Hurry," Bael snarled.

Ursula's sword bounced against her thigh as she clambered down. Another blow slammed into the statue, and claws ripped through the top of the torch, knocking the ladder loose. Ursula lost her grip, tumbling off the ladder in an avalanche of falling debris, dust, and fragments of steel and copper.

Her heart skipping a beat, Ursula plummeted lower. Frantically, she grasped around, her fingers tightening around a rung. Pain tore through her shoulder as she barely held on. Coughing through the dust, she squinted into the shaft of light streaming into the ruins of the arm. There was no sign of Bael.

"Bael!" she shouted.

Silence greeted her—until Cera's voice broke it from below. "Jump. We'll catch you!"

Just as she let go of the rung, the dragon's head peered into the hole. The creature opened its jaws and screamed, the sound sending a shudder of dread up her spine.

* * *

ZEE's ARMS nearly broke her fall, but Ursula slipped through them, slamming onto a metal catwalk that rattled violently. Pain splintered her hip, but at least the walkway had broken her fall, and she still had her sword.

Coated in dust, Zee peered down at her. "Are you all right?"

Slowly, Ursula sat up. "Yeah."

Cera knelt, helping Ursula to her feet. "Where is the lord?"

Ursula peered up at the shattered torch, the sunlight streaming through the dust. The dragon had disappeared—for now. She shook her head. "He was still in the torch. The dragon ripped him away."

Ursula's heart thundered, her legs shaking. What had happened to Bael?

Cera grabbed her arm. "We must find the lord."

Ursula's pulse raced. "The bats. If Bael were falling through the air, Sotz could have found him. Bael rides the lunar bats better than anyone."

From above, the screech of shearing metal echoed off the walls—and then, the bloodcurdling sound of a dragon's scream as the creature ripped away another chunk of the statue.

"We need to get out of here!" Ursula shouted.

Zee flashed a blade—a delicate, mother-of-pearl dagger inlaid with gold. "Agreed. I'm just not sure I brought a sufficient weapon."

"Not to worry." Straining her eyes through the dust and debris, Ursula eyed a locked door at the end of the catwalk. "I've got the only weapon we need." She crossed to the door, unsheathing Excalibur. She swung her sword at the lock—once, twice—steel clashing against steel. She smashed the lock, then kicked the door open into a curved hall of crisscrossing metal beams: the crown of the statue, where sunlight streamed through narrow windows onto a metal walkway. Just as Ursula hurried to the window, desperate to catch a glimpse of Bael, a claw came into view, heading right for them. The sound of screeching metal pierced her eardrums again, and she stared through the window as the dragon peeled off a layer of metal like he was peeling an orange.

Ursula whirled, pointing to a spiral metal staircase. "This way." Gripping her sword, she ran to the stairs, with Cera and Zee close behind.

They sprinted down the steps into the darkness, spiraling lower into the depths of the statue, while above them, the dragon sheared off portions of the statue. The sound of tearing metal was deafening. Ursula's footfalls pounded the stairs, her body propelled forward by an irresistible force, the song of Excalibur singing in her blood. *The past doesn't matter anymore. Only what lies ahead.* As she ran, she tuned out the sounds of shearing metal.

At last, as they neared the bottom, new voices echoed off the metallic walls—the voices of young women.

"What is going on?" someone was shouting.

Another answered. "It's Wiglaf. He tore out of here hella fast."

Ursula slowed her pace, listening to the voices from below as the stairwell reached a large hall.

"Why would Wiglaf tear everything apart like this? It must be the girl, don't you think?"

"He's coming!" someone shouted.

Ursula stopped walking, peering over the railing. Just below her, twenty women stood on a concrete floor, surrounded by makeshift cots.

Despite the shabbiness of their surroundings, they were all dressed glamorously—short gold cocktail dresses, black strapless gowns—each one as gorgeous as a supermodel, most nearly six feet tall. A dragon's harem of sorts.

Ursula gripped the railing, surveying the danger. An enormous guard, his shoulders the width of a refrigerator, stood guarding a door, gripping a battle-axe. His muscled body oozed menace—but the dragons were nowhere to be seen. She could almost *feel* their power, their ancient, primal magic vibrating through the building, and she needed to find them. More importantly, her *sword* needed to find them.

Another screech of shearing metal echoed through the hall as the dragon tore at the statue.

An idea sparked in Ursula's mind, and she turned to Zee. "Can you glamour us to look like supermodels and movie stars?"

Zee chewed her thumb. "I think so. I'll just need to fix your clothes and makeup. Your face is good enough, I guess." She frowned at Cera. "But I'll need to change nearly everything about this one."

Ursula stroked the hilt of Excalibur. "Just don't change the sword."

Cera glared at Zee, who lifted her hands, her body glowing with a pale, pearly light. With her eyes closed, she muttered under her breath. As the pale light curled around her, Ursula felt her leather clothing transform into silk that slid against her legs, and she stared down at a plunging neckline. From the waist down, folds of tulle and silk hid her sword. From the corner of her eye, she could see that Zee had darkened her hair to a deep brown.

She glanced at Cera, who grew taller—her hair now a long, platinum blonde, her eyes changing, now almond-shaped and hazel. Cera straightened, flicking her long hair over her shoulder.

Zee merely gave herself a few more inches, transforming her outfit into a short cocktail dress, her eye-makeup glittering, lips a deep blood red.

Ursula touched the sheath under the folds of her gown for reassurance. "Let's go."

Standing tall, they walked down the final turn of the stairwell. While the guard stared up at the destruction above—the dragon tearing through more of the statue—Ursula and her friends slipped into the crowd of women.

The guard gripped his battle-axe, his eyes blazing red as he stared at the women. Dark, shadowy magic curled off his body. "Get to the warren, now!" his voice boomed. "All of you!" He flung open the door into a dark hall.

A dark smile curled Ursula's slips, and Excalibur hummed by her side. *The warren.* Exactly where she needed to go.

The women scrambled around, hurrying, and in the chaos, Ursula slipped into their ranks right behind Cera. She kept her head down as she moved toward the guard by the door. But before they could go through the threshold, the guard's hand shot out, and he grabbed Cera's arm, his eyes blazing red.

"I don't remember you." He growled. "Did Lucius bring you here?"

Cera smiled at him sweetly. "Yes. Of course."

The guard slowly looked her up and down. "You look like one of his."

Cera winked at him, and his grip on her arm eased up. Ursula kept her head down, passing through the door into a dark hall. All around her, the dragon's magic thickened the air, a shimmering, metallic glow. Her sword seemed to vibrate by her side.

Here, in the bowels of the statue, the dragons had dug a large tunnel. As they moved closer, a low growl vibrated off the walls. Ursula shuddered as a dragon's head appeared in the opening. A ray of sunlight pierced the hall, sparking off the beast's shimmering scales. Its magic grew sharper, and the dragon seemed to glow as if lit from inside like a lantern, eyes beaming with pale light. An icy shiver of fear snaked up her spine. But this time, she had the sword.

The dragon blinked slowly, then nodded once.

From behind them, the demon guard stepped into the hall. "Follow me, captives!" His voice boomed.

As the dragon turned and moved into the tunnel, Ursula and the other women filed after him into a passage the size of a subway tunnel.

With the dragon's back toward them, Ursula considered drawing Excalibur from its sheath under the folds of her dress, and she ached to carve its blade into the reptile's flesh. She could probably get in a good swing or two before the dragon turned around, assuming she didn't kill it outright. Still, she hesitated. It wasn't time yet. She needed to get into the warren itself.

Its movements serpentine, the dragon slithered through the hole, further into the warren's interior. Among the women, a nervous energy buzzed—almost terrified.

A tall blonde woman by Ursula's side was staring at the ground, muttering under her breath as she walked, her entire body shaking. "The Drake. The Drake was here... He has complete control over everything."

What was she talking about? Ursula cleared her throat. "The Drake?" she prompted.

The woman's eyes widened, her beautiful face smudged with mascara, and she put a finger to her lips. "Shhhhh..."

From Ursula's side, Zee grabbed her arm. "Ursula," she whispered. "This isn't good. Drakes aren't supposed to exist. King Oberon killed the last one."

"What the hell is a Drake?" Ursula whispered back.

"In fae lore, they were the leaders of the dragons. Immensely powerful, imbued with the magic of gods—"

The blonde glared at them, raising her finger to her lips again. "Shhh-hhh. Don't speak of him."

Behind the dragon, they rounded a corner, and the tunnel expanded into a cavernous hall. Carved from the bedrock, it was shaped like an amphitheater, with giant concentric platforms of stone that led down to a stage. Three sleeping dragons reclined on the stones, their scales shimmering in golden torchlight. A metallic scent hung in the air, so thick she could taste it on her tongue.

The demon guard led them down the stone ramp, and Ursula glanced at the massive dragon bodies, their hides slowly expanding and contracting as they slept. Her fingers went to the hilt of her sword. *Not yet, Ursula.* The Drake was the dragon she needed to defeat first. Cut off the head of a serpent...

As they moved down the ramp, a man stepped from the shadows. He was gigantic, at least eight feet tall, and clad in a suit of armor. He gripped a massive broadsword. But it was his hair that drew her eye—a bright red, the color of poppy flowers. It glowed with an inner light, shimmering even in the dim light of the warren.

And here he was—the Drake. Ursula reached for her sword.

CHAPTER 25

"Thank you for coming down on such short notice." The Drake spoke in a deep baritone, his voice oozing with power.

Battle fury began to race through Ursula's blood, making her body tremble—and yet something about his presence stilled her, willed her to obey his unspoken commands. As if drawn by a magnetic pull, she stepped forward.

The Drake's eyes glowed with an amber light, and he lifted his hands. "I am Lucius Artorius Castus. The last Drake. Leader of dragons." His eyes blazed with magic, and they locked right on Ursula. "And I do not remember seeing you before. Or have I?"

His eyes flashed, and her mind clouded. The words *kneel before me* rang in her mind, and Lucius drew his sword.

Zee elbowed her in the ribs. "Ursula!"

Lucius's eyes darted to Zee, and as soon as his gaze was off her, Ursula's mind cleared again. Her body blazing with power, she drew Excalibur, and she could feel her body humming with ancient magic. By the time the Drake turned back to her, she was ready for him.

Snarling, he lunged for her, but she parried his blow. Their swords clashed, echoing off the stone walls, and the Drake's eyes burned into her. "Do you think you can invade my home?"

Around the hall, sleeping dragons began to stir.

"I command a clan of dragons," his voice boomed.

"Is that right?" As she fought, Ursula summoned her fire magic, channeling it into the blade. She could feel Zee's glamour fading, as her body began to glow.

Lucius's eyes widened, flashing for a moment with fear. "The mystery girl."

"You can call me Ursula." Ursula slashed at him with Excalibur, her limbs blazing with a primal surety, as if she knew where each one of her muscles needed to be, each precise stroke of her blade.

"Where did you get that blade?" The Drake slashed at her, but she parried. Emerazel's fire seared the sword, igniting it with power. Around her ribs, her armor began to materialize, spreading around her torso, then moving down her arms. With this power burning through her body, she wanted blood and vengeance, slaughter and victory. She wanted to feast on stars, to grind monsters into dust. "You mean Excalibur? Viviane gave it to me. Did I mention that I know how to wield it?"

Lucian's eyes blazed. "That whore."

As he backed away, Ursula pressed in on him. "Where is Bael?"

"Bael?" Confusion flickered across his features. "Oh, you mean that monstrous demon that was creeping around here? He's been dealt with."

From behind her Zee shouted a warning, but it was too late. A dragon's talon slammed into her side with a loud crack. Ursula flew across the floor, slamming into a stone bench. Pain splintered her body.

"Good girl, Esther," said the Drake as he crossed to Ursula's crumpled form, his sword ready.

Ursula moved her legs. The blow should have killed her—and yet, after an initial flash of pain, she felt fine. The magical armor had protected her. Best not to let Lucius know that.

He pointed his sword at her head, a grim expression on his face. "The prophecy cannot be fulfilled. As protector of Mount Acidale, it is my duty to destroy the Darkling." He lifted his sword for a strike, but as he brought it down, she rolled to the side, and his sword rebounded off the granite.

Ursula crawled to her feet, raising Excalibur, her blade burning brightly, now ten feet of fire.

"I don't give a shit about your prophecy, and I'm not sure I'm your Darkling. I have no interest in destroying the world." She slashed at him, not entirely sure if she meant it. "I asked you nicely before. Now tell me where Bael is!" she roared.

Lucius retreated, his face paling. Slowly, a dark form rose behind him, then two more. The dragons stared at her with yellow eyes.

"Kill her!" the Drake screamed.

The closest dragon lunged, fast as a cobra. Ursula leapt back, and the dragon's jaws snapped the air where she'd been standing.

She brought up Excalibur, channeling more of Emerazel's fire into the blade until it burned like a super nova.

The dragon lunged again, but this time instead of dodging, she slashed at its head. The beast screamed, rearing back, blood pouring from its neck.

And yet it was hard to think clearly, hard to focus on death and destruction when her mind kept turning back to one thing—those pale gray eyes. "Tell me where Bael is!"

In the chaos, she'd lost track of Lucius. It seemed he'd slipped into the shadows. When another dragon lunged for her, she slashed her blade through its chest, feeling the hot thrill of victory as her sword found its mark. *This* was what she was meant to do, her destiny. And yet she couldn't keep her mind off Bael. What had the Drake meant when he'd said Bael had been *dealt with?* What the fuck did that mean?

When the next dragon lunged for her, Ursula wasn't quite ready, and the creature caught her in its jaws, violently jerking her into the air. The dragon's mouth closed over her head, and it shook her from side to side. Her head slammed against the inside of the beast's mouth like a bell clapper, her bones rattling within her.

The armor protected her from the dragon's teeth, but the movements rattled her body. For just a moment, the shaking stopped and its slimy tongue brushed over her, pulling and sucking her into its gullet. Gravity shifted and suddenly she was upside down in a narrow fleshy passage, in complete darkness, struggling to breathe.

* * *

729

PANIC SET in as she clawed at the dragon's esophageal lining, and she lost her grip on Excalibur. Instantly the magical armor surrounding her disappeared. Around her the dragon's throat constricted, like the coils of a snake, squeezing the air from her lungs. She squirmed and wriggled, but the clenching motion of the monster's muscles pushed her downward, toward its stomach. Swallowing hard, Ursula closed her eyes, her heart thundering against her ribs.

Fear claimed her mind. She'd imagined how she might die any number of times. Since Emerazel had conscripted her into service it had become almost an obsession. Usually in these morbid fantasies she was locked in combat with a particularly lethal demon, and she'd missed a parry. The resulting sword thrust severed an artery. Given her profession, bleeding to death was the most logical outcome, and death by magic was a close second. Never in her most disturbing visions had she imagined dying of suffocation and stomach acid inside a dragon's gut.

Her body pushed through some sort of internal draconic sphincter, and she was able to move again—but this freedom came with a big splash of stomach acid. Ursula screamed, expelling the last of the air from her lungs. She thrashed in the beast's gut as bile and acid burned her skin, her mind ripping apart with panic, lungs blazing with pain.

She was hardly conscious when her fingers brushed Excalibur's hilt, but she grabbed it reflexively. The sword seemed to draw the magic from her as if of its own accord, and it cast a glowing light over the folds of the creature's stomach lining. What had the words on the side of the blade read? *Take me up.* Her fingers tightened around the leather grip.

Golden light radiated up her arm as magical armor spread over her skin with a rush of power. Once the armor covered her face and head, she found that she could breathe again. As flames began to lick along the blade, the beast's stomach muscles convulsed. She was thrown back and forth as she slowly brought her free hand to the sword's grip. As soon as she did, the sword lengthened into a fiery pillar.

Around her, stomach acid hissed and steamed, spraying over the visor of her armor. She was thrown around again as the fire charred the monster's stomach lining. She pushed the blazing sword forward, burying it in the dragon's entrails. Then she carved to the side with all her strength.

With a hiss of burning flesh, the sword cut effortlessly through the dragon's guts. Ursula continued to be tossed violently, but she kept the sword moving until, above her, light pierced through a gap in the lining.

As the gap widened the spasms grew fainter. When the gap was big enough for her to fit through, she slowly climbed to her feet, her body glowing with magic armor.

The dragon lay dead in a pool of blood and bile. She stepped from its steaming carcass onto the stone floor, her eyes focused right on Lucius. A mix of draconic stomach acid and blood hissed along Excalibur's flaming blade as she leveled it at the Drake and the two remaining dragons who crouched behind him.

She arched an eyebrow. "Which one of you fuckers is next?"

"Impressive," said the Drake. "No one but the Darkling could have survived that."

His eyes burned with cold fury, but with Excalibur's magical armor surrounding her, they seemed to have lost their ability to command her. She needed to block out everything—everything now—but the Drake.

She took another step closer. "*Now* tell me where my friend Bael is."

"No."

It was then that Ursula noticed Zee standing next to him, Lucius's sword pressed to her throat.

"You will put down that infernal weapon." His voice was pure ice, and his sword twitched. Zee yelped in pain.

Zee stared at Ursula, her jaw clenched with determination, a few drops of blood stained the steel blade.

Pure, molten fury burned in Ursula. She wanted more than anything to carve Lucius's skin from his bones, but there was no way she'd be able to do that with Zee as his hostage.

"Drop the sword," said the Drake.

Slowly, she lowered her blade, dropping it on the stone. Sorrow and regret threatened to crush her chest as she let go. Was this it? As soon as her fingers left the sword's hilt, her magic armor vanished from her skin in wisps of pearly smoke.

The Drake grinned, kicking away her sword. "That was far too easy. You should really take care not to let your emotional attachments get the better of you. You just lost a battle that you could have won, if only you hadn't been hampered by human weakness."

He flicked his sword away from Zee, pointed it at Ursula.

Ursula folded her arms. "Well. You have your Darkling. Let my friends go."

"I cannot do that."

Emerazel's fire licked at her ribs. She might not have the sword, but she still had hellfire in her veins. Fire began to ignite her torso, blazing down her forearms.

The Drake shook his head. "Oh, dear. Without Excalibur you cannot hurt us." He nodded at one of his dragons, who crossed to her. The monster snatched her up in his hand, claws piercing her ribs. Hellfire erupted from her, but the dragon ignored it. The beast lifted her into the air, then turned and presented her to Lucius.

The Drake stood only a few feet from her now. He'd dropped his own weapon. Now, he leveled Excalibur at her head. "This *is* a fine weapon. I can see what all the fuss is about."

Anger ignited. "It's not meant for you."

"Is that right?" Lucius sliced the sword sharply through the air. There was no hitch in his stroke. He conducted the blade like it was an extension of his body.

"How—" Ursula started to say, but Lucius interrupted with a disdainful laugh.

"You don't know who I am, do you?"

A total knob-end? Ursula studied him. There *was* something familiar about him. Her eyes were drawn to his shock of red hair. *Was that it?* No, she would have remembered meeting a man with hair that color—that glowing, coppery red. Still there was a niggling sense of familiarity. The color of his hair was almost identical to the red scales of the dragon that had attacked Avalon.

Her eyes must have widened in recognition because Lucius grinned. "Sometimes it's more convenient to assume a human form."

He inclined his head and the dragon dropped her on the ground. Lucius kept Excalibur trained on her while the dragon began to transform, its neck shortening and its scales retracting into its skin. A moment later, a man stood in its place. He looked exactly like the guard who had led the gaggle of models down to the Drake's lair.

"Stop toying with her, Lucius," said the guard. "She has killed some of our own. She is the Darkling. She must be destroyed."

Lucius shook his head. "King Midac said we are to bring to her to Acidale alive. Lock her up. We will deliver her in the morning."

Lucius turned back to the captive, and Ursula could feel the fear ripple through the room. "Now, my beauties. Who would like to be my personal guest this evening?"

Ursula couldn't see his face, but she was pretty sure his eyes were glowing with that cruel, commanding magic.

CHAPTER 26

The guard led her down a dark, rocky tunnel toward a metallic door, its border suffused with a golden glow. Ursula gulped. She'd seen a door like that before. When she'd first arrived in New York, Bael's room had been protected by a similar magical barrier—nearly impenetrable.

As they approached, the guard spoke in Angelic—too softly for Ursula to hear the words. At the last word, the barrier around the door shimmered, then disappeared, enshrouding them in darkness.

The sound of an unsheathing sword pierced the quiet, followed by the guard's footsteps. "Open the door."

Ursula cautiously stepped closer, her pulse racing. Whatever monstrous creature lurked behind the door seemed to have the guard on edge. Slowly, she pulled open the door to a dark interior, and the tip of the guard's sword pressed into her back. She took a step forward into the blackness, and the door clicked shut behind her.

Instantly, a body slammed into her, nearly knocking her to the ground. A pair of powerful arms surrounded her. She struggled against them, but they pinned her arms to her sides—until she heard the deep inhale of breath.

"Ursula." It was Bael's voice, and his seductive sandalwood scent enveloped her. *He's alive. He's here.*

His grip loosened but he kept his arms around her, and he leaned down, whispering into her hair. "I'm sorry. I thought you were a guard. I didn't recognize you right away. You smell different. You smell like death." Warmth from his body radiated against hers.

"I ended up inside a dragon for a few moments."

His body tensed, and he released her. "What?"

"I got out."

He loosed a breath. "Thank the gods you're okay. They trapped me behind that gods-damned door. If anything had happened to you, Ursula..." He trailed off.

"What?"

"I would have had a lot of dragons to kill." He flicked a match, lighting a candle on a rough wooden table. Amber light flickered over a surprisingly large room, the floor covered in Persian rugs.

Ursula took a deep breath. This wasn't what she'd been expecting. "Where are we?"

Bael lit a candle in a silver sconce, and its light danced over the stone walls, some of them hung with paintings. An enormous, low bed stood in one corner of the room. "I think this was one of the dragons' quarters. They don't seem to have proper cells. I don't think they tend to leave their prisoners alive very often."

In the dim candlelight, Ursula surveyed the paintings on the walls. The one closest looked strangely familiar—a vibrant vase of yellow poppies in a post-impressionist style. She narrowed her eyes. "Is that a Van Gogh?"

Bael cocked his head. "Yes."

Next to the yellow poppies hung another painting, this one encrusted with gold leaf. Ursula strained her eyes in the dim light. It looked something she'd seen in the Tate Britain on a school trip. "I've seen that, too."

"Klimt. Dragons are obsessed with material wealth and beauty." He pointed at a far wall. "There's a Caravaggio over there."

Ursula plucked a candle from the table, and crossed to the other side of the room, her breath catching in her throat. Even in the light of the guttering candle, the painting was hauntingly beautiful—an androgynous man, draped in sheets and vine leaves, drinking wine. Dionysus, probably.

Ursula frowned at it. "I'm surprised the dragons aren't affiliated with Emerazel. She seems to have an endless supply of gold bullion."

"They were once, a long time ago, but Emerazel betrayed them. They've been mortal enemies ever since."

"What happened?"

"I don't know." The air seemed to thin. "Emerazel makes many enemies."

"So which god do the dragons serve?"

"None. Dragons roamed the earth before the gods fell. Like the fae, they have no divine affiliation."

Ursula turned away from the painting. Her body ached with fatigue, muscles burning, but despite the opulent furnishings the dragons hadn't bothered to include any seating. She crossed to the bed, sitting on the edge. "We need a plan to get out of here."

Bael crossed his arms. "You could create a sigil. We could return to the Plaza."

Ursula shook her head. "The dragons have Zee and Cera. I can't leave them behind."

Bael's arms tightened across his broad chest. "Then we wait until morning."

"Do you think you can fight the dragons?"

"I've killed one before." Bael cocked an eyebrow. "And I understand you killed one this evening."

"More than one."

"Tell me."

"Well, Zee glamoured us to look like the captives. And one of the guards—" She bit her lip. "Did you know that the dragons can take on human forms? Well, one of the guards led us down in their warren—that's what they call this place—and Lucius was there."

Bael stiffened at the mention of the Drake's name. "Lucius? The Drake is here?"

Ursula nodded. "Yes. He was the red dragon in Avalon."

Bael growled, the sound sending a ripple of primal fear up Ursula's spine.

"What's the matter? Who the hell is he?" asked Ursula. "Do you know who Lucius is?"

Bael's voice rumbled in her core. "He was Viviane's lover, once. He helped Oberon forge Excalibur."

Ursula's stomach dropped. "So that's why he could wield it. He seemed pretty certain I was the Darkling, you know."

Bael's body completely stiffened, his hands clenching into fists.

"What do you mean *'he could wield it'*?"

"I had to give him the sword. He was going to hurt Zee."

His expression darkened. "The sword will allow him to channel dragonfire again. With Excalibur in his hand, he could raze the earth to the ground. I don't believe he thinks you are the Darkling, but I think *he* could be the Darkling."

Dread bloomed in her chest. She'd brought Excalibur right to the Darkling.

Bael paced. "No single person will be able to defeat Lucius while he possesses Excalibur. We have only one option. We must go to the fae. They are our only hope. You must call on Emerazel's fire so we can escape."

"What about Zee and Cera?"

"Every war has casualties," he snarled.

Ursula rose. "I can't leave them behind. They've both saved my life more than once. They've saved your life too—"

"When they forced me to drink from your veins."

"You would have died if they didn't."

"Maybe I should have died." He said it so softly Ursula nearly didn't hear him. "Do you honestly think I want Cera to die? She's been practically the only person I've spoken to for centuries, but we have very few options now."

"Back up." Ursula glared at him. "What do you mean you should have died? Does this have anything to do with your tendency to charge into fights? You were the Sword of Nyxobas once, the leader of his army, yet you throw yourself into danger with no regard for your personal safety."

Shadows whispered in his eyes. "Sometimes there is no time for calculation. One must act whatever the consequences."

"*That* is your explanation for your death wish?" Ursula shook her head. "I don't believe you. There's more to it. Nyxobas wouldn't have put you in charge of his legions if you were simply rash and headstrong. Something happened. In the Shadow Realm, everyone says you are broken. Why?" Her mind raced. She had almost put it together. Having just cut her way out of a dragon's belly, Ursula was feeling a little rash herself. It was time to ask him for the truth. "What happened to Elissa? Why did you kill your wife?"

Bael turned from her, unable to meet her eyes, and she grabbed his arm.

"Tell me," she said softly.

He stared at the ground for a long time, and she could practically feel the emotions whirling off him. At last, without meeting her eyes, he spoke, his voice ragged. "It was a long time ago. Not long after I'd become immortal. I had been away, checking on our vineyards."

The vision of the ruddy, flower-dappled fields burned in Ursula's mind. "You were coming home—there was a fire."

Bael's pale eyes slid to her, and the pain etched on his features nearly broke her heart.

"How?"

"I saw a vision from your memory when you drank from me. It looked like an ancient city."

His entire body was rigid with tension. "It was Emerazel's vengeance."

A cold, dreadful understanding began to bloom in her mind. "What was?"

"I chose Nyxobas over her. When you deny the gods, it doesn't end well. She burned half the city of Gubla. When I ran home to save my wife, Emerazel was waiting for me. I wasn't strong enough to fight her. I let her take over my mind, let her draw my sword, with my hand. And I watched myself drive it into Elissa's heart. She was screaming for mercy. She didn't understand why I wanted to kill her—the terror in her eyes, the betrayal..." And then, so softly she nearly couldn't hear him: "She'd been carrying our child."

The weight of his grief pressed down over the both of them, and Ursula wanted to pull him from this exquisite pain. She wrapped her arms around him, bringing him close. She had the strongest urge to feel his beating heart, so grateful that he'd survived all this time. She pressed her hand over his chest, feeling his heart thud against her palm, then rested her head against his chest. "It wasn't your fault, Bael. I know people worshipped you as a god, but you are not one. You couldn't have stopped it. You couldn't have fought her. This was Emerazel's doing, not yours. She did it to break you. Don't let her win."

Slowly, his powerful arms wrapped around her, and he touched his forehead to hers. "Ursula," he said in a whisper. "I won't let anything happen to you."

* * *

LIGHT BLINDED her as the door to the chamber was flung open, and she pulled away from Bael.

The silhouette of a guard loomed in the doorway, two more behind him. "The Drake will see you now."

"No," Bael snarled.

Ursula held out a hand. She *needed* Excalibur back. Maybe the Drake was the Darkling, but the sword was meant for her. She'd been able to feel it. "I'll be fine, Bael." She looked into his eyes, searching them.

Bael's fists tightened. "You're not going without me."

One of the guards nodded at Bael. "It won't matter. You're both unarmed, and the Drake will decide your fates." He flashed a crooked grin. "And given what you did to his dragons, I can't wait to see how he kills you. The only question is which of you dies first, and which of you has to watch the other suffer."

CHAPTER 27

With her arms shackled behind her back, Ursula followed the guards back into the amphitheater. Bael walked grimly by her side, and she could almost feel the rage curling off his body. On his golden throne, Lucius sat in the shadows with Excalibur resting on his knees. It looked so *wrong* there in his lap, and its steel blade called to her, like a child who needed his mother. If her hands weren't bound behind her back, she'd have snatched the fucking thing from him.

Across from him on the stone benches, the captive women huddled next to each other. Ursula caught Cera's eye, and she heaved a sigh of relief. But Zee was nowhere to be seen.

Ursula glanced at the central dais. The dragon's carcass had been removed, and hastily arranged carpets now covered the stone. Still, blood and bile from the dragon seeped through the fabric, and the room smelled of death. If she'd come here on her own—if she hadn't needed to worry about Zee and Cera—perhaps none of this would be happening. If Lucius hadn't been able to use them as leverage, she'd never have given up the sword. They'd been her weakness.

Lucius quirked a smile. "The Darkling, and the Lord of Abelda. How intriguing." He crooked a finger. "Come closer."

Ignoring him, Ursula stood right where she was. Bael didn't make a move, either.

Lucius's expression darkened, and he cleared his throat, then frowned at one of the guards. "Gaderian, King Midac is late. Go above and check that he hasn't gotten lost."

At the mention of King Midac's name, Ursula heard a low growl rise from Bael's throat, nearly imperceptible.

The guard's footsteps echoed off the room as he crossed to the passage at the other end of the chamber. With a sharp crack of elongating bone and the scrape of burgeoning scales, he transformed into a dragon. His green, scaly body disappeared into the tunnel.

Lucius glared at Ursula, his fingertips lazily stroking Excalibur. The gesture was borderline obscene. "The king of Acidale will decide your fate. He has been looking for you for a long time, Darkling."

A million questions raced through Ursula's mind. "What does the king of Acidale want from me?"

Lucius shrugged. "I imagine it's because of the powerful magic that lives within him. But I am only his servant."

"His servant?"

"It is my sworn duty to protect Mount Acidale and to obey its king."

"And what about Excalibur?" Ursula stared at the blade, her body aching to snatch it from him. "I thought the one who yielded it was the Darkling, according to the prophecy." She closed her eyes, recalling Merlin's words.

> "The end starts when magic thickens the air,
> The lost, as if unburied from the soil
> Uncovered from the dankest roots of oaks.
>
> Darkling, remember. Will you ring death knells
> for Mount Acidale, kingdom of fire?

"The sword was lost. The Darkling gets the sword, and rings the death knell for Mount Acidale. You appear to have the sword. You are capable of wielding it, and I have no intention of destroying anything. If anyone is the Darkling, it's you."

"The sword is safe with me. I will keep it from the dark one's grasp." Lucius's eyes blazed as he looked at Ursula, until a commotion by the tunnel broke his gaze.

A pair of heralds in gold-accented crimson doublets strode into the room, blowing a short fanfare on brass trumpets. Lowering their trumpets, they shouted in unison, "Please bow for His Royal Highness, King Midac of Mount Acidale."

They stepped to the side, and eight men entered, carrying a litter on their shoulders. It was painted blood-red and embellished with gold leaf. Seated on a chair in the center was a thin man with a long, brown beard, which he stroked with bony fingers. A robe, embroidered with gleaming, colored gems, covered his thin frame. At the sight of him, her heart began to race.

Lucius had risen from his throne. Before the king had come in, he'd hidden Excalibur somewhere, and Ursula yearned to see it again. What the hell had he *done* with it?

Lucius bowed deeply. "Welcome, your Highness."

Ignoring him, King Midac flicked his long fingers. "Bring me closer."

The men, dressed in simple black clothing, moved slowly under his weight, until they stopped about halfway down.

Slowly, King Midac's gaze swerved to Ursula. A long, pointed tongue darted out, and he licked his lips. "Is this the girl? Come closer, girl." Venom laced his voice.

From behind, a guard pushed her forward, and Bael snarled. She peered up at the king, at his giant cheekbones and the ruddy skin that nearly matched his robe. He squinted at her, knitting his overgrown, curling eyebrows. "You are Ursula?"

She studied him, her pulse racing. *He knows more about me than I do.* He was the king of the land where she was born. For reasons she didn't understand, she was important to him—and most disturbingly of all, something about him seemed eerily familiar. A warmth that radiated from his skin. She stepped back involuntarily. Emerazel's fire.

The king grinned, exposing long, widely spaced teeth. "You can sense my power, can't you? The fire flows in my veins, just as it does in yours. Is it true that you now work for the Goddess of Fire?"

She straightened. "I am a hellhound, bound to collect the souls of those who've made a pact with Emerazel."

"Excellent. You will return with me and teach me what you know."

What? "So... this isn't about me being the Darkling?"

"No."

The king glared at the Drake. "Bring the sword to me, as well."

Lucius inhaled sharply. "The sword?"

"Don't play games with me, Lucius. I know you recovered Excalibur."

Lucius paled, then slunk back to the throne. His body trembled as he bent down and picked up the sword from the ground. Slowly Lucius drew the blade, his hand shaking.

"Bring it here." The king's voice boomed.

"How did you know I had the sword?"

The king chuckled, a dry, rough sound. "I'm not going to take it from you, Lucius. I merely wanted to *see* it."

Relief washed over Lucius's face, and he sheathed the sword again. As he did, a dragon's shriek echoed off the stone walls. Ursula whirled. From the mouth of the tunnel, a dragon's head rolled into the room, blood spewing from its severed neck. *What the fuck is going on?*

Immediately, hooded figures stalked from the tunnel, moving with a preternatural grace that seemed oddly familiar. Ursula didn't have time to study them closely, because Lucius charged past, knocking her to the ground.

And that's when all hell broke loose. The dragon guards transformed with the snapping of bones, the growing of scales. King Midac's chair-bearers nearly dropped him, and the captive models screamed, running around the room.

With her hands still bound behind her back, Ursula rose. Icy fear licked up her spine as a new figure walked into the room, his body shrouded in dark magic. She *knew* that magic, that power. With the enormous, leathery wings cascading through the haze of shadow magic, there was no mistaking Abrax in all his demonic glory. Abrax, demigod, son of the God of Night. Abrax—the powerful incubus who wanted her dead. Or worse.

The shadows thinned around him, and his pale eyes pierced the dim light. "I've come for the girl."

Bael stepped forward, his body taut with fury. "I have claimed her, as you know."

Abrax's eyes turned to Bael, his eyes blazing with pale light.

"I said, bring me the girl!" Abrax's voice echoed off the hall.

Two guards grabbed her by the arms, their fingers digging into her flesh as they dragged her forward. Abrax's lips curled in a smile. "Then kill the Lord of Abelda."

The men behind Abrax threw back their hoods, revealing the blank, gray, featureless faces of golems. Just as they rushed for Ursula, two of the dragons lunged for them, swiping at them with their claws.

Bael's voice boomed from behind her, "Run!"

Ursula swung her body, freeing herself from the guards. She kicked hard, taking out one of them, then she ran for Bael. Just as she was about to reach him, tendrils of shadow lashed out and wrapped themselves around his chest.

Abrax landed next to him, his leathery wings outstretched. "Still hanging around with Emerazel's cur. You have the most extraordinarily bad taste in women."

Bael strained against his bonds, but they held him fast. Then Lucius stepped from the shadows.

"What are you doing here, Abrax?" asked the Drake.

"Taking what is mine," Abrax growled.

"You want the Darkling?"

A ghost of a smile crossed Abrax's lips. "Is that what you think? That Ursula is the Darkling?" He cocked his head. "Actually, I don't really care what you think. It's time for you to die, Lucius."

Lucius shook his head slowly. "I'm not going to die." He unsheathed Excalibur. With his eyes locked on Abrax, he slowly raised the blade. The hair on his head glowed brightly, like a lit torch, and a deep red flame began to flicker along the blade, covering his arm. Ursula sucked in a breath. Even Abrax would have trouble fighting a man ensconced in Excalibur's armor.

In the next moment, he was grunting, his body hunching over as the blade disappeared underneath him. The hair on his head blazed red, and crimson scales sprouted from his skin. Claws grew from his fingers, and his body expanded. When he lifted his head, Ursula stared into the face of a dragon, its eyes glowing like embers.

Abrax flapped his wings, lifting into the air. "Kill the dragon!" he shouted at the golems.

The faceless creatures charged the Drake, leaping on him. They hacked at his scales with their knives, but their blows merely bounced off.

In what seemed like slow motion, he twisted his neck, looking up at the ceiling, then opened his mouth to scream.

Only this time instead of a piercing shriek, a gout of orange flame raced into the air, pouring from the Drake's throat in an unending stream. The golems leapt and tumbled to avoid the fire, and the room blazed with heat.

Bael growled, still bound by Abrax's magical cords. Ursula turned to help him, but he shook his head. "Get out of here. Leave me. I'll be fine." Shadows darkened his eyes. *"Now, Ursula!"*

The flapping of wings turned Ursula's head, and her world tilted as she looked up at Abrax in his terrifying demon form, with sharp, dark talons curling from his hands. Before she could run, he snatched her, lifting her up, his powerful wings beating the air.

"Ursula!" Bael's voice echoed off the hall.

Fear raced up her spine as Abrax carried her higher, and she gaped at the chaos below her. The Drake and the other dragons battled the golems. King Midac's litter lay smashed, surrounded by the bodies of his bearers. He'd disappeared, and a pentagram burned in the center of the wreckage. *He escaped using Emerazel's sigil.*

And Bael—he still struggled on the floor. He'd ripped one arm free, and three golems surrounded him, knives drawn. Her heart climbed into her throat, and Abrax's talons pierced her flesh under her ribs. *He's unarmed. Mortal. There is no way he's going to survive this.*

"Bael!" she shouted.

He looked up. If she wasn't dangling in Abrax's grasp she would have hit him. She'd seen that look before, the one that said *I've accepted my fate.* But this time, she thought he might be right.

Abrax leaned down, whispering in her ear. "How will it feel to watch your lover die?"

Ursula thrashed in his grip, but as she did, another figure rushed onto the stage—long legs moving in a torn black cocktail dress, pale hair streaming behind her. *Cera.* As she raced for Bael, she reached into her purse and pulled out a black ball. No, not a ball. An apple. The one filled with Bael's shadow magic. What the *hell?* Hadn't he said he couldn't find it?

"Bael!" Cera shouted as she tossed the fruit to him. In his free hand, he caught it, and in a single motion brought it to his mouth, biting just as the golems leapt. As soon as the apple touched his mouth, his eyes blazed a deep red.

Abrax snarled, and shadow magic wrapped over Ursula's head like a shroud.

CHAPTER 28

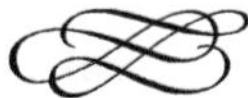

Ursula could see nothing but shadows. Chilly wind whipped at her skin, and she shivered in Abrax's grip. Why had Bael told her that he wasn't able to get his magic back? With a sinking feeling, she had a feeling that it had been *her*. With his magic, he thought he was a danger to her, driven by bloodlust. So he'd given up his magic for her, and the thought tightened her stomach. If he'd had his magic when they'd stormed the dragon lair, the dragons wouldn't have stood a chance.

Abrax's powerful wings beat the air like a war drum, the rhythm melding with the pounding of her heart. Frigid air rushed over her skin, and as they flew, she pushed out the talon tips piercing her flesh—pushed out all thoughts, in fact—except for Bael. The dragons, the golems, the Drake—they all wanted him dead. But Ursula had seen him fight, and she knew he had a chance.

They must have been flying for ten minutes at least when the beating of Abrax's wings began to slow. Her stomach lurched as they descended, and her feet brushed the ground, then she stumbled to her knees.

"Abrax?" She hated herself for showing weakness, and he didn't respond. Still blinded by shadow magic, she crawled to her knees, grasping around on the damp earth, feeling only pine needles beneath her fingers. The air smelled sharply of evergreens. So she was in a forest.

Figuring that out didn't exactly help—the fact remained that she couldn't see and was shackled.

"Get up." Abrax grabbed her cuffed wrists, roughly pulling her to her feet.

He pushed her forward, and she stumbled over roots and the uneven forest floor. It took all her concentration just to stay upright. "Where are you taking me?"

He didn't answer, but she could feel the roots start to thin, the ground growing more bare, and a breeze rushing over her skin. A clearing, perhaps.

Abrax pushed her forward, and she stumbled over a wooden step. The breeze stilled as they entered a stairwell of some kind—a damp space that smelled of wood. Abrax's dark magic crawled all over her body, making her shiver as she climbed the stairs. At the top of the stairs, Abrax leaned past her, and a shudder ran up her spine. The sound of a door creaked.

"Move," said Abrax, pushing her forward again.

She stumbled forward onto a wooden floor that creaked beneath her feet, and into a room that smelled of mold and decay. Her heart thundered against her ribs. *Where is he taking me?*

After ten paces, Abrax opened another door. "Watch your step."

He shoved her and she tumbled down, her body flailing against wooden stairs, until she slammed against the ground. At least it was soft—dirt—but even so it hurt. Her arms and ribs were bruised, and she'd smacked her head on the dirt. The smell of mold nearly suffocated her. As she pushed herself to her feet with a grunt, her pulse raced. She was in a basement. This was not good.

She tried to turn, to run back the way they'd come, but Abrax shoved her again. *Arsehole.*

"Don't worry," he snarled. "We're almost there now."

"Almost *where*?" When he didn't answer, she said, "If you hurt me, Bael will come for you. And Emerazel will send Kester after me."

Abrax merely dragged her forward by one of her elbows. After only a few steps he stopped. For just a second, his fingers brushed her check. In the next instant, those same fingers were around her throat. He reached behind her, breaking through the shackles that bound her wrists. Her hands were free, but she still couldn't see. Already, he was pushing a blade against her belly.

"I need you to strip," he said.

Ursula's heart threatened to gallop out of her chest. What was he playing at? He'd never shown any real sexual interest in her. The one time they'd kissed, he'd been oddly repulsed by the experience.

"Why?" she asked.

His blade cut into her hip. "I won't ask again."

A portal. He wanted to take her through a portal. To the Shadow Realm? No fucking way. "I'm not going to take off my clothes." Abrax stepped back, but the next thing she felt was a powerful force slamming against the side of her skull. And then, nothing.

* * *

THE ICY CHILL of the water woke her with a start, and she thrashed about wildly as it closed over her head. She tried to swim, but the currents pulled her down deeper. Her hands were bound again with magic shackles, and water rushed into her lungs. She gagged, thrashing frantically in the dark, sinking to a watery grave.

Something brushed against her skin, and voices began to whisper in her ear. "You have been away so long, little one." Icy cold fingers stroked along her thigh. "She has more of that delicious fire."

Ursula bucked, twisting away from the touch.

"No, little one. Stay with us awhile. We are so cold. We need your warmth."

Ursula thrashed in the water, desperate to escape from the Forgotten Ones.

Her lungs burned, but a force seemed to tug her upwards, and the fingers that brushed over her skin slipped away. As her head breached the surface, she gasped. Abrax's shadow magic still blinded her, but the creosote smell in the air told her exactly where she was. The Shadow Realm. The fucking moon.

Rough hands—Abrax's?—dragged her out of the water and onto a cold stone floor. Ice dripped down her back. She was naked. The tension on her bonds slackened, and as she scrambled to pull her knees to her chest —shivering uncontrollably, her teeth chattering—the shadow magic obscuring her vision fell away.

Curled on the floor, she rubbed her eyes, surveying the room. It looked like the water portal room in Bael's manor, with a pool of water in its center and narrow windows revealing a stark lunar landscape. Abrax stood in the center of the room, pulling a dark robe over his shoulders to shield his body. Without looking at her, he tossed one to her. She'd been right. He had absolutely no sexual interest in her—even if he was an incubus.

"Put this on," he commanded.

On the floor, Ursula struggled to pull the robe over her shoulders with her hands bound, resorting to using her damn teeth. Abrax flicked his wrists, and dark shadows curled from his fingers, wrapping themselves around her. Slowly, she felt the manacles behind her back weaken, until they crumbled away. Quickly, she wrapped the dark robe around her, still shivering.

"Follow me." He crossed to a tall obsidian door.

Ursula flexed her fingers, then padded across the floor, her bare feet leaving wet footprints. She stepped outside into the frigid air, her heart sinking at the sight of the sharp, violet spire that jutted out of the center of the lunar crater.

Abrax led her through another black door into a hall. From a door opposite appeared a pair of oneiroi guards, their eyes blazing like starlight. Each held a sword.

"Kill her if she tries to use her fire," said Abrax.

The two oneiroi closed in on her, swords drawn as she followed Abrax down a long hall. The manor looked like Bael's, with a central hall ringed by balconies, but it was also different—darker, the windows smaller and narrower. While Abrax maintained a similar sparse aesthetic, he had decorated his manor with artwork and gems of silver, black, and purple. Lined by sleek, black doors, the hall ended with a balcony open to the lunar air, and icy winds whipped over Ursula's skin.

Abrax turned to look at her.

"I must prepare the interrogation chamber."

Ursula's knees went weak. *He's going to torture me.* "I won't tell you anything."

"And I'm not interested in what you have to say. For now." He shot a glance at the oneiroi. "Put her with the other one."

Abrax stepped to the edge of the balcony, and a crack sounded in the air as a pair of wings sprang from his back. With two mighty beats, he disappeared into the gloom above them.

One oneiroi drew a key from his pocket and carefully opened a narrow door, while the other gestured with his sword that she should enter. Shaking, she stepped inside. As she did, the first guard kicked her in the back, sending her sprawling across the floor.

Quickly she scrambled to her knees, but the door slammed behind her, and a key clicked in the lock. Ursula's heart thudded in her chest, the blood rushing in her ears.

Swallowing hard, she looked around the room. A pale stream of pale light illuminated gray marble walls—and a silhouette. Ursula gazed up at the figure as he stepped into the light.

Kester.

"Ursula. Fancy meeting you here."

Her lips curled in a grim smile. "Kester. I've been looking for you. Unfortunately, I guess I can't count on you to save me."

He shook his head. "No, Ursula. We're in this together."

C.N. CRAWFORD

SHADOWS
&
FLAME
SERIES

Eternal Magic

A DEMONS OF FIRE AND NIGHT NOVEL

CHAPTER 1

Ursula lay on the cold stone floor, dressed in a mud-spattered gown and bare feet. Her head throbbed painfully as she tried to get her bearings in the Shadow Realm prison.

Across from her, Kester sat on the edge of a low cot. His right fingers drummed on his knee in irregular twitches, like the movements of a wounded spider. When he saw Ursula staring, he quickly crossed his arms over his chest, but he didn't meet her eyes.

This wasn't the brash Kester she remembered. Something was wrong.

She winced at the sight of him. "Are you okay?"

"I'm fine," said Kester, before adding more strongly, "What's happened while I've been in here?" He rose, wearing only a pair of dingy trousers, and crossed to where she lay on the floor. Shirtless, his muscular frame was leaner than Ursula remembered, and dirt darkened his face. It was hard to reconcile this haggard version of Kester with the cocky playboy she'd first met in London.

He extended a hand, and she allowed him to pull her to her feet.

"I'd been hoping I might get a roommate," he said. "It's lonely around here."

Ursula shook her head, trying to accept the fact that she and Kester were now Abrax's prisoners. "How long have you been here?"

"On the moon? A couple of weeks."

"But..., how? I thought you were on a special mission for Emerazel."

"I was." Kester frowned, lines about his green eyes creasing the handsome planes of his face. "But Abrax caught me when I tried to infiltrate Lucius's dragon warren."

"Balls," said Ursula. Over Kester's shoulder, she could see through the iron-barred window that gave a view of the lunar landscape beyond. Slowly, she pushed herself to her feet and crossed to the window. So much had happened in the last hour—the fight in Lucius's warren, Abrax attacking and abducting her. Dread crawled over her skin as she tried to process it all. She could hardly believe she was back here on the moon.

She sucked in a slow breath as she peered out. Beyond the bars, enormous cliff walls curved off in either direction—the walls of a caldera so massive the far side was barely visible. Below her nestled the city of oneiroi dwellings, stacked on top of each other like shoeboxes. And looming over everything was the violet crystal spire of Asta, where Nyxobas lived—God of Night. She shivered, thinking of how she'd nearly died more than once the last time she'd visited the Shadow Realm.

"Ursula?" Kester prompted.

"Right. You want to know what you've missed." Ursula took a deep breath before turning to face him, then swallowed hard. "I followed you to Avalon, and ended up with Excalibur. Then I lost track of Zee in a dragon's lair when the world's creepiest incubus abducted me."

"Abrax. Of course." Kester studied me for a long time. "Why do I feel like there's something important you're not telling me?"

She cleared her throat, then mumbled, "I'm engaged to Bael, fallen lord of the Shadow Realm."

His green eyes widened. "What?"

"I'm engaged to Bael!"

A chill fell over the room, Kester's large eyes piercing the gloom. "Are you out of your *mind?* Bael leads the Shadow God's legions. He was once the Sword of Nyxobas. He murdered his own wife long ago, and he's second in command to Nyxobas himself. He is *not* your friend. He would rip your heart from your chest—or worse—if that was what Nyxobas asked of him."

Ursula turned back to the window as she tried to decide how to best describe her relationship with Bael. Kester was wrong, of course. Bael wasn't a threat. If he'd wanted to kill her, he could have done so any number of times. For an instant, she remembered how he'd pressed her against the wall of her room in Marazion, his teeth on her throat. He could have torn her jugular wide open, but he'd resisted the call of the old way. Whatever Bael's motivations were, killing her wasn't one of his priorities.

She turned back to Kester, crossing her arms. "Bael isn't our enemy. He's fighting Abrax too. He—"

"Bael is ruthless and unmerciful." Kester's expression was incredulous. "I cannot emphasize this enough. You cannot trust him."

"No," said Ursula, shaking her head. "He's changed. He's lost his wings. Hothgar and the other lords want him dead." Her mind burned with the memory of Bael kneeling over her on the dusty floor of the arena, as the lords brayed for her blood. She could practically feel the sand on her cheek, hear the jeering crowd and Bael's strong voice as he asked for her hand. "He saved my life when he claimed me as his wife."

Kester snarled, the sound rumbling through Ursula's gut. "Don't tell me you consented."

"I didn't exactly have a choice at the time."

Kester's voice was as sharp as one of Cera's obsidian blades. "Just because you're in the Shadow Realm living amongst demons does not give you carte blanche to start marrying them."

"I had to agree to his proposal to live, and we've been allied since. That's all. Anyway, Emerazel seems okay with it."

"Right, she was so *happy* with this situation that she broke the window in your portal room? Don't think I didn't notice that." Kester's voice was ice when he spoke again. "I have seen Bael in battle. He is lethal and remorseless. You can't trust him. Ever."

Ursula turned back to the view beyond the window. She remembered how the Shadow Realm had seemed when she first arrived—so foreign to her, so terrifying. Surely this was part of Kester's problem. Fear of the unknown. And the solitary confinement. *How long has he been imprisoned here?* She wished more than anything she could get them both out of here.

The sound of footfalls turned her head—Kester pacing back and forth over the floor like a caged animal. Something was off about him.

She squinted, studying his gait. He moved awkwardly, favoring one leg. "What happened to your leg?"

"I'm fine."

"You're limping."

"Abrax was trying to get me to tell him where you were."

"And he hurt your leg?"

"Yes." Kester stopped pacing to sit again on his cot. Violet light from the window caught his face, and Ursula sucked in a breath. Kester wasn't just dirty. His face was covered in a patchwork of bruises.

Instinctively she went to him, kneeling on the stone so she was at his level. He lowered his head, avoiding her gaze. *This explains everything: the fear, the anxiety.*

"It's okay," she said, gently brushing his hair to the side. The bruises ranged from deep purple to greenish yellow. This wasn't the result of a single beating. Abrax had tortured him more than once.

"What did he do to you?"

"It doesn't matter. He won't do it again."

"What do you mean? You're still his prisoner." *Just like I am.*

"He wanted *you*. Now he has you. He won't have more questions for me."

He winced as she traced her finger over his cheek. "Why haven't you healed yourself?"

"I did at first, but then Abrax drained my fire. Starkey's Conjuration doesn't seem to work properly without it."

"Oh right, I'd forgotten about that," said Ursula. "Well, I still have my fire. I can heal you."

Kester smiled for the first time since she'd entered the cell.

Slowly, she incanted Starkey's Conjuration. She could feel Emerazel's fire churn within her, then Kester's face transformed, the skin lightening to a healthy pink. He leaned back against the wall, and let out a slow breath.

"Thank you," he said softly.

"No problem."

Ursula sat on her haunches as she studied him. Resting his head against the gray stone of the wall, with his eyes closed, he looked more like the Kester she remembered. Rakishly handsome, even if his hair looked frightful.

"So why were you looking for Excalibur?" she asked.

"To fight the dragons," said Kester absently, his eyes still closed. "It's the only way to kill those bloody reptiles."

"But the Lady of the Lake wouldn't give it to you?"

"She would not." There was just enough disappointment in his voice to make Ursula suspicious.

"So the only reason you were searching for the blade was to fight the dragons?"

"I had to do something," said Kester, his eyes still closed.

Kester's face remained all innocence, but Ursula plowed ahead. "The Darkling prophecy had nothing to do with it?"

Kester's eyes flashed open. "Who told you about the prophecy?"

"Merlin."

"That daft old bastard." Kester sighed. "That stupid poem of his has caused more trouble than this supposed Darkling character."

"You don't believe it's true?"

"I haven't seen any evidence. Anyway, there are plenty of terrible people in the world. Whether one is the Darkling or not seems immaterial."

Ursula caught his gaze before he had a chance to look away. "But I got the sword. You don't think I'm the Darkling?"

Kester traced his thumb slowly over his lower lip, his gaze boring a hole into Ursula. "I wouldn't rule it out."

Ursula sucked in a deep breath. "Merlin and Nimue sensed something strange about me. I frightened them. But the Darkling is supposed to be evil, and… Well, I really can't remember if I was evil or not for the first fifteen years of my life, but for the past three, it didn't get a lot worse than tutting loudly at people who walked slowly in Tube stations."

"Until your engagement to a Shadow Lord, I'd never pegged you as evil. And what's more, the Darkling is supposed to destroy the gods. I don't suppose Emerazel would have given you her fire if that were in your destiny. She did sense something unusual in you. I just don't know what it was."

Ursula loosed a relieved breath. Of course Kester was right. Abrax was probably the Darkling. Abrax certainly seemed hell-bent on leading a rebellion against the gods. "I still have my fire. We could escape, fight our way out."

Kester grimaced. "I tried that already, but Abrax has these creatures. They move like nothing I've ever seen—"

"Golems. Good point. I barely managed to kill one of them."

"You killed one?" Kester didn't bother to hide his surprise.

"It's not easy, but they can get over-confident and make mistakes. Fatal ones."

"I want to know how you did it. I'm sure I can improve on the technique."

Apparently not even Abrax can beat the cockiness out of him.

Before Ursula could tell Kester how she had goaded the golem into attacking, the door to the cell opened with a rush of frigid air.

Flanked by a pair of oneiroi, Abrax stood in the doorway, shadow magic flickering about him.

CHAPTER 2

*E*ven in his human form, Abrax sent an icy trickle of fear through Ursula's chest. He wore a black velvet jacket buttoned up to the neck and dark gray pants. He moved like a predator, each step calculated to require the barest minimum of effort. Like a cat preparing to pounce. His gunmetal-gray eyes pierced the dim light of the cell, cold as death. "Ready for a little chitchat, Ursula?"

"I don't have anything new to tell you," said Ursula, remaining exactly where she was.

"We'll see about that," Abrax snarled as he motioned for his oneiroi to enter the room. The guards split, one to either side of the room, so that they flanked her.

Ursula felt fire kindle in her veins, but before she could summon her power, Abrax flicked his wrist. Tendrils of shadow magic leapt from his fingers, wrapping around Kester's throat.

Shadows slid through Abrax's eyes as he turned to Ursula. "Either you extinguish your fire, bitch, or the hound dies while you watch."

Kester clutched the tendrils at his throat, his lips already turning purple. It took all of Ursula's self-control to quench the fire in her blood.

"Fine, we can talk." She took a step closer to Abrax, desperate to beat the shadows right out of him.

"That's close enough, Ursula darling," Abrax purred. "Kneel and hold out your hands."

Ursula hesitated, but a choking noise from Kester's throat spurred her to her knees. She knelt on the stone floor. When she lifted her hands, one of the oneiroi drew a pair of glowing manacles from under his cloak. Once Abrax clasped the manacles on her wrists, he smiled at her.

His pale eyes glinted in the gloom. "This is going to be fun. We have so much to talk about."

"I suggest you release Kester." Flames began to flicker around her fingers. "These manacles might be immune to my flames, but they won't prevent me from burning you to a crisp."

"I'm bored of this now." Abrax flicked his wrist again, and the cords of shadow magic that bound Kester disintegrated. "But start any fires, and the hound's dying cries will haunt your nightmares."

Ursula studied Abrax as she considered her options. Obviously, going with him wasn't optimal. For one thing, he'd tried to consume her soul on multiple occasions, and then there was the whole *torture* thing she'd just learned about. Time spent with Abrax probably was unlikely to be among her happiest memories.

Her chest tightened. What else could she do? She wasn't about to let him kill Kester.

"All right. I'll come with you," she said through gritted teeth.

She followed Abrax into the hall. Once through the cell door, the oneiroi guards assumed positions on either side of her. Each held a short sword with a lethal-looking edge.

Abrax walked ahead. His shadow magic had receded, giving him an almost human appearance. Still, she'd seen him assume his demonic form enough times to know he could eviscerate her in an instant if he felt like it.

As Ursula followed, she allowed her fire to begin to kindle in her veins. Not enough for anyone to notice, but enough so she'd have it ready at her fingertips if anyone attacked her.

Her footsteps echoed off the sleek walls, and she surveyed her surroundings. Abrax's manor was sparsely decorated, the bare walls a sterile gray. Maybe Abrax took Nyxobas's edict for austerity and asceticism seriously.

The manor was deathly quiet, and she would have thought it empty if not for a few glimpses she caught of oneiroi servants slipping into door-ways as they approached. Even with Emerazel's fire warming her, she shivered. Abrax's own servants found him terrifying.

When they reached the central hall, Abrax led them down a staircase with steps of black marble. At the bottom of the staircase, they stepped onto the floor of the great hall. While Bael had decorated his floor with an enormous mosaic of a lion's head, Abrax's was lined with simple slate tiles.

As if reading her mind, the incubus gestured at the gray stone. "Orna-mentation and embellishment are for the weak-minded."

"Wanker." Frankly, right now, she couldn't think of a better response.

The oneiroi to her right made a little noise that sounded remarkably like a laugh, though Abrax didn't seem to notice as he started across the room. Ursula frowned at where they were going. A jumble of scaffolding stood propped against the cliff face at the far end of the room.

"After my visit to your boyfriend's manor, I decided to do a little exca-vating myself. I think you'll want to see what I found." Abrax reached the scaffolding, then lifted a tarp to reveal the mouth of a tunnel.

Ursula glared at the ragged hole cut into the rock. "Where exactly are you taking me?"

"Someplace private where we can chat."

Bollocks. "We can chat perfectly well right here. Just send your guards away, and I will tell you anything you want to know." She channeled a bit more of Emerazel's fire into her blood.

Abrax flashed the guard next to her a look, and instantly the cold steel of a sword pressed against her spine.

"We'll chat where I say that we'll chat."

She grunted with frustration, her gut churning with nerves. With the blade directing her, she followed Abrax into the tunnel.

Inside, Abrax conjured a glowing orb, revealing crudely carved walls and a floor littered with debris. Ursula sniffed. It had that familiar lunar smell: creosote and rock dust. Abrax hadn't been lying—this tunnel had just been hewn from the cliff face. A cold fear threatened to quench the fire in her veins. *Where is he taking me?*

Abrax led them farther into the bowels of the cliff. After a hundred yards, the walls seemed to close in. Ursula had to duck as they passed through a narrow gap in the rock and into another tunnel. Here, the floor was clear of debris and the raw smell of rock dust much fainter. Ursula reached out to touch the smooth stone walls. In this part of the tunnel, they were moving through an older space. She glanced behind her, seeing only impenetrable darkness.

Abrax led them deeper into the side of the cliff, the light from his orb revealing curling patterns and runes carved into the rock. The same ones she'd seen in Bael's manor, carved by the same people. The passage twisted and turned, deeper and deeper into the side of the cliff.

Ursula's jaw clenched as they walked. She hated the idea of ending up in a remote place with this smarmy, torturing prick. But she wasn't holding any cards in this scenario.

Around them, veins of violet crystal began to streak the rock, and Ursula reached out to touch one. Icy shadow magic hummed against her fingertips. For a moment, she glimpsed Nyxobas's void yawning before her. A voice rose from the depths of her own mind. *Who are you, Ursula? Who are you really?* Fear washed over her. She wasn't sure she wanted to know who she was—she craved the pure, sweet oblivion of the void. The emptiness—the freedom.

As suddenly as the vision had arrived, it was replaced by a vision of Emerazel's infernos—so realistic she could taste bitter ash on her tongue. She yanked her hand back as though burned.

She must have yelped, because Abrax spun round.

"Keep your hands at your sides," he growled.

Ursula felt the sharp point of a sword at her back again.

As they moved deeper down the passage, the cool hum of shadow magic flickered over Ursula. More of the purple crystals glinted in the rock around them. Emerazel's fire thrummed in her veins, yet her skin felt frigid—like she was standing outside on the coldest day of winter.

Something wasn't right. Shadow magic had never felt this icy, this foreign, before. When Bael had taught her how to wield it, to shadow run, it had been a powerful energy flowing within her. Now, it was something entirely different, as alien to her as the harsh lunar landscape.

Just up ahead, Abrax disappeared from view as the tunnel cut sharply right. When she reached the turn, her breath caught as a wave of frozen air washed over her. *I could really use a warm coat right about now.*

The tunnel opened up into a large cavern. Like the interior of a geode, violet crystals lined the floor, walls, and ceiling. In between the crystals grew enormous luminescent mushrooms. Their light shone through the translucent stone, illuminating the room with indigo light.

Abrax strode to a platform in the center of the cavern, his arms folded over his chest, and mounted it. Despite the stillness of the air, thick clouds of shadow magic swirled about him. Violet light sculpted his exquisite face. He was striking—except the fact that he was a murderous arsehole kind of detracted from his beauty a bit.

"Now, this is a nice place to talk," he said.

A frigid chill rippled over Ursula's body, and her teeth began to chatter uncontrollably. Shadow magic wafted and curled between the crystals like swamp gas among the roots of ancient trees.

Slowly, the magic seemed to penetrate her body, filling her with an icy, gnawing emptiness. Ursula's legs gave way to quavering spasms, and she fell to her knees.

"Now you see the true power of Nyxobas," intoned Abrax.

"What is wrong with me?" Ursula managed. Her body was shivering uncontrollably, her teeth chattering so hard she thought they might break.

"That is what I intend to find out," said Abrax.

One of the oneiroi guards grabbed the chain between her manacles and began to drag her toward the center of the cavern. As she neared Abrax, Ursula saw that he stood on a platform carved from pure shadow-crystal. Shadow magic floated over its surface in a dark miasma. Every fiber of her being wanted to run, to sprint back down the tunnel, but her entire body trembled uncontrollably, like a fish flopping on a fisherman's dock.

She was unable to so much as throw a punch as the guards lifted her up. When they dropped her onto the crystal platform, shadow magic seared her skin, as if she'd been thrown into a bath of liquid nitrogen. Pain screamed through her body. *Get me the fuck out of here.*

With the chain that bound her wrists, Abrax yanked her into a sitting position. "Who are you?"

"Ursula," she said through chattering teeth. "You know this, you useless knob-end."

Quick as a snake, Abrax slammed his boot into her chest and pushed her down to the crystal. "Tell me where you come from."

"I-I don't know," Ursula stammered. The icy shadow magic was so cold she could barely string the words together.

"Who taught you to use shadow magic?"

"Bael…" He'd trained her to channel shadows. Once, it had seemed second nature to her. She had no idea why it was *hurting* her so much now.

"I'm asking you again. Where are you from?"

"I've told you before. I have no memory before the age of fifteen."

"Don't lie to me."

"Look, a hag woman from the river told me something, but I have no idea if it's true," Ursula blurted out as a searing pain lanced between her shoulder blades. The crystal was so cold she could hardly breathe. "She said I'm from Mount Acidale."

Abrax lifted his foot slightly. "Where in Mount Acidale?"

"I don't bloody know!" said Ursula frantically. If he didn't let her up, she was certain the air was going to freeze in her lungs.

Abrax pressed down again with his heel, and pain screamed through her chest, so sharp she could hardly take a breath. "If you want the pain to end, you will answer my questions. Where are you from in Mount Acidale?"

"I…don't…know," said Ursula, her mind swimming with agony. "I can't breathe. If you don't let me up—"

Abrax shook his head. "Pathetic. Kester put up more of a fight."

With a jerk on the manacle chain, so hard it threatened to rip her arms from her sockets, Abrax pulled her to her feet.

She shivered in the frigid air of the cavern. *Someday, Abrax, I'm going to stop your withered heart.* "You know I'm engaged to Bael. The laws of Nyxobas protect me."

Abrax jerked her chain so hard she stumbled toward him. He grabbed her hair, so that her face was only inches from his. "Let me be clear, Ursula. In my domain, nothing protects you." He traced the sharp edge of a fingernail along her throat. "No one even knows you're here."

"Kester—"

"Kester will be dealt with." Abrax pushed her away. "If you want to live, you're going to need to start answering my questions. Tell me about Mount Acidale."

Ursula shook her head. "I don't remember anything. Agnes gave me a piece of my mother's blouse. Covered in blood."

Abrax's eyes narrowed. "Agnes? The hag of the Thames you mentioned?"

"Yes."

Abrax stepped toward her. "What did Agnes tell you?"

"She told me she was dead." She should have felt a bit more of a pang at that memory, except Ursula couldn't remember her mother at all. It was hard to grieve for someone when you didn't even know what they looked like, couldn't remember their voice or their smile.

"Is that all?"

"Agnes only allowed me to ask three questions."

Think, Ursula, think. She needed to find a way to get out of here.

Abrax paused, his eyes unfocused as he considered what she had said.

Now standing, Ursula took the opportunity to scan her surroundings. They stood on a platform in the center of the cavern, entirely ringed by violet crystals. The platform itself had been carved from the stump of an enormous crystal, its surface inscribed with more of the twisting runes she'd seen in the tunnel. If it weren't for the freezing shadow magic, it would have been astonishingly beautiful.

Ursula glanced at the pair of oneiroi guards stationed at the base of the platform. They watched her with silver eyes, their faces expressionless. If she made a run for it, she'd have to get past them. And she was nowhere near full strength right now.

Before she could conceive a plan, Abrax pulled her hair so that she looked into his steel-gray eyes. "You said Agnes showed you a piece of your mother's blouse?"

"Yes. She had a rag that she said had been my mother's. Why do you care?"

"What did it look like?"

Ursula tried to envision the scrap of material. Everything from that time on the shore of the Thames seemed blurry, as though she'd been wearing glasses with the wrong prescription. The hag had given her the scrap of blouse, and later she'd stuffed it into a plastic bag. *What had it looked like, exactly?* Slowly, the memory bloomed in her mind.

"It was purple, I think. With gold embroidery. Covered in blood."

"Your mother was a member of the royal guard?" Abrax's face cracked into a vicious smile. "One killed in uniform. I wonder if she was the one Nyxobas recruited."

"Recruited for what?" Ursula stared at Abrax, trying to decipher what he was talking about.

"Now I understand why Kester and Emerazel didn't tell you anything."

"What are you talking about?" Panic crept into Ursula's voice.

"In the battle of Mount Acidale, we turned one of the king's guards. The woman worked for us. When Bael gave the signal, she attacked the king, just as she was supposed to. She only managed to kill the queen. If Kester hadn't been standing next to King Midac, she would have killed him, too."

Ursula's pulse raced. Bael had ordered her mother to kill a king? When she cast her mind back, she remembered Bael's disturbed reaction to learning she was from Mount Acidale. But was this even true, or just more bullshit from Abrax? "You're telling me that my mother tried to kill the king."

Abrax's voice was as smooth as a serpent's hiss. "Exactly. And that blood you saw on her shirt came from Kester's blade running through her heart."

CHAPTER 3

"No." The air seemed to have thinned around her. "You can't possibly know it was my mother just because there was blood on the fabric. She could have died any number of ways."

But even as the words left her mouth, she began to doubt them. When she'd told Bael she was from Mount Acidale, he'd seemed to freeze and his gaze had shuttered—as if he'd been putting something together. Maybe Abrax's version of events wasn't the complete picture, but there was *something* there.

Still, this was Abrax she was dealing with. Not exactly a trustworthy source. And yet it made a certain sense. This could explain why Emerazel had been so interested in her, why Kester was so distant.

Ursula glared at Abrax. "You said Bael ordered my mother to kill the king?"

Abrax smiled. "Indeed. Bael was the one who gave the order. I'm sorry to be the bearer of bad news, but I think your lover hasn't been entirely forthcoming about his role in your mother's death."

Ursula narrowed her eyes at Abrax. She wasn't going to believe a thing he said until she got to speak to Kester and Bael herself. At least—*if* she was getting out of here alive. She'd never felt this defeated before, out of options. And as if to punctuate the point, Abrax sent a stream of shadow magic curling around her.

Pain pierced her ribs, and she found herself peering into Nyxobas's void, darkness claiming her vision and mind.

"Nyxobas!" she screamed into the abyss. "Your charming son wants me to believe you killed my mother. Do you have anything to say about that?"

Silence greeted her. The last time she'd entered the void, Nyxobas had come to her. He'd helped her defeat Abrax.

"Nyxobas!" she shouted. "Tell me the truth."

The voice that responded wasn't Nyxobas's, but that of another god—dry, scratchy, full of rage—and female. *Ahhh, the goddess of fire.* Slowly, from the gaping darkness, a female form arose, one hewn of dancing flames. Was this a welcome visit, or were things about to get a whole lot worse?

"Consorting with the Night God?" Emerazel's voice sizzled over her skin. "You are bound to be *my* servant."

"Maybe you could help a little, Emerazel. I'm kind of in a tight spot here."

"Find a way to get out of there alive. You *will* work for me until I release you from your bondage. Your soul is mine."

"I'm just pointing out that if you chose to kill Abrax, it would be helpful." Honestly, the gods were wildly irrational and pretty much insane as far as Ursula could tell.

Infernos blazed in Emerazel's eyes. Around her, gouts of fire erupted. She towered over Ursula, her skin incandescent, like the surface of the sun. In each hand she held a whip.

* * *

Ursula's arms jerked upward, golden manacles cutting into her wrists. She'd ended up on the cold, crystal floor. Luckily for her, she'd snapped right out of that trance before she'd had the misfortune of finding out what Emerazel had planned with the whips. In any case, it didn't seem like she'd taken on board Ursula's suggestion of killing Abrax. It was entirely possible that Emerazel had no power in the Shadow Realm. Or, she was just batshit.

"Lift her up," Abrax growled.

The oneiroi guard jerked the chain again, pulling Ursula into a kneeling position.

Was Emerazel really about to whip her, or had that been a screwed-up dream?

Abrax's lips curled in a dark smile. "Now you see why we must fight them. To the gods, we are but pawns in their game of power and domination. We will only be free once we overthrow them. We will force the magical realms into submission, replacing their gods."

That is exactly what the Darkling would say. Abrax wanted to rule over the earth and the magical realms as a single god.

Abrax loomed over her. "If you join me, we could do great things. Together, we can vanquish the gods. We can usher in a new era. An era led by mankind, without the seven gods."

Ursula stared dumbly at Abrax, unsteadily rising to her feet. *Is he really suggesting that I join him?* "You've got to be kidding me. First of all, since when did you care about humanity?"

"They existed on earth before we did. They just need a strong hand to guide them."

Ursula straightened her shoulders, her wrists chafing against the manacles. "And I presume you're going to be this leader."

A slow shrug. "I am the most powerful of Nyxobas's demons. And I can be very convincing. Who better than I to deliver mankind from their subjugation?"

Ursula studied Abrax, trying to determine if this was some sort of elaborate trick. "Then what's in it for me?"

The incubus stepped forward and brushed a cool finger along her cheek. "Me. I will give you power like you've never experienced. We will rule over the earth, over Mount Acidale, over Maremount and Lilinor."

Bloody hell. This guy is certifiable. "I still don't understand why you need my help with this. I thought you wanted to kill me."

Abrax's smile broadened. "Oh, absolutely. You will have to sacrifice your mortal body to join my fight, but I can't see how that would be much of a sacrifice. Once you get rid of that pointless vestige, your soul can unite with mine."

The air in the cavern began to cool. "Yeah, I'm going to be a hard no on that one. Has it occurred to you that dragging someone into a dungeon and torturing them isn't the best way to initiate a proposal for a lifelong partnership?"

Abrax moved closer, his icy eyes blazing. A strange warmth began to spread over Ursula's skin. "How could you refuse? I am offering everlasting life. When you shed this grotesque form, you will live for all eternity within me. Also, I'm not really asking for your consent."

She gritted her teeth. "Of course not. Consent isn't really your thing."

Again, Abrax brushed a finger along her cheek. An oddly disturbing sensation tingled through her skin at his touch, and she shuddered. She tried to find the words to say *no,* but his incubus power was already paralyzing her.

Abrax grinned. "When our souls combine, complete and utter ecstasy will overtake you."

Every ounce of her being told her to run, but her body was frozen under his powers. Beneath the soothing calm created by Abrax's magic, disgust roiled in Ursula's mind.

He looked at her sympathetically. "That little stunt you pulled in Lacus Mortis won't work again. I have complete control of you now."

Abrax stroked her cheek again. She sucked in a sharp breath as an alien warmth burned at his touch. Inside, a war raged, desire clashing with disgust, but she couldn't bring herself to move.

Abrax leaned down. "Don't worry," he whispered. "Immortality is moments away."

Fuck off, you rapey arsehole. Her heart began to thunder against her ribs, fear spreading through her chest, but she'd become immobilized.

He leaned in, gently nibbling her ear, and a shiver rippled up her spine. He slid one hand to her forehead and one between her breasts. He began to speak in Angelic, and a wild ecstasy pooled in her gut. Now, pure panic began to overtake Ursula's mind, and something inside her screamed wildly to get out of this. This couldn't be happening.

And yet, it was. Shadow magic gathered around them as Abrax continued incanting. Although her body remained fixed in a state of frozen rapture, she could feel shadows begin to crawl along her skin. Icy cold, they slipped into her pores.

Her body convulsed in a baffling mix of pleasure and pain. Cold shadows coursed through her blood. Abrax chanted louder, and Emerazel's fire began to fade. She tried to open her jaw to scream, but her muscles refused to respond.

Tears pooled in her eyes. Not because she was able to cry, but because Abrax's paralysis prevented her from blinking.

Abrax lifted his hand from her forehead, and wiped the tears away. "There there, the hard part is over. Your soul is almost mine."

No. Adrenaline and raw panic snapped through her nerve endings.

He leaned in close, his mouth only inches from hers. Then, fixing his eyes on hers, he began to draw her soul out. Silver threads passed through her lips, wafting into the air. Abrax reached for them with a thin tongue. As he pulled the first of the threads into his mouth, his eyes widened in surprise. Then his brow furrowed and he winced, like he was tasting something vile.

His tongue flicked out again and drew in another strand of her soul. Instantly, his shoulders hunched and he gagged, his eyes bulging.

Instinctively, she reached for her fire, only to find it wasn't there. Abrax's shadows had extinguished it. Worse, her body remained transfixed.

Above her, Abrax wiped at his mouth in disgust. "My shadows have quenched Emerazel's fire, yet I am unable to consume your soul. You have the distinct honor of being the first person whose soul has repulsed me." His lip curled in disgust. "I've never been so revolted. I'm sorry, Ursula, but it doesn't look like you're going to be joining me after all."

Her relief only lasted a moment, because already Abrax was reaching into his velvet jacket to withdraw a thin blade. It glinted in the violet light of the cavern, the edges of the crystals reflecting its mirrored surface. Frantically, Ursula reached for her fire, but her veins were empty.

Time seemed to slow, and Ursula could feel every beat of her heart. Each one threatening to be its last. The crystal at her back hummed with shadow magic. Strangely, it no longer felt ice cold. Familiar shadows whispered below its surface. Shadows she'd used before. Shadows that now flowed through her veins, since Abrax had tried his little soul-meld.

As Abrax moved for her, she let the shadow magic flow through her. Instinct took over. Her body just moved, three feet to the right, and Abrax's blade splintered on the crystal. Shadow running had become second nature to her now.

Abrax whirled. "How?"

But Ursula didn't have time to respond. As soon as she had broken contact with the incubus, Emerazel's fire had come raging back, clashing with the shadow magic in her body. The two things were never meant to mix. She grunted in pain as a burst of fire and shadows erupted from her.

On the plus side, the magical explosion threw Abrax across the cavern.

Abrax shouted at his guards, "Stop her!"

Ursula tried to draw her magic back, but the mix of freezing shadows and infernal fire was uncontrollable. Magic continued to blaze from her like an incandescent geyser. It sprayed into the crystalline ceiling, and broken shards fell around her in a razor-sharp rain.

An oneiroi guard lunged for her. Before she could direct her fire at him, he slammed the toe of his boot into the side of her head.

CHAPTER 4

Ursula flinched as someone touched her shoulder.

"It's okay," said a familiar voice. "But you look terrible."

Ursula opened her eyes to find Kester crouching next to her, his handsome features creased with worry.

"I look terrible?" she repeated. "Charming as always."

The cot's rough fabric scratched her cheek, and she blinked, taking in her surroundings. Back in the cell. She tried to sit up, but dizziness whirled in her mind.

"What did he do to you?" An edge laced Kester's tone.

"Slammed me with shadow magic. Then I fell into the void, tried to speak with Nyxobas, and ended up with Emerazel instead."

"And what would you have to say to Nyxobas?" asked Kester.

Ursula pushed herself up onto her elbows, considering just how to bring up Abrax's little "Kester killed your mum" story. While she was debating this, Kester looked back at her with a mix of confusion and worry. If he'd killed her mother, he certainly didn't seem concerned about it now.

"I was actually trying to find out—" She bit her lip. She'd need to think about this before she launched into it. "Never mind. There's more. He wanted to unite our souls or something and rule over mankind, but apparently my soul repulsed him."

Kester's lip curled. "Your *soul* repulsed him? That's a bit of a personal insult, I'd say."

"I've never been so happy to repulse someone. Speaking of which, what do you mean I look terrible?"

"Pale bags under your eyes, a bit like someone sucked the life out of you. Time for Starkey's Conjuration Spell again, I think."

Ursula winced, her body groaning with pain. "I've been getting a lot of use out of that one."

She allowed her head to fall back on the scratchy cot as she incanted the spell. With the final word, a soothing magic filled her body, imbuing it with strength once more. Blinking, she sat up.

"Why Urusula, you look simply ravishing now." A sly smile. "Did you know you have beautiful skin when you don't look near death?"

"Are you really flirting with me right now?"

Kester shrugged. "I don't see why not. We're both alive. Things could be worse."

Ursula leaned back on her hands. "I don't understand *why* we're both alive. Why didn't Abrax kill me after he failed to get what he wanted?"

As she spoke, she studied Kester. If Abrax had been telling the truth, did Kester know? Had he put it all together, the way Bael might have?

Probably best to just lay it all out there and see how he responded. "Kester, Abrax said—"

Just then, the door opened with a bang, and Abrax stood in the center, flanked by his usual pair of oneiroi guards.

Ursula rose, already summoning Emerazel's fire.

"Which one of you told him?" Abrax shouted, his voice sharp with rage.

What now? "What are you talking about?"

"Hothgar. He's demanded an audience. Someone told him you were here."

"And you think it was us?" said Ursula, heat rising in her chest. "The two people who've been chained and imprisoned the whole time? There's something very wrong with you, you know that?"

Abrax's eyes narrowed. "No one else knows you're here."

"Last time I spoke to Hothgar, he told you to kill me. He wants me dead. Even if I'd managed to find my way out of here, Hothgar wouldn't exactly be first on my list of people to visit."

"Obviously you have a leak in your manor," said Kester. "One of your guards, perhaps?"

"That is impossible." Abrax's icy voice echoed off the walls.

Ursula folded her arms, still a bit ticked off about the whole "manacle torture" thing. Not to mention the attempted soul-reaping. But she wasn't wearing manacles now. One incubus—two guards. She may not get a better moment to fight back than this.

She cocked her head. "If the Sword of Nyxobas found out you've been keeping us imprisoned without his knowledge, you've got no one to blame but yourself. What is the punishment for disobeying his orders?"

With a roar of rage, Abrax lunged for Ursula. She dodged out of the way like a toreador evading a bull. As Abrax reached her, Ursula slammed into him, sending him sprawling to the floor.

Flames sprang from her hands as she leapt on Abrax. She pressed her palms to his chest, and he screamed as smoke rose from between her fingers.

As she seared Abrax's chest with her fire, Kester lunged for the nearest oneiroi, catching him off guard. In a single motion, he drew the guard's sword from its scabbard. In a blur of speed, he severed the guard's head. Hot blood sprayed across the wall of the cell.

Under Ursula's firm grip, Abrax writhed, until he vanished beneath her fingertips—only to reappear across the room in a swirling cloud of shadows. Ursula shouted a warning to Kester, but she was too late. Already, Abrax was sending strands of shadow magic twining around Kester's ankles. He yanked them, and Kester slammed to the ground.

Ursula started to rush for him, but the remaining guard leveled his sword at her throat. The blade pressed against her skin, and the oneiroi's large eyes gleamed, promising death if she moved. As she raised her hands, Abrax sent shadows snaking across the room, and they slid around her chest.

Abrax's shirt was smoking where she'd burned him, but that didn't stop him from kicking Kester hard in the gut.

Ursula tensed, waiting for Abrax's attack. Instead, he beckoned her forward.

"You're coming with me, little dog. Hothgar asked for you specifically."

Ursula winced as she stepped over Kester's prone body and into the hallway, but she knew a kick to the ribs wouldn't keep Kester down for long. Still, she needed to find a way to get him out of here. Even if Abrax was snapping a fresh pair of glowing manacles to her wrists right now.

"This way," said Abrax, and she begrudgingly followed him down the sleek-walled hallway.

As Ursula padded barefoot over the floor in her ragged gown, she couldn't help but think of Bael. Once, Bael had been Nxyobas's Sword, living for years in isolation. She had the feeling that he hadn't let anyone in at all, for all those millennia—until he'd met her. Could he really have been involved in her mum's death?

She didn't have long to think about this, because the hallway opened up into Abrax's stark atrium. This time, a cage-like elevator stood in the center. Ursula felt a pang of sadness as she saw that it was almost an exact replica of the one at Bael's manor. She followed Abrax into the metal cage, avoiding getting anywhere near him. The door slammed closed.

Inside the elevator, the chain clanked and rattled as they rose toward the roof, passing by floor after floor of obsidian walls and doors. When she'd first come to Bael's manor, she'd been terrified of him, and the surroundings hadn't helped. The Bael she'd come to know over time seemed so different than the terrifying Sword of Nyxobas she'd first encountered, brooding on his dark throne. But he still held secrets he hadn't revealed to her.

When they reached the roof, Ursula shivered as an icy lunar breeze slipped through the remains of her dress. Like in Bael's manor, the view from the roof was magnificent. The great walls of the caldera curved thousands of feet above them, and the violet spire of Asta sparkled in the distance.

Abrax, of course, didn't stop to admire the view, immediately striding toward a black carriage at the far end of the roof.

Footsteps clacked over the roof, and a new set of guards flanked her. She walked between them, following Abrax to the carriage. When they reached it, Abrax stopped to open the door. Ursula climbed inside, her chest tightening. Being in the Shadow Realm without Bael felt completely wrong. She shuddered as Abrax sat next to her and the oneiroi guard.

As they rose into the sky, Ursula got a final view of Abrax's manor in all its glory, the gleaming glass and steel. But the hair on her arms prickled as she got a good look at the roof. Lurking in the shadows stood a large contingent of oneiroi—and behind them, at least five golems.

CHAPTER 5

The lords' chamber fell silent as they entered, heels echoing off the marble hall. At a semicircular granite table sat Hothgar, flanked on either side by the ten other demon lords. Hothgar—Sword of Nyxobas—wore a thin chain-mail shirt, his hoary beard and eyebrows giving him a wise appearance. Which, based on what Ursula knew of him, was completely misleading. He gripped a gavel, his petty little symbol of power.

Ursula cast her gaze over the other demon lords—high demons, each one. The luminescent mushrooms lining the hall cast a faint, violet light over their bestial faces. If Ursula had any hope of breaking out of here, it was snuffed out when she noticed the phalanx of guards standing behind the lords.

For their part, the lords—including Hothgar—were glaring at both Abrax and Ursula, hatred gleaming in their dark eyes. It took her a moment to realize the God of Night himself sat in the room, towering over all of them in his dark throne, dark magic curling around him in shadowy tendrils, black eyes gaping wide. He probably had no idea what the hell was going on here. Lost in the void, as usual. Even in a trance, he was a creature of nightmares, cloaked in darkness.

Abrax grabbed Ursula's arm, pulling her forward until Hothgar held up a hand. The old Sword of Nyxobas nodded to his guards, and five of them began marching toward Ursula and Abrax.

"What's this about?" Abrax started forward.

"Stay where you are, incubus." Hothgar didn't bother to hide the anger in his voice.

Abrax let out a low growl in response.

The five guards encircled the pair of them, and one of the oneiroi pulled Abrax's sword from his scabbard.

Abrax's shadow magic whipped around him in sharp coils. "I am a son of Nyxobas. How dare you treat me this way?"

"Your soldiers attacked my family at the Lacus Mortis—"

"Oh. *That.*" Abrax sighed. "Are you still whining about that? I told you that was an accident. I briefly lost control of my men—"

"People died."

"People die sometimes. In any case, I made reparations. It is time we put this behind us."

His diplomacy skills were somewhat lacking, Ursula thought.

Hothgar continued to stare stonily at Abrax.

One of the guards by Abrax's side grunted, then held up a lethal-looking dagger. "He was concealing this on his person."

"It is for my personal protection," said Abrax. "Look." He flicked his wrist, producing another knife from his sleeve. "I have another blade here." He held up a thin needle of steel. "One can never be too careful."

The guard's eyes widened, and he snatched the blade from Abrax.

Abrax shoved his hands in his pockets. "Now may I take my seat at the table?"

"No, you may not," growled Hothgar.

"And why is that?" Abrax straightened, throwing his shoulders back slightly.

"You have brought a hound of Emerazel's into our realm without permission." Hothgar looked pointedly at Ursula.

Abrax shook his head. "And what of it? She already knew of the realm. She spent considerable time here."

"I am done with your excuses. You will remain quiet while I interrogate the cur."

Hothgar turned his dark gaze on Ursula. "Why have you returned to the Shadow Realm?"

"I just love it here so much."

Hothgar continued to stare at her.

"Abrax abducted me," she continued. "I'd never have come here will-ingly, considering the last time I was here, everyone tried to kill me."

Hothgar's eyes narrowed. "The bitch lies. You will tell us the truth."

From behind, a guard shoved her hard in the back. She fell, sprawling to the stone floor. *Arsehole.* Her hands still manacled, she scrambled to her feet again.

Hothgar stood. "You will have one chance to name your co-conspira-tors. If you want a clean death, you will not lie."

Why is he not getting this? "What are you talking about? Abrax kidnapped me. He was holding me against my will. I want nothing to do with you and the Shadow Realm."

Hothgar nodded at another one of his guards—a demon with a massive barrel chest and a neck like a tree trunk.

"Bring out the prisoner," said Hothgar.

Kester?

Ursula stared as the guard disappeared into a tunnel that led out of the hall. When she glanced at Abrax, he looked as perplexed as she was. *So he doesn't know what's going on either.*

After a few minutes, the doors slammed open, and the guard returned, leading a demon with a chain attached to an iron collar on his throat.

Not Kester—the muscular form draped in tattered, dark clothes was far too large. Enormous golden manacles clasped his hands, thicker than any Ursula had seen before. A black hood covered the man's head. She took in the beautiful, golden color of his skin—

But she didn't have long to admire it. The prisoner pulled on his chain, fighting and snarling like a wild animal, and she almost wondered if he'd rip through it. As the guard dragged him past the granite table of lords, the prisoner lunged for them. A sharp pull on his chain from the prison guard stopped him in his tracks.

Abrax spoke, his voice disdainful. "I cannot believe this creature is your source. How can you believe a man who has betrayed his god?"

The guard yanked the hood from the prisoner's head, and Ursula gasped. It was Bael, dark and powerful shadows whirling off his body. The former Sword of Nyxobas—and her betrothed. Except, he wasn't exactly looking at her with love in his eyes. In fact, he was staring at her with a feral hunger, his eyes blood-red. Bael had been corrupted by the *old way*, the feral state that overtook shadow demons when they drank blood. And right now, he kind of looked like he wanted to rip his fiancée's throat out.

Ursula hardly noticed the burning pain of Emerazel's fire as it filled her veins.

"Where did you get him?" Abrax's voice boomed across the room.

Hothgar gripped his gavel. "A guard found him wandering around his manor. He said you're plotting against the realm. That you'd kidnapped the bitch."

"He's insane. Obviously, he drank the bitch's blood and is corrupted by the old way."

Hothgar raised an eyebrow. "But he was right about the bitch—"

Ursula raised a manacled hand. "You do realize that I'm standing right here? My name is Ursula."

Hothgar glared at her. "And you're also a female hound. Which makes you one of the goddess's *bitches*. I am merely addressing you using our technical term."

Ursula smiled pleasantly. "Sure. That's the technical term. Having spoken to your wife, I believe the technical term for you is something like 'conjugal disappointment,' but you don't hear me banging on about it."

"Let's stick to the point." Abrax pointed to Bael. "He's gone feral. He's lost his wings and his seat at the lords' table. We should be discussing the best way to put him down. And yet, you're telling me that you believe his word over mine?"

Hothgar's eyes narrowed. "He didn't lie about the hound."

Bael growled, a low, inhuman sound that sent an icy shiver dancing up Ursula's neck. Was the real Bael under there somewhere, buried beneath the feral rage?

Hothgar laid his hands flat on the granite table. "Is there anything else you've been keeping from us, Abrax?"

Abrax cocked his head. "No, there is nothing else."

Liar! Ursula wanted to scream. Should she tell them what she knew now?

Hothgar's eyes narrowed, and his lips flattened into a line. "Are you sure there is nothing else you'd like to confess?"

Abrax stood with his hands in his pockets, perfectly relaxed. "I may have indulged in a few too many gin and tonics last night. Is that the sort of thing you're looking for? In my defense, they were made with Harris gin and a hint of coriander. Nearly impossible to resist overindulging, as I'm sure you'd agree."

Hothgar's lip curled. "Bring out the other prisoner!"

The guards around Abrax drew their swords, pointing them at his throat, but he never shifted from his relaxed posture. The doors slammed open again, and the guards dragged in another prisoner. Just as with Bael, this prisoner wore ragged clothes and a black hood. Not as large as Bael, but struggling just as hard against his bonds. The guards shoved him until he stood a few feet from Bael.

Kester.

When the guard pulled the hood off his head, Ursula stared back at her green-eyed friend, a rag stuffed into his mouth and tied behind his head.

Every powerful ally she had was now in this room, chained up as prisoners. And one of them was raging with bloodlust.

Well, this is a pretty little mess we've got ourselves into.

CHAPTER 6

"Remove the gag. I want to hear what he has to say," said Hothgar.

The guard drew a short knife from a scabbard on his belt. With a dexterous flourish that belied his impressive girth, he sliced Kester's gag.

Kester spat the rag onto the floor.

"Who are you?" asked Hothgar.

Kester glared at the hoary-faced demon. "You know who I am."

Hothgar loosed a sigh. "For the rest of the room."

"I am Kester." His voice boomed over the hall. "Hound of Emerazel."

Hothgar pointed at him. "In fact, he is the one they call the Headsman. He is the one who slew Innas the Black, the one who carved out Bothrop's eye, the one who murdered Vesper the last succubus of Maremount." Chatter buzzed among the demon lords before Hothgar held up his hands to quiet the room. "And, do you know where he's been for the last month? He's been a prisoner in Abrax's manor. The incubus has been holding him captive. A prize such at this should be shared. Each lord should carve a piece of his flesh."

Ursula's stomach tightened into knots. *Well, that does not sound wonderful for us.*

A hush fell over the room. Hothgar's outstretched finger moved to point at Abrax. "He has hoarded the greatest prize for himself. He has prevented the course of justice. He has lied to the lords. *He* is a traitor to the realm!"

The guards around Abrax stepped closer, their swords inches from his throat.

"Hothgar," said Abrax almost nonchalantly. "Stop acting like a prat. First of all, must I remind you that I am immortal. Your demons and their little swords cannot kill me. Secondly, I am the son of Nyxobas. I only want what is best for the realm. You're a fool to question my motives. You have no right to interfere with my business."

Hothgar shook his head. "The lords have cast their ballots. You are to be imprisoned."

The air in the room dropped to a frigid temperature, the violet lights seeming to dim, suffocated by shadows.

"No," Abrax barked, but Ursula could see fear in his eyes. "I will not be imprisoned again."

Hothgar didn't reply, simply nodding at the guards.

So much happened in the next few moments that it was almost hard for Ursula to process it.

Wings sprouted from Abrax's back as he transformed into his demon form, talons emerging from his feet and hands. As his wings beat the air, a chorus of screams erupted. Abrax's oneiroi were attacking the other guards.

If Ursula's eyes hadn't been instinctively drawn to Bael, she might not even have noticed what he was doing in all the chaos of the battling guards. But as it was, he drew her gaze like a magnet.

Across the room, Bael grabbed the chain attached to his collar and ripped it from his jailor's hands. Once free, he raced across the room, his wrists still bound. The chain dragged behind him, clanking over the stone. Ursula's blood roared in her ears at the sight of him, a confusing mixture of relief and fear.

"Ursula!" he rasped, his throat hoarse and his eyes burning like embers. He'd gone completely feral. And yet...

Even though her pulse raced wildly and her heart pattered like a frightened rabbit, she stopped herself from moving away from him. *Bael won't hurt me. Not even when he's twisted by the old way.*

When he reached her, he clamped his fingers around her waist—a little possessively, but not too hard. "Ursula. Are you all right?"

She blinked, taking in his stunning features—the beauty of a Greek god, all golden skin and black hair sweeping over his forehead. And despite the red bloodlust tinging his eyes, he actually sounded concerned. "Are *you* all right?"

"I will not hurt you." He stared into her eyes. "I'm in control."

Ursula could see a war raging within him—a desire to drink her blood combined with a need to protect her. "Are you sure?"

He nodded solemnly, and she breathed in the faint scent of sea air that curled off his powerful body—and under that, the scent of sandalwood. The smells of his homeland, where he'd once lived as a human, before the gods dragged him into their wars. Tightening her fingers, she resisted throwing her arms around his neck. Gods, it was good to see him, but he was clearly pretending to be feral, and she wasn't going to blow his cover.

Around them, chaos reigned. Abrax's oneiroi fought Hothgar's guards in a whirlwind of clashing blades. And above it all, Abrax hovered above them, leathery wings beating the air rhythmically.

"We need to go," said Bael.

"We need to bring Kester."

Bael scanned the chaos. "There." He pointed with his manacled hands. Across the room, Kester fought a pair of demons. Blood flowed from a cut on his arm, but he'd managed to grab a sword.

Ursula sucked in a sharp breath. "Let's grab him and get the hell out."

She made a move for Kester, hurrying across the room by Bael's side. But before they could make any headway, Hothgar's guards leapt into their way. Unarmed, Ursula dodged. Bael snarled, twirling the chain attached to his neck over his head like a cowboy's lasso until he slammed it into the closest guard's face.

"Kester!" Ursula shouted.

Kester turned to look at her, green eyes flashing while two oneiroi guards surrounded him. "There are too many! I'll find you outside."

Before Ursula had a chance to argue, Bael grabbed her arm. "This way. He'll be fine."

With guards closing in around them, she didn't have time to debate. On her way to the doors, she caught one last look at Kester. He leapt into the air. In a single spinning move, he decapitated the two guards who'd surrounded him.

Oh. That's why they call him the Headsman. And apparently Bael was right. He'd be fine.

Without looking back, Ursula turned to follow Bael's enormous form. He led her through the melee, clearing a path with brutal but precise lashes of his chain. By the time they reached the tunnel, the crowd had thinned.

Bael and Ursula raced down a granite passage that opened into the cold, lunar air. From here, Ursula caught a glimpse of the carriage at the end of the platform. But ten yards from the tunnel's opening, Bael pulled her in close to him, pressing her body against his.

She stared at the tunnel's mouth, where five lunar bats swooped onto a platform. Each one carried a rider dressed in black. And as the riders slipped off the lunar bats, Ursula recognized their eerily smooth movements. A shudder danced up her spine. *The golems from Abrax's roof.*

"Bael," she whispered. "They're golems."

Bael put his fingers to his lips, whistling. At the piercing sound, the golems swiveled to look at them.

"What are you doing?" Ursula hissed. "They'll tear us to pieces."

As if he didn't hear her, Bael was already charging toward the golems, spinning the chain above his head.

Ursula raced after him. *Bloody hell, Bael. There is no way we can defeat five golems armed only with a piece of chain.*

The golems spread out at the tunnel's mouth, moving as gracefully as dancers. Ursula knew the slim blades they held in their hands made them absolutely lethal.

Just as Bael moved within range, he cut sharply right, sprinting toward the edge of the platform. Ursula followed, running as fast as she could with the manacles around her hands, and with the stupid gown trailing at her ankles.

A shadow passed over their heads as another bat winged into view, heading right for them. Ursula's heart plummeted—until she recognized the silver hair fluttering behind the rider, the wide eyes. *Cera—riding on the back of her lunar bat, Sotz.* Ursula's chest unclenched just a bit at the sight of her little friend.

"Ursula, get over here!" shouted Cera as she swooped along the edge of the platform.

The dusty lunar air burned Ursula's lungs as she raced full speed toward Cera, golems close behind her. From the periphery of her vision, she could see Bael's enormous form slamming golems off the side of the platform.

"Ursula!" Kester's voice boomed behind her, and she whirled to see him bursting from the tunnel, a horde of guards behind him.

"Now!" yelled Cera. "We'll get Kester on a second pass."

Ursula's throat tightened. *No. I'm not leaving him here.* Golems were surrounding him, and he had no idea how dangerous they were.

"Kester," Ursula shouted. "Watch out."

She reached into herself, channeling her rage. Her mind blazed with images of Abrax, of Emerazel—everyone who wanted to control her—until hot wrath simmered in her blood. With a volcanic explosion of fury, flames erupted from her body, searing hot. Good thing flames wouldn't burn a hellhound like Kester.

The fire raced for the golems until a fireball engulfed them. She didn't stop to watch their bodies melt, or to wonder if they felt pain, she simply screamed for Kester to run to Cera's lunar bat. She heaved a sigh of relief as he made it aboard.

Overhead, wings beat the air. On a second lunar bat, Bael swooped lower, slowing the flight just long enough for Ursula to jump on in front of him. Frantically, she swung her leg over the bat's body, struggling in her long dress, until the hem hiked up to her thighs. She was barely clinging onto the creature, completely unsteady. But bloodlust or not— she knew Bael wouldn't let her fall.

CHAPTER 7

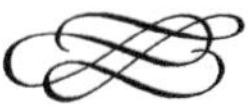

 rsula nestled into Bael's powerful body as they soared into the air, the wind whipping at her red hair, and he curled his arms protectively around her. With her wrists still bound, all she could do was hunch over and grip the bat's fur, but Bael's muscled arms kept her in place.

Around them, lunar moths fluttered—a wild murmuration of glowing. Bael guided the bat between the streams of enormous moths, and Ursula gaped at the strangely familiar beauty of the lunar landscape.

Ursula leaned back into Bael, breathing in his delicious smell. "How did Cera know to be outside?"

"I told you I was in control." His breath warmed the shell of her ear.

Distracted by his allure, it took Ursula a moment to piece together what he was getting at. "So when Hothgar found you wandering his manor, consumed by the old way—" She looked back into his eyes, finding that they'd returned to their natural color—a pale gray that stood out sharply against his dark eyelashes.

"I was faking it."

"And how did you convince him that Abrax had me prisoner?"

"That was easy. I let them torture it out of me."

Urusula's stomach clenched. "Bael! Are you all right?"

"I'm fine."

"But how did you know about Kester?"

"I didn't know about Kester. I only told them about you. Hothgar must have searched Abrax's manor after he requested the audience with Abrax."

Ursula glanced at the lunar bat soaring through the air just behind them. Cera sat crouched around Sotz's shoulders while Kester clung to the fur on the bat's back, his expression grim. Hellhounds weren't exactly meant to fly. Ursula's pulse raced when she caught a glimpse of the enormous flock of lunar bats in hot pursuit of them.

Ursula whistled to catch Cera's attention. "Bats! Behind us!" she shouted over the wind. Good enough to get the point across.

Bael leaned in closer to his bat, his body pressing against Ursula's, and he whispered into the bat's ear. They picked up speed, winging for the sheer cliff face that ringed the crater. As the cliff surged into view, Kester called out a warning. At the last moment, they plunged downward along the cliff's face. Bael steered his bat sharply into a dark passage carved into the rock.

Ursula pressed her head against Bael's chest as they flew through the darkness, trusting only the bat's sense of echolocation to not slam them into the rock. After what felt like an eternity, violet light began to fill the passage again.

Ursula sucked in a deep breath, stunned by the strange beauty around her. The mushroom cavern was just as she remembered it. A forest of bioluminescent fungi on the floor, and above them, the distant sound of the bat colony. Up ahead, she recognized the path that led to Bael's manor.

"Bael. Are you sure the manor's a good place to hide? Seems like the first place they'd look."

Bael grunted. "You need to trust me, Ursula."

Of course. How could she forget Bael's favorite habit of failing to tell her anything in advance?

But as they came to the entrance to Bael's manor, they simply flew on past, soaring deeper into the forest.

Nearby, Cera whistled, pointing back toward the mouth of the cave at a lunar bat pursuing them.

"Hang on," shouted Bael.

Ursula clutched the bat's fur as they nosedived into the mushrooms. Ursula's pulse thundered in her veins at their speed. They swooped between the massive trunks of the fungi, until—with a jarring bump—they landed beneath a large cap, skidding in the dirt, Ursula clinging to the bat's fur.

For just a moment, they caught their breath, then Bael dismounted, pulling Ursula off after him. He walloped the bat on its rump, and the creature soared into the air again, past the tops of the mushroom caps.

Just a few feet away, Cera and Kester landed with an audible thump. Kester slid off Sotz, while Cera stayed crouched on her bat's shoulders.

Bael nodded at her. "Led 'em on a proper chase."

"Of course, my lord," said Cera.

Cera whispered in Sotz's ear, and a moment later they were winging into the air, leaving Bael, Kester, and Ursula under the giant mushroom.

Bael beckoned Ursula and Kester closer, until they were huddled around the mushroom's base. He whispered softly, "We need to wait until Cera draws them off. No talking. You must be absolutely still. A bat's hearing is excellent, and they will signal to their riders if they can sense us."

Bael knelt on the ground, closing his eyes, apparently listening for the sound of bats. Ursula glanced at the manacles still binding her wrists. At some point, she'd have to get the bloody things off of her.

For just a moment, she caught Kester's eye as he rested his back against the flesh of the mushroom. Blood flowed from the wound on his shoulder, and he looked exhausted. She wanted to heal him, but she'd have to wait until all the bats were out of earshot before she began chanting anything.

She looked between the two men, who studiously avoided each other's gazes. How strange to have Kester and Bael in the same place—two ancient enemies, forced to work as allies, but not making eye contact with each other.

And on the off chance that Abrax had been telling the truth—both of these men had been there when her mother had been killed. Could it really be true, or had Abrax just been screwing with her?

After a few minutes, Bael rose, holding out his hand to Ursula. "I think they're gone. We need to move."

With Ursula's manacled hand in his, he started into the mushroom forest, leaving Kester to follow.

"Wait," said Ursula. "Kester's hurt. I should heal him first."

Bael stopped, but didn't turn around. "Be fast. If he can't keep up, we will have to leave him. We cannot afford stragglers."

Nice.

Ursula turned to Kester, who rolled his eyes. With her hand hovering above Kester's shoulder, she incanted Starkey's Conjuration as quickly as she could, watching as his skin healed, knitting together without so much as a scar.

"Thanks," said Kester. "We need to stop making a habit of this."

"Let's go." Already, Bael was taking off at a stiff pace between the mushrooms, slipping between the stalks with a practiced stride.

Ursula's bare feet sank into the rich soil as they walked. She kept her eyes peeled for the carnivorous caterpillars that had almost eaten her on her last visit. But after a while, she realized that in this part of the forest, the only caterpillars crawled high above their heads on the ancient, towering mushrooms.

They moved without speaking, the silence deafening. Ursula's few attempts at conversation were met with monosyllabic answers from both men. It wasn't clear if Bael was still worried about being heard by their pursuers or if he just didn't want to talk in Kester's presence. It *did* seem like they had a past, and their awkwardness around each other was quickly giving credence to Abrax's claims.

Every few minutes, Bael would slow, directing them up the nearest slope. As her thighs began to burn, Ursula cursed him mentally. *Is it just me, or is he choosing the most difficult course?* As their path continued, the giant mushrooms began to thin, until at last they approached the edge of a ridge.

On the slope that curved off below them, a few faintly glowing mushrooms trailed off into darkness. Strangely, the air had an antiseptic smell. It took a few sniffs for Ursula to identify it. Ammonia.

"The Cavern of Night," Bael said quietly.

"The what?" asked Ursula.

In typical Bael style, he declined to explain, instead turning to walk along the rim of the ridge. "Follow me. Stay close."

He moved more slowly than before, holding his chain carefully so it didn't make noise.

"Where are we going?" Ursula whispered.

"Someplace safe," said Bael. Then he added, "Keep your eyes on the darkness. Let me know if anything moves."

When Ursula looked down the slope, beyond the last of the mushrooms, she saw only darkness. Anything could come out of those shadows. Just to be safe, she began to summon a little fire into her blood.

At last, Bael stopped as they reached a narrow path. Ursula's heart tightened in her chest. The path simply led down the hill and into shadows—or the Cavern of Night, as Bael had called it.

"Listen carefully to my instructions." Bael's gray eyes glinted in the dim light, and he lifted his palm into the air. Right now, Bael was all general—all Sword of Nyxobas. "If I raise my hand, you are to drop to the ground and stay perfectly still. No matter what happens, do not move again until I signal." He met Ursula's gaze. "Keep your fire extinguished. It won't help you where we're going."

Of course, a general never explained himself to his troops. Bael started down the hill, and Kester and Ursula walked quietly behind him. The path wound between a few knee-high mushrooms—then into darkness. Ursula reached out, touching Bael's muscled back as they walked. After a while, her eyes began to slowly adjust. As they followed the path, Ursula saw that despite its name, it wasn't entirely black in the Cavern of Night. A few glowing mushrooms sprouted among the gloom, and the path itself seemed to have a bioluminescent glow.

Above them, the sound of lunar bats grew louder, their squeaks and squeals piercing the darkness. More than once, Ursula's stomach lurched when one of the lunar bats shrieked particularly loudly. The pungent stench of ammonia thickened in the air around them, and she was sure that it concealed something worse, the fetid smell of death and decay.

Bael stopped abruptly, and Ursula nearly bumped into his back.

"What is it?" she whispered.

Bael put his finger to his lips, and she tuned in to a distant wailing—a high-pitched sound, like a baby crying.

A shudder danced up Ursula's spine. *A baby?*

"I'm going to investigate," Bael whispered, his gaze locked on Ursula. "Stay here until I return. Whatever happens, don't move, and get low."

Hunched over, Bael slipped into the darkness.

Ursula and Kester knelt on the path, surrounded by shadows. Only the path's pebbles cast a dim light. When Ursula picked one of them up to look at it, she realized it was a tiny piece of mushroom.

She and Kester waited in silence, her knees pressed into the squishy mushroom path, until an unearthly scream pierced the silence. The hair on the back of Ursula's neck stood on end. *What the hell?*

The noise echoed in the stillness of the cave until it slowly wound down into silence. Ursula glanced at Kester, his face illuminated by the faint glow from the path. He simply put a finger to his lips.

A deep, rumbling noise turned Ursula's head, followed by a heavy *thud* on the ground. A cold fear began to tighten Ursula's gut. Silence yawned, then another *thud.* Closer this time.

Ursula crouched lower, fear rippling over her. They were completely exposed on this featureless plain, unable to see as well as the creatures that lived here.

A movement in front of them sent terror racing through her veins, until she smelled Bael's familiar presence again.

As if from nowhere, he was crouching next to her, warmth radiating off his body. He leaned down, whispering in her ear, loud enough for Kester to hear. "The Molok has woken."

From the shadows, Kester's green eyes widened.

Of course he knows what the hell is going on. Everyone but me.

Thud. This time, Ursula could feel the dirt and stone shudder underneath them.

Kester glared at Bael. "Are you trying to get us killed?"

Thud. Another impact in the darkness shook the ground.

Bael grabbed Ursula by her manacled wrists, pulling her to her feet. "Run!"

With her bound hands, Ursula yanked up the hem of her dress, running awkwardly with the ridiculous constraints. *For crying out loud, I don't even have shoes on.*

Together, they sprinted deeper into the Cavern of Night. *Thud.* What the hell was that noise? Falling mushrooms? Someone hurling trees at them?

Bael charged forward, swinging the end of his chain above his head like a lasso.

They dodged to the side as a large shape suddenly loomed ahead of them. Ursula caught a glimpse of a small bat splayed out on the dusty ground. Blood flowed from a wound on its head. As they neared, an enormous insect-like creature scuttled off its back.

They sprinted past, just as the bat's body exploded in a spray of gore. *Thud.* A giant tree trunk—or something—had smashed through its abdomen.

They raced along the path, Bael in the lead, Ursula just behind—running as fast as she could with her manacled hands, her breath ragged in her throat. Kester brought up the rear. Darkness enveloped them, and thudding impacts shook the ground. Ursula's lungs felt like they were on fire, her legs burning with the exertion, and sweat trickled down her brow.

Thud. Another impact slammed down, this time just inches in front of Bael, and Ursula's heart skipped a beat. *Tree trunks. Definitely someone throwing tree trunks.*

Far up ahead, Bael slammed into the trunk at full speed. Ursula tried to dodge to the side, but that only meant that she slipped and fell, her balance thrown off without the use of her arms. Kester tripped over her, stumbling onto his hands and knees.

He scrambled to his feet, but another tree trunk slammed into the ground next to him. As Ursula crawled to her knees, she glimpsed the closest trunk, illuminated by the faint glow of the path. With a stab of horror, she realized it wasn't made of wood, but of a thick chitinous armor.

Not a tree trunk. A giant leg.

Ursula turned to run, but Bael's voice stopped her. "Don't move!" he barked.

From the forest floor, Kester tugged sharply at her dress, his finger to his lips. Slowly, he raised it and pointed. Adrenaline snapped through Ursula's nerve endings. Twenty feet above her head, another monstrous leg was poised to strike. If she ran, it would crush her.

Ursula's stomach dropped as the head of a massive insect slid into view. It took all of her willpower not to scream at the pale arachnid monster looming above her.

The spider was enormous, at least the size of a small house. Its skin was the color of bleached bone, but her gaze froze on a lethally sharp pair of fangs. They were bracketed by a pair of longer appendages that twitched like giant fingers.

Ursula's mind raced. She stood below it unarmed, her wrists bound by golden manacles. No way to defend herself. Even though Bael had cautioned not to use fire, it sparked to life in her veins anyway.

Kester stood next to her, watching the spider intently. Bael was maybe twenty feet from her. Just like her, he stayed perfectly still, then slowly pointed to his eyes.

Eyes. That's a signal we did not discuss, so...

The spider's head lurched lower, so that the twitching appendages touched the dirt in front of them. Unlike its massive legs, these appendages moved delicately over the cavern floor, tapping the soil like a drummer tuning a timpani. Ursula's muscles tightened as she realized it was searching for them.

That was when she understood what Bael was trying to tell her. *The spider has no eyes. It can't see us.*

Bael's eyes were wide as he pointed frantically at the cavern floor. *Another gesture I need to interpret.* The air behind her moved, and she ducked instinctively as one of the giant appendages passed over her head.

From the ground, she met Bael's gaze. He held up one of his hands, letting all five fingers dangle like legs. With his other hand, he made a walking motion on the top of his knuckles.

You've got to be bloody kidding me.

CHAPTER 8

Ursula shook her head vigorously *no*, but Bael ignored her, kneeling to pick up a handful of dirt from the floor. *No, don't do it.* In a slow, underhand motion, he tossed it about ten feet in front of her. As soon as the dust hit the floor, one of the twitching appendages flicked over to touch it.

"Now, Ursula!" Bael hissed.

"I'm going to kill you," Ursula snarled as she leapt. But she was too slow, the manacles and the long gown throwing her off. The spider's appendages snatched her in midair. *Oh balls.* Her pulse raced wildly.

Claws of fear pierced her rib cage. Above her, the spider's fangs stabbed downward, aiming straight at her head. Instinctively, she summoned her flames. As the venom-soaked fang plunged toward her face, she caught it in her burning fingers.

Her blazing hands melted through the tip of the chitinous fang like butter. The arachnid's head jerked back with a dry scream. The severed end of the fang narrowly missed puncturing her leg as it spun past her. The loss of its fang sent the arachnid into a sort of frenzy as the remaining fang flexed and pulsed.

Ursula's heart slammed hard against her ribs. She pulled the heat from her hands, and reached above her head in an effort to pull herself up one of the spider's legs.

From the darkness below, Bael shouted, "Ursula, are you all right?"

"Sort of. I melted one of its fangs."

"Can you climb any higher?" asked Bael.

"I'm trying, but my hands are bound." *Seriously, what the fuck were you thinking?*

The appendage moved, and she swung out over darkness. In the dark cavern, she had no idea how high up she was.

"Maybe try moving the leg lower," Bael suggested.

"Does it look like I'm in control of this thing?" she shouted.

"*This* was your idea?" Kester asked.

"Can you two be quiet?" yelled Ursula. "I need to concentrate."

A light blazed below her—Bael had called up a glowing orb. While she could now see what she was doing, she could also see that she was at least fifty feet in the air, and her stomach swooped. A fall from this height would kill her.

Ursula stared down at her body—her torn, mud-spattered gown practically hanging off her, draping to her ankles. Frankly, the damn thing was encumbering her. Ankle-length gowns weren't made for climbing spiders any more than they were made for running through mushroom forests. *Time to give the gown a trim.*

She summoned fire into her body—enough to burn the fabric off the lower half of her dress, until the flames quickly snuffed out again in the damp air. She now wore a dress that reached just below her arse—much better. She kicked her legs forward so that she was able to wrap them around the appendage. Slowly, she began to shimmy upwards, blocking out the fact that her inner thighs were rubbing against the spider's disgusting skin. At last, she made her way up onto the spider's head.

The spider must have worked out what she was trying to do, because the other appendage swung back to pinch her. And yet, this time she was ready. As it neared, she cinched her legs tightly. When the approaching appendage was about five feet away, she let go with her hands. She only had to think of Bael and this asinine plan to channel enough heat into her fingers to melt a deep hole in the exoskeleton of the incoming appendage. The spider unleashed another eerie howl that keened throughout the cavern. *That's for trying to smoosh me.*

She shimmied upwards, making it maybe ten feet, when the spider suddenly began to swing its head from side to side like a terrier shaking the life out of a rat. It took all of Ursula's strength to hold on.

"Can you try burning it again?" Bael shouted from below.

Ursula's stomach was churning, her nerves blazing, but she channeled some fire into her hands, letting it flow through her fingertips. The spider shrieked, then raised its head into the air like a trumpeting elephant—bringing her up with it.

Ursula's blood roared in her ears. *Okay, this isn't ideal.* For a moment, she felt almost weightless, suspended a hundred feet above the floor of the cavern.

Then, the spider flung her down.

The fall felt like slow motion, her hands slipping loose, her body tumbling backward, plunging into darkness.

Midair, a powerful set of arms caught her, absorbing her impact with a shocking grace—and hurtling back upward with her. Shadow magic whirled around them, propelling them through the air. Her blood thundered in her veins, and she gripped tightly to Bael's shirt, clinging on for dear life.

They raced toward the giant arachnid's carapace, shadow magic flowing around them in dark wisps. They landed hard on the spider's body, Bael clinging tightly around her waist to keep her steady. Ursula gasped as the impact knocked the wind out of her. The spider screamed, lurching upright.

Bael grabbed tightly to a ridge of exoskeleton with one hand, and with the other, he pulled Ursula close. "Are you all right?"

"You almost got me killed."

"But you survived."

When we're off this thing, we're going to have some stern words. They were sitting on the back of the spider's body now, and it shifted beneath them, stalking into the darkness. Up here, and with her dress shorn, it wasn't quite so difficult to balance.

"So what's the plan?" asked Ursula.

Bael crouched on the spider's back. "Are you ready?"

Ursula was rapidly losing patience. "I asked you for the plan. I'm not ready until you tell me the plan. If you ask me to battle this spider again—"

"Molok," said Bael.

"Spider, Molok, whatever. I almost died."

Bael smiled. "I think you're going to like what I have in mind. Do you remember how to call Sotz?"

"Do you think he can hear us from here?"

Bael nodded. "We're right under the rookery. He's up there somewhere."

"And the plan is—"

Her question was cut off by a lurch from Molok as the spider lumbered on. *Okay. No time to ask about the plan.*

While Bael helped steady her on the creature's back, Ursula put her fingers to her mouth and whistled. A moment later, the sound of bat wings rhythmically beat the air, and Sotz swooped out of the shadows. Ursula's chest unclenched at the sight of the enormous bat.

Sotz kept pace alongside them as the spider trudged through the cavern. She could probably jump onto Sotz from here, but they were missing someone.

"What about Kester?" she asked.

"The Headsman? We could just leave him behind."

"Bael." Her voice was growing sharper. "He's a friend."

A wry smile from Bael. "Of course. I'll get him. Tell Sotz to take you to the Grotto. We'll meet you there."

Before she could say another word, Bael leapt off the back of the spider into the darkness below.

CHAPTER 9

*B*ael's orb flickered above her like a guttering candle. In a few seconds, it would extinguish. With a final whistle for Sotz, Ursula leapt off the spider. The bat caught her expertly, and she clutched his soft fur, clenching her thighs around his body.

Pressing her face against his neck, she whispered, "Take me to the Grotto."

Sotz's wings pounded the air as he flew through the darkness. For the first time since she'd arrived on the moon, Ursula felt in control, losing herself in the familiar rhythms of lunar bat flight. Despite being a hellhound, she was at ease in the sweet oblivion of the shadows. Above her, the bats' shrill voices loaned a sense of place to the otherwise pitch-black Cavern of Night.

Ursula peered over Sotz's side, but she could see nothing. Here, the cavern lived up to its name—reminiscent of Nyxobas's void. Why the hell did she find the void oddly comforting, strangely alluring? Sweet oblivion, boundless freedom. An escape from her true self.

A voice rose from the depths of her own mind. *Who are you, Ursula? Who are you really?* She pushed the voice out of her mind, tuning into the sounds and scents around her instead. The bats rushing above her, the wind whipping at her hair, Sotz's familiar smell... Here, she felt at home.

Sotz banked sharply, and a vortex of lights greeted her. Arrayed in a massive spiral, the lights twisted around like the gyre of a distant galaxy. Not stars, but rather tiny mushrooms growing on the cavern floor. Sotz glided lower, his speed slowing until they landed gently on a giant boulder.

"Is this the Grotto?" asked Ursula.

Sotz chirped in what she thought was an affirmative answer, and she slid off his back onto the damp soil. The lunar bat launched himself into the air, leaving her alone again among the faint light of the mushrooms. Where exactly was she supposed to meet Bael here?

At the base of the rock, a glowing path led toward the spiral of mushrooms she'd seen from her flight. While she was waiting for Bael, she began walking quietly along the path. It sloped downward, weaving between the mushroom caps. Goose bumps rose over her bare legs, and she would have rubbed her arms for warmth if only her hands weren't still bound. The slope steepened, until she found herself walking along a path that wound along a cliff's steep face. The path twisted between giant boulders and ran along narrow ledges that kept the yawning precipice only a single misstep away.

Ursula's lungs and thighs were burning when the path stopped at a massive onyx boulder, blocking the mouth of a cave. Ursula drew in a short breath at the sight of the stone. It looked exactly like the one in Bael's manor, and when she ran her fingertips over it, she found it smooth and cool to the touch. Is this where she was supposed to go? Bael was able to push his boulder to the side, but Ursula couldn't get this thing to budge. She'd need shadow magic to move it.

Exhausted, Ursula sat on the damp earth, the soil cool beneath her bare thighs. She rested her back against the cliff face, pulling her knees up to her chest for warmth. *I guess I'm going to have to wait for Bael and Kester after all.*

She nearly jumped out of her skin when the boulder suddenly rolled to the side, revealing the cave entrance.

A familiar voice pierced the silence. "Ursula, is that you?"

"Cera?" Ursula hopped up.

"Ursula!" The little oneiroi woman hurried toward her, frowning at her singed dress. "What *are* you wearing?"

"Is that really your biggest concern right now?" She lifted her hands. "Not, you know, the manacles binding my wrists?"

Cera hopped from one foot to another, muttering to herself as she stared at the singed hem, her silver hair cascading over her back. Apparently the hem was the main concern.

Ursula nodded at the cave's opening. "Cera, can you tell me what's going on? Where are we?"

"We're at the Grotto. You're perfectly safe here."

"Is there any chance we could go inside? I'm freezing."

"Of course. It will be an honor. Everyone is very excited to meet you."

"Everyone?"

"You'll see." Cera hurried back into the tunnel, and Ursula followed, ducking her head to pass under a low stone archway.

"Bael hasn't arrived, I take it?"

"He'll be joining us soon," said Cera. "Not to worry."

Cera led Ursula down the tunnel, carved straight through the side of the cliff. It looked similar to the tunnels in Bael's and Abrax's manors—narrow with smooth walls. Glowing fungi illuminated strange runes and twisting designs engraved into the walls. Voices began to carry through the cave, growing louder as they walked. The tunnel curved sharply, then opened to a large, well-lit cavern.

Ursula gasped. This cavern teemed with people.

Not people, she realized as her eyes adjusted, but oneiroi. They moved among a small collection of stone dwellings, like a miniature version of the city at the foot of Asta.

Cera began to lead her down a rock slope, and toward the closest structure.

"What is this place?" asked Ursula.

"This is the Grotto."

"Why is it here?"

Cera stopped, turning to look at her. "It's the last free city of the oneiroi. I'm taking you to Xarthra. She'll explain everything."

As Ursula digested this information, Cera led her into the city. Oneiroi filled the streets, each one wearing thick robes, with hoods covering their silver hair. Ursula's eyes widened. *I know these outfits.* When she'd seen a group of oneiroi reviving a golem in the mushroom forest, they'd been wearing these robes.

Cera led her through winding streets until she stopped at a small stone dwelling.

"This is where Xarthra lives?" asked Ursula.

Cera laughed. "No. But there is absolutely no way you can go to an audience with Xarthra wearing mud and a singed dress."

Cera opened the door, revealing a modest bedroom. A small bed and dresser nestled in one corner. Dominating the center of the room stood a table covered in myriad colorful fabrics, sequins, and sewing equipment.

"Have you always lived here?" asked Ursula.

Cera shook her head, her eyes darkening. "No. I used to live in the great crater. After Bael went into exile, my little home in the crater was destroyed. Punishment for serving him. So, Xarthra moved my belongings here. I had nowhere else to go."

Ursula bit her lip. "I'm sorry. That must have been hard."

Cera shrugged. "It's all right. I didn't have much." She yanked out a patch of green tulle from the pile on the table. "And they saved all my dresses and sewing supplies." She loosed a long sigh. "Let's get you something to wear."

She turned, rummaging through a basket of clothing at the far end of the room, muttering to herself the whole time. While she searched, Ursula peered outside the window, hoping to catch a glimpse of Bael and Kester. No such luck so far.

After a moment, Cera scrubbed a hand over her mouth. "Somewhere, I've got a cream silk dress for you. I hope that will be suitable?"

"Cera. You are amazing, and I'll wear anything you have. Assuming you can get it on me."

It took Cera only a few minutes of rummaging before she pulled out a long, pearly gown—strapless, and slashed up to the thigh.

Ursula blinked at it. "Are you sure it's not too...fancy?"

Cera tutted. "You cannot meet Xarthra looking like you might plan to assassinate her. And most importantly, it's strapless. Your manacles won't get in the way."

She had a point. Ursula turned her back, and Cera ripped the tattered, singed dress off her. Cera spent a minute scrubbing the dirt and grime off Ursula's body while Ursula shivered in the center of the room, goose bumps all over, until Cera directed her to step into the dress. Cera helped to pull it up her body, and it fit like a glove. A pair of cream high heels were the finishing touch.

"There," Cera said, stepping back. "That looks gorgeous. But before we leave, we just need to fix your hair and face situation."

"My face situation?" Ursula bristled.

Cera smiled. "You just need some cosmetic enhancements."

Ursula's stomach clenched. At this point, she just *really* wanted to get off the moon, and submitting to Cera's meticulous grooming might be the only way forward.

era led Ursula into the heart of the city, along a winding path that curved between humble homes, their facades lit by glowing mushrooms.

In the center of the Grotto was an open cobbled square that reminded Ursula of an Italian piazza. At one end stood a tall building carved from a single pillar of rock, beneath a peaked column that hung from the grotto ceiling, nearly touching it. *A giant stalagmite.*

Violet light glowed over the swooping runes and sigils that covered its surface—similar to the ones she'd seen in the tunnels, but with pictographs: curling creatures that looked like caterpillars and bats. Ursula shivered at a carving of an eight-legged beast: the Molok.

Cera led her up a flight of sloping steps carved into the stalagmite, and Ursula's new heels clacked off the stone. At the top stood a pair of oneiroi guards dressed in blood-red cloaks and holding spears tipped with silver axe-heads. They nodded curtly at Cera. *I guess we're expected.*

Teetering slightly in her heels, Ursula followed Cera inside the stalagmite building, where she found herself in a single room. An ancient oneiroi woman with long, silver hair and glittering violet jewelry sat on an onyx throne on a dais. It took Ursula a moment to realize that Bael and Kester were standing in the shadows near the dais, and she smiled with relief at the sight of them.

Cera bowed before Bael. "My lord. I'm sorry to have kept you waiting—"

"Cera," said Xarthra. "The demon's name is Bael. He is not your lord within the Grotto."

Cera scowled. "Yes, of course, Xarthra. I forgot."

If Bael was upset about the lack of honorific, he didn't show it, instead giving a short bow. "Thank you for brining Ursula here." He smiled at Ursula, his eyes gleaming with that deep, familiar gray. "We were just making introductions. Xarthra, this is Ursula. She and Kester are here to help us restore the moon to its rightful owners."

Ursula smiled, nodding as if she had any idea what the hell Bael was talking about.

Xarthra stared at her, tapping the armrests of her throne. "I have heard of your exploits, Ursula. Is it true you defeated Abrax at the Lacus Mortis?"

Ursula shivered, thinking of how she had almost died that day. "I was able to drain his magic, but I'd be lying if I said I knew how."

Xarthra cocked her head. "A stupendous feat in any case. Abrax poses a great threat to our society. If we are to retake the moon, he must be defeated."

"Thank you." Ursula cleared her throat. "Sorry—where exactly *are* we?"

"I am Xarthra. Daughter of Zeth. Oldest living descendent of the Shining-Haired." Xarthra's eyes flashed. "And I will rid the moon of the demons and lead my people to freedom once again."

Ursula stared at her. "Right. Of course. And Bael and I are helping you."

Xarthra blinked slowly, retaining her regal bearing. "As you know, Bael has his own reasons for assisting."

Ursula smiled, nodding again. *Of course I don't know. That would involve Bael having filled me in.*

Bael stepped forward into the candlelight. "When I returned to the moon after Abrax stole my wings and attacked my manor, I was lost. Alone. Eventually I would have succumbed to Hothgar and the other lords. But, with Cera's help, Xarthra showed me a new path."

Okay. Ursula couldn't quite play along any longer. "Let me get this straight. You've been working with the oneiroi resistance this whole time?"

Bael nodded. "I didn't see any reason to fill you in. After all, you work for Emerazel."

Frustration simmered in her chest. "Any of you happen to know which oneiroi planned the attack on my room the last time I was here? The bomb with the note?"

Bael looked confused. "A bomb with a note?"

"An oneiroi on a white bat threw a bomb through my window. There was a note too. It said that I wasn't welcome on the moon, and that next time they wouldn't miss."

Concern furrowed Bael's brow. "I don't know who that was."

Xarthra raised a wrinkled finger. "That was my doing. I sent one of my men to try to scare you away. We worried that your presence—" She paused as she carefully considered her next words. "We worried that you might *distract* Bael from more important matters."

"Can someone tell me what the fuck is going on?" Kester interrupted. He looked exhausted, with his hair plastered to his face and smudges of dust on his cheeks.

Ursula let out a long sigh. "Demons and oneiroi are working together to defeat Nyxobas. That's the long and short of it."

"Righto," said Kester, looking down at his cuffed hands. No one but he and Ursula seemed bothered by the cuffs.

Ursula turned back to Xarthra. "Is there any chance you could get Kester something to eat and drink? He's had a rough couple of weeks."

Xarthra nodded at the nearest guard, who scurried off. Then, she tapped her fingertips together. "Bael and I will raise an army of oneiroi to defeat the demon invaders."

Ursula frowned. "What about Abrax's golems? He has his own army."

Xarthra smiled for the first time since Ursula had met her. "The golems will be neutralized."

"Neutralized?" Ursula stared. "I nearly lost my life to one. A single golem killed at least three of Nyxobas's most powerful demons with nothing but a knife. How are you going to neutralize them?"

Bael scrubbed a hand over his stubble. "She's not going to believe us unless we show her."

Ursula lifted her manacled hands. "As much as I want to see the golems straight away, I don't suppose anyone could help with this situation?"

"Oh. That." Xarthra narrowed her eyes. "We'll get there." Without another word, Xarthra rose and began striding over to the piazza, her movements shockingly smooth for someone who looked so ancient. "And you've probably never seen exactly how the oneiroi can really fight, either. Follow me, and I will show you."

CHAPTER 11

With a regal bearing, Xarthra led them toward the cobbled piazza, where violet light gave the dark stone an eerie hue. As they walked, two oneiroi servants bustled up to Ursula and Kester, thrusting cups of water and mushroom sandwiches into their arms. Ursula did her best to tuck the water into the crook of her elbow while chomping into the sandwich, but it wasn't her most elegant moment. Crumbs littered the top of her cleavage in her strapless gown.

At the edge of the piazza, lined with stone buildings on all sides, Ursula took a seat by Kester's side on a bench. Kester looked exhausted as he bit into his sandwich.

"Are you feeling okay?" Ursula asked.

Kester nodded. "I'm fine. It's just that Abrax enjoyed starving me. Between the missing calories and all the running from giant spiders, I'm a tad fatigued."

Ursula smiled faintly. "I'm just glad I found you."

Kester flashed her a sheepish smile, his cheek dimpling.

Movement at the far end of the piazza turned her head, and Ursula watched as a pair of guards led a hooded figure over the cobbles. Ursula's stomach clenched. Those creepy, fluid movements were definitely the movements of a golem.

The guards led the hooded golem into the center of the piazza, where a stone block stood with an iron loop attached to it. The guards tied the golem to the block, then slowly backed away.

"I need volunteers." From just in front of Ursula, Xarthra's voice boomed over the square.

On cue, three oneiroi guards in blood-red robes stepped forward. Chained to the cube, the golem strained against its bonds. Ursula's stomach clenched. She knew how lethal the bloody thing was. She and Bael had barely defeated one, and she couldn't see how three little oneiroi could fight the beast. Hard to defeat something that can't feel pain.

Between mouthfuls, Ursula leaned in to Kester, whispering, "I'm not sure this is the best idea."

Xarthra apparently overheard it, because she shot Ursula a sharp look. "My soldiers are highly trained."

Before Ursula could reply, one of the oneiroi reached into his robe and withdrew a small dagger. Ursula's eyes widened. The blade was identical to the ones the golem had used to carve Sallos into a quivering mass of flesh. The oneiroi tossed the blade at the golem's feet.

Like a serpent striking, the golem pounced on the weapon. Simultaneously, the three oneiroi dropped their cloaks. Ursula had been expecting a trio of men, but these oneiroi were all female. They wore tight-fitting black outfits, each with a small sword at her hip. With a rasp of steel, they drew their swords in unison.

With the sound of shearing metal, the golem ripped free from its bonds. It held its dagger lightly in one hand, then froze completely. Slowly, the oneiroi women approached it, and Ursula's pulse raced. If Xarthra was wrong—if her oneiroi weren't a match for the golem—the creature would attack them next. And Ursula and Kester were still stuck in the bloody cuffs.

The hair on Ursula's arms rose, as a low keening growl emerged from the back of the oneiroi's throats. Like a pack of wild dogs, they encircled the golem. Ursula's knuckles clenched around the remains of her sandwich. She was no longer focusing on her food. The golem's movements looked predatory, almost bestial.

Then, with a shout so sudden that she nearly jumped, the oneiroi attacked.

The golem swung for the nearest oneiroi, but the woman was faster, dodging under the golem's blade. With a vicious scream, the oneiroi sliced her sword upward, severing the golem's arm at the elbow. Simultaneously, the remaining pair of oneiroi tore into the golem's opposite side. In a blur of black cloth and silver hair, they slashed the golem's free hand from its wrist. Without any arms, the golem had no way to defend itself. An instant later, the three oneiroi had pinned the golem to the ground and pulled back its hood. Ursula shook her head in disbelief. The entire attack had taken less than ten seconds.

Xarthra's clapping echoed off the cobblestones. "Well done."

Bael nodded solemnly, but didn't speak.

A few more oneiroi guards came out, then bound what remained of the golem with rope. Moving swiftly across the cobblestones, the three oneiroi fighters approached Xarthra, heels clacking off the stones. They moved stiffly—almost as if they were fighting against their bodies. They didn't speak, instead making growling noises in the back of their throats.

The hair rose on Ursula's arms again as she realized where she'd seen oneiroi like this before. Cera's blood-crazed brother had acted like this when he'd attacked Bael.

Bael rested a gentle hand on her shoulder. "They won't hurt you, I promise," he said. "But you're going to need to hold out your hands."

"They're corrupted," Ursula hissed.

"Xarthra has trained them to control their hunger. The corruption is what allows them to defeat the golems. It gives them extraordinary strength."

"Bael speaks the truth," said Xarthra. "The oneiroi are in control of their bloodlust. In fact, they have made a great sacrifice. For as long as they live, the craving will curse them." She nodded at the three oneiroi. "They took the curse willingly—to fight for the freedom of their people. Do as Bael asks and hold out your hands."

Ursula flicked a quick gaze at Bael. She *did* trust him. Slowly, she extended her manacled wrists. The oneiroi walked toward her, their bodies twitching, growling louder. Hunger flashed in their silver eyes. When they'd moved within reach, all three of them grabbed her manacles. Gritting their teeth, they began to squeeze all at once.

The manacles glowed brighter and brighter, but they were no match for the vise-like grip of the oneiroi. With a blinding flash, the manacles disintegrated. Already, they were moving on to Kester's golden cuffs.

Ursula rubbed her wrists, loosing a long breath. "Thank you so much."

As the oneiroi freed Kester, Xarthra reached into her tunic and pulled out a roughly carved obsidian bowl, about the size of a large mug. She crossed to the oneiroi, then knelt and placed the bowl at their feet.

Ursula stared as Xarthra drew a short obsidian dagger from her belt. She tightened her fingers around the blade, then ran it sharply through her palm without hesitation.

Blood flowed into the bowl, and the oneiroi stared on hungrily. When the bowl was filled, Xarthra passed it to the first oneiroi. The oneiroi took the bowl to her lips and drank.

Each oneiroi took a sip of their queen's blood. As they swallowed, they visibly relaxed, the tension in their limbs softening, eyes lightening to a pale silver.

When they'd finished, they handed the bowl to Bael, and he brought it to his lips.

"What are you doing?" Ursula blurted.

Bael lowered the bowl. "*This* is how I was able to manage my own bloodlust."

CHAPTER 12

At the simple wooden table in Cera's home, Ursula sat across from Cera and Kester. To her right, Bael leaned back in his chair with his eyes closed, the candlelight wavering over his perfect features. Kester still hadn't managed to fill his stomach, and he sipped soup from a large mug. The domestic scene should have been relaxing, but tension gripped Ursula's muscles. She couldn't stop thinking about what Abrax had said about her mother's death.

Kester finished his soup, leaning back in his chair. "Bael and I just followed the glowing path until we got to the Grotto. Honestly, I could have done it myself."

Bael slowly opened his eyes, narrowing them at Kester. "It is easy to get lost in Cavern of Night. You really have no idea."

Kester arched an eyebrow. "I'm a hound. I don't get lost."

Bael snorted.

Ursula pinched the bridge of her nose. "Okay, enough with the competitiveness. Anyone know what happened to Zee?"

"No," said Cera. "I was able to flee the Drake's warren in the chaos of Abrax's attack. Zee didn't make it out with me. She's either with the dragons still, or she's found a way out."

Kester's lips curled wistfully. "She's extremely resourceful. My money is on an escape."

Ursula blew a strand of red hair out of her eyes. "Should we try to find her now?"

"No." Bael's eyes darkened. "We must help the oneiroi. We have to wait here until we are ready to attack Hothgar."

"And when will that be?" asked Kester.

"A year at least," said Bael.

"A year?" Kester rose abruptly, nearly knocking the table over.

Bael nodded. "We need to recruit more oneiroi to the cause. At this point, our army isn't big enough to defeat Abrax and the rest of the demon lords."

"So we're just going to wait down here in this pit?" If Kester had had any of Emerazel's fire, his eyes would have been blazing.

"It's the safest place," said Bael. "Abrax has no idea how to find us here."

Ursula shook her head. "I'm with Kester. I know you made a promise, but we can't hide here for an entire year."

Bael's jaw clenched. "What do you propose that we do?"

"I'm going to Mount Acidale." Ursula hadn't even realized the full extent of her plan until the words were out of her mouth.

Bael's eyes widened. "That's absurd. It's far too dangerous."

"I agree," said Kester. "You can't go there."

Ursula straightened. "I'm not asking your permission. I want to find my family. I need to find out who I really am." She looked sharply between the two men. "Abrax told me about the Battle of Mount Acidale..."

She let the sentence trail off into what was now a deathly quiet room. Bael studied her intently, his slate-gray eyes unreadable. Kester's face had paled. They did know something.

"What did Abrax tell you?" asked Bael.

"He claims that you've been lying to me. That you knew who I was the moment you met me."

A line formed between Bael's straight eyebrows. "That's not true."

Kester cut in. There was steel in his voice, but also sadness. "Her mother was a member of King Midac's senior guard. The one who killed the queen and tried to murder the king."

Bael's eyes whirled with shadows. "You knew this all along and you kept it from Ursula?"

Kester gripped his water glass. "Emerazel forbade me from telling her. I had no choice."

"You killed Ursula's mother." Bael's voice was pure ice.

Ursula's stomach lurched, and she wanted to be sick. *Abrax was telling the truth.*

A clang of metal interrupted them, and Ursula jumped—Cera dropping a spoon to the floor.

"It was the middle of a battle. Death was all around us. I saved the king's life from an assassin who had been brainwashed by shadow demons." Kester glared at Bael. It was as if Ursula wasn't even in the room. "I did my job. Besides, it's not as though your hands are clean. I heard you were the one who recruited her."

"What's going on?" Ursula demanded.

Bael's eyes were black as the void, his entire body stiff with rage. "If you weren't Ursula's friend, I would tear your arms from their sockets and feed your corpse to Molok. I don't know who recruited Ursula's mother. It wasn't me."

Kester shook his head as he drew an obsidian blade. Bael's eyes twitched in recognition. "You didn't think I was armed, did you, demon? Maybe you shouldn't leave blades lying around. Come over to that table and I'll carve out your heart"—he lowered his voice to mimic Bael's—"and feed it to Molok."

Ursula's own sense of rage was building, roiling in her gut, ready to erupt.

Bael growled, his voice rising into a roar. "Hound of Emerazel—"

Ursula leapt up, knocking the table over and stepping between the two men. "Enough already!" Her voice boomed off Cera's low ceiling. "We've had enough bloodshed. I forgive Kester for killing my mother. I don't even remember her."

And that was messed up, wasn't it? Ursula craved oblivion, wanted to flee from something disturbing in her past—that instinct existed in the depths of her mind. But it wasn't right. She needed to remember her mum. She needed to care, or she could never really know who she was.

Flustered, she folded her arms, unsure how to be angry about the death of someone she couldn't remember at all. "Just fill me in on things in the future, will you? Both of you. Don't leave me in the dark. And I need to find out who I am. I might have other family still in Mount

Acidale, and I want to go to see if they are still alive. And we need to look for Zee."

The truth was, she didn't feel much for her mother. Hard to feel anything when you couldn't remember, when your mum was just an abstract concept.

Bael's eyes were the color of the void, his knuckles white as snow, but he sat down in his chair. Across from him, Kester slowly lowered the blade.

"All right," Bael said after a few moments, his voice cracking with rage. "I'll speak to Xarthra, and I'll take you to Mount Acidale. We'll look for Zee and your family."

* * *

Ursula awoke in the morning. At least, she thought it was morning. Not like there was daylight in the Grotto, only the perpetual glow of the bioluminescent mushrooms that grew along the cavern walls. Still, the smell of sizzling bacon wafting through Cera's house suggested that it was probably morning.

She clambered out of the bed she'd been sharing with Cera, and crossed barefoot into the main room. Cera stood over the stove, steam curling from a cast-iron pan. Cera pushed the bacon around.

"Good morning," Ursula mumbled.

"There's no coffee," said Cera in a voice that was far too chipper for Ursula's current mental state. "But there's some black mushroom tea in the kettle."

Ursula smiled faintly, nausea fluttering in her gut. *Sounds...delicious.*

On the other side of the room, two bodies stirred. Kester and Bael lay stretched out on the floor. Despite their loathing for one another, they'd been chivalrous with the sleeping arrangements. They'd both insisted that the ladies got the bed while they took the floor. In theory, this was also so they could guard the door, but given that the smell of bacon hadn't roused them, Ursula had to question their usefulness as guards.

Ursula sat down at the kitchen table. "How did you sleep, Cera?"

"Well enough, but I got peckish, so I thought I'd fix some breakfast."

"The bacon smells amazing."

Cera grinned, then bustled over to the table with a steaming plate of rashers. "There might not be any eggs in the Grotto, but there's always bacon."

Kester sat up on the floor, stretching his arms over his head. "How's that?" He looked tired, but the bags under his eyes seemed less heavy. "I haven't seen any pigs."

"Oh." Cera beamed. "This bacon is chiropteran. The bats are good for other things than riding, you know."

Ursula's stomach curdled, but she plastered a smile on her face. "How wonderful." Maybe mushroom tea wasn't such a bad idea after all. She grabbed the ceramic pot in the center of the table, then poured a few steaming cups for the table.

She sniffed it cautiously before taking a sip. It wasn't Earl Grey, but it didn't have the dank, fungal flavor she was expecting. "This is pretty good."

Cera nodded vigorously. "It has lots of caffeine."

Kester pulled out a chair next to her, already reaching for the bat bacon. "This looks amazing."

Cera flipped three more sizzling strips of meat onto a plate. Without hesitating, Kester dug in.

Wood squeaked over stone as Bael pulled out a chair and sat down. Immediately, Cera was by his side filling his cup with tea and slapping down slices of bat bacon.

Bael plucked a piece for himself. "Thank you, Cera."

Ursula leaned back in her chair. "So what's the plan?"

Bael bit into the crispy meat. "We leave for Acidale in an hour. Just us. Kester isn't coming."

Ursula sucked in a sharp breath. She hadn't been expecting things to happen quite that fast. "You know the way?"

"No," said Bael, shaking his head. "But he does." Bael gave a Kester a sharp look.

Kester stared at Bael over his steaming tea. "There's a sigil in Mount Acidale. I can tell you the name."

Ursula nodded. "And we just travel there by Emerazel's fire?"

"Exactly."

Anticipation rippled over Ursula's skin. Three years ago, she'd simply turned up in a burnt-out church in London, with nothing but her name and a little note in her pocket. She'd never known who she was, why she seemed to have magical powers. She'd never known why her memory had disappeared in the first place. Would she finally get some answers?

Kester put down his tea. "There are some things you should know. First, Mount Acidale is ruled by King Midac."

Ursula inhaled sharply. "I know. Apparently my mum tried to kill him."

"He's an arrogant despot," said Kester. "In Mount Acidale, hellhounds are to be killed on sight."

"And the dragons will recognize you if they find you," Bael added. "They saw you use Emerazel's fire in the warren. Lucius knows what you are."

Ursula frowned as she processed all the new information. "I thought King Midac had Emerazel's power?"

"He does," said Kester. "But after the battle, he decreed that he was the *only* one allowed to channel her flames. Anyone else caught with Emerazel's fire is put to death."

Wonderful. "Let me guess. This is why no one is allowed to enter the kingdom?"

"Exactly," said Kester. "It's how he maintains his grip on power."

"So is there a way to move around the city?" asked Ursula.

"Don't use your fire, and we stay out of sight," said Bael. "I have a contact who will help us."

"Do you think he could help me find my family?"

Bael nodded. "And he might help us recover Excalibur from the dragons. With the blade, we can defeat Hothgar. Just like I promised Xarthra." Bael's gaze slid to Cera. "Can you assist Ursula's preparations?"

"Of course, my lord—"

Bael lifted his hand. "Here in the Grotto, you may call me Bael." He rose, slouching so his head didn't hit the ceiling. "I must collect some things for our trip. I will return shortly." He stepped outside and closed the door behind him.

Cera began dragging a basket of clothes out of the corner. "Ursula. You will need something to wear in Mount Acidale."

Kester threaded his fingers behind his head. "Find your most outdated clothing, then. Stiff olive silk. Awkward bustles. Mount Acidale is not like New York. They've been isolated for hundreds of years. Their sense of style is, to put it nicely, dated."

Cera's body tensed. "I can't dress Ursula in something ugly."

Kester shrugged. "She needs to blend in. If you clothe her in Francesco Sforza, she'll stand out like a sore thumb. Do you want her to be caught and tortured?"

"Fine," said Cera.

"Then I suggest you search for something like a moth-eaten wool cloak."

Glumly, Cera crossed into another room. She returned a few minutes later clutching three pairs of thick woolen stockings, a pair of black lace-up Victorian boots, a stiff crinoline dress—the color of plums—and a gray, woolen cloak.

"My, my," said Kester. "You *are* good."

Just then, the door opened with a bang. Bael stood in the entrance, and Ursula sucked in a breath. He wore dark wool trousers, a gray waistcoat, and a heavy wool frock coat. A thin sword hung from a black leather belt. In his hand, he held a black top hat. He looked like some sort of down-on-his-luck, time-traveling Victorian gentleman.

"Don't you look dashing!" said Cera. "Where did you get that from?"

"Consignment shop," he said simply.

Cera shooed him outside. "Give the lady a few minutes to dress."

While Bael and Kester waited outside, Ursula pulled on the woolen stockings and the crinoline dress. Despite the drab appearance of the clothes, Ursula had to admit they were comfortable and warm. Cera helped her tighten the corset until she could hardly breathe, and Ursula leaned down to lace the boots up to her knees.

As she threaded the laces through their holes, she felt like she was doing something oddly familiar, her fingers working expertly on the old-fashioned boots. Of course, she'd probably once worn something exactly like these boots around Mount Acidale, and she'd probably worn a corset just like the one that squeezed her ribs right now.

When she'd fully dressed, Kester and Bael pushed through the door again. By the doorway, Kester plucked a golden flask from his pocket, then began the familiar task of pouring liquid over the floor in the shape of Emerazel's sigil.

Bael stared at the floor, and Ursula could tell from the tension in his shoulders that the fire still made him nervous. "Are we ready?"

"Almost." Kester thrust the flask at Ursula. "You might need this to return."

As Kester knelt to light the sigil, Cera ran to Ursula and threw her arms around her. "Be careful."

"I will," said Ursula. "And you keep an eye on Kester."

Cera pulled away from the hug. "I will. And I'll fatten him up too."

Kester cracked a smile, before looking at Ursula more solemnly. "Cera's right. Be careful. Mount Acidale is dangerous enough as it is, and Midac and Lucius would like nothing more than to kill you. Now go. The sigil will take you to the Church of Laverna."

The flamed burned brightly, and Ursula stepped into the flames. Warm firelight danced over Bael's skin. He wouldn't be immune to the flames like she was, but her magic could protect him—as long as he stayed close.

Ursula launched into the traveling spell, grabbing Bael's body to pull him close as the flames erupted around them. And with Bael in her arms, she felt her body crumble into ash.

CHAPTER 13

Ursula barked a cough as they reconstituted in a small room, their ashy bodies solidifying over a rickety wooden floor. Coughing, Bael brushed a few bits of ash from his jacket.

Ursula surveyed the space. Dim, silvery light streamed through long, slatted windows in stone walls, highlighting ash and dust motes floating in the air. An enormous brass bell hung above them.

"It looks like Kester put us right into the bell tower of Laverna," said Bael.

Ursula crossed to the closest window, peering between the slats. She squinted as an icy breeze blew against her cheekbones. Okay. Maybe it hadn't been morning in the Shadow Realm, because the moon hung in the sky here in Mount Acidale, and no one moved on the dark streets below.

Far below them sprawled a tangle of timber-frame houses—built close together, with sharply peaked roofs. Smoke curled from their chimneys. Ursula sniffed, taking in a sulfurous scent that tickled something dormant in the back of her skull.

Bael stood by the window. "Mount Acidale is not known for its beauty." He touched her elbow. "But let me show you the castle."

He led her to the opposite side of the tower room. Peering through the slatted windows, Ursula could see more of the Mount Acidale slums, but also the looming mass of a larger structure—a ruin, really. A crooked jumble of stone that might have once looked like something stately.

What may have been beautiful towers were now roofless stumps, dark soot scarring the walls. Ursula couldn't help thinking it looked like the partially decomposed carcass of a monstrous creature.

A scream pierced the air, and Ursula's body stiffened. Hard to mistake the shriek of a dragon.

Ursula pointed to the ruined castle. "Did the dragons do that?"

"No," said Bael. "That was Kester's and Emerazel's doing. In the Battle of Mount Acidale, Emerazel's followers torched Calidore Castle, almost razed it to the ground."

"Does the king still live there?"

"As far as I know," said Bael. "Not all of the castle burned. Many of its rooms are still habitable."

As Ursula studied the ruin, Bael moved around the room behind her. She jumped at the sound of creaking hinges, turning to see him lifting the top of an ancient trapdoor.

"I think this is the way down," he said simply.

Ursula followed him down a short wooden ladder, then down a dark staircase that wrapped around the interior of the tower. Their footsteps creaked as they walked, and Ursula shivered at the eerie atmosphere. The air smelled of mold and damp leaves.

At the bottom of the dank tower, Bael tried a doorknob. When he found it locked, he broke it with a sharp kick just above the lock. The door swung open to reveal the interior of a church. Or a temple, perhaps —one covered in dust and cobwebs, with symbols of flames etched into stained-glass windows.

They crossed into the center of a sanctuary, where Emerazel's sigil hung above them. Rows of church pews faced them. Carved into the stones on the far wall was a Latin inscription: *Hodie mecum eris inferno.*

"Well, we're in the right place," said Bael.

"How do you know?"

"The inscription," he said, pointing at the Latin text. "'This day you shall be with me in the infernos.' The words Emerazel speaks to her followers when she personally reaps their souls. This is definitely the Church of Laverna."

Given that the king had forbidden the use of fire magic, it was no wonder the place seemed a bit shabby.

Bael started down the central aisle toward a pair of large wooden doors, and Ursula followed, her crinoline gown practically trailing on the dusty floor.

As they neared the exit, the sound of creaking wood pierced the silence, and a small door opened in one of the walls. A man stepped into the sanctuary, dressed in a dark robe. He looked like a priest, but apparently he was a priest of Emerazel. One forbidden from using her magic.

"Who are you?" he asked. Ursula could sense the fear in his voice.

"We were just leaving," said Bael, starting toward the doors.

The priest's eyes widened as he looked past them toward the sanctuary and the broken bell tower door. "You must leave at once," he said in a sharp whisper. "If Midac were to learn of the sigil—"

"Just on our way out," said Ursula.

And with that, Bael pushed open the church doors. Outside, a bitterly cold wind nipped at Ursula's skin, and they crossed onto a narrow street, the houses crowded over a cobbled road. Mist curled through the air. Ursula shivered, pulling the wool cloak tightly around her.

"Should we be worried about the priest?" she asked.

"No," said Bael. "Laverna is a goddess of thieves and deceivers. He won't be compelled to tell the truth."

"Well, that is reassuring."

If Bael heard her, he didn't show it, instead starting across the small churchyard at a brisk trot. Graves jutted out of the bumpy grass at odd angles, and Ursula hurried to catch up with Bael.

"What now?" she asked.

Bael paused for a minute, squinting his eyes. "This way."

Ursula walked briskly to keep up with him, taking in the scene around her. Three-story, rickety houses loomed over the street, built so close together they blotted out most of the moon. Although they'd left the Grotto, Ursula still felt that sense of dark claustrophobia. She followed Bael down streets so narrow she could practically touch both sides if she stretched out her arms. Not that she had any desire to actually do so. A misting rain had left the cobbles slick with ice, and it took her full concentration not to slip on the stones.

Bael peered at her, his gray eyes glinting in the gloom. "Do you recognize anything here? Anything familiar?" His voice was nearly inaudible.

She shook her head. "Maybe a vague sense that I've been here before, but that's about it."

"I haven't been to my home in centuries," he said. "My real home. I don't like what it makes me remember." He slid his gaze to Ursula. "You might not like what you remember here, either."

A chill snaked up Ursula's spine. "I know. But I have to try. You once told me I shouldn't run from my painful memories. I think you were right."

Silence fell over the pair again. As they made their way through the maze of streets, Ursula felt a familiar prickling of the hair on her arms. Somewhere in the darkness behind them, someone was watching.

"Bael," she whispered as loudly as she dared. "I think we're being followed."

Bael's hand immediately went to the blade at his belt, and they both picked up their pace as the street opened onto a larger avenue. The fog thickened around them, and a misty rain fell. Bael grabbed Ursula's hand, pulling her into the shadowy entrance of a store. A horse neighed in the distance.

Ursula was pressed up close to Bael's powerful chest. Warmth radiated from his body, and the intoxicating scent of sandalwood curled around her.

"What are you doing?" Ursula whispered, half tempted to just rest her head against his body and close her eyes.

Bael pressed a finger to his lips.

A clattering sound echoed off the buildings, and Ursula peered around the corner. A black carriage was emerging from the fog. Pulled by a brace of horses, it barreled over the cobbles. From its roof, a coachman slapped the reins, urging the horses onward.

Bael pulled her closer, enveloping her in his shadowy magic to cloak her. It took Ursula a moment to see why. Armed with a long rifle, a footman rode next to the coachman. As the carriage passed, Ursula caught a brief glimpse of a young couple sitting inside. Then the carriage disappeared back into the fog.

She rested against Bael for a moment, drinking in his soothing smell and enjoying the feel of his powerful arms around her.

Still, she couldn't really enjoy the close contact when she realized that across the avenue, stood a pair of men dressed in long black coats. One wore a bowler hat, while the other sported a thick set of muttonchops. Bowler Hat's hand moved inside his coat and drew out a revolver. Ursula's pulse raced.

"Thieves, I think," said Bael. "They must have followed us from the Church of Laverna."

Bael spoke softly, his voice nearly husky. "We should go." Almost reluctantly, he pulled away and peered onto the street. *"Now."* He grabbed her hand and pulled her after him.

About twenty feet into their sprint, a voice interrupted them.

"Don't move," Bowler Hat barked.

Bael stopped, turning to face them. "Put down your gun," he said slowly.

The mugger laughed, moving closer. "You'll have to pay first. Empty your pockets." He had an old-fashioned sort of Cockney accent—one Ursula had only ever heard used by the octogenarian set in London.

"I'll only say it one more time," said Bael. "Put down your gun."

Muttonchops muttered something to his partner, who began to raise his revolver. Fire began to kindle within Ursula, but Bael was already moving in a flicker of shadows. Breaking bone cracked the air—then a scream—as Bael snapped Bowler's wrist. The revolver skittered into the street. Bael stepped behind the man, then pressed the edge of his sword against his throat in a blur of shadows and steel.

Bowler's hat fell to the cobbles, revealing thinning hair. He struggled, but Bael pressed his sword harder against the man's throat. Muttonchops scrambled around for the revolver.

"Stay where you are," said Bael, his voice glacial. "Or your friend dies."

Muttonchops lifted his terrified eyes to meet Bael's. "Let him go."

Bael's sword remained pressed against the man's throat.

"We are only trying to feed our families," Muttonchops whined.

"You would have killed us," said Bael.

"We had no choice. There is no food." Tears welled in Muttonchops' eyes, and his voice was thick. "Don't kill my brother."

Ursula looked from Bowler to Muttonchops. She had to admit, they seemed genuinely upset. Of course, Bowler had a sword pressed to his throat, but Muttonchops's tears looked authentic.

Ursula bent to pick up the revolver from the cobbles, finding the metal grimy and wet with rain. Rearing back, she threw it with all her strength down the empty street. It disappeared into the fog and gloom with a distant clatter.

"I think we should let them go," she said.

Bael studied her for a moment, as if trying to determine if she was serious, then released the pressure on his sword. As Bowler moved away, Bael shoved him hard, sending him sprawling into his brother's arms. Both men fell onto the mucky street.

"If you follow us, I *will* kill you both," said Bael. "And it won't require any effort on my part."

He nodded at the winding road, and led Ursula away into the thickening fog.

CHAPTER 14

They walked along the avenue for a few blocks, and Ursula's skin no longer prickled with the sense of hidden eyes.

"You don't hear accents like that often," she said softly.

"This place never really left the nineteenth century." Bael's eyes seemed to be searching the fog for signs of hidden danger.

"So if I open my mouth, everyone will know I'm not from here?"

Bael shook his head. "No, they'll think you're rich. Your accent is courtly. Not that that's a good thing. A courtly accent means they will rob you, and worse. Before they kill you."

They reached an intersection, and Bael stopped to study the misty road.

"We're in Spickwithe. We're close," he said to himself.

"Beg your pardon?" asked Ursula.

"The Black Friars."

So he's just speaking in ominous-sounding phrases now.

Bael cocked his head, his eyes flashing. Then he grabbed Ursula's hand. "Run!"

They sprinted along the new road, and were just ducking inside an alley when a gunshot rang out and a bullet whistled over their heads. Down the road, Ursula caught a glimpse of a soldier—dressed in purple and gold. The king's uniform. Shadows whirled around Ursula and Bael—Bael's magic. But it was too late. They'd been spotted.

"This way," Bael hissed, sprinting down the alleyway.

More gunshots echoed in the rainy night.

"Why are they shooting at us?"

"There's a curfew," said Bael. "Anyone out after sundown can be shot on sight."

Ursula raced after him, her lungs burning as she struggled to run in the stupid crinoline dress. Next time, she'd come in disguise as a man.

A gunshot rang out again, and the whistling noise of a rifle ball. Plaster splintered a few feet above their heads. As they turned a corner, Ursula shot a quick glance behind them at a small contingent of soldiers.

Bael grabbed her arm, pulling her into another tiny alley.

"They'll find us in here," she whispered frantically.

Bael shook his head, and pointed to a sign above their heads. Despite the flaking paint, the shape of a man dressed in a black smock was clearly visible. *The Black Friar.*

She lifted her skirts, hurtling down the curving alley behind Bael until it ended abruptly at a red door. Bael knocked sharply on the wood. After what seemed like an eternity, a panel was pulled aside.

"What do you want?" said a woman's voice.

"*Qui bibit, sanctus est,*" said Bael.

The window snapped shut. And the shouting of soldiers echoed off the buildings. It was only a matter of time before they were found.

"Bael, we can't stay out here," she whispered frantically.

"It's an old password." Bael met her gaze. "She needs to confirm it in the ledger."

"Ledger?" Ursula said incredulously. It seemed an entirely inappropriate concept for the current situation.

A moment later, the door swung open. Bael grabbed Ursula by the hand, pulling her inside with him. The door slammed shut behind them.

Ursula blinked, then coughed. Thick smoke filled the room, its scent drowned by an overpowering floral smell. A kerosene lamp flickered on a table next to them.

The dim light fell on a skinny young woman standing before them. "You got brass?" She crossed her arms over her chest. With a shock of red hair, she might have been pretty once, but now her front teeth were missing, and pink blotches mottled her skin. The poor thing looked like she hadn't slept in a week.

Bael pushed past her. "We're here to see Pasqual."

The woman touched Bael's arm. "Wait here, love."

She slipped past him, disappearing into the smoky haze.

Ursula grabbed Bael's arm. "What is this place?"

"The Black Friars."

Ursula sighed. "I know that. I mean *what* is this place?"

Before Bael could answer, the girl returned through the gloom. "This way."

They followed her into the miasma, and Ursula resisted the urge to cover her mouth and nose with her forearm to mask the smell. Wouldn't exactly be polite.

She nearly tripped over the first body—a man sprawled across the floor. At first she thought he was dead, until he slowly moved his leg out of her way, mumbling something incomprehensible.

She followed Bael and the toothless woman into a second room, where the smoke grew thicker. She rubbed her eyes. Here, the pungent floral odor only grew stronger. A light flickered near her knees, and she glanced down to see a small man crouched next to another sleeping body. He held a candle in one hand, which he used to light a long pipe.

Understanding began to dawn in Ursula's mind. *Oh. Is this an opium den?*

"This way." Already, the woman was leading them onward, through a narrow door and into a red-walled room. A flickering oil lamp stood on a small desk, and stained, shiny pillows littered the floor. A black door stood inset into one of the walls.

"Wait here," the woman said before disappearing back into the hallway.

It was only another moment before a man appeared out of the curling smoke. He wore a dark purple robe, and a small velvet hat sat atop his dark hair. He had long, thin fingers, and lips that appeared a little too red against his olive skin. Ursula stepped back instinctively. *Definitely a vampire.*

Bael put his hand reassuringly on her shoulder as he greeted the man. "Hello, Pasqual."

Fangs glinted when he smiled. "Bael, what brings you to my home?"

"My friend and I need a place to stay."

"You can't stay in the Silver Lair?"

"We're here in secret," said Bael.

Pasqual nodded. "So it's true what I hear from the Shadow Realm? You've lost your wings?"

"Unfortunately."

Pasqual's dark eyes fell on Ursula, studying her. "Who is she?"

"A friend of mine," said Bael.

Pasqual frowned. It was obvious to Ursula that he wasn't satisfied with this response.

"A friend," Pasqual repeated.

Of course, anyone who knew Bael at all would know that he didn't have any friends.

"Well," the vampire drawled, "I guess you can stay in my quarters."

"Can I have your assurance that you'll keep our presence discreet?" asked Bael.

"You have my assurance."

"Thank you, Pasqual."

"This way." Pasqual pulled open the black door.

Ursula tried not to grimace as she imagined how the vamp's quarters might look. The state of the opium den didn't give her high hopes for the blood den, but she followed the two men into the soporific haze.

The door led to a narrow stairwell, and the stairs groaned under their weight as they climbed upward through the murky air. At the top of the stairs, Pasqual pushed open a creaking door into a single loft-style room.

Oak cabinets nestled in one corner, and a few high-backed chairs stood around a circular table. Moonlight streamed over a loft bed that overhung bookshelves, crammed with old tomes. But it was the row of windows spanning the far wall that drew Ursula's eye.

"This is beautiful," said Bael. "And familiar."

"Thank you. I hope you aren't offended, but I was most impressed with one of the rooms in your manor. The space you kept for Elissa after she left this world. I always loved that room, and her portrait."

That's...weird.

"You've been in Bael's manor?" asked Ursula. Even though Elissa had died millennia ago—in ancient Canaan—Bael had kept a little space for her in his manor on the moon. Since Emerazel had forced Bael to murder his own wife, the guilt must have eaten at him terribly over the years, every time he walked into her quarters. Did it hurt him now to be here?

Bael and Pasqual exchanged a look. "Yes. I was Bael's servant for many years," said Pasqual.

So they *did* go back a long way. Ursula crossed to the window, running a finger along the cool glass. Here, she had a full view of King Midac's ruined castle—closer now than Laverna's church. Ursula could clearly see the burnt husks of what once had been splendid towers.

"You should have seen it before the great fire," said Pasqual from behind her. "It was magnificent."

Ursula nodded. "I can imagine."

Pasqual sighed softly—a strangely human sound. "In any case, my home is your home. You must sleep here."

Ursula raised her eyebrows. "And where will you sleep tonight?"

Pasqual grinned. "You mean when the sun comes up? I'll be in the basement. I have a cozy little coffin down there." He grinned, flashing a razor-sharp pair of canines. "But trust me when I tell you, you don't want to see it."

Bael smiled from where he stood near the doorway. "Thanks, Pasqual. We'll be fine up here."

Pasqual sauntered over to one of the oak cabinets, pulling out a bottle of wine and two glasses. "Would either of you care for a drink?"

Bael nodded. "We'd love a drink."

In a series of graceful moves, Pasqual drew the cork from the bottle. As he poured the wine, Ursula read the label: Chateau Margaux 1983. With wine like that, she had a feeling Kester would be disappointed he'd been left behind to recuperate in the Grotto.

Pasqual sat at the table, motioning for each of them to join him.

"So. What is your business in Mount Acidale? After the great battle, I never thought you'd return."

"We're here to retrieve Excalibur from Lucius, and to find Ursula's family."

Pasqual's eyebrows flicked up at Ursula. "You're from Mount Acidale?"

Ursula looked to Bael, not sure how much she should say. Slowly, almost imperceptibly, he nodded.

"I think I may have been born here." Ursula took a sip of her wine. It tasted delicious: a bit woodsy, with hints of rosehips and berries.

"Do you know where Lucius may be found?" Bael seemed eager to get the conversation back to Excalibur.

"Lucius doesn't often leave his warren under the castle."

"Doesn't he hoard women, like most of the dragons? He must leave to satisfy his cravings somehow," said Ursula.

Pasqual laughed. "You certainly seem to know a lot about Lucius."

"I had the misfortune of meeting him recently."

Pasqual swirled the wine in his glass. "King Midac has decreed that the dragons are not to abduct the women of Mount Acidale."

Bael frowned. "And Lucius has agreed to that?"

A slow shrug from Pasqual. "Lucius has taken to visiting Leopold's in secret."

Bael's eyes sparked with excitement. "Ah. Are you sure of this?"

Pasqual's expression darkened. "Bael. If you cause trouble at Leopold's, it will be bad for my business. Madam Moncrief is ruthless."

Bael nodded. "I'll speak to her first. I can be very diplomatic, you know."

Ursula looked between Bael and Pasqual. "What is Leopold's?"

Pasqual steepled his fingers as he turned to her. "Madam Moncrief runs Leopold's, the preeminent brothel in Mount Acidale. Lucius likes to hold—how shall we say—private events there. I can arrange a meeting with Madam Moncrief, if you want to find Lucius and this sword of yours. You've both had a long journey. Why don't you rest for a few hours?"

Taking his wine with him, Pasqual rose and crossed to the door. Ursula shivered. Despite his generosity, she found something entirely unnerving about the preternatural grace of a vampire.

Bael looked at Ursula with concern, his shoulders stiff.

"Leopold's is the best way to get to Lucius. I don't want you to think…"

"Think what?" Ursula quirked an amused eyebrow, enjoying Bael's discomfort.

"Think that I frequent brothels. Madam Moncrief is a good source of information. She's also on Nyxobas's payroll."

A smile curled Ursula's lips. "I didn't say a thing, Bael. If you want to frequent brothels in your free time—"

His eyes darkened. "For work."

"If that's what you want to call it."

It seemed to take him a moment to catch on that she was teasing him, before a faint smile appeared on his lips. His shoulders relaxed, and he took another sip of his wine.

Ursula snatched her wineglass and walked back to the window to study the view. "You seem to know Pasqual pretty well."

"He's an old friend," said Bael. "In fact, he helped in the battle of Mount Acidale."

"And he used to work in your manor?"

"Yes. He's very protective of me."

"How did he end up in Mount Acidale running an opium den?"

"Vampires don't tend to do well in Nyxobas's ascetic environment. They are pleasure-loving creatures. Opium doesn't have any effect on vampires, so it was a good business choice for him." Bael drained the last of his wine. "It's late. We should sleep." When he met her gaze, a sort of confusion clouded his features.

Ursula mirrored his perplexity, her skin warming as she stared at his perfect features. She could imagine herself lying next to him in bed, running her fingers over his chiseled muscles, losing herself in his powerful embrace. Should she invite him to join her in the loft? Would he even accept? What would happen if she pulled off her crinoline dress and crawled into his lap? She could almost imagine his powerful hands around her waist, his tongue exploring her breasts…

Just as she opened her mouth, working up the courage, Bael cut her off.

"I'll sleep on the couch."

Her mood fell, and she crossed sullenly to the loft's ladder.

CHAPTER 15

*P*ale light streamed through the window, washing over Ursula's face. She rubbed her eyes. It took her a moment to remember she was in Pasqual's apartment in Mount Acidale, her legs tangled in the bedsheets. She wore only a slip, one that came to just below her arse. She wasn't getting dressed in the stiff Victorian garb until she actually had to.

Still rubbing her eyes, she climbed down to the main level. Bael lay asleep on the couch. He'd done his best to scrunch himself onto the cushions, but he was simply too big. Both his legs and one of his arms trailed on the floor. His enormous chest rose and fell slowly.

Ursula crossed to the cabinets, hoping to find some food. Unfortunately, vampires didn't eat, so she was shit out of luck. Her stomach rumbled.

"You're up?" Bael asked sleepily from the sofa. "What happened to your clothes?"

He was one to speak. He'd stripped down to a T-shirt and underwear, and Ursula's gaze lingered over his body.

"The sun's too bright," she said. "I can't sleep."

She turned to find Bael staring at her bare thighs. Good. She wanted him staring at her legs. In fact, she wanted to wrap them around his abs. *Ursula. Control yourself.*

She cleared her throat. "I was hoping for something to eat, but vampires aren't known for their cuisine."

Bael rose, pulling open the door. "But you don't know Pasqual like I do. He's an incredible host." He leaned down, then picked up two steaming, paper-wrapped packages.

The smell of ham wafted into the air, and Ursula's mouth watered. "What did he bring us?"

"Sandwiches. Wild boar, if I had to guess," said Bael. "Mount Acidale is famous for them."

"Here in the city?" said Ursula, looking confused.

Bael laughed. "Mount Acidale got its name from the Akidnor Mountains. You can't see them through all the smog, but north of here is an enormous mountain range. Wild boar are plentiful on its slopes." Bael handed her a package. "I hope you'll like it more than the lunar bat bacon."

Ursula was already tearing through the paper. "I love bacon. I just didn't want to eat bat because of Sotz. It would feel like eating a friend."

Amusement danced in Bael's eyes. "That's what I've always liked about you. Your devotion to your friends. Kester, Zee, Cera—even Sotz. It's a trait I admire."

"Is that why you're still friends with Pasqual?"

"Yes," he said.

"Is this also why you are helping Cera and the oneiroi?"

Bael took a long time to respond. When he spoke, his voice was thoughtful. "At first I just wanted allies, a way to get back my wings, but over time, I saw how the oneiroi were mistreated." His gray eyes slid to the window. "When I killed Cera's brother in the Lacus Mortis, I felt terrible. I'd thought he was just another oneiroi—one of Abrax's tricks. When I saw Cera's face, it pierced me to the bone."

"There was no way you could know. You were defending yourself," said Ursula.

"I know." Bael turned his face back to her, his mouth firm. "But that was the turning point. I care about what happens to Cera and the oneiroi. They weren't just servants and soldiers to me. When I learned Xarthra had a cure, a way to cure the corrupted, I had to help."

Ursula wanted to hug him, to wrap her arms around him, to tell him he was a good man no matter what had happened with Cera's brother.

Something stopped her, and she just nodded instead, swallowing her boar sandwich.

"Is it strange for you," asked Ursula, "finding yourself in a room modeled after Elissa's quarters?"

"I'm used to dwelling in the past, brooding in my old memories," he said. "For me, love is tragic. A curse almost."

Ursula's stomach tightened. "You still believe that? After all these years, you still think love is a curse?"

Bael's eyes darkened. "When I regain my wings, I will be immortal. If I fall in love, it will only be for the briefest moment of my existence. For me, love will always be tempered by the pain of knowing that I'll lose the other person, that I'd watch them grow old and die. The pain of loss is eternal."

Ursula opened her mouth, then closed it. Although death was a long way off for Ursula, she was ultimately mortal. Freedom from Emerazel—when she'd satisfied the demands of the fire goddess's bargain—came with death. She hadn't really thought about it until now, and everything seemed to be crashing around her, the light from the window suddenly blinding. Her stomach churned.

"Are you all right?" asked Bael.

"Totally fine," she lied.

Of course, when Bael was talking about falling in love with a mortal, he meant her. Bael was an immortal demon. Technically, he was her mortal enemy, and their engagement could never be real. She would play along with the engagement until she'd helped him defeat Abrax and recover his wings. Then, she'd return to Emerazel and work like crazy collecting souls to pay her remaining debt. And when she'd finished that —she'd wither and die.

Bit of a mood killer, these revelations.

Ursula cleared her throat. "When do we leave for Leopold's?"

"The king's forces will be crawling the streets during the day. Sundown is our best bet."

Ursula blinked, suddenly overwhelmed with fatigue and images of her own face withering in her mind. She crossed back to the ladder.

"Where are you going?" asked Bael.

Darkness weighed on her mind. "Back to sleep until it's time to take some action."

* * *

As the last of the ruddy afternoon sun slanted through the window, Ursula rifled through a garment bag—something Pasqual had dropped off. Apparently, she needed to dress the part in order to worm her way into Leopold's—which meant dressing like a Victorian prostitute, of course. Ever the gentleman, Bael turned his back to her while Ursula stripped off her slip, the apartment's cool air whispering over her naked skin.

When she tugged the outfit out of the bag, it confirmed her worst fears. Black, lacy, and short as hell, it could *maybe* be considered a dress in some cultures. Still, she slipped it on over her naked body. Technically, it fit. The lace covered just enough of her anatomy so she wouldn't flash anyone—as long as she didn't sit down, or bend, or move. A corset tightened her chest, lifting her breasts practically up to her chin.

"Is this it?" asked Ursula.

"Did you find the necklace? Pasqual said you'd find one."

"A necklace? I was more focused on my tits hanging out." Ursula investigated the bag again, finding some black beads coiled on the bottom. A choker. Ursula clipped it around her neck.

Bael coughed. He was wearing a new ensemble of his own: a perfectly fitted black tailcoat, pants, a gray silk shirt, and black leather wingtips. "Let me know when I can turn around."

She had to admit she detected a certain eagerness in his voice.

She looked down at herself, at the skimpy black lace and the swell of her breasts. Worst of all, the delicate stiletto heels she was wearing felt like they could snap at any moment. "I'm ready."

Bael turned to face her, and his jaw dropped. His pale gray eyes roamed over her body as if he were memorizing every curve. "You look..." He cleared his throat. "We have masks," he said abruptly.

He held up a large mask in the shape of a lion's head, covered in pale yellow feathers shaped to look like fur, ruby-red eyes, and a formidable set of teeth.

He handed Ursula her own mask—black lace formed into the image of a cat, including long, silver whiskers and rubies around the eyes. She slipped it over her head, finding that it fit perfectly.

Bael seemed to be making a considerable effort to meet her gaze, to tear his eyes off her cleavage. "Pasquale hasn't left us undefended. Apparently, your choker is made of wire coated with diamond shavings. And watch this." He picked up an umbrella from the floor, and gave the handle a few twists. A moment later, he pulled out a steel blade, grinning. "Are you ready for this?"

Ursula swallowed hard. "Dressing up as a Victorian prostitute to hunt a dragon? No problem."

CHAPTER 16

*B*ael and Ursula sped through the streets of Mount Acidale in a black carriage. Pasqual had stayed behind at the Black Friars, entrusting them to the coachmen. The damp Mount Acidale air chilled Ursula's bare skin, raising goose bumps on her thighs and arms.

On the roof rode a grim-faced footman armed with a rifle. The carriage raced at a breakneck pace, pulled by a pair of black horses.

"Fill me in a little on the plan," said Ursula.

"We go inside. Madam Moncrief will direct us to Lucius. Then, we will steal Excalibur."

"How do you know Madam Moncrief will help us?"

Bael's reply was almost ominous. "She'll help us."

The carriage rounded a corner sharply, and Ursula peered out the window at Midac's crumbling castle. Massive gray towers rose toward the sky like the broken legs of a monstrous elephant. They passed a grand gate, its portcullis guarded by a small contingent of soldiers. Before, when they'd been running from the soldiers, Ursula hadn't been able to get a good look at them. Now, as they zoomed past, she could see they were dressed in dark purple uniforms trimmed with gold—just like her mother had worn. Rifles rested on their shoulders, and curved swords gleamed at their hips.

A moment later, the avenue turned back into the city, and rain began hammering the windows. After a few blocks, the coachman slowed the horses, and they turned down a narrow alley, nearly scraping the carriage on the buildings' rickety facades. About half a block later, the footman banged on the roof with what Ursula imagined was the butt of his rifle.

Bael pulled his coat about him, then opened the door. A gust of chilly wind ruffled Ursula's hair and rippled over her exposed skin as she followed Bael onto the street. The coachman had hopped down from his place on the roof, handing her a heavy fur coat. Gratefully, she pulled it around herself, stepping over the cobbles. She stood just behind Bael as he knocked on a rough wooden door. When it cracked open, an old woman peered out.

"Madam Moncrief is expecting us," said Bael.

Without answering, the woman pulled the door wider, her wiry gray hair radiating around her head.

Warm air greeted them as they slipped into a small receiving room. Gaslight flickered over dark maroon wallpaper and thick Persian rugs on the floor. The old woman stood expectantly, staring at them with large, dark eyes.

Bael shrugged off his coat, handing it to her, and Ursula followed suit. As she did, Bael's eyebrows flicked up at her ensemble.

It took Ursula a moment to realize that despite the brevity of their passage from coach to cloakroom, Mount Acidale's frigid wind had done more than leave goose bumps on her skin. Bael looked away as she crossed her arms over her chest.

The old woman bowed low, still without speaking, then disappeared down a dark hallway.

Ursula moved closer to Bael. "Who was she?"

"One of Madam Moncrief's ladies-in-waiting. I imagine she is informing the madam that we've arrived."

As if on cue, the old woman returned and beckoned them to follow her. They walked down a dim hallway, then through a mahogany door into a larger room. It was dimly lit, its dark walls hung with gilt-framed paintings.

A woman in a silk kimono-like dress sat on a chaise longue, her heart-shaped face framed by soft, blonde curls. She might have been in her early forties—beautiful, but with a certain coldness to her features that sent a shiver up Ursula's spine. Her unnatural stillness gave her a sort of reptilian air, as if she were conserving all her energy.

"Bael, is that really you?" she asked, her voice low and melodious, her neck oddly stiff.

"It's been a long time, Madam Moncrief."

"Oh, Bael." A joyless smile. "You know you can call me Anne."

An uncomfortable silence fell over the room, until Lady Moncrief rose. Ignoring Ursula, she glided languidly to Bael and wrapped her arms around his neck. She drew a finger along the line of his jaw.

Ursula's fingers tightened into fists. *What the hell?*

"You know I've missed you terribly," Anne purred. "Mount Acidale just isn't the same since you left." Her finger trailed down his neck and onto his chest. "You really haven't changed at all, have you."

"I'm here on business." Bael gently pulled her hands from him.

"Oh, business can wait. We need to get reacquainted. It's been *such* a long time since your last visit."

Bael shot a sharp, panicked look at Ursula. "May I introduce you to my fiancée?"

Madam Moncrief's body didn't move. While her arms remained draped over Bael's shoulders, her gaze flicked to Ursula. Not even trying to hide what she was doing, she traced her eyes over Ursula's body, from the hem of her black lace skirt, along the curves of her breasts, until she met Ursula's eyes for the barest of moments. Her attention flicked back to Bael.

"What do you want?" She slowly withdrew her arms from his shoulders.

"I need a favor."

Madam Moncrief's lips curled up, in the barest hint of a smile. "You know I don't do favors, even for someone as beautiful as you."

"I need to speak to Lucius. I was told he would be here tonight."

Madam Moncrief stepped back. "I cannot help you. I am not a philanthropist."

Ursula spoke. "The Drake has stolen something from us. If we don't—"

Madam Moncrief's head snapped to look at Ursula. "I wasn't speaking to you. Do not interrupt me."

Irritation simmered in Ursula's chest, but she shut her mouth anyway.

"Have you noticed how polite Ruth is?" Madam Moncrief slowly beckoned the older, gray-haired woman, curling her long finger.

Ruth shuffled over to her side.

"Open your mouth, dear." The Madam patted the older woman on the head.

Ursula cringed as the woman opened her mouth, revealing yellowed teeth and an empty cavity where her tongue should have been.

"Ruth spoke back to me once, twenty years ago," said Madam Moncrief with a sigh in her voice. "So I cut out her tongue. She has never spoken back since. Isn't that right, Ruth?"

Ruth nodded solemnly.

"As I was saying." Madam Moncrief turned back to Bael. "If you want my help, you're going to have to pay me."

"How much?" said Bael.

Madam Moncrief's eyes sparkled. "Oh, I don't want your money. I have plenty of money."

Shadows slid through Bael's eyes. "Then what do you want?"

"I want you," said Madam Moncrief, tracing a finger along his chest.

"No."

"Oh, not like that!" said Madam Moncrief with feigned indignation. "I would never jeopardize something as beautiful as a marriage. I merely wish to engage your company for a period of time."

"And in exchange, you will help us reclaim the Excalibur that the Drake stole?" asked Ursula.

"Of course," said Madam Moncrief. Her eyes narrowed, and she looked at Bael. "So do we have a deal, demon?"

Bael nodded.

"Splendid," said Madam Moncrief, snapping her fingers. "Ruth, you will show Bael to my boudoir."

Ursula's stomach churned as Bael left with Ruth. What *exactly* was he going to do?

Madam Moncrief returned to her chaise lounge, and she picked up a small book to read. "Bael has agreed to the deal. So that means you're free to go," she said without taking her eyes off the book.

"Was I supposed to follow him?"

Madam Moncrief sighed. "No, little sparrow. You may make your way to my salon. When Ruth returns, she will show you where to go."

As if on cue, Ruth appeared at the doorway.

"Is Bael settled?" asked Madam Moncrief.

Ruth nodded, her dark eyes wide.

"Then please take the girl to the salon." The madam handed her servant a small knife with a mother-of-pearl handle. "You have my permission to use this on her face if she tries to misbehave."

Ursula's fire kindled. *I really don't like her.*

Ruth nodded, her expression blank, then turned to lead Ursula out of the room.

Ursula followed Ruth down a dark, wooden hall. Without Bael, she felt suddenly vulnerable, and the skimpy outfit didn't help. Or the fact that Madam Moncrief's mute servant had just been directed to potentially stab her in the face. Still, in the dimly lit hallway, the shadows provided their own sense of security. Hellhound or not, Ursula always felt best in the shadows.

At the end of the corridor, Ruth opened a door into a warmly lit room. It took Ursula a moment to figure out they'd wandered into a small, sparsely attended theater. On a stage, a raven-haired dancer wore a large feather boa and not much else. She swayed to the sensual music of a jazz combo. As the dancer slowly adjusted the position of the boa in time to the music, Ruth led Ursula to a seat upholstered in red velvet.

Ursula sat carefully, so as to keep as much of herself covered by the lace of her skirt as possible. Plus, who the hell knew what bodily fluids stained these seats. When she looked up, Ruth had disappeared into the shadows.

The music intensified, and the dancer threw her boa into the audience. With a dazzling smile that warmed Ursula's chest, the dancer began spinning her tasseled breasts, the movements strangely hypnotic.

Ursula smiled. *I want to learn how to do that.*

The small crowd clapped appreciatively, and Ursula strained her eyes to try to get a better view of the audience. Unfortunately, it was hard to see with the single spotlight focused on the stage.

Ursula swallowed as she realized that it was also impossible to know if Ruth had returned to Madam Moncrief's chambers or if she was sitting directly behind her, ready to plunge the silver dagger into Ursula's face if she moved from her seat.

With a brilliant smile, the burlesque dancer gave her tassels a final twirl, then stepped out of the spotlight. On cue, the band stopped playing, and the lights blinked out, leaving Ursula in pitch darkness. All around her, whispers filled the air, until at last, the lights blinked back on again.

A tiny man stood on a stool in the center of the stage. He couldn't be more than three feet tall, dressed in a specially tailored three-piece suit and a top hat. Throwing out his chest, he shouted to the crowd in a surprisingly deep voice.

"I hope you all enjoyed Fanny and her boa." He winked broadly. "And who could forget her tassels!"

The crowd clapped again as Fanny stepped back into the spotlight, a new boa wrapped around her talented bosom. She bowed deeply.

"But," the little man continued, "have I got a treat for you! Mistress Berezina will be putting on a special performance this evening."

The volume of the clapping doubled as a tall woman stepped into the light, her appearance totally intimidating. Mistress Berezina wore knee-high boots, a black leather corset, and matching knickers. Her ice-blonde hair had been pulled back tightly into a bun, her expression severe.

Glaring at the audience, she stamped her foot hard on the stage floor. Ursula jumped as the boot heel clacked like a gunshot. Immediately, the spotlight expanded as the dwarf wheeled out a wooden rack. Artfully displayed were a variety of whips, ropes, and handcuffs.

"I'll be giving demonstration of whip," she announced loudly, in a thick Russian accent.

The dwarf disappeared into the darkness.

Mistress Berezina stamped her foot again, the sound echoing through the now perfectly silent theater. The dwarf entered the light first, then behind him appeared a hulking man in a leather mask. Apart from the collar and the mask, the only thing he wore was a pair of black briefs. The dwarf directed the man by means of a steel chain attached to a tight-fitting collar. With a click of metal, the dwarf connected the chain to an iron bolt in the middle of the stage.

Ursula's eyes lingered over the hulking man's deep, olive skin and muscled form as a cold understanding began to dawn in her mind. When she made out the medley of savage tattoos on his chest—a crescent moon and swirls of stars—it only confirmed her fears.

Oh gods. Bael.

Mistress Berezina gave the chain a sharp tug. "On your knees, enormous slave-man."

Bael obeyed, dropping to his knees. Ursula's hand covered her mouth in disbelief.

Mistress Berezina stared at him. "You have been very bad boy, large night demon."

Bael didn't answer.

Mistress Berezina jerked the chain. "Is true?"

This time Bael tried to respond, but the mask made it impossible for him to speak clearly.

"Do you know punishment for offending Madam Moncrief?"

Bael mumbled something into the mask.

"You *don't* know?" said Mistress Berezina with feigned incredulity. "Then I show you, muscle man."

From the rack she selected a long riding crop. She smacked it hard against her leather boot.

Ursula felt a mixture of fear, excitement, and an overwhelming urge to burst out laughing. It wasn't that she was worried that Lady Berezina would hurt Bael. She'd seen the shadow demon endure a lot more than a few smacks from a riding crop. But she'd never seen him submit to anyone. Bael was always in charge, and here was this blonde woman looming over him, just so he could find out about Excalibur. Would he play his part, or would he lose it and throw Mistress Berezina into the crowd?

The dominatrix extended the riding crop so it caught Bael under the chin.

"Stand up to receive punishment, muscle demon man," she said.

Bael rose, now towering over her.

Mistress Berezina spoke to the audience. "My technique is inflict pain but leaving no marks." Like a serpent striking, she flicked the riding crop so it smacked Bael hard in the chest. "Did you feel that, large slave?"

Bael didn't move.

She smacked him again. This time on the shoulder. Still Bael didn't react.

"I see we have stoic one," said Mistress Berezina. "But let us test just how sensitive your large body is."

She smacked him hard across the chest with the full length of the riding crop. Bael didn't move.

Mistress Berezina frowned. "On your knees."

Bael knelt.

"Shall I teach large demon a lesson in obedience?" she asked the audience. Without waiting for a response, she returned the riding crop to the rack, and selected a whip. Ursula grimaced as the mistress pulled out a cat o' nine tails. She twirled it expertly in her hand, the leather whips making an ominous whirring noise.

If Bael heard the sound, he didn't react.

Mistress Berezina paced across the stage, heels clacking off the floor, until she stood directly behind Bael. Without warning, she struck him hard on the shoulder. The sound of the whips slapping against his skin echoed loudly in the silent theater, and Ursula grimaced. *My poor large demon man.*

Mistress Berezina struck him again, then three more times. With each strike, Ursula expected Bael to flinch, but he remained as still as a statue.

Mistress Berezina held up the whip. "I was told the demon slave brought consort. Perhaps she can make him feel pain."

A blinding light shone in Ursula's eyes, and it took her a moment to realize the spotlight had been cast on her. As she blinked, the dwarf appeared by her side. He gripped her hand, pulling her from her seat. *Oh gods. Please make this end.*

Ursula straightened her mask as she followed the dwarf down the aisle, up a short flight of steps, and onto the stage.

"She's pretty thing, isn't she?" said Mistress Berezina.

The crowd cheered its approval.

Bael still knelt on the floor, rivulets of blood trickling down his back, and Ursula winced at the sight. The woman had aimed directly for the raw wounds where his wings had once been attached. Ursula's muscles clenched with anger, but if Bael wanted to go ahead with this, it wasn't her place to argue.

Mistress Berezina raised her hands. "Do you think this little one can handle bullwhip?"

As the crowd continued to cheer, Mistress Berezina reached for an enormous whip that lay coiled around one end of the rack like a giant snake. The dominatrix pressed it into Ursula's hand with a stern expression. Then, she took Ursula's wrist in an iron grip and pulled her closer to Bael.

Mistress Berezina spoke softly into Ursula's ear so the crowd couldn't hear. "Madam Moncrief will have her satisfaction." Her Russian accent had completely fallen away—now pure Londoner. Gripping Ursula's shoulder, she glanced pointedly into a dark corner of the stage. Ruth stood there, a blank expression on her face, the sliver blade glinting in her hands.

Okay, okay, okay. Ursula could take any of these women in a fight, but she'd come here for a purpose—to get Excalibur—and kicking people's arses might not get her what she wanted. If they kicked the shit out of everyone, they'd only end up on a frigid street in nothing but their underwear. Minus the magic sword.

Throwing back her shoulders, Ursula held out her hand and took the whip. It was heavy, but instantly she was aware that she'd used one before. Had Former Ursula—*F.U.*—been involved in some kind of Mount Acidale BDSM? That was one question she wouldn't ask her family if she ever met them.

She flicked the whip, and it uncoiled with a sharp snap.

"We have natural," Mistress Berezina declared.

The crowd roared its approval.

The spotlight beamed on Ursula, and she squinted in the bright light. She held the whip tightly, trying not to think of all the unseen people in the audience. Bael knelt on the floor, blood streaming down his back.

"Sorry, Bael," she muttered under her breath. She flicked the whip. It cracked as it wrapped around his torso.

"Good! Now strike again. Harder!" shouted Mistress Berezina.

Ursula flicked the whip, the crack as loud as a gunshot. The tip slapped into the center of Bael's back, but he didn't so much as flinch.

"Again, small ginger woman!" yelled Mistress Berezina, stamping her foot.

Ursula tried to aim the whip a little higher so she wouldn't hit Bael in the same spot—but she aimed too high, and the whip wrapped around his neck.

The crowd roared its approval.

Ursula tried to pull back the whip, but it had wound around itself tightly and wouldn't budge. Bael's head pulled back, and the whip lifted up the bottom of his mask.

Ursula grimaced. *Bloody hell. I'm no good at this.*

Scowling, Mistress Berezina snatched the whip from her and flicked it in a sideways twisting motion. After the end unwound from Bael's neck, she handed the whip back to Ursula. "Now you punish muscle demon man better."

Ursula cracked the whip, wincing as it struck Bael hard on one his wounds. He grunted. *I'm sorry, muscle demon man.*

Mistress Berezina's eyes blazed. "He felt that. Hit him again like that."

Ursula cracked the whip again. She'd tried to aim away from the open wound but only succeeded in striking the one on the opposite shoulder. The audience roared its approval, and Bael grunted again.

"Again!" shouted the dominatrix.

She grabbed Ursula's hand, trying to force her to crack the whip again. Blood poured from Bael's back.

Ursula's jaw clenched, anger rising in her like a volcanic eruption. *Okay. That is enough.* "No more."

The woman grabbed Ursula by the throat, squeezing hard. "I said hit again."

Ursula punched the woman's arm out of the way. "I said no more. Do not *touch* me."

A pop of shearing steel sounded in the theater as Bael ripped his chain from the bolt on the floor.

At the same time, Mistress Berezina tore the whip from Ursula's hands and lashed out with it. The end wrapped tightly around Bael's throat, like the coils of a serpent. She tried to pull him down, but Bael grabbed the whip with his hands and jerked it roughly. Mistress Berezina sprawled hard on the stage floor, and Bael ripped off his hood.

Ursula ran to him, reaching for the whip that still wrapped around his neck. She helped him uncoil it.

"Are you all right?" Bael asked.

"I'm fine," said Ursula.

Bael held her close. She could smell sandalwood and feel the heat that radiated from his bare chest. His breath was hot on her neck.

"Bael, your back—"

He leaned down, pressing his lips against hers in a searing kiss—a hot desire, like burning coals that needed to be extinguished. Dimly, she could hear the crowd cheering wildly. But as quickly as it had begun, the kiss was over, and Bael pulled away.

Then the spotlight went out.

CHAPTER 18

From the darkness came a familiar voice.

"Bravo!" said Madam Moncrief. "You two put on quite a show."

As Ursula's eyes adjusted to the darkness, she made out Madam Moncrief's form.

"My fiancée was not part of the deal," said Bael. "You had no right to bring her on stage."

"No, but it will be the talk of the town," said Madam Moncrief. "The people loved it."

Given the crowd's frantic cheering, she wasn't wrong about that. *Doesn't change the fact that she's an arsehole though.*

Bael's gray eyes pierced the darkness. "Enough time-wasting. Now it is time for you to follow through on your end of the bargain. Where is Lucius?"

Madam Moncrief sighed, just as the lanterns began to glow with orange light once more. "I could have made you famous. But, as you wish. Ruth, take them to the Royal Suite."

"The king has a suite here?" asked Ursula.

Madam Moncrief laughed, her voice tinkling. "No, that's just what we call it. It's the largest private room. But you'll need to change. You look like you just visited a slaughterhouse. Ruth will return you to my boudoir. You can clean up there."

Ruth beckoned them forward with her mother-of-pearl blade, which she seemed a little *too* fond of.

They followed her back through the smoky warren of corridors, into a large room decorated with colorful silks. A tuxedo had been laid out on a pink, fluffy bed.

Ursula frowned at the wounds on Bael's back. "Can you get some bandages, please?"

Ruth nodded, then slipped out of the room.

"Does it hurt?"

Bael grunted. "I've had worse."

Ursula moved closer, studying his skin. Blood oozed from the pair of wounds Abrax had left when he stole Bael's wings. And over those scars, welts where the whip had struck him.

"Sorry about the whole whipping thing."

Before Bael could reply, Ruth opened the door and handed Ursula a roll of gauze.

Using one of Madam Moncrief's pink towels, Ursula wiped the blood from Bael's wounds as gently as she could, while Bael stood perfectly still. When his back was clean, she bound the wounds tightly with gauze, stretching her arms to reach all the way around his enormous chest. Ruth stared on, dagger in her hand.

Psycho.

"Thank you, Ursula," said Bael.

Ruth opened her eyes wide, pointing at the tuxedo on the bed. She made no move to turn around or leave the room while Bael changed, instead staring at him, wide-eyed. He disappeared into the hall. Ruth and Ursula stared at each other in silence.

A minute later, Bael reappeared dressed in his tuxedo and lion mask. "Take us to the Drake."

Ruth led them up a long, creaking flight of stairs to a small landing. Ursula was sure her delicate heels would snap at any minute, sending her tumbling down the stairs. A large door stood at the top, emblazoned with a golden crest that featured a topless woman. *Ah. The Royal Suite. Classy.*

Ursula adjusted her mask as Ruth knocked on the door. After a few moments, a giant man opened the door.

The hair rose on the back of Ursula's neck. *And we're on the right track.* She recognized him from the dragon's lair—he was the dragon shifter who'd been in charge of keeping an eye on the captive supermodels. Some dragons hoarded gold. Other dragons hoarded women like they were possessions. Lucius happened to like both.

"We asked not be bothered," said the large man.

"I was told there were gentlemen here playing whist," said Bael. "I was hoping for the opportunity to play a few hands."

The guard took a moment to size Bael up. With an almost imperceptible nod, he said, "Let me confer with my party."

The dragon shifter closed the door, and Ursula and Bael waited in silence until the shifter pulled open the door again.

He met Bael's gaze. "The buy-in is one hundred and fifty pounds."

"That is perfectly acceptable," said Bael. He reached into his jacket pocket and handed the guard a leather purse. "You can hold this for the duration." The guard opened the purse and peeked inside. He nodded again, then slowly opened the door wider.

Bael crossed inside, but when Ursula started after him, the guard blocked her path.

"Just you, sir."

Bael didn't blink. "But the woman brings me luck. If she can't come, I'll have to take that money back." He started to reach for the purse.

From behind him, another voice called out. "Oh, let him in, Harry. Someone needs to replace Hamish. He's completely trollied, as usual."

Another voice slurred in a thick Scottish accent. "Who took my fuckin' bottle a gin, you fuckin'..."

The guard opened the door wide enough to allow Ursula to enter. Around a table sat four enormous men. Like Bael and Ursula, they also wore masks, but theirs were the scaled faces of dragons. Three wore masks in varying shades of green. The fourth's mask was dyed a deep red. *And that would be Lucius—the Drake.*

When he spoke, his voice confirmed his identity. "As I was saying, you may take Hamish's seat. He was just popping out for a fag break." Lucius said it with the firmness of an order.

Immediately, one of the green-masked shifters stood and stumbled away from them. As Bael took his seat, Ursula got a better look at the room. Behind the dragons, flickering lantern light washed over an oak bar and a small stage. Jazz played from an ancient-looking gramophone, and a topless girl, who couldn't have been much older than Ursula, danced halfheartedly, her eyes glazed. As she hadn't been invited to sit, Ursula stood awkwardly in the corner of the room.

The rest of the room was richly upholstered in cream and gold-colored fabrics, along with more of the thick Persian rugs she'd seen in the brothel. Rows of windows surrounded them, and as she watched, Hamish struggled to open a pair of French doors to a rooftop patio. Ursula could find no sign of Excalibur, but she supposed Lucius was unlikely to just leave it lying about.

"Let me deal you in." Lucius shuffled a deck of cards, and began to toss them out to Bael and the other shifters. Once he'd finished, he leaned back in his chair. "We will be playing by Hoyle's rules. You may bet after every trick."

Lucius looked at his cards, then laid a small pile of gold sovereigns on the table. They began playing their cards one at time. It took Ursula a minute or two to deduce that Bael was paired with one of the green-headed dragons, while Lucius was paired with the other. As the game went on, Bael began to win trick after trick.

Lucius laid down his final card. "Well played, sir."

Bael quietly raked his gold sovereigns across the table.

As Lucius dealt the next hand, Ursula realized she'd been forgotten, and she surveyed the room again. The topless dancer continued to gyrate listlessly. Hamish stood on the balcony, smoke rising from his cigarette.

Ursula crossed to the bar, her gaze flicking to Lucius as she passed him. Her heart leapt. She recognized the pommel of the sword strapped to his waist as Excalibur's. *Bingo. Now we just need to find a way to steal it.*

She tried to catch Bael's eye, but he was focused on the game. She poured herself a glass of wine at the bar, lifting it to her lips to mimic drinking it. *I'm getting the distinct impression that Bael might end up gambling for the sword itself.*

He lost a crucial trick in the next hand, but in the following hand won back all the money he'd lost. A few hands later, Lucius stopped the game and asked the topless dancer to bring over an ancient-looking bottle of scotch and some whisky tumblers. After pouring everyone three fingers of the amber liquid, he dealt another hand. Hamish returned from his smoke, stumbling over to lean on the bar next to Ursula.

"It's time I won some money," Lucius announced to no one in particular. He threw down all of his remaining coins. "I'm all in on this trick."

Ursula looked to Bael, but again he ignored her. Without speaking, he pushed in a matching number of coins, scraping them over the table. Lucius flipped over his card, revealing the king of clubs, and the other shifters followed. Bael was last. He took a sip of his scotch. Then he flipped over his card.

Ace of clubs.

Lucius growled a swear, throwing his drink across the room. Glass shattered against the wall.

"Well, that does me for the night," Lucius announced, trying to regain his composure.

"You're finished?" asked Bael.

"That's right," said Lucius, smoothing out his bright red hair. Even with his face hidden behind the dragon mask, Ursula could tell he was on the edge of flying into a rage.

"Perhaps you would consider gambling something else?" Bael proposed.

Lucius paused. "You wish to make a non-monetary wager?"

"Perhaps," said Bael, deftly setting the trap. "What else of value do you have?"

Lucius leaned forward. "If I am to make a gamble such as the one you propose, it will have to be on equal terms."

"Of course," said Bael.

"Then I'll wager this sword for your lucky kitty." He pointed at Ursula, licking his lips, and her stomach turned.

Bael reached across the table, shaking Lucius's hand. "I believe we have a deal."

"Excellent."

Lucius collected all the cards, and began to reshuffle. "We play one trick. If I win, I add your woman to my collection. If you win, you take the sword." He dealt the cards, until at last, he flipped over the last card. Hearts was trump. As Lucius studied his hand, his foot moved under the table. Gently, he tapped his partner's calf.

Cheating, of course.

Bael's partner went first, leading with a jack of hearts. Lucius's partner followed with a ten of hearts, followed by Bael with the king of hearts.

Ursula held her breath as she waited for Lucius to play his card. As long as he didn't have an ace, Excalibur was all theirs.

Lucius flipped over his card, and Ursula sucked in a short breath as she glimpsed the ace of hearts.

CHAPTER 19

Okay. Time for a Plan B. And this was probably going to be the arse-kicking plan.

"No." Ursula stepped out of the shadows. "I saw you cheat."

"Is that true?" Bael rose, pushing back his chair.

Lucius sputtered for a moment. "Are you questioning my honor?"

"I saw you tap your partner under the table." Ursula crossed her arms. "You were communicating."

Lucius glared at her, and Bael lunged for the sword. Surprisingly, Lucius was faster. Spinning, he slammed his foot into Bael's chest, knocking him to the floor. Instantly, the other two shifters at the table jumped on him. Bael strained against them as they pinned his arms.

Ursula started forward to help, but Hamish grabbed her by the forearm in an iron grip.

The shifters pulled Bael to his feet, each gripping one of his arms with their considerable dragon strength.

Ursula's stomach clenched. *Bollocks. I'd say this is not going well.*

"I always like to know a man before I kill him." Lucius pulled away Bael's mask. As he did, Bael lunged forward, smashing his forehead into Lucius's face.

"Gods dammit," Lucius snarled. Blood streamed from his nose, and his red hair flashed like a torch. He stared at Bael for a long moment, then slapped him hard on the cheek.

"I should have suspected you'd try something like this." He pivoted, staring at Ursula, his eyes piercing. "Hamish, is that the ginger tart who killed Vortigan?"

Hamish pinned her arms with one arm, wrestling off her mask with the other. He reeked of gin. "It's her."

Ursula struggled against Hamish, but he pulled her closer, roughly grabbing her hair. Ursula jammed her heel into his foot, hard enough that she heard something crack. Hamish grunted, his grip slackening. That was all Ursula needed. She drove a knee into his groin.

Hamish went down hard, and she snatched the wine bottle off the counter, smashing it until it shattered against the wood. She drove the jagged stumps into Hamish's shoulder, and he yelped.

Ursula spun. Bael still struggled against the pair of shifters. Ursula charged, but one of her heels snapped mid lunge. She fell flat in front of Lucius. Before she could stand, he'd pressed the tip of Excalibur into her throat.

"You poor thing. Was it his idea to dress you up like a whore?" Lucius cocked his head. "Live like a whore, die like a whore." He lifted the sword as he prepared to strike.

Behind her, Bael roared. The sound was deafening, like standing next to a jet engine. Even though she knew it was Bael, that he'd never hurt her, a primal fear slid through her bones.

Lucius's sword plunged down. Ursula tried to roll out of the way, but Lucius's aim was true. He stabbed her shoulder with Excalibur and yanked it out again for another strike. The pain ripped her mind apart, and she braced herself for another blow, unleashing a wild scream. Only when her own voice died out did she hear the *thunk* of bodies colliding. Lucius flew overhead, slammed into the side of the bar.

Bael stood over her. "Ursula!"

Ursula gasped, the pain leaving her breathless. She rolled over, catching sight of Excalibur on the floor. She tried to reach for the sword, but her arm wouldn't move properly. Bael grabbed the sword, just as Lucius charged him. He swung the blade, but Lucius managed to dodge it.

Ursula moaned, pain screaming through her shoulder. Blood was pumping from the wound. Her vision began to dim.

Bael roared again, and another shifter flew over her head, shattering a glass window.

"Kill them," yelled Lucius.

Bael knelt next to her, scooping her into his powerful arms. The room swam as Bael charged for the doors to the balcony. He didn't seem to be slowing as he approached the glass. Ursula closed her eyes, flinching as Bael smashed right through it.

Outside, icy rain lashed her face, and she shivered.

"Stay with me, Ursula," said Bael.

Distantly, she was aware of Lucius's bellowing, and the shrieking of men shifting into dragon form. She caught a glimpse of a shifter overhead, leathery wings sprouting from his back.

Then the world tilted, and Ursula's stomach lurched as she felt a rush of air over her skin, a sense of falling. In the night sky, storm clouds swirled above them, and they plunged into darkness. Shadows curled around her, sweet oblivion pulling the pain from her body. She was floating, close to the void now.

"Ursula." Nyxobas's voice wrapped around her, and she yearned to fall into the void.

Reality yanked her back into focus, and she was back in Bael's arms, breathing in his sandalwood scent. Cold rainwater soaked her skin, and she shivered uncontrollably.

"Almost there, Ursula." His voice sounded like it was coming from far away, over the sound of hooves pounding a stony pavement.

"What happened?" Pasqual's voice.

"Do you have sal ammoniac?" Bael asked.

The sound of crunching glass pierced the air.

"I'm sorry, Ursula." Bael's voice.

The vile stench of cat piss forced her eyes open.

"Incant Starkey's Conjuration," commanded Bael.

Her head swam as she began muttering the words in Angelic. Bael gripped her hand, his fingers interlacing with hers. She tried to focus on his face, but her eyes wouldn't cooperate. At the final line, pain burst through her body.

* * *

Ursula awoke with the milky light of the sun washing over her, burning into her brain, and she lifted her hand to shade her face. Pain lanced down her arm.

"Mmmght," she moaned.

Someone shifted in the bed next her.

"Ursula?" It was Bael's voice.

"Am I dead?"

"We're in Pasqual's apartment."

A few memories came drifting back to Ursula. "Why did you make me sniff cat pee?"

"That was sal ammoniac—smelling salts. I needed you to wake up."

Ursula shivered, her body aching. "I feel like death."

"You lost a lot of blood," said Bael.

"I didn't even get to kill anyone." She inched closer to Bael's warm body, wrapping her arms around him.

Bael brushed her hair from her face. "You should really sleep."

"The sun is too bright," Ursula murmured. "And I'm cold."

Bael wrapped his arms around her, pulling her in close until his smell and his soothing magic enveloped her. When she closed her eyes, images from Bael's past bloomed in her mind—the red sands and blue skies of ancient Byblos, a briny ocean wind sweeping over sandy temples.

* * *

Bael touched her cheek.

"Ursula?" he whispered.

She opened her eyes. Bael looked down at her, ruddy light sculpting the chiseled planes of his face. Her head lay on a pillow, and a thick blanket was wrapped around her body. She was on the sofa now, moved down from the loft bed, and Bael knelt beside her.

"I know you want to sleep, but you need to eat something. I brought you some soup." He held a steaming bowl that smelled rich and fragrant.

"What kind is it?"

"French onion."

Ursula's stomach growled. She tried to sit up, but Bael stopped her. "You're still hurt. Let me help you."

He reached under her back and effortlessly lifted her into a sitting position, and a sharp pain stabbed her shoulder blades. Even with Bael's assistance, Ursula winced.

"Why do I still hurt?" asked Ursula. "I incanted Starkey's Conjuration, right?"

"Getting stabbed by a sword like Excalibur is different than getting stabbed by an ordinary blade."

"Because it's magical?"

Bael reached for the soup. "Yes. If you hadn't been able to incant Starkey's Conjuration, you would have died." He handed Ursula the bowl, his gray eyes shining in the dying sunlight. "It's hot."

Ursula took a sip of the soup. It *was* hot, but it also tasted amazing. "Thank you for saving me."

"I figured I owed you."

Ursula cocked her head. "I suppose you did." She took another sip of the soup. The rich broth warmed her stomach. She was almost too scared to ask the next question. "Did we get Excalibur?"

Bael shook his head. "No. And even worse, we've lost the element of surprise. Lucius will be expecting us next time. I don't think it's safe for us in Mount Acidale at this point."

Disappointment welled in Ursula's chest. She still hadn't discovered anything about her family.

As the last of the setting sun dipped below the buildings, a knock sounded on the door.

"Bael? Ursula?" Pasqual's voice pierced the wood.

"Come on in," said Ursula.

The door creaked open, and Pasqual frowned at her with concern. "How are you feeling, dear?"

"Could be worse."

"Glad to hear it. You were bleeding like a pig last time I saw you."

Ursula grimaced. "I hope I didn't make a mess of your carriage."

Pasqual smiled broadly, his fangs glinting in the semidarkness. "Darling, I'm used to a bit of blood on my belongings."

Okay. That was creepy as hell.

"In any case," Pasqual went on, "I wanted to warn you that the guards are about in full force, searching for Ursula. They say she is the daughter of the would-be King Killer. They're offering an enormous reward."

Ursula's stomach lurched. So she was a bit famous here. No wonder she'd escaped to London.

Bael rose sharply. "We need to leave at once."

Pasqual rubbed his hands together. "That's not all. Someone already knows where you are." He handed Bael an envelope.

Bael tore it open. Ursula couldn't see the text from where she lay on the bed, but she could see the blood-red wax seal. There was no mistaking King Midac's royal arms.

Bael read the note out loud.

"Dearest Ursula,

You're in terrible danger. If I could find you, it is only a matter of time until Lucius does, too. Meet me on top of the Light Tower in the Necropolis. The undertaker will escort you tonight.

Signed,

A friend."

Ursula stared at the note. "Where is the Necropolis?"

Bael scrubbed a hand over his mouth. "I don't think you're in any condition to go. Whatever this is, it's too risky."

Ursula arched an eyebrow. "I'll be the judge of that."

Pasqual coughed. "If I may interject, I don't think you have much of a choice. The king's guards will be watching Laverna Church for you, expecting you to leave from there."

Ursula smiled grimly. *Looks like we're staying, then.*

CHAPTER 20

Ursula was pretty sure Pasqual's solution was the worst idea she'd ever heard, and yet Bael had agreed, and she went along with it because at least Bael wasn't demanding they leave Mount Acidale anymore. In any case, the end result was that she was now standing in a dark basement between an open grave and a pile of corpses, holding her nose. The stench was like nothing she'd ever experienced—far worse than the cat-piss smelling salts. She inched closer to Bael. At least her shoulder had begun to feel a bit better.

"I'm sorry." Pasqual cleared his throat. "I would have cleaned up down here if I'd known you'd be visiting."

"Why is your basement filled with dead bodies?" asked Ursula. Her voice was nasal due to the fingers holding her nostrils shut.

"They were opium addicts."

"So they all overdosed?"

"You might say they got a bad batch," said Pasqual. He grinned, flashing his fangs.

"You mean you killed—"

Pasqual cut her off with a wave of his hand. "Let's not dwell on the particulars of who killed whom."

"When does the undertaker arrive?" Bael interjected.

"Should be here any minute," said Pasqual.

As they waited, the corpses did not get any less rotten. It took all of Ursula's willpower not to hurl.

At last, a knock sounded on the wooden doors, and Pasqual pulled them open. A gaunt man with a face like a mummified dog stared at them, gripping a long pitchfork. Behind him stood an open-topped wooden cart.

"Good to see you, Victor," said Pasqual.

Victor just stared.

Seems like a fun bloke.

"I have some bodies for you," said Pasqual. "Also, my friends would like a ride to the Necropolis."

Victor nodded slowly, his eyes shining and mournful. He didn't blink once.

"Excellent," said Pasqual. He stepped out onto the cobbled street, and quickly looked in both directions. He gestured for Ursula and Bael to follow him out. "Hurry, hurry." He pointed to the cart.

They hopped in the back, ducking down so they couldn't be seen.

"Bael," Ursula whispered. "If someone looks in, they'll see us."

The undertaker appeared in front of them. On the end of his pitchfork, he'd skewered a body. Ursula gagged. With a single motion he tossed it in front of them, and Ursula held her breath, trying to tune out her disgust while bodies filled the cart.

The undertaker climbed onto a seat in front of them. Without speaking, he handed them a wool blanket. Bael pulled it over them, and gently pushed Ursula down. Through the blanket and the pile of bodies, Ursula heard the undertaker slap the reins on his horse, and the cart began bumping over the cobbles.

After a few blocks, a shout pierced the quiet. "Who goes there?"

The cart slowed to a stop, and she felt Bael stiffen next to her.

"It's a patrol," whispered Bael. "Close your eyes and don't move."

Ursula lay perfectly still. Outside of the cart, horse hooves clopped over the pavement, and the sound of male voices floated above them. King Midac's soldiers.

"You know there's a curfew?" said one of the men.

If the undertaker responded, Ursula didn't hear it.

"It's the undertaker," said another. "Do we really want him out during the day?"

Hooves echoed off the cobblestones, moving around the cart as one of the horses circled.

"Carry on," said the first voice.

The cart lurched forward, and one of the bodies flopped into her. She clenched her jaw tightly, then clamped her eyes shut as they bumped along the street. With each bump over the cobbles, she felt a dull throb in her shoulder where she'd been stabbed.

They traveled through the city for what must have been at least an hour. Fortunately, no more patrols intercepted them. A faint breeze picked up, giving Ursula some breaths of fresh air, even in the corpse wagon. Throughout the journey, she kept her eyes shut, focusing instead on the warmth of Bael where he lay next to her. Once again, her thoughts drifted back to the beautiful, sun-scorched fields of Byblos where Bael had once lived.

She nearly jumped when he gently nudged her. "I think we've arrived."

When she opened her eyes, a dead man's face stared back at her, until Bael gently pulled her up out of the corpse wagon. They were still bumping along the road, and she held on to Bael for stability.

"Look," he said.

In front of them stood an old stone wall. Broken crenellations, like gnarled teeth, lined the top. Victor directed the cart through an iron gate. On the other side, tall monuments of pale stone pierced the thick mist. They stood at odd angles, like broken teeth.

The cart stopped at a low building of gray stone, and the undertaker turned in his seat. He gestured for them to get out, and Ursula was more than happy to comply.

In the fresh air, she sucked in a deep breath and hopped down to a gravel path. Bael followed, and the undertaker slapped his reins. The cart rolled off into the fog, leaving them completely alone.

Ursula loosed a long sigh. "That may have been the most disgusting experience of my life. So glad I could spend it with you."

A faint smile. "Are you ready to go?"

"Yeah." The fog seemed to thicken in the air around them. "Any idea where we're heading?"

Bael pointed to a knoll in the distance, where a tower loomed above the hill. "That's the White Tower." He started into the mist, his footsteps crunching over the gravel path until he turned off into the grass.

Dressed in a simple woolen skirt, button-down shirt, and shawl, Ursula followed Bael between the gravestones and obelisks. Ursula's clothes grew damp in the thick mist, and she pulled her cloak tighter around her.

Eventually they ran into another gravel path, and Bael picked up the pace until they reached the base of the hill. As they climbed it, Ursula wished she'd brought a sword instead of the small dagger Pasqual had given her. She was good with a sword—a dagger might not get her very far. What if it was some kind of trap?

The White Tower stood in a small clearing of oaks at the top of the hill, built of pale marble with only narrow windows interrupting the stone. Cautiously, they encircled the monument, searching the shadows for signs of their mysterious "friend." A door was inset into the stone tower, but no one seemed to be lurking around the place.

"Do you think he's already here?" Ursula whispered.

"There's only one way to find out." Before Ursula could respond, Bael charged at full speed into the tower door. He slammed through it, wood splintering around him.

So much for the stealth approach.

Taking a deep breath, she rushed in after him. Already, Bael seemed to have disappeared into the tower, and she stood alone on a marble floor. As her eyes adjusted to the dim light, she made out a marble staircase that curved upward.

Drawing out her dagger, she began to climb the curving stairwell, winding her way up the interior of the tower. The arrow slits illuminated brief portions of the stairs, but for the most part she was hidden in shadows. Of course Bael had to rush ahead on his own.

As she neared the top, more silver light began to filter in from an open doorway that she thought led to the roof. Her fingers tightened around the hilt of the dagger. From her position in the stairwell, she had no way of knowing who or what was on the roof.

Keeping as low as she could, she peeked out.

The first thing she saw was Bael's body lying on the stone only a few feet from her. As she stepped out onto the tower's balcony—about to kneel down next to Bael, a metallic clicking sound stopped her. From behind, something hard and cold pressed into the back of her head. *Not good.*

"If you move, you die," said a man's voice. Gruff and cold as the night itself.

Bloody hell. Ursula remained still, but the muzzle of the gun pressed against the base of her skull.

"Drop the blade."

Ursula let go of the dagger. It struck the tower stairs, then spun off into the darkness below.

Ursula stared at Bael's prone body on the stone balcony, and panic clawed at her chest. "What did you do to him?"

The man didn't answer, instead pushing the gun harder into the base of her skull. His intent was clear—leave the relative safety of the stairs.

Slowly, she climbed onto the roof of the tower. A pair of glowing manacles lay on the stone.

"Cuff yourself." He pushed the barrel of the gun harder into the back of her skull.

She knelt and clasped her wrists together. The man pushed her forward, toward the edge of the tower, and her gaze flicked to Bael. He lay face down, and the sight of glowing manacles on his wrists eased some of the panic in her chest. If he'd been cuffed, he was still alive. A rope had been tied around his feet, and white cloth was wrapped around the back of his head. He didn't move as she passed.

The man directed her forward, until she reached the crenellations that ringed the tower's edge. Her muscles tightened. *What does he want from me?*

"Don't move, or I will have to pull the trigger," said the man. He pulled the muzzle of the gun from the back of her head.

Ursula stood as still as she could. Far below her, the gravestones rose from the mist like the stumps of an ancient, petrified forest. In the distance, the gray slate roofs of Mount Acidale pierced the fog beside the broken towers of Calidore Castle. A cold wind nipped at her, and she shivered.

From the opposite side of the tower roof, the man spoke. "Now. Turn around slowly."

CHAPTER 21

$\mathcal{U}$rsula turned to survey her assailant. Dressed in a soldier's uniform, he was older than she expected, his hair a shock of white in the darkness. One of his arms was missing, but with his other hand, he pointed a pistol at Ursula. Narrowing his eyes, he moved closer to her, staring at her face as though trying to memorize it.

After a moment, his eyes widened, and his jaw dropped slightly.

"It's really you…" said the soldier, sounding stunned. "I'm sorry, but I had to be sure it was you." He lowered the gun.

Fury rippled through Ursula's mind. *Might as well gain the upper hand while I can.* She charged across the tower and slammed her left side into the soldier's chest, pain splintering her own shoulder. His pistol flew over the side of the tower, and he fell hard on the marble. He stared up at her, stunned. Her hands were still manacled, but she pressed them to his throat anyway and began to channel fire into her palms.

The soldier gasped. "Gods below, Ursula. What are you doing?"

"I want you to answer some of my questions. Starting with—who the hell are you?"

He stared at her. "You don't know?"

Ursula continued to let the fire simmer in her veins as she studied the man's face more carefully. He looked about sixty, with a long, white scar that bisected his left cheek. Still, he might have been handsome once, with a strong jaw and blue eyes. There was something familiar about those eyes.

She gasped, realization dawning. They were the same deep blue as her own eyes.

"How did you know my name?" She couldn't keep the tremble out of her voice.

"I've known your name for as long as you've been alive, Ursula Anne Thurlow. Please stop trying to burn me."

Ursula's mind whirled. He had her eyes. He knew her name. He'd just said her full name, in fact. A name she hadn't remembered.

She blurted the only thing that came into her mind. "What was with the gun bollocks?"

The man sighed. "I just had to be sure it was you. I thought you were dead. I'm your grandfather, Ursula." He looked at the fire licking about her fingers, then he ran his fingers through the flames. "Your fire doesn't hurt me. It runs in my veins as well. I pledged myself to Emerazel, too."

Ursula fell back on her haunches. "Are you my mother's father?"

"Yes."

She swallowed hard. "Then you managed to survive even after she committed treason."

Her grandfather laughed, but there was no joy in it. "I'm a tough old codger."

He slowly crawled to his feet. His collar was scorched at the edges, but he was otherwise unharmed, the skin of his neck unblemished.

Ursula stood, and a million questions flowed through her mind. What had happened to her mother and the rest of her family? Why hadn't he looked for her? *Okay, Ursula. One question at a time.*

She swallowed hard, staring at him. "How did you find me?"

"I'm the head of King Midac's guards. I was there when Lucius told the king that he'd been attacked by a demon and a woman who fit your description. Fortunately, the king's spies report directly to me. I was the first to learn your whereabouts." He paused to look at her, concern showing on his face. "But here's what I don't understand. You don't seem to recognize me at all."

"I have no memories of my childhood. When I was fifteen, I turned up in London with complete amnesia. Nothing but a scrap of paper with my name on it, and a warning about turning eighteen."

Her grandfather stepped toward her. He limped, but it was his expression that unnerved her, sadness shining in his blue eyes. "You've been in London all these years? I thought you were dead. Hard to believe it's really you here."

"I was in London. No idea how I got there. They found me in the smoking rubble of St. Ethelburga's Church."

Her grandfather nodded. "There was a sigil there. It stopped working. Was the church completely burned?"

"There was nothing left after I arrived."

"Why can't you remember anything?"

She shook her head. "I have no idea. I thought you might."

"Then you don't know about your mother?" he asked softly.

"I know she died."

Her grandfather nodded without looking at her. "My daughter did a terrible thing. I believe she deserved her fate." When he looked back at her, his eyes shone with tears. "What happened after you arrived in London? How did you find your way back here?"

"On my eighteenth birthday, Emerazel sent a hellhound for me. I've been working for her ever since. I was supposed to collect souls, but I had a bit of a detour in the Shadow Realm, and I got caught up in an incubus's plan to overthrow the god of night. You know how it goes." She folded her arms. "How is it that you came to have Emerazel's fire? Isn't it outlawed here?"

The old man sighed. "Before your mother died, King Midac had a magical dagger that allowed him to carve people with Emerazel's sigil. He used it to build a great army." His eyes seemed to burn into Bael. "When Nyxobas learned of what Midac was doing, he sent his demons to attack—"

Something shifted behind Ursula and she spun. Bael had rolled onto his side, and he glared at them. Her grandfather had wrapped the white cloth around Bael's mouth as a gag.

Her grandfather spoke gruffly. "Do you want the honor of killing this shadow-creeper? I can't imagine what the demon did to you while you were his captive."

Ursula blinked in surprise. "He made me soup, for one thing. I'm not his captive."

"You are aware of what he is?" Ursula could sense confusion in her grandfather's voice.

"I am. He's a friend. He saved me in the Shadow Realm." Probably best to leave out the whole *engagement* bit.

Her grandfather's brow furrowed. "So he didn't kidnap you?"

"No. He's helping me." Ursula suddenly remembered what her grandfather had said about being the head of the king's guard. "We're trying to steal Excalibur from Lucius, the Drake. We think the Darkling has arisen, and only Excalibur can defeat him."

Her grandfather's expression was indecipherable. "Do you really believe the prophecy is being fulfilled?"

Ursula nodded. "Have you heard of Abrax?"

Her grandfather nodded. "He and this one"—he pointed to Bael—"led the assault on Mount Acidale."

Ursula sucked in a deep breath. "We're pretty sure he's the Darkling. He's trying to overthrow the gods. He says he wants to free mankind, but honestly, he just wants to rule them. He's got a bit of an ego problem."

Her grandfather shook his head. "Even if that's so, it would be impossible to take Excalibur from Lucius now. He's shifted into his dragon form. The blade is part of his body."

"The prophecy says, *Darkling, remember. Will you ring death knells for Mount Acidale, kingdom of fire?* If we don't stop Abrax now, he will destroy the Shadow Realm, and then he will attack Mount Acidale."

Ursula's grandfather thought for a long moment, stroking his chin. "Well, there is one possible way—"

From the ground, Bael slowly rose to his feet, clearing his throat loudly, but Ursula ignored him.

She held her grandfather's gaze. "Tell me how I can defeat Lucius. I've been told no one's ever defeated him."

"That's not entirely true. The White Dragon defeated him."

Hope rose in Ursula's chest. "And how do I find the White Dragon?"

Her grandfather shook his head. "She hasn't been seen in millennia."

"Is she dead?"

"I don't think so. Dragons are immortal as long as they aren't killed by man. No one has claimed to have killed her."

"So where do I find her?"

"That's the problem," said her grandfather. "She is believed to live on Mount Acidale itself."

Ursula glanced at the city's gray roofs.

"No," said her grandfather. "Not the city. Hidden behind all these clouds and smog is a great mountain. It's where the White Dragon is said to dwell."

"Do you believe the rumors?"

"I don't know…" said her grandfather. "But people disappear every year. There are tracks, markings in the snow—"

Bael grunted, his pale eyes gleaming in the darkness.

"Maybe I should take off the gag now," said Ursula.

Her grandfather stepped back, and Ursula crossed behind Bael, reaching all the way up to untie the gag from behind his head.

Bael glared at her grandfather, his eyes pure ice. "The White Dragon is a myth. And even if she were real, she would kill us in an instant should we find her."

Ursula's grandfather's eyes narrowed, and Emerazel's fire began to dance about his fingers. "The only reason you're alive right now is because my granddaughter said you were her friend."

Ursula held up a hand. "It's already decided. Bael, I'm going to look for the White Dragon."

Bael cursed under his breath.

Her grandfather raised his hoary eyebrows. "It's not the worst thing in the world. You're not safe here. Midac will learn who she is, if he hasn't already. Once he does, his guards will search every house in the city until he finds her. Go up to the mountain for a few weeks. Let things cool off down here, and then you'll be able to leave."

"Or, maybe we'll have found the White Dragon by then," said Ursula.

Neither Bael nor Ursula's grandfather looked exactly convinced, but they didn't argue either.

CHAPTER 22

$\mathcal{U}$rsula's grandfather managed to convince Bael to swear on Nyxobas's void that he wouldn't hurt Ursula, and only then would he release them. After they made their way down to the bottom of the tower, Ursula collected her dagger from the gravel path. The mist had thickened, and a chill rippled over Ursula's skin, even through her shawl.

Her grandfather disappeared into the fog, returning a few minutes later in a carriage. He stepped out, opening the door for Bael and Ursula. "This should get you where you need to go. My ancestral home is in Saint Meratz. Can you find your way there?"

Bael nodded. "Certainly."

"When you arrive, tell the owner of the Three Pigs that you're guests of mine. They'll lead you to my chalet. I'll send a pigeon to him, so he should be expecting you."

Bael climbed onto the front seat, collecting the reins to drive the carriage.

Ursula's grandfather looked at her, his blue eyes bright in the darkness. "Ursula," he started to say. "I'm so glad you're alive. When all this is over, I hope we can find each other again."

A strange, empty sort of guilt pierced her chest. She didn't remember him at all. "Of course. You called me Ursula Anne Thurlow, but I don't know your name."

He smiled. "My name is Frank, but as a girl you always called me Papa."

She cocked her head. "I'll be back soon, Frank." She couldn't bring herself to call this stranger Papa. "And then I want to hear everything about my life before I escaped to London."

With a dull ache in her chest, she climbed up onto the front carriage seat with Bael. The void seemed to blossom within her, a gnawing emptiness. When she'd cut off her memories, she'd severed an important part of herself, and now she missed it like a phantom limb. She peered at Frank waving goodbye, and Bael led them down the gravel path into the mist.

"You don't remember him at all?" asked Bael.

Ursula shook her head. "No. And it's like I'm missing something. Like I'm not complete."

Bael's gaze slid to her. "You'll remember, Ursula, if you want to."

As the carriage picked up speed, they raced through the darkness, bumping over stones and pits in the road, and Ursula stared at the sky. A faint glow had spread across the horizon, the rising sun tinged the clouds with pink, and a dusty rose color stained the rocky landscape. They were moving away from the city, over rolling hills dotted with trees. She shivered in the cold, and Bael shifted a wool blanket over her legs. Ursula pulled it up tight, but she found herself leaning against Bael for warmth anyway.

"Not much farther," said Bael softly.

Amber sunlight illuminated an alpine forest of pines and firs. To the east, the landscape fell off steeply into a deep valley. Snow dusted the tops of the trees, sparkling brightly as they caught the first rays of the sun. At the far end of the valley, a small town nestled into the hillside. Inhaling the cold mountain air, Ursula could smell the faint wood smoke from their chimneys. A significant improvement on the corpse wagon they'd taken to get here.

Bael pointed at the village. "That's Saint Meratz."

"Oh," said Ursula. "It's beautiful."

A huge peak towered above them. It rose into the sky like a massive pyramid, its slopes a mix of white snow and sheer cliffs of stone. Snow blew off the summit in a high-altitude wind, puffing into the air.

"That's Mount Acidale?" she asked.

"Yes," said Bael. "You used to be able to see it from Calidore Castle, but in recent years, coal fires have left the city shrouded in smoke and smog."

The road curved, and they raced into the aspen forest toward Saint Meratz.

* * *

By the time they arrived, the sun had fully risen. Bael steered the horses toward a brown, three-story building with a peaked roof and curling white eaves.

A boy ran to the horses as they stopped, and Bael handed him the reins. A sign above the building's doors read *Three Pigs.*

Ursula stepped down from the carriage, then followed Bael through a creaking door into a small, crooked-walled tavern.

Three Pigs was a quiet place—or, more likely, sunrise wasn't its most popular time of day. A pair of older men sat at a table playing backgammon.

An elderly bartender nodded to them as they approached, cleaning a pint glass with a cloth. "You must be the friends of Frank's?"

"Yes," said Ursula. "He said you could direct us to his chalet."

"Certainly," said the bartender. "My boy Callum will show you the way."

Ursula turned, jumping a little to find that a young boy had appeared seemingly out of nowhere.

A smattering of freckles covered his nose, and he blinked at Ursula. "Are you Frank's guests?"

"Yes," said Ursula. "And you're Callum, I take it."

The boy nodded, turning to lead them out of the tavern. Outside, in the milky sunlight, Callum led them down the road and onto a path that turned up the hillside. As they hiked, Callum kept up a steady stream of chatter.

"Frank's pigeon is named Jack," he said very seriously, but to no one in particular. A little farther on, he pointed to a picturesque stream. "That's Giggling Brook."

"It's beautiful," said Ursula.

Callum glared at her. "A girl drowned in one of its pools last year." His tone suggested she should have known.

885

Ursula shuddered. *Weird kid.* The path led them back into the forest, and the scent of pine invigorated Ursula.

Callum grinned. "There are bears in the forest, but they hardly ever eat people."

Bael spoke quietly. "Have you ever seen a bear?"

Callum shook his head. "No, but my grandad has. He says they're as big as a horse."

"Callum, do you know anything about the White Dragon?" asked Bael.

Callum stopped, and his eyes grew wide, his face paling. "No one's seen the dragon in a hundred years." He hissed the last word, sounding eerily like an old woman.

"Do you think it's still out there?" asked Ursula.

Callum slowly nodded. "At night sometimes..." He shivered as if remembering something terrible. "I can hear screaming. Monsters come when it's dark out." Without another word, he turned and ran back toward town.

"Well, that was unnerving," said Ursula.

Bael shrugged. "People are afraid of dragons."

Ursula's footsteps crunched along the path, until the forest ended abruptly and they stepped out onto an alpine meadow. At the far end stood a picturesque chalet, its roof gabled with large decorative moldings. But it wasn't the beauty of the building that made Ursula fall to her knees.

In the meadow before her, the morning sun illuminated hundreds of flowers of gold and blue and pink—just like the wildflowers of her dreams. Corncockles, anemones, daisies and chickory... Smudges of periwinkle and honeyed hues.

Just like the wildflowers she'd painted on the walls of almost every place she'd lived.

CHAPTER 23

The next morning, Ursula stood shivering on a small balcony. She'd slept late, the mountain air having a soporific effect. Her shoulder had now completely healed. On the mountainsides, a thin dusting of snow coated the trees. Frost glinted on the stems and petals of the wildflowers, and she realized she was lucky to have seen them at all.

In addition to the wildflowers, the chalet had sparked its own set of memories. Inside, she found black-and-white pictures on the walls. A man who looked like her grandfather, a pretty woman, and a little girl. There were no labels on the photos, but Ursula had known at once that the woman was her mother, and that the girl was her. A dull memory had flashed in her mind—a ginger-haired woman teaching her to fight with a sword.

But that wasn't all. In a room in the back, she found a rack with a collection of weapons: swords, daggers, and spears. When she picked up one of the blades, she'd recognized its familiar weight. These were the weapons her mother had taught her with.

Yet so much remained missing. She still couldn't remember any specific details from her childhood beyond the vague glimmers of training sessions. Bael had pointed out that there were no pictures of anyone who might be her father.

Bael joined her on the balcony and handed her a steaming mug of tea. "Did you sleep all right?"

"I did." She'd been tucked under a thick down comforter, and it had kept her warm even as the night brought with it a frigid chill. But not as warm as when Bael had slept next to her. She'd woken to find herself curled around his muscled body, her legs embarrassingly wrapped around one of his.

"I slept pretty well," he said, adding, "I've made breakfast."

She crossed back into the chalet, greeted by the rich scent of bacon, and her stomach rumbled.

Bael grinned. "I made a visit to town this morning for supplies. No bat meat this time, I promise." He'd laid out two plates of eggs and bacon. A steaming pot of tea sat on a trivet in the center of the table.

Ursula sat down, her mouth watering, then dug into the food with a quiet ferocity. "This is delicious. Thanks for cooking."

He cleared his throat awkwardly. "I was unable to make breakfast properly. In the Shadow Realm, servants wait on the lords. And in ancient Byblos, men never cooked. I went through at least a dozen eggs and a pound of bacon before I went outside to find someone to cook for me." He nodded at a young man who sat in the corner of the room.

Ursula jumped. She hadn't even noticed him, but now that she looked at him, she saw fear etched across his pale features. Bael, apparently, scared the shit out of him—enough that he had agreed to come into the chalet to cook for them.

"C-can I go now?" the young man stammered, his voice plaintive.

Bael nodded curtly. "You may leave. Thank you for your assistance."

The young man rose on shaking legs and tripped over them to get out of the chalet.

Ursula held up a hand, stifling a laugh. "You're ten thousand years old, and you never learned to cook eggs?"

Bael's dark eyebrows rose up. "I was busy being a warrior of legendary strength."

"Mmm. That does sound time consuming. Quite a lot of demands on your warrior time."

"And I never needed to learn to cook. There was always someone to do it for me."

Ursula suppressed a smile, imagining Bael's perplexed face as he tried to scramble eggs that morning. Defeated by the unrelenting heat of a frying pan. "I can teach you how to cook someday, if you want to learn."

"It does seem a useful skill."

Ursula stifled another laugh. In ten thousand years, this had only just occurred to him.

* * *

A FEW HOURS LATER, Ursula and Bael were hiking up the slopes of Mount Acidale. Ursula's lungs burned in her chest, and her legs felt like they were loaded down with lead weights. She didn't know the exact altitude, but the air was definitely thinner. Fatigue burned through her muscles. Not that she was about to admit this to Bael.

Now they hiked through an aspen grove. The trees had lost their leaves, leaving only trunks of pale bark. To Ursula, if felt like they were walking through a forest of bones.

"How are you doing?" Bael's eyes skimmed up and down her body.

"I'm fine," Ursula lied, as she tried to hide her heaving chest.

They reached a ridge line, and from here, Ursula could see the roof of the chalet. It looked so small from here, like a toy. In the distance, thick clouds hid the city of Mount Acidale.

Directly above them was Mount Acidale itself. It looked like a peak from the Swiss Alps, with great snowy fields, jutting cliff faces, and massive cornices of ice. Ursula didn't want to admit it, but she could see now why Bael had said finding the White Dragon—if she did exist— would be an impossible task.

Bael handed her a canteen, and she took a swig of ice-cold water. They'd now left the aspen forest behind and started up the edge of the ridge. A cold wind blew down from the mountain, but the exercise kept Ursula's body warm. As she acclimated to the thin mountain air, she moved at a comfortable pace alongside Bael.

"What did you think of Frank?" she asked.

"He seemed interesting."

There was something about his response that raised Ursula's hackles. "Interesting? That's all?"

Bael didn't respond.

"He loaned us his carriage, and is letting us stay in his chalet."

Bael stopped hiking and turned to face her. "He's one of Emerazel's." Venom laced his voice.

Ursula stared at him in disbelief. "*I'm* one of Emerazel's."

"I trust you," said Bael. "I don't trust him."

He turned, picking up the pace now, and Ursula had to push herself to keep up with him. Her lungs began to burn in her chest again as they reached another ridge. Apparently, Bael hadn't quite overcome his rage toward Emerazel's hounds. But given that the fire goddess had forced him to murder his wife, she supposed a bit of unresolved anger was understandable.

A broad snowfield spread out below the ridge. She peered up the mountain slopes. High above them, an enormous cornice of snow curved over them on the ridge, glinting in the light. Without stopping, Bael began to make his way onto the ridge.

Ursula chased after him. Even with the hiking boots, her feet slipped in the snow.

"Bael—stop!" she called after him, gasping for breath.

Bael slowed, then turned to face her. His eyes looked as cold as the snow. "I fought your grandfather in the Battle of Mount Acidale."

She wasn't getting his point. "Right. So?"

"Did you see his arm? I was the one that severed it. I almost killed him."

"It was a battle," said Ursula, starting toward him.

Shadows slid through Bael's eyes. "You don't understand. We're locked on different sides of a war that has been raging since before I was born. Since the seven gods first fell to earth. Emerazel forced me to kill my wife. You're mortal, too, and eventually, she will force me to kill you too. She still loathes me for choosing Nyxobas over her, and when she's finished with you, she will try to use me to slaughter you." He paused as his eyes faded back to their usual slate gray. "I love you, Ursula, but I can't protect you. You aren't safe with me."

Ursula gasped at his confession, her chest warming and heart racing at the same time. She started toward him, but a loud *crack* stopped her in her path.

When she looked up, her heart paused. A monstrous piece of cornice had cracked off and was barreling toward them.

<h1 style="text-align:center">CHAPTER 24</h1>

"Avalanche!" shouted Bael. He sprinted toward her.

She turned to run, knowing they'd never make it in time. As the cornice bounded toward them, it broke into smaller pieces of ice, setting off more floods of snow. Bael caught her about the waist and plowed forward, tumbling off the ridge, but it was too late.

The avalanche hit with the roar of a jet engine. They tumbled down the slope amid blocks of ice the size of small houses. Bael tried to hold on to her, but a massive piece of ice smashed into him, and he spun away. Ursula tumbled through the snow, which pulled at her legs like frozen quicksand. Somewhere in the back of her brain, she remembered that to survive an avalanche, you were supposed to swim on top of the snow. She swung her arms and kicked with her legs, scrambling to keep her head above the surface.

"Bael!" she shouted, her voice drowning in the roar of the churning snow. Through the sea of white, she glimpsed a grove of pine trees hurtling toward her at breakneck speed. Panic ripped through her mind as she approached the trunks—and slammed directly into one. Tree bark pressed into her face, and snow from the avalanche piled up and over her. In an instant, the sun disappeared, and she was plunged into a frigid darkness.

She struggled against the snow, but it packed in tighter and tighter, entombing her in a frozen embrace. Oddly enough, despite her terror, there was something strangely peaceful about the soft sound of sliding snow and the scent of pine needles.

Although snow was packed into the back of her jacket and up her pant legs, she felt no pain beyond an icy trickle down her spine as it melted. She wiggled her toes and fingers. She didn't appear to be hurt at all. She took a breath, but the snow didn't allow her to expand her lungs much.

I'm not going to die like this.

She tried to move her arms and legs, but she found them frozen in place, like she'd been dropped in cement that had instantly solidified.

A stiff pine branch pressed into her cheek, its needles sharp as pins. She tried to move her head out of the way, but only succeeded in driving it into her mouth.

Okay. I'm going to become one of Callum's unnerving stories.

Ursula forced herself to relax as she tried to focus. *I need to think of a plan.* But her mind wasn't quite working properly, and her fingers and toes were starting to grow numb. She gritted her teeth as another icy trickle of water dripped down her back. It was then that the first inklings of an idea came to her.

Slowly, she began to channel Emerazel's fire, the heat warming her veins. Her toes and fingers burned as the fire thawed them. She summoned the flames along her arms and into the snow itself. Steam misted past her face until she was able to move her arms. Slowly, she brought them forward until she was able to grab onto some of the tree branches. Then she did the same thing with her legs.

As the snow melted, it dripped along her back and down her thighs in icy rivulets. She forced herself not to flinch. Eventually, she was able to move both feet close to the tree.

"This is going to suck," she muttered to herself as she channeled fire into her head and shoulders.

Icy water poured over her, dripping between her breasts. She ignored it, pulling hard on the tree branch with her arms. Her body moved up a few inches. She waited for snow to fill in under her feet, then repeated the procedure. It took her ages, but eventually she was able to inch her way up the side of the tree.

At last, her head broke the surface, and she sucked in sharply, breathing in the clean mountain air.

On the snow's surface, she threw herself down, catching her breath until she felt ready to climb to her feet. Her jacket and pants were scorched, and the soles of her boots smoldered. All around her, enormous boulders of ice jutted from amidst the splintered tops of trees.

"Bael!" she shouted, her voice echoing across the remains of the snowy field. Almost immediately, she put her hand to her mouth and turned to look back up at the cornice. Nothing else was falling, at least.

Slowly, she began to make her way through the snowy field, searching the white expanse for Bael. Her pulse raced when she found his pack on the snow. It had torn open—its contents spilled across the snow. At last, she found Bael resting against a large chunk of ice. His chest was above the snow, his lower half buried. There were deep scratches on his face, and his eyes were closed.

She ran to him, and his eyes opened. "Ursula. I was terrified you were—"

"Dead?" Ursula laughed. She knelt to touch his cheek. "I'm fine. I was buried. My fire got me out. That's all."

She looked down at the snow packed around him. "Let me dig you out."

Bael shook his head. "No. You can't."

"What are you talking about?" she said, pulling at his arm. "You can't stay here. You'll freeze to death." She looked up at the darkening sky, and the red rays of sunlight.

Bael looked at her with gray eyes. "Ursula. Both my legs are broken. Strong as you are, you won't be able to carry me. You'll need to go back to the village. Have them send a rescue party." A trickle of blood dribbled from his lip. His eyelids fluttered, then closed.

"Bael?" Concern pierced her chest. She touched his shoulder, but he didn't move.

I can't leave him. I just can't. As quick as she could, she channeled what remained of Emerazel's fire into her hands and began digging him from the snow.

CHAPTER 25

As she dug into the snow, steam rose around her. She tore into the frozen landscape, her hands melting all the snow and ice. It took her ten minutes, but she was able to clear enough snow to get a good look at Bael's body.

What she saw made her want to cry.

Both of Bael's legs had been shattered, and his back was bent at an awkward angle. She touched his face again, but he didn't respond. His chest rose and fell slowly.

Ursula looked up at the darkening sky. The last rays of sun cast the clouds in a deep orange light. On any other day, it would have been beautiful. Now, it only added to the urgency of the situation. Night was falling, and if she didn't find someplace warm, they'd freeze to death. Without his wings, Bael could die here.

She reached under Bael's shoulders and began to pull him up onto the snowfield. Blood oozed from the wounds on his back while she tugged him, struggling with the weight of his body. He left smears of blood in his wake, and his broken legs slid over the snow. Her lungs burned and her body ached. Still, this was her only chance to save him.

If it came down to it—if it were life and death—she'd have to use Starkey's Conjuration spell on him. But she almost thought Bael would rather die than allow her to heal him that way. He'd forbidden her from healing him with magic, because it would seal up the wounds on his back. He'd never get his wings back.

It was dark when she reached the path. Or, where the path once was. The avalanche had torn through the aspen forest, smashing the tree trunks into an impenetrable thicket of splintered logs.

Ursula's pulse raced. She dropped her grip on Bael's shoulders, her lungs heaving. The sun had fallen, and the wind nipped at her skin through the holes that had been torn in her clothes. She looked back to the snowfield, streaked with red. Another forest on the opposite side had avoided the majority of the avalanche. She squinted into the remaining light, finding a dark opening in the trees. Ursula reached under Bael's arms. *Maybe I can find some shelter there.*

She was dead tired by the time she reached the far side of the snowfield, so cold that her body had begun to shiver uncontrollably. She peered into the darkness of the forest, at the path leading into its depths.

Dragging Bael behind her, she pressed on through the deep snow. It took all of her strength to pull Bael even a few feet.

Part of her wanted to lie down in the soft snow, to burrow underneath the flakes and curl up until spring. She could hibernate, like one of the bears Callum had told her about. Emerazel's fire would keep her warm.

A low moan from Bael snapped her out of her fantasy—a quiet sound, but one laced with pain, and it brought her back to reality.

She lifted her head and refocused her eyes. The frozen forest was perfectly still, but for a few drifting snowflakes. Inside the tree line, dark green pine boughs blocked out the sky, and the trunks of the trees were as thick as titans' legs.

Ursula's breath caught in her throat as she caught a glimpse of something large looming in the shadows. After a moment, she made out the shape of a chimney and a peaked roof.

Hope leapt in her heart. Using the last of her energy, and still dragging Bael behind her, she pushed through the drifts until she reached the steps of a small wooden cabin. She lay Bael down in the snow, then knocked on the door. Her breath froze in the air as she shivered uncontrollably. No one answered, and the tiny windows were too grimy to see through.

She tried to turn the doorknob, but it wouldn't open. A cold winter wind blew through the treetops, dusting her with snow. An iron lock hung from the latch. She tugged it, but it didn't open. She slumped against the door. Exhausted. So close to safety. Bael moaned in the snow at her feet. *Think, Ursula, think.*

She reached out for the lock again, finding the metal ice cold. Digging deep within herself, she summoned her fire, and flames flowed into the lock. She gasped as the heat thawed her frozen fingers. The lock cracked as it broke, and the door swung open.

She'd hoped to hear a worried voice call out with an offer to help, but she was greeted only by a puff of dust and a faint musty odor. She inched forward. *I need to get warm.*

Her eyes fell on a small cast-iron stove, and she instinctively crawled toward it. Its door was shut, but when she pulled it open, she found a few half-burned logs. Hardly thinking, she channeled the last of Emerazel's fire into them, and they burst into flame.

She fell back, nearly spent. Show drifted in from the open door. She still needed to bring Bael inside.

One final push, Ursula.

She crawled toward him, now too tired to stand. Somehow, she latched her arms under his and pulled him in behind her. With the very last of her strength, she shut the cabin door.

* * *

SHE AWOKE SHIVERING on the cabin floor when the fire died down, and the winter chill began to settle over her again. Bael lay next to her, his face gray. Crawling to her knees, she put her cheek to his mouth. The slimmest of breaths brushed her skin.

I'll help you as soon as I can.

She stood, her legs shaking. She made her way to the stove, where she found a small pile of logs. She threw a few more on, then turned to survey the room. Judging by the light that shone through two small windows, one on either side of the door, it looked to be midmorning. A small table stood by the stove, and a small bed sat in the corner. A thin layer of dust covered everything in the room.

Her stomach rumbled.

On a shelf on the far wall, she found a few cans of stew, a can opener, and an old pot. *This will have to do.* She opened the soup—some kind of beef stew with carrots—and dumped two cans into the pot.

897

As the stew warmed on the stove, she crossed back to Bael, pressing her hand over his heart to feel his heartbeat. His gray eyes fluttered open.

"Ursula?" he muttered, his voice husky with pain.

"Bael, you're badly hurt, but I found us someplace warm."

"Ursula..." he said again, but his voice trailed off, and his eyes rolled back into his head.

Fuck.

In the rush to find safety, Ursula hadn't had time to process Bael's injuries. Now, she knelt by him for the first time, forcing herself to take in the horror of what the avalanche had done to his body. Grief hit her like a fist to the throat. Both legs had been shattered, broken in multiple places. But that wasn't the worst of it. His hips were twisted at an entirely wrong angle. His back was broken.

Ursula looked to the bed. That would be the most comfortable place, but with his back broken, she worried that she would make things worse if she moved him onto it.

Instead, she crossed to the bed and pulled off the sheets. Returning to Bael, she began to remove his clothes. "Don't leave me yet, Bael. I still need to teach you to cook."

She pulled off his shoes first. His trousers were another matter—with his legs mangled and his back broken, pulling them off would be risky. After searching around the cabin, she found a small knife. Carefully, she cut his trousers off him, revealing a mess of purple bruises.

When she got to his hips, she undid his belt, then cut off the rest of the fabric. Under his trousers, he wore a pair of black boxer-briefs. Throughout all of this, the only movement from Bael was the slow rise and fall of his chest.

Next, she carefully cut off his navy sweater. His chest was bare underneath, and without thinking, she ran her fingers along the dark tattoos inked onto his skin. As she removed the fabric at his stomach, she swallowed hard, her throat tightening. The skin there was a deep purple, and not from tattoo ink. Massive bruises wrapped round his muscular core. This must have been where the chunk of cornice hit him.

Tentatively, she touched the purple skin. Bael's eyes flashed open— black as the void. He grabbed her wrist in one of his massive hands.

"Nooo," he growled.

"Sorry," whispered Ursula.

Bael released his grip, and his eyes closed. As gently as she could, Ursula removed the rest of his sweater. She didn't try to turn him over, but she could see his back was wounded as well. Blood seeped onto the floor.

She sat back on her haunches and surveyed him. He'd been injured so badly, she didn't know where to start. The temptation to use a conjuration spell was overwhelming, but Bael would never forgive her for ruining his chance at getting his wings back. She'd only use that as a last resort. Maybe she needed to go back to town after all, to find a healer. She pulled the steaming pot of soup off the stovetop. *I'll come back for that later.*

Carefully, she covered Bael with the duvet. Then, she crossed to the door and unlatched it.

Except, when she pulled open the door, her heart fell as a snow drift slid into the room. She slammed the door closed against it. It had snowed while she'd been sleeping, burying them in the cabin. Leaving here right now would be virtually impossible.

Gods damn it. She needed to think clearly, but she could hardly focus. Her stomach rumbled, and she poured the stew into a ceramic bowl. Maybe she could feed a little to Bael, too.

When she returned to Bael, his skin had gone even paler. He moaned softly. When she touched his forehead, she found it hot with fever. Taking a bite of stew, she studied him for a few minutes. Then she sighed and put down the bowl.

There was *one* way she could save him without ruining his future as a winged demon—but it wouldn't be pretty. She shivered in her freezing clothes, drenched with snow.

First, to get dry. She peeled off her sodden clothes, stripping down to her underwear, and hung them by the warm stove to dry. In nothing but a skimpy lace bra and knickers, she set about collecting everything she needed.

Five minutes later, she laid out a coil of old rope she'd found hanging from a nail, and a small knife. First, she unwound the rope. Then, as gently as she could, she tied his feet together. The spare end she secured around one of the legs of the cast-iron stove.

She crouched by his head with the blade in her hand.

"Sorry about this, Bael. This will be messy." She cut into the palm of her hand, then let a little of her blood dribble into his mouth.

The effect was immediate. Bael's eyes flashed open—red as her blood, and intent on her wrist. She'd planned to pull her hand away, but Bael was faster. He grabbed her arm, drawing it to his lips. His mouth was hot on her skin, and she could feel the blood begin to drain from her.

Bollocks. I am quickly losing control of this.

CHAPTER 26

Ursula's eyes snapped open. She was no longer in the cabin on the side of Mount Acidale. Instead, she sat in an immense hall. Servants bustled around her, carrying trays of roast chicken, baskets of steamed prawns, and piles of meat pies. Someone spoke in her ear, and she turned her head to see Abrax dressed in an indigo uniform. His silvery eyes shone with excitement. She opened her mouth to scream, but instead of a shout of terror, out came a deep male voice. Bael's voice.

"This is quite the feast, don't you think?"

Abrax nodded. "For humans, the food is exceptional."

"So we're on the same page," continued Bael. "After dinner, we sign the armistice. The king gives up his disciples, and we retreat."

"Correct," said Abrax.

In Bael's body, she felt herself stand, carried along with him, in his memory. He raised his glass.

"A toast to King Midac," he said. "This armistice will bring peace to Mount Acidale. A truce to the war between Emerazel and Nyxobas."

The room cheered, but Ursula's eyes went to the king's table at the far end of the room. A man in a ruby-flecked golden crown sat at the far end of the table—King Midac, presumably. His golden hair curled from beneath his crown, blue eyes taking in everything. To his right sat the queen, her dark hair stark against her white gown.

And to his left—Kester. A sword hung at his hip, and he scanned the room.

But it was the woman next to the queen that drew Ursula's attention. Her auburn hair tumbled over a purple velvet gown. With her bright blue eyes and heart-shaped face, there was no mistaking that this woman was Ursula's mother. Ursula's blood roared in her ears.

She wanted to shout, to run across the room and ask the woman a million questions, but of course she couldn't. This was Bael's memory. She had no control as it unfolded.

Instead, she sat quietly and began to eat. With Bael's eyes focused on the meal, Ursula couldn't see anything beyond an enormous steak and a pile of potatoes. *Please look up. Please look up.*

A scream pierced the peaceful atmosphere, and Bael's eyes flashed up. A fracas had erupted at King Midac's table. Everything seemed to slow, growing quiet as Bael's eyes moved from person to person. First, his gaze flicked to Kester, who reached for his blade. Then they moved to the king, whose expression was one of abject horror. When Bael looked at the queen, the source of the horror was obvious. Blood bloomed from the center of her chest, where a steak knife stuck out. Bael's gaze slid to Ursula's mother. Her hands dripped with blood as she lunged for the king.

The scene slowed further as, for the briefest of instants, Ursula's mother turned toward Bael. Where Ursula would have expected to see some sort of grimace, the woman's face looked instead strangely calm. And then she saw her eyes—black as Nyxobas's void.

Ursula shrieked in silent agony.

Then everything sped up again. Bael leapt over the table. Across from him, Kester drew his sword. Pushing the king aside, Kester drove his blade into Ursula's mum's stomach.

Bael reached her a moment later, but Kester leapt into his path. "You betrayed us."

"No!" Bael shouted.

King Midac pushed forward, standing next to Kester and drawing his sword.

"I saw her eyes," roared the king. "One of your night hags. There will be no armistice. This was an assassination." The king's voice was thick with emotion, his eyes blazing with rage. "Kill the shadow demons!"

Bael started to charge, but a king's guard intercepted him. With a single swing, Bael hacked off his head. When Bael's eyes refocused on the king, more guards had moved between them. Led by Ursula's grandfather, they closed in around Bael and Abrax.

The memory skipped forward. Now, Bael and Abrax were fighting back in a wild blur of shadows and fury. Around them, the floor had grown slick with blood. Still, the guards pressed in. Bael and Abrax continued to eviscerate them, hacking through necks and pressing closer to the king's table.

When they reached it, Abrax leapt on top. Bael knelt to examine Ursula's mother. She lay on the floor, blood oozing from the wound in her side.

"Who sent you?" asked Bael.

Ursula's mum stared back at Bael. Her eyes had returned to blue—no longer reflecting the darkness of the void. She didn't answer.

Bael pressed his hand to her wound, putting pressure on it. "I said, who sent you?"

Ursula's mother moaned softly, but she didn't answer.

A shout turned Bael's head. A young girl was charging for him, a sword aimed at his throat. Abrax lunged for her, blade extended, but Bael blocked the attack with his own sword.

The girl pressed on, coming for him anyway. In a flash of shadows, Bael dodged under the girl's blade. With a chopping motion, he batted it from her hands, then wrapped his arms around her tightly. Nearby, Abrax was playing defense, fighting any king's guard who approached.

"Who are you?" said Bael.

The girl looked up at Bael, and Ursula nearly screamed. The blue eyes, the auburn hair, the fierce expression she'd seen a million times in the mirror. It was her own face that looked at Bael. *F.U.'s face—Former Ursula.*

"Don't hurt my mother." Her own eyes streamed with tears, looking back at her.

"I need to know why she betrayed us," said Bael.

F.U. struggled against his grip. "My mother is a follower of Emerazel."

Bael shook his head, gripping her tightly. "I saw the void in her eyes. She's a follower of Nyxobas."

"N-no..." F.U. stammered. "My mother would never betray King Midac. She loved the queen."

Bael looked at the queen's body where it lay on the floor. The handle of the steak knife still protruded from her chest.

The rising of Bael's wings behind him cast a dark shadow over Ursula, and she pulled herself from his grip.

Flames began to rise around them.

CHAPTER 27

$\mathcal{U}$rsula opened her eyes slowly. Outside, storm winds howled around the cabin, and the fire crackled in the stove. She was pretty much naked, apart from her lacy bra and knickers. Bael lay next to her, his eyes closed, his mouth no longer pressed to her wrist. Her hand lay on his chest, and as she started to move it away, his eyes opened: two orbs, the color of blood.

"Ursula," he said, his voice rough. His body was full of tension, like it was taking every ounce of his strength to keep himself from tearing her to pieces. Slowly, he began to push himself up.

Ursula remembered his broken body. "Don't move."

She looked at his legs—the ripped flesh and shattered bones now completely healed over. His hips looked aligned. She might have turned him into a cannibal with a personal fixation on her blood, but at least she'd healed him.

She looked again, and fear prickled through her. Bael's legs were no longer bound with rope. Before she could scoot out of range, Bael grabbed her by the waist, his fingers gripping her tightly. He pulled her to his muscled chest, pure steel, and his blood-red eyes bored into her.

Her blood raced through her veins. She was acutely aware of every inch of skin that touched him, her breasts pressed against his chest.

She was also aware that he could rip her throat out at any moment, but she couldn't seem to focus on anything except his powerful body under hers, his fingers on her waist. His breath warmed her neck, his mouth dangerously close to her throat. Without entirely realizing what she was doing, she arched her neck in a silent invitation. She intuited that she had to let him take control right now, to give in to what he wanted.

His teeth skimmed her throat. "You healed me," he growled. "With your blood."

She felt her hips pressing against him. "There wasn't any other way."

"I told you to get help."

The first time he had drunk from her, he'd become bestial and demonic. This time he seemed more in control. *Maybe Xarthra's blood is still helping him.*

Ursula touched his cheek. "I saw you. In the battle of Mount Acidale. We've met before."

Bael's voice purred against her throat. "What are you talking about?"

"I saw your memory, after my mother attacked the queen. I was there. Abrax tried to attack me, but you parried. I tried to kill you. You let me live. So consider us even."

Bael's breath was hot on her cheek, and his sandalwood scent curled around her like a dangerous caress. Ursula's skin heated. His eyes had faded to a pale gray again, now full of questions. His skin felt smooth against hers, and the entirety of her world narrowed to every point of contact between them—the tops of her breasts skimming against his chest, his fingers possessive on her waist. She wanted them to move lower, to explore her body.

As if reading her thoughts, Bael pressed his mouth to hers in a searing kiss. She parted her lips, her tongue brushing against his. Her skin heated, chest flushing, and molten heat pooled in her core. She hooked her leg around him, silently demanding more from him. She felt as if her breasts were swelling, her body readying itself for him.

For just a moment, he pulled away from the kiss. "I love you, Ursula," he said. His voice was perfectly even, like this statement was nothing more than a comment on the weather outside. But as she looked into his gray eyes, she knew this couldn't be further from the truth. With this statement, he was telling her his devotion was complete. With these simple words, he was telling her he would follow her to the ends of the earth, that he would protect her in any way she desired, that he would die for her if he had to.

She held his gaze. "I love you too."

Bael pulled her close again, enveloping her in his arms. His dark, powerful magic whispered over her skin, and his chest swelled with each breath.

Ursula laced her fingers through his thick hair, and warmth surged within her. She wanted him to tear off the last scraps of fabric between them, to press his mouth to her breasts. She unhooked her bra, letting her nipples brush against his body, and she felt his muscles stiffen as he tried to restrain himself.

He pressed his mouth to her neck, teeth skimming her throat, until his warm tongue replaced it, swirling over her skin. As Bael's hands slid upward along the curve of her ribs, she let out an involuntary moan. Her breasts brushed against him as they kissed, her nipples hardening. Gently, he pushed her onto her back. Of course he wanted to be in control here. He ran his hand down her body until it reached her panties, and she lifted her hips as he pulled them off.

His eyes drank in her naked body, hungry and desperate, swirling with dark shadows. He was fighting hard to restrain himself. She didn't want him to hold back. She wanted him to completely unleash himself on her. She reached for him, pulling off his boxer briefs.

"Ursula," he started to say, but she arched her back, her legs falling open to entice him.

A low, animal growl escaped his throat, and Bael let go of his restraints. He gripped her hips, his mouth hot and possessive on her neck. She gasped as he filled her.

"Bael…"

Heat suffused her. Not the burning pain of Emerazel's fire, but a fever that threatened to overwhelm her very being as they moved together. Bael's breath was hot in the cusp of her ear. An incandescent flame lit in her very core until pure ecstasy claimed her mind.

CHAPTER 28

Wearing nothing but her underwear, Ursula stood by the wood stove, stirring a pot of stew. Bael sat on the bed, his jacket slung over his shoulders for warmth. In his lap, he held Ursula's torn shirt. He'd found a needle and thread on one of the shelves, and he'd busied himself by carefully stitching a patch onto the shoulder.

"How long do you think this storm will last?" asked Ursula.

"The wind is beginning to wane. I think it will finish tonight," said Bael.

Her stomach rumbled. "Good thing we've got food here." The thick stew was just beginning to bubble. "I think it's hot. Are you hungry?"

"I'm starving," said Bael. "That smells amazing. How did you manage to cook it?"

"I opened the cans, dumped the contents into a pot, and heated it up. It's very complicated. Someday I'll show you my technique." Ursula filled two ceramic bowls with steaming stew, then brought them over to Bael. She sat next to him, eagerly digging in. Maybe it wasn't a complex recipe, but it tasted delicious all the same.

After a few minutes of eating in silence, she said, "I don't understand how you were able to resist the old way. Last time you consumed my blood, you nearly killed me."

"Xarthra's blood acts as an antidote. I'll need more, but for the time being, I'm in control."

"That's handy, considering we're trapped in a small space for now."

Bael slid his stew onto the table, then handed Ursula the shirt he'd been patching. "Try this on when you're ready."

Ursula pulled on the shirt and buttoned the front. All the holes had been fixed, and it fit perfectly.

Bael rose and crossed to the door. He cracked it open, and a burst of snowflakes blasted into the cabin, followed by icy wind. Night had fallen outside, but Ursula could see that snow had piled at least halfway up the doorframe.

Ursula's heart sped up. "Bael," she whispered, "I think we're trapped here. There's four feet of fresh snow out there, and the avalanche destroyed the path back to the chalet. We can't go back that way."

"We'll find a way around," said Bael absently. All of a sudden, his gaze seemed intent on one of her hands, and he crossed to her and lifted it to inspect it.

"Care to tell me what you're doing with my hand?"

He met her gaze, holding up her hand like it might be diseased. "I'm trying to understand how you're able to wield a sword with something so small."

She dropped her soup onto the table, and pulled Bael back down to the bed.

* * *

EVEN CURLED UP NEXT to Bael, Ursula could tell the cabin was freezing cold. Propping herself up, she looked to the stove. The barest wisps of smoke rose from the remains of the fire. Next to her, Bael slept soundly, completely unmoving.

Wrapping her sweater around her bare shoulders, she climbed out of bed. As Bael continued to doze, she added some fresh kindling and blew on the coals until flames licked over the twigs. She crouched in front of the open stove, alternating between warming her fingers and stoking the embers.

"Thanks for starting the fire," said Bael from the bed.

"No problem."

A moment later, she felt Bael's arm on her shoulder as he crouched next to her, and she leaned into him.

"How did you sleep?" she asked.

"Like a man saved from the brink of death." He raised his arms over his head. "But I think we can try leaving now."

Ursula rose and pulled on her dried clothes. Bael had patched everything, and while they wouldn't be as warm as before the avalanche, they were at least waterproof again.

Fully dressed, Bael reached for two strange-looking objects that stood next to the door. Made of fresh saplings, they looked like a failing final project for Basket Making 101.

"What are those for?"

"You haven't seen a pair of snowshoes before?"

Her eyebrows shot up. "Those are snowshoes?"

"The owners of this cabin didn't see fit to leave any behind. While you slept, I slipped out and made some. Here, give me your foot."

While she stood by the door, Bael crouched down, tying the improvised snow shoes to her feet. They were a little wide, forcing Ursula into a sort of bowlegged gait, but when she stepped out into the snow, she found that she only sank in a few inches.

"These are amazing!" She clomped in a small circuit.

Bael appeared a moment later, a larger pair affixed to his feet, "Are you ready?"

"Slightly reluctant to leave our little haven, but yes."

They hiked back toward the path of the avalanche. The storm had smoothed everything out, turning the ice-scarred snow into a veritable winter wonderland. Ursula was about to start across the field when Bael caught her arm.

"I don't think it's stable."

"Oh right," said Ursula immediately, feeling foolish.

Bael looked up at the cornice, and shook his head. "Unfortunately, I think our way home is over the top of that monster."

Ursula gaped at him. "You want to hike up there?"

"I don't see any other way."

"What about continuing further along the path, past the cabin?"

Bael shook his head. "I investigated it this morning. There's another exposed snowfield. If we want to find the dragon, we need to go up."

Without waiting for Ursula to respond, he started up the side of the snowfield, sticking to the trees.

Ursula followed behind, her makeshift snowshoes crunching over the snow. They walked through the pine forest. Above them, fresh snow weighed down the tree boughs, sparkling in the sunlight. The rising sun lit a bluebird sky, and sunlight glinted off tiny snowflakes still suspended in the air. It felt like magic, even if it wasn't.

With aching legs, Ursula climbed beside Bael for hours. It must have been about noon when they reached the top of the forest. Bael handed her his canteen, and she took a long drink of the ice-cold water.

Ursula stared at the towering cornice. "So do you know a path over it?"

Bael shook his head, his gray eyes thoughtful. "I was hoping we might find a crack we could slip through."

Ursula scanned along the ice, but it appeared to be a single sheet of uninterrupted cliff.

"Looks pretty smooth to me," she said. "We'll need to climb it."

"We don't have the right equipment. You'd need crampons, a rope—"

"Or a pair of hands that can melt handholds right into the ice?" Ursula channeled flames into her hand.

Bael's eyebrows rose in admiration. "Do you think that would work?"

"I know it will," said Ursula. "I used these very hands to climb out of a deep tree-well before I saved you."

CHAPTER 29

About fifty yards of snowfield lay between the edge of the forest and the cornice. If a chunk of cornice broke off, they would immediately be swept away by sliding snow. Assuming they weren't crushed by the cornice itself.

Bael held a finger to his lips, then started across the snowfield.

After a few agonizing minutes, they reached the bottom of the ice cliff.

"I'll start climbing first," whispered Ursula. "Then you follow along behind me, using the handholds that I make."

She crouched, then channeled flames into her fingers. Steam hissed from the ice as she carved holds at knee level, waist level, chest level, and then a pair just above her head.

Grabbing onto the holds above her head, she slipped her feet into the hollows at the base of the cliff. Once her feet were solidly in place, she reached up higher and melted a new hold. Slowly, she began to scale the cliffside.

She'd worried about being cold, but there wasn't any wind, and the sun warmed her back. If anything, she felt a little hot. The cliff sloped out, and her forearms began to burn as she climbed, Bael following behind her.

How much farther do I have? She leaned back, but the lip of the cornice obscured her view. It could be only a few more feet, or it could be three hundred. Her arms shook with the effort of holding on. She glanced down, her stomach immediately clenching. It was at least one hundred feet to the snowfield from here. Too far to drop safely. The only option was up, assuming her arms could keep up.

She pressed on, one hand at a time. Her arms felt like they were on fire. Slowly, more and more blue sky appeared above her head. With a final push, fatigue burning her muscles, she pulled herself over the lip of the cornice. She lay on the snow for a few minutes, catching her breath under the bright blue sky. She crawled to peer over the edge of the cornice, and she caught sight of Bael looking up at her, thirty feet below on the snowy cliff face.

She waved, afraid to shout. Bael waved back, then disappeared under the edge of the cornice as he climbed up the curve. Ursula sat back. Her forearms ached, and she rubbed them through her jacket.

She stood, slowly turning to survey the scene at the top of the cliff. Another snowfield, but flatter and without a looming cornice. *At least I don't have to worry about avalanches.* A cold wind blew over the snow, exposing the ice in some places, shifting it into enormous drifts.

At the far end of the snowfield, a rocky cliff of brown basalt rose a thousand feet up the side of the mountain. She squinted. A thin tendril of smoke seemed to rise from the very base of the cliff. Hope and fear thrilled within her. Was this the dragon's lair?

Ursula turned back to the cornice to check on Bael's progress. As she did, the crack of breaking ice blasted through the silence. Ursula's heart leapt into her throat, but a moment later, Bael hoisted himself up onto the snowfield in a puff of snow.

Bael rose, his face pale. "Ursula," he shouted. "Run!"

What is he doing?! He's going to set off an avalanche. But the snow beneath her was already moving. A sharp report rang out, like the sound of a cannon firing, as the ice ruptured. Ursula turned to run as the cornice began to break up beneath her feet.

In front of her, a chasm formed in the ice. She sprinted toward it, the ground under her feet sloping upward as it began to fall toward the snowfield three hundred feet below.

She leapt when she reached the edge, hurling herself toward the side of the newly forming cliff face. Even as she pushed off, she knew she wouldn't make it over the wide expanse. She began plunging downward, her fingers raking along the ice. She channeled Emerazel's fire into them, trying to make handholds, but her superheated fingers only served to carve gouges that she couldn't grip.

She slammed into a protruding chunk of ice, tearing her jacket. White-hot pain lanced her chest, and she knew that she'd broken ribs. Still, the icy protrusion had stopped her fall, and she managed to carve a hold before she slipped off completely into the abyss.

Below her, the chasm expanded, deepening into an icy crevasse. The chunk of cornice continued to tilt away from her. For a few moments, it looked like it might slow—until it fell away with an enormous crack.

Ursula clutched tightly to the hold she'd carved in the cliff, as the chunk of cornice slammed onto the snowfield below her, releasing a great cloud of snow into the air. It looked soft as eiderdown as it bloomed toward her in the afternoon sun. Then the roar of the avalanche hit her, shattering the moment of peace.

She could only imagine the unseen horror unfolding within the cloud as the cornice disintegrated into a thousand blocks of ice. As the flakes settled, Ursula scanned the snowfield frantically for any sign of Bael. She couldn't find so much as a mitten or hat darkening the barren expanse of ice and snow.

"Bael!" she shouted, ignoring the danger of another avalanche. Only the echoes of her own voice greeted her.

She winced as she surveyed her position. She lay on her side on a thin ledge. With one hand, she clutched a hold she'd melted into the ice. Peering down, she had a view of the snowfield—at least two hundred feet below her. Much too far to jump. Craning her neck to look up, she could see the melted scars her superheated fingers had carved in the ice. Above them, the wall of cliff rose sharply to the sky.

Ursula shivered, but not with cold. Dark clouds had gathered in the sky. The start of another storm? A snowflake drifted past her face, and dread bloomed in her chest. *I can't stay here.*

She sucked in a painful breath, before slowly incanting Starkey's Conjuration. She grimaced in pain as her ribs knit together. Slowly, she pulled herself up. Channeling some of Emerazel's fire into her free hand, she carved another hold into the cliff.

She glanced down again, but she already knew there was no way out of this by going down. She didn't have the strength to climb that far.

Panic gripped her, but she tried to think clearly. Bael was down there somewhere, and the snow was beginning to fall. If she didn't get off the cliff, she'd freeze to it.

Carving holds into the ice, she began to climb again, her heart hammering. This time at least, the cliff didn't lean outward, and she was able to support her weight with both her hands and feet. Her muscles burned, but she pressed on. She was breathing hard when she climbed over the top of the cliff.

Snowflakes fell around her, drifting through the late afternoon air. The wind had picked up, and she shivered as it sliced through the new tear in her jacket. A tear slid down her cheek when she thought of how Bael had so carefully patched it up that morning. *Don't lose it, Ursula. There's a chance he's still alive, but you can't help him by standing around.*

Pulling her jacket tightly around her, she started onto the windswept snowfield. Her feet crunched over the ice as she wandered between the giant snowdrifts. They loomed over her in strange curving forms, and she wondered what sort of frozen beasts they might be hiding. When she brushed the snow off one, she discovered a giant boulder.

After ten minutes of walking through the snow, she realized she didn't really have a plan in place. *I should have been following the edge of the cornice —to look for a way down.*

But when she turned to go back, she realized the drifting snow had covered any tracks she'd left behind her. She shivered, the wind knifing into her, as she tried to decide what to do. The snow fell more heavily now, but she could still see the distant outline of the mammoth cliff of rock. *If I'm going to find shelter here, that's where I'll find it.*

As she walked toward the distant cliff, the snowstorm picked up. Snow whipped over the frozen hillocks and swirled about her in twisting gusts that tore at her clothes. Ursula pulled her jacket tighter, but snowflakes blew into her eyes. Her hands grew numb, and her toes felt like they were frozen. Still she trudged forward. Her teeth chattered uncontrollably.

"Stay moving, stay warm," Ursula whispered to herself. The mantra helped keep her going.

Slowly, the stony cliff crept closer, like the dark side of a ship in a stormy sea. She was half frozen by the time she reached the wall of basalt. It towered above her, disappearing into the winter sky. Exhausted, she slumped against it as she looked for a crack or a crevasse she could crawl into, but the stone was completely sheer.

"Stay moving, stay warm," she whispered, willing herself back to standing. Slowly, she began to walk along the base of the cliff, putting one foot in front of the other. Her eyes searched for some hollow she might shelter in, but the stone remained unblemished.

She was shivering uncontrollably now, her mind focusing on the mantra. "Stay moving, stay warm…"

She stumbled, falling to her knees. *So cold. Need to rest.* She leaned against the side of the cliff. The wind whistled in her ears, and snow whitened her legs. She channeled some of Emerazel's fire into her palms, marveling at the flames as they warmed her face. Their heat brought with it a throbbing pain as it thawed her fingers.

She thought of Bael, how he'd warmed her only a night ago, his naked body pressed against hers. Now, as darkness fell, that memory seemed so distant. Flames danced over her hands, twisting in the wind before snuffing out.

Her teeth chattered. "Stay moving, stay warm…" But she couldn't stand. *I'm too tired.* She pulled her legs up to her chest, shivering.

I'll just rest here a while, wait the storm out.

Around her, the blizzard howled, and snow drifted against her. Ursula closed her eyes, the cold piercing her mind. She couldn't remember a reason to keep them open.

* * *

I'M ON FIRE. Someone has lit me on fire.

Ursula's eyes flew open. Frantically she swatted at herself to put out the flames, but her hands, bound with rags, were like soft clubs.

"Shhh…" said a gentle voice. A young woman knelt next to her, her hair the color of snow.

"My hands…" said Ursula. "Fire?"

"Be still," said the woman, grabbing Ursula's wrist. "You're safe now."

"Bael?" said Ursula, looking into the woman's eyes—eyes so blue they might have been carved from glacier ice.

The woman held a finger to her lips, white hair flowing over an ice-blue dress. "Shhh…" she whispered, before beginning to incant in Angelic.

CHAPTER 30

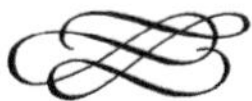

A low whistling woke Ursula. Slowly, she opened her eyes. She no longer sat against the cold stone of the cliff face. Instead, she lay in a soft bed, under layers of thick blankets. Only the air on her face still had the bite of winter. As she surveyed the room, she could see that it appeared to be carved from ice. The ice walls ranged from a blue-lavender near the ceiling to darker teals and ultramarines near the floor. For a moment, she thought she might have fallen into a glacial cave, but as she studied the walls, she could see deep gouges and scratches in the ice. This cave had been carved.

"You're awake?" A low, female voice.

Ursula turned her head to find a woman seated on a small chair near the stove. Her gleaming white hair hung to her shoulders in neat braids. She faced away from Ursula, watching steam rise from a tea kettle. This apparently was the source of the whistling that had woken her.

Ursula struggled to sit up, discovering that her hands were wrapped in rags so thick they looked like boxing gloves. *So I wasn't dreaming.* "What have you done to my hands?"

"Your fingers were nearly frozen when I found you. The bandages are to protect them. Would you like some tea?" Slowly, she turned to face Ursula.

Ursula's stomach clenched. The woman's skin was so pale as to be nearly translucent, and was marred by a blood-red scar that sliced from forehead to cheek. She looked at Ursula through a single, glacier-blue eye. She hadn't noticed that before, when she'd briefly woken from her sleep.

"Wh-where am I? Where is Bael?" stammered Ursula.

"The demon?"

"Yes."

"He's fine." The woman frowned for a moment. "You must be Ursula, then?"

"How do you know my name?"

"The demon is wandering around in the snow, calling your name."

Ursula's chest tightened. "He's still out there? Is he okay? He was hit by the avalanche." Her breath caught as she waited for the woman to respond.

"He was swept down the mountain, but he's otherwise unharmed. He's a strong one." The woman crossed to Ursula, holding a steaming cup of tea between delicate fingers.

Ursula took it from her, breathing in the scent of chamomile and lavender. Without hesitating, she took a small sip. It tasted as delicious as it smelled. "How did I end up here?"

"In my cave? I saw the flames as you tried to warm yourself. It's not often that a follower of the fire goddess wanders into my domain."

"Your domain? Who are you?" But Ursula realized she already knew the answer. The gouged-out walls, the woman's pale complexion. She'd found the White Dragon. Or rather, the White Dragon had found her.

"I can see from your face you've figured it out on your own," said the woman. "You may call me Grisial."

"I wasn't sure if you were real. I'd heard stories…"

"Oh, I'm very much real." Grisial leaned over the bed to stare at Ursula with her single eye. "Why are you here?"

"I need your help."

"Why?"

"Lucius has Excalibur."

"So?" said Grisial, leaning back on her haunches. "The sword has always been his."

"I need it to defeat the Darkling, or he's going to take over the world."

"And you think I'm going to help you get it from him?" Grisial started to stand and turn away.

Ursula pushed herself up, and spoke as forcefully as she dared. "You are the only one who can defeat Lucius."

"No. I will not help you—I cannot help you." Grisial backed away from her.

"Why?"

"Because I value my life. Just as you should value yours." Genuine fear trembled in Grisial's voice. "Lucius cannot be defeated if he holds the blade."

"But you defeated him..."

"And look what it cost me," said Grisial, pointing to her blind eye.

"Lucius did that?"

Grisial nodded, pain etched in her features.

"So I came all the way here. Nearly dying—"

"You'd be dead if I hadn't saved you," Grisial pointed out.

"And you're telling me that you can't help." Frustration simmered in her chest, building to something like anger. "You don't understand. If the Darkling comes to earth and enacts his plan, we'll all be dead. You need to fight Lucius. You're the only one who can help."

Grisial stared at Ursula with a deep sadness in her eye. "I didn't defeat Lucius. Lucius was in love with me. He let me win."

"I don't understand. He ripped your eye out, then let you win?" Ursula sat back on the bed, stunned. "Maybe you should start from the beginning."

Grisial sighed. "Female dragons are very rare. I was the first born in a thousand years. As his right, as Drake, Lucius claimed me as his. He raised me in his harem, hidden and separate from the other dragons. I didn't know what I was, and he didn't tell me. He wanted to keep me as his own."

Ursula's lip curled. "So he kept you as a slave."

Grisial shook her head vigorously. "Not exactly. He didn't lay a finger on me. I think he hoped I'd fall in love with him. It didn't happen that way. I fell in love with one of his guards, Ben. Ben told me what I was. He showed me how to transform into my dragon form. When Lucius found out..." Grisial heaved a sob. "He killed Ben. I tried to fight him. You can see what he did to me. It wasn't so much that I defeated him as I managed not to die."

Grisial looked so forlorn, so vulnerable, that Ursula nearly gave her a hug. This was *not* what Ursula had expected of the White Dragon. "Well, he stole Excalibur from me, so apparently I made his power worse."

Grisial's eye widened. "Lady Viviane gave you the sword?"

"Yes."

"You weren't lying about the Darkling. Sit still." Grisial moved closer to Ursula, standing just in front of her. Gently, she placed her fingers on Ursula's temples. She closed her eye, concentrating. After a few moments, she pulled away.

"Who are you?" Grisial's voice sounded worried—sharp.

"I'm Ursula Anne Thurlow," said Ursula, remembering the name her grandfather had told her.

"No, I mean *who* are you?"

"That's all I know. I lost all my memories of my childhood. They called me the mystery girl in London."

Grisial crossed her arms over her chest. "Why should I trust you if you don't know who you are?"

"My grandfather is the head of the king's guards."

Grisial sucked in a sharp breath. "Your mother is the queen killer?"

"That's me. I don't remember her at all. I think someone magically wiped my memories."

Grisial shook her head. "That's impossible. I know of no magic that can erase memories."

Ursula held out her hands, palms up. "But I can't remember anything."

"Then try harder," Grisial snapped.

"It won't work," said Ursula with a frustrated sigh. "I saw a million psychologists back in London. I was hypnotized, fed special diets, but none of it could help me recall anything."

"That's because you didn't want to remember."

Ursula frowned. "What do you mean?"

"When Lucius killed Ben, I completely lost it. I attacked Lucius. Spilled his blood. At first, I remembered none of it. It was like one moment Ben was dying, and the next I was here on Mount Acidale."

"So how do you know what happened?"

Grisial laced her fingers together. "I kept going back to the last thing I saw." She shook her head at the memory. "It was awful—Ben bleeding on the floor—but I forced myself to push past it. To recall what I did next."

"That won't work for me. I don't remember anything before I arrived in London. There's no 'last thing'—it's just blackness, then waking up in a burnt-out church in London. To be honest, I hardly remember the church, just the hospital after."

Grisial thought for a long while before speaking. "I think you start with your last memory, even if it is the hospital, then work backward."

"If I can tell you more about my past, will you help us get Excalibur?"

"Maybe."

Well, it doesn't look like I have any other options. Ursula closed her eyes. She concentrated on the moment her eyes opened in the Royal London Hospital.

"Focus on the minutiae," said Grisial. "The details will help place you in your memory."

Ursula summoned up the memory of the hospital room, the rough cotton sheets, the beeping of the heart monitor, the dueling scents of antiseptic and floral arrangements...and the moment she opened her eyes. Then she focused on earlier, when the firefighter pulled her from the rubble.

"I remember the firefighter," she said excitedly.

"Good," said the White Dragon. "Now go further back."

Ursula closed her eyes again. Slowly, the firefighter came back into focus. Her head on his shoulder. The acrid smell of smoke in the air. He moved backward, and she realized her memory was like a movie in reverse, watching the firefighter carry her in slow motion back into the flames. Pieces of a shattered beam rose from the floor until no longer broken, and they fitted themselves into the ceiling. Smoke and fire surrounded her. She couldn't breathe.

She opened her eyes, sucking deep breaths. Panic roiled within her.

"Is it working?" asked Grisial.

"I think so. I could see the firefighter carrying me."

"Good. Now try again. Further back."

Ursula closed her eyes, and the smell of smoke curled into her nostrils. She could taste ash on her tongue. The firefighter carried her deeper into the flames, moving backward. Heat seared her skin. Her heart raced. Slowly, he lowered her to the ground. As she descended, she could see the outline of a sigil on the floor. The firefighter straightened. Then he began backing away, disappearing into the flames. She was alone. An inferno raged around her.

Ursula curled her legs inward, so that her knees touched her chest. Her eyes closed, and the memory skipped.

She was standing outside now. On top of a castle wall, maybe. A row of stone crenellations rose in front of her, and flames licked about her feet. Emerazel's sigil. She could hear herself incanting the traveling spell in reverse, pain throbbing in her shoulder. When she looked down, she could see blood seeping through her shirt, blossoming like a flower. *Did someone stab me?*

Her heart slammed against her ribs, and ice-cold grief threatened to overwhelm her.

As she finished the spell, she crouched, then drew the sigil in reverse, using a bottle of perfume. Everything was backwards, the liquid pouring upward from the stone and into the bottle. She shoved the full perfume bottle into her pocket as she walked backward to the crenellations.

The smell of fire curled through the air. As she peered over the side, she could see an inferno raging beneath her. Her chest heaved in panic, sorrow slamming into her. She reached into the air, and a dagger zoomed out of the flames and into her hand, flying in reverse. It took her a moment to understand what had happened—that she was now holding a dagger she'd just thrown off the ramparts.

A gold blade, encrusted with jewels.

With one hand, she pulled down the collar of her shirt. With the other, she pressed the blade into her skin. Burning pain lanced through her, and she slowly un-carved Emerazel's sigil, moving backward through time. When it disappeared, she shoved the dagger back into her sheath. Tears streamed down her face—crying for her mother. Sobbing for the life she'd lost.

She uncrumpled a piece of paper, pressing it against the flat stone on one of the crenellations. For an instant, she could see the text, but she didn't even need to read it—she already knew what it said.

On your 18th birthday,
March 15, 2016,
ask for a trial.
- Ursula (You)

Then she began un-writing it, the ink flowing from the page into the pen.

* * *

With a gasp, Ursula opened her eyes. Grisial stood next to the bed. All at once, memories began trickling back to her—her mother, teaching her to fight with a sword, striding purposefully across a field, teaching Ursula to read. And yet—despite the memories, the images, it all felt strangely distant, as if she was watching a stranger's life. Not her own. She still didn't understand. What had happened to her memories? Why had she blocked everything out?

Her chest tightened. "It-it was my choice to forget the past, but I don't know why. I was the one who carved the sigil into my shoulder. I wrote myself the note," Ursula stammered. "I was the one who wrote the note. I wanted to forget."

The dragon looked at her sympathetically. "You needed to escape your memories."

"Yes, but I still can't feel anything, so I'm not sure why." She looked into Grisial's single sapphire eye. "Do you trust me now? Will you help me defeat Lucius?"

"I will help you, but you know I cannot defeat him. Not when he possesses Excalibur. The most I can do is protect you while you plead your case. Maybe you can convince him."

Ursula stood. "Then what are we waiting for?"

CHAPTER 31

Ursula wrapped her legs tightly around the dragon's neck, while her hands each gripped a bony horn. In her dragon form, Grisial was a massive beast, at least the size of the Drake. Her scales were as white as ermine fur and camouflaged perfectly with the mountain snow. It was obvious, now, why she hadn't been seen in hundreds of years.

With a scream, Grisial launched herself into the air. Ursula clung on for dear life until she adjusted to the massive beats of the dragon's wings. They flew out over the snowfields, and Ursula recognized the cliff she'd huddled against the night before, trying to warm herself. Grisial had given her new gloves and a jacket, and the soft wool warmed her body even as the wind whipped at her hair.

Grisial dove, and Ursula gripped tightly as they plummeted toward a snowfield. The dragon's wings billowed out as they landed, blowing clouds of snow into the air. When the snow cleared, Ursula glimpsed Bael standing fifty yards from them. He glared at the dragon, his dark magic slicing the air sharply around him.

Ursula waved to him, laughing as his eyes widened when he saw her perched on Grisial's spine. Then Grisial's neck lurched awkwardly, and Ursula fell to the snow. By her side, Grisial transformed into her human form.

Ursula rose, brushing the snow off herself as Bael charged toward her. When he reached her, he swept her into his arms.

"I thought I'd lost you," he said, his voice hoarse with emotion.

"Sorry to disappoint you." Ursula smiled, but she immediately regretted the comment when she saw the tears in Bael's eyes. "Oh, I'm sorry. You must have been so worried."

She pressed her face into his neck. Bael didn't speak as he held her tightly, but she could feel his chest heaving. At last, he cupped her chin with a calloused palm. "I am so glad to see you," he said, before kissing her on the lips.

"Are you two quite done?" asked Grisial.

Bael's grip on Ursula slackened as he turned to look at the dragon shifter.

Ursula gestured between them. "Grisial, this is Bael. Bael, this is Grisial."

The demon and the dragon eyed each other warily.

"Grisial saved my life. I would have frozen to death if she hadn't found me. She has agreed to help us negotiate with Lucius."

Bael frowned. "Negotiate? Not fight?"

Grisial shook her head. "Without a legion of demons behind you, he'd defeat you in seconds if he's in his dragon form, with Excalibur. I can at least guarantee your safety while you negotiate. I can fly us to Calidore Castle. You two must convince Lucius to help. If he gives you trouble, I will help you escape."

Bael's eyes glinted in the sunlight as he nodded. "Let's go."

WHILE THE RIDE in Frank's carriage had taken them most of a night, the flight to Calidore Castle lasted less than an hour on Grisial's neck. Ursula sat in front, with Bael behind her, his muscular arms gripping the dragon's horns while keeping her from falling off. In the cold air above Mount Acidale, his embrace kept her warm.

Urusula stared wide-eyed at the view as the sun set, bathing the trees in buttery yellow light, washing the rural towns in amber and pink. It was only as they reached the city of Mount Acidale and its haze of smog that the beauty of the land began to fade.

Grisial dove into the smog, aiming straight for the broken towers of Calidore Castle. With the sixth sense of a homing pigeon, Grisial burst from the dirty sky directly above the castle.

As the White Dragon landed in a courtyard, the king's guard charged toward them. Grisial spun, and with a draconic scream, breathed a stream of icy water at the men. As the water contacted the ground, the walls, and the guards themselves, it instantly froze into solid ice.

As rifles began to fire from the roofs above them, Bael pulled Ursula behind a bronze statue of King Midac. He covered her with his body, but most of the bullets were aimed at Grisial. They zinged off the dragon's scales like hail.

Grisial turned, breathing more ice at the attacking guards. As the men began to freeze, a captain yelled for them to retreat.

"Block the doors," shouted Bael to the dragon.

Grisial directed her icy breath so that it froze all but one of the entrances to the courtyard. With all the guards either frozen or blocked from entering, Grisial morphed back into her human form.

"This way." With her one blue eye flashing, she beckoned them toward the remaining door.

"Wait." Bael ran to the nearest frozen guard, and with a crack, ripped the man's cutlass from an icy grip.

Ursula gagged at the sound. There was no question that Bael had snapped the man's wrist. He was already reaching for the guard's rifle when Ursula shouted for him to stop.

She rushed to the guard. Beneath the ice, she could see the man was still alive. His eyes rolled in their sockets, and he grunted in fear, unable to speak with his jaw frozen in place. Quickly, she began channeling Emerazel's fire into her hands.

"What are you doing?" said Bael.

"These are my grandfather's men. You can't go about snapping their limbs off." With a quick burst of heat, she melted the rifle from his grip.

"Here." She handed the rifle to Bael. "You wanted this."

She turned to thaw a second cutlass from another guard. *Feels good to have a real blade again.* "I'm ready."

Already, shouts penetrated the stone walls—soldiers readying for an attack. They had to move quickly.

Bael used his shoulder to ram into the wooden door, splintering the wood with his enormous body. Ursula followed close behind him, and the three of them sprinted through the outer gate, then through a series of halls. Shouts rang out nearby, but they managed to avoid the guards, moving quickly down a stone corridor and up the steps into King Midac's great hall.

Ursula froze in the hall. It was the same one she'd seen in Bael's memory. Rows of columns lined the hall, supporting a three-story ceiling. Where banquet tables had stood during the armistice, she now found a stone floor and a red rug leading up to two thrones. She swallowed as the memory flashed through her mind. She'd watched her mother die here. She'd watched her own dreams bleed out on the floor.

Guards clustered around the thrones, blocking the king from view and raising their rifles. But Grisial was already shifting, the massive girth of her reptilian form shielding Bael and Ursula in a barricade of white scales.

Ursula lifted up a hand. "We aren't here to hurt you."

But the guards ignored her, firing their rifles. Grisial screamed. Like ten thousand claws drawn simultaneously along a granite wall, the sound pierced Ursula's marrow, and she instinctively pressed her hands to her ears, dropping her cutlass to the ground. Above her, windows shattered, glass spraying into the air in a million tiny fragments. Even the marble columns vibrated. After what seemed like an eternity, Grisial quieted, and a deathly silence fell over the room.

Her ears ringing, Ursula peeked around Grisial's side. Like Ursula, the guards had dropped their rifles. As they bent to retrieve them, Bael shouted, "Put down your rifles. We wish only to speak with Lucius."

"A shadow demon!" hissed one of the guards.

"Why have you attacked my men?" said another voice. Softer than the guard's, but filled with confidence. Unquestionably King Midac.

"The Darkling is building an army," Ursula called out. "He plans to conquer everything. We need to speak to Lucius."

"Lucius isn't here," said Midac.

Before Ursula could reply, a tremendous crash trembled the hall as the ceiling was punctured by the bulk of a massive red dragon. The beast tore through oak beams like they were matchsticks. There was no mistaking Lucius, the Drake, as he slid through the ceiling into the great hall.

Still in his dragon form, Lucius turned to face Grisial. With a piercing scream, he charged. He was bigger than the White Dragon, and she dodged to the side, leaving Ursula and Bael exposed. The Drake could have devoured them then, but his eyes were fixed on Grisial. She spun, breathing frigid water at Lucius. Ice solidified on his chest and forelegs, and for a moment, he was frozen in place. Then, he wrenched one of his legs upward, and the ice shattered. He stalked toward Grisial.

The Drake inhaled, and his chest began to glow with fire. Ursula could see the shape of Excalibur, the outline of the blade embossed on his breast —a part of him. With a shriek, he unleashed a gout of flame at the White Dragon. It raced across the room, a horizontal geyser of fire. It would have immolated Grisial had she not simultaneously breathed an icy stream of water. Ice and fire collided with a tremendous cracking sound.

Ursula and Bael dove behind one of the marble columns. The king was bellowing something about dragons fighting in his castle, but the noise from the dragons practically drowned him out.

Lucius and Grisial continued to spew their elemental flames in a storm of ice, fire, and steam. Still exhaling fire, Lucius dug his claws into the marble floor and began advancing toward Grisial. She breathed ice at him, but began to falter, her massive sides heaving as she expelled the last of her frozen reserves.

"Stop, Lucius!" shouted Ursula. "Your fight is not with Grisial. We only wish to speak with you."

One of Lucius's golden eyes rolled in her direction. Ursula stepped from behind the column, her heart beating a wild rhythm in her chest.

"We have met before, Lucius, here in Mount Acidale, but also in your warren in New York. You saw Abrax abduct me. He's the Darkling. If we don't stop him, he will bend mankind to his will. Mount Acidale will fall to his armies. You will have failed in your duties to protect the realm."

Lucius stopped breathing fire. He growled, a deep rumbling sound that shook the room, trembling over Ursula's skin. Across the hall, the guards trained their guns on her.

"I come in peace. Grisial, if you transformed into your human form, it might help to show them that we mean them no harm."

Grisial's icy blue eye studied her for a moment, then the dragon shook her head. Before Ursula could say anything more, she reared back, but instead of attacking leapt into the air. With a single beat of her wings, she disappeared through the hole in the roof.

"Bollocks," said Ursula under her breath. *There goes our ride.*

Across from her, Lucius was already transforming. Red hair sprouted from his head as his legs and arms shifted into their human form. Then he was striding toward her, pointing Excalibur at her throat.

"Bring them to me," commanded King Midac from across the room.

Lucius's gaze slid to Bael, who still held a cutlass and rifle. "Drop your weapons, or the girl dies."

Slowly, Bael lowered the sword and rifle to the flagstones.

"Now follow me," said Lucius.

Ursula followed Lucius across the shattered stones of the hall toward the king's throne, their footfalls echoing off the flagstone floor. Around her, beams from the roof burned among steaming puddles of water. King Midac sat in his golden throne, staring at them. Dust whitened his hair, and the guards encircling him trained their rifles on Ursula and Bael with extreme intensity.

"Are you the ones who attacked Lucius?" said the king, his voice hard.

"Do you mean just now, or when he was at the brothel?" said Ursula, as confidently as she could manage.

"Do not speak of such filth in my presence." The king's gaze swiveled to Lucius. "Is that true? You were dining with strumpets when they attacked you?"

Lucius flushed, his cheeks turning a surprisingly bright shade of pink. "It was my leisure time, Your Majesty."

The king glared, leaning forward in his throne. "Your job is to protect Mount Acidale. Not to consort with harlots and whores."

The Drake's cheeks reddened further.

"Look, I realize that appearances are important, but Mount Acidale is in danger," Ursula interjected.

King Midac's anger turned to her. "Mount Acidale is not in danger. Despite his caddish ways, Lucius and his dragons are excellent protectors."

Ursula's jaw clenched. "Abrax is seizing power in the Shadow Realm. He plans to topple the gods, then seize the kingdom of men. You saw him in New York—"

"What happens in the Shadow Realm is of no consequence here."

"Abrax is the Darkling," said Ursula, desperate to emphasize the enormity of the situation. "He's coming for all the gods, because he wants to rule the earth *and* the magical realms."

King Midac pointed a finger at her. "The Darkling is only a story made up by a conniving wizard, created to keep the simple-minded afraid, and in his control."

"Lady Viviane gave me Excalibur for the specific purpose of fighting the Darkling."

"You lie."

"I do not."

"Then why does Lucius have possession of the blade? If the Darkling were real, you would never have allowed him to steal it from you."

Ursula stared at the king, dumbfounded. He was willfully ignoring her. Abrax was readying an army of demons and golems to enslave mankind, including those in Mount Acidale, and no one believed her. Her fingers clenched.

King Midac's eyes narrowed. "The girl wants to harm me. Seize her," he shouted.

Before she could move, Lucius threw her face-first onto the flagstones. While he pressed the blade of Excalibur to her jugular, a pair of guards clasped her hands with a set of golden manacles.

Behind her, Bael bellowed like an enraged bull, and when she glanced back, she found him surrounded by five guards, their swords trained on him.

"If you fight, demon, I won't hesitate to kill your friend," hissed Lucius.

Ursula's eyes slid away from them, focusing on the flagstones. This was where her mother had died. Still, Ursula couldn't quite connect to the memory, as if it weren't her own. Emptiness—a dark oblivion—gnawed at her chest.

With a painful jerk, the guards lifted Ursula to her feet. Bael stood across from her, his hands also bound behind his back.

"Imprison them," said the king. "I'll decide their fates in the morning."

Lucius led them from the hall, and Ursula had a strange sense of *déjà vu* as they were marched down a twisting staircase and into the bowels of the castle.

CHAPTER 32

In a dank antechamber, the guards peeled her clothes off, forcing her into what could best be described as a burlap tracksuit. It smelled of death, like it had once been stored in Pasqual's basement. The guards blindfolded her, then led her over a cold, stone floor.

"Put her in with the other girl," said a gruff voice.

The sounds of other prisoners rose around her—muffled, moaning, calling out. After a hundred yards, she heard a key scraping in a lock and the creaking of iron hinges. A guard pushed her forward, and the door slammed shut behind her.

In retrospect, we should have come up with a better plan.

Hands touched her shoulders as she clawed at the blindfold.

"Ursula, relax. I'll get this off you."

A moment later, Ursula was blinking at an emaciated woman in the dim light. Dressed in rags, with matted gray hair and yellow teeth, she looked like she could be the river hag's sister. Light from an oil lamp wavered over her gaunt features.

"Do I know you?" asked Ursula, backing away.

"Oh sorry, I totally forgot about the glamour," the old woman chirped. Her skin shimmered, then the illusion fell away to reveal a dirty—but much prettier—face. One that Ursula recognized immediately.

"Zee! What are you doing here?" She threw her arms around her friend, hugging her tightly.

"Oh, you know. It just seemed like a fun place to hang out. I really like talking to the walls and drinking my own urine when they forget to give me water. What are you doing here?"

"It's a long story."

Zee cocked her head. "We've got nothing but time here, sister."

"I came here to try to get Excalibur, but King Midac didn't seem to like me. How exactly did you end up in here?" asked Ursula.

"Same way you did. I tried to steal Excalibur, but Lucius caught me. That freaking sword is hard to hold. It's like…heavy." Zee stepped closer, her cheeks gaunt. "You don't have any snacks on you, do you?"

A banging interrupted them, followed by a shout. "Ursula!"

"That sounds like Bael," said Zee, raising her eyebrows in surprise.

"He came here with me."

Ursula crossed to the door, peering out a window at eye level with a pair of iron bars through it. She could see into the grim corridor. Across from her stood a row of doors, each with a similar opening. Three down to the right, she could see Bael's face looking through a window.

"Ursula," he called out. "Are you all right?"

"I'm fine. I could have done without the burlap clothing, but on the plus side, Zee's in here with me."

"Zee? Your fae friend?"

"Yeah, she's stuck in here with me."

Bael frowned slightly. "Well, she could be useful to us."

"I'll let her know." Ursula pressed her hand against a bar, already missing him. "I'll talk to you soon."

Bael nodded. "Soon."

Ursula turned back to Zee, who had a hint of a smile on her lips. "You both seem quite close. What's going on there?"

Ursula crossed her arms. "Well, he *is* my fiancé."

Zee's eyebrows shot up. "Did you sleep with your own fiancé? I'm horrified."

Ursula tried to smile innocently, but based on Zee's expression, she had apparently failed.

"You had relations with a demon?" Zee whispered. "What was it like?

I've heard Nyxobas endows his prized demons with more than physical strength—"

"Zee!"

"But of course Bael doesn't have his wings, so it might not be quite as—"

"ZEE!"

"Okay," said Zee, leaning back against the wall of the cell. "It's just, you know, I've had no one to talk to in here except some woodlice, and they're not wonderful conversationalists."

Another round of banging interrupted them, and a pockmarked guard peered in at them through the window. "Lights out," he growled.

"Yes, sir." Zee reached for the oil lamp. With a sharp exhale, she extinguished it.

The door clicked as the guard slid a panel over the window, plunging the cell into darkness.

"The guards are awful," said Zee.

"So what happens now?" asked Ursula.

"Well, they'll have us keep the lights out until *morning*." Zee enunciated *morning* the way she might if she'd been miming air quotes. For all Ursula knew, Zee was actually making air quotes, but it was impossible to tell in the dark. "But sometimes I think they have us keep the lights off for days on end."

Something pressed against Ursula's side, and she nearly jumped, until she realized it was Zee.

"Sorry," said Zee. "It gets cold in here."

Zee rested her head on Ursula's shoulder and spoke softly. "Do you know how long I've been imprisoned?"

Ursula tried to tally all the time that had passed since they'd been separated at Vortigan's warren under the Statue of Liberty. "I'm not sure. A week or two maybe?"

"Oh," said Zee. From the tone of her voice, Ursula couldn't tell if she was relieved or horrified.

"Well, it could be worse. At least you weren't tortured in prison like Kester was."

Zee stiffened. "You saw Kester?!"

"Abrax had him. He's fine. Recuperating with Cera right now."

Zee sighed audibly. "I was worried about him."

"He can more than fend for himself." Ursula was glad for the darkness, so Zee couldn't read the expression on her face as she remembered Kester stabbing her mother.

* * *

URSULA WOKE IN THE DARK. She could feel Zee's small form next to her. Although it was pitch black, she could hear by Zee's slow breathing that she was asleep.

The lack of sensory input should have bothered Ursula, but it didn't. The darkness felt safe and clean, like she didn't exist. Like nothing could hurt her—no memories of her mother's shirt, stained with red, or Kester driving a sword through her ribs….

Ursula closed her eyes and opened them, blinking a few more times. The blackness remained the same. Just her and her thoughts. She closed her eyes again, and sucked in a slow breath.

Maybe she shouldn't run from her memories anymore. She'd come here to learn who she really was, hadn't she? She'd never be whole until she remembered everything.

It was time to revisit her arrival in London.

Slowly she began unwinding the memory. She started with the scratchy sheets of the hospital bed, then the firefighter carrying her through the burning rubble of Ethelburga Church. A moment later, she was reconstituting out of ash on the palace roof. She slowed down the mental images, studying F.U.'s agonized face, then the strange reverse carving of Emerzel's sigil into her skin.

She wanted to know why she'd done this to herself, but in this memory she was merely an observer. She could watch each moment, see every detail, but she couldn't feel the emotions. Even in her memories, she was keeping a distance. *Why?*

She scrolled back further. New memories began to unfold before her —memories she hadn't seen before. F.U. sprinted backward through a door, into a dark stairwell. Down and down it wound, and she bounced backward down the stairs. F.U. was gasping for breath, tears streaming from her eyes. *What had upset her?*

F.U. burst through a door into a cacophony of screams and shrieking steel. Men were fighting, bleeding all around her. She was in the midst of some sort of battle. Looking down, she found the gold dagger in her hand as she ran backwards, moving into the battle. The reverse nature of the memory was disorienting as she dodged swords and halberds, moments before they swung over her head.

Out of the corner of her eye, she caught sight of demonic wings beating the air—Abrax's wings. Fear nearly sent her fleeing back to reality as she realized where she was. This was the beginning of the Battle of Mount Acidale—the throne room.

F.U. ducked down, falling to the floor, and began sliding in reverse under a table. Her hands reached for something, and Ursula nearly screamed at the sight of her mother's corpse.

F.U. cupped her mother's head in her hands. Red hair draped over Ursula's shaking fingers, as her mum's dead eyes stared at the underside of the table. Ursula nearly screamed again as they suddenly focused, and the corpse drew in a shaky breath.

"No, Mother. Stay…" she heard herself say. F.U.'s eyes were blurry with tears. She looked at her mother with an expression of abject horror.

Ursula could see the love in her mother's eyes, and her mum reached up to touch her cheek. The memory twitched and jerked like an old silent film. F.U. leaned in as her mother whispered in her ear.

Then the memory went dark as if the film had run off the reel.

Ursula opened her eyes, gasping in the dark, quiet cell. Next to her, Zee continued to breathe softly.

Ursula's mind raced. What had she just seen?

F.U. had been at the battle. She'd seen it in Bael's memory, and now her own. She'd been at her mum's side when she died. Was this what had sent her running from Mount Acidale? Did she know that King Midac would blame her too? Maybe her mum had told her to run. Those seemed reasonable possibilities. But why did she feel the need to rid herself of her memories? There was something more there she didn't yet understand.

She was just considering whether to revisit the memory when the door burst open. Zee screamed, as Ursula blinked in the light. A figure stood in the doorway: a giant of a man, with shoulders that nearly spanned the doorframe. *Bael?* Ursula squinted.

No, the hair wasn't right, not dark enough.

"I wish to speak to the queen-killer's daughter," Lucius's voice boomed.

CHAPTER 33

$\mathcal{U}$rsula stood slowly. Her eyes still hadn't adjusted to the light. Instinctively, she began to channel fire into her palms.

"I told you, your fire won't hurt me." Lucius grabbed her by the wrist.

He dragged her from the cell, throwing her onto the rough floor of the hall. As she scrambled to her feet, she heard a shout, muffled through four inches of solid oak. Unmistakably Bael's voice.

"Looks like I woke your boyfriend up," said Lucius. "A pity. The condemned deserve their sleep."

Horror slammed her in the gut like a fist. *Condemned?*

Lucius's hand was at her wrist again, pulling her up in a vise-like grip. He yanked her to her feet and began dragging her down the hall. Her pulse raced wildly.

"What do you want with me?" Ursula shouted, struggling against him.

Lucius turned to her, his eyes the color of molten steel. "Obey me, and I'll give you a painless death." He squeezed her wrist so hard that she was sure her bones would snap. She grunted with pain, wishing her fire could do some damage to him. Lucius continued to drag her down the hallway, while the sound of Bael's assault on his cell door grew more distant, until they turned a corner and she could no longer hear it.

She'd expected Lucius to lead her upward, to some sort of bird's-nest-like dragon eyrie. Instead, he led her downward, deeper into the bowels of the ravaged castle.

At last, they pushed through a doorway, into a massive corridor. A giant tube, hewn straight from the bedrock. Ursula shuddered when she saw the walls, deeply gouged by dragons' claws.

They followed the tunnel as it twisted downward. At last, it opened into a familiar cavern. Here, massive dragons rested on tiers of stone, their sides moving in slow breaths as they slept. There was no question that this was Lucius's Mount Acidale warren.

Lucius led Ursula past the sleeping dragons, into a smaller, human-sized corridor.

"Where are you taking me?" she hissed.

"Someplace private, where we can talk."

Ursula glanced at Lucius with surprise. His voice had lost its brutal edge. While it didn't exactly sound kind, it also didn't sound like he planned to eviscerate her the instant he got her alone.

He pushed through a heavy oak door into a living room of sorts, but one that gleamed brightly. Just as she had when stepping from her cell into the hallway, Ursula had to shield her eyes. As her pupils constricted, Ursula gasped with astonishment. Gold filled the room. Gold coins littered the floor like confetti, and bars of bullion lined the walls behind golden armchairs. Solid gold sarcophagi stood against the walls. Even the walls and ceiling were papered with gold leaf.

"You reek of death," said Lucius, reminding her that she still wore the soiled prison uniform. He pointed to a door, covered entirely in gilt, like a museum picture frame where the picture was simply more gold. "There's a shower in there. Clean yourself up. Then we'll talk."

Like in the living room, gold lined every inch of the bathroom. Lucius had even eschewed a porcelain toilet for one made of solid gold. Not that Ursula spent a lot of time judging. She practically tore her dirty clothes off as she made a beeline for the shower. Steam filled the space.

The water was piping hot, but Ursula spent a good ten minutes under the scouring stream, scrubbing at her hair and body with gold-flecked soap. Finally clean, she stepped out into a steam-filled bathroom, toweled her hair dry, and slipped into one of Lucius's robes. Whatever he had in store for her, at least she wasn't dirty.

In the living room, Lucius sat on a gilt chair, Excalibur on his lap.

Ursula frowned. He wore a black shirt and dark navy pants. The only gold on him was a thin chain around his neck.

"Is there a problem?" asked Lucius.

"I was just surprised that you weren't wearing a gold shirt."

Lucius shrugged. "That would be ostentatious."

"Look," said Ursula, "I appreciate the shower, but what do you want with me?"

"I wanted to hear your side of the story."

"My side," she repeated, dumbfounded by this change in his behavior.

Lucius cleared his throat. "Grisial. Please join us."

From between two of the sarcophagi, a door creaked open, and Grisial stepped into the room, her white hair draped over a bright red gown. "Hi, Ursula."

Ursula blinked. "What are you doing here? I thought you escaped."

Grisial smiled. "I thought so, too, but Lucius caught up with me."

"So you're a prisoner as well?"

"No," said Lucius. "Grisial is free to go if she so wishes."

Ursula crossed her arms. "Can you fill me in a little? The last time I saw you two in a room together, you were trying to kill each other. And that was a matter of hours ago."

"We have a complicated history. But you're the one who makes me nervous. If I recall correctly, you disemboweled my friend Dreq," said Lucius solemnly.

"Well, he ate me," Ursula sputtered. "What was I supposed to do?"

"Most humans consider it a great honor to be eaten by a dragon. Dragon bile is said to cleanse the soul of sin and free you of any earthly bonds. If you'd allowed yourself to be digested, you could have lived a glorious afterlife."

Glorious afterlife, my arse. "Right…" said Ursula.

Lucius leaned forward, fixing her with his amber eyes. "Grisial told me your story about getting Excalibur. I'd like you to understand that I spent years as a torturer. I know when people are lying and telling the truth. Tell me. Is it true you spoke to Viviane? That she gave you Excalibur?"

Ursula didn't have any idea what was going on. "You mean the Lady of the Lake?"

Lucius pierced her with his gaze. "I assumed you'd stolen the blade from her."

"No. She gave it to me to fight the Darkling."

Lucius stared at the blade in his lap. From where Ursula stood, she could see the words *put me down* engraved in the steel. "Vivane was my great love. Were it not for this blade, she would not have died," said Lucius softly. Slowly, he raised his eyes from the steel. "Is it also true what you told Grisial about the Darkling?"

"Yes," said Ursula. "Abrax is gathering power as we speak. He says he intends to free mankind, but he only wants to rule them. If he succeeds, he will subjugate the human world, and the magical realms."

Lucius nodded slowly. "I'll help you." Lucius looked from her to the blade. "I'm sorry," he said, "but the blade is mine." He rose, sliding Excalibur back into its sheath.

Lucius was turning toward the door when it burst open. Five guards rushed into the room. They trained their rifles on Ursula.

From behind them, Ursula's grandfather stepped into the room. "The king requests an audience with all three of you."

CHAPTER 34

With the rifles trained on her back, she crossed into the great hall. From his throne, King Midac stared at her. "Why is the prisoner out of her cell? Why are you consorting with her?"

Lucius strode up to the king's throne. "Sir, I believe the girl speaks the truth. That there is an immediate threat to the kingdom."

The king cocked his head, his lip curling. "*I* decide when there is a threat to the kingdom." He rose from his throne, "Am I not the king?"

"Yes, Your Majesty," said Lucius, casting his eyes down.

The king glared at the shifter, then pointed at Grisial. She tossed her white hair over her shoulder in what looked like an act of defiance.

"Who is that?" the king bellowed.

"That is Grisial," said Lucius.

Midac's face blazed with rage. "You captured the White Dragon, and you did not immediately tell me?"

"Your Majesty," said Lucius. "I was in the process of interrogating—"

"It is *my* job to determine the fate of our prisoners," Midac shouted. He pointed a thin finger at Grisial. "Bring her to me."

The guards leveled their rifles at Grisial's head. Slowly, she walked up to the edge of the throne.

"Why did you try to kill me?" growled Midac, rage palpable in his voice.

Ursula was impressed at how genuine Grisial was able to make her smile. "I came to deliver important news. News crucial to the survival of the kingdom. The Darkling—"

"Do not speak of the Darkling!" A vein throbbed on his forehead as Midac yelled, "He does not exist, and even if he did, we are perfectly safe here in Mount Acidale. I have a legion of dragons to protect us. We repelled the last attack, when the shadow demons tried to slaughter us."

This guy has drunk too deeply from the goddess's fires, and he's lost his mind.

Ursula took a step closer to the king. "I have seen the Darkling, and you have too. Here in your kingdom. He was part of the attack that killed the queen. He abducted me from New York to try to force me to join his cause. He is building an army in the Shadow Realm. If he's able to bring them to earth, he will overrun your realm—"

"Who are you to interrupt me?" Emerazel's fire blazed in Midac's eyes. "I am king of this realm. You are but a—" King Midac froze as he looked at her. "Y-you—" he sputtered, his voice quavering. "This girl. I recognize her."

Oh bollocks. Ursula's stomach dropped.

"The queen slayer's daughter. How dare she speak to me with such insolence?" The king's face had gone red, spit flying from his mouth. "Her mother murdered my wife. She was a traitor."

King Midac gestured to Lucius, who dragged Ursula up the steps to his throne. He stepped closer to her, Emerazel's fire streaming from his right hand in great gouts of flame. His eyes burned with insanity, crazy as the gods themselves.

"You will burn for what your mother did," he roared.

Before Ursula could step away, the king grabbed her by the shirt and pulled her toward him. Then he pressed his hand, blazing hellfire, into her face.

Heat and pain exploded into her vision. Midac's palm must have been a thousand degrees as it pressed against the bridge of her nose. She screamed, fighting to escape his grip. Midac held her for what must have been at least a minute, until he dropped her to the marble flagstones.

"No!" Midac gasped. "That is impossible." He stared at her in horror.

"Wh-what?" Ursula stammered, her heart slamming against her ribs.

"Your skin. It didn't burn."

Ursula touched her nose. Her skin felt smooth under her fingertips. His flames hadn't actually burned her.

"Emerazel's flame immolates all flesh. Unless—" Midac's eyes narrowed as he studied her. "Unless the goddess's fire flows in your veins as well."

Ursula began to step away, but the king grabbed her. His fingers wrapped like manacles around her bicep. With a jerk, he tore her shirt open, exposing her collarbone. "Just as I thought. She carved herself." Still gripping her bicep, he drew a small dagger from his belt and held it to her face.

"Remember this?" he asked. The blade was kinked, its golden handle melted.

The same blade she'd seen in her memory. "I don't think so—"

"This was once the athame of infernos. Emerazel's dagger. Only the chosen were allowed to taste its power." Unadulterated rage contorted the king's features. "You stole this from me. You illegally carved yourself. Then you destroyed it." The king lifted the broken blade so its point was inches from her right eye. "You are a thief, with purloined fire in your veins," Midac hissed. "The penalty for this transgression is death."

Lucius moved into the corner of her vision. "Your Majesty, she came to us at her own peril. She has not attempted to harm the kingdom. Death is not an appropriate punishment."

Releasing Ursula, Midac turned to glare at Lucius. His eyes blazed with the heat of Emerazel's infernos, and Ursula finally understood the source of his rage. The goddess's blood filled his veins, her fire driving him mad. Of course—because the gods themselves had lost their minds.

The king jabbed the dagger at Lucius's face, but the shifter dodged it effortlessly. Midac's hands began to glow with hellfire.

"Stay back, dragon," Midac shouted. "Do not forget that you are bound to protect Mount Acidale."

"It is a duty I hold with great honor. Now tell me, Your Majesty," said Lucius. "Was my oath to you or to the kingdom?"

King Midac sputtered, his eyes flashing wildly.

Lucius leaned closer, so that his eyes were on the same level as Midac's. "That's right, Your Majesty. My oath was given long before you were even born. It binds me to the kingdom. To Mount Acidale. Not to a particular king." Releasing Ursula, he grabbed the king by the wrist. "Your

Majesty, the pressure of your job is affecting your judgment. You will take a brief sabbatical from your duties."

"Noooo!" shrieked the king, as Lucius's other hand clamped around his remaining wrist. Emerazel's fire erupted from Midac's fingers, and he tried desperately to burn Lucius.

"Sir," Lucius continued. "May I also remind you that I am a dragon and am immune from Emerazel's fire?" Like a python coiling around its prey, Lucius's arms slowly wrapped around Midac's chest. "Have you ever seen my chambers, Your Majesty? I believe you will find them exceptional. Fully provisioned and decorated most tastefully. A few days in my rooms away from the stress of this court will do wonders for your well-being."

Turning to the entrance of the throne room, Lucius began to drag King Midac from the room.

CHAPTER 35

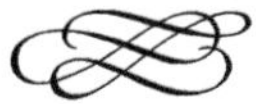

As Lucius disappeared out the door, Ursula and Grisial stared at the guards who surrounded them, rifles pointed at their heads. Had Ursula just witnessed a coup? And if so, were she and Grisial about to take the blame for it?

"At ease, men," shouted a familiar voice. Slowly, the guards lowered their weapons.

Ursula stared as her grandfather stepped in front of the throne. "As you can see, the king is temporarily indisposed, but I am certain he will return in a few days. You may return to your stations."

Frank's order seemed to relax the guards, and they began to creep away from Ursula and Grisial.

When they'd moved out of earshot, Frank stepped down the stairs, nodding at Grisial. "I must say, I am impressed that you managed to find her."

"It wasn't easy," said Ursula.

"No, I imagine not."

"Your granddaughter can be very convincing," said Grisial.

"She always has been."

Ursula wrung her hands together, wondering if she could summon up some of that persuasive ability. "Frank? My friends are still imprisoned. Bael and Zee." She bit her lip. "Any chance you could free them?"

He arched a white eyebrow. "We can talk in my office."

* * *

FRANK SHOWED them to a large room above the main gate to the castle and told them to wait there. Once inside, Ursula sat on a worn leather couch, listening to raindrops pattering against a row of glass-paneled windows. Through the wet panes, Ursula had a misty view of the moat and the cobblestone street.

With a creak, the door to the office opened, and Frank stepped inside, followed by Zee and Bael, each still wearing their burlap prison outfits.

Bael was already in attack-planning mode. "We will need enough swords and shields to arm ten thousand soldiers."

"The armory is well stocked," said Frank.

As Bael nodded a curt approval, Zee caught Ursula's eye. "Are you okay? I thought Lucius was going to kill you."

Ursula shook her head. "He's an arsehole, but he's on our side for now. He's imprisoned King Midac in his quarters."

"He didn't hurt you?" Bael's eyes shone brightly.

"He was an excellent host. Even got a shower and golden robe. More importantly, how are we going to take on Abrax? Are we bringing these swords and armaments into the Shadow Realm?"

"Precisely," said Bael.

"You'll have the support of my soldiers," added Frank. "You'll need them."

Ursula could see the concern etched on Bael's face. A large-scale invasion of the Shadow Realm by an army sworn to the fire goddess had never been on his agenda. Still, he kept his mouth shut. It wasn't as if they had a ton of options.

"Good," she said. "Now that that is settled, can we get Bael and Zee some clothes that don't smell like the bottom of a grave?"

* * *

THIRTY MINUTES LATER, they all sat squished together on Frank's sofa, gripping steaming cups of tea. Bael's and Zee's prison uniforms had been carted off while they showered, and they now wore simple black clothing.

Frank sat on the edge of his desk. "It will take me a few days to notify my men and collect the weaponry."

Bael nodded. "Good. That will give us time to prepare for your arrival." He stood, turning to Ursula and Zee. "We should return to the Grotto. Ursula, will you be able to bring the two of us along with you through the sigil?"

Before Ursula could answer, the door to Frank's office burst open. Lucius filled the doorway, his hair seemingly brighter than normal, and gripping a long, cloth-wrapped object. *Seriously, does he ever knock?*

"Leaving already?" he said, his voice a low growl.

Bael faced Lucius head-on, his broad shoulders larger even than the shifter's. "We must return to the Shadow Realm."

"And you plan to take our soldiers? Leaving Mount Acidale undefended?"

Frank straightened. "Bael and Ursula will need all the men I can round up to fight the Darkling. If we defeat him there, we don't need to worry about him invading here."

"But I do believe you'll be needing my sword," said Lucius, touching the pommel at his belt.

Ursula smiled. "That we do." *I'd rather wield it myself, but I suppose this will have to do.*

Lucius puffed out his chest. "And one more thing. I believe you lost this." He handed her the cloth-wrapped object in his hands.

Ursula took it from him, and her jaw dropped open as she unwrapped it, revealing a gorgeous, gleaming katana. One she knew very well— Honjo, in fact.

"H-how? Where?" she stammered, gripping it by the hilt.

"You stabbed me in the leg with it," said Lucius. "When we first met in the skies above New York. I'm not giving you Excalibur back, but I suppose you can have that one."

Frank put his hand on Ursula's shoulder, staring into her eyes. "Give us a little bit of time to get our forces organized and trained for the Shadow Realm. But we will be there to fight by your side. Make sure you're ready for us."

CHAPTER 36

A cold wind ruffled Ursula's hair as she surveyed Cera's home—or what remained of it. With the roof torn off and the door caved in, it hardly counted as a house anymore. She found no sign of either Kester or Cera. Behind her, Zee and Bael coughed, ridding their lungs of ashes, staring at the ruins.

Dread whispered in Ursula's skull. *What happened while we were gone?* "Cera? Kester?" she called out softly, but silence greeted her. It felt colder than she remembered.

Bael spoke in a low voice. "Draw your blade."

Ursula was already gripping Honjo, and she lifted him defensively.

"Stay where you are." He crossed to the bedroom, pushing through the door and poking his head inside. He returned a moment later, shaking his head.

"Nothing?" asked Ursula.

"Just the burned outline of Emerazel's sigil."

"Kester must have taken Cera out of here," said Zee.

"Where would they have gone?" asked Ursula.

"I don't know," said Bael. "But the mark looked at least a day old."

A chill rippled over Ursula's skin. "Apparently, someone found the Grotto. I think we need to explore."

Already, Ursula was pushing through Cera's front door, Zee and Bael following behind her.

The scene that greeted them was pure devastation. Where once had stood a city of stone houses, now she found a pile of rubble. A few wisps of smoke rose from the ruins, and a deathly quiet enshrouded the place. Ice snaked up Ursula's spine. This was all wrong.

Her chest tightened. "Either Abrax or the lords must have found them."

Something glinted in Bael's hand—an obsidian blade he must have taken from Cera's house. "Let's get to my manor." He pointed to the path out of the grotto. "We can go that way, to the main cave."

Zee looked Bael up and down. "Wait a second. You can't go around looking like that." Immediately, Bael's massive form shimmered, his skin twisting until he no longer resembled a massive demon. Instead, he appeared considerably smaller, with a stooped back and thin wisps of hair sprouting from his chin.

Ursula's eyebrows shot up, but within moments, her skin was shimmering as well, deep wrinkles developing along the tops of her hands. "Let me guess. I look like a hag."

Zee smiled. "I had lots of practice doing hags in the prison. Kept the guards away from my cell." As she spoke, she transformed into a weedy demon with a single green horn that sprouted off-center from the middle of her forehead.

Glamoured to look like the ragged end of Abrax's army, they began to hike up the side of the grotto.

Despite the destruction of the hidden city, the path itself was clear, and they were able to move quickly.

When they reached the boulder blocking the city entrance, it only took a single push from Bael to roll it aside. They slipped out onto the cliffside path in the dim violet light. Ursula shuddered, remembering that the Molok lurked somewhere in the darkness below.

As they stood on the side of the cliff, Bael put his fingers to his lips and whistled. A moment later, the soft, rhythmic sound of bat wings beat the air.

Sotz swooped before them.

"You go on," said Bael. "I'll take Zee with me."

Ursula wasn't sure if Zee's horned demon scowled or if the frown on its lips was simply its natural resting face.

In any case, when Sotz circled back, Ursula leapt onto his back, grabbing his fur with one hand and clutching Honjo with the other. Together, they lifted off into the darkness, the cool air whipping at her hair.

* * *

THEY REACHED BAEL'S MANOR, soaring through a hole in the ravaged wall, where great beams of metal twisted into the darkness like steel innards. Starlight shone through cracked shards of shattered windows, and ragged holes interrupted the sleek walls. Burn marks marred the marble floors.

It had been damaged the last time she'd been here—but it now looked considerably worse.

"Thanks, Sotz." Ursula slid off the bat.

As Sotz launched himself back into the lunar sky, she surveyed the room. The demon lords had ransacked the place, leaving only the half-smashed stones of the mosaic. Scorch marks streaked the floor where some sort of bomb had exploded. An icy breeze blew through the holes in the walls, the familiar creosote smell mixing with the more recent scent of fire.

A screeching of claws turned her head. She watched as the bat carrying Bael and Zee skittered to a stop on the tile.

Bael offered Zee a hand, and she hopped off, looking a little shaken.

"You okay, Zee?"

"I'm fine." She rubbed her green horn as though soothing it. "Just not used to riding these creatures."

"It's a bit of an acquired taste," said Ursula. "But then it's amazing."

Without another word, Zee closed her eyes, pulling the glamour off the three of them.

As he took in his manor, Bael stiffened, his darkening eyes seeming to focus on one of the ravaged upper levels. Ursula followed his gaze to a balcony cloaked in shadows.

"What is it?" asked Ursula.

"There's someone up there," said Bael. "Draw your sword."

Ursula looked at the sword in her hand and inwardly rolled her eyes.

Asking her to draw her sword was clearly some sort of nervous habit of Bael's at this point.

"Who deigns to invade my manor?" Bael bellowed.

Never a fan of stealth, that one.

His voice echoed in the darkness. Then a shadow shifted on the balcony, revealing a familiar silver-haired oneiroi.

"My lord. Is that you?" Cera's voice rang out in the darkness.

"Cera," shouted Bael. "You can stop calling me *my lord.*"

Cera's pale eyes went wide. "Zee, is that you?"

"Yes, it's Zee." said Bael. "Could you send down the cage?"

Ursula was pretty sure she heard Cera softly say "Yes, my lord" as she disappeared into the shadows.

A few moments later, a creaking sound groaned through the manor as the cage-like elevator began to descend. When it reached the floor, they stepped inside, and Bael shut the door behind them. Within moments, the lift began to rise slowly, groaning as it swung from side to side, and they passed one dark, dusty balcony after another. Ursula grabbed the bars with one hand, and the chilly manor air whispered over her skin. She'd once felt so intimidated here. Now, it felt strangely like home—broken walls and all.

Instead of rising all the way to the roof as Ursula was used to, the elevator stopped at Cera's level. The door creaked open onto a small marble platform. Cera stood at the far end, and as soon as the elevator door opened, she rushed forward to give Ursula a hug.

Bael stepped out onto the platform. "It's good to see you again, Cera."

Cera released Ursula, running to hug Zee. "Zee, are you all right? You look skinny. Did the dragons hurt you?"

Zee shook her head. "I'm fine. Where's Kester?"

Cera's muscles stiffened as she released Zee. "There was an attack. Abrax and his golems captured him."

Ursula's stomach sank, worry blooming in her chest. She'd already seen what Abrax had done to him the first time he'd been captured. She couldn't imagine he'd be treated any better now.

CHAPTER 37

Ursula sat next to Bael in his living room—one of the few intact rooms remaining in his manor. Zee sat cross-legged on the floor, while Cera busied herself making tea.

The oneiroi sighed over the steaming tea kettle. "After you all left, Abrax and his golems attacked the grotto. Xarthra led the defense against them, but there simply weren't enough oneiroi to fight back. Abrax's forces are too strong."

"What about her new soldiers?" asked Bael. "The ones who've been drinking her blood?"

Cera shook her head sadly. "All killed in the battle. The rest of the oneiroi are hiding in the mushroom forest. Others are in the deep caverns below the grotto. Abrax is hunting them like animals. That's how he thinks of us, you know."

"Why did you come here?" asked Ursula.

Cera handed her a hot cup of mushroom tea. "Because I knew this is where you'd go first when you returned."

Ursula rubbed a knot in her forehead. "We can train here in your manor. Zee can help to glamour us from prying demon eyes."

Bael nodded. "This is the last place Abrax would look anyway."

Ursula frowned, not understanding. "But your manor is in shambles, and worse, it's completely exposed. The first demon that flies by on a bat will see us."

Zee ran a hand through her short, blonde hair. "I can glamour the exterior, but not indefinitely."

"We'll only need a few days," said Bael.

He stood, his perfect jaw firm. "Cera, do you think you can rendezvous with the remnants of Xarthra's army?"

Cera nodded. "Yes."

Ursula found herself staring at Bael, at his deep golden skin. His dark hair swept over his forehead, and his straight black eyebrows furrowed as he fell deep into thought. Eyelashes dark as the void, and eyes pale as the morning sky over Byblos. Bael had looked this beautiful for ten thousand years. Ten thousand years of perfection.

And if she was going to stay with him, he'd watch her grow old, wither, and die. A cold shudder danced up her spine. She had more immediate concerns than her future mortality, but it chilled her to the bone nonetheless.

* * *

URSULA WOKE TANGLED in the bedsheets, in what might have been morning. It was always hard to tell on the moon. Last night, she'd slept wrapped in Bael's powerful arms, dreaming of Byblos.

When she woke, she found herself alone in his stark, gray room. Starlight streamed through the window, bathing his room in silver.

Hunger drew her out of bed—hunger and the scent of food. Given that it smelled delicious, she knew for certain Bael wasn't cooking.

Wrapping a soft, black robe around her shoulders, she opened the door and walked down the stairs to the kitchen.

Cera knelt over a small stove, stirring something in a pot. "Hungry?" she asked.

"Famished," said Ursula.

"Well, come here, then," said Cera. "It's mushroom stew. Your favorite, if I recall." She ladled a heaping portion into a chipped ceramic mug, then handed it to Ursula. "Drink it. It's good for you."

Ursula took a long sip. The stew was warm, with the same rich mushroom flavor she remembered.

With the stew warming her stomach, she dropped into a chair across from Cera. "I thought you were going to look for survivors."

"I only just returned."

Ursula blinked. "How long have I been asleep?"

"A day at least. Bael said not to disturb you. That your journey to Mount Acidale had exhausted you."

"Where is he?" asked Ursula.

"In the caves, helping find the remnants of Xarthra's army."

"And Zee?"

"On the roof. Glamouring the whole place."

Ursula took a sip of her stew, crossing her legs. It seemed everyone had a role to play.

"You want something to do, don't you?" asked Cera.

"Bingo."

Cera clucked her tongue. "Well, you can't go around just wearing a robe."

"Not a lot of options." Ursula looked down at the bathrobe she'd taken from Lucius's quarters. It was now covered in soot and bat sweat.

"Come with me." Already, Cera was bustling into another room.

Ursula slid her soup onto the counter, then followed Cera into the next room, where a number of baskets and hampers lined the wall. Cera muttered to herself, rummaging about in one of the hampers until she produced a pair of leather pants, a form-fitting black top, and a pair of boots.

Ursula smiled. "Ah. Perfect. I believe I left these behind the last time I was here."

"I thought they might be useful."

"I'm going to grab a shower." She frowned, remembering something Bael had told her the night before. "Bael said the hot water was broken?"

Cera let out a long sigh. "Now that he's decided that we're all on equal footing around here, he insists on doing everything himself, except he doesn't know how." She followed Ursula into the dark-tiled bathroom, then fiddled with the knobs, and steam began to fill the room. "Let me know if it's not warm enough."

Ursula laid her clothes on the tile counter and pulled off her robe. She stepped into the scalding water, watching her skin turn pink under the punishing stream. She grabbed a bar of silver-flecked soap and began scrubbing at her skin.

After a few minutes, she stepped out of the shower, water dripping down her body. After drying off, she pulled on her clothes.

She found no sign of Cera when she crossed back into the living room —just Honjo, sheathed and lying on the sofa. She strapped her sword around her waist, feeling herself again with her blade on her.

From the floor below, voices in the atrium drifted through the air. She crossed to the balcony, catching a glimpse of Bael and a small group of oneiroi, some of them lying on cots, bleeding.

Bael looked up, catching Ursula's eye, his forehead furrowed with concern. "Ursula. Can you help?"

Ursula's pulse raced at the sight of blood, and she ran to the elevator, pulling open the metal door. As the elevator creaked down to the atrium, she wrapped her hands around the bars, staring down at the pitiful scene on the tiled floor.

The closer she got, the worse it seemed. Blood leaked through hastily wrapped bandages, and some of the oneiroi on the litters appeared to be missing limbs.

When the elevator reached the floor, she yanked open the door. "What happened?"

Bael shook his head. "One of Abrax's golems found their hiding spot. These are the survivors. They need to be healed."

Without responding, Ursula crossed to the closest oneiroi. Blood oozed from a deep wound on his scalp, and his eyes held a dazed look. She knelt by his side and began incanting Starkey's Conjuration, the magic tingling over her skin. As she spoke, the man's wounds began to knit together. He didn't speak when she finished, instead staring at her with clear, silver eyes.

Another oneiroi moaned nearby, and she turned to help, the words of Starkey's Conjuration already on her tongue.

Slowly she moved through the group of oneiroi, incanting the spell as quickly as she could, the magic tingling over her body. Bael helped, too, bringing in more wounded oneiroi and directing the process.

By the time she'd finished, her limbs felt completely drained, and the sensation of Emerazel's fire in her veins held a dull pain of its own.

Worry nagged at the back of her mind, and she met Bael's gaze. The golems were ruthless. "We need to fortify the manor. It's only a matter of time before Abrax realizes we're here and sends his golems in."

Beal scrubbed his hand over his mouth. "Already working on it. And I expect there will be more injured survivors." He pointed to a group of oneiroi clustered around a table. "Cera has already set up a food station for survivors."

From the crowd of oneiroi, Cera bustled over to Ursula, thrusting another mug of hot soup into her hands. "You never finished yours. I won't let you starve here."

While Ursula sipped her soup, Bael got to work directing some of the oneiroi to help fortify the manor. She watched him directing one group to fill in holes with rubble, and another to erect scaffolding near a particularly precarious part of the manor's walls. Cera was right. Bael was a natural leader, but she knew it wasn't enough. An army this size made up of injured oneiroi could never defeat Abrax.

Where the hell is Lucius?

CHAPTER 38

$\mathcal{B}$ael and the oneiroi worked for hours, filling in holes and constructing fortifications. Ursula had continued to heal groups of oneiroi as they straggled into the refuge, exhausted and hungry. After a few hours, Zee had wandered down from her perch on the roof. She'd looked exhausted as well, and Ursula had wondered just how much effort she was expending to maintain the glamour on the entire manor.

It wasn't long before Bael was directing people into rooms to sleep. Then, he went out to search for more survivors.

Exhausted, Ursula climbed into his bed on her own. She closed her eyes, mentally reviewing all the possible outcomes of a battle with Abrax. Tonight, as her mind whirred over battle scenarios, the image of her mother's dying face did not haunt her dreams.

Instead, a thunderous bang jolted her from sleep. She flew upright in bed, her heart galloping at the sound. The entire building shook, and her pulse raced. *Abrax?*

Grabbing Honjo, she ran to the balcony, finding the atrium in chaos. One of the scaffolds had been ripped out, and a horde of oneiroi was pouring in through the gap. Dressed in black uniforms, they wielded swords and daggers. Ursula's blood thundered in her ears. *Abrax's army has found us.*

She could hear Bael shouting as she scanned the balcony for a way down. The metal elevator wasn't on her level, and she didn't relish the idea of getting stuck inside it with a pitched battle going on five levels below.

She rushed to find a stairwell, when a door at the far end of the balcony burst open. A pair of golems stepped out—followed by Abrax himself. Like ink in water, dark shadows swirled around him, and his eyes shone like starlight through the gloom. Her stomach dropped at the sight of him.

He shouted, pointing in her direction.

Even with Honjo in her hand, Ursula knew this wasn't a fight she was going to win. Two golems would eviscerate her in moments.

So—the only option was to run. She turned, sprinting over the balcony, only to find that it ended abruptly, torn apart as though by a massive talon. As she neared the end, she realized this was one of the portions of the manor Bael had been trying to repair. Bits of scaffolding spanned the gap three floors below. Her heart slammed against her ribs, and she turned to look back at Abrax.

The incubus had disappeared, but his golems loped toward her with easy movements that belied their speed. She had only seconds to decide what to do, and adrenaline burned through her nerve endings.

Sliding Honjo into her sheath, she crouched at the edge of the broken balcony. A bit of iron bar poked out horizontally into the gap. With her heart in her throat, she gripped it with both hands and swung out into space.

She hung for a moment, suspended above the throng of violence below her. Bodies surged in the small space of the atrium, and oneiroi screamed as they stabbed and bled onto the floor.

Kicking her legs, she swung her body—once, twice, three times.

A golem appeared above her as she leapt onto the balcony below. With a quick glance, she confirmed that the balcony was empty. When the golem's legs swung into view, she slashed at them with Honjo. The blade ripped through bone—or clay, or whatever it was golems were made of. The golem didn't make a sound as its legs fell to the ground. It just silently pulled itself up to the upper balcony.

From the lower balcony, Ursula considered her options. If she could leap about ten feet across, she could make it to an even lower balcony. She should be able to find a way down from there.

Battle fury began humming in her blood. *I can do this.*

Holding Honjo tightly, she sprinted, leaping into the air. Time seemed to slow, and she hung suspended above the drop. Then she was landing, rolling on the rough balcony a full floor lower.

As she clambered to her feet, a thumping sound jolted her, like the whirring of a helicopter's blades. She knew that sound—detested that sound.

Slowly, Abrax rose into view, his black wings beating the air. His eyes blazed with an otherworldly light, and talons had replaced his hands and feet.

Ursula's heart slammed against her ribs, and she turned to run. She sprinted down the dusty balcony, but Abrax swooped behind her. She reached another break in the floor—a second place where Bael's manor had been fractured. This one too far to jump.

"You can't escape me," Abrax hissed from behind her.

With two beats of his wings, he was ahead of her, alighting on the edge of the fractured balcony. The floor shook as he landed on it and began stalking toward her.

Ursula trained Honjo on him, battle rage filling her blood.

"I see you've got your pretty sword back." Abrax prowled closer, his movements eerily smooth. "But you and I both know it's not going to help you."

"I've stabbed you before, demon. And I'll do it again."

"And you've discovered I'm immortal. You cannot kill me. Not even with that lovely piece of steel. Give up now, and your death will be painless."

Abrax prowled closer, and Ursula took another step back, fury igniting in her blood. Below her the battle raged on. She considered jumping over the railing, but she was still four stories from the floor of the atrium, too high to make it.

Fight or flight, Ursula. First, fight.

With a familiar power roiling through her body, she lunged for Abrax. He shifted, and she sliced his wing. She attacked again, striking him between his ribs, and he roared.

"Ursula," he bellowed. "You can't defeat me."

True, but at least she'd hurt him.

Black magic began snapping around him—and that would be her cue to get out of there. *Flight time.*

She turned and ran. From behind her, Abrax lunged forward, his talons raking on the balcony floor. Her heart fell as she saw a golem blocking her path, holding a dagger in each of its hands. *I can only win by trickery.*

She lunged forward, gripping Honjo. She feinted, at the last instant diving right. She flew past the golem, her momentum carrying her over the edge of the balcony and into the abyss.

CHAPTER 39

She had no time to correct her position as she smashed into the scaffolding. An audible crack sounded as her shoulder rammed a piece of wood. Blinding pain lanced through her, and she clawed for purchase on the scaffolding. But her hand wouldn't work properly, and she slipped, plummeting toward the tiled lion mosaic of Bael's atrium.

And yet as she hurtled toward the floor, the night wind whipping through her hair, she felt strangely at home—even in mid fall. Time seemed to slow down. She belonged in the air, in the darkness. As if she had phantom wings, she directed her fall—aiming for one of Abrax's men to cushion her impact.

But before she could slam into him, a pair of strong arms caught her. With a shock of horror, she looked up into Abrax's ice-cold eyes.

"That wasn't very smart," he said coolly. "Almost got yourself killed."

He gripped her hard, his wings thumping the air, and he started to rise. Didn't he know that getting this close to her was dangerous?

Fire kindled in Ursula's blood, and as flames licked about her arms, Abrax's face contorted with pain, his clothing burning. As he began to summon his own icy magic, she slammed Honjo's hilt into his throat. A crack echoed over the atrium. She'd crushed his larynx.

The temperature in the room plummeted, and Abrax dropped her. She began to fall, this time tumbling awkwardly to the floor. She braced for impact when Bael slammed into her with a blur of shadows.

He knocked the breath from her lungs. Instead of splattering on the floor, they crashed onto a balcony. Flat on her back, Ursula groaned, as pain lanced through her injured shoulder. Her chest heaved as she sucked in air.

"Are you all right?" asked Bael.

Ursula grimaced. "That hurt my back. On the plus side, I managed to light Abrax on fire."

"Can you stand?" Bael held out a hand.

Ursula grabbed it with her good hand, and he pulled her up.

"Where's Abrax?" said Ursula, scanning the atrium. She smelled his burned flesh, but found no sign of him. "I crushed his larynx." She smiled darkly. "He won't be able to command his soldiers very well without a voice."

Bael returned her smile. "Beautiful work." He picked up Honjo from the floor and handed it to her. "He flew off after you injured him."

For the first time, Ursula noticed the blood covering Bael's body. "Are you okay?" she asked.

He looked down at himself. "Of course. None of this is mine. We should get out of here. Abrax will be back once he heals himself."

By Bael's side, she crossed to the balcony's railing. Here, they were just one story above the atrium floor, and she peered over the side, staring at the oneiroi battling below them. Abrax's horde had pushed Bael's soldiers back, cramming them near the entrance to his chambers.

Without another word, Bael leapt over the balcony's ledge, landing gracefully on the floor. He spun like a lethal gyre, his sword clearing a circle in the seething mass of oneiroi. Blood misted the air as his blade cut through his enemies.

"Jump. I'll catch you," he yelled.

Ursula rolled her eyes. She didn't need him to catch her. She'd felt something earlier, the first time she was falling—a sense that she belonged in the air, that phantom wings could carry her. Ursula sucked in a breath, then she leapt, carefully directing her flight so she landed next to Bael.

She still gripped Honjo. "Thanks. I'm good."

By Bael's side, she sprang into action, carving her sword into Abrax's oneiroi. Battle fury imbued her body, and she felt herself moving at the speed of a night wind, every footstep falling into the right place, every arc of her sword finding its mark in her enemy's flesh. After Mount Acidale, she understood why. She'd been a warrior once—one of the king's guard. Trained by her mother to fight. The muscle memory, the skill had never left her, and she felt completely herself as she carved her sword into her enemies. They pushed forward, swords clashing with Abrax's men.

A scream pierced the air, and Ursula looked up. Abrax's demonic form appeared above Bael's fortifications. His army surged forward, crashing into Bael's remaining force. Screams and blood filled the air as they fought.

By her side, Bael led the vanguard, fighting with a ferocious brutality. Shadow magic flowed about him like a midnight cloak as his blade carved through oneiroi and golem alike. Ursula moved with nearly the same speed, and she felt a similar dark magic whispering through her body.

More of Abrax's forces poured in through the broken fortifications, but instead of leading them toward a possible exit, Bael led them toward the sheer cliff at the back of the manor—where the black onyx stone stood, protecting the entrance to his secret chambers. When he reached the stone, Bael put his shoulder against it. It rolled to the side.

"Inside," he shouted.

The remaining allied oneiroi surged into the tunnel, and Ursula joined them.

Bael's shout echoed off the wall, followed by a resounding clash of steel. Then, the stone rolled back in front of the entrance. For a moment, the interior of the tunnel was completely pitch black, until an orb sparked in the darkness. The oneiroi cheered reflexively, as light shone on Bael's bloodied face.

CHAPTER 40

Ursula sat on the platform in Bael's chambers, her feet dangling over the abyss. She'd spent the last hour healing the remnants of Bael's force, and fatigue burned through her limbs—even if there hadn't been many people left to heal. Seventeen, in fact, if she included everyone. Less than ten if she included those still capable of fighting.

Her head throbbed.

She tried not to think of the oneiroi who'd died. A woman with short silver hair—one who'd eaten mushroom stew in Bael's living room just the day before—had bled out in the first few minutes after they'd sealed themselves in. Two of the dead oneiroi now staining the floor with blood looked like they'd only just gone through puberty.

But worst of all, Cera and Zee weren't here, and Ursula wouldn't allow herself to imagine the worst. She refused to believe they were among the dead out there.

She sat at the edge of Bael's stalagmite platform, staring into its impenetrable darkness, until she felt Bael's powerful arm wrap around her. His soothing, briny, sandalwood scent enveloped her body, making her muscles relax.

"Are you all right?" he asked quietly.

"I just wish we could look for Cera and Zee. I hate sitting here."

"Zee's glamouring powers are formidable," he said. "I have faith in her ability to disguise herself and Cera well enough that they'd go unnoticed."

"True." She leaned against his shoulder, somewhat reassured.

"Sir," said a quiet voice. A young oneiroi stood next to them. It was difficult to judge an oneiroi's age, but on a human scale, she'd have pegged him as fifteen at best. The boy cleared his throat. "We have a problem in the tunnel."

"They cannot move the stone. The ancient oneiroi glyphs prevent it."

"It's not the stone. It's the cliff face itself. They're digging into it."

Ursula's blood turned to ice. They had no army left. And what the hell had happened to Lucius and her grandfather's reinforcements?

Bael stood, cursing under his breath, and Ursula pushed herself up beside him.

Following him, she walked over the stone bridge that spanned the void, then crossed into the tunnel. The sound of digging echoed through the tunnel even before they reached the stone—a heavy slamming sound, like a jackhammer banging in slow motion.

"Any idea what they're using to make that noise?" asked Ursula.

Bael shook his head. "I don't know, but it sounds big. I don't think the oneiroi are wielding it."

Ursula's mind raced through possibilities. "Maybe Abrax conjured a giant golem."

"Maybe." Bael crouched in the tunnel, a sword in one hand and an orb floating just above the other. "Whatever it is, it can't get in. The wards on this place are too strong."

As if on cue, the hammering sound stopped. The tunnel fell silent, with only the sound of their breath and the beating of their hearts. The onyx stone glimmered in the darkness.

Dread rippled up Ursula's spine. "Something's happening." Slowly, she approached the stone. The air around it flickered and shimmered like sand under a desert sun. She could feel heat on her face.

"Bael. We need to move the boulder."

"What are you talking about.?"

Ursula pressed her hands against the stone. Though the stone was black as a starless sky, putting her hands against it felt like touching Emerazel's inferno. She pushed, and slowly it rolled to the side. Fire licked around its edges, smoke billowing.

"It's me, Ursula!" she shouted.

The flames died down, and when the smoke cleared, she stared at the reptilian head of the Drake.

CHAPTER 41

They sat on the platform near the entrance to Bael's chambers, watching the few remaining oneiroi as they worked to clear the floor of the atrium. Lucius had singlehandedly decimated Abrax's forces with his dragon fire. Ursula tried not to envision how it must have gone down—in the confined space, his flames would have been inescapable, instantly incinerating any oneiroi and golems in his vicinity.

Bael peered at her. "How did you know it was Lucius?"

Ursula looked at him, a bit flummoxed. "Dragons dig their own tunnels, and the noise sounded too—I don't know how to describe it—too practiced. The superheated stone confirmed it, the particular feel and smell of the flames. I knew it had to be Lucius trying to break in."

Lucius brushed ash off his body. "Clever one, isn't she?"

Bael frowned. "But how did you move the boulder? I should be the only one able to move it."

Ursula shook her head. She hadn't really thought about it—she'd just done it. And yet the last time she'd tried to move it, it hadn't budged. "Maybe because Lucius was trying to melt it?"

Bael arched an eyebrow, apparently unconvinced.

Lucius crossed his arms. "So what's the plan?"

"We need to rebuild an army," said Ursula.

Lucius snorted. "That's going to take months, and you have nowhere to do it. Abrax will attack again as soon as he discovers what you're up to. We need to do something immediately. Why do you think I flew all the way here?"

Ursula was about to ask how Lucius was able to fly to the moon, when Bael spoke.

"You're going to help us?"

"Yes," said Lucius. "If Abrax is the Darkling, he needs to be put down." Lucius touched Excalibur at his hip. "You said you needed Excalibur."

"You'll let me wield the blade again?" asked Ursula.

"Don't be ridiculous," Lucius snarled. "I'll fight alongside you."

Bael's dark magic curled around him in wisps. "Lucius, I appreciate your offer, but we cannot accept."

Emerazel's fire flickered in Ursula's veins. "Are you out of your mind? We have a dragon willing to fight on our side. He wields Excalibur, and the prophecy says that only that sword can defeat the Darkling."

Bael shook his head. "The prophecy was made up by an addled egghead of a mage. The only thing accurate about it is that the Darkling exists. That's it. If we're going to defeat Abrax, we can't depend on a legend. We need a proper army. What about Frank's soldiers?"

Lucius pressed his lips into a thin line. "I don't think they're going to make it here any time soon. Many are still loyal to King Midac."

Disappointment welled in Ursula's chest. She'd been counting on those reinforcements. "We can't wait to find out. A sword in the hand is worth a thousand in the…bush. Okay, that's a terrible expression, but my point is—we have Excalibur here now, and it's worth a shot. Or else we need to form an army of the shadow demons here."

Bael stared at her, waiting to hear the rest.

"The lords are as much at odds with Abrax as we are. None of them want him to take over the Shadow Realm. He'd imprison them all in the void."

Bael nodded, mulling this over. "Hothgar would never form an alliance with me. He'd be too threatened by the idea that I was seeking my former position as the Sword of Nyxobas. But if we could get him out of the way…"

A shrill shout from the far side of the manor interrupted them. Lucius reached for Excalibur just as the dark form of a bat flew in through one of the cracks in the walls, carrying two people on his back.

Ursula held up her hand. "Easy, Lucius. He's a friend." Warmth sparked in her chest as she recognized the two riders. "And so are his passengers."

Ursula hurried over to Sotz.

"Ursula!" cried Zee and Cera in unison.

As they slipped off Sotz, Ursula wrapped her two friends in a hug. "I was starting to think the worst. What happened to you two?"

Cera pushed her silver hair off her face. "Zee glamoured us to look hideous, and we escaped among Abrax's forces."

Lucius crossed to them, staring at Zee. "Fae girl. I recognize you." He nodded at Cera. "But who is this tiny one with the sharp teeth?"

Lovely manners on him.

"This is Cera," said Bael. "She's worked for me for a long time."

"You don't remember me?" Cera asked, looking Lucius full in the face. "I was in your warren in New York. Granted, Zee had glamoured me to fit in among the human women. I was taller. Blonde hair."

Lucius's eyes widened. "You were *that* Cera? You kept me entertained with stories about dressmaking mishaps. Patches on clothing that went awry, and something called wardrobe malfunctions."

Ursula blinked. "You were entertained by stories about dressmaking mishaps?"

Lucius lifted his chin. "It's not often that anyone tells me stories." A hush fell over them as Lucius studied the little oneiroi. He bent lower, meeting her gaze. "Cera, would you be willing to give me a tour of this place? I've only just arrived."

Cera nodded. "Of course. And you must be hungry."

Lucius nodded solemnly. "Fighting makes me very hungry."

"I'll fix you something." Cera beckoned him toward the elevator.

"He's not going to eat her, is he?" asked Ursula, a little worried.

Bael spoke in a low rumble. "Cera can fend for herself."

Ursula clamped a hand on Zee's shoulder. "So where did Cera and you go after you escaped?"

"Cera took me down to her home on the crater floor," said Zee. "When we saw Lucius flying toward the manor, she called that bat—"

"Sotz," Ursula corrected.

"Right, she called Sotz, and we flew up to see what was going on." Zee nodded at the ash-covered bodies on the floor of the atrium, wrinkling her nose. "It looks like Lucius helped out, in his own way."

"He saved us," said Ursula. Next to her, Bael grimaced. It was obvious he wasn't thrilled about Lucius's entry into their fight. "And it's a good thing, too, because my ancient demon-warrior over here can't die yet. He still hasn't learned to make a grilled cheese sandwich. Or, like, toast."

Bael's dark magic thickened the air around him. "Lucius was helpful, but we are still going to need an army. He can't defeat the entirety of Nyxobas's legions on his own."

Zee's eyes twinkled with excitement. "You need to see this." She grabbed Ursula's hand and pulled her toward the wall, where a ragged gap overlooked the lunar crater outside.

Ursula sucked in a slow breath, looking out onto the stark landscape, the cool air rushing over her skin. In the city below, oneiroi filled the quiet streets between their stone houses. Silver hair glinted in the starlight, as did a mishmash of blades and weapons in their hands. It took Ursula a few seconds to realize they were marching, in a great flood of bodies, toward the remains of Bael's manor.

Bael spoke from behind her. "The oneiroi are rebelling."

Ursula shouted into the atrium, "We have an army!" Her voice echoed off the walls.

"Cera!" called Bael. "Lucius! We're going to parlay with the oneiroi from the villages."

Around the room, the heads of the few remaining oneiroi popped up. Cera and Lucius appeared from one of the upstairs rooms.

What had they been doing up there?

Bael put his finger to his lips and whistled. Moments later, Sotz swooped in through the gap in the walls and landed on the atrium floor.

Ursula slid onto Sotz's back, and Bael climbed on behind her. With a few beats of Sotz's wings, they launched through the gap in the wall, soaring over the lunar crater. Ursula gripped tightly to Sotz's fur as they zoomed above the crowd of oneiroi. From the corner of her eye, she spotted a flash of bright red—Lucius had shifted, and he was flying alongside them. Of course he wouldn't miss an opportunity to be the center of attention.

They plunged toward the biggest crowd of oneiroi, a thousand feet below at the base of the manor. The lunar wind whipped at Ursula's hair as they flew, and they landed on an enormous boulder.

Bael climbed off Sotz, and Ursula joined him.

He stepped forward, starlight washing over his golden skin. "For those who do not know me, I am Bael, Lord of Albelda, and this is my betrothed, Ursula of Mount Acidale. We bring grave tidings."

He looked at Ursula, and she surmised she was supposed to take over. "The Darkling lives among you. You know him as Lord Abrax, and he wants to rule instead of the seven gods."

The crowd murmured below her.

Bael's eyes shone as he spoke. "Abrax has forsaken his sacred pact with his father, Nyxobas. He now schemes to overthrow the gods themselves. And worse, he has poisoned the council of the demon lords with lies and falsehoods."

The crowd of oneiroi watched them silently now, their eyes focused entirely on Bael. Given the ease with which he could control a crowd's attention, Ursula could see why Nyxobas had chosen him to be his second-in-command. He was a born leader.

Or maybe the giant red dragon on the boulder behind him just scared the ever-loving shit out of them.

"But all is not lost," Bael continued. "The lords themselves are in chaos, and that means they are weak. Their legions are inactive, their manors unguarded. Abrax is powerful, but if we attack the lords, we can appropriate their legions and build an army large enough to defeat Abrax. Together, we can defeat the Darkling."

The crowd of oneiroi cheered again, but when they fell silent, a high-pitched voice keened over the crowd, screaming about the dragon. The fear in the woman's voice was palpable.

Ursula crossed back to Lucius and ran her hand over the scales on his neck. "He looks terrifying and he breathes fire, but he is not our enemy. He saved us in Bael's manor, saved the other oneiroi. Lucius, the Drake of Mount Acidale, will fight on our side."

"He'll incinerate our enemies," added Bael.

As if on cue, the Drake reared back his head and breathed a stream of flame into the dark sky. It arced across the caldera like the tail of a comet.

A deathly silence fell over the crowd for a moment. A pale, pinkish light had begun to tinge the sky—the first signs of the sun rising after weeks of darkness.

All at once, the crowd erupted with cheers, shouting and waving their weapons in the air.

Bael raised his hands to quiet them. "Our task is simple. We will take Hothgar's manor. If he falls, the rest of the demon lords will join us." Bael raised his sword. "For an oneiroi to attack a demon lord is a death sentence. If you will help me, I will grant you your freedom as Sword of Nyxobas."

At these words, the crowd went berserk, screaming and surging forward. They chanted Bael's and Ursula's names like mantras, and a shiver rippled over Ursula's skin at the weight of their responsibility.

CHAPTER 42

Three hours later, the slowly rising sun sent rivulets of sweat trickling down Ursula's neck, and her legs burned with tiredness as they reached Hothgar's manor. By Bael's side, she marched at the front of the oneiroi rebels.

Hothgar's manor looked completely impenetrable—a fortress of steel and stone that clung to the cliff face a thousand feet above them. Still, they had a dragon on their side, at least, and they'd formulated a plan on their march.

When they reached the base of the manor, Bael climbed another boulder to address the crowd, holding out his hand for Ursula to join him. Under the slanted rays of the rising sun, Ursula looked out over the oneiroi horde.

"We will commence our attack in five minutes," Bael's voice boomed over the crowd. "Those of you who own bats should call them. Pull one of your brothers or sisters on the back if there is room. Do not worry about Hothgar's forces." He looked at Ursula, indicating she should go on.

"Lucius will protect us as we breach the manor's walls," she announced. "Once inside, fight like hell." *Fight like hell* was about the extent of their plan.

Bael's bat swooped lower, and Bael slid onto his back. Sotz was next, swooping lower, and Ursula climbed on, gripping his fur. She beckoned another oneiroi fighter on behind her, then tightened her thighs around Sotz. He lifted off into the air.

Soaring above the horde, with the lunar wind in her hair, Ursula directed Sotz around in a wide arc. As she did, she surveyed the oneiroi below her, leaping onto their bats. With her knees, she directed Sotz toward the manor, just as Lucius was blasting an enormous hole in the walls, shearing metal with the intense heat of his flames.

Sotz's wings beat the air, and they rose higher, toward Hothgar's manor. Around them, scores of lunar bats swarmed, each packed with two or three oneiroi. They clutched all types of weapons—swords, spears, and outlawed stone daggers with blades sharp enough to cut through rock. Ursula's limbs trembled with a battle fury as ancient as man, her heart pounding like a war drum.

As she neared the manor on Sotz's back, Ursula's adrenaline surged. Thick smoke bloomed from a hole, and oneiroi began streaming in. With a gentle nudge, Ursula directed Sotz toward the opening. Inside, the smaller oneiroi rebels clashed with larger shadow demons. With her blood racing, Ursula swooped down to land amidst the clashing of steel, the screaming of warriors. Somehow, she belonged in battle. As she leapt to the floor, she drew Honjo.

A massive demon lunged for her, his head painted blue and shaved as smooth as a river stone. In one hand, he held an iron blade with a nasty serrated edge. "I will feast on your entrails, bitch."

He launched his sword hard at Ursula's head, but Ursula swung, parrying. Sparks flew in the smoky air as her sword clashed against his.

Blue Head was rearing back for a second strike when a shadowy power surged in Ursula's body, moving through her like a night wind. She drove her sword up into his chest, then ripped it out again, watching the monster fall to the ground.

That was when she noticed Bael standing over him, staring at her. "How did you learn to fight like that?"

"My mother taught me."

Bael narrowed his eyes. "There's more to it than that. Sometimes, you move like an ancient warrior."

Ursula shrugged. "No idea."

A shout interrupted them, and the thumping of demon wings. Hothgar soared above them, shifted into a fully demonic form. His ivory horns gleamed in the rays of sunlight, and a downy fur covered his wings, giving them an almost feathery appearance. He carried a long spear, and he opened his mouth to screech, the sound curdling Ursula's blood. He waved his spear in a complex set of patterns, and shadowy magic gathered around its tip.

"Hothgar," roared Bael. "How good to see you again."

Hothgar fired a bolt of shadows in their direction, but Bael blocked it with his sword.

A movement sounded behind Ursula, and she whirled, her sword ready. She caught a demon in the gut, nearly carving him in two. Her blood roared in her ears at the crimson arc that spewed from him. She glanced up at Hothgar, who twirled his spear, magic crackling at its tip.

"Stop playing with your spear, and come down and fight us," said Ursula.

Hothgar's response was to unleash a bolt of shadows from his spear, and they tore through the air in her direction. She dove to the side, and Hothgar's magic shattered the marble floor by her side.

Hothgar hovered above them, his downy wings thumping in the air. Ursula's blood boiled as she looked up at him. She needed to lure him closer, within sword's range, so she could actually fight him. As she tried to think of a way to bait him down, an enormous crash sounded behind her, and she pivoted. Lucius's draconic head slipped through a new hole in the wall, his red eyes flashing.

"Oh, Hothgar," Ursula shouted, all innocence. "I forgot to mention that I've made some new friends."

The sound of shearing steel pierced the air, and the floor of the manor shook as Lucius pushed his way into the atrium.

Hothgar turned, flying away from the new threat and swinging his spear frantically. He unleashed bolts of shadows at Lucius, but the magic seemed to have no effect, bouncing off the dragon's ruby scales as if they were made of mirrors.

Fast as a viper, Lucius struck. With a crunch, his teeth snapped onto one of Hothgar's wings. He swung the demon violently, like a terrier with a rat. Hothgar screamed, and the sound of breaking bones filled the air. For a moment, she thought the Drake would devour him, but when Hothgar fell still, Lucius dropped him. Ursula winced as Hothgar slammed into the atrium floor with an audible crunch.

"Your lord is defeated," shouted Bael at Hothgar's remaining forces.

"You have two choices: drop your weapons," Ursula cried out. "Or feed our dragon with your bodies."

Around them, swords slammed against the floor as shadow demons rushed to drop them.

Bael raised his sword and boomed, "If you are a demon, surrender yourself, and I will show you mercy. If you are oneiroi, I ask you this: join us and fight for your freedom. It is time to take back your rightful place on this planet. It's time for you to stop living as slaves."

A cheer erupted in the hall, the oneiroi raising their fists. When Ursula looked at the demons, she found their eyes burning with anger. And yet, each one knelt, their fists held together as they allowed themselves to be manacled.

But Ursula's gaze moved back to Hothgar, his body spilling blood onto the floor. An ancient demon like him wouldn't die easily. When she noticed his leg twitch, she ran to him, her sword drawn. She stood over his prone body, his blood staining the marble. His legs lay shattered and one of his arms had been torn clean off, but her gaze homed in on the slow rise and fall of his chest.

"Bitch," he growled when he saw Ursula.

A burst of dark shadow magic from Hothgar's body knocked Ursula backward, and she slammed down hard on the floor. Reeling from the impact, she leapt up again, finding Hothgar standing over her. *The wings.* To make him mortal, she needed to go for the wings.

"I will have my vengeance," Hothgar roared, his downy wings spreading out behind him. "Nyxobas's magic will destroy you."

A dark battle fury surged in Ursula's blood, and she lunged swiftly behind Hothgar. Over his wings, her gaze met Bael's. He'd had the same idea, and together they brought down their swords hard through Hothgar's wings. Blood sprayed over Ursula, and Hothgar's back arched. He shrieked toward the ceiling, then fell to his knees.

Ursula raised her sword. "Hothgar is defeated."

The crowd cheered, and a small group of oneiroi grabbed hold of Hothgar, dragging him away as his blood streaked the floor. He was shrieking at her, at Bael, at everyone around him. But his wings now lay as dusty, gossamer scraps on the floor, and he was no longer a threat.

A heavy hand pressed on her shoulder. "To the winner go the spoils," Lucius's voice rumbled in her ear.

Is he talking about the wings? She could hardly think clearly over the wild, excited cheers of the oneiroi.

Ursula met Bael's gaze. "What happens to the wings?"

He looked surprised. "The wings are Hothgar's."

"So you're not going to use them?"

Bael inhaled sharply, his lip curling with disgust. "Each lord's wings are given to him by Nyxobas himself. Hothgar's wings are powerful, but only the wings Nyxobas gave me himself will ever touch my skin."

* * *

AT THE GAPING hole in Hothgar's manor, Ursula was just preparing to whistle for Sotz when a woman's scream ripped through the air. She whirled, her gaze landing on a balcony above them. A pair of oneiroi were pulling a woman with long blonde hair onto a balcony.

"Help!" she shrieked, then elbowed one of the oneiroi in the face. Freeing herself, she ran to the balcony, peering over the ledge.

"Ursula? Is that you?" Hothgar's wife—an enormous woman with platinum braids Ursula knew as The Viking—turned and punched an oneiroi coming up behind her. "Don't touch me. I'm with Ursula."

"It's okay," Ursula shouted. "I know her."

As some of the oneiroi streamed back out through the gap in the manor, Hothgar's wife joined Ursula and Bael on the atrium floor.

Her platinum braids draped over her long black gown. "Where is my husband?"

Ursula cleared her throat. "Alive, but we took his wings. He's imprisoned."

The Viking snorted. "Serves him right. This is a man who animated dolls to worship his manhood. How can I help?"

Ursula shook her head. "We don't need help, but thank you. If I heal his wounds using magic, Hothgar will never get his wings back. He'll live, but he'll no longer be Sword of Nyxobas."

And with a quick glance at Bael, Ursula set off to heal the man who'd called her *bitch.*

CHAPTER 43

Flanked by Lucius and Bael, Ursula stared up at Abrax's manor. Behind them, the hastily constructed army camped out, waiting for their next command.

Abrax's black monolith towered over them, its windows replaced with an undulating black magic that shimmered in the sunlight. It had been three days since the attack on Hothgar's manor, and the forces of two more lords had joined their alliance. But it seemed attacking the manor of a demigod wasn't as easy as an attack on the manor of a regular lord. Nyxobas's magic flowed in Abrax's veins, and he was no ordinary shadow demon.

So far, the shimmering magic had repelled every attack, even Lucius's fire. Worse, Abrax's soldiers launched black magic missiles at them if they came too close.

Lucius stood by her side, arms folded and red hair gleaming in the sunlight. "Maybe we can distract them long enough to tear a hole."

Bael squinted in the sunlight. "Abrax's manor is well fortified, but if we focus our forces on a single point, maybe we could break through."

Ursula looked between the two men. "That's just what he wants us to do. He'll tear our army to pieces."

Bael shook his head. "That's the only way inside. The crater will run with blood, but we'll breach his walls."

"The cost is too high," said Ursula. Her fingers tightened into fists as she racked her brain for another way. "Bael, do you know if all the manors in the cliff have a secret entrance like yours?"

"What do you mean?" he asked.

"Abrax has a tunnel in his manor that leads to a room constructed entirely of shadow crystal. But there was a second tunnel that Abrax had blocked. Do you think that could lead to the mushroom forest?"

"It's possible," said Bael. "We can certainly look." He held his fingers to his lips and unleashed an ear-piercing whistle.

From the bright lunar sky, two bats swooped lower, landing between Bael and Ursula.

Ursula hopped onto Sotz's back and whispered in his ear. He scrambled forward, then launched himself off the edge of the cliff. Two strong beats of his wings sent them rising into the thin lunar air, and Bael soared into the sky behind her.

A deep thrumming rumbled through her gut, like the sound of distant thunder. In his dragon form, Lucius soared next to them. His red scales gleamed with the promise of fire, but it was the small person perched on his neck that caught Ursula's eye. Cera smiled over at them.

Ursula's stomach tightened. *That's...unexpected.*

Bael turned in the air, soaring for a crevasse in the cliff face, and Ursula flew in after them.

Darkness enveloped them, until the glow of the mushroom forest drew the world back into focus. Ahead of her, Bael banked hard, directing his bat along the cavern wall. They skimmed above the mushroom caps, and Ursula caught a few glimpses of the carnivorous caterpillars that lived among them. She shivered, remembering the sharpness of their teeth.

"There!" shouted Cera, pointing to the wall of the cave.

Ursula followed Cera's outstretched finger to a pitch-black rock high on the cavern wall. Using her knees, Ursula directed Sotz in a tight turn, to just above the rock. Close up, it looked nearly identical to the one in Bael's manor. But unlike the other obsidian stone, no path led to the rock. It sat perched alone on a terrifyingly narrow ledge that overlooked the cliff.

"I think this might be it," Ursula called out.

As Sotz cut back for another pass, Bael leapt from his bat, landing effortlessly on the narrow ledge. Sotz banked his wings, and Ursula soared lower. They glided toward Bael, and her stomach fluttered at the idea of landing on the tiny ledge.

"Jump!" shouted Bael.

With her heart in her throat, Ursula leapt. Her stomach plummeted, until Bael's powerful arms wrapped around her, catching her on the cliff's edge.

"Nice jump," he said quietly.

"Thanks." Ursula's pulse was racing out of control.

Wings thumped the air as Cera and Lucius approached, then Cera leapt through the air onto the narrow ledge. Grinning, she landed on the ledge next to Bael, dirt clouding around her feet. As she stood, Lucius circled around, heading toward them. Ursula tensed. There was no way a dragon would fit on the ledge.

She backed up against the cliff wall, staring at Lucius as he transformed in midair. His massive wings shrank, scales receding. Red hair erupted again from his scalp. He landed next to Cera with a heavy *thunk*.

"So is this it?" he asked, without blinking an eye.

Bael heaved his body against the boulder. Shadow magic shimmered, and it rolled to the side, revealing the dark mouth of a tunnel. Bael muttered in Angelic, and a glowing orb appeared above them.

His footsteps crunched over the path, and the others followed him. Ursula drew Honjo as she walked, staring at the amber light that glowed over runes and glyphs inscribed in the walls. An ancient oneiroi tunnel. In here, the air seemed to coat her tongue with a stale dust.

They walked for ten minutes in the darkness, with the orb light wavering over the walls. In here, Ursula found herself relaxing, as if she were at home. The darkness and the narrowness of the corridor felt almost protective. She was tracing her fingers along one of the carved glyphs when she nearly bumped into Bael's back.

He'd stopped, now staring at something in front of them.

"What is it?" asked Ursula.

"A cave-in, I think." With a flick of his wrist, he directed the orb higher. Its dim light illuminated a jumble of enormous rocks and stone that blocked their path, crammed up to the tunnel's ceiling.

"Can we dig through it?" asked Ursula.

Bael's brow furrowed. "We have no idea how deep it goes."

Lucius stepped into the light. "I can dig through. No problem."

Ursula waved at the narrow walls. "There's hardly any room for you to transform. What if you used Excalibur to melt the rocks?"

Luciius scratched his cheek. "Excalibur doesn't work that way for me. It allows me to breathe fire, but I can't turn it into a flaming sword."

"I can do that," said Ursula.

Lucius took a step back, gripping his hilt protectively. "No."

Cera nudged him gently. "You can trust her, Lucius. Let her try it."

Lucius's frown deepened, giving him the appearance of a petulant, overgrown child. "The sword is mine."

"Lucius," said Cera more sharply. "We're in a confined tunnel. She's not exactly going anywhere."

Lucius sighed as he slowly drew Excalibur from its sheath. He turned it so the pommel faced her, handing it over.

Ursula lifted the ancient blade, and its power seemed to hum through her blood. She closed her eyes, exhaling. It felt good to hold Excalibur again.

In the dim light of the tunnel, the steel seemed to shimmer with an internal light. *Imagine how it would feel to wield this in battle.* She would be an avenging goddess. Flame would bloom from the blade in an endless stream as she carved enemies into burning piles of limbs. She found herself smiling at the blade, turning it over in her hands.

Lucius cleared his throat. "You said you could melt the rocks."

"Right, of course. I wasn't just…having disturbing and violent fantasies, if that's what you think." Ursula motioned for Bael to step aside, and she walked up to the rock. Closing her eyes, she summoned Emerazel's fire, and it burned through her limbs, her bones. She felt the delicious lick of flames moving along her arms, snaking down to the sword's hilt. The steel sucked hungrily, drawing Emerazel's fire from her as if it were quenching an insatiable thirst. When she opened her eyes again, she was staring at ten feet of incandescent sword billowing out before her. The scent of burning hair filled the air around her as her eyebrows singed from the heat.

She pressed forward, pointing the blade at the wall of rubble. She cut the blade through the rock, and Excalibur sliced through the stone like a hot razor through butter. She cut the blade sharply, over and over, melting rock, clearing the way.

At last, molten rock slid down toward her feet, and a new tunnel appeared in front of her.

"Good," said Lucius from behind her. "You've cleared the way. Now return my sword."

Ursula turned, fire still licking along Excalibur. The blade hummed in her hands, hot and lethal. The Lady of the Lake had been right. This blade could defeat Abrax, and she didn't want to give it up.

"Put the sword down," said Lucius, his eyes blazing. "I won't ask you again."

Ursula stared at Lucius, with his broad shoulders and shock of red hair that looked like a lit match. There was something about him that pissed her off.

"Ursula!" Cera cried, her eyes flashing. "Give him the sword back. You *promised* to return it." Dodging Excalibur's flames, Cera thrust the hilt of Honjo at Ursula. "*This* is your sword. Honjo, remember? If you give us Excalibur, I'll give you Honjo."

Ursula curled her lip in a snarl. It was true—she *had* promised to return the blade, and she wasn't going to slaughter everyone in here to keep it. She sucked in a sharp breath, letting the flames die down. Excalibur went cold, and Ursula lowered the blade to the floor.

It had hardly touched the stone before Lucius snatched it back. Without looking at her, he began inspecting the blade.

"Sorry," she mumbled. "But it belongs with me."

Lucius didn't answer as he ran a finger along the edge of the sword, checking for nicks.

Cera thrust Honjo into Ursula's hand. "That was good work."

In the narrow tunnel, Bael pushed past her, his light illuminating the space. With the rubble cleared, the tunnel seemed to continue on until it reached an intersection with another passage.

"Bael." Ursula stepped in beside him. "I know this place. That tunnel leads to Abrax's manor."

Bael's eyes gleamed in the dim light. "Good. Then our new goal is to break open one of his walls. Are you up for it, Lucius?"

The dragon nodded. "As long as there's enough room for me to transform, I'll happily tear this manor apart."

Their footfalls echoed off the tunnel walls. When they reached the intersecting tunnel, Bael extinguished his light. They crept into the new tunnel, treading lightly on the rough gravel.

Bael and Lucius slid through the opening into Abrax's manor first, moving swiftly ahead of Ursula. She paused for a moment at the opening, gazing into the dark space. When her eyes adjusted, she could see the scaffolding that still stood around the entrance to the tunnel. Within the atrium, she could see that a metallic barrier covered the windows.

Her stomach dropped. Within the atrium, there was no sign of either Bael or Lucius.

Something is wrong.

She started to call a warning to Cera, but inky magic entangled her limbs, snaking around her arms and legs like boa constrictors. Abrax stepped out from the shadows in a corner of the room. *Oh, balls.*

His hands were in his pockets, a stupid smirk on his face. "Well, fancy running into you again."

Ursula struggled against the bonds of magic, trying to maintain a grip on her sword. Her limbs were completely immobilized. "What's going on?"

His footfalls clacked over the marble floor. "Did you think I would leave the rear entrance guarded only by a pile of stone? I'm the son of Nyxobas. I'm a demigod. I'm not an idiot. Wards screamed in my quarters as soon as you stepped into the tunnel." Abrax prowled closer, his icy eyes shining with a wicked glee. "You must be wondering what happened to your big strong friends."

Grabbing her by her collar, he lifted her so she faced the opposite wall. Two bodies lay on the floor.

Ursula's blood roared in her ears. "Did you kill them?" Her own voice sounded strangely distant.

"Not yet. What would be the fun in killing them without an audience?"

He nodded into the atrium, and a pair of golems stepped out of the shadows. Rage and panic surged in Ursula's chest, and she tried to jerk her limbs against the bonds of shadow magic. But all she could do was stare on as the silent automatons advanced on Bael and Lucius.

"Don't worry. They're not going to die just yet." Abrax lifted his chin. "Bring them to me," he commanded the golems.

The golems dragged Lucius and Bael over the floor, their bodies wrapped in shadow magic, limbs struggling against the constraints. Despite the immense power of these men, Abrax's bonds held tight.

Abrax flicked his fingers, and the golems began to kick Bael's and Lucius's supine bodies.

"Stop it, you talon-handed fuckstick," Ursula shouted.

Abrax lifted a hand, signaling that the beating should stop. "Manners, my dear. A follower of Nyxobas is never uncouth." He paused, cocking his head like a bird. "But of course you are all vile, debased creatures." He crossed to Bael and jabbed at his ribs with his toe. "This one allows his servants to call him by name." He moved to Lucius. "And this one beds the oneiroi. Vile."

Lucius's eyes flashed with rage, but he couldn't speak with the shadow bonds clamped over his mouth.

Ursula's eyes strained as she scanned the shadows. *Where is Cera?*

Abrax's pale gaze turned on her. "So which one should I kill first?"

"N-no," Ursula sputtered. "No."

"No?" Abrax parroted. "That's not an answer to my question, I'm afraid."

"Don't kill them."

"Silly Ursula! That wasn't an option. I am going to kill them. You get to choose who dies first. Those are your options."

Ursula stared mutely. She wasn't going to play his game.

Abrax sighed, as though the whole situation were taxing for him. "Fine. I'll do it myself." He drew a long, thin blade from a sheath on his hip. A wave of horror slammed into Ursula, and she opened her mouth in a silent scream as Abrax drove it into Bael's shoulder.

"Stop!" shouted Ursula.

Abrax drew out the blade. Blood gleamed on the steel. "But the fun is only just getting started."

Ursula's heart slammed against her ribs. "What do you want?" Her voice echoed off the ceiling.

Abrax turned to her with a small smile. "You know what I want. I want you to join me. Fight with me. Rule with me."

"Why me?"

Abrax's eyes pierced her. "Because untapped power lives inside you, and I want it."

"If I join you, will you release them?"

"Of course," said Abrax. "They will be free to go." His smile was a rictus grin.

Ursula glanced at Bael, his blood pouring over the floor. She couldn't simply stand here and watch him die. Grief ripped through her mind. This was it, wasn't it? This was the end. She just wanted to know that Bael would make it out alive.

"All right," she said slowly. "I'll join you, on the condition that you release my friends."

Abrax's eyebrows rose slightly. "You know, I had always taken you for a fool, too devoted to your earthly desires to comprehend the full magnitude of my offer. But I'm heartened that you seem to be learning. When I consume your soul, you will live forever. Eternal life, Ursula, is a glorious gift."

Abrax stroked her cheek, and bile rose in her throat. Already, the incubus's dark power was washing over her. Even as the bonds that wrapped around her loosened, his icy magic slid over her skin, skimming her body.

"I thought you hated the taste of my soul."

Abrax's eyes shone in semidarkness. "Yes, but it will be only a momentary inconvenience."

He leaned in closer to her, his lips hovering just above hers. The bonds of his inky magic slipped off her, and yet she was still completely immobilized by him, her body electrified by his magic. She was drawn to him and repulsed by him at the same time, completely transfixed.

Her pulse raced, and she tried to remember what her plan was. Did she have a plan? No—her only plan had been to stop Abrax from killing Bael. Now, Abrax had her completely enthralled with his incubus magic, and it curled around her ribs in seductive tendrils. She felt as if silk had wrapped around her body, until she didn't want to move. He wasn't pressing his lips against hers, but he was close enough that his magic washed over her all the same.

A sound nagged at the edge of her consciousness.

Abrax's magic still enthralled her, but an insistent sound, like a klaxon, hammered at the back of her mind.

"Ursula!" It took her a moment to recognize her own name.

She opened her eyes. Abrax's face hovered over hers, his eyes closed. A stream of golden magic flowed from her mouth into his. But she read something on his features—something an incubus wasn't supposed to display.

Pure, utter disgust.

"Ursula!" Cera stood near the bodies of Bael and Lucius, her sharp teeth flashing. "Catch this!" she shouted, throwing something at Ursula. The object seemed to move in slow motion as it arced through the air toward her. Light refracted off a blade, a jeweled pommel. Excalibur.

Drawing on the last of her strength, Ursula lunged for the sword, grabbing it by the hilt. Shadow magic poured from Abrax's body, but she sliced through it with the blade.

The connection severed. Abrax's eyes burst open. Staring at the blade in Ursula's hand, he roared, "I offered you immortality, and still you try to kill me? So you will sicken and die, like all the other peasants and mortals. Your flesh will grow old and decay. Is that what you want?" His face cracked into a wicked grin, and his eyes flashed a deep gold.

She carved the blade through the air, and it felt like a perfect extension of her. But she couldn't summon Emerazel's fire, couldn't get the sword to burn like it had before. *That is a problem.*

Abrax's eyes danced with amusement. "Your fire courses in my veins now, so I might as well kill you."

Ursula's muscles tensed, and her fingers clenched around Excalibur's hilt. She raised the sword. "Abrax. Have you ever encountered Excalibur? It's mentioned in the Darkling prophecy."

Abrax snarled, and the sound rumbled through her bones. With a cracking and lurching of his body, he began to transform. Wings sprouted from his back, and talons curled from his feet.

Ursula gripped the sword tightly, desperately trying to summon her fire magic. Abrax lunged for her, and she swung, the sword's steel deflecting his raking claws. Rage simmered in her body, and she slashed at the incubus, driving him back.

Distantly, she was aware of the sound of Cera screaming. And when she turned her head, her heart stopped. Golems stood over Bael and Lucius—and one of the creatures was driving a blade into Bael's back.

Ursula's world tilted. She was hardly aware of her own screaming.

Without his wings, Bael was mortal.

"Too late." A gleeful, sing-song declaration from Abrax.

Ice-cold fury slid through Ursula's veins, and she raced for the golems as fleet as the night wind. With speed she didn't realize she possessed, she sliced through their bodies, then spun to face the demon.

A wicked smile, arms crossed over his chest, leathery wings rising above him like a funeral shroud. "Maybe you shouldn't have betrayed me."

Ursula pointed Excalibur at his chest, her arm trembling with a simmering fury.

Abrax sighed. "You and I both know you're drained. You have no fire left to fight me." He shook his head. "I'd been thinking about killing you, but now I think I might just let you live. So you can feel pain in your heart until your sad little mortal body withers and dies."

That was what Bael had worried about. Watching her grow old while he remained in his prime. And now he was dead. Something cracked within Ursula, and hot wrath erupted in her body.

The last dregs of Emerazel's power burned through her veins, flowing into Excalibur. Fire leapt from the blade, forming a massive sword of flame.

She lunged forward, and it pierced Abrax's chest. He moaned, falling to the tiles, clutching his ribs. Pure rage consumed Ursula as she stalked over to him, flames flickering around the tip of the blade.

"You filthy bitch," Abrax moaned.

"Still had some fire left. You really should have drained all of it." Ursula pointed Excalibur at Abrax's throat.

"N-no—" sputtered Abrax as he frantically tried to get away. His legs didn't seem to be working properly, and blood smeared the tiles under him.

Ursula pinned his throat with her blade. "You said you didn't believe the prophecy. Was that a lie?"

Abrax's eyes flashed with terror. "I will give you anything you want. Money, power..."

Hot anger ripped through her mind. "You just took from me the only thing I want." She slashed the flaming blade downward, opening up another deep wound in his chest. The smell of burning flesh darkened the air.

Abrax's back arched, and he writhed in agony. "Wait! Wait!" Frantically, he dug into his pockets until he pulled out a wallet between his fingers.

"You think you can buy me?" Ursula snarled.

"It's not money," Abrax rasped. "Wings."

"Wings," Ursula repeated, as understanding began to dawn.

"If you want to save him, you can use these." Abrax cracked open the billfold, giving Ursula a view. Folded inside were two golden wings that glowed with an otherworldly light. "But first you need to be a good hound and fetch." He threw the billfold across the room.

"Pull your magic off him," Ursula growled, her blade piercing his skin.

The inky magic receded from Bael's body. Then Ursula slashed at Abrax's throat, cutting through his jugular, a gurgling noise rising from the wound. But her attention was already elsewhere.

Ursula stared at the billfold on the marble floor. Bael's wings, the source of his immortality, rested twenty feet away. Dropping Excalibur, Ursula sprinted for them, hope blooming in her heart.

CHAPTER 44

She snatched the billfold from where it lay on the floor, then sprinted to Bael.

"Cera!" shouted Ursula as she ran. "I'm going to need your help. I have his wings."

"Flip him over!" Cera shrieked. She ran over to where Bael lay and grabbed the wallet from Ursula's hands.

As Cera carefully withdrew the wings, Ursula turned to Bael's still body. His chest wasn't moving. Could she really still save him? Grunting and using all her strength, she pushed Bael's body over, so he lay flat on his front.

"Hurry," shouted Cera.

Ursula grabbed the fabric at Bael's shoulder and began to pull.

"Wait." Cera pulled out a knife, then began cutting the shirt off his back, and drew the blade through his bandages. Fresh blood oozed from the wounds where Bael's wings had been.

Looking at his ravaged back, Ursula snatched the wings from Cera. The wings were featherlight and transparent, glowing with a pearly magic. "What do I do?"

Cera chewed her lip. "I think you just put them on the wounds."

Slowly, Ursula pressed a wing onto the closest wound. She paused for a full second, but nothing happened.

"I think it needs to be both of them," whispered Cera.

"Right." Holding her breath, Ursula carefully placed the remaining wing on the second wound.

For a moment, nothing happened. Then the wings began to glow brighter, with a silvery light like a burning star, until they shone so brightly Ursula had to cover her eyes. Relief bloomed in her chest. *It's working.* A wild joy bubbled through her.

When she opened her eyes again, Bael was sitting before her. His bare, tattooed chest glowed with an unearthly light, and the room filled with the scent of sandalwood. He drew in a deep breath, standing and extending his hand to Ursula.

"Thank you," he said, the light fading. Shadows began to swirl about him once again, and dark wings cascaded behind him.

He looked like a god, and Ursula's jaw dropped.

"You returned my wings to me." He pulled her closer, enfolding her in his powerful arms.

Ursula could have hardly thought it possible, but his body felt even stronger, like steel cables now reinforced his muscles. He kissed her, and she melted into his embrace.

A deep cough interrupted them.

Lucius was pulling dead fragments of shadow magic off his body. "I'm sorry to intrude, but where is Excalibur?"

Ursula whirled, turning to find Abrax. But he wasn't there.

In fact, where he'd been lying, she saw only a smear of blood. Hadn't she slashed his throat? And his chest?

"How did he survive that?" she cried. "I thought the sword could kill him."

A sound somewhere between a growl and a roar rumbled in Lucius's chest. "That sword is mine."

"So we will retrieve it," said Bael.

Lucius gripped his hair. "The demon could be anywhere now."

Ursula frantically racked her brain. What use would Abrax have for Excalibur?

That was when a terrifying realization sparked in her mind. "I know where he's gone. He wants to kill his father. He'll be at Asta, hunting for Nyxobas."

* * *

At Asta's spire, Sotz landed on the platform. The violet crystal glowed faintly in the bright light. Bael climbed off from behind her, and Ursula followed, her gaze flicking to Cera and Lucius as they landed gracefully.

With a sickening snapping sound, Lucius shifted into his human form. He clapped his hands together, his face reddened. "Let's get my sword, shall we?"

They stalked into the tunnel, and Ursula reached out to touch the walls of the passage. Without Emerazel's fire in her veins, the crystal didn't feel ice cold. If anything, she could feel the deep hum of magic thrumming all around her, seeping into her veins.

Ursula could hear the distinct sound of hammering when they entered the hall of the lords, and she strained her eyes in the dim light. The faint indigo gleam of the crystal cast a pale glow on the empty stone tables of the demon lords.

Ursula's gaze flicked to Nyxobas's throne, where he sat, as usual, in a dark-eyed daze. But he wasn't alone, and that was where the sound of hammering was coming from. Abrax stood just before the sleeping god, gripping Excalibur. He grunted, rearing back to swing for his father's head. But his aim was off, and it slammed into the stone next to Nyxobas for what must have been at least the hundredth time. The rock sparked, and shards of crystal sprayed onto the floor of the throne room.

"Put it down, fool," Lucius bellowed. "You cannot handle the blade. Only Excalibur chooses who may wield it."

Abrax turned, his face a mask of fury, blood streaming from his throat, his chest. "I am the son of a god. I can do what I want."

"Surrender yourself," said Bael. "You are outnumbered and half dead."

"No." Abrax stumbled toward them, his pale eyes wide.

"No?"

"Did you not think I would have a contingency plan?" He pointed to a dark form in the corner. A man, wrapped in shadow magic.

Ursula's stomach clenched when she recognized Kester's sandy hair.

Abrax grinned. "All I have to do is snap my fingers, and the shadows will coil around his throat."

"Do you think we won't sacrifice Kester?" said Bael.

"She won't." Abrax pointed to Ursula.

"Bael," said Ursula. "Let me talk to him."

Bael's dark wings cascaded gracefully behind him. "Ursula, wait."

But she was already striding across the marble floor.

Abrax smiled at her as she approached. "I knew you would save your friend."

"Release him." Nyxobas's power thrummed over her body, coiling between her ribs. Maybe her fire magic was gone, but now she felt the thrill of night magic—cold, ancient, and strangely familiar.

Abrax narrowed his eyes. "Your soul for his."

"Ursula!" shouted Bael in warning, but Ursula was already leaping, the shadows carrying her as if on a phantom wind.

She appeared next to Abrax. Before he could strike her with Excalibur, she drove Honjo into his ravaged chest. Abrax's eyes widened as she jerked the sword upward.

"You cannot kill me. I am immortal."

"I know you can feel pain." She twisted the blade, watching his face contort with agony.

Abrax's body began to quiver, his bones contracting, his face becoming demonic.

"No you don't," said Ursula, grabbing him by the throat and pulling his face closer. "You were right. I'm drained of Emerazel's fire. But that only leaves room for Nyxobas's shadows. They're drawn to me, like they belong to me. I'm a creature of the night. I always have been. Do you remember what happened when you tried to kill me on the sands of Lacus Mortis?"

There was fear in Abrax's eyes now. "I am immortal—"

"But that won't stop me from consuming your magic."

Ursula breathed in, sucking Abrax's shadowy magic into her body. Dark and wispy as smoke, it imbued her body, pooling around her skull, her ribs. She felt herself lured into the void, that clean expanse of nothingness, where she didn't have to feel. She fought to stay focused, drawing Abrax's magic from him.

Abrax's pale eyes widened. As Ursula drained him, a voice boomed all around her, penetrating her skull. "Enough!"

She looked at Nyxobas where he sat on his throne, his eyes now sharp and clear as rays of light.

She stared into the god's ancient face, and the darkness of the void drew her under.

1003

CHAPTER 45

She drifted in the void, darkness enveloping her.

"Ursula." Nyxobas's voice rumbled through her bones, his voice reverberating in the darkness, seeming to come from every direction. Or maybe from within her mind.

"Why are you fighting Abrax?" his voice boomed.

If she hadn't been floating in a void, Ursula would have sighed in frustration. "He was trying to kill you. I was trying to save you."

"Do you know why you are here, in the void? Do you know why my power imbues you?"

A thought, an idea from the back of her mind, blazed to life. Something she'd known for a long time, but that she'd refused to really entertain. "I come from you, don't I? My mother was one of your followers. I saw her eyes—black as the void."

"She was my lover."

"And I'm your daughter." How long had she known this for? It was the first time she'd allowed herself to think it, and yet it seemed so crystal clear to her now. The night had always called to her. She'd felt the power of shadow magic flowing through her veins. She felt a distant horror at the realization that Abrax was her brother.

Emerazel had known all along, hadn't she? When Ursula had first met the fire goddess, Emerazel had forced her to kneel with a gleeful sense of dominance.

"If you can find your way out of the void, I'm pulling the mark of that bitch from you," said Nyxobas, as if hearing her thoughts. "You won't belong to her anymore. You're a demigod, Ursula. And that's why I needed to test your ability in combat at Lacus Mortis. You did not disappoint me."

"You sacrificed my mother, didn't you? You used her as a pawn in your war against Emerazel's followers."

"Your mother was a powerful warrior, like you. She made her own choice. She was very devoted to me," said Nyxobas. "She made her own decisions. She chose to try to kill the king for me. He was a follower of my greatest enemy, Emerazel. He needed to be stopped, his bloodline ended. In his quest for power, he was converting too many souls. I couldn't allow Emerazel that sort of advantage. Your mother understood."

In the void, Ursula's emotions were dulled, and yet she felt a distant sense of betrayal. Her mother had chosen Nyxobas over her. Her mother had left her alone. Still, here in the void, that clean, soothing emptiness pulled her under, that freedom from the pain of memories. If she could just stay here forever…

"I need to get out of here," she whispered.

"But you prefer it here, don't you? You long to escape. There's nothing in your memories but the darkness. You did that to yourself."

"I remember some things… I remember watching my mother die. Her eyes were filled with your shadows." Still, Ursula couldn't *feel* the memory —until all at once, she found herself back in Mount Acidale.

It was the floor of King Midac's hall, and her gaze went to the king's table. King Midac sat at one end of the table, near the queen and Kester.

But it was the woman next to the queen that drew Ursula's attention, her auburn hair tumbling over a purple velvet gown. Bright blue eyes, a heart-shaped face—the woman who'd once rubbed her back at night when she had nightmares about dragons. The woman who'd baked her favorite bread on her days off, who'd patiently taught her to wield a sword. The woman who'd pulled Ursula onto her lap, reading her stories about faraway lands, before she went to bed at night. *My mother.* Ursula wanted to run to her, to ask her not to leave.

She knew what was coming next, and a sense of betrayal pierced her ribs like a dozen arrows.

Ursula stared as her mother drew a steak knife, driving it into the queen's heart. Blood poured from her chest.

Why did you choose to leave me? They'd been members of the king's guard together. Ursula had been proud of her uniform—the purple and gold. She'd been a proud soldier, like her grandfather. Her mother was ripping her world apart.

The woman who'd combed her hair, who'd soothed her tears when the other children had called her a *fatherless child.*

Once, her mother had been her world.

Time seemed to slow down, and grief slammed into Ursula. Her mum lunged for the king, but Kester was already reaching for his blade. For the briefest of instants, Ursula's mother turned toward the hellhound, her eyes black as Nyxobas's void. Ursula's mind screamed.

Then everything sped up again. Bael leapt over the table. Across from him, Kester drew his sword. Pushing the king aside, Kester drove his blade into her mother's stomach.

The world went dark again.

"How did that feel?" asked Nyxobas. "Now you see why you rid yourself of your own memories."

"She left me," said Ursula. "She betrayed me, and I was ashamed of her. But I can't stay here." Grief threatened to swallow her whole—but she could take it. She didn't need the void now.

Gasping, she pulled herself from Nyxobas's shadows once more, and light shone in her eyes again. Across from her, Abrax lay stunned, his eyes filled with shadows. Still lost in the void.

Those emotions from her memory—the shame, the pure sorrow—still ripped her mind apart, threatening to drive her mad. *My mother was once my world—and she left me.*

Ursula snarled, picking up Excalibur from the marble floor. She swung it once—clean through Abrax's neck. Blood arced over the floor, and his body slumped to the marble.

"Sorry, Dad," she whispered. "But he had to go."

When she looked up at Nyxobas, she found him lost in the void once more. She slid her fingertips under the collar of her shirt, finding the skin smooth.

The mark of Emerazel was gone.

CHAPTER 46

Ursula sat at the dining room table in her old apartment. Across from her, Cera sipped from a glass of wine, her eyes locked on Lucius.

The chandelier bathed them in warm light, and Ursula relaxed into her chair. By her side, Zee twirled a champagne glass, marveling at the pink flower in the bottom. "Let's not leave New York any time soon, okay? I've had enough mushroom stew and disgusting prison food to last me a lifetime. And more importantly, the humans have already rebuilt my favorite Thai place."

Since the dragons had destroyed half of New York, humans were already reconstructing the city, piecing their lives back together, one building at a time.

At Zee's side, Kester ran his finger over the rim of his wineglass, meeting Ursula's gaze. "You do realize that since you no longer work for Emerazel, you won't be able to keep this apartment, right? You're off the payroll, darling. No more gold for you."

Ursula frowned. "But you can keep it, right? Maybe I can just…sublet from you. Except without the exchange of money, because I won't have any."

Kester arched an eyebrow. "I suppose there's not much work available for an ex-hellhound demigod of night, is there?"

Ursula shrugged. "I don't suppose there are any demigod temp agencies."

Lucius leaned back in his chair, folding his fingers behind his ginger hair. "Tell me again how you freed yourself from the bonds of Emerazel."

Ursula took a sip of her Châteauneuf-du-Pape, rolling it around on her tongue. "Nyxobas did that for me. It seems that all this time, he'd wanted me to prove myself before he was willing to step in. He wanted to test my mettle in the battles of Lacus Mortis, and he needed to see if I was willing to accept my own memories, or if I belonged in the void with him."

Cera blinked, her silver eyes wide. "He's not angry that you slaughtered his son?"

Ursula nearly felt a twinge of guilt. She'd executed her own brother, right in front of their dad.

Nearly felt guilty—but not quite. "Abrax would have found a way to kill his father at some point if he'd lived," said Ursula. "In any case, Nyxobas has been lost in the void. Didn't have to feel a thing."

Since she'd killed her brother, Nyxobas had become even more remote than ever.

She understood. He was escaping. *Like father, like daughter.*

Cera cocked her head. "Do you think Nyxobas even knows that the oneiroi have been freed in the Shadow Realm, and that some of us sit on the council of lords now?"

"No," said Ursula. "I don't think he'll be coming out of the void for quite some time."

"Bael is Nyxobas's Sword now," said Kester. "Shouldn't he be in the Shadow Realm? And you with him, if you're his bride-to-be?"

Ursula shook her head. "If I have anything to say about it, we'll simply finish rebuilding in the Shadow Realm, and then we'll leave. The longer we spend there, the more time there is for some other lord to decide it's his turn to be Sword, and then I have to kill more people. And granted, I may be a demigod—"

"Are you going to keep mentioning that?" Zee cut in.

"I may be a demigod," Ursula continued, ignoring her. "But I don't want to have to keep killing people. I'd rather just live out my immortal, demigod life in peace."

The scent of acrid smoke curled through the air—a mixture of burning flesh and something else—something bitter. Ursula's stomach clenched.

Cera leaned across the table, her silver eyes shining with concern. "Do you really think the lord is ready for this? For what you're asking him to do?"

Ursula sucked in a deep breath. "I don't know. But we had to try."

In the next moment, Bael glided into the room, carrying an enormous oak tray crammed with silver domes. Before each of them, he laid out a covered plate. The smell nearly choked Ursula as Bael slid a dish in front of her, his gorgeous face beaming with pride, gray eyes shining.

"Smells wonderful," Ursula lied.

Across from her, Lucius was mumbling something that sounded like, "Smells like Pasqual's basement."

Ursula pulled the dome off her plate, staring wide-eyed at what she found. In a small bowl, Bael had poured half a can of Spaghettios. By the side of the bowl, Ursula found small pieces of hot dog, cut up and charred. At least, she thought they were hot dog pieces. They sat next to a lump of blackened marshmallows and three graham crackers, smeared with butter and crushed peanuts.

A heavy silence fell over the room, broken only by the scraping noise of Cera pushing marshmallows around on her plate.

Ursula swallowed hard. "Maybe I should have helped you a bit more. I thought with the simple recipe books…"

Bael's dark eyebrows rose, and he dug into the Spaghettios. "I didn't look at the books. Is this not right? I got these food products from a human supermarket. Is this not typical food for your realm?"

Zee sighed. "I'm calling the Thai place."

* * *

Ursula lay on Bael's chest, staring at the ceiling of the room that had once been hers. His powerful torso rose and fell slowly beneath her head. It seemed like ages ago that they'd first met, when she'd found him chained to a table upstairs. She'd been terrified of him then, the ancient and wounded warrior. Now, he felt like home.

Bael stroked a hand down her hair, and she breathed in the scent of sandalwood.

So maybe he couldn't cook. He was perfect all the same.

Ursula shifted, her gaze trailing over the wildflowers she'd once painted on the walls. The memory had always been there under the surface of her mind—the forget-me-nots and golden aster, the smudges of periwinkle and honey-hued blossoms, exactly like the fields in Mount Acidale. She'd always had glimpses—the flowers, the auburn-haired woman who taught her to wield a blade.

And there—on the ceiling—the image of the star-flecked, midnight blue zodiac that had made her feel at home. Now, she knew why. Once, she'd been the Mystery Girl—a lost and adrift outcast. Now, she saw that she'd found little ways to keep her parents around her. To root herself in her past, in her history.

Her gaze trailed over the flowered fields once more, and a vivid image burned in her mind—her mother's face. Her mum was leaning over her, brushing a strand of red hair from her face. It still hurt that her mother had chosen Nyxobas over her, a betrayal that even now gnawed at her chest. Once, her mother had been her world.

Bael stroked his hand over the back of her hair again, and she reached behind him, lightly touching the tip of his black wings. His dark magic thrummed over her body, mingling with her own power, her own shadows.

A sly smile curled his lips. He liked that. "When will we marry?" he asked.

She looked up at him, her gaze lingering over his chiseled features, his stormy gray eyes, the color of the skies over Byblos. "We're both immortal. We have all the time in the world."

"Soon," he said. "I don't want to wait."

She smiled. "Soon, then."

Ursula wasn't the same person she had been in Mount Acidale. Now, she was strong enough to feel, to let herself remember. In this life, she had Bael—and Kester, Zee, and Cera. And she intended to keep them close.

* * *

THANK you so much for reading the Shadows & Flame series. If you want to see more of Bael, he plays a role in the Shadow Fae series. If you would like to continue with the next series in this world, pick up **The Vampire's Mage Boxed Set.**

ALSO BY C.N. CRAWFORD

For a full list of our books, check out our website.
https://www.cncrawford.com/books/

And a possible reading order.
https://www.cncrawford.com/faq/

ABOUT

C. N. Crawford is not one person but two. We write our novels collaboratively, passing our laptops back and forth to edit each other's words.

Christine (C) grew up in New England and has a lifelong interest in local folklore - with a particular fondness for creepy old cemeteries. Nick (N) spent his childhood reading fantasy and science fiction during Vermont's long winters.

In addition to writing fiction, we love to hear from our readers and can be reached at any of the following links. We always reply to our readers.

www.ingramcontent.com/pod-product-compliance
Lightning Source LLC
Chambersburg PA
CBHW051746020826
48982CB00015BB/813